Dear Reader:

Welcome to *Sunsational!*

It's summer and although the sun beats down, a cool breeze caresses you. You relax on your favorite lounge—this is *your* time. You reach for your book.... But wait, didn't you finish it yesterday?

There's nothing worse than finishing a novel without having the next right there to begin. That's why we created *Sunsational*—four much-loved Harlequin Presents novels in *one* volume.

It means you'll have four exciting romances, by four of your favorite authors—Emma Darcy, Emma Goldrick, Penny Jordan and Carole Mortimer—within easy reach. Let them carry you away to a secluded beach near Sydney, to the bustle and excitement of London.... Let these stories make your summer sunsational!

We wish you continued happy reading.

The Editors
Harlequin

EMMA DARCY nearly became an actress until her fiancé declared he preferred to attend the theater *with* her. She became a wife and mother. Then she tried architecture, designing the family home in New South Wales. Next came romance writing—"the hardest and most challenging of all the activities," she confesses. But one she's clearly at home with. Emma's newest Presents novel, #1385 *The Colour of Desire*, will be available in August wherever paperbacks are sold.

EMMA GOLDRICK describes herself as a grandmother first and an author second. She was born and raised in Puerto Rico where she met her husband, a career military man from Massachusetts. Emma uses the places to which her husband was posted as backgrounds for her romances. *Mississippi Miss*, Emma's latest Harlequin Presents novel which is on sale now, is rich with the warmth and humor of life in a small southern town.

PENNY JORDAN'S "first half-dozen attempts at romance writing ended up ingloriously," she remembers, "but I persevered and one manuscript was finished." She plucked up the courage to send it to a publisher, convinced her book would be rejected. It wasn't and the rest is history. She is married and lives in Cheshire. Penny is a regular contributor to the Harlequin Presents line and her stunning new novel, *The Hidden Years*, will be released in October.

CAROLE MORTIMER, one of our most popular—and prolific—English authors, began writing in the Harlequin Presents series in 1979. She now has more than forty top-selling romances to her credit. Carole writes strong traditional romances with a distinctly modern appeal, and her winning way with characters and romantic plot twists has earned her an enthusiastic audience around the world.

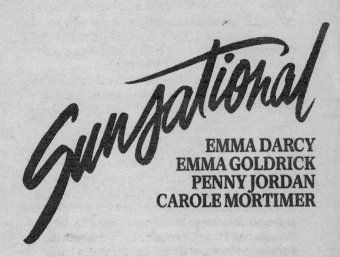

Sunsational

EMMA DARCY
EMMA GOLDRICK
PENNY JORDAN
CAROLE MORTIMER

Harlequin Books

TORONTO • NEW YORK • LONDON
AMSTERDAM • PARIS • SYDNEY • HAMBURG
STOCKHOLM • ATHENS • TOKYO • MILAN

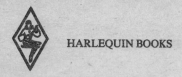

HARLEQUIN BOOKS

SUNSATIONAL
Copyright © 1991 by Harlequin Enterprises Ltd.

ISBN 0-373-83236-2

SUNSATIONAL first printing July 1991

The publisher acknowledges the copyright holders of
the individual works as follows:

FANTASY
Copyright © 1985 by Emma Darcy
Harlequin Presents Edition 1985

RENT-A-BRIDE LTD.
Copyright © 1985 by Emma Goldrick
Harlequin Presents Edition 1985

YOU OWE ME
Copyright © 1985 by Penny Jordan
Harlequin Presents Edition 1985

LOVERS IN THE AFTERNOON
Copyright © 1985 by Carole Mortimer
Harlequin Presents Edition 1985

CONTENTS

FANTASY
Emma Darcy

CHAPTER ONE

THE car lurched from one pothole to the next. Steering a steady course was fast becoming impossible. Dense bush-scrub crowded in on the dirt track and just as Eve began to think she had made a mistake, it thinned out and there was the sea.

She brought the car to an abrupt halt. As she leant forward to switch off the headlights, another light seemed to wink at her from the darkness ahead. She closed her tired lids, squeezed some of the strain from her eyes, then looked again. Nothing. The darkness around her was complete. Relief poured its soothing oil on over-stretched nerves. She was alone. Not only alone but well away from any human contact. She could stay here without fear of anyone coming to question or look at her with curious eyes.

For a long, weary moment she rested her head on the car-door. The tangy crispness of sea air drifted through the open window and teased her nostrils. It smelled clean. The peaceful drone of lapping waves washed through her fretful mind. Eve did not want to think any more. Every thought brought a bitter sickness. As another shudder of revulsion cramped her stomach, she thrust the door open and almost fell out of the car.

The sound of the sea drummed in her ears, rolling out its sonorous invitation. She walked towards it, kicking off her shoes as sand dragged at her feet. Frothy crests glinted in the moonlight, endlessly moving, spilling on to the beach, beckoning her closer before coyly retreating. Wet sand squelched between her toes. It felt good. Cool water washed around her feet, sucking at them persuasively.

Eve's hands moved instinctively, ridding her body of clothes. She trod them underfoot, a grimace of disgust on her face. Such clothes did not belong in this place. There was nothing corrupt here, no perversion of nature, no trace of a sick, twisted society. Her gaze swept slowly around the cove. The sea had been beating on these rocks and sand for thousands of years and would probably do so for many more thousands of years, unchanged by so-called civilisation.

Again water swirled around her feet, seductively inviting. She followed its drag, welcoming the cold sting of the next wave as it broke against her legs. Urged on by a blind need to rid herself of tonight's events, Eve struck out past the breakers to where the water rose and fell in soft swells. Here it was peaceful, soothing, and she floated with the tide, bobbing mindlessly like a piece of driftwood.

An alien sound filtered through her ears. Its message tapped persistently on her brain until reason insisted it was the sound of a voice, a human voice. She rolled her head sideways, not quite believing that it was so. The sight of a man ploughing into the surf towards her was nerve-jolting.

Eve thrust her legs down, frantic to avoid facing anyone. She kicked out jerkily and just as she began to swim, her leg-muscles cramped with paralysing pain. Her mouth opened to emit a scream of agony. Water gushed in, choking the sound in her throat. Her legs were useless. She was sinking. Her arms flapped in panic. She broke surface for a moment but not long enough to gulp in air. Pain crippled her and the water was all around, endless pain and water. Her lungs were bursting with the need to breathe. She had to breathe.

Consciousness came with more pain. Her chest heaved convulsively as she coughed out sea-water. Eve whimpered in agonised protest as nausea compounded the torture in her legs.

"Stupid bitch! If you want to drown yourself, go do it on someone else's beach!"

The harsh invective was lost on Eve. She struggled to reach her legs. "Oh God!" she sobbed, clutching at the knots of pain.

Other hands swept her feeble grasp aside. Eve collapsed back on to the sand while strong fingers massaged the cramped muscles. Slowly the tension eased until only a bearable ache remained. Eve unclenched her teeth and opened her eyes. The man was kneeling beside her, a huge, dark blur.

"Thank you," she whispered.

He slapped the loosened muscles once more and stood up, a towering figure of a man, completely naked. Only then did Eve remember her own nakedness. She shivered as his gaze raked her from head to foot.

"The mermaid act is over for tonight. Get on your feet," he ordered peremptorily.

Before she could gather strength enough to make a move he had leaned over and pulled her up. Eve's legs wobbled and she would have fallen if he had not caught her in time.

"Goddammit!" he muttered. "I suppose I'll have to carry you."

There was no gentleness in the arms which cradled her. Eve's breasts were crushed against a hair-roughened chest and the sand clinging to her body rubbed its gritty discomfort into her flesh. The enforced contact between her nude body and his brought a flood of embarrassment to add to her discomfort.

"Please. I can walk if..."

"Shut up!"

The sharp impatience of the man made her squirm. He held her more tightly.

"Please..." she began again.

"I'm not spending the whole bloody night on a cold beach pandering to you."

"If you just let me go you won't have to worry about me."

He ignored her, striding purposefully towards the road but not towards Eve's car, which was now some hundred metres behind them. Discomfort and embarrassment quickened into fear.

"Where are you taking me?" she squeaked, panic catching at her voice.

He reached firm ground and abruptly stood her on her feet. His hands gripped her waist, holding her steady while he drew in a deep breath and expelled it. Then he spoke, biting each word out with sharp emphasis.

"Look, lady! I'm not interested in you. Neurotic women are a bore. To put it plainly, you're just a headache. I'm tired. Because of you, I'm also wet and cold. I'm going back to my cabin to have a hot shower, get warm, and if it's at all possible, get some sleep. And you're coming with me."

"I've got my car. You don't have to—"

"No way!" he snapped impatiently. "If you think I'm giving you another chance to drown your woes, you can think again. I can do without a body washed up on the beach, not to mention the hassle of calling the police."

"But I didn't mean to—"

"You're wasting your breath."

"No, truly. I—"

"Oh, for God's sake! I saw the headlights come down the track and I watched to see what you were up to. You went straight for the sea and you weren't figuring on putting those clothes back on again. You churned right on in without a backward glance. A dead-set suicide if ever I saw one. You ignored my shouts and when you saw me coming you sank out of sight."

"I got cramp and..."

"So it was cold. I'm cold. And I'm not going to stand here arguing. What you do with yourself tomorrow or next week is out of my hands, but tonight you came to my beach and made yourself my business, so just shut up and walk since you don't like being carried. My cabin is just behind that grove of trees."

He had swung her around and pushed her in the right direction. Eve stumbled along. The hand on the pit of her back did not allow any choice in the matter. She did not have the strength to fight him, and besides, she was now shivering with cold. A small building loomed out of the darkness ahead. Obviously this had been the source of the flicker of light she had seen earlier. It was a log cabin, small and primitive. The front door was open. She hesitated on the step, panic attacking her once more at the thought of being shut in, alone with a hostile stranger and both of them naked. The man swept her inside and closed the door.

"Stand still while I light the lamp," he ordered curtly.

Eve stood rooted to the spot, her mind too numb to direct any other action. It was an old-fashioned kerosene lamp. The man's face sprang to life in its yellow glow. It was a hard, imperative face, framed with thick, shaggy black hair. Straight eyebrows beetled over deeply set brown eyes. His nose was slightly hooked. The jawline was strong and square. Deep lines ran from cheeks to mouth, an attractive mouth which gradually thinned in irritation as he looked at her.

"I'll get the water-heater going. Grab a blanket off the bed and put it around you."

Her eyes skittered away from his very masculine nakedness. The powerful physique was intimidating. A double bed stood in one corner of the room. A mohair rug lay across the foot of it. The man moved to a back door and disappeared outside. Released from his presence Eve snatched up the rug and wrapped it around her. She sat down on the bed. Her legs were trembling too much for her to do anything else and she needed to rest and recover some balance.

Haphazard thoughts darted in and out of her brain. She was too exhausted for any coherent thinking. It was much, much easier to simply sit still and wait for the man to tell her what to do. He had saved her from drowning. But for him she would be dead. Right now she was not sure if she was glad to be alive or not and she could not find the will to care about the immediate future.

"Come on. Water's running warm."

She glanced numbly at the man, not heeding his words. The towel around his hips was reassuring. And he was older than she had first thought. His features had a settled maturity. Closer to forty than thirty, she mused, yet his body was that of a young man.

"Move, dammit! I've done enough carrying for one night."

Eve forced her legs to obey. He beckoned her outside and she followed him along a short verandah to a room which was also lit by a lamp. It seemed to encompass several purposes. Fishing gear was stacked along one wall, laundry-tubs and work-table against another, and a makeshift shower at the end. Water was spraying down. The man felt its temperature before whipping off her rug and pushing her under it. He handed her a washer.

"Hurry up! I haven't got water to waste."

Her slow movements annoyed him. With another exasperated mutter he slung his towel aside, stepped into the shower with her and reclaimed the washer. There was nothing gentle about the brisk way he set about wiping her free of sand. Her neck, back and legs were given a quick rub-down. Then he roughly swung her around to face him.

"Why, in God's name, would a woman with a body like yours want to risk drowning?" he demanded curtly.

The washer encircled her breasts and moved down, over her stomach, between her thighs.

"Wasn't thinking of drowning," she mumbled as a treacherous warmth tingled through her body.

She grew more and more aware of the hand behind the washer and the masculine strength of the body so close to hers. Here was a real man. Not like Simon.

This man was well and truly aware of her as a woman. She stared in fascination at the undoubted evidence of his male arousal.

With his self-appointed task completed, the man straightened and the powerful thrust of his loins was even more awesome. Her fixed gaze elicited a further sigh of exasperation.

"What the hell! I don't take a shower with a woman every day and you're not exactly ugly."

His explanation fell on deaf ears. A wild mêlée of emotions was churning inside Eve. The shattering disillusion of finding the man she loved in bed with another man forced every instinct to cry out that she was a woman who wanted to be loved as a woman. Loved, desired, taken as a woman. To know, to feel how it would be, how it might have been if Simon had been the man she thought. If he had wanted her, been excited by her, like this man. She had been looking forward to her marriage night, the marriage night that would never come now. Frustration and thwarted curiosity and a thousand crying needs forced her hand out. She touched him, her fingers soft, tentative, wondering.

His swift intake of breath was followed by an instant rejection. He knocked her hand away, stepped out of the shower and hastily knotted the towel around his waist. He turned back to her with a glare of contempt.

"What are you? Some kind of nymphomaniac? Or do you simply get a kick out of living dangerously? The package might be tempting, but I'm not so starved for sex that I'll take anything that offers." He turned off the taps and threw her a towel. "Dry yourself and cover up. I'll make us some coffee. It might bring you to your senses.''

Eve knew she should be ashamed, knew that she should be shocked at herself, but the dull, empty feeling was back again. Somewhere in the back of her mind she was shocked but it did not seem to matter. It did not matter what this man thought of her either. He was a stranger, not of her world, here tonight and gone tomorrow. It was quite ironic, really. Far from being a nymphomaniac, she was a virgin whose virginity had never been even threatened.

She knew now why Simon had never wanted to make love to her, why he had insisted that her wardrobe consist of boyish clothes, why he had liked her hair kept short. He had explained his reluctance to consummate their love by claiming that he wanted a true bride. She had been flattered by his old-fashioned romanticism, pleased and proud that he valued her so much.

Eve sourly wondered what excuse he would have given on their wedding night, whether he would have been able to sublimate his true sexual inclinations and keep fooling her. It was lucky that she had found out before she was legally tied to him. But she did not feel lucky. She felt badly used. And yet she was not used. Here she was, all untouched, and likely to remain so. A bitter irony curved her mouth into a grimace. She was certainly safe from being touched by the man inside the cabin. She wrapped the mohair rug around her once again and returned to the main room.

The man had pulled on a pair of jeans and a sweater. He was standing at a gas stove, waiting for a kettle to boil. Two mugs were sitting on a roughly hewn wooden table. Eve pulled out a chair and sat

down. Neither of them spoke. Clearly he did not like
the situation and Eve had nothing to say to him. She
was not about to explain her behaviour. He had taken
control and brought her here. If he did not like it he
had only himself to blame. The kettle whistled. He
poured steaming water into the mugs and pushed one
towards her.

"There's sugar there. No milk," he stated flatly.

"I don't take either," she muttered.

Models could not afford excess weight. Simon had
drummed that into her. He had approved of her slim
hips and long legs but had always been critical of her
full breasts, even demanding that she wear a bandeau
to flatten them for some photographs. "Top models
are not cows," he had said disparagingly. A whole
parade of his words and actions marched through her
mind, stamping out a new dimension of meaning. She
had been a blind, naïve fool not to have guessed
something was wrong in their relationship. Simon had
never been a manly man, not like the brooding figure
across from her. His chair creaked. She glanced up to
find him studying her with cold objectivity.

"I seem to know your face. Should I?"

Alarm screeched through her brain. The last
thing . . . the very last thing she could afford was to be
recognised. Her break-up with Simon would cause
comment enough. A rumoured suicide attempt would
hit the headlines. She forced her voice to be dull and
careless.

"I don't see how. We've certainly never met before."

He could have seen her face on magazine-covers
whenever he passed a newsagency, on television ad-
vertisements, hoarding boards. But not quite the face

he was seeing tonight, not a face washed clean of its artful make-up. He stared at her for a moment longer then gave a dismissive shrug. His glance fell to her hands.

"Not married?"

She shook her head, relieved that the danger was over.

"Man trouble?"

Her mouth twisted with disgust. "You could say that."

"It figures."

The dry comment brought a painful flush to her cheeks. He was obviously applying her answer to a lot more than she had meant. That mad impulse to touch him must have seemed blatantly wanton.

"I'm sorry that...that I've disrupted your night and been so much trouble to you. I...I didn't think there was anyone here."

"Lucky for you I was here. And still awake."

"Yes. Lucky," she echoed dully.

He sighed and stretched back in his chair, making it tilt backwards. "Didn't he want you?"

Her gaze flickered up and for a moment the whole depth of her disillusionment was there in her eyes before she tiredly hooded them. "No, he didn't want me. He wanted the image. Not me."

There was puzzlement in his voice when he spoke. "What image? You mean the face and the figure? Or are you someone..."

"No, no," she said quickly, not wanting him to probe out her identity. The sick débâcle of her love for Simon billowed through her mind and all the bottled-up horror of the night burst out of her in tortured words.

"He doesn't want a woman. Not a real woman. We were going to be married. Next week. And to-night...he wasn't expecting me at his apartment. I went...the music was so loud he didn't hear me ring. I used my key. There was a smell—heavy, sweet—incense, pot, I don't know. It worried me. I went into his bedroom. He was with...with another man...and they were...they were...I...I ran out and just kept driving until I found this place."

The tears which Eve had kept choking back for hours began trickling down her cheeks. The large green eyes were pools of misery, blind to everything but her inner grief. She did not see the flash of recognition on his face, nor the comprehension which brought a soft compassion to his eyes. Having found release, the tears continued to well up and overflow. Eve slumped forward, propping her head with one covering hand as she wept uncontrollably. Her heart seemed to swell to breaking point. Great racking sobs eased the constriction in her chest, and it was a long time before the sobs deteriorated into shuddering little sighs. She dabbed the wetness from her eyes with the back of her hand.

Only then did she become aware of fingers drumming a restless tattoo on the table. Her chest heaved once more as she struggled to pull herself under control. A furtive glance at the man caught the dark frown which pulled his eyebrows together into a heavy line. The fingers stopped tapping and she felt his gaze on her. Having bared her soul as well as her body, Eve felt even more naked. Her hand clutched the rug more closely around her, subsconsciously grasping for a protective cloak.

"Want to lie down?"

The quiet question brought a self-conscious flush to her cheeks. She hung her head, not knowing what to answer. All along the man had judged her harshly and she could not tell if he was being kind or critical.

"You must feel completely wrung out. It's been a very rough night on you, and I haven't made it any easier." He sighed and his hand spread open in a gesture of appeasement. "I'm sorry for having been so...so unsympathetic."

She darted a glance at him. He seemed sincere. She swallowed nervously and forced herself to speak.

"I really didn't think of drowning. It was just...I felt...I needed..."

He waved a dismissive hand. "You don't have to explain." Then in a softer voice, "You're well rid of him, you know."

"I know," she whispered, but her eyes were haunted with the pain of emotional surgery.

He pushed himself to his feet, rounded the table and gently squeezed her shoulder. "Come on. Into bed. You'll feel better in the morning."

Taking it for granted that she would follow his suggestion, he leaned forward and turned off the lamp. Eve was slow to react. An arm slid around her shoulders, lifting her upright and supporting her for the few steps to the bed. It was not until he tried to relieve her of the mohair rug that Eve felt driven to protest.

"Please..."

"A little late for modesty, don't you think?" came the dry comment. "You won't need it in bed," he added as he pulled back the bedclothes for her.

Eve hesitated, then realising that the darkness cloaked her anyway, she let the rug go and quickly slid between the sheets. The soft comfort of the pillow and mattress felt incredibly good. She stretched her legs and sighed before languidly moving into her usual sleeping position. The slight rustle of clothes whispered in her ear. Her head whipped around, her eyes wide open in alarm. The dark silhouette near the bed was tossing a garment aside.

"What . . . what are you doing?" Eve choked out. It was perfectly obvious what he was doing but she did not want to accept it.

"Coming to bed."

"With me?" she squeaked.

"There's only one bed. You surely don't object to sharing it with me," he said reasonably.

"But . . ."

"Look! I was wrong earlier and I made you feel bad. I didn't understand what you were feeling, the rotten kind of sexual shock you'd been through. No woman deserves to be hurt like that."

He climbed into bed and before Eve could shrink away, his hand reached over and gently cupped her cheek. He propped his head up with his other and looked down at her.

"And you are very much a woman, a beautiful, desirable, totally feminine woman."

She stared back, her mind exploding with the certainty that he meant to have sex with her. His hand trailed down her throat. She swallowed convulsively. It stroked across the line of her shoulder, featherlight in its touch. Her skin leapt with the prickles of tiny, electric shocks.

"Relax. I won't hurt you. Just unwind and let go. I'll give you the kind of loving you need."

Eve's cry of protest turned into a strangled gasp. His hand had moved from her shoulder. It was closing over her breast, gently squeezing the soft fullness, his thumb brushing lightly across her nipple. Then his mouth was on hers and his body was moving, touching, pressing.

CHAPTER TWO

SHE had invited this. Nothing could have been more
blatantly inviting than her action in the shower. So
how could she stop him? What could she say? She had
to say something. Eve opened her mouth. Any words
she might have spoken were stolen from her tongue.
The kiss which had begun as a tantalising touch on her
lips, became a deep, sensuous exploration which took
her breath away.

Her fingers blindly plucked at the hand which held
her breast captive, but the sweet pleasure emanating
from that hand weakened their purpose and they grew
still. There was a strange exhilaration in feeling the
hard length of his body against hers. Her skin was
prickling with excitement and a treacherous hum of
anticipation danced along her veins. Did she really
want it to stop? Hadn't she wanted to know what it
was like? All she had to do was let it happen.

A tiny voice of sanity screamed that it was wrong.
She did not even know this man, let alone love him. It
was wrong to let this intimacy go on. But her brain was
being flooded by other messages, fascinating messages of unimagined pleasure, and slowly but surely
they seduced that tiny voice of reason into compla-
cency. A worm of guilt remained. With one of those
odd side-steps the brain performs when a decision be-

comes too hard, Eve shut her eyes and pretended this was her wedding night.

He was not Simon, but Simon had cheated her. His love had been a deception. The sensations sweeping through her now were no deception. She had been holding back her response, but wanting now to feel the passion which had been denied her, Eve returned the kiss with fervour. Casting all inhibitions aside, she let her hands roam, finding that she liked the springy thickness of his hair, the muscular strength in the neck and shoulders above her, the firm flesh which was such a contrast to her own softness.

Her body arched its invitation, demanding his touch, wanting his exploration, begging to know the whole range of feeling that he promised. And he gave her what she needed with all the delicacy and finesse of a very experienced lover. Eve did not think of him as a person. He was touch, awakening her body to a life it had never known, fine-tuning it to a high pitch of pleasure, his mouth and hands finding and exploiting erotic zones she had read about but scarcely believed. She had been unable to imagine the incredible sensitivity which tingled with increasing pressure, demanding more and more satisfaction. There was an urgency which became a compulsion, so that her whole being was concentrated on one need, and the need had to be fulfilled. It was right, necessary, imperative.

Her body trembled in anticipation, every nerve-end aching for the entry which had been delayed for so long. She held her breath as it began. There was a hesitation, a withdrawal. Her breath rushed out in a sob of need. Her hands pleaded for it to be finished. There was a hard, driving thrust, a tearing pain, then body owning body in an act of possession which was totally dominant, throbbing with its own vibrant life, all-demanding until its demand was ultimately met, and Eve was floating on a different sea, her body bathed in a sweet, warm ecstasy she had never known existed. She sighed and the sigh was utter contentment, a beautiful measure of peace and satisfaction and total relaxation.

The man sighed also. He lifted himself away and Eve had a twinge of regret that it was over, that he was separating himself from her. There was a touch on her stomach, a light, sensitive touch which made her shiver.

"Are you all right?"

The deep voice held concern and Eve prickled with sudden embarrassment. She was lying here with a stranger, having just experienced the most intimate relationship with him. She wished he had not spoken. The words had broken into her self-absorption, forcing her to acknowledge him as a person. He stirred. She had to answer him.

"Yes. Yes, thank you."

The words came out stilted, too formally polite for a situation which cried out for precisely the opposite. She choked down a bubble of hysteria as she faced up to the actual reality of what she had done.

"You could have stopped me at any time. I would have stopped. You had only to speak up."

The edge of accusation in his tone struck her jarringly. Why was he blaming her? She had not seduced him. She would have kept rigidly to one side of the bed, left to herself. He had not seduced her either. Honesty demanded that she admit that truth.

"I didn't want you to stop." Then understanding dawned. "Don't worry. You won't be accused of rape."

It was an ugly word, rape. It soured the pleasure he had given her. She rolled on to her side, turning away from him, but before she could settle comfortably he had pulled her back and was leaning over her again.

"Rape doesn't enter into it, as well we both know. But you should have told me you were a virgin. Goddammit! You didn't act like a virgin and it never occurred to me that you might be one." He sighed and shook his head, and when he spoke again the anger had been replaced with a soft wryness. "Well, I hope you enjoyed it because I can't roll the clock backwards. The devil of it is, I meant to help you, not create another problem." He dropped back down on his pillow, moving his head restlessly until he put his hands behind it. "And the truth of it is, I didn't want to stop either. I just hope you don't regret it."

She had enjoyed it. Her body melted with the remembrance of pleasure as she recalled all the nuances of feeling. No, she did not regret the experience he had given her. She knew it all now. Knew how it felt to be a woman.

"I wanted to know," she murmured, more in confirmation of her thoughts than in answer to his words.

Silence stretched between them, a more solid wall than any partition, yet their very separation forced a greater awareness of the man on to Eve. He lay very still and there was a quality of tension about him, of hard, concentrated thought. It suddenly struck her that Simon had been obliterated from her thoughts for a longer time than would have seemed possible a little while ago.

"Well, if it was what you wanted, why the hell should I care?" The words were muttered as if they underlined the final say in an argument. His breathing became more relaxed as if he was settling for sleep. Suddenly his head turned towards her. "Why were you a virgin anyway? You're not so very young."

"You know why." She wished he would stop harping on the subject of her virginity. It recalled Simon too painfully.

"But surely there've been other men who wanted you," he persisted.

"I loved him. No one else. Please don't go on. It doesn't matter."

Eve thought how strange it was, lying here with a man she did not know, just voices in the darkness. The whole night had been strange, isolated from a life which used to make sense to her. Nothing seemed to make sense any more. Simon had turned into an alien and she herself had acted completely out of character.

"Tell me about yourself."

She glanced sharply at the man, resentful of his intrusion into her reverie. He knew too much already, far too much to be admitted to her real life. She would die of embarrassment if she ever met him again away from here. What she had shared with him had been wonderful, a beautiful experience, and she did not want it spoilt. It was the one good thing that had happened to her this night. But it had to stop here.

"Do you live here all the time?" she asked, wanting the assurance that she was unlikely to run into him elsewhere.

"I come and go," he answered vaguely. "Where do you live?"

"In Sydney." That was vague enough. It was a big city.

"What will you do tomorrow?"

"I don't know. I'll work it out as I go home," she said despondently, hating the thought of explaining to her mother that the wedding was off.

"It's not going to be easy, is it? Better for you to stand back from it for a couple of days. You can stay here if you like."

"I couldn't do that," she said quietly. Her involvement with this man was too deep already.

"You need a breathing space. Time to get your head together. Ever gone fishing? It's a very restful occupation. Empties the mind of pressures."

Memories from her childhood flashed into her mind and a wave of nostalgia softened her voice. "I used to go fishing with my father. That was a long time ago."

"Is your father at home?"

"No. He died when I was fourteen."

"Do you live alone?"

"No. With my mother. She and I…" Eve clammed up, suddenly realising he was drawing her out.

"Do you good to stay a while…go fishing," he said temptingly.

Suspicion wormed into her mind. "Why should you invite me to stay? You didn't want me here before… before…"

"Before I found out that you weren't what you seemed to be? No…you're quite right. I would've shot you out of here as fast as possible." He sighed and his voice took on a soft lilt of self-mockery. "Maybe I want to make amends…maybe I feel a kind of responsibility…I don't know. I guess I'd like to make sure you're all right."

"I'll be all right," she muttered, rejecting his interest in her. That could only develop into complications she did not need. All the same, it was a tempting idea, to stay here, go fishing, postpone the moment of stress, the tears and argument which were inevitable...a temporary escape, not long, just long enough to build up some strength of purpose so she could cope. "Do you think..." she hesitated, torn between caution and temptation.

"Do I think what?" he prompted.

"Could we...if I stayed here tomorrow...could we remain strangers? I mean...just being here...no questions asked," she finished limply, hoping he would humour her but expecting him to laugh at her unease.

His silence made her feel like a silly child.

"Oh, forget it! I'll go," she said decisively.

"No. I want you to stay. And you want to leave it all behind you for a while. I'll play along with that. After all, I come here for the same reason," he said slowly.

"That's...that's kind of you."

He gave a short laugh, a slightly derisive sound. "Perhaps it's easy to be kind to a stranger," he mused. "Are you feeling cold over there?"

"Not really."

"I thought you shivered just then."

"I'm not used to sleeping in the nude."

He rolled on to his side and scooped her back against him, curving her body to his. One hand cupped a breast familiarly as his mouth grazed over her ear. "Relax now and go to sleep. I'll keep you warm."

Warmth flooded through her but she was far too aware of his masculinity to relax and go to sleep. He did. She heard his breathing grow lighter and his hand slackened its hold. She lay snuggled against him, marvelling at the comfort another body could give. Eventually sheer weariness took its toll and she drifted into sleep.

She woke suddenly, aware of a tingling caress on her cheek. Her eyes widened in shock at the strange face above her. It spoke and memory surged back in a hot flood of embarrassment.

"Perfect skin. You really are a very beautiful woman, even in the morning. I doubt that I've ever seen such true blonde hair, except on a child . . ."

Child! Had he recognised her? Her fingers flew in agitation to her hair. Last night it had been wet, uncombed. It was a relief to feel the loose curls. Without the careful blow-waving which smoothed a frame for her face, she was not instantly recognisable as Eve Childe.

"Classic cheekbones, perfect features, and those sea-green eyes. Enough to steal a man's soul. Maybe I did catch a mermaid last night."

The possessive note in his voice brought a sharp awareness of her vulnerability. Fear jabbed at her mind. She had been crazy last night, completely reckless to have put herself in the power of a stranger. So very intimately. She knew nothing of him. Nothing at all. Except that he was a good lover. Fear cut deeper. Did he now expect a repeat performance? She clutched at the bed-clothes, pulling them up around her chin. Her eyes darted around the room even while common sense told her there was no immediate escape from him.

"What . . . what time is it?" she asked, swallowing
hard to combat a very dry throat.

"Almost lunch-time." Amusement gleamed in his
eyes. "And I'm not the big, bad wolf come to gobble
you up. In fact, you could call me quite house-trained.
I even found your clothes on the beach and washed
them for you." He nodded towards the end of the bed.
"Look for yourself."

The silk culottes she had discarded last night were
neatly folded.

"Not very practical for going fishing," he added
drily.

Going fishing! Eve choked back a hysterical little
laugh. She really had been out of her mind to even
contemplate such irresponsible behaviour. "Thank
you, but I really must go," she said quickly. "My
mother will be worrying where I am."

"I doubt it."

Eve's breath caught in her throat as wariness jan-
gled into alarm. What did he mean? Her eyes flickered nervously over the strong physique. His jeans and
Tee-shirt emphasised the broad chest and muscular
limbs. This was a lonely, out-of-the-way place and if
he wanted to keep her here . . .

"My mother will be worried. If I'm not home this
morning she might call the police."

He shrugged and stood up, eyeing her with lazy
mockery. "Why should she worry? Weren't you with
your fiancé last night? She'll draw the natural conclusion and not be overly concerned. After all, you're
getting married next week."

"I'm not . . ." Eve began in a fluster.

"We know that, but she doesn't. Why be in a hurry
to tell her? Indulge yourself. You had a shock last

night and it won't hurt anyone if you take a day off. Besides, you need the time to take stock of where you're going from here," he said matter-of-factly. "I'll go clean the fish for lunch. There's an outhouse beyond the laundry. Get dressed and take a stroll. No rush."

She watched him cross the room to the door on to the verandah. His calm, unhurried air did much to soothe her nerves. He did not seem to pose any threat to her. She remembered their conversation last night after...her hand slid across her stomach and her thighs quivered as physical memories tingled around her veins. A warm glow suffused her body. Crazy it might have been, but she did not regret last night's madness. Not yet, anyway.

It took a concentrated effort to shrug off the languor which tempted her to lie there. She forced herself out of bed. Her eyes skated around the room. It was certainly spartan in its furnishings. The floor was cobble-stoned and the only real concession to civilisation was the gas-stove and the insect-screens on the windows. Her gaze dropped to the silk culottes at the end of the bed. She eyed them with distaste. Simon had chosen them, insisting that they showed off her cute behind. Grimacing at the thoughts which that conjured up, Eve snatched them up and pulled them on. They were hopelessly creased. She wished there was something else she could wear. With a sigh of irritation she did up the zip and fastened the halter collar at the back of her neck.

Now was the time to leave. The man was out of the way. The sensible thing to do was walk out the front door, return to her car and drive back to Sydney. To stay was to risk...She opened the front-door and a light sea-breeze wafted over her skin. Her eyes drank in the glittering blue of sunlight on water, white, white sand, a cloudless sky, marked only by swooping seagulls. She breathed deeply, savouring the salty smell. It was the smell of freedom from all the shackles of society. What would she risk by staying here? Just for a day. One lost day could not hurt.

The man did not know her. He seemed friendly and reasonable. In all honesty she could not say that he had pressed himself upon her last night and his concern over her virginity suggested a man of sensitivity. Surely such a person could not represent any danger. And she would enjoy going fishing.

Her gaze followed the dirt track back to her car, still parked on the beach verge. Last night she had not even considered that the road might lead to a house, but last night her mind had been too distracted for clear thinking. Even now it shrank from the prospect of dealing with explanations and argument. She did not want to face up to the repercussions of the inevitable split with Simon. Not yet. Not when she could stay here for a while.

She walked outside and surveyed the house with curiosity. The log cabin fitted so snugly into the grove of trees that it looked to be part of the landscape. At one side were two large water tanks, partially camouflaged by native shrubs. She strolled around the back and spotted the small outhouse. It provided a decidedly primitive sanitary arrangement. Eve mused that civilisation did have its advantages, particularly in the plumbing department.

She hesitated over her return to the house, the impulse to stay becoming undermined by the necessity of confronting the man again. It was difficult to ignore the fact that she had slept with him. Her empty stomach growled its demand for food and the smell of cooking fish added its persuasion. The door leading on to the back verandah stood open. She approached it with caution, treading lightly so as to make no sound. There was still time to change her mind and go.

The man was standing at the gas-stove, watching a sizzling pan of fish. Again Eve was struck by his strong masculinity. He had none of Simon's litheness, the quick grace of movement which she had thought of as refined elegance. Even in casual clothes Simon had had style, not that he would ever have worn old workman-like jeans. The man across the room looked at home in them. It occurred to Eve that he would look at home in anything because it was not the clothes which drew the eye, but the man himself. He carried an air of self-assurance which suggested he could handle anything that came his way. He was the sort of man one would choose to have as a companion on a deserted island.

A smile twitched at Eve's lips. For all intents and purposes this was a deserted island, and he was obviously cooking fish he had caught. His head suddenly turned. Dark, piercing eyes scanned her quickly and caught the trace of a smile on her lips. The hard face relaxed. His smile was rich with satisfaction. Eve's heart thumped a warning but the reckless mood of last night had taken hold again.

"Smells great."

His smile widened into a grin. "Nothing like fresh fish."

"I'll just wash my hands," she said, nodding towards the all-purpose laundry.

"Don't be long. These are ready to eat."

"I'll be right back."

It was not until water was splashing over her hands that Eve realised her own facial muscles were stretched into a grin. It surprised her. Yet on second thoughts, it was not surprising. She had thrown her cap over the windmill with a vengeance and the resulting light-headedness was having its effect. Today she was going to enjoy herself and the rest of the world could revolve without her. It would catch her up eventually. That was unavoidable. But not today. A printed sign flashed into her mind. GONE FISHING. She laughed as she dried her hands. She was ready for breakfast, lunch . . . anything.

CHAPTER THREE

THE fish was delicious; tender, full of flavour, cooked to perfection. Eve ate with relish and poked at the bones for the last shreds.

"Want some more?"

She looked up at the man sitting opposite her. His eyes were crinkled in amusement. They were attractive eyes, dark, intelligent and very expressive.

"No. I'm just being greedy." She put down her knife and fork and sighed with satisfaction. "I can't remember the last time I ate so much for breakfast."

"You had a very empty stomach."

The wooden chair creaked as she leant back against it. It did not alarm her. The chair was strong and solid, like the rough-hewn table and the rough-hewn man. She observed him curiously as he lit a cigarette.

"Do you smoke much?"

He threw her a careless look. "Do you object?"

She shrugged. "I'm hardly in a position to object. It's your home."

He exhaled the smoke slowly. Then his mouth curved into a dry little smile. "So it is. I enjoy a cigarette after meals but no, I don't smoke much. Do you?" He nodded an invitation to the packet.

She shook her head.

"What would you like to do this afternoon?"

The question surprised her. "Aren't we going fishing?"

"Tide's wrong. We'll try later on."

His matter-of-fact tone dispelled the prickle of unease. Her gaze was drawn to the window, to the age-old appeal of sand and sea. "I'd like to walk along the beach. Are there any shells?"

"Some."

"I used to collect shells. I had a whole shelf of them."

"Don't you still have them?"

She turned back to him with a wistful smile. "No. When my father died we sold up and moved into the city. Mum insisted it was time I left childish things behind. And the apartment was too small for a lot of clutter. I missed them though. I always liked the sound of the sea and I could hear it in the shells."

"Then maybe you should start another collection." He stood and picked up their plates. "I'll go wash these and we'll be on our way."

Eve rose quickly to her feet. "I'll do them. You cooked. Just tell me where to put the bones."

He did not relinquish the plates but stood there looking her up and down in a slow, measuring way. Eve blushed, all too conscious of how well he knew her body.

"I could lend you a Tee-shirt if you want to save those clothes for later."

"Thank you." It was an embarrassed whisper and she forced more volume into her voice. "You're very kind."

His lips quirked sardonically. "It'll hardly be high fashion but a belt might help. You'll find them in the chest of drawers near the bed."

His crack about high fashion made her look sharply after him as he strode out on to the verandah. The suspicion that he knew her identity crawled uncomfortably around her mind. Uncertainty made her nervous and she stood there, her fingers absently pleating the silk of her culottes. The texture of the material gradually impressed itself on her mind and she remembered that he had washed them. He would have seen the designer label. Surely that had prompted his remark. Relief washed through her. She hurried to the chest of drawers, found a Tee-shirt and quickly discarded high fashion for casual sloppiness.

Laughter gurgled up in her throat as she took stock of her appearance. The sleeves began just above her elbows and flapped above her wrists. The crew-neck hung loosely around her shoulders and the hem drooped unevenly around her thighs. The soft cotton clung to her breasts, but barely touched her anywhere else. She found a belt and gathered in a waist, making a most inelegant mini-dress.

"Ready?"

He was leaning against the door-jamb, amusement written all over his face. Eve knew she looked ridiculous but she did not care. Today it did not matter how she looked. Today Eve Childe did not exist. In her place was a carefree woman. Carefree for a little while, anyway. She almost skipped over to the front door and flung it open in her eagerness.

"Let's go," she called to him, a lilt of childish excitement in her voice.

They walked along the beach. Seagulls swooped overhead, the only other living creatures in sight. The breeze plastered the Tee-shirt around Eve's body and made it skirl around her thighs as she ran ahead of her companion. She was completely unaware of the sexiness of her makeshift dress. Her eyes were fixed on a large, spotted shell at the water's edge.

"It's a good one!" she shouted triumphantly, holding it aloft like a trophy. Then with a happy smile of anticipation she pressed it to her ear. The echo of the sea was distinct. Her face lit with pleasure as the familiar drone reverberated through her brain. Satisfied, she brushed the sand from her newly found treasure and polished it on her Tee-shirt.

"See! Isn't it beautiful?" she crowed in delight.

"Yes. Very beautiful."

The deep appreciation in his voice carried overtones which jolted Eve out of her reverie. She glanced up into eyes which were not fastened on the shell in her hand. For a long moment their gaze locked and Eve's pulse beat louder than the drum-roll of the sea. He did not touch her, yet she could feel his touch. Her skin crawled with sensitivity and an aching weakness invaded her thighs. Her chest felt constricted and only when it became painful did she realise she was holding her breath. She expelled it quickly and forced herself to turn away from him, taking a few jerky steps before darting a glance back at him.

"Please don't," she begged.

"Don't what?"

He had not moved but the dark eyes threw out a challenge which had to be answered.

"Last night..." She took a deep breath to steady her voice. "Last night—I don't regret it but it would be wrong to repeat it."

"Why?"

Even his stance was a challenge. He was not threatening her but he was so very much a man, and his eyes told her she was very much a woman, and they were here alone, together, and he knew she would respond to him.

"I don't love you," Eve explained, a note of fear in her voice as she fought his strong attraction.

"That didn't worry you last night," he reminded her with relentless logic.

Her hands fluttered helplessly. "I don't...I'm not..."

"Not in the habit of making love with strangers?" he finished for her. "No one knows that better than I. But it was good, wasn't it?"

The soft words were seductive. Eve's body shivered, a traitor to her will. "Yes, it was good," she admitted reluctantly, "but you're a real person now and I don't love you."

He frowned. "A real person?"

"Don't you see?" she rushed in anxiously. "It was like a fantasy, an answer to a need."

For what seemed an eternity his eyes burned into hers, demanding that she recall the intense reality of their bodies joined in intimacy. At last he turned his gaze out to sea, releasing Eve from the tension of conflict.

"A fantasy!" he muttered and gave a derisive little laugh. "Funny! I've thought of myself as many things but never a fantasy." He sliced her a wry smile. "Comes with fishing a mermaid out of the sea, I guess."

The fire of desire was quenched. Eve smiled her relief. "I'm not a mermaid."

"No." His eyes gently mocked her. "You're more of a child."

The word jarred. Her smile faltered until she remembered the shell in her hand. She looked down at it and sighed. "Perhaps that's what I'd like to be today. A child with no worries."

"Then so be it."

The warm indulgence in his voice lifted Eve's heart. She threw him a grateful look and he laughed a deep, throaty chuckle.

"Perhaps innocence is bliss. Shall we paddle along? You can pass me any shells you want to keep."

It was pleasant strolling along the edge of the water. Eve stooped now and then to pick up a promising shell. None was as perfect as the first one she had found. The man had rolled up the legs of his jeans and was following her in a lazy fashion, not too close but close enough to be companionable. Occasionally he drew her attention to something; a bird, a ship on the horizon, a pair of porpoises beyond the line of breakers.

A light piece of driftwood floated in on a wave and Eve picked it up. She drew hop-scotch squares in the firm sand and tried to throw a broken shell into the top corner. It slid across the line. The man retrieved it, pushed her to one side, took careful aim and landed it dead-centre. She grinned at him.

"Don't tell me you played hopscotch as a kid."

"When my elder sister dragged me into it. She was a dreadful bully."

Eve laughed. "I can't imagine you being bullied."

He smiled a very self-assured smile. "I did get the better of her eventually."

"Strange how times change. You don't see kids playing hopscotch any more."

"They're inside watching television. The whole world watches television. It's easier than living," he remarked cynically.

"But you prefer living," she murmured, understanding now why he had failed to recognise her. Any regular viewer would have known her face.

"I prefer to make my own pleasure, yes."

And he was very good at making pleasure, Eve mused before stifling the thought. She liked his company. He was an easy man to be with but she did not want to think beyond that.

"Let's bask in the sun for a while."

He did not wait for her agreement but stretched himself full length on the warm sand above the waterline. She sat down near him, drawing her knees up and hugging them. He put his hands behind his head and closed his eyes.

"What do you do for fun and relaxation?" he asked lazily.

"I don't have much free time. I like reading."

"What?"

"Travel books mostly. You can pick them up and put them down without losing the thread of a story."

"Done any travelling?"

"No. Not yet. I will though. Have you?"

"Mmh. Too much. Too many places. Too many people."

She eyed him curiously but his lids remained shut and his face was relaxed, revealing nothing. "Is that why you've settled here?"

He did not answer immediately and Eve turned her gaze back to the endless fascination of the sea.

"I like it here," he said slowly. "It's peaceful. Natural. Unspoiled."

"Yes," she agreed dreamily. "It's like we were on an uninhabited island and civilisation is far, far away."

He gave a soft chuckle. "But you don't want us to play Adam and Eve."

She threw a wary glance at him but the gleam in his half-opened eyes was sheer devilment.

"That might invite Satan into Eden," she retorted lightly.

"Get thee behind me, Satan," he intoned, then added curiously, "Are you religious?"

"Not in any formal way, but I believe in the Christian code of behaviour."

"Do unto others as you would have done to yourself?"

"Yes. It's wrong to hurt people. To be dishonest. Lying and cheating," she added bitterly, the image of Simon rising sharply to mind.

"Forget him," came the terse order. "Tell me where you would most like to travel?"

They talked of other countries, other people, other ways of life. It was pleasant, impersonal talking, taking Eve's thoughts away from herself. The afternoon sun beat into their skin. Eventually the man beside her stirred and climbed to his feet.

"Think I'll go for a swim. Coming?"

He had stripped off his shirt before Eve found her voice. "You know I haven't a costume."

He laughed. "Neither have I, but who's to see? There's only us."

"I...I don't think so," she mumbled, averting her gaze from the hands which were unzipping his jeans.

"You're not likely to get cramp again. The water won't be so cold in the heat of the day. Besides, I'm here to look after you."

The jeans were pushed down and he stepped out of them. Her gaze was irresistibly drawn to travel up the strong, muscular legs and higher. She flushed as she met his questioning eyes.

"Does nudity bother you? It's much more pleasant to swim naked than with clothes on, you know. A child wouldn't hesitate," he added persuasively.

She privately acknowledged the truth of his argument but she was frighteningly aware of the body which had taken hers in such total possession. "I'm not a child," she muttered.

"No, you're a woman. An adult woman who shouldn't be choked up with fears and inhibitions. Why don't you let yourself feel free? It won't hurt anyone."

He turned and strode towards the water, leaving her to make her own choice. He ploughed through the first line of breakers to where the surf was deep enough for him to dive. Eve watched his dark head bob up and down and thought about what he had said. The conventions which shackled her seemed foolish and unnecessary here. The water looked inviting. The sun was hot. She wanted to swim naked and feel the wet coolness on her skin.

She pushed herself up, took off her clothes and ran into the surf, not giving herself time for second thoughts. She felt gloriously alive, her whole body tingling with sensuous pleasure as the cold water slapped and caressed her. She let herself sink under its surface, enjoying the total submersion. A hand grabbed her arm and yanked her up.

"I'm all right," she spluttered in protest.

"Just making sure. Keep your head above the waves for my peace of mind. Okay?"

"Okay," she gave in readily, not wanting him to hover around her protectively.

He did not crowd her but stayed within easy striking distance. Eve swam, floated, wallowed in the freedom which she found so delightful. Only when her fingers started crinkling did she move back towards the beach.

"Had enough?"

"Yes. I'm turning blue."

Over-conscious of his watching eyes, Eve kept her back turned to him. Consequently she did not see the wave which bowled her off her feet and churned her around. Strong arms lifted her up and held her steady while she coughed out the water she had swallowed.

"You got well and truly dumped. Didn't you see it coming?"

"No. I wasn't looking," she gasped out between coughs.

"Need the kiss of life again?" he teased.

She threw him a look of reproof and having looked at him she could not tear her eyes away. The sheer vitality of the man held her captive. He was so big, so strong, so dominatingly male. Beads of water shivered on the powerful chest as it breathed in and out. Her mesmerised gaze lifted slowly to the mouth which knew how to kiss. She saw his smile die and a long breath whistled out from the barely parted lips. The hands which had steadied her took a more possessive hold.

He stepped towards her, closing the small gap between them so that the tips of her breasts pressed lightly against his deeply tanned skin. The contact was like an electric shock. Eve jerked away. Her hands lifted and pushed against his chest to prevent a repe-

tition, but his hands had also moved, sliding down
from her shoulders, down the curve of her spine and
closing over the roundness of her hips. He thrust her
lower body against his and the potent force of his desire defeated any defence she might have managed.

Her body had a will of its own and it responded instinctively, exulting in the excitement of sexual
arousal. Dazed by the strength of her own desire she
looked up at the face above hers as if searching for an
explanation, something which might justify this tu-
mult of feeling inside her. She knew so little of the
man and yet he could awaken her most primitive instincts so that they clamoured to be satisfied.

His eyes demanded that she yield to him. They
blazed with the exultant light of the victor on the edge
of victory. They conceded nothing and Eve felt what
little will she had to resist drain away. She wanted him
to take her and as if he perceived that mental surrender, his mouth came down and claimed hers.

Eve's hands slid up around his neck. Her fingers
thrust into the wet thickness of his hair, blindly urging on the passion which was leaping through her
veins. His mouth devoured hers in an invasion which
had her senses reeling. A wave crashed against them,
forcibly ending the kiss. Churning water sucked at her
legs. She was lifted and held tightly against his chest
as he took her beyond the breaking surf to the calm
swell of deep water.

It lapped around her breasts as he kissed her again,
and she clung to him as he swept her with him into a
whirlpool of sensuality. Then he was lifting her higher,
arching her back so that his mouth could trail down
her throat to her breasts. He licked the salt water from
her nipples and so distracting was the fierce wave of

pleasure that she was barely aware of the hand parting her legs, pushing them to either side of him where
they drifted, weightless, and the firm muscles of his
stomach felt good against her softness.

Slowly, slowly he guided her down until she felt
hard flesh probing upwards. She cried out as he entered her but the penetration was swift and his mouth
was on hers again, his hands moulding her body to his,
and the sheer eroticism of that movement inside her
stilled any thought of protest.

Eve was unaware of the sea, the sky, the birds which
wheeled around them. Her whole being was concentrated on an inner world which suddenly exploded like
a volcano of molten lava, and the blissful warmth of
it pervaded her whole body, melting her bones with its
exquisite pleasure. She wound her arms around the
body which supported her. Its strength was hers. They
were one being and there was a wonderful sense of
peace in their union. For a long time they stayed together, wrapped in their shared warmth, moving only
with the gentle roll of the waves.

"Stay with me."

The husky whisper slid into her haze of contentment. Lips brushed against her ear, making it tingle
with awareness.

"Forget the whole damned world. Let there only be
us."

He lifted her face to his and kissed her, a long,
drugging kiss of sweet persuasion. Eve wanted it to go
on and on, blotting out reality, but even as she responded to the spell he was casting, Eve knew it had
to end.

She had stepped too far out of her normal existence as it was. This wild, abandoned loving was to-

tally foreign to her cautious nature yet she could find no shadow of regret in her heart for anything that had happened. She had wanted to shed all responsibility, be a free spirit following impulse and instinct without reason, without care. But to stay with this man would be like trying to prolong a dream. It could not last forever. Sooner or later reality would intrude, the dream would crumble.

"I have to go back."

It was a mournful whisper and his arms tightened around her, pressing his claim. "Let it go," he urged. "This is more real than anything you'll find back there."

She sighed and laid her head on his shoulder. The temptation was great. Yet she had her career and time was a model's worst enemy. She had to go back. Her gaze swept slowly around the cove and came to rest on the small log-cabin. It had been a resting-place. The man had salved her emotional wounds and shown her what it was to be a woman, but this was lotus-land. It was time to leave.

She reached up and kissed him, a soft kiss of gratitude, a kiss meaning goodbye. "Thank you, but I can't stay. I have obligations, people to be seen, and my life to sort out. You've been very kind, and understanding. I appreciate, very much, all that you've shared with me. I'll never forget it."

She was withdrawing from him and he knew it. The sense of finality in her words was unmistakable. For a moment she thought he was not going to accept her decision. His hands cupped her face and his eyes burnt into hers, demanding recognition of what they had just experienced together.

"You must go?" It was more a challenge than a question, denying that her departure was necessary. She had a choice.

Eve was sorely tempted but the very strength of his attraction struck panic in her heart. She had already succumbed to him twice. To stay was to throw aside her whole upbringing, all the threads which had been the fabric of her life. And where would it lead? What would become of her? It was a gamble she could not take, yet the thought of leaving was suddenly very painful.

"I have to," she cried, and it was a plea against the sense of loss which sharpened even as she spoke.

The dark brilliance of his eyes clouded. He slowly released her from their intimate contact and a helpless kind of despair clutched at her as his withdrawal cemented her decision.

"I'm sorry."

"Don't be sorry. You're free to go. You were always free to go," he stated in a calm, expressionless voice.

"Yes I know. But I..."

His hand lifted and soft fingers brushed across her lips, silencing her. He shrugged off the hard, impassive mask which had shuttered his thoughts and a smile lightened his face.

"It was beautiful while it lasted. Don't be sorry. Do you want to go now?"

She nodded. He was making it easy for her, just as he had made the whole afternoon easy, letting her do as she liked. Having made the decision it was better that she go quickly, yet she could not force her legs to move. She was suddenly and poignantly aware of having destroyed something precious, something of great value which she might never find again.

He took her hand and pulled her with him, helping her through the roughness of the surf to shallow water. "You won't mind if I don't come up to the cabin with you?" he said casually. "I'll go along the beach and pick up my clothes."

"I...all right," she agreed awkwardly and watched him stride away from her.

The separation was complete. Eve trudged up the sand, agonising over her decision with every step. She had come to this beach to escape, and she had. Only somehow the escape had gone too far, becoming an entity of itself which had irrevocably changed her life. Now as she walked to the cabin she felt dislocated, caught between two different worlds, belonging to neither. Yet the heavier weight of years and custom had demanded her return to what she knew.

The cabin seemed very empty without the man to dominate its space. It really was a comfortless place, bare and primitive, a stark contrast to the luxury of home. She hurried over to the bed. It took only a minute to don the silk culottes. Her gaze lingered briefly on the rumpled pillows, remembering how he had cradled her into sleep last night. Again she felt the wrench of parting. Tears pricked at her eyes and she moved blindly to the door, shutting the memory quickly behind her. She took a deep, steadying breath and set off down the track.

He was standing by the car, the Tee-shirts slung across one shoulder, the powerful chest still bare, his jeans clinging damply to the strong, muscular thighs. His eyes held a wry gleam as they looked her up and down, but he smiled as he lifted a hand towards her.

"Your shell. I thought you might like to keep it."

She took it and a huge lump rose in her throat as she fingered its perfection. "Thank you," she choked out huskily.

"Eve, if you want to come back..."

The use of her name stilled her heart in mid-beat. Shock deafened her ears to what he was saying.

"You called me Eve!"

The strangled accusation brought no denial. He frowned in irritation but there was no puzzlement over her words.

"You know who I am!" she cried in hurt protest at his knowledge.

"So? What does it matter?" he said carelessly, as if the whole point was irrelevant.

But it did matter. She had not been a stranger to him, not just a girl who had happened along. He had known she was Eve Childe.

"When did you recognise me?"

He shrugged. "Sometime last night while we were sitting at the table. You do have a well-publicised face, you know," he added with a touch of irony.

Last night. Before he had made love to her. It was like a punch in the stomach. Her memory darted back over the sequence of events. He had been almost brutal to her after he had fished her from the sea, not one kind word or action. It wasn't until just before they went to bed that his manner had changed. She felt sick. All the loving and kindness had been for Eve Childe. She had wallowed in a fool's paradise while he had amused himself with her.

"Just what did you hope to gain by this?" she demanded bitterly, her eyes blazing with scorn.

"Gain?"

The surprise in his voice grated over the rawness of her humiliation.

"Oh, don't pretend you didn't expect to gain something! It's been a great game, hasn't it? Feeding me enough rope to hang myself?"

He frowned and his feigned puzzlement incensed her even further.

"You couldn't climb into bed fast enough, could you? Not when you realised who I was. It didn't matter a damn that I was too worn out emotionally to care what happened to me. That only made me an easier mark. Did it boost your ego to know you were making it with Eve Childe? Or were you already thinking of how you could work the situation to your advantage? No doubt you thought I'd be a good meal-ticket for you to latch on to. Or failing that, you could set up a red-hot story to sell."

His face had tightened and hardened during her wild tirade. He waited for her to run out of breath then spoke with cutting coldness. "Eve Childe holds no attraction for me whatsoever. The last thing I would want or need would be a woman to support me, and I can pay my own way without stooping to selling scurrilous stories."

Eve was too worked up to heed the dangerous glint in his eyes. "Huh! I suppose you live like this out of choice!" she scoffed. An ugly laugh of self-derision grated out of her throat. "God! I must have looked like pennies from heaven to you! A lay-down gift just asking to be exploited. But let me tell you, you'll only make trouble for yourself if you take this story to a scandal rag. I'll deny it categorically and if you come after me I'll—"

He slapped her.

She stared at him, open-mouthed, her hand instinctively covering the sharp sting on her cheek.

"You blind, stupid fool!"

His biting anger frightened her more than the slap. She shrank back against the car, terrified that he meant more violence. His lip curled in derision at her fear and the dark eyes stabbed her with contempt. He waved a curt dismissal as if she was unworthy of his attention, then swung on his heel and began striding away.

"Go home, little girl!"

He had not bothered turning his head but the savage mockery in the words reached her nonetheless. Eve snapped out of her shocked daze. A turmoil of emotion churned into seething life.

"You...you bastard!" she screamed after him and hurled the shell in a frenzy of hurt and frustration.

Her aim was hopelessly astray. He kept on walking without so much as a hesitation in his gait. Recognising the futility of expending any more energy on a man who was ignoring her, Eve flounced into the driver's seat, revved up the engine with angry emphasis and spun the wheel for home.

CHAPTER FOUR

LITTLE girl indeed! She had been woman enough for him last night. And this afternoon. He had not hesitated to take full advantage of her pliancy. Fool that she had been, letting a stranger make love to her! She had recklessly disregarded all the tenets of common sense. The fantasy of freedom had beckoned and she had tested it to the full. Crazy not to realise that the dregs were bound to be bitter!

Damn the man! He had been amusing himself with her. She remembered with smarting clarity the "high-fashion" remark, and his deliberate use of the word, "child". She had been so easily deceived, a gullible dupe, wanting to believe her secret was safe. She should have guessed last night when he suddenly stopped considering her a neurotic bore and saw her as a desirable conquest.

Eve Childe! He had made love to the image, not the woman. The age-old allure of the boy-girl image, that's what Simon had fashioned. It had been a hit success; the slightly fey quality, the teasing mixture of youthful innocence and sexiness. Her long, coltish legs had always been emphasised in shorts or slacks of one kind or another, a provocative contrast to the soft femininity of her face and the hint of vulnerability in the green eyes. The image had sold well, at very high fees, but the stranger had got it very cheaply. A gift.

No wonder he had been surprised at her virginity!
No doubt he had thought that all models slept around.
It was true that propositions were commonplace in her
line of work. He was not to know that her mother and
Simon had always protected her from men like him,
men who took sex for granted.

Tears stung her eyes. She had given herself to him
so...so unreservedly. It had seemed right, unbelievably beautiful, an experience to be treasured. There
had been something idyllic about two people coming
together like that with no outside considerations in-
fluencing them, a pure attraction where names and
backgrounds didn't matter. Eve gritted her teeth to
prevent a sob emerging from the tightness in her
throat. She would not cry over him. He had deceived
her. For what purpose she did not know, could not
even guess and did not want to. She had to forget him,
put the whole incident behind her as if it had not happened. She had to get on with her real life, and to do
that she had first to get home.

She forced herself to think ahead. Her mother
would have to be placated and Eve could not tell her
the truth of her prolonged absence. Then there was
Simon. Pure hatred burned across her mind. No matter how much it might affect her career she was going
to sever all connection with Simon. Pride and self-
respect demanded that.

She concentrated on making plans for the future
and gradually the long drive soothed her ragged
nerves. It was almost dark when Eve finally garaged
her car underneath the apartment building. Her tired
gaze noted Simon's Volvo in the visitors' bay. She felt
physically and emotionally exhausted and the thought

of confronting Simon right now triggered a dangerous mood of angry rebellion.

She pushed herself out of the car, locked it, then
strode towards the lifts, eyeing the Volvo balefully as
she passed it by. She wondered how long it had been
there and what Simon had told her mother. Certainly
not the truth. The truth would be far too unpalatable
for Marion Childe's digestion, despite her cast-iron
constitution. A lot of things could be stomached along
the road to success, but there was a limit to what one
could swallow. Marion Childe had deliberately encouraged Simon's interest in Eve but even she would
see that marriage was out of the question.

Eve summoned a lift and stepped inside, automatically pressing the button for her floor. It suddenly
struck her that she had been thinking of Simon without pain, with disgust and contempt, but without even
a twinge of the pain she had felt last night. She was
surprisingly calm, almost as if the ugly scene in Simon's apartment had happened years and years ago,
to someone else. The floor bumped to a standstill. The
doors opened. Eve gave herself a mental shake and
walked out. Her apartment key had barely touched the
lock when the door was flung open.

"Eve!" Marion Childe gathered her daughter in.
"You're home, thank God! I've been at my wits' end
worrying what to do." The flood of anxiety was
abruptly interrupted by a critical frown. "And look at
your lovely clothes! What on earth have you been doing all this time?"

Eve made no immediate reply. Simon was coming
forward, a mute appeal in the vivid blue eyes. She
found herself observing him in a curiously detached
way. It was the same Simon she had fancied herself in

love with; the same golden tan skin, streaked blond hair and blue, blue eyes; the same handsome face and lithe body, elegantly clothed as always, yet he had lost all his attraction. In fact she found his dress rather effete, too consciously perfect, as if too concerned with projecting an image. Of course! Simon dealt in images. Specialised in false images. Just as their oh-so-romantic love had been false.

"Eve."

She recoiled from his outstretched hands. He smoothly waved them in a placating gesture.

"You shouldn't have rushed away like that," he began softly, indulgently, as if she was a child who had acted without thinking.

Eve bridled at the tone even while recognising it as a tone which Simon and her mother had often used when she was being difficult. And she had all too frequently given in to it, accepting that they were older and wiser than she. Not any more would she give in to them. Eve gritted her teeth and turned to her mother.

"I'm sorry, Mum. I should have called and told you I was all right. It was selfish of me but I needed time alone to think." Her voice sounded cool and calm, so self-assured that Eve was amazed at herself. Had the last twenty-four hours wrought so much change in her?

Marion Childe showed her surprise at the unexpected command in her daughter's manner. "Well, so long as you're safe and sound. But your clothes, dear, you've ruined them. They'll never be the same—"

"Is that all you can think about, Mum? My clothes!" Eve flared, and all the bottled-up resentment of years came seething out. "All my life it's been clothes, clothes, clothes! Don't play, Eve. You'll get your dress dirty. Sit up straight, Eve. Your skirt will crease if you slouch. What am I? A doll or your daughter? Did you ever consider that a person lived inside the clothes you dressed me in? Did you, Mum? Do you even care what I'm feeling now, or is a pair of silk culottes more important to you?''

"Eve!" The shock on her face was countered by the reprimand in her voice. "Of course I'm concerned about you. It's just that your clothes cost so much. You know that!''

"Yes, I know," Eve sighed, knowing full well that her outburst had been futile.

Appearances would always be of first importance to Marion Childe. However much anxiety she had suffered today, it had not stopped her from being immaculately dressed. The tailored pantsuit was not the least bit crumpled. Her long, ash-blonde hair was smoothly groomed into a French roll. An artful makeup hid the few wrinkles which aged the lovely face. For the first time in her life Eve felt sorry for her mother. Marion Childe would never know the heady delight of freedom from all social restraints.

"Well, I won't be wearing these culottes again, Mum, so you'll have to write them off as a dead loss," she added decisively, determined now to cast off the habit of following her mother's dictates. She was a person in her own right, and no longer a little girl to be told what to do. Certainly not a little girl!

She turned a cool face to Simon who had backed off from the line of fire. "I wasn't expecting to find you here. Since you are, we might as well use the opportunity to settle everything right now."

"Eve, now don't be too hasty," her mother warned. "Simon has been very distressed about last night's argument and I'm sure..."

"Argument, Simon?"

The green eyes mocked his evasion. An unbecoming flush spread up his neck, making him look surprisingly callow.

"Eve, I swear to you that if you'll let me explain..."

"No explanation is necessary. Our relationship is finished, Simon. Permanently."

His expression hardened as his self-interest was threatened. "You need me, Eve. Without me—"

"Like hell I need you!" she retorted scornfully.

"Eve! For goodness sake, will you listen to reason?" her mother demanded.

Eve turned on her. "No! I won't listen to any damned reason for continuing with him." She stalked away from them, impatient with the whole scene. The seeds of rebellion had been sown on a beach a long way from here but their growth was rapid in the cloying atmosphere in this room. She seated herself carelessly on one of the lounge-chairs in the living-room and faced them with an air of complete self-possession.

There was a short, fraught silence while her mother took stock of the defiant determination Eve had shown. She glanced worriedly at Simon then pasted a conciliatory smile on her mouth.

"Eve dear, you're obviously overwrought..."

"On the contrary, I am perfectly clear-headed. In fact, I doubt that I've ever seen things so clearly. If you'd like to sit down, Mum, I'll tell you what I have in mind."

The smile shrivelled. Marion Childe sighed and fluttered an apologetic gesture at Simon. Eve resented the apology but made no comment.

"I'll make some coffee," her mother said, clearly playing for time. "Would you like something to eat, dear?"

"No thanks, and I don't want coffee. I'm tired and I'd much prefer Simon to leave. Right now."

"Now look here, Eve—" Simon began as he stepped forward aggressively.

"I looked, Simon, and I finally saw a great deal," Eve whipped back at him. "I don't owe you a damned thing!"

"I made you."

"Into what you wanted. Am I supposed to be grateful for that? So the image was successful. You made as much out of that as I did. As of now the partnership is dissolved. Come Monday I'll be giving my name to the top agents in town and I'll take my luck with them."

"Eve, that's not fair," her mother protested. "Simon has—"

"Mum." Eve's eyes flashed a warning. "I'm through with being pushed, your way or his. I'm twenty-two years old. I have a mind of my own and I intend to do what I want. I appreciate the fact that you've both worked hard at turning me into a success, but it wasn't so much for me as for yourselves. You wanted the success, much more than I did."

Her mother looked at her as if her daughter had turned into a stranger. She shook her head and sank into the nearest chair. "I don't understand what's happened to you, Eve. Why are you acting like this?

I'm your mother and I've only ever done what's best for you."

"I know you think that, Mum," Eve said more softly, but the truth had to be said. "The problem is that what you think is best for me is not what I think. It's time you stopped living through me. I have to live my own life. I'm not your little girl, Mum. I'm a woman."

For one sharp moment her mind flashed to another place, sand and sea and a hard, demanding man who had known her as a woman. It took a concentrated effort to push the memory away.

"A woman!" Simon burst out angrily. "You've no more sense than a baby! You're not seeing anything clearly at all. Your ego's had a knock and you're suffering from a swelled head, thinking you can launch out on your own. It's my photographs that've made you. Do you think any tin-pot photographer can capture the same effect?"

"We'll see, won't we?" Eve replied silkily, not rising to his taunt.

The handsome face twisted with disgust. "God! If you weren't such a stupid innocent you'd see which side your bread was buttered on. Together we can go right to the top and I don't mean here. New York...London...Paris."

"No!" The green eyes filled with contempt. "I'm not so innocent, Simon, thanks to you. And it so happens I prefer margarine to the butter you're offering. Go find yourself another girl to mould into what you want. I'm not available, not even for the promise of New York, London or Paris."

"You're cutting off your nose to spite your face," he hurled at her in exasperation.

"It's my face," she stated coldly.

Her stubbornness made him bare his teeth in frustration. "You'll come crawling back to me when you find yourself a flop."

"Don't count on it."

"It's not good practice to burn your bridges before you cross them, Eve," he said tightly. "I can see there's no talking sense to you now. Try a little fling on your own. See how far you get without me." He strode to the door, then turned to her with a sour smile. "I'll even forgive your ingratitude when you finally admit you're wrong."

Eve disdained to make any reply to his exit line. She could only feel relief at his departure.

"He's right, Eve," Marion Childe said reproachfully. "You just don't realise..."

"Don't I, Mum?" She turned soul-weary eyes to her mother. "Then I'll have to find that out for myself."

Her mother held out placating hands. "Eve, let's talk about it."

"No." Eve knew that tone from old. It meant Mother knows best. She pushed herself to her feet. "I've said it all, Mum, and I meant every word. I'm going to have a long bath. Later, if you want to talk about us, we'll talk. But not about Simon."

As she lay soaking in a tub of warm water, memories of other water seeped into her mind and for a little while she gave them full flood. It was easy to rationalise the foolishness of her first surrender to the man's love-making. She had been off-balance, too emotionally disturbed to counter his physical persuasion. But she did not understand what had driven her into that second wild passion. Time, place, circumstances; she simply did not know.

It was fortunate that she had decided to leave before she had irrevocably placed herself in the man's power. He had deliberately deceived her and whatever motive he had nursed in keeping back his knowledge of her identity, one thing was certain. He could not have been trusted any more. Grimly Eve wondered if any man could be trusted.

She heaved herself out of the bath and slowly dried herself. Her body reacted sharply to touch and Eve wondered how long it would take to forget the physical magic it had been taught. At least there was no risk of her becoming pregnant from this mad escapade. Her preparation for marriage provided an inbuilt safeguard from her folly.

Her mouth thinned as she thought of Simon. Never would she crawl back to him, not in a million years. She put on a house-robe and walked out to the kitchen, hungry now, and ready to do battle with her mother if necessary. She wanted to be friends with her but she would not accept domination.

Marion Childe began by treating her daughter as an invalid, someone who needed to be cosseted and indulged. Eve was wryly amused by the tactic. She did not fight it. Only time would make her determination clear and eventually her mother would have to come to terms with an adult daughter. Marion Childe's ambitions had to be steered away from Eve and on to herself. She was a very good-looking woman and still young enough to do something constructive with her life. It had been blindly obsessive to channel all her energy into pushing Eve forward. Now that the first step of independence had been taken, there was no need for Eve to give more hurt by rushing too far too soon.

On Monday Eve cancelled all the wedding arrangements, then took portfolios of photographs to the top modelling agencies in Sydney. Their enthusiasm over adding her name to their lists was slightly dimmed by Eve's insistence that she would not work with Simon Trevaire. She remained adamant against reasoning even though she knew the arguments were valid. Her name had been linked with Simon's from the outset of her career. They had been a team, Eve Childe and Simon Trevaire. The agents were doubtful of selling her name without the photographer who had given it its individuality, and even more doubtful when Eve told them she did not particularly want to continue with the image Simon had created for her.

In the frustrating weeks which followed, Eve found that their doubts were justified. The offers came, but always with the proviso that Simon be behind the camera. She turned them down flat. She was warned that she was committing career suicide and Eve began to despair that she could make it on her own. She found no sympathy at home.

"Headstrong foolishness!" her mother ranted, having decided that Eve was not an invalid after all.

Marion Childe was equally headstrong, determined to steer her daughter back on to the course which she had set from the time Eve was a teenager. It was she who had sought out Simon Trevaire and virtually presented him with Eve, and while she now deplored his duplicity, she was still prepared to insist that Eve work with him. Eve ignored her mother's nagging but she felt very much alone as each fruitless day passed.

And rising in ever stronger waves from her subconscious, came the wish that she had not returned to this life at all. That one stolen day retained its spell despite how many times Eve reminded herself of its sour ending. The man could not be forgotten and her memory of their brief relationship always brought with it a deep, uncontrollable yearning. She had not felt alone with him. He had known her on a level which no one else had ever shared. If only it was possible to go back. But it wouldn't be the same—couldn't be—not after the way it had ended. Yet sometimes the call of sand and sea... and the man, was so strong it squeezed her heart unbearably.

There seemed no way to counter it. She told herself she was indulging in fantasy. Even if he had spoken the truth and there had been no crass ulterior motives in his action. Even if she crawled back and apologised and they could recapture their feeling for each other... and if all those ifs were fulfilled, there was still no real future with him.

He had not offered a future. Just—stay with me. And what had that meant? How long could one live an aimless existence, drifting around a beach, fishing, making love? Making love. She had to wrench her mind away from the seductive memories and transplant them with practicalities. One could not ignore the facts of life. Somewhere in her future she wanted marriage, children, and in the meantime she had to find work and make a living. Only there was no joy in the facts of life. Not like on the beach with the man.

There was certainly no joy from the modelling agencies either. Her career was fast becoming a non-event. When one of them finally called with a glimmer of hope she was ready to accept anything. It was not a firm offer. The Lamarr Corporation had only requested an interview with her but the request at least showed interest. An appointment was quickly arranged and Eve felt a prickle of excitement.

The Lamarr Corporation was the most prestigious cosmetics firm in Australia. As long as Eve could remember their products had been promoted by international stars, actresses and top-name models from the United States, Britain or Europe. If this interview meant they were considering Eve as the next Lamarr girl, it was the opportunity of a life-time. If they chose her there would be no lack of offers in the future. Her name would be well and truly made, not only here but on the international market.

Eve did not tell her mother about the appointment. If the interview was successful it would be soon enough to share the news. Then Marion Childe would have to eat all the negative words she had thrown at her daughter. Eve hid her excitement but her resolve to keep the interview a secret crumbled on the night before the appointment.

Simon Trevaire came to visit. It was immediately apparent to Eve that her mother had invited him. She faced them both with seething resentment as they hammered facts at her, demanding that she bend to reason.

"Be sensible, Eve. Publicity is everything in this game," Simon insisted ruthlessly. "Unless your face is seen continually you'll lose your buyer appeal. Put aside the personal element and work with me on a strictly business basis. You're losing more than I am, you know. My work's always in demand."

"He's right, dear. You've been stubborn long enough," her mother backed up predictably.

Eve retaliated with the only weapon in her armoury. "Is that so? Well it might interest you to know that I have an interview with the Lamarr people tomorrow. And that, I might add, promises to do more for me than you ever did, Simon."

"An interview is not a contract," he scoffed.

Nevertheless his certainty in her need for him was shaken and Eve pressed her advantage. "But you don't know that, do you, Simon? I'll take my chances with them, thanks very much."

He sent her a malevolent look as he stood to go. "I won't come again, Eve."

"I didn't ask you to come at all," she replied pointedly.

Marion Childe saw him to the door and they stood muttering their mutual exasperation for a minute or two. As soon as Simon had left her mother turned on Eve accusingly.

"Why didn't you tell me?"

"Why didn't you ask me if I wanted to see Simon?"

"Someone had to take a hand in getting you back together," she explained curtly.

"I don't want your hand directing my affairs, Mum."

"You're letting it all go down the drain with your stupid wilfulness."

"I don't care if it does. I won't go back to Simon."

But she did care. She desperately wanted a chance to prove she could make it on her own. After all, she was not trained for any other work and the future was beginning to look very uncertain.

The same sense of desperation dragged her feet as she walked up the wide terrazzo steps to the Lamarr building the next morning. They had to like her. Her gaze lifted to the gold emblem on the large glass doors. If this prestigious firm decided to use her then the fear which had begun worming around her heart could be banished. Eve pushed one of the doors open and walked into the coolness of marble, a high vaulted ceiling and cascading water. The fountain was a statement of pure luxury and that was the hallmark of Lamarr products. They were luxury items, outrageously expensive but in a quality class of their own.

Eve glanced nervously at her watch. Still ten minutes before her appointment. She checked her appearance in the mirrored wall behind the fountain. The soft green of the silk suit emphasised the colour of her eyes and the hairdresser had done his usual professional job. The Eve Childe of her photographs looked back at her, perfectly constructed for this most important interview. She was not quibbling about her image this morning.

Satisfied that she could not have presented herself any better, Eve headed for the bank of elevators on the side wall and pressed the button for the Public Relations Floor. John Lindsey headed the department and he was the man she was to see. Eve took several deep breaths to steady her nerves as the compartment lifted and moved silently upwards. When the doors slid open she had fixed a smile on her face and for once she was pleased to see the gleam of envy in the receptionist's eyes. It boosted her confidence.

John Lindsey greeted her with more reserve than she was accustomed to receiving from PR men. He was tall and slender, well presented in the young, executive style. He was not handsome but not unattractive either. His smile held charm and the quick, appraising eyes glinted with appreciation. He was the kind of man who could readily put both men and women at ease.

"Miss Childe, I've looked forward to meeting you in person," he said politely as he saw her settled in a chair. He returned to his desk with a brisk step then flashed her a disarming grin. "Sometimes the camera lies but that is assuredly not the case with you."

"Thank you," Eve murmured, grateful for the compliment.

The grin disappeared. He assumed a business-like air and launched into crisp speech. "I'll come straight to the point, Miss Childe. We've developed a new perfume and we want the right girl to sell it to the public. It has been our standard policy to use big-name stars for publicity campaigns, but..." He paused as if choosing his next words cautiously. "...this perfume is different, unique. We thought a different approach might be more effective. Your name was put forward as a possibility and we would like to explore that possibility. I say explore because our board of directors is not convinced that you can present the right image."

He threw her a little smile of encouragement as if to reassure her that he thought she would be right. The waggle of his eyebrows said it was out of his control. Eve appreciated the byplay of expression but it only increased her inner tension. He continued.

"What we'd like to do is make a pilot commercial with you. We'll pay you your normal fee but there's no guarantee that the commercial will be used. You may not care to waste your time without such a guarantee, but on the other hand, if you win approval with your work, the rewards will obviously be great. Apart from its financial aspect, a contract with Lamarr is quite a reckoning force in the fashion world, a fact I'm sure you appreciate.''

"Yes, I do,'' she agreed quickly.

"Then perhaps you would like time to consider our proposition,'' he invited magnanimously.

There was nothing to think about. Eve had no other choices in the offing. The opportunity to prove herself was dangling in front of her and she grasped it with eager hands. "No. I'm quite happy to go along with that arrangement.''

"You understand it may lead nowhere,'' he repeated insistently, almost apologetically. He really was very charming.

Eve smiled, unable to contain her excitement over the offer. "On the other hand, it's a chance worth taking, isn't it?''

He smiled back. "I thought you'd see it that way. Our Legal Department has an agreement drawn up for you to sign but Mr Lamarr would like to see you first. Excuse me a moment.'' He leaned forward and pressed a button on his desk intercom. "Please inform Mr Lamarr that I'm bringing Miss Childe up now.'' He stood and there was no doubt that he was pleased with the situation. "If you'll just accompany me?''

Eve rose gracefully to her feet. "You said Mr Lamarr. I thought Margot Lamarr...''

"The queen has abdicated in favour of her son,'' he explained with a touch of dry amusement. "Margot Lamarr retains the title of Chairman of the Board and still fronts for the business, but it's Paul Lamarr who runs the company. It's not commonly known but make no mistake about it. He's the one you have to satisfy in order to seal a contract. And he's a hard man to please,'' he added with a telling sigh.

Eve's nervousness returned as they rode an elevator up to the Executive Floor. Her stomach cramped into knots and she frantically tried to relax. It was clearly so important to impress this man. She had to be calm, self-assured, and above all, she had to convince Paul Lamarr that she was the right girl to sell his perfume.

She barely took in the sleek expensiveness of the reception area. John Lindsey nodded an acknowledgement to the woman at the desk. She waved towards a door and Eve was led straight to it. The PR man knocked before opening it but he ushered Eve inside without waiting for an answer.

It was a huge, streamlined office but Eve had eyes for nothing but the man who slowly rose to his feet. The grey suit was tailored perfection but he might as well have been dressed in jeans and Tee-shirt or nothing at all. It made no difference. He was the man from the beach, the man she had slept with in a primitive log-cabin, the man who had haunted her dreams ever since. And he was Paul Lamarr.

CHAPTER FIVE

HE stood there, tall, powerful, so clearly master of the situation, as the head of such a company would be expected to look. He acknowledged the formal introduction with a faint smile then addressed his PR man with all the confidence of a man who knew his instructions would have been carried out to the letter.

"It's been brought to an agreement?"

"Yes."

"Then I want to talk to Miss Childe alone."

Eve had not moved or spoken. Shock held her rigid while wave after wave of emotion churned up conflicting thoughts. He was Paul Lamarr, not a drifting fisherman. And oh God! She had virtually accused him of being a gigolo, a beach-bum on the make. He had told her that her identity held no attraction and why should it when he was Paul Lamarr.

Had he brought her here to show her that? Ram it down her throat? He looked so much in control. Stay with me... stay with me... the words pealed around her brain. What had this powerful man wanted? A part-time mistress for his beach-cabin hideaway? Why had he manoeuvred her into coming here now? To take up where they had left off? Where she had left off. She had walked away. He had not wanted her to go. He had been so angry, contemptuous. And had every right to be. Except he could have told her who he was. He could have settled her fears with a word. But he hadn't. He had let her go with a wave of disgust. And now...

The thud of the door closing behind John Lindsey triggered the words which were uppermost in her mind. "What do you want?" Her voice was sharp, edged with panic.

A quick frown cut a V between the straight dark eyebrows. "I'm sorry this has been a shock to you. Circumstances change..."

"They couldn't have changed more, could they?" She gave a hysterical little laugh. "The high and mighty Paul Lamarr is putting me in my place. Well and truly."

The frown deepened. "It was not my intention to lord it over you in any way."

"N-no?" The word was a quaver of disbelief. Eve was too blinded by the vast change in circumstances to see the situation any other way.

"No." The answer was firm, just short of explosive.

There was no further explanation. The dark eyes bored into hers with an intensity which was wholly discomforting. She could feel his power winding around her. He seemed to be waiting for some signal from her and suddenly she was afraid of her vulnerability to this man. Afraid of where it might lead if she revealed how deeply he affected her. In helpless agitation she walked over to the large picture window, turning her back to the disturbing force which was Paul Lamarr.

Her mind clamped on to the job offer and chewed it into meaningful little bits. A trial commercial. No guarantee of a contract. Unless Mr Lamarr was satisfied. Satisfied. The word stuck and billowed with images. He wanted her back. But on his terms. A powerful man flexing his power. Maybe he even knew how desperate she was for work. She had insulted him, walked away. A man like him, a man used to getting his own way, snapping his fingers for a woman, any woman...

"It's...it's not a real job is it?" She could not bear to look at him but she had to know the truth. "You're just dangling out the bait so I'll play along with you."

There was an excruciating silence. Her words hung in the air, vibrating with ugly meaning, spreading out tentacles which clutched at her heart, squeezing mercilessly.

"And will you play along with me, Eve?"

The question was soft, yet its overtones struck her like hammer-blows. There was no sound from him but intuition screamed that he had moved up behind her. Her skin prickled with alarm. She swung around to face him and he was close, suffocatingly close. Her breath caught in her throat. Every nerve was electrified by his nearness.

She opened her mouth to speak but his hand brushed her cheek in a soft caress and the cry of protest dried up on her tongue. The insidious magic of those finger-tips sent a wave of heat through her body, re-awakening memories she had tried to erase. Her heart fluttered like a captive bird. She pressed a hand to it, desperate to quell its wild tattoo.

The shattering truth burst across her mind, tearing aside all the imposed veils of convention. There was no right or wrong about it. She yearned to feel this man's arms around her again, his body pressed to hers, belonging together as they had in the sea that afternoon, an incredible joining of two people into a unit where nothing else existed.

"The contract is yours, Eve. If you give me what I want."

His voice was a low, seductive murmur. He moved as he spoke, his hands sliding over her hips, sensuously relearning the curves as he fitted her lower body to his. The hard strength of his thighs made her legs tremble with weakness. Eve could not believe this was happening here and now, in this office, yet intuition told her that this man could make it happen anywhere, and she was mesmerised by her instinctive response to him. Her body had a will of its own and it revelled in the sensations which only he had ever aroused.

He took her handbag. She heard it thud on the floor but the slight noise was strangely distant, over-ridden by the louder thud of her heart-beat. Then his hand was at her waist, underneath the loose tunic-top of her suit. Finger-tips lightly traced the curve of her spine. Up and down, up...a shiver of pleasure crawled across her skin. The touch roved further, across her back, under her arm, lingering over the soft swell of her breasts.

Her own hands lifted, instinctively drawn to him. They spread over the fine silk of his shirt, following the contours of the powerful chest she knew so well. Had never forgotten. She felt his sharp intake of breath and looked up into eyes which were dark with unfathomable depths. She did not know that her own eyes were a green haze of desire, that her lips were parted, quivering with anticipation. Not until his mouth came down on hers, harshly plundering, did she even question the need which had driven all sense of time, place and circumstances from her mind.

There was a split second of resistance. Then the violent passion of his kiss sparked an overwhelming response. Hard hands thrust her closer, savagely possessive. She melted against him, exultant in her surrender, revelling in the rawness of his desire. Her arms wound around his neck, owning him as fiercely as he owned her.

His fingers thrust roughly through her hair, clutching her head too tightly for a moment, then sharply pulling it back. Eve gasped in hurt protest at the painful wrench. She lifted her eyes in puzzled appeal and stared disbelievingly at the blazing anger in his.

"I don't trade business for sexual favours, Eve, but it's interesting to know how far you'll go for the sake of your career." He straightened her tunic-top and stepped back, sweeping her with a look of utter contempt.

"I . . . I don't understand you," she cried. It was a plea from the heart carrying all the agony of confusion.

"You couldn't even begin to understand me."

The coldness in his voice chilled the heat from her body. She shuddered. Her hands lifted automatically, rubbing at her arms to restore feeling. She was completely dazed, unable to come to grips with the situation.

"Why?" she choked out in bewilderment.

One eyebrow rose with cynical emphasis. "You think you're irresistible, Eve? You think that because I once found you exciting, you have only to offer me your body and I'll be putty in your hands?" He made a sharp sound of disgust and turned away.

She watched him walk around his desk and settle himself in the comfortable leather chair. His scathing words had whipped away the last trembling traces of desire. He was indeed a stranger now, a cold, unfeeling alien. He sat behind his executive desk, a man of power and authority who did not hesitate over cutting others down to size. He had just reduced her to dirt under his feet.

"Don't underestimate me again, Eve. I don't play with my work. There's nothing I want from you except your professional services as a model. The other directors of the company don't think you can do the job. If you satisfy them, and me, the contract's yours."

It was a curt statement of fact, completely emotionless. His eyes sliced through her as though she was meaningless fodder for the cameras.

"Why choose me?" It was more an accusation than a question, a spark of defiance rising out of the ashes of her humiliation.

He leaned back in his chair, surveying her with hooded eyes. "Because you can do the job. I've seen a side of you the others haven't."

A painful tide of hot blood scorched up her neck as his words conjured up too many painful memories of how much he had seen of her.

"And strange as it might seem, I wanted to please you," he added with a savage twist of self-mockery.

"Please me," she echoed in a strangled voice.

He smiled a thin, pleasureless smile. "You showed me how much you valued your career when you walked away that afternoon. This contract should set you towards international success. You could say I'm returning a favour. You gave me something I valued.

I'm now giving you something you value... free of charge. All you have to do is perform for the cameras.''

Eve felt sick. The blood drained from her face as the full impact of his words sank in. Too late she recognised that what they had shared together had been of irreplaceable value, a magical affinity so rare that it had seemed a dream. Her own uncertainties and suspicions had ended that dream. A few moments ago it had lived again for her, but not for him. She had poisoned it with rash, frightened words which had risen out of the terrible vulnerability she had felt. There was no way back now. He had judged and condemned her.

"You think I'd sleep with you just to... to further my career?'' she asked in faltering protest even while knowing it could do no good. There was nothing she could do or say which would change his view of her.

His mouth twisted with distaste. "It's hardly a new idea, is it? Shall we get down to business? I prefer not to waste my time on irrelevancies.''

He waved her to a chair. She took an unsteady step towards it. Her foot knocked against something. It was her handbag, still lying on the floor where it had been dropped. Tears stung her eyes as she bent to pick it up. A wave of desolation accompanied her move to the chair but she concentrated hard on sitting with all the conscious grace of a trained model, her legs folded to one side in the approved sitting position. The only thing she had left to cling to was her career, and it was in a shambles because of her break-up with Simon. It was necessary to swallow her pride and listen to what Paul Lamarr had to offer.

"First let me explain that we're not interested in your professional image. We're after something fresh and original to sell our new perfume."

Eve showed her puzzlement. "But if you don't like my work..."

"I'm sure you've been very effective but the Lamarr girl has to be all woman, not a provocative teaser."

Eve blushed a fiery red and was furious with herself for reacting to the label. Paul Lamarr was only stating the truth. The image created by Simon had been a deliberate sexual tease.

"What precisely do you have in mind?" she asked stiffly.

"I want a woman whose beauty is entirely natural, unaffected. A woman with a dream-like quality of innocence. In short," his voice dropped to a flat monotone, "I want the woman I saw on a beach one afternoon. If you're a good enough actress to deliver that on film, then the contract is yours."

Eve was stunned. She had revealed so much of herself that afternoon, believing that her secret inner self was safe with the understanding stranger. She had let herself be a free spirit, uncaring of consequences, and it had been wonderful. To even contemplate commercialising that private magic seemed a monstrous betrayal of trust, yet that was what Paul Lamarr was suggesting. Not suggesting. Demanding.

"You'd ask that of me?" she choked out. It was too much. How dared he be contemptuous of her for supposedly selling her body when he was prepared to peddle her soul for a perfume.

Surprise flickered in his eyes. It was abruptly quenched. "Aren't you a good enough actress to reproduce that mood?'' He turned the question into a deliberate taunt.

She hated him in that moment. Hated him with all the force of her being. She had been mistaken. The feeling had all been on her side. That afternoon meant nothing to him. Perhaps a pleasant interlude. Nothing of value. He had not cared. Did not care. She was a model to be used. That was all it could ever have been for him, a man who had obviously known so many beautiful women. A bleak desolation hollowed out her heart and shadowed her expression.

''Eve...''

The harsh demand in his voice barely registered. She looked blankly in his direction, wondering why he had said she had given him something he valued. The answer which sprung to mind brought a twist of irony to her lips. Her virginity. Of course. Didn't men prize virginity in a woman? So odd that it should matter one way or the other. It was only the loving which mattered.

''Eve.''

His voice was more insistent, slicing through her reverie. His eyes had that probing intensity again and he had leaned forward with a tautness in his body she had not noticed before.

''Do you mean...'' he hesitated, ''...did that afternoon mean something special to you?''

How could she admit that now? He had made it impossible. Shaming. ''Only in so far as any fantasy is special,'' she replied carelessly. ''But if that's what you want, Mr Lamarr, I'll do my best to—how did you put it—reproduce the mood? At least I can try,'' she added wryly.

She had to try. If she walked out on Paul Lamarr's offer she would have to admit failure to her mother. And Simon.

"Ah yes! Fantasy!" The words were breathed out on a sigh. Paul Lamarr sank back into his leather chair and relaxed. His mouth curved with grim amusement. "That's the name we've chosen for our new perfume. Fantasy. I'm sure you'll be able to do it justice, Eve. After all, I know you can make a fantasy... almost real."

Only the most rigid self-control prevented Eve from hurling the job back in his face and walking out. Hatred fired her blood to boiling point but somehow she kept the steam locked in, gritting her teeth with fierce determination. She would show him she was a professional model, all right. She would show them all; her mother, Simon, the whole damned world, but Paul Lamarr most of all. Pride insisted that he never know how deeply he had hurt her.

"I hope you'll be satisfied," she grated out through her clenched teeth.

"Our first objective is to demonstrate your suitability for the role to my fellow directors," he said blandly. "Are you free tomorrow morning?"

"Yes." There was no point in pretending she was busy.

"Good. I'll arrange a meeting. Be here at nine o'clock. Or is that too early for you?"

"No."

"You won't need to go to a hairdresser first. I want to present them with the new Lamarr girl so wash out that sleek style and let your hair dry into its natural curls. And please refrain from using any make-up whatsoever." His eyes skimmed over her in cold appraisal. "Have you something more obviously feminine in your wardrobe?"

"What would you suggest?" Eve asked tightly. He was stripping her down to the bone.

He shrugged. "A form-fitting dress perhaps? I want your breasts to be seen. Your photographs tend to make them appear negligible."

Her control broke. "Why don't you ask me to prance naked?"

There was a flare of irritation in his eyes. Then his mouth twitched into a sardonic smile. "Lamarr aims for sensuality and excitement. Women don't appreciate the obvious and my fellow directors are women. I'm sure you can show off your natural attributes without being crudely obvious."

Eve flushed. His smooth riposte had turned her impulsive jab into a very crude shot. She realised how stupid it was to show her vulnerability. Misdirected pin-pricks were futile. Paul Lamarr had all the big guns in this situation. He did not need her but she needed what he was offering.

"As you wish," she said flatly, knowing that surrender was the only course to take. "Is there anything else you would like me to do?" she added with a semblance of sweet reasonableness. She lifted clear green eyes behind which was a steady wall of defence. The surrender was very superficial.

His face seemed to grow harder, all harsh lines and angles. The stab of his eyes was edged with fine contempt. Inwardly Eve returned his contempt, measure for measure, but she kept her gaze limpidly submissive. It gave her a feeling of triumph. He could no longer wound her with his contempt.

"No. There's nothing else I want of you," he stated with almost insulting precision. "If you're ready to sign the agreement now, Lindsey can take you along to the legal department." He leaned forward.

"One thing, Mr Lamarr," Eve flashed at him before he made contact with the intercom.

He raised questioning eyebrows.

"I understand that this agreement is on a purely professional level?"

"I thought I'd made that eminently clear."

"Then I insist on being addressed in a purely professional way Mr Lamarr. I resent your familiar use of my personal name. You have no right to call me Eve."

The dangerous flare in his eyes gave mute warning that her challenge had been foolish. Anger suddenly exploded out of him.

"Just who the hell do you think you are to dictate terms to me?" he thundered at her, exasperation driving his voice up several decibels. "You don't rate even a glimmer of recognition on the international scene. There's a whole list of women . . . natural drawcards for this campaign! But I risk time and money to give you your chance at the big-time and what bloody thanks do I get! First you insult my integrity and intelligence. Then your God-almighty ego gets pricked on a few necessary instructions. And on top of that, you have the incredible impudence to stand on your dignity and tell me what I should call you!"

He dragged in a harsh breath and his tone dropped to a low, biting sarcasm. "Well, hear this, Miss Eve Childe! I'll call you any damned name which comes to mind. You should be thanking your good fortune that you're here to be called anything at all. If you don't like it, get up and keep walking, because in God's name, you are instantly replaceable! You've already cost me more trouble than you're worth. Do I make myself clear, you silly little girl?"

Tears welled up in her eyes and a huge lump of unrelieved emotion constricted her throat. Her brain admitted the damning facts. Looked at from his point of view she had been very silly, but from the moment she had entered this room, Eve had been incapable of any clear focus on the job offer. There had been too many distracting tangents scattering her thoughts.

"I'm sorry," she choked out. It was barely a whisper and she threw him a despairing look of appeal.

He sighed and ran a hand over his face, casting off the stiff anger. His expression sagged into weariness. "I'm sorry too. It's no good. It was a mistake bringing you here."

"No, please. I do want the job and I am grateful for the offer. It was just...I couldn't..." she sought helplessly for an explanation, then gave up. "I'll do my best really I will," she pleaded anxiously.

For long, taut moments he stared at her in silence. Eve had the forcible impression that he was not seeing her at all, yet he looked directly at her.

"Fantasy," he finally muttered and his lips curled around the word in soft derision. He seemed to give himself a mental shake and the heavy eyelids came down, reducing his gaze to narrowed slits. "Well, the agreement is ready for you to sign. Unless you have something else to say we might as well get on with it."

She shook her head.

He activated the intercom. "Send Lindsey in."

The door opened to admit the PR man almost immediately. Paul Lamarr rose to his feet and Eve followed suit.

"Sign up Miss Childe and proceed with the necessary arrangements." He nodded a dismissal. "Nine o'clock tomorrow morning, Miss Childe."

He did not move from behind his desk. He stood straight and tall, a commanding figure of power and authority. She had been dealt with and now she was being summarily dismissed. Eve drew in a deep, steadying breath and walked over to John Lindsey. He smiled his charming smile and held the door for her. She could not return the smile. It was all she could do to make her retreat with dignity.

It was a retreat in more ways than one. Paul Lamarr's angry outburst had cleared her mind. He held all the cards and she had to play his way if her career was to survive, let alone climb to the top. Maybe it would have been better to go back to Simon, she thought defeatedly, but the more rational part of her brain denied this. The job for Paul Lamarr was a short-term arrangement. It would soon be over. And maybe she would be successful. By herself. For herself. Surely that was worth a bit of heart-ache.

As for the rest, that day she had spent so intimately with him was a closed episode. Far distant, forever locked in another dimension which did not even relate to the present. Yet when he had kissed her... Forget that, she ordered herself sternly. Paul Lamarr was... Paul Lamarr. That was the end of it.

CHAPTER SIX

"YOU'RE not going like that!"

Eve sighed and threw her mother a look of exasperation. "Mum, I told you all the details of the proposition. I don't intend to jeopardise this chance by ignoring instructions."

Marion Childe sniffed her contempt. "What do men know about presentation? You'll be seeing Margot Lamarr this morning. The queen of cosmetics! She won't expect you to turn up bare-faced."

"It's Paul Lamarr who runs the business, Mum," Eve reminded her curtly.

"He wouldn't notice a touch of blusher. Or a subtle eye-liner for that matter. A bit of cheating won't go astray," her mother argued. "Black's not black and white is certainly not white in the cut-throat world of business. You've got to shade things your way. It's about time you learned that, Eve."

"I don't think Mr Lamarr appreciates shades of grey, Mum," Eve said with a touch of irony. She suspected black was very black to Paul Lamarr and cheating would most certainly be black. "He said no make-up and I'm following his instructions to the letter."

Marion Childe's lips thinned in disapproval. "Stubborn," she muttered as her eyes ran critically over her daughter's appearance. "Well, at least the dress has style. I hope he appreciates that."

Eve hoped so too. She had spent all yesterday afternoon searching through boutiques for just the right dress. Pride demanded that Paul Lamarr should find nothing to criticise this morning. It was a pretty, feminine dress and the clinging fabric hugged every curve. The high, rounded neckline was deceptively modest because the overall effect was sensuality personified. The shell-pink of the elongated bodice ran to her hips, tightly form-fitting all the way. The gored skirt featured zig-zag borders of a delicate mauve and a pastel sea-green.

It was a dress which high-lighted Eve's natural colouring. Her silky, blonde curls suited its femininity and the startling green of her eyes was quietly emphasised. She was pleased with her choice. High-heeled, pink sandals added stylish elegance as did the pouched leather handbag which had been dyed to match. The novelty of appearing her natural self secretly delighted her, and to her mind, she looked better than she had for a long, long time.

She said a firm goodbye to her mother, blithely letting all the repeated advice flow over her head. She set off with the lightness of step she had experienced that day on the beach. This morning she was free of the old Eve Childe image. This morning she was herself. The only disturbing factor was the man she was going to meet. Eve knew it was necessary to curb her emotional reaction to Paul Lamarr, yet every time she thought of him it was physical chaos. Her stomach fluttered haphazardly, her skin prickled with apprehension and her nerves played a devastating game of catch-me-if-you-can. As she made her way to the Lamarr building, Eve worked on preparing herself for their meeting, intent on presenting a calm, confident surface.

By the time she arrived in the reception area on the Executive Floor she felt reasonably pleased with her composure. She could even smile at the surprise in the receptionist's eyes. Yet as she was shown into Paul Lamarr's office, her nerves stretched to screaming pitch. He was standing in front of the picture window, apparently oblivious of her entrance. She willed him to turn around, take the initiative, give her some hint of his mood. He did not move.

"Good morning," she forced out stiffly, determined that he not find her lacking in civility.

Paul Lamarr swung around and immediately his dominating presence projected its aura of power. His eyes swept over her in sharp appraisal. Eve's stomach cramped as she waited for the inevitable comment.

"Good morning," he nodded, whether from courtesy or approval Eve could not tell. His expression gave nothing away. His gaze lingered on her breasts. "You're wearing a bra."

Eve was not sure if it was a statement or a question. "Yes, of course," she answered quickly, aware that her pulse had jumped into an erratic rhythm.

"Take it off. You don't need it and my sister will immediately assume it's padded."

"But..." Eve mentally cringed at the hard implacability on Paul Lamarr's face. "You said not to be obvious," she finished limply.

"The dress fabric is not transparent. Don't tell me you've never gone without a bra, Miss Childe."

The cynicism in his voice brought a hot tide of embarrassment flooding up her throat. Paul Lamarr was not going to believe a denial. Eve glanced around helplessly. "Where can I go?"

"Go?"

"To take it off."

The dark eyes mocked her request. "I haven't time to waste on coyness, Eve. Your body holds no secrets from me, as well you know. Take it off here while I check if my mother's ready to receive you."

A wave of hatred gorged her throat as he turned his back on her and strode over to the desk. How dared he treat her so cavalierly! As if... as if she was a model, Eve reminded herself savagely. There was no time to waste. Paul Lamarr was already speaking into the intercom. She spun around and dropped her handbag on to the nearest chair. With as much speed as her fumbling fingers permitted she unzipped her bodice, removed her bra, stuffed it in her handbag, then readjusted the dress so that it fitted her snugly.

Her hands were reaching for the zipper again when other, stronger hands performed the service for her. Her skin crawled with sensitivity as his fingers fastened the hook and eye at the nape of her neck. Her body played traitor to her feelings, the nipples of her breasts hardening and becoming prominent under the clinging material.

"Ready now?" His voice was toneless, seemingly disinterested.

Eve furiously cursed her physical vulnerability to the man. "Yes, thank you," she added stiffly, making a slow business of picking up her handbag. She willed him to move away but he was still close to her when she turned around.

Two angry spots of colour burnt in her cheeks. She lifted her thick eyelashes and glared defiance at him.

It rattled her composure even further to find an un-expected softness in his eyes. For one confused moment the office drifted in a haze and the memory of sea and sand was overwhelming.

"You look...very beautiful." The words were dragged out, as if spoken against his will.

She caught her breath as he seemed to lean towards her.

"Eve."

What was it in his eyes...torment...desire? Strong, intense feeling wrapped around Eve, holding her captive. Every nerve in her body tingled with anticipation, acutely aware that he was about to say something vitally important. Then the moment lost its vibrancy. She felt his withdrawal before he took the half-step backwards.

"Not the time," he sighed, and the electric intimacy was gone like a phantom which had never existed.

"Come." He took her elbow and began steering her towards the door. "You'll have to maintain the calm control of a Daniel this morning. You're about to walk into the lion's den, or rather the lioness's lair. My mother clawed her way to the top and age hasn't blunted her claws," he added drily.

It was a friendly warning. Eve's confusion grew. She did not understand Paul Lamarr at all. His manner to her now contrasted so sharply to what had gone before that she accompanied him in a dizzy state of puzzlement. His touch on her arm did nothing for clarity of thought either. Despite all the negative emotion he had stirred, he had only to be close to her and she reacted positively to his physical magnetism.

They walked through the reception area to a door, then into another reception area. The change in decor was dramatic, from streamlined modernity to all the elegance of a past age. Eve's high heels sunk into the deeply piled peach carpet. The furnishings were rich and exquisite, velvet and lace curtains, antique furniture, tapestry and polished wood and opulent vases of roses. Even the receptionist's desk was beautiful. Eve's eyes were inevitably drawn to the gold-framed portrait on the far wall. The imperious face of Margot Lamarr was warning enough that she would not suffer fools gladly.

Paul Lamarr murmured a casual greeting to the immaculately groomed receptionist as they moved past. The woman's eyes glowed with interest. Eve was given no time to speculate on relationships. She was steered straight in to an office which could have been the drawing-room in a palace. Or throne-room. Margot Lamarr sat in a high winged armchair behind a magnificent Chippendale-style table, very much the Chairman of the Board. A second woman sat to the left hand side of the table, her chair turned outwards, towards the newcomers.

Eve was immediately the focus of sharp, speculative eyes. Neither of the two women moved or spoke, but the silence was thick with questions. That they were mother and daughter was obvious. The likeness was startling. Both were large-framed and strong-featured, handsome rather than beautiful with their dark eyes, creamy skin and thick auburn hair. Margot Lamarr's heavier eyelids and slight looseness around the jaw betrayed her age, but the facial bone-structure of both women made age relatively painless as far as looks were concerned.

"Margot Lamarr, Kristen Delaney . . . Eve Childe."

It was more of an announcement than an introduction. It seemed odd that he should put their names on an equal basis without titles to differentiate their positions.

"I'm very pleased to meet you," Eve said with cautious politeness. Their watching silence had already begun to unnerve her.

"No doubt," the younger woman muttered waspishly.

"Kristen!" The tone and the glance was reproof enough. Margot Lamarr was accustomed to command. She returned her gaze to Eve. "I have been looking forward to meeting you, Miss Childe. I can now see that your previous image was very misleading. To be frank, I would never have given you a moment's consideration. But Paul does sometimes come up with the unusual. Rest assured that you'll now be given fair consideration. You may sit down."

"Not so fast, Mother. I might have been outvoted but I won't be ignored. We haven't even seen how she moves."

The resentment in Kristen Delaney's voice sent a tingle of apprehension up Eve's spine. Paul Lamarr left her side and strolled over to the chair on the right hand side of the table. As he settled into it he made a lazy, uninterested gesture to Eve, clearly advising compliance.

"Walk up and down, Eve."

Her modelling career had been concentrated on the camera. Eve had never experienced the pressures of the cat-walk, eyes dissecting her body in clinical detail as she moved. It was difficult to maintain a pose of indifference in the face of such critical attention.

"Enough!" Margot Lamarr's voice was decisive.

Eve was relieved to come to a halt.

"Well, Kristen?"

Eve glanced towards the younger woman, hoping for a sign of approval. Kristen Delaney's expression lightened but it was a malicious smile which curved her mouth.

"I'd like to see her play out the fantasy. A body is one thing, the ability to project a mood, quite another."

"Miss Childe has not yet received a script of the fantasy, Kristen. Lindsey has organised a meeting with our film director later this morning."

The cool statement by Paul Lamarr brought a flare of triumph to his sister's eyes.

"You see, Mother? Not even an audition!"

The old lady's face was as unreadable as her son's. "Your brother is not a fool, Kristen. No doubt he has reason to believe Miss Childe is capable of performing."

"He has reason!" The words were tossed out scornfully. "Well, there's no proof available of that, is there? He's signed this..." She waved an airy hand in Eve's direction but disdained to give her the courtesy of recognition. "This parochial model up for a pilot commercial which is going to cost the company a minimum of twenty thousand dollars, and I say we're entitled to some proof that this investment is not money down the drain."

She turned to Eve, her dark brown eyes glinting with malice. "Well, Miss Childe, I'll tell you what we want and you give it to us. You're walking along a beach collecting shells. One of the shells is the Fantasy perfume. You open the bottle, apply the perfume and dream that you're a mermaid who is surprised by a fantasy lover. His kiss turns you into a woman.'' She picked up a small box from the table and held it out. ''Here's the perfume. Let's see you put it on and dream. Your face should tell it all.''

Eve's heart had shrunk into a tight ball as Kristen Delaney spelled out the details. Her whole body shrieked a protest. Paul Lamarr was not only demanding that she be the woman on the beach, he was intent on replaying that afternoon with all its personal nuances.

''I can't!'' It was almost a sob of protest, a harsh, strangled sound.

''You can't?'' Kristen Delaney taunted. ''What do you mean, you can't? It's a reasonable request. Here.'' The small black box was offered more insistently. ''Do please get on with it.''

Eve could not look at Paul Lamarr. She glanced at the queenly figure behind the table, hoping desperately that Margot Lamarr might release her from this impossible task. There was no help from that quarter. The dark, obsidian eyes were observing Eve with cold detachment. There was no help from Paul Lamarr either. His continued silence emphasised that she was totally alone in this.

Eve forced herself to step forward and take the perfume. The square black box carried the gold Lamarr emblem. She removed the lid. On a soft bed of peach satin lay a scalloped shell. It was sculptured from plastic but tinted a mother-of-pearl sheen which made it look real. Two seed pearls formed the opening catch. Eve's fingers trembled as they snapped it apart. Inside was a tiny shell-shaped bottle of perfume.

She knew it was no earthly use, unstopping the perfume and dabbing it on. Her eyes lifted to Margot Lamarr, appealing for understanding but expecting rejection. "I'm sorry. I can't do it. I'm not an actress who can switch a mood on and off. I have to feel it...and I can't. Not in this room," she explained haltingly.

"Oh that's brilliant, that is!" Kristen Delaney scoffed, slapping her hand down on the armrest in disgust while sending a scathing look towards her brother. "A fine choice, Paul! You've budgeted for two days' shooting. Two days! What if she can't feel the mood? How far over the budget do you intend to indulge this whim of yours?"

The sneer brought a flush of pride to Eve's cheeks. "I'll do my best within the time, Mrs Delaney."

"Your best!" the woman jeered, not the least bit mollified by Eve's tentative assurance. "And what guarantee do we have that your best is even adequate?" She turned to her mother with a smug air of having settled the matter. "I don't know how you can tolerate Paul's judgment in this affair. I'll remind you again, Mother, that bringing in an unknown is totally against company policy. When this pilot study fails I expect my opinions to be given more weight. And I'll be demanding some very stringent accountability for this mistake."

Margot Lamarr arched her eyebrows in haughty disdain. "Don't presume to tell me what I should do, Kristen. It has yet to be proved a mistake, and it's not good business to allow policies to become stagnant. New blood can be exciting and productive. It could be that Paul has found a star who will give us the advertisement of a decade."

"A star! Good God! No one outside of Australia has even heard of her. You'll see I'm right, Mother." She rose to her feet and grew more formidable with all the puffed-up confidence of her rightness. "Since I've been outvoted on this matter I see no point in staying. I have no doubt that the results of this ill-thought-out foray into the unknown will confirm my judgment. I'll leave you to humour your new star." She strode over to the door with a sniff of contempt at Eve as she passed.

"Kristen..."

The authority in Margot Lamarr's voice was muted but very real nonetheless. She emitted power with effortless ease. Her daughter turned reluctantly, one hand remaining on the doorknob in a gesture of defiance.

"...you were wrong about one thing. Miss Childe does have pretty breasts."

Frustration glared out of the younger woman's eyes. Her lips thinned with the effort to retain control. Then with one venomous look at her brother she wrenched the door open, stepped out and slammed it after her.

Eve lowered her lashes and wished the floor would open up and swallow her, anything to be out of this dreadful scene.

"You shouldn't goad her, Mother." Paul Lamarr's tone was bland, untroubled. "It doesn't make for peace."

"There's no peace with Kristen. She can't see beyond her emotions," came the flat retort. There was a heavy sigh, a rustle of movement. "You may sit down, Miss Childe."

Eve glanced apprehensively at the old lady. Margot Lamarr had settled further into her chair, her head tilted back against the studded velvet. The gleam in the hooded eyes seemed coldly reptilian.

Eve sank into the nearest chair, intensely relieved to have been given that concession. She had felt pinned like a trapped butterfly while Kristen Delaney had unleashed her weapons in the fight for power. Eve had been made acutely aware that Paul Lamarr had put his position on the line in employing her, but his motives seemed even more indistinct.

Questions buzzed around Eve's mind. Did he hope to cement his authority by vindicating his judgment? Or did he have some real, personal interest in Eve herself? Nothing seemed clear at all. Her nerves quivered in anticipation of another inquisition. Eve had been lacerated by the cub's claws but the lioness had kept hers sheathed so far.

"I'm sorry you were subjected to that distressing scene," she began with smooth civility, "but it's as well for you to realise you're very much on trial. I respect Paul's judgment. I wanted to meet you simply to see what he sees in you. Having done that, I find myself intrigued. Where did you first meet Paul?"

The question slid out, catching Eve completely unprepared. A swift tide of embarrassment scorched up her neck and a confusion of painful thoughts made speech impossible. Her lips tried to form words but her tongue was paralysed.

Paul spoke. "I saw her on a beach some weeks ago."

Eve gulped at the direct answer. She darted a desperate look at Paul Lamarr, an agonised plea for discretion. He was facing his mother, his expression completely neutral.

"She was as you see her today, Mother, only her natural beauty was even more evident when I saw her. Unbelievable and quite entrancing. In fact, it took me quite some time to identify her as Eve Childe. She would not give me her name and she had no idea who I was until she walked into my office yesterday."

"Ah!" It was a hum of satisfaction. "That explains a great deal." The gimlet eyes returned to Eve. "Were you expecting to hear from him?"

"No!" Surprised whipped out the negative. "I thought…" Eve stopped, the colour draining from her face as quickly as it had risen. The attack from Margot Lamarr was not aimed at Eve's work but at Eve personally. "I thought it was you who was interested in seeing me," she finished limply.

There was a protracted silence. Eve marshalled her defences to counter the next thrust but she was unexpectedly given a reprieve. Margot Lamarr turned her gaze on to her son. A tired cynicism drew lines of age on her face.

"I hope you know what you're doing, Paul. Kristen does have a point. It's company time and money you're using."

"It won't be wasted," he replied shortly.

She rolled her head back and closed her eyes. "The pieces fit together. Never take me for a fool, Paul. I've given you a free hand. Go and get on with your gamble. I hope Miss Childe is worthy of it."

Paul Lamarr slowly unfolded himself from his chair. He walked over to the still figure behind the table and placed a hand on her shoulder. "I'm not a fool either, Mother," he said softly.

Her hand reached up and covered his, the beringed fingers clutching tightly for a moment. She lifted heavy lids and for the first time Eve saw her eyes soften.

"I know what it is to gamble. I've had to do it many a time, and often with everything against me." She smiled. "I wish you luck."

He hesitated, apparently about to say something, then turned to face Eve. They both looked at her and their eyes held the same probing intensity. Eve suddenly perceived the close relationship between mother and son, a kinship of spirits that Kristen did not share, would never share. The daughter had been bypassed for the son, the natural inheritor of his mother's life-force.

Eve felt transfixed under that strong, mutual gaze. It took considerable will-power to rise to her feet and step forward to return the box of perfume.

"Keep it, my dear. I'm sure you'll like it. It's the best we've ever produced."

Eve was flustered by the gentle tone. "Thank you. You're...you're very kind."

The old lady sighed. "There's little room for kindness in the cosmetic business. I hope, very sincerely, that you don't let my son down, Miss Childe."

"I would be letting myself down even more if I don't succeed, Mrs. Lamarr. I shall do my best," Eve said flatly.

A smile broadened the old lady's mouth. She patted her son's hand in an indulgent way. "I'm certain you will, my dear. Absolutely certain. You have my best wishes. Both of you. I've seen worse gambles pay off."

Eve's heart gave a funny little lurch at the linking of herself to Paul Lamarr. It was done in such an oddly knowing way.

"Thanks, Mother," Paul Lamarr murmured.

The interview was obviously over. He stepped around the table and took Eve's arm. What would have seemed merely a courteous gesture in other circumstances, now seemed a deliberate reinforcing of a link between them. They walked out of the room together and Eve felt so emotionally disturbed, she did not even question where they were going. The door of Paul Lamarr's office had closed behind them before she began to collect her wits.

"My mother never ceases to amaze me. I didn't expect her to don kid gloves. But since Kristen ran true to form you're probably in urgent need of sustenance," he added with a wry little smile. "What would you like; coffee, tea, or a strong draught of alcohol?"

The smile scraped over sensibilities which had been well and truly clawed. The pressures of the last twenty-four hours had mounted inexorably and Eve felt herself abused by them, physically, mentally and emotionally. She stared at the man who had devised the whole torture, outraged that he could calmly smile at her and ask if she wanted a cup of tea.

"You are an out-and-out bastard, Paul Lamarr, and I don't care if you tear up that agreement right now," she stormed at him.

The smile disappeared and any suggestion of softness which had been on his face went with it. "A little late for second thoughts, Miss Childe," he stated coldly.

"A little late in letting me know precisely what you wanted, too," she hurled back at him. "Why don't you use the whole damned lot?" Her mouth twisted in contempt. "But of course, the great Lamarr name wouldn't want anything so obviously crude as intimacy! Oh no! A kiss will suffice, provided it's delivered with bare breasts and passion. Well, if that's the scenario you can forget it. I don't do nude shots.''

"You won't be required to," came the tight retort.

Eve glared at him, hating his knowledge of her body. She could not bear the memories he had so callously evoked. She swung on her heel and paced away from him, spitting out the hurt in uncontrolled bursts.

"Do all your one-night stands provide inspiration for your work, Mr Lamarr? Is it your customary practice to get the women you bed to replay the...the mood for you in front of a camera?'' She turned, eyes blazing with scorn. "How low-down crude can you get? To use what I felt that day. To exploit something which was totally private and..." She stopped. With a stab of anguish she realised that the words trembling on the tip of her tongue were far too revealing.

"And what?"

The soft invitation made her shiver. She was suddenly aware that he was not affronted by her outburst. He was watching her intently, his body poised as if ready to spring at her.

"What did you feel, Eve?" Soft, insidious words, slicing through to her heart.

You know damned well what I felt but I won't give you the satisfaction of hearing me say it, Eve determined in grimly set silence. He stepped towards her and she tensed. He waved a careless hand.

"If it meant nothing to you, what's all the fuss about?"

"It was private...personal," she declared in resentful protest.

He shrugged, but still there was that watchfulness in his eyes. "You had no trouble walking away from it. In fact you were relieved that I gave you the opening to manufacture reasons for putting it all behind you. It was easier if I was an out-and-out bastard, wasn't it?"

She flinched at the accusation, knowing it was untrue but unable to find words to deny it with credibility. She had walked away because too much had happened too soon, turmoil following on turmoil, charged with wildly varying emotions. It had been necessary to get back on to some steady plateau, to get everything sorted out and in perspective.

The shock of discovering he had known her identity all along had twisted her perspective. The mistrust she had learnt from Simon's betrayal had still been a very fresh wound, fertile ground for infection. She had not thrown those insults at Paul Lamarr as excuses for her departure. The poison of disillusionment had fed them to her.

"I'm sorry I said those things to you," she choked out. "I was terribly wrong. But you...you could have told me who you were."

His mouth curled with cynicism. "Given you my name, rank and an itemised account of my wealth? Would you have stayed with me then, Eve?"

Truth whispered from her lips. "I don't know."

The dark eyes mocked her savagely. "You'd already chosen to go back to your career. And now I'm a bastard because I'm not letting you keep that day behind you. I'm dragging it right out in front. So what? Why be so sensitive about it, Eve? You can turn it to good account. A success-hungry model like yourself should not expect to keep her privacy. And as to your personal life, it'll become very public once you achieve your ambition. So why should you quibble now? Success is what you want, isn't it? What you want more than anything else? To be Eve Childe, international model of the year?''

Behind the words was a heightened intensity which set her nerves on edge. He was only an arm's length away and if he touched her Eve knew she would give herself away. And what then? A confusion of emotion ripped through her. She wanted to feel again what they had shared together but this was not the man from the beach. This was Paul Lamarr, a cold, ruthless man.

"Yes, that's what I want," she agreed in despairing defence.

The tension eased away. When he spoke his voice no longer held a dangerous undercurrent. It was soft with a dull weariness. "Then there's no argument, is there? You do what the script demands. It should be easy for you. Just dredge it out of your memory."

The intercom buzzed. Without another word Paul Lamarr strode to the desk and stabbed his finger on the switch.

"Mr Lindsey is on the line, Mr Lamarr. He says it's urgent."

"Put him through."

With Paul Lamarr's attention withdrawn, Eve sagged with the hopelessness of the situation. Tiredly, aimlessly, she stepped over to the picture window and gazed out over the city rooflines, seeing only the painful edges of her thoughts. It had been so simple without names. Just a man and a woman reaching out to each other. The importance she had placed on her name had severed their easy communication, and now the name of Paul Lamarr and all which that encompassed, stood as an insurmountable barrier to ever bridging the chasm between them. If she said she wanted him he would despise her, just as he had despised her yesterday for a response which had been completely natural, instinctive. Any appeal would fall on stony ground.

He had her legally locked into a job which was going to drain her emotions, but if she did not go on with it, what alternatives did she have? Every answer was bleak with emptiness. At least this job could lead to a career.

"Eve!' The call was sharp, peremptory.

She swung around, her feelings carefully guarded.

"Are you available all next week? If not, what days?"

"I'm free whenever you want me," she answered briefly.

He stared at her for a long moment. Then with a wry grimace he began speaking into the telephone again. "It might as well be done as quickly as possible. Check with the Weather Bureau and the Wardrobe Department, then arrange what you can. And Lindsey, you know where your orders come from. In future, you will take no notice of Mrs Delaney's demands until you refer the matter to me." It was a cutting reproof. There was another pause then, "Keep me informed of progress and send someone up for Miss Childe."

He frowned as he put the telephone down and was still frowning when he faced her. "Eve, should Kristen try to apply any kind of pressure on you directly or indirectly, I want to know. Tell Lindsey if I'm not available. I won't tolerate interference at this stage. Will you do that?"

She nodded.

He smiled but it was a tight, cold smile. "I have no doubt that you'll make a success of this."

"I hope so." It was a husky whisper. Her throat was dry and she had no confidence.

He hesitated then spoke with brusque efficiency. "Lindsey has the head of the film-crew with him. He'll give you a complete script and a rundown on camera angles. You'll be taken to the wardrobe section for measurements and so on. By the end of the morning Lindsey will have worked out a schedule so you'll know what time's involved."

There was a knock on the door.

"That'll be your escort." Again that tight smile. "No doubt I'll see you on the beach in due course."

On the beach. Eve felt sick but she did her best to cover her reaction as Paul Lamarr led her to the door. She had been lashed enough by his scepticism. Self-protection demanded that she hide her vulnerability from him. He passed her over to the waiting man with barely a nod.

Eve took a deep breath. Paul Lamarr had dismissed her in all but a professional sense. That left her nothing but to be professional. So be it then, she decided firmly as she walked towards the first practical beginnings of the job ahead of her.

CHAPTER SEVEN

THE moment of truth was fast approaching. The rehearsals had not gone badly but Eve knew that Lloyd Rivers was not impressed with her performance. The rotund film-director had coaxed and prodded and pleaded, then snuffled behind his luxuriant beard at the results of his efforts. His hands had rubbed more agitatedly at the impressive paunch as the blue eyes had gradually lost their sparkle. His final words of praise had lacked enthusiasm. They had been trotted out with synthetic approval. He obviously thought she could do no better.

Eve was not sure of it herself. She knew the beach was inhibiting her. She tried to tell herself it was not the same. Caravans and various other vehicles were parked around the log-cabin. There were people everywhere, busy on their various tasks. John Lindsey danced close attendance, ensuring that no problems arose. Eve had been given courteous attention by all the staff. And Paul Lamarr had stayed away. All she had to do was throw more of herself into the role. But that involved remembering too much. And the memories hurt.

Nan Perkins stood back, her pencil-slim body poised at an uncomfortable angle as she scanned the mirror in front of Eve. She pushed irritably at the wave of strawberry-blonde hair which flopped over

her forehead. The large brown eyes narrowed in critical judgment. "I think a deeper shade of lip-gloss,"
she muttered and rummaged in the make-up box for
the right tube.

Eve sat very still, her lips slightly parted while the
beautician applied the gloss with swift, skilful strokes.
Nan Perkins was in charge of costume as well as make-
up and she was extremely efficient. All the Lamarr
people were efficient. The whole programme had gone
ahead like clockwork. In a few minutes Eve would be
dressed ready to shoot the first scene. She would leave
the caravan, walk down to the water's edge and cameras would begin to roll.

Nan Perkins drew back and studied the mirror
again. "That does it. You'll look completely natural
on film." She glanced at her watch. "Time to dress."

Eve stripped to her briefs. She was not to wear a bra
under the Tee-shirt mini-dress. The garment was a far
better fit than Paul Lamarr's Tee-shirt but the effect
was similar. Instead of a man's belt she wore a pretty
girdle of shells. Her only other prop was a clear plastic bag containing a variety of shells which she had
supposedly picked up along the beach.

There was a tap on the door of the caravan. "Ready,
Nan?" It was John Lindsey keeping everything on
schedule.

"Ready!" Nan Perkins gave Eve a friendly pat on
the back and a smile which held satisfaction at a job
well done. "You look lovely. Good luck!"

"Thanks," Eve croaked, a lump of nervousness
rising in her throat.

John Lindsey greeted her with a wide grin as she
stepped out of the caravan. "Time to get it in the can.
The sun's about to set."

Eve glanced at the horizon. Sea and sky were bathed in glorious colour. The cameras were to capture the last shimmering hues of the sunset before panning in on Eve as she strolled along the beach. She saw that the film-crew were all at their stations. It was not until she and John Lindsey had begun walking down the sand that she noticed the tall, powerful figure standing next to Lloyd Rivers. Her hand clutched the arm swinging next to hers.

"Forgotten something?" the PR man inquired anxiously.

"No." Eve drew in a sharp, steadying breath. "That is Mr Lamarr, isn't it?"

"With Lloyd? Of course. He wouldn't miss the shooting. He's ridden this project all the way."

Eve's nerves screwed a little tighter. She should have expected him. He had said he would see her on the beach, but his absence up to this point had been one pressure removed. To have to perform in front of him—now—when there was no longer any time for trial and error, produced mind-bending pressure. She could not do it. She had to. She was committed and there was no way out. There was no way she could even ignore his presence. John Lindsey steered a direct line to the two men.

"Eve..." Paul Lamarr nodded an off-hand greeting, his eyes skimming over her in quick appraisal. "You look the part. Rivers tells me the rehearsals went smoothly."

Eve darted a look at the film-director but his attention was on the camera-crew. A self-conscious flush crept into her cheeks. "They were all right," she murmured.

"Time to take up position, Eve," Lloyd Rivers cut in abruptly. "We might need several takes and I don't want to run out of light. When I give you the signal just take it smooth and easy like we practised. Okay?"

She nodded, avoiding Paul Lamarr's intent gaze.

"And walk up the dry sand. We can't have footprints near the water's edge," was the final instruction as she turned to go.

She could feel those dark eyes following her. The hand holding the bag of shells grew clammy. The sand dragged at her feet. The memory of that other afternoon was suffocatingly close. She tried to push it away, tried to concentrate on the job which had to be done, but Paul Lamarr was watching her and his presence thwarted any possible attempt to act naturally.

With a dull sense of fatalism Eve took up the rehearsed position where dry sand met the damp graininess left by dying waves. She fixed her gaze on camera three which was to pan in on her face at the critical moment.

"Ready to roll?"

The director's call was answered by each camera-crew.

"Eve?"

"Ready," she called back. She was as ready as she ever would be, under the circumstances.

"Action!"

Eve forced her legs to move in a relaxed stroll. A wave gently rolled the shell which was her first stop. She bent down, picked it up, held it briefly to her ear to listen to the sea's echo, then dropped it into the bag she was carrying. The Fantasy shell was several paces further on. She pounced on it, tried to project excitement as she opened it. The rehearsed movements were carried out one by one. No fumbling. No mistakes. At last she could close her eyes as she caressed the perfume down the line of her throat.

"Cut! That's a take," the director confirmed in his unenthusiastic but decisive voice.

It was over. Relief was sending out tenuous threads of relaxation when another voice sliced through them, bringing instant tension.

"Everyone please stay in position. Rivers, a word with you." It was a harsh, peremptory voice, the voice of command. Paul Lamarr was not pleased.

A sigh of defeat drained Eve of all caring. She stood there listlessly, her fingers idly replacing the perfume stopper. A sideways glance showed the two men in earnest conversation. She knew she had done what Lloyd Rivers had expected of her. He would be assuring Paul Lamarr that the take was as good as any he would get.

"It's not what I want!" Frustration exploding.

"She hasn't got it to give." Decisive judgment.

Eve dropped her gaze to the Fantasy shell in her hands. The perfume held no magic for her. Only Paul Lamarr had given her the magic she craved and somewhere the spell had been lost, dissipated on the winds of mistrust.

She was unaware of the pathetic picture she made, head bowed, shoulders slumped, one toe drawing aimless squiggles in the sand as she struggled with her inner pain. She was unaware of Paul Lamarr's purposeful approach until his words cut into her heart.

"What in hell do you think you're playing at? Wooden mannequins?"

Her head snapped up as if jerked by a string. His hands fell on her shoulders, strong, impatient hands which swung her around to face him. His mouth was a thin, angry line, his eyes puzzled, probing.

"It doesn't live, Eve. You didn't put any feeling into it. Don't you want to make a success of this?"

She stared at him, her eyes bleak with the memory of what had been lost. Her lips moved in a defensive mumble. "I told you I wasn't an actress."

"You don't have to act. All you have to do is remember." His fingers tightened their grasp, digging into the soft flesh of her shoulders. "Don't you remember that afternoon, Eve? Wasn't it good?" His eyes burned into hers, demanding that she relive the memory.

"It wasn't real," she choked out, fighting to counter the turmoil he was provoking inside of her.

"It was real!" he insisted vehemently. "You were here. On this beach. Paddling through this water. You found a shell and you were in love with the dream of freedom. You can't have forgotten," he added passionately.

"No," she whispered, caught up in the emotion which throbbed through his voice.

"Then live it again! Do it for the camera. Isn't that what you love more than anything else?"

Pain twisted across her face. "Oh God!" she sobbed and tried to wrench herself out of his hold. "You don't understand," she begged helplessly.

"What don't I understand?"

She shook her head, blinking back the tears.

"Eve..."

The hard urgency in his voice brought a surge of hysteria. "Let me go! I'll try. I'll try again. But you've got to leave. I can't do it in front of you. Just go away and let me get on with it. Please!''

The wildness of her speech brought a heavy frown to his face. "I'm affecting your performance?"

"Yes...no!" she cried out in confusion, desperate for him to leave but equally desperate not to reveal how deeply he affected her.

His hands gentled their hold and ran caressingly down her arms.

She shivered and shrank away from him. "Please don't touch me."

He stared at her, disbelief struggling with some other, stronger emotion which stirred her pulse-rate into leaps and bounds. "All right. I'll go," he said with slow, almost strained deliberation. "You'll give me what I want, Eve?"

"If...if I can." She could not promise, yet she could not deny the tortured demand of his eyes.

He nodded and turned away, striding back to the film director who was standing patiently near one of his camera-crews, waiting for further orders. They were given with sharp, decisive gestures. Paul Lamarr called John Lindsey to his side. More words were spoken. Then Paul Lamarr was walking up the beach. There was no backward glance. He made straight for the four-wheel-drive Land-Rover which was parked on the grass verge.

"Righto! Let's move everyone!" Lloyd Rivers barked out. "Get those footprints wiped off the sand, shells back in position, film ready to roll. Come on! Come on! Action stations and fast about it!"

He beckoned Eve over to the dry sand. She moved on leaden feet, still watching Paul Lamarr's departure. The Land-Rover roared into life, turned in a tight circle and headed off up the bush-track to the high-way.

"You okay?" the film-director asked softly. He stroked his beard and pursed his lips before stretching them into a wry curve. "You look a bit shell-shocked if you'll pardon the pun."

"I'm okay," she assured him. "How long have I got?"

"Maximum ten minutes. The light's going fast. We can cut in the sunset from the last take but it's better if we don't have to. Think you can do it?"

"I'll get into place." There was a limit to her assurances.

Eve spent the time immersing herself in the memories of that one magical afternoon. Fears and doubts were ruthlessly locked away. She did not allow herself to question why she should do this for Paul Lamarr, why she should give him this gift of her inner self. Some deep, basic need in her demanded that he see and understand what she had felt that day.

"Action!"

The word prompted her to move. She felt the inner tensions drift away as the sea-breeze wafted through her hair. She could do it for him. She could feel it now, the heady sense of freedom. Only sand and sea around her... and there was the shell. Childish delight in its perfection. The sea-roar reverberated through her brain, mingled with the echo of words telling her she was beautiful. And another shell. Pink fantasy. Perfume. Its scent sharpened by salt air. Enticing. Beautiful. Caressing her skin. And the memory of tender hands stroking her, loving her. And she wanted that love again. So much. So very much.

"Cut!"

Slowly, reluctantly, Eve dragged herself out of the self-induced dream. A heavy wave of depression washed over her as reality returned with all its emptiness. Remarks flew around the film-crews. She was vaguely aware of excitement on the air but was untouched by it.

"Get that in the can and hold it with kid-gloves!" Lloyd Rivers roared above the hubbub.

"Sure you don't want another take, Lloyd?" someone yelled.

"Drown that idiot!" the film-director retorted with a laugh. He strode over to Eve and wrapped her in a boisterous bear-hug. "That was great! Great!" he boomed. "We'll have this commercial wrapped up in gold if you play it like that tomorrow. Beautiful! Absolutely beautiful!"

Eve flushed with embarrassment and wriggled out of his arms. "I'm glad you liked it," she muttered.

"Liked it! My God! It sent shivers up my spine." His grin faded as he sensed her detachment from his jubilance. "Hey..." he breathed softly, "you're not feeling so good, are you?"

She shrugged. "I'm not an actress. The feeling has to come, and now I'm tired. If it's all over for now, I think I'll go up to my caravan."

"I'll take you up," he offered, quick to pamper her needs now that she had proved worthy of special attention.

"No. I'd rather go alone, and you must have work to finish up here," she added tactfully.

"As you like," he agreed with an easy shrug.

Eve turned to go but his hand suddenly snaked out to stop her. She glanced back at him questioningly.

"Mind telling me something?"

The curiosity in his eyes sparked a defensive wariness. "That depends on what it is."

"I've been in this game a long time and I'm no fool at my job," he stated matter-of-factly. "I know how to get the best out of the material I have to work with. This afternoon I used up my whole experience on you and you gave me only the mechanics. Nothing more. Not even a glimmer of the response Paul Lamarr got out of you. So what did he say? I'm always ready to learn new tricks."

"Ask him," she said more curtly than she meant to.

His eyes narrowed speculatively. "He's not a man I care to cross."

A wry smile curved Eve's lips. "I guess I don't care to cross him either. Thanks for your forbearance. And I hope I can please you tomorrow."

He let her go without further comment but Eve was not allowed to go alone. John Lindsey fell into step with her.

"Lloyd sounded pleased," he remarked with his easy charm.

"Yes."

"He obviously got what he wanted."

"What Paul Lamarr wanted," Eve corrected flatly.

They trudged a few steps in silence.

"You sound a bit down. Anything I can do for you, Eve?"

She threw him a weary glance. "No. I just want to change out of these clothes and go to my caravan. Be alone for a while. Does that have your approval?"

"It's not a question of my approval," he protested. "I simply want to ensure that . . ."

"That there are no problems. I know," Eve sighed. "Well, he's got what he wanted so there's no prob-

lem. I just have to live with it, that's all." Tears filmed
her eyes, turning them into a green haze of pain as she
turned to the PR man. "And you know what the worst
of it is? He doesn't even know what he's got."

John Lindsey's face was a caricature of incompre-
hension. He gestured his frustration. "If you'll explain..."

They had reached Nan Perkins' caravan. Eve
dashed the moisture from her eyes and took a deep
breath. "It doesn't matter. Take no notice. I'm only
maundering. Put it down to the artistic temperament.
Please leave me alone now."

Before he could say any more Eve opened the caravan door and stepped inside. Nan Perkins was not
there. Eve quickly changed into her own clothes, put
the mini-dress on a hanger in the cupboard and was
about to leave when the beautician came hurrying in.

"Sorry! Didn't realize you'd come up. Need any
help?" she asked breathlessly.

"No, thank you. I put the dress away. I was just
going."

"Are you all right, Eve? John thought you might
need company. I'll come along with you if you like. A
chat might help you wind down. Even old hands like
ourselves rarely see a performance like that."

Eve could not help a dry smile. "Does John Lindsey always fuss around like a mother hen?"

Nan Perkins returned the smile. "You can't blame
him. I've never seen Mr Lamarr so uptight. Of course,
Mrs Delaney would love to see him fall flat on his face
over this project. That bitch has..." She paused as if
suddenly realising she had been indiscreet. "Well,
never mind Company politics. And congratulations!
Lloyd's walking around with his stomach puffed out

and everyone's terribly pleased. We all respect Paul Lamarr. And like the way he runs the Company. His sister is a bitch," she added feelingly.

"I can't say I cared much for Kristen Delaney either," Eve commented. "Thanks for the offer of company, Nan, but I really would prefer to be alone."

"Okay. I'll see you at dinner then."

Eve hesitated. Dinner was to be served in the log-cabin. She cringed at the thought of sitting in there for any length of time. Her memories had been brought too close to the surface. "I think I'll make myself a snack in the caravan and go to bed early. Will you make my excuses to the others please, Nan?"

A frown creased the other woman's forehead as she peered anxiously at Eve. "Sure you're all right?"

"Yes. Don't worry. I'll be fine tomorrow." She threw a reassuring smile over her shoulder as she stepped outside then shook her head at John Lindsey who was hovering near the log-cabin.

The caravan which had been supplied for her private use stood at the back of the cabin to the left of the water-tanks. She climbed into it and shut out the world with a vast feeling of relief. The cupboards and refrigerator had been provisioned. There was no need to face anyone this evening, no need for polite smiles and pretended interest. She could indulge herself to her heart's content, only there was no contentment in her heart.

The caravan had a comfortable double bed. She crawled on to it and buried her head in the pillows. The tears she had repressed were given free flow and they flowed for a long time, great welling tears, pushed out by surging waves of misery.

The knock on the caravan door was an intolerable intrusion. Eve dragged a pillow over her head and ignored it. To hell with them all, she thought rebelliously. Whatever was wanted could wait until tomorrow. She had done all that was required of her today. A sharper rap carried impatience and insistence but Eve stubbornly clung to silence.

"Eve, I know you're in the caravan. Either you open the door or I'm coming in anyway."

A chill ran through Eve's blood. That was Paul Lamarr's voice. But he had gone. She had seen him leave. How could it be his voice? Unless he had come back to check on her performance. But Lloyd Rivers would have reassured him so what did Paul Lamarr want now? Hadn't she given him enough of herself today?

"Eve, I'm coming in." Hard. Purposeful. Relentless.

"No! Wait!"

Panic shot her off the bed. She couldn't let him see her like this, tear-stained, dishevelled, her defences in tatters.

"I'll only be a minute. Please wait," she called out, concentrating fiercely on pulling herself together.

She whirled over to the sink, slapped her face with water and briskly towelled it dry, hoping to put colour in her cheeks. Suspecting that he would not give her time to change out of her crumpled clothes, she straightened them as best she could, ran a brush through her hair, took a deep breath and stepped over to the door. No sooner had she pushed it open than Paul Lamarr was brushing past her.

She pulled the door shut after him and immediately berated herself for not having the presence of mind to get out of the caravan. Paul Lamarr dominated its small space and he was too close to her, suffocatingly close. In a bid to minimise his disturbing presence she slid into one of the bench-seats behind the table and only fluttering a side-glance in his direction, gestured an invitation for him to take the opposite one.

"Please sit down, Mr Lamarr."

The words were stiffly polite, too obviously ill-at-ease and he made no move. Eve was forced to look up at him. The dark eyes burned into hers, anxiously probing. She swiftly lowered her lashes, speaking quickly in an attempt to hide her inner agitation.

"Why did you want to see me? We've finished for the day. Mr Rivers was satisfied with the last take."

"More than satisfied," came the soft reply. "Why are you so upset?"

"I'm not upset," she flashed back resentfully. "I'm tired. That's all."

She could not hold his disturbing gaze without giving away the lie and she would not accept the humiliation of the truth. She stared down at the table.

"Rivers, Lindsey, Nan Perkins, they all said the same thing. You're wound up tight. Too tight. Not the usual reaction to success, Eve."

Anger rose to the insidious taunt and flared off her tongue before she could stifle it. "I did what you wanted. I haven't wasted your money. What do you want now? Just say it. Say it and leave me alone."

Was it merely the reflection of her own agonised eyes in his? For one vivid moment they seemed to be one again and Eve was tempted to reach out and beg him to understand. The need to recapture what they had once shared hammered through her body and he seemed to be generating the force behind the feeling. But no...no...it couldn't be so. Not after all he'd said and done. Eve wrenched her gaze away, and lest she be drawn into some weak stupidity, she propped her elbows on the table and covered her face with her hands.

"Eve..."

Was it a plea? The rough urgency in his voice suggested it might be so but she could not let herself believe it. She heard the sharp intake of breath and the whisper of a sigh before the touch came on her shoulder. She automatically shrank from it, remembering all too well how he had reviled her for responding to him that first morning in his office. The touch was withdrawn.

"Eve, if you don't want to go on with it. If what I've asked is...if it's hurting you, I'll release you from the contract. It wasn't my intention to hurt you, Eve."

The soft, caring words bit into her heart, painfully recalling the man he had been on the beach. Fantasy, she reminded herself. This could only be compassion for the emotional strain he had inflicted on her. Tears pricked her eyes but she resolutely forced them back. Dear God! She didn't want to go on with it but what else could she do now? Where was she to go? Back to her mother and Simon and admit failure?

"I have no other choice. I must go on with it," she choked out despairingly.

His silence shrieked along her nerves. Go away, go away, she cried in wordless torment. At last he spoke, and his voice sounded as strained as Eve felt.

"I'm sorry. I didn't mean to place more stress on you by this visit. I only wanted to...to let you know there would be no question of demanding recompense if you wished to walk out on the contract. I hope it goes well for you tomorrow."

Then he was gone, the caravan door rattling on the emptiness he had left behind. Eve felt like a hollow shell, as if he had taken her life-force with him. Why had he softened? What had made him regret tying her into this contract which he had planned so ruthlessly?

Eve shook her head in hopeless confusion. She would never understand why he had done anything, why he had even bothered to save her from the sea. At least death was peaceful, she thought grimly. But so very final, the voice of sanity whispered, and while there was life there was always hope of something good turning up...sometime.

She dragged herself up, made a pot of tea and cut some cheese on to biscuits. The crumbs had to be washed down her throat but she munched on. There was no point in making herself faint from lack of sustenance. She had to get through tomorrow. Paul Lamarr would have the commercial he wanted. Kristen Delaney would have to admit defeat. And Eve...she would have her career, her meaningless, empty career, full of bright lights and inner darkness.

She undressed. The night air had turned unexpectedly chill. With a little shiver she pulled on a nightie, snapped off the light and climbed under the blankets. She turned the damp pillows over and settled herself comfortably. Still sleep would not come. She opened a window and listened to the soothing drone of the sea. It should have soothed her but it didn't. She tossed and turned, her body restless with too many frustrated yearnings.

She heard the muted voices of other people going off to bed. In an attempt to block out disturbing thoughts she concentrated on picking out the sounds of nature; the hum of insects, the intermittent birdcalls, the rustle of leaves. Eventually sleep stole over her but it was full of shadows, nameless, frightening things which tormented her subconscious and gave her no rest.

CHAPTER EIGHT

EVE woke, tired and listless. A buzz of activity told her the day had begun outside. The final scenes of the commercial would not be shot until after sunset but preparation for those crucial minutes would go on all day. Eve dreaded those few minutes. They loomed ahead of her like another nightmare.

Once she had dreamt of being a star, famous, fêted by other celebrities, admired across the world. She had never dreamt of the price that had to be paid for stardom, the sheer personal cost which stripped her life of the privacy she valued. It was too high a price. To perform what had to be performed this evening would leave her emotionally barren.

She could not do it. Would not. Paul Lamarr would have to be satisfied with less than he wanted, even if it meant she forfeited her chance of a contract. She did not want a contract with him anyway. His presence always brought pain and confusion.

"Eve! Breakfast in twenty minutes. Are you awake?" It was John Lindsey, rounding up his wayward chick for the main event.

"Yes. I'll be out in time," she called back, resigning herself to the inevitable.

She brooded through breakfast, eating little so as to be out of the log-cabin as quickly as possible. She took her coffee outside to where some folding chairs had been set up under the trees. John Lindsey joined her, his forehead puckered with concern.

"Are you all right, Eve? You look a bit pale this morning."

"No make-up," she smiled, not wanting to discuss how she felt.

He did not respond to her smile. His eyes scanned her worriedly. "Any problems I can deal with?"

She avoided his intent gaze, looking past him to the sparkling sea. "No. It's a lovely morning, isn't it?"

He sighed and dropped into the chair next to her. "Should be a lovely day. If all goes well."

Eve sipped her coffee while John Lindsey checked over the work programme with her, making sure she knew where she was expected to be and when. It was an unnecessary exercise but Eve let him talk on, preferring the conversation to be impersonal. Eventually she excused herself to change for the morning rehearsals.

The mermaid scene required her to be in the water. Eve pulled on a comfortable maillot. It was cut high on the thighs for easy leg movement and while it had no real support for her breasts, the stretch fabric held them firmly. She hesitated over a beach-coat then decided it was useless. The sun was already warm and once rehearsals began it would have to be discarded anyway. She picked up a large beach-towel and returned to John Lindsey.

The burr of an approaching vehicle had drawn his attention. Eve followed his gaze and immediately tensed as Paul Lamarr's Land-Rover bounced around the last turn of the rutted track.

"That'll be Halliday now."

Eve glanced sharply at the PR man. "Not Mr Lamarr?"

He threw her a curious look. "The Land-Rover's a Company vehicle. Were you expecting Mr Lamarr this morning?"

"No. I . . . No."

She shook her head and once again took refuge in looking out to sea, fiercely telling herself to put Paul Lamarr out of her mind. It was impossible. The whole environment conspired to remind her of him. However, by the time the Land-Rover pulled up beside them she had succeeded in masking her inner tension.

Eve recognised the driver as John Lindsey's man from the PR Department. His passenger alighted with all the cocky confidence of a man who was used to and expected adulation. He filled the tall, dark and handsome mould in every category; lustrous black curls, flashing eyes, white, white teeth, and a body which had been poured into skin-tight jeans and Tee-shirt, all the better to show off the very male muscularity of his undeniably splendid physique.

His eyes gloated down Eve's body and up again. One wickedly arched eyebrow accompanied his opening remark. "You're Eve Childe? The legs I recognise but the body and face are something else again. The nymphet has definitely turned into a delectable woman. Something tells me I'm going to enjoy being your lover."

Never, Eve flung at him silently. She was repulsed by the blatant ego of the man and even more repulsed by the thought of being intimately handled by him.

John Lindsey performed the formal introduction. Eve nodded coolly and very pointedly turned her attention to the conversation between the two PR men.

"Any messages?"

The driver shook his head. "I have to get straight back. I've got some news for you though. I'll be driving out this afternoon with none other than the old lady herself."

"Margot Lamarr?"

"And Mrs Delaney. They're both coming."

There was a short speculative silence which was broken by Rick Halliday, preening himself with self-importance. "The ladies obviously want to see the action, and there's no way I'm going to disappoint them. Nothing like a V.I.P. audience to get the adrenalin running."

"Well, it seems you'll have it," John Lindsey said blandly, but his eyes darted anxiously at Eve for her reaction.

Her carefully impassive face revealed none of the nervous tension which had just tied another knot in her stomach.

"Thanks for the tip-off, Dave. Be sure to give the ladies a very smooth trip."

"No worries," the driver grinned. "It's not every day I get to be the Queen's chauffeur. Be seeing you."

He climbed back into the Land-Rover, gave a jaunty wave and was off. John Lindsey sighed with some feeling, then turned back to his two charges. Before he could say anything a shout from the beach demanded their attention. Lloyd Rivers was beckoning them down.

Rick Halliday draped his arm around Eve's shoulders and leered at her. "No rest for the wicked. Let's go, baby."

Eve stiffened. Her initial antagonism deepened to loathing. This obnoxious man was to play her fantasy lover! The whole concept now seemed doubly impossible. How could she pretend any positive feeling at all when her whole body was screaming negatives?

"We're not rehearsing yet, Mr Halliday," she said coldly and shrugged off his arm. She fixed her gaze on Lloyd Rivers and strode ahead, kicking the sand with angry feet.

Rick Halliday quickly caught up with her, completely unabashed by her coolness. "This is our big chance, baby-doll. World-wide circulation! And am I going to make the most of it. Rudolph Valentino, here I come!"

And the awful part was, he took himself seriously. He really did think he was the world's greatest gift to women and his conceit extended into the rehearsals. His attempt to turn the kiss in the mermaid scene into a full-scale assault on her mouth made Eve shudder with revulsion.

"No time for all that, Halliday," Lloyd Rivers cut in drily. "Make it short and sweet. We're not running to a full-length movie. Let's just get the action flowing. Finesse can come later."

It took considerable practice to get the second scene timed correctly. Having been lifted from the water and kissed, Eve had to push away from her lover, dance a few steps to show the joy of having legs instead of a tail, perform an ecstatic pirouette, then rush back to her lover for the final, exultant lift into the air and slide-down embrace. Rick Halliday made the most of that slide-down embrace. His hands relished the exploration of every curve. By the time Lloyd Rivers was satisfied with the routine, Eve was sickened by their lecherous touch.

"Lunch and rest now."

The words were a welcome release. Eve picked up her beach-towel and wrapped it around her. She felt cold right through to her soul.

"Eve, walk up with me," Lloyd Rivers ordered rather than invited.

She fell into step beside him, stonily silent.

The film director puffed along, finding the dry sand hard going with the weight he had to carry. His slow progress ensured that the rest of the company was soon out of earshot.

"Eve, if I thought I was going to shoot that sequence as you just played it, I'd walk into the sea and drown myself. I've let it pass because you've got the mechanics right. But I'm telling you now, if you don't come up with the feeling when we shoot this evening, we've got dead film. And all the magic of yesterday will be wasted. You do appreciate that?"

"Yes."

He glanced sharply at her, not liking the brief answer. "This is important to me, Eve. A man gets tired of making hum-drum commercials even if he makes them well. This is something special. Can you reproduce the mood?"

They were Paul Lamarr's words. Empty, meaningless words, asking the impossible. She had only had one lover. Alone she might have been able to relive those intense emotions which the fantasy required. But with Rick Halliday...never!

"I can try," she answered evasively.

Lloyd Rivers showed his frustration by pulling up and frowning heavily at her. "There's time for more rehearsals this afternoon."

"No. No more." Her tone was too emphatic for any argument. She tried an appeasing smile to gloss over her sharpness. "It wouldn't serve any purpose. As you said, I've got the mechanics right."

"Yeah! The mechanics!" he said disgustedly and gave a defeated sigh. "Well, play it your way. God knows it seems I have no say in it."

They had almost reached the log-cabin. Eve excused herself and sought the balm of solitude in her caravan. At least there she was free of questions and Rick Halliday could not bother her. She stripped and washed herself clean, made some lunch, ate it without appetite, then lay down on the bed.

Sheer weariness dragged her into sleep. It was deep and dreamless. An insistent call demanded that she climb out of it but her subconscious did not want to respond. She clung on to the dark nothingness until someone was shaking her shoulder. Her head swam with reluctance but she opened her eyes. For a moment she felt completely disorientated, but then she recognised the woman who stood over her and reality swept back with a vengeance. She groaned and turned over.

"Sorry, Eve, but you'll have to get up now," Nan Perkins warned kindly. "We don't want to run short of time."

Eve heaved herself off the bed and headed for the sink. She splashed water on to her face, had a quick drink, then gestured her readiness to Nan Perkins.

"You look wrecked," the woman said sympathetically, "but we'll soon do something about that. Didn't you sleep well last night?"

"Too restless," Eve explained shortly.

"Too worked up," came the knowing comment. "Never mind. It'll be all over today. Let's get on with it."

Nan stood guard at the laundry door while Eve showered and shampooed her hair. She hurried the ablutions. There were too many memories here, just as there were in the main room of the cabin. She wrapped herself in the towelling beach-coat then accompanied Nan to her caravan.

In contrast to yesterday there was much to be done. Eve's hair was more carefully arranged into its soft curls. Her fingernails and toenails were varnished a pearly pink. After that, the make-up; a delicate blusher on her cheeks which gave her skin a luminous quality, frosted pink on her lips, and an other-worldly emphasis given to her eyes. A tiny sprinkling of glitter highlighted the arch of her eyebrows. Deep, sea-green shadow on her lids gradually faded to the lightest suggestion of silver-green above her eyes. Below the lower lashes the silver-green was repeated, along with a few minute touches of glitter.

Fitting Eve into the mermaid costume took considerable time. First there was the foam-rubber padding to fill out her legs to a smooth tapering shape. The tail itself was moulded from plastic which was rolled on and pulled snugly to her hipline. With her lower body turned into that of a mermaid, the final costume could be drawn on.

Constructed from a stretch fabric, the tail section was heavily sequinned to give the effect of gleaming green scales. Once it passed the hipline, a finer, transparent fabric formed the bodice. It was flesh-coloured and barely visible. The sequins of the tail became less and less concentrated until only a modest sprinkle high-lighted the rounded thrust of Eve's breasts.

The last adornment was a pendant necklace. Tiny miniatures of the pink Fantasy shell were threaded on a silver chain with the full-size perfume container as a central pendant. This was Eve's one prop for the mermaid scene. She was to finger it dreamily until her fantasy lover surprised her.

"Now you look fantastic!" Nan grinned at her, having taken stock of the finished product.

Eve lay on a dust-sheet on the floor, feeling like a stuffed turkey which was destined to be fed to the lions, or rather, lionesses. Nan had reported the arrival of Margot Lamarr and Kristen Delaney some ten minutes ago. Paul Lamarr had not been mentioned and Eve had not asked about him. She did not want to think of Paul Lamarr. She did not want to think of anything. She just wanted this whole thing finished, behind her.

John Lindsey knocked and entered. "Ready to go?" His eyes glinted appreciation as he took in the fairy-tale quality of Eve's mermaid. "That costume is a work of genius, Nan. Sexiest damned thing I ever saw. No offence, Eve," he added quickly.

"No doubt it'll help get me through this first scene," she answered drily.

He beckoned outside and the driver of the Land-Rover climbed into the caravan.

"Wowee!" the younger man goggled at her. "Maybe I ought to take up fishing."

"Enough of that!" Nan Perkins laughed, pleased with their reactions to her work. "You tear off one sequin as you carry Eve down and I'll have your heads."

With Nan directing the operation the two men picked Eve up, manoeuvred her outside and carried her down the beach.

Lloyd Rivers detached himself from Rick Halliday, shouted orders at the camera-crews and set about directing Eve's exact positioning at the water's edge. He had obviously been watching the run of the waves. Eve was placed so that her tail was just lapped by the water. He checked her pose, moved her supporting arm a little further out so that she was sitting with more of a lean, then waded to the camera platform to make sure that the angle was exactly right.

Eve did not glance around. She had seen the watching group which stood outside the camera-lines but it was easier to pretend it had nothing to do with her. People moved around her, washing out footprints. Lloyd Rivers came ploughing back. He stood over her, a grim look of determination on his chubby face.

"Well, it's up to you, my girl. You look gorgeous enough to stun the viewers anyway, but I want more than that. You've got five minutes to think yourself into the role. For God's sake, do it!"

Eve's fingers sought the Fantasy shell which hung around her neck. She stared out to sea, trying to blot everything from her mind, all the twisted, painful thoughts which had tormented her. Gradually the sea rolled over them, the primitive, powerful force of nature which dominated all horizons.

"Action!"

But the sea was empty. She needed something, someone to share the emptiness of her world. Someone to bring her alive. There was so much feeling in her aching to be let out, given, shared, waiting only for the right touch.

The touch when it came was of hot, grasping hands, lifting her up to a hot, demanding mouth which determinedly invaded hers. Instinctively she struggled, frantically pushing at hard, muscular shoulders, bending her head back, fighting desperately to escape that loathsomely questing mouth.

"Cut!"

She kept clawing her revulsion even as he thrust her back.

"You bitch!" Rick Halliday snarled down at her. "You've ruined the whole bloody scene! What in hell were you fighting me for?"

"Shut up, Halliday!" Suddenly Lloyd Rivers was there, taking her into his arms, supporting her with a gentleness which was in total variance to the sharpness of his order.

"It wasn't my fault!" Rick Halliday protested angrily. "She came at me like a hell-cat. God! You'd think I was trying to rape her or something."

Eve shuddered and hid her face against the wide expanse of shirt above Lloyd Rivers' paunch. "I'm sorry," she mumbled.

She received a comforting pat on the head. "Don't you worry about a thing," the film-director assured her softly. "We can edit that last bit out. The rest of it was brilliant. Brilliant! That's all that matters for now. We'll go on to the next scene."

Tears swam into her eyes. "I can't do it. I can't," she choked out.

His arms tightened around her. "Yes, you can. You've got to do it. God! A woman who can emote as you just did can do anything. Now you just calm yourself down while Nan Perkins gets you ready for the finale." He ruffled her hair in a tender gesture of encouragement then raised his voice. "Lindsey! Get moving! And handle with care. This is valuable merchandise.''

Eve was once more carried over the beach. She shut her ears to the babble of voices around her. Fortunately John Lindsey and his helper had the tact to remain silent. They laid her carefully on the dust-sheet in the caravan and swiftly departed.

Nan Perkins set to work, quickly stripping off the sequinned outer garment. Eve helped her roll the plastic tail down and remove the padding. It was a physical relief to be free of that uncomfortable constriction but there was no relief from the ordeal which stretched ahead of her.

With quick, efficient skill Nan repaired and touched up the intricate make-up on Eve's face. Then she held the sea-green dress while Eve stepped into it. Bikini briefs were stitched on to the hipline where a band of sequins supported the filmy, chiffon skirt. The bodice was an exact replica of the mermaid costume so that the transformation from sea siren to woman had visual continuity. Nan repositioned the shell necklace and Eve was ready for the final scene. Ready as far as all outward appearances were concerned. She would never be ready to respond to Rick Halliday with the emotion expected of her.

John Lindsey escorted her back down the beach. Eve darted a nervous glance at the V.I.P. group. Margot Lamarr was speaking to Lloyd Rivers. Kristen Delaney was chatting to Rick Halliday who was wearing a very smug smile. Eve winced and let her eyes skate over Paul Lamarr. He stood slightly aloof from the others and she knew he was watching her approach. Lloyd Rivers tapped Halliday's shoulder and broke away from the group, relieving Eve of the necessity to meet and speak to anyone.

He met her, wrapped his big hand around hers and squeezed it in a conspiratorial fashion. "One more effort, Eve. That's all we need. We'll pick it up from where you were pushing at Halliday's shoulders. The camera will run down your body to capture the moment when your toes hit the sand. Then up again, and your body has to look pliant, yielding, for that one long shot before you break away."

"No kiss," Eve demanded stonily.

Lloyd Rivers took note of the rebellious storm in her eyes and made the concession without argument. "No kiss. We'll turn you three-quarter on so that it need only be simulated. That won't throw you off?"

Eve dropped her lashes, unable to answer the anxious question in the film-director's eyes. "It'll help," she muttered.

They had walked down to the water's edge. Eve was in position for the final shoot. Lloyd Rivers patted her hand. "Wait here. I'll get Halliday sorted out. We'll have one brief practice of that embrace and then we'll shoot. Okay now?"

She nodded.

It was several minutes before he was back. Eve had not watched him. She did not want to look at Rick Halliday... or anyone else.

"All right. Now let's get this embrace looking smooth."

Eve sensed Rick Halliday's hostility before she turned around. His hands gripped her waist too tightly. She followed the director's instructions as best she could, trying to ignore the revulsion she felt.

"Relax, you silly bitch!" The words were a venomous hiss and his fingers dug cruelly into her flesh.

"Shut your mouth, Halliday, and keep it shut!" came the harsh rebuke. "Do your part precisely as I said, and Eve will do hers. I'll give you a countdown, Eve, so you can be prepared. Once I call action, you have to give."

They were left alone. Rick Halliday glared after the retreating figure of the film-director then looked down at Eve with hot contempt.

"You know what you need," he jeered at her. "You need someone to grind you into a bed until every last bit of ice is melted. And oh man! Would I love to do it!"

"Five. Four. Three."

Eve placed her hands on his shoulders and began pressing away from him. Rick Halliday took the opportunity to ram her lower body into his as he lifted her up.

"Two. One... action!"

There was no way Eve was going to be persuaded into a repetition of this scene. Spurred on by that thought alone, she carried through the routine action-perfect.

"Cut!"

"Get your hands off me this instant!" Eve snapped at Rick Halliday, her eyes fiercely rejecting him.

His hands slid around with slow insolence and flipped across her breasts as she drew away from him. She barely restrained herself from flying at him tooth and claw.

Lloyd Rivers came charging in, shouting orders in readiness for a replay. He strode up to Eve, heaving dissatisfaction. "Well, what else do you want? That

was useless! You know damned well it was useless!
You've got to put that feeling into it. So what's the
problem now? There's no point in your giving me that
mechanical doll again.''

"That's all you'll get," Eve bit out angrily, too
churned up to even consider his words. She turned on
her heel, blindly intent on escape.

Lloyd Rivers caught her arm and swung her back.
"Are you mad? You can't throw it all away! We're
two-thirds there. Just one more effort from you
and—''

"I won't do it!" she cried wildly.

"You won't do it?" Lloyd Rivers repeated incredulously. He took hold of her shoulders and shook her
as he thundered, "By God! You will do it! We'll shoot
that scene again and again until whatever it is inside
you cracks and I get what I want. You're under contract, my girl!"

"I won't have that load of slime touch me again!
And get your hands off me!" she screamed, flinging
off his grasp.

"What the hell . . ."

"What's the trouble?" Paul Lamarr's voice cut in
with sharp authority.

Lloyd Rivers threw up his hands in disgust. "The
trouble is she's throwing a temperament fit and won't
see sense!"

"Sense!" Eve shrilled. "There's no sense in continuing. If that filthy gorilla comes near me again, I'll
vomit!"

"Halliday?"

She swung on Paul Lamarr, almost beside herself
with fury. "Yes, Rick pig-almighty Halliday! Your
marvellous choice of a fantasy lover, who's so damned

full of himself that fantasy's not good enough for him! Oh no! Full-scale sexual assault is his style, and if you think I'm going to let him paw me again..."

"Now look here, you stuffed-up little snob! If you..."

"That's enough, Halliday," Paul Lamarr directed sternly.

"I haven't even started. She's been pulling against me from the word go. Tell him, Rivers! She isn't even professional enough to do a kiss."

"You'd have to be a professional whore to stomach your kisses," Eve spat at him.

"Why you..."

"I said enough!" There was no arguing with that steely tone. Paul Lamarr raised his voice. "Lindsey, over here!"

The PR man hurried forward, closely trailed by Kristen Delaney.

"See that Mr Halliday leaves immediately. Halliday, we no longer require your services. You'll be paid the agreed fee."

"Now just a Goddamned minute..."

"Immediately!"

"Why is he to leave?" Kristen Delaney demanded.

"It's my decision, Kristen. Don't interfere. Please go, Halliday. There is no percentage in arguing."

"All right, I'm going!" Rick Halliday snarled. "But you're making a big mistake. She's the trouble. Not me!"

Paul Lamarr was unmoved. Lloyd Rivers gesticulated despair as Rick Halliday tramped away.

"Where do we go from here? You saw what we shot just then. She might as well have been a wet rag for all the emotion she showed. It ruins what could have been..."

"We get another man."

Paul Lamarr's pronouncement sparked a tirade of protest from his sister. "Another man! Are you mad, Paul? It takes time to get another man. And more time to set all this up again. Two days' shooting, you said. And who's to say Miss Childe won't object to the next man, and the next? You can't keep on with this obsessive whim of yours. To make it open-ended is sheer pigheadedness. I say she's had her chance. You've used up your budget. It finishes here!"

"Kristen has a valid point, Paul."

He swung around to face his mother. "You saw the film last night. It's worth going on."

"I wouldn't like to throw this one away," Lloyd Rivers spoke up earnestly. "I could fit another shoot into my schedule in a fortnight's time."

"A fortnight! Out of the question!" Kristen Delaney snapped. "Even you can't justify gambling that far, Paul."

He turned sharply to Lloyd Rivers. "Can you shoot it differently? Minimising the man's role. I know he has to be there but the emphasis was always on Eve. I don't think we'd lose much if the emphasis is even more on her. Providing he's reasonably well-built he could be anyone."

"Like more of a prop than a player," came the eager retort. "Yes, it can be done. But you'd better choose someone fast if it's to be done this evening. The light won't last forever."

Paul Lamarr wheeled on Eve. "It's up to you. Look around and pick a man."

"So now we're down to amateur dramatics," his sister sneered. "If she can't co-operate with a professional actor then—"

"Shut up, Kristen! Eve…this is your only chance."

Eve had barely taken in the argument which had whirled around her. Once the abominable Rick Halliday had been removed she had sunk into a dull stupor, too sickened to care what was decided. She did not care about the film, the future, or her career. The last two days had been a nightmare of churning emotions and she only wanted to be released from any continuation of it.

She did not want another chance. Another chance meant dredging around her soul for more feeling and she was all used up. Worn out. Soul-weary. She stared at Paul Lamarr, her eyes pained with the burden he had laid on her.

"Come on, Eve…choose," he urged insistently.

Her mind sought frantically for an escape. And found one. The choice which Paul Lamarr would never accept. "I'll do it with you."

CHAPTER NINE

THE stunned silence was broken by a high-pitched laugh which ended in a gurgle of derision. Kristen Delaney was amused. Her brother wasn't.

"For God's sake, don't be absurd! We haven't time."

His curt impatience only served to reassure Eve that this was indeed the best retreat open to her. "I'll do it with you or not at all," she stated decisively.

"An ultimatum! Your star is not very accommodating, Paul, but since this is your private little gamble, why don't you accommodate her?" Kristen jeered.

He ignored his sister. "Be reasonable, Eve. Don't forget your career. This is make or break time!"

His words no longer had the power to stir the heavy pall of apathy around Eve's heart. She remained silent.

Her passive resistance angered him into a sharp gesture of frustration. He spoke with uncontrolled harshness. "Then that's an end to it if you won't change your mind!"

Her only response was to sag with relief. He had released her. She could leave.

"Paul . . ." Margot Lamarr's voice slid into the impasse with all its imposing authority. "—we have a large investment in this commercial. In business terms,

we are now in a position where we lose everything... or take the one possible course which might
show us a profit. If Miss Childe can do it with you the
Company wins.''

Alarm shrieked through Eve's nerves as she realised that Paul Lamarr was considering his mother's
advice. He could not. Surely he would not.

''Rivers, have the angles worked out before I return. I'm going to change my clothes.''

A broad grin lightened, the director's face. ''Yessir!'' Instantly he was off, shouting orders and wildly
gesticulating.

''Paul, you're not going to demean yourself by...''
Kristen's disbelieving voice petered out as her brother
strode up the beach towards the log-cabin.

Eve could not believe it either. She had been so sure
he would refuse. Despair compressed her heart into a
small heavy lump. How could she do it with him? She
had thrown down the gauntlet, so confident that he
would not pick it up. Now there was no avoiding the
inevitable result. If only he had not been prompted by
his mother. Eve cast a resentful look at Margot Lamarr and caught a gleam of—what was it—heightened watchfulness? Did the old lady know that Eve's
gambit had been a bluff? That she had not anticipated being taken up on it?

''Come, Kristen,'' she said in her not-to-be-ignored
tone. ''We shall withdraw to the sidelines and leave
Miss Childe to compose herself for this crucial scene—
now that she has the partner of her choice.''

A painful surge of blood burnt into Eve's cheeks.
There had never really been a choice. She had come to
this beach and he had been here. A stranger. Her lover.
The man who had shown her what it was to be a

woman. He had taken her along new pathways, opened wonderful doors and led her into a new dimension of feeling. He had been a partner in a deeper sense than she had believed possible. And yes! If the clock was turned backwards she would not wish for it to be anyone else, and if the choice was hers again, she would never have left him.

But he had shed the mantle of lover, partner, understanding friend. The sharing had stopped on this beach and now she had to play out a travesty of what they had known together. He would be with her and yet not with her, acting from business necessity, forced into a partnership he did not want, a partnership from which he recoiled.

"Eve! Over here!"

Lloyd Rivers was summoning her. She forced herself to respond. The film-director was bubbling with confident enthusiasm.

"We'll do it, by God! We'll have it in the can tonight, come hell or high water. A man waits a lifetime for something like this, so don't let me down now, Eve. You've got your man. For one bloody awful minute I thought we'd had it. Thank God for the old lady! There's a woman with a business head on her shoulders. Didn't get where she is on airs and graces. A real tiger, that one!"

Lion. Lioness. Queen of the jungle, Eve mentally corrected him, wishing fiercely that she had never come into the old lady's stamping ground.

Lloyd Rivers drew breath and plunged down to business. "Now when Lamarr gets down here we'll have a quick run-through of the actions. You do exactly what we've rehearsed. The camera will catch you three-quarter on as you run back to him and change to full-face as he lifts you up. Only Lamarr's back view will be in the picture. Understand?''

She nodded.

''That means the whole focus is on you, Eve, so now is the time to produce everything. Give me the whole works and you'll be a star everyone'll want to see.'' He glanced over her shoulder. ''Ah, there's Lamarr coming now. I'll go up and brief him.''

He hurried off and Eve's gaze was irresistibly drawn to the man who was approaching. Paul Lamarr was dressed in the same clothes he had worn that day so many weeks ago, the Tee-shirt emphasising the powerful breadth of his chest, workmanlike jeans rolled up to the muscular calves of his legs.

Memories shivered over her skin and pumped a frightening rhythm through her veins. She grasped desperately for the dignity of self-control but control was a will-o'-the-wisp, evading her completely when Paul Lamarr took up the position directed by Lloyd Rivers. He was so close, barely centimetres away. And in a matter of moments there would be no space between them.

Lloyd Rivers said the fateful words. ''Now to start, you have to hold Eve so that her feet do not touch the sand. Once she curls her arms around your neck you let her slide down. When her feet hit the sand you let her go and she'll push into the dance routine. Okay, let's try it.''

She could not look at him. Her heart was beating like a drum gone mad. He lifted her and pinned her against his heart, the heart which had once beat in joyous unison with hers. She pressed her hands against his shoulders, keeping her eyes determinedly shut as her body trembled its treachery.

The first touch of his mouth was like an electric shock. She jerked her head back, her eyes wide open in alarm as nervous tremors shook her even more visibly. Instinctively her fingers strained against his strength in a vain attempt to halt the chaos he was provoking.

Dark eyes mocked the fear in hers. "Aren't we supposed to be kissing?"

"Ah, well, um," Lloyd Rivers waffled in his beard.

"There's no need to change the script," came the curt comment.

Action followed on the words before Eve had time to voice a protest. One arm easily supported her as the other hand slid up and held her head steady. Warm, sensuous lips closed over hers, teasing, tantalising, creating havoc with her defensive resistance, until of their own accord her hands crept up around his neck. She did not even realise he was lowering her. The seductive excitement of his kiss consumed her senses. Her head swam with dizzy warmth. Not until cold water washed around her toes did the touch of wet sand register. Then she tore herself out of his embrace, a clamour of self-protective instincts demanding that she follow the script. It provided a respite, necessary space for the madness coursing through her body to be halted.

"Good! Good!" Lloyd Rivers boomed approval. "Hold it there for a minute, Eve."

She had reached the point where she pirouetted before running back. She glanced sharply at Paul Lamarr. He looked calm, unmoved, as if nothing had happened. And nothing had! Just a kiss, a short, meaningless kiss to him. Oh God! she thought despairingly. Had she given herself away? Did he realise how he had shaken her? Even now she was still trembling.

"Now, Mr Lamarr. While Eve pirouettes you move down a couple of steps and turn so that you won't be in profile as she returns."

He followed Lloyd Rivers' instructions.

"Right. You saw how Halliday lifted her up high. Do the same, then turn with her in that position so that she's silhouetted against sky and sea...like this...before she slides down. The camera will follow her. Got it?"

"I think so."

"Okay, Eve! Take it from the pirouette!"

She took a deep breath and ordered her feet to perform their practised steps. If she managed it right this first time, maybe there would be no need for further rehearsals. The sooner this scene was accomplished, the sooner she could escape from the emotional and physical turmoil aroused by Paul Lamarr.

He caught her securely, lifted and turned precisely as Lloyd Rivers had demonstrated. Her feet dangled against his thighs. Then she was sliding down and he watched her all the way, not with the hard, impassive eyes of Paul Lamarr, but with eyes which gleamed with intimate memories, their bodies sliding together, in his bed, in the sea, need answering need.

"Splendid!" Lloyd Rivers declared excitedly. "We won't need to waste any more time. Move back for the start and I'll have the sand cleared ready for a take."

He clapped his hands and roared commands. Eve was in a state of shock. She did not understand what was going on in Paul Lamarr's mind and her own was incapable of reasoning. Her eyes darted around. Any target was better than the man beside her. It jolted her

even further to see that the whole camp had gathered
to watch. Paul Lamarr's involvement had obviously
stirred a lively curiosity.

Lloyd Rivers demanded a retreat and the onlookers
moved back out of range of the cameras but the
heightened interest made Eve painfully self-conscious.

"Block them out."

She glanced up, startled by the strained tone of the
command. This was not the Paul Lamarr she was accustomed to seeing. This was the man who had loved
her. His hand cupped her cheek, a gentle touch which
awakened poignant memories.

"Pretend we're alone. Remember the feeling you
had with me then. Give it back to me, Eve. Just this
once."

His voice had dropped to a husky murmur and there
was a deep yearning in his eyes, a hunger which grew
and enveloped her in its need to be fed.

"Why? For a film?" she choked out, not quite believing what she saw and voicing the harsh cynicism
which he had taught her.

"A man can dream," he said enigmatically, and the
need became more tangible as his arms took her pris-
oner and he pressed the dominance of his body on to
hers. "You were a beautiful dream, Eve. It might be
madness but I want to live that dream again. If it only
lasts a few seconds, let me feel what we once had together."

Her heart gave a great leap of hope. "Then . . . then
it did mean something to you. It wasn't just a . . ."

"Action!"

The words she had tried to voice withered under the
fire of his desire, a fire which simultaneously burst
through Eve's veins. Somehow she remembered to

press her hands against his shoulders as his mouth claimed hers. Then he was lifting her, moulding her body to his, and her hands rushed around his neck, fingers thrusting into the thick hair, urgently pleading for the passion she had known with him, only with him. And it was there, exploding between them, in them, body calling to body with all the craving for fulfilment, for the appeasement of lonely, aching need. An exultant joy sprang alive and bloomed in all the empty places.

"Eve!" A hoarse murmur.

"Yes." A breath of surrender.

Conflict…torment…desire in his eyes. "Eve, you must go. Go and come back to me."

Her feet were on the sand. She remembered what she had to do. It would only take a few moments. She danced away, flying with happiness, free of the darkness, free to love and be loved. She pirouetted with the sheer joy of being alive, brilliantly beautifully alive.

His arms were stretched out to her, wanting her back. She ran with the ethereal lightness of thistle-down and he lifted her high, high, wheeling, and she arched her body against the sky in ecstatic delight, offering it as her gift to him. And slowly, melting with each moment of anticipation he gathered her down to a kiss which branded her his, a fierce claim of possession, burning into her soul, taking all she had to give. And she gave unstintingly, wanting, inviting, needing the ultimate sharing which would seal their union.

Then unbelievably he was withdrawing. His head lifted. Hard fingers dragged her apart from him. She clung on, bewildered by the abrupt severance. Firmly he took her hands and pulled them down to her side.

Only then did the alien sound of applause clap into her ears, shocking her back to reality.

She stared around her, appalled by the number of witnesses. Grinning faces seemed to leer at her. They had seen. They all knew what she felt for Paul Lamarr. She shrank closer to him, instinctively seeking his protection. Lloyd Rivers was almost upon them. The director was flapping his arms with excitement.

"Thank you, Mr Lamarr," he rolled out with relish, then lifted his hands to heaven. "And praise be to whatever artistic muse it is which smiles upon us tonight. We have that finale locked up tight and I promise you both that I, and only I, shall edit that film with hands of reverence. Eve, you were magnificent. Mag-nificent! A privilege to watch you my dear, dear girl."

He patted his paunch with smug self-indulgence. "Ah, what an advertisement this'll be! Not only for your perfume, Mr Lamarr, but for Eve, for me, for the art of film-making. An achievement, by God! A shining jewel among the old, trite formulas. No cup of tea at this commercial! They'll be calling in people to watch the box, eyes drinking in the beauty of it. Grand stuff! Grand stuff! Well worth your trouble, Mr Lamarr. A generous gesture standing in for us. Yessir. And well done too."

"Thank you, Rivers, but of course, Miss Childe is the star," he said with an emphasis which held no pleasure in its tone.

Before she could even send him a questioning glance, Eve was clasped roundly to a swelling paunch, then held at arm's length as the film-director voiced his elation in even more grandiloquent terms.

"And what a star! Such feeling! Such expression! My dear you were utterly, utterly superb. I thank you from the depths of my artistic soul. And I shall do you justice," he concluded with a bow which had all the flourish of a maestro.

"You're very kind," Eve muttered, hopelessly embarrassed by the fulsome praise. It was totally undeserved. She had not acted. The film's requirements had been the last thing on her mind. If Paul had not prompted her...she glanced back shyly, her eyes aglow with the warmth of loving.

He was not there. He had gone. A sudden chill swept her heart until she caught sight of him near the closest camera-crew. He was speaking to John Lindsey. Again she became conscious of the large number of spectators. This was no place for private conversation, but she wished he had waited for her. Perhaps he would take her home. Her work here was over. They could go together. There was so much to say, explain, satisfy.

Nan Perkins was coming forward, a beaming smile on her face. "Well done, Eve. I'm so glad it all worked out. I sure didn't want to see those costumes wasted."

"Great costumes!' Lloyd Rivers chimed in, clearly in the mood to lavish praise on everyone.

Paul Lamarr was moving over to his mother. He said a few words to her, nodded as she replied, then without even a glance in Eve's direction, he set off up the beach towards the cabin.

"Eve?" Nan's voice, curiously inquiring.

"Pardon?"

"I was suggesting that you come up to the caravan and change."

"Oh!" Eve tried to collect her wits. Of course Paul Lamarr was going to change back into his business suit. She had to get out of this costume also. "Come on then."

If Nan had not been accompanying her, Eve would have sprinted across the sand. As it was the other girl protested her hurry. Eve was too consumed with a sense of urgency to care what anyone thought. Her hands were reaching for the back fastenings of the dress as the caravan door closed.

"Hold on! I'll do it," Nan insisted.

No sooner had Eve stepped out of the dress than she was thrusting her arms into the beach-coat. She was at the door again before Nan stopped her.

"Don't you want me to remove that make-up? It could be tricky."

"Yes. Yes, of course. Sorry." Eve forced herself to sit down. "Please hurry, Nan," she said anxiously as the other woman wasted precious time in hanging up the dress.

"You've got me almost out of breath as it is. What's the rush? We won't be pulling up stakes here for another hour or so."

"I just want to... to get back to normal."

Nan sighed and set about creaming Eve's face. "I don't know. You're a funny one, Eve. Are you always so uptight? Not once have I seen you relaxed. Except when you were asleep. And then it only took a few seconds of consciousness for you to be drum-tight with tension again. You ought to take up yoga. Good for the body. Good for the mind."

The advice fell on deaf ears. Eve's mind was racing, feverishly trying to hurdle the doubts which had suddenly grown out of her anxiety.

Surely he could not switch passion on and off, as if it had never been. Yet he had put her aside so abruptly at the end. And he had moved off without one personal word to her. How could he go like that? The feeling had been mutual, a deep, urgent reaching for each other. He had to be waiting for her out there. He had to be.

Yet there had been room in his mind for the film. His kiss had completely swept it from hers. He had not forgotten where he was and what they were supposed to be doing. When the cameras had stopped rolling...no...no! her brain screamed. It couldn't be so. He could not have aroused her emotion with such cynical deliberation. Not just for a film. He had wanted her. Really wanted her. As it had been on the beach that afternoon so long ago, the sweet sense of utter belonging. He could not turn his back on that.

But she had, Eve reminded herself painfully. He had asked her to stay and she had gone. Gone for a whole lot of muddled up reasons and with a cutting rejection on her lips. A beautiful dream. That's what he'd said. He did not believe it could last. Last for him? Or for her? she had to speak to him. She had to know.

"That'll do!" She sprang up from the chair, almost knocking it over in her haste.

"There's still some glitter..."

Eve was already stumbling down the caravan steps, her pulse hammering out its panic. The door of the log-cabin was opening. Paul Lamarr came out. He glanced towards her. Eve held her breath. His eyes met hers but there was no spark of recognition, acknowledgement, anything personal. Just darkness. Like ashes whose flame had been thoroughly extinguished. Dead.

The hard mask of authority stamped his face, cold, ruthless, impenetrable. The distance between them was not only physical. He had removed himself from her, mentally and emotionally. If somewhere inside him there beat a soft spot of vulnerability, it did not show. He was Paul Lamarr. Head of the Company.

Eve could not bring herself to speak. She did not have the strength to batter at the wall between them. It was too high, too formidable, and she was not even sure if there was a vulnerable spot.

He gave her a distant little nod, walked straight to the BMW which had been parked next to the Land-Rover, and drove away. She watched until it disappeared behind the thick scrub.

A beautiful dream. A fantasy. Locked into film but its substance thrown away. The man on the beach was lost to her forever.

CHAPTER TEN

DEAR Miss Childe,

Margot Lamarr requests your attendance at a private screening of the promotion film for Fantasy perfume. It is to be held in the Conference Room of the Lamarr building at 5.00 p.m. this Friday, 23rd March.

Refreshments will be served and you are invited to bring a guest if you so wish.

Yours sincerely,
John Lindsey.

"Well?"

The expectant ring in her mother's voice grated on Eve's ears. Marion Childe had thrust the letter into her daughter's hands, demanding that it be opened immediately. The Lamarr emblem on the envelope had obviously given rise to feverish speculation while Eve had been out shopping.

"Nothing definite," Eve replied flatly.

"It must be something. They wouldn't write for nothing," her mother insisted.

Marion Childe's fingers were fidgeting. Eve sighed and passed her the letter. There would be no peace until her mother had read it, and probably no peace afterwards. Until a contract was offered or refused by the Lamarr Corporation her mother would endlessly nag on the subject.

Ever since she had returned from the beach, Eve had lived in an emotional limbo, unable to stir herself to excitement or enthusiasm about anything. The future was a dull, grey, amorphous blob and she did not want to think about it, let alone discuss plans for it. Her mother had been frustrated by Eve's reluctance to talk about the filming. She had kept digging for more details, questioning and speculating on the answers until Eve had completely closed up, refusing to speak about it any more.

"But this is marvellous, Eve!' Marion Childe's eyes glowed with excitement. "They wouldn't bother showing a film they're not interested in. And they wouldn't invite you unless they intended to sign you up. Read between the lines. You've got it!''

"There's no commitment, Mum. Don't get carried away. It's only an invitation.''

"But the invitation speaks for itself. I don't know how you can be so cool about it, Eve. Think of what it can mean to you.'' Her eyes glowed even more brightly. "Oh, I can't wait until Friday! To see your work and meet Margot Lamarr. It'll be—''

"I don't want you to go, Mum.''

Shock and hurt chased across Marion Childe's face. "Eve, you can't mean that. The letter says you can bring a guest.''

Eve sighed. "To tell you the truth, I'm not sure I'll sign a contract, even if I'm offered one. I couldn't do a job like that again.'' To her intense mortification tears filled her eyes and trickled down her cheeks. She hurriedly dashed them away but more kept coming.

"Eve..." The hurt bewilderment on Marion Childe's face suddenly cracked and the mother in her rushed to comfort. She hugged her daughter close, patting her back, stroking her hair, murmuring soothing words as deep, heart-wrenching sobs came tumbling out in uncontrolled bursts.

Eve finally dragged herself away, ashamed of her breakdown and apologising in a string of incoherent words. Marion Childe led her into the living-room, sat her down on the sofa and took her hands, rubbing them in gentle sympathy.

"Eve, you've locked me out ever since the break-up with Simon," she began tentatively.

Eve shook her head. "You wouldn't listen."

"I'm sorry. I thought I knew what was best for you. I don't know what's going on any more," she admitted despondently. "You've insisted on going out on your own and maybe I have been too...too domineering in the past, but you didn't have any direction of your own, Eve. You needed looking after. You looked to me to make decisions."

She dragged in a deep breath and plunged on. "Now you want to make your own decisions. I have to accept that. But please, can't we talk about them? It's a very lonely place out there and I want to help. You may not think I've been a good mother but I do love you, Eve, and I care very, very much, what happens to you. Please don't lock me out."

"Oh, Mum, I don't know what I want," Eve poured out in a rush, then gave a shaky little smile. "But it has been very lonely these last few weeks."

"Why don't you want me to go on Friday, Eve?" her mother asked softly, and hurt was still there, mixed with a need to understand.

"It's . . . you'll see . . ." How to explain that she felt too embarrassed by the naked emotion which would be on show. Eve sighed. "You can come, but please don't push anything, Mum. I'm not sure I want to have any further connection with the Lamarrs. They demand too much."

Her mother frowned. "What do you mean?"

"All they care about is selling their product," she said bitterly.

"But, Eve. That's business."

The green eyes became even more bleak. "I know. But I didn't like being a pawn in a power-game, prodded and fought over and knocked aside when I'd been used to give them what they wanted."

"But it works both ways, dear. You use them to get what you want. You shouldn't take it so personally."

But it was personal. Terribly personal. Only Eve could not bring herself to explain that. It hurt too much. "You're probably right, Mum. It's just that I can't cope with it."

"Will you let me help? I can stand between you and the Lamarrs, Eve. What you need is an agent to protect you," her mother said eagerly.

"Mum, don't push. Please just let it ride for now. Wait until Friday and I'll see how I feel about it after the film is shown."

For once Marion Childe did not pursue her own point of view. She went out of her way to pamper Eve, cooking tasty meals to tempt her appetite, buying tickets for a musical which had won acclaim on Broadway and had just opened in Sydney, making bright conversation and being generally indulgent towards her daughter. Eve appreciated her mother's efforts. There was still a large gap in their understanding but that was not something that could easily be bridged. Their outlooks on life were too diverse but at least there was sympathetic communication and Eve's loneliness was eased.

Friday came and as the day wore on Eve became more silent and tense. Her mother tried to fuss her into wearing something the Lamarr people had not seen but Eve chose the pink and green dress she had worn to the interview with Margot Lamarr. It gave her a perverse satisfaction to wear a bra underneath it. No one was going to tell her to take it off this time, Eve thought grimly. Nor was she going to be intimated by any of the Lamarrs.

She applied a subtle make-up, designed more to disguise her pallor and the slight shadows under her eyes than to enhance her natural beauty, but it served both purposes. She left her hair in its natural curls. It was easier than going to a hairdresser for a more formal style. She even dabbed on the Fantasy perfume which Margot Lamarr had given her. The scent was fresh and oddly definable. It made one want to smell it again and again. No doubt it would sell well, Eve thought bitterly.

Marion Childe had dressed with her usual, impeccable taste. Her cream silk suit was teamed with a yellow and cream blouse in a soft crêpe de chine. She looked very elegant with her upswept blonde hair and carefully subdued make-up and she smiled with genuine pleasure when Eve told her so.

They arrived at the Lamarr building with five minutes to spare. John Lindsey met them in the lobby and escorted them up to the Conference Room, answering Marion Childe's questions along the way with his easy charm. He ushered them into a room which already seemed full of people. Eve recognised some faces but by no means all. The gathering suddenly parted and Margot Lamarr swept down the room towards them with all the stateliness of a queen.

"My dear Miss Childe, a pleasure to have you with us again. And this is . . ."

"My mother, Mrs Marion Childe."

"Indeed? You're very welcome, Mrs Childe. This is a gathering of the people who have been involved in the production of our new perfume, from laboratory to publicity. I will not waste time in introducing you now. I'm sure you're as impatient to see the finished film as everyone else is. Come, sit with me."

It had been an extremely courteous greeting and Eve smiled at the gratified look on her mother's face. There was an excited hum around the room as they moved forward. Those people standing quickly seated themselves. Eve saw Paul Lamarr lead an obviously pregnant lady to an armchair. Her heart gave a sickening lurch and she looked away.

Kristen Delaney gave Eve a thin smile from across the room. She was talking to Lloyd Rivers who beamed with bonhomie. Nan Perkins gave a little wave. Other faces seemed to peer curiously at her. Eve was glad to sit down in the front row of seats. Even though she was placed next to Margot Lamarr, at least she had her back to the crowd. Eve fixed her gaze on the large screen which dominated the end wall. She wished it was smaller, wished even more fiercely that she had not come at all. To see what was going to be shown could only give her pain.

The lights went out. The darkness was comforting. The few murmurs died into an expectant hush. The

screen flashed blue. Black and gold lettering boldly
spelled out:

LAMARR
presents
FANTASY

Then instantly there was the sound of the sea and
behind it a flute, beginning a haunting melody. The
sea rolled out of the blueness on the screen, shimmering into a horizon of glorious colour. The camera followed the fading hues around the sky until suddenly
there was Eve on the beach with her bag of shells.

Her first instinct was to shut her eyes but there was
a dreadful fascination in watching the emotional play
of expression on the face up there on the screen, and
the emotion seemed to be intensified by the flute in the
background, trilling, swooping, interpreting every
feeling with its purity of sound.

The sea-haze which was used for the transition from
girl to mermaid was brilliantly done, a waver of misty
colour accompanied by one long, drawn-out note
from the flute. The editing had been masterly. It was
impossible to tell where Paul Lamarr had taken over
from Rick Halliday.

Eve cringed as the focus fastened on her face in the
last sequence. It was all there, the joy, the excitement,
the ecstasy of loving and being loved, the exquisite
anticipation of fulfilment. And if it wasn't plain
enough the music told the story, rising and rising in an
exultant crescendo. Mercifully the film ended on a
shot of the Fantasy shell around her neck as she slid
down to the last embrace. If it had included the final
kiss she would have died of embarrassment. The

screen blacked out. The lights were switched on. Eve squirmed in the ensuing silence.

"Am I or am I not a genius?" Lloyd Rivers demanded in fulsome tones.

Somebody laughed and then applause broke out, loud, enthusiastic, almost deafening applause. Lloyd Rivers swaggered up to Eve, pulled her on to her feet and held up a hand for quiet.

"You're right! I am most certainly a genius," he declared patting his stomach with affection before throwing out his hand in a sweeping gesture. "But I present to you a star who could rival the young Ingrid Bergman... if she could cure herself of being a director's nightmare."

More laughter and even louder applause. Eve blushed furiously. The film-director would not let her go. He had centre-stage and he was not above to give it up.

"And let me say, if that doesn't sell your Fantasy perfume, nothing will. I thank you all for your contribution to my art."

A mood of happy triumph hung over the following uproar. Eve took the opportunity to slide down into her seat as John Lindsey called the room to order.

"I believe Mrs Lamarr would like to say a few words."

The old lady stood and the hush was instant.

"I congratulate all of you who have worked on this project to bring it to fruition. The Lamarr name is enhanced by this new perfume, the best I think we have ever produced. It was worthy of a new concept in publicity and I congratulate my son on his imaginative idea, and his foresight in selecting Miss Childe to play the starring role."

Eve darted a glance at Paul Lamarr who had not moved from the side of the pregnant lady. His eyes were hooded and his face could have been granite for all the expression it showed. Nothing had changed. She had not expected it to but the pain in her heart stabbed a little deeper. Not even a graphic reminder of what they had shared could pierce his inflexible will.

"I congratulate Mr Rivers," a dry little smile was bestowed on him, "on his genius. The camera-work and editing was indeed brilliant." A warmer smile was directed at the pregnant lady. "I thank Mrs Knight, perhaps better known to the public as the song-writer, Jenny Ross, who very graciously consented to compose the music which so beautifully expresses the mood of the film."

There was a stir of interest, a craning of necks to see the woman whose name conjured up so many memorable songs. Eve now understood why Paul Lamarr had been so attentive. Jenny Ross was a guest of very special note. A mere model paled in comparison. She sighed and wished once more that she had not come.

Margot Lamarr looked directly at Eve as she continued. "As you all know, it has been company policy for many years to use established stars for publicising our products. This time we gambled with Miss Childe. Some of us held grave doubts about her ability to project the mood we envisaged, but I don't think any of us anticipated the sheer, poignant beauty of a performance which will be memorable for many years to come. It is our incredibly good fortune that for some time at least, she will be spoken of as the Lamarr Fantasy girl."

Eve was too stunned to resist when Margot Lamarr took her hand and drew her to her feet again. There

was a nerve-tingling silence. Everyone was staring at
her and she suddenly realised they were seeing her, not
as the woman who stood before them, but as the girl
on the screen. Something like a collective sigh ran
around the room. Eve writhed in self-conscious agony. This was far worse than applause. Instinctively
her eyes sought Paul Lamarr's and this time he too,
was looking at her.

It was for you, only for you. Don't you know that?
she cried silently. He closed his eyes and bowed his
head as if he did not want to receive her message.

Margot Lamarr concluded her speech. "I now invite you all to stay and celebrate the culmination of
your work with the refreshments which are being
wheeled in."

It was a signal for more clapping and a general
hubbub followed as people rose to their feet. Eve was
grateful to everyone who stood. It made her feel less
conspicuous. The light pressure on her hand signalled
that Margot Lamarr had not yet finished with her. She
turned to the old lady, wary of any personal talk.

"A contract has been drawn up, Miss Childe. It only
awaits your consideration and subsequently your signature. John Lindsey will be fixing an appointment
with you before you leave this evening. I hope it gives
you satisfaction."

"I'll consider it, Mrs Lamarr," Eve said quietly.

The black eyes sharply probed Eve's guard but her
defences were firmly in place. She was not going to be
drawn into a commitment here and now.

Margot Lamarr switched her gaze to Marion Childe
who was rising to her feet in a slightly dazed fashion.
"You must be very proud of your daughter, Mrs
Childe."

Marion Childe shook her head as if to clear it. "I don't know what to say. I never imagined..." She looked at her daughter in obvious wonderment. "Eve, you were just amazing. I never realised that you could act so expressively."

"Yet your daughter stated flatly that she is not an actress," Margot Lamarr remarked with an oddly questioning look at Eve. "It was, one might say, an illuminating performance, and one which, perhaps, carries its own reward. Ah, Kristen." She turned to her own daughter who had descended on them with a forced courtesy on her face. "This is Mrs Childe, Eve's mother. My daughter, Kristen Delaney."

"How do you do?" Marion Childe murmured weakly, still rather overwhelmed by the occasion.

Kristen Delaney inclined her head in regal fashion before turning to Eve. "What a surprise package you turned out to be, Miss Childe! But then, there's nothing like having the advantage of inside knowledge and Paul certainly had that, didn't he? Lloyd Rivers has just been telling me how..."

Margot Lamarr interrupted with all the smoothness of a very sharp knife. "Kristen, sour grapes never go down well." Then she smiled, the lioness baring her teeth. "Have a glass of champagne. It's much more suited to the occasion."

A waiter had arrived with a tray of drinks. Behind him came Paul Lamarr and another man, Robert Knight, who was not only Jenny Ross's husband but a producer for television. Lloyd Rivers descended once again. John Lindsey and Nan Perkins joined the cluster of people. Toasts were made, congratulations passed around, but not a word from Paul Lamarr. Eve smiled and nodded like an automaton, only vaguely conscious of what was being said. She was intensely aware of Paul Lamarr's silence. She willed him to say something, anything, open up even the most tenuous thread of communication.

He was watching her with a chillingly detached air. Robert Knight expressed interest in contacting her agent. Marion Childe stated that she was managing her daughter's career. Lloyd Rivers expounded on Eve's future in glowing terms and her mother lapped it up, adding her own ambitious comments.

Career. Career. Career. A sledgehammer striking at the wedge between them, driving Paul Lamarr further away. His withdrawal was almost tangible. Eve wanted to reach out, stop him, scream that a career had no meaning to her. What she had shown him up there on the screen…that was the only reality. She did not want the bright lights, only the warmth of his love.

Desperation overrode pride. She looked at him with all the torment of need in her expressive green eyes. There was one startled flicker of response before he wrenched his gaze away, his face stiff with rejection. He muttered a couple of words to his mother and smoothly extracted himself from the group around Eve. He skirted the crowd with quick, purposeful strides and left the room.

John Lindsey touched her arm and said something about a contract. Eve's heart was beating an agonised protest, pleading for, demanding one last chance. Her feet followed its dictate, taking her past people, automatically choosing Paul Lamarr's path, quickening with urgency as she reached the doorway.

The corridor outside was empty. She ran around the corner to the bank of lifts. The indicator showed one going down. She jabbed at other buttons. She had to catch him. Tell him. Make him listen. Tears of frustration filled her eyes as the steel doors remained shut.

"Eve! Wait!"

She turned to John Lindsey in a frenzy of impatience. "I don't want your contract," she hurled at him. Her hands reached feverishly for the buttons again.

"Stop her, John!"

Restraining hands caught her shoulders as the elevator doors opened.

"Let me go! I have to go!" Eve sobbed frantically.

"Mrs Lamarr?"

Heels clicking on the corridor. "Thank you. I won't need you any more."

Surprise held Eve rooted to the spot for a moment. Then she realised she was free. She rushed into the lift and slammed her hand on the DOWN button. The doors rolled shut but not before Margot Lamarr had stepped into the compartment.

The old lady eyed Eve with age-old experience. "Do you know what you're doing?"

"I don't care. I don't care about a career," Eve flung at her, her own eyes darting desperately to the flashing numbers. Fourth floor...third...the lift was crawling down. Oh God! Make it go faster, she begged.

"My dear, one should always keep options open. The contract will still be waiting for you on Monday if you change your mind."

"I won't change it." Second floor. Come on. Come on, she screamed silently.

"No. I don't think you will. By the way, if it means anything to you, he told me he was going fishing."

Going fishing. Eve's heart swelled with emotion. She turned to the old lady, tears of relief trickling down her cheeks. "I must go. I love him," she whispered.

Margot Lamarr gave a tired little smile. "I'll tell your mother where you've gone."

Eve's smile was wobbly. "Thank you."

The lift doors opened on to the lobby. Eve walked out, hope soaring high as her mind and heart leapt ahead to the man on the beach.

CHAPTER ELEVEN

No light winked at her from the cabin. Panic pressed her foot down on the accelerator. The car leapt forward, almost bouncing out of control on the rutted track. He had to be there. Had to be. The headlights picked out the Land-Rover by the side of the cabin and relief coursed through her veins. He was there. She brought her car to a screeching halt, then sat for a few moments, gathering her courage into determined purpose. He was not going to turn her away. She would not let him.

Even so her steps grew hesitant as she approached the cabin. It took every bit of her will-power to push open the door and walk inside. The darkness held no sound. The room felt empty. She forced herself to speak.

"Paul? Where are you?"

No answer.

The beach. He would be on the beach. She kicked out of her sandals and rolled off her panti-hose, tossing them on the nearest chair. Bare-footed and with her heart pumping out its urgency she ran outside. Her eyes immediately caught the dark silhouette at the water's edge. She could not tell if he was turned towards her or the sea. He stood motionless. She kept running, the heavy sand underfoot slowing her progress but not until she could see that he was facing her did she falter to a walk.

Still he did not move. Not one step towards her. He could have been a statue but for the dark glitter of his eyes. His hands were thrust into the pockets of a windcheater, his head thrown back a little at a proud, forbidding angle.

Eve stopped and caught her breath. His stance held no invitation yet she sensed that he was waiting, wanting her to speak. She swallowed and chose her words carefully, reaching back to a time of beautiful harmony.

"Can I... can I stay with you?"

His chin lowered sharply and she heard his breath hiss out as if he had held it for a long time. Tension shrieked around her nerves as she waited for his answer.

"If you want to."

Still he made no move towards her. Only the four soft words, barely audible above the sound of the sea. Then slowly he drew one hand from a pocket and held it out to her. She took it as one would a life-line, her fingers winding around his in a tight grip. There was a look of disbelief in his eyes. Eve smiled assurance, but it was a tremulous smile, affected by too many uncertainties.

"Let's walk," he suggested gruffly.

It was enough to begin with. To be beside him, arm brushing arm, in step together, knowing he accepted her presence. Dying waves curled around their feet just as they had so many weeks ago. The innocence had been lost and there was much pain to be appeased, but it was a beginning. A shell rolled against her foot and she paused to pick it up.

"Don't!"

The sharp command stabbed out, a cry of torment. She straightened instantly, looking up at him with anxious eyes. He shook his head and dragged in a deep breath.

"Eve, I don't want a fantasy. I've tramped this beach too many times, wanting you to come back. When you ran down to me it was like a dream come true, but—"

She placed a silencing hand on his lips. "No buts. I'm not a dream. I'm here. Feel me. Love me as you did before. I want you to." She pressed her body close, wound her arms around his neck and lifted her mouth to his. "I love you, I want you, I need you," she murmured in a litany of longing.

He groaned, a deep, primitive sound which she smothered with her kiss. Then his arms were around her, crushing her against him as he took her offering with passionate hunger. His hands moved over her in restless possession, thighs, hips, waist, back, hair, needing to confirm her reality. She savoured every touch, wanting more and more.

"Let's go up to the cabin," she whispered.

He seemed reluctant to move.

"Here then. It doesn't matter where."

She slid out of his hold and stripped in front of him, dropping her clothes carelessly on the sand, inviting his desire with every sensuous move of her body. She felt free, uninhibited and exultant that he could not tear his eyes away from her. Her pulse beat faster and faster but she knew the race was almost won. He wanted her every bit as much as she wanted him. Surrender was just a breath away. She unzipped his windcheater, pressing her naked breasts against his warm skin and running her hands over his broad shoulders as she pushed the restrictive material aside.

"Eve...not here." Hands tightened around her waist and dragged her back so that his gaze could feast on her. "My God! I want to drown in you all night."

Elation bubbled up into a triumphant little laugh. "The sea then."

He caught her wild mood and laughed also. "No, not the sea, my little mermaid. You're far too much woman for a cold bed."

"I'll race you up to the cabin."

She had broken free of his hold and was metres away in moments. She glanced back to see him still standing there, a bemused grin on his face.

"Come on. There's just you and me and the sea. Let's be free," she sang in excitement.

He laughed, a sheer, boyish whoop of laughter, then scooped up her clothes and gave chase. She had almost reached the road when he dived and caught her ankle. He cut off her shriek with his mouth and their kiss grew in urgency. It was he who broke it, breathing harshly as he pulled himself up and lifted her to her feet.

"You're not a mermaid. You're a witch. Let's get this sand off us."

He hurried her to the cabin, led her through the main room to the laundry. Water hissed down from the shower. It was cold but Eve did not care. Warm hands caressed the sand from her body. There was no rough washing this time and he did not jerk away when she touched him. He turned off the taps and reached over a towel. She took it from him and slowly wiped the moisture from his body, loving him with her hands and lips until he groaned and tore the towel away.

In an instant she was scooped up in his arms and held against a wildly thumping heart. She kissed the leaping pulse in his throat as he carried her to the bed, then lay with her body open to him, pulling him down on top of her.

"No. Let me look at you."

A pale moonlight streamed through the window. Slowly his fingers traced the curves of her body, tantalising her skin with their light touch.

"You are so very beautiful," he murmured and there was gloating pleasure in the soft tone.

He kissed her breasts, trailed his tongue down to her navel and lower, paying a devastating homage to her body. The intimate stroking set her trembling with feverish pleasure but her need to hold him, own him, be him, was far too great to savour the erotic sensations he was arousing.

"No more," she gasped. "I need you now."

And he was hers. She joyfully wrapped her arms around him and lifted her body to meet his. He entered her slowly and the movement inside her was exquisite. This was no impatient thrust but the loving possession of a connoisseur intent on savouring what he owned to the fullest extent. Eve writhed on the edge of ecstasy, pleading incoherently to be taken further.

Then there was no more control. Their hearts beat in wild exultation as they abandoned themselves to each other, reaching for that peak of fulfilment where at last their bodies melted together in the liquid warmth of ultimate unity. And there they clung, physically sated yet holding on to the emotional security of their oneness, reluctant to let it end.

He rolled on to his back, carrying her with him so that her head lay over his heart. He stroked her hair, her back, long, lingering caresses which made her shiver with sensitivity.

"How long have I got, Eve?"

The flat resignation in his voice drove a needle of uncertainty into her heart. "What do you mean?" she asked in a nervous rush.

He sighed and it was a shudder running through his body. "One day? Two? Will you stay with me 'til Sunday night?"

She slid her hands around and under his chest, hugging him tightly to her. "For as long as you want me," she promised huskily. "I don't want to ever leave you."

She felt the sharp intake of his breath and the odd little skip of his heart. His fingers wound through her curls, absently tugging them.

"You mean this weekend. I know you're to sign the contract on Monday." His voice was carefully stripped of emotion, too carefully. He was hiding from her.

She hauled herself into a sitting position and bent forward to look into his eyes. They were black depths of stillness, waiting, expecting nothing, just waiting. She touched his cheek in a tender caress, sending out her love through gentle finger-tips.

"I don't want a career. I told them before I followed you that I didn't want a contract. The only Lamarr girl I want to be is yours. And yours I'll be for however long you want me... a weekend, a month, a year, all my life... if you'll have me."

She kissed him, using soft, persuasive lips to convince him that her offer was no transient thing but a need which could only be answered by him.

He took her head between his hands and lifted it away. "Don't! Don't say what you don't mean, Eve." There was emotion now. His voice was raw with it, eyes glittering with a vulnerability she had never seen before. "I've got to know what to expect. You can have your career. I wouldn't try to take that from you. I don't know how I'll bear the separations but I'll adjust. So long as you love me like this when we're together."

"Oh, Paul! I'll always be your love," she assured him tenderly. "I'm no actress. I don't even like being a model. It was something my mother pushed me into because of my looks. It was her ambition, not mine. I just went along with it because I didn't know what else to do and it pleased her. It was you who kept pushing career at me and I agreed with you out of pride. That first day in your office when you touched me, all I wanted was to feel again the magic we shared on the beach. It had nothing to do with the job."

The struggle between belief and disbelief brought a pained tautness to his voice. "You cannot conceive how hard it was for me to reject you that day, Eve, but you had already rejected me and the magic we shared to go back to your career. I thought you could not have felt what I felt. Otherwise you couldn't have walked away as you did...right after we had made love...how could you?"

She sighed and gently smoothed the lines of pain from his forehead. "Remember how I was when you found me? I was terribly hurt and disillusioned. What happened between us came too fast on the heels of that. It really did seem like a dream to me. It wasn't until I was back in my real life that I understood what I had left behind."

"But you could have come back. You couldn't have really believed that I'd set out to use you for gain. I was here, every night for weeks, waiting for you."

The lonely yearning in his voice stabbed her with guilt. She was ashamed of the truth but it had to be said. "I was frightened. I didn't know who or what you were. I was too much of a coward to take a blind plunge."

His silence was ominous. His next words were even more so, quiet, deadly words. "But it's all right now that I'm Paul Lamarr."

The man she loved had suddenly been supplanted by the cold, ruthless Paul Lamarr of the Lamarr Corporation. Eve felt as if she had been slapped again. She shrank away and curled into a tight, lonely ball. The bed creaked as he moved. She flinched from the soft touch on her shoulder.

"It doesn't matter. I don't care why you're with me as long as you are. Don't turn away from me, Eve." He curved his body around hers and gentled her stiffness with loving hands. Warm lips nuzzled the curve of neck and shoulder. "Nothing in my whole life has equalled what I felt for you that day. Do you know what you were like? A little girl lost. I wanted to comfort you, ease your pain, give you whatever you wanted. It was a delight to see you emerge from the shadows in your mind. You were like a butterfly, climbing out of its chrysalis and spreading its wings to the sun."

His hand cupped her breast and his voice deepened with husky longing. "I wanted to capture and hold you but I couldn't spoil your flight. You glowed with such a special kind of joy. When you gave yourself to me, it was magic beyond my wildest dreams, like embracing all the elemental things of life and knowing they were yours. I thought I had everything a man could ever want... But you went away."

He sighed and it was a long, wavering breath through her hair. The desolation which had echoed in his voice brought tears to her eyes. She had no doubt now that he loved her but it still hurt that he doubted her love. She turned and slipped her arms around his neck, giving him the reassurance of her body.

"I won't leave again. Not unless you send me away. I didn't mean to hurt you, Paul. I just couldn't think straight and I didn't trust my own feelings. Don't you see how confusing it was for me? I thought I was broken-hearted over Simon's betrayal. I had believed myself in love with him. Then suddenly you had blotted him out of my mind. I couldn't understand how I could be so fickle. It was as if the whole world had turned around and I had slipped off its axis. I felt I had to climb back to reality.

"And when you turned out to be Paul Lamarr and set me up for the film, I was even more confused. I had dreamed of the man on the beach but I hated you as Paul Lamarr. I hated what you were doing to me. If there had been a viable alternative I wouldn't have gone on with it. As it was, I didn't seem to have much choice."

"What do you mean? You could have refused."

He was frowning. She sighed and drew a smoothing hand across his forehead. "Didn't you know I couldn't get work?"

He shook his head, the frown cutting even deeper.

"Oh, Paul! I was just about desperate. No one wanted to use me without Simon behind the camera. We'd been a team, you see. But I couldn't go on working with him. Not after... well, you know. Anyway he'd come around trying to tell me I was a silly fool, and Mum was backing him up, nagging at me all the time. Then the Lamarr offer came along and I kind of waved it in their faces, showing them that I could be independent. I didn't know you were behind it. I thought it was a genuine offer and it seemed my only chance to get back on my feet, all by myself. I was thrown completely off-balance when I walked into your office and saw you."

"I didn't know," he muttered. "I didn't even consider such a factor."

He rolled on to his back and lay in brooding silence. The abrupt separation alarmed Eve. She slid a tentative hand across his chest, wanting to reinforce her presence. He caught her hand and squeezed it.

"So you felt trapped into playing the role. You didn't really want to do it," he said with slow deliberation.

She sighed and nestled against him. "It was either accept the job or admit failure. It sickened me that you should want to commercialize what had been very special and very personal, but I reasoned that since it had meant so little to you, I shouldn't let it mean so much to me. But it hurt, and in the end I couldn't do it... at least, not until you stepped in and took Rick Halliday's place. I didn't mean you to, you know. It was just a way out. I thought you'd refuse."

He cradled her more tightly. "I've been a fool, a blind stupid fool," he stated with a fine edge of self-contempt. "The signs were all there if only I'd had the eyes to read them from a difference slant."

He stirred and leaned over her, eyes begging forgiveness as he tenderly brushed the curls away from her temples. "And you had to come to me. I don't deserve you, Eve. I've been so damned full of myself, pride, ego, call it what you will...all this time I've thought only of what I wanted."

"That's not true," she contradicted softly. "You thought you were giving me the career I wanted."

"No." He dragged in a deep breath and let it out slowly. "All I thought of was making you come back to me. The film had nothing to do with selling perfume or lifting you to stardom. It was only to remind you of what we had shared, make you want it again. I was too proud to beg...at least I was until I had you in my arms for that last scene. Then I couldn't stop myself. I wanted you so badly that any crumb would do."

"Then why did you walk away afterwards?" The remembered hurt drove a note of accusation into her voice. "You must have known I wasn't acting, Paul."

"Your response threw me into complete turmoil. I hadn't expected you to give yourself like that. I didn't know if you were teasing me, exulting with your power, or what. I was angry at myself for begging and angry at you for putting a career ahead of what we had together. I'd shown you how much I wanted you but I wasn't going to grovel at your feet. When I came out of the cabin and you were standing by the caravan, my damned pride insisted that you take the first step towards me. But you didn't move. You just stood there."

"I was waiting for a signal from you," she explained. "I was churning...I thought you might have done it just to get the film. It was such a turnabout. I didn't know what to think and you looked so cold and distant. Even tonight I wasn't sure. I tried to show you what I felt after the film was shown but you turned away and left.''

"I had to go. I couldn't stand another minute of hearing about your career. I knew that you wanted me, Eve. I saw it in your eyes. But I wasn't sure if I could stand being your part-time lover, always craving for more than you'd be prepared to give me. I didn't want to come second to a camera. I drove here to sort it all out in my mind.''

"And what conclusion did you come to?" she asked softly.

He smiled, a wryly tender smile. "None. I just walked along dreaming of a girl I once knew, wishing it was possible to go back in time. Then she arrived.''

Eve teased the corners of his smile with a tracing finger. "Were you surprised?''

He considered for a moment, then shook his head. "It seemed like I'd been waiting for you so you came. I didn't really question it. I'd dreamed of it so often that when it happened, I felt I was still dreaming.''

"I was terrified that you would reject me," she confessed, sure now that rejection was no longer even a remote possibility.

He grinned. "You had a very persuasive way of sorting me out. In fact you can sort me out like that anytime you feel like it.''

Her cheeks burned at the reminder of her blatant wantonness. "I thought action might be better than words," she said shyly.

"Much, much better," he agreed and kissed her very thoroughly. He came up for air and added, "Mind you, some of those words were pretty powerful. Would you say them again?''

"What?''

"Oh, things like...I love you, I want you, I need you. And...I never want to leave you... The trouble was I didn't quite believe you earlier on tonight."

The warmth in her heart flooded into her voice as she repeated what he wanted to hear.

"And you'll marry me?" he prompted softly, with a wealth of feeling which more than matched hers.

Tears of happiness filmed her eyes. "If you want me to," she whispered huskily.

He planted little kisses all around her face then hovered over her mouth. "Eve, you are my love and my life. I never want to be without you again." And his kiss demonstrated all the fervour of his declaration. It sparked the desire for more intimate possession and as their passion grew, so did their joy in each other. "This isn't a fantasy, is it, my darling?" Paul murmured provocatively.

"No." Eve laughed in exultation. "No, it's real. Oh, Paul! It's beautifully, wonderfully real."

RENT-A-BRIDE LTD.

Emma Goldrick

CHAPTER ONE

SHE started shivering just as the airplane banked and turned out over the calm surface of Lake Waco, to the west of the central Texas city of the same name. She wrapped her arms around herself to keep control, but it was difficult. Her eighteenth birthday had passed without celebration or comment, and the quick trip to the law offices in Dallas had left her more confused than before. Aunt Ellen had prodded and poked at her without mercy, until finally Stacey had signed all the papers without reading any of them, just to find a little peace.

"Now all that's settled," her aunt had said, "we can get back to the ranch. George will be waiting for you." She spoke in a nasal simper. The sound irritated Stacey as much as the words did. Yes, of course, her dulled brain snarled at her, George will be waiting for you. And so will Uncle Henry. And of the two, her uncle was the one she feared most. Dear Uncle Henry, who had come down the pike with hardly a shirt to his back, and married Aunt Ellen for the money she didn't possess! As soon as he had found out that it was all Stacey's money, that was when son George had popped up.

"He'll make a fine husband for you," Aunt Ellen kept insisting. "And it will knit the family together. Won't that be lovely?" Of course, Stacey muttered under her breath. Lovely for George, or for Aunt Ellen? Poor Aunt Ellen, whose face was disfigured by a huge strawberry birthmark on her left cheek. And who seemed to fear her husband more than she loved him.

Poor Aunt Ellen, who, in all the confusion, had come to the Dallas airport, only to find that the power of attorney she wanted was still in their hotel room. So, somehow or another, Stacey found herself boarding the plane alone. Making her first adventure outside the boundary of Rancho Miraflores since her—what?—fourteenth birthday. But of course Uncle Henry would be waiting for her at the terminal in Waco. "And here, take your pills while I'm watching," her aunt ordered.

Stacey swallowed them down without protest. Her pills were no longer something she fought over. They had just seemed to appear, without a doctor's visit, two years before. Well, she kept telling herself, they *did* reduce her tensions, relax her. In fact, they usually put her to sleep. Except at times like this when she was violently excited.

The touch of a hand on hers snapped her back to reality. The young man in the adjoining seat was trying to prise her clenched fingers loose from the arm that separated them. "It's a perfectly normal landing," he assured her. "Relax! Is this your first flight?"

Her eyes moved slowly down to where his right hand clasped her left. His thumb smoothed the skin on the back of her hand, gently, warmly. Almost in a daze her eyes wandered up to his face. He topped her five foot seven by a good head, she noted. Wide-set dark eyes, under a fringe of curly brown hair. Craggy. Not handsome, just—vibrant.

"Lord help us, you'll shake yourself to death, girl!" With one easy motion he flipped up the separating arm and pulled her close up against him. For a microsecond she struggled, her innate anger driving, but then a combination of events took over. She recalled the last time she had been enfolded in strong loving arms. When she was thirteen, and her father had hugged her tight and then gone off to Vietnam—and never returned. Her muscles relaxed as she savoured the warm comfort. She leaned her head over against his chest, and the steady rhythm of his heart comforted. One of his hands tangled in her hair and gently stroked her into a hypnotic state. The wheels of the aircraft touched ground, squealed, and began to run true as the nosewheel made contact.

"There now, everything's home safe." He pushed her slightly away, but still in the circle of his arms.

"I wasn't afraid of the plane," Stacey half whispered, staring at him. Look! She commanded her hazy mind. Look at him! The corners of his mouth seemed perpetually turned up into a grin. He's got a strong nose—a Roman nose. What is he? A displaced centurion? Why am I wandering like this? She snatched her eyes away from him and looked out the window.

The plane had taxied off the runway on to the concrete apron in front of the terminal, and a couple of baggage handlers came out of the building and headed for the parking area. The high-winged twin engine commuter plane trundled up to the same area, swung around in a half-circle, and stopped. The motors roared once, muttered to a stop, and coughed. The triblade propeller just outside Stacey's window twirled for a time or two, then it too came to a stop.

There was a bustle up and down the aisle as the passengers moved towards the forward door, where the stewardess struggled with the complicated handles. The man beside Stacey started to get up, and then sat back down again.

"You don't get off here? I thought it was the end of the line."

"Not quite," she sighed. "They go on down to Temple, too. But I have to get off here. I don't want to, but I have to."

"There's plenty of time. Relax." He settled himself back in his seat as an example. "This crowd will mill around for another ten minutes or so before the doorway is cleared. Cigarette?"

She shook her head, and the long thick blonde hair swung gently around her face, obscuring its soft creamy oval, and the grey eyes. "I don't smoke," she said, and then, driven by her fears, "Why am I so scared? They can't make me marry him!"

"I suppose not," he answered. "Marry? Want to tell me about it?"

"I—no, I can't." She turned her head away from him to hide the incipient tears. Why am I doing this? she screamed at herself. Why am I so—frightened? I never was like this before! Why so suddenly, in the past two years, have I become such a rabbit? They can't make me marry him, can they?

Outside her window she could see the other passengers straggling away from the aircraft, moving into the chill of the air-conditioned building. Now that the plane had stopped, the heat closed in on them, beating off the silver fuselage, and threatening to bake everything inside. The baggage handlers moved slowly, pulling luggage out of the belly compartment, tossing it carelessly on their battery-powered cart. Nobody else was in sight. For just a brief second Stacey felt elated. Maybe Uncle Henry couldn't come? But deep down, she knew better. It was a typical south Texas summer day, when even the crows were walking, but Uncle Henry would be there. Have no doubts about that, little lady!

"I wish I could just keep on flying," she mused wearily. "Just keep on going, and never come back. I wish I had a ticket to some place ten thousand miles from here."

One of his hands came to her shoulder, the other offered a handkerchief. She snatched at it and dabbed her eyes before she turned to face him. "I'll bet you think I'm a fool," she suggested warily.

"No, not a fool," he answered. His deep voice rumbled in the almost-empty aircraft. "Just a scared kid. Look, my name is Harry. Sometimes it helps to talk to a complete stranger. If it would help you—?" The rest of the invitation floated on empty air as the stewardess came back to urge them off the plane. He stood up and moved out into the aisle to let her pass.

Stacey chewed her lip, watching the subtle movement of his muscles as he slid away from her. It's no use delaying, she told herself. They'll be out there, waiting to pounce. And I might as well get it over. She was still shaking slightly, but having made her decision, she could feel the invidious effects of the pills take over, leaving her languid and dispirited. Like a condemned woman she stood up in the narrow space between the seats, brushed down her blue linen skirt, rearranged the simple lace-stippled blouse, and moved out into the aisle.

"Thank you," she offered softly as she brushed by him and strode down the aisle. Her long slender legs wobbled as they carried her towards the exit, but her shoulders were squared, and she held herself as regally as any queen. If only I had the courage, she lectured herself. That's all I need, courage. I had it all once—Daddy called me his brave little girl. And look at me now! I'm the one who owns everything, not them! But as she stepped out of the gloom in the cabin into the bright sun, she knew very well that courage was exactly what she did not have.

Uncle Henry was not, as she had expected, standing at the foot of the ramp. Only the stewardess was there, holding her clipboard. The heat was like a slap in the face. A slight breeze brought in a touch of coolness from the lake. Stacey could almost see, almost taste Uncle Henry standing there. Somebody called from inside the terminal, and the sound reverberated off the aluminum skin of the airplane, and sent a shock wave through her. Her feet were frozen to the top stair, and she began to shake again. Good God, she screamed at herself, I'm coming apart at the seams! They can't do this to me. There *has* to be some place to run!

Warily, like a fox trapped in a covert, she backed slowly away from the rim of the stairs. One trembling step, and then another, before she backed into someone behind her, someone whose voice penetrated the fog of terror in her mind.

"There's nobody there!" Harry—the deep comforting voice, the craggy comfortable face. Stacey whirled around and buried herself against his chest, still shaking. His welcome arms came around her again, warm and supporting.

"Here now!" He bent over to bring his lips close to her ears. "Whoever they are, they're only people." His lips teased the lobe of her ear.

"Not people—relatives." He could hear the cry of anguish in her words, and a frown flashed over his face.

"Ah!" There seemed to be a million miles of understanding in that one word. Her slender figure clung to him like a limpet. Both her arms went around his waist, as her eighteen years of shy reserve were dissolved by her immediate fear.

"Of course." He offered her the handkerchief again, and gradually her stomach settled, and the tears stopped. He released his hold just enough so that she could wipe her eyes and blow her nose. "Relax," he instructed. "Just look pretty. Leave everything else to me. We'll get our luggage. You are not to be afraid!"

It was like a command from on high. *You are not to be afraid.* And very suddenly it all seemed so simple. Of course—leave everything to him. I am *not* afraid. Do you hear that, Uncle Henry? I'm not afraid of you!

They went down the steps together, side by side, Harry's arm thrown protectively around her shoulders as he reduced his long stride to match hers. Halfway down he pulled her to a halt and turned her into his arms again. "For the audience," he whispered, as his head came down slowly over hers. His lips brushed hers casually, then returned, gently and warmly. As the pressure gradually increased, her arms stole upward, struggling around his neck. Her hands buried themselves in the thick hair at the nape, pulling him into more intimate contact. Violently unclassified feelings ran up and down her spine, longings she knew from another life, perhaps. And when he broke the contact, she released her grip with strange reluctance.

"Remember now," he cautioned her, "let me do all the talking. You just look happy and pretty, smile a lot, and agree with everything I say, right?"

"I—yes," she muttered, still deep in her daze. He fumbled with her left hand, and she felt cold metal against one of her fingers, then he was leading her down the stairs, with one arm hugging her closely.

They walked almost in lockstep across the steaming tarmac and fought their way inside, to the coolness of the air-conditioners. The luggage was already on display on the carousel. All their fellow passengers had disappeared. Outside Stacey could hear the engines of the commuter plane warm up again. Her eyes searched the terminal lobby. It was easy enough to stand on the stairs of the plane and say, I'm not afraid of you, Uncle Henry, but here on the flatland, moving closer and closer to meeting with him, was another story indeed.

She pointed out her single bag, and Harry pulled it off the carousel, along with two immaculate cowhide bags of his own. Gold initials sparked at her. HJM. I wonder what it means, one part of her mind asked, while the other directed her eyes into dark corners.

"Hey," he said softly, and pulled her close, "remember what I said."

"I—I'm finding it hard to," she stammered. "I wish I had another pill!"

"Pills? At your age?" Another frown rode across his craggy face.

"Well, I—Aunt Ellen said I was—hyperactive, or something, and the pills—"

"Aunt Ellen?" he asked gruffly.

"She—my father's sister. She's my—my guardian, I guess."

"Forget about the pills. Want anything here?"

What she wanted, she recognised, was not to go out that door. The lobby was empty of Delanos—any kind of Delano—which meant they must be waiting outside, in front. And all I want to do is stay in here, her conscience told her. "A newspaper," she muttered at Harry, for want of anything else to say.

He knew what she was up to, she could see, for a tiny smile played around the stern corners of his mouth. But his hand snatched up a copy of the *Waco Tribune-Herald,* and tucked it under her arm. "Nothing else?"

"I—" Courage is what I need, she told herself desperately. There's no time for lesser measures. "Would you kiss me again?"

His tiny smile became a wide grin. "It's addictive," he said softly as he leaned down and administered another one, like the first, but longer this time. Stacey's hands refused to release him until she had run completely out of breath. Her feet were inches off the floor, and her head miles above—or at least it seemed that way. When he finally dropped her, she could feel the warm imprint of his hand on the middle of her back, as if he had branded her for life. She leaned her head against his chest, just long enough to catch her breath. When he pushed her slightly away she could see he was laughing—not at her, but from the joy of it all.

"You surprise me," he chuckled. "And I thought I'd done it all!"

She dared not ask what he meant. She bowed her head and ducked behind her swinging hair, using her fingers to bring everything back to its normally pristine fall. It was all an excuse, an attempt to give herself time to sort out her startled emotions, which refused to be sorted. Nothing like this had ever happened to her before. Nothing.

"Your ghosts aren't here?" He was searching the terminal himself.

"They're bound to be," she sighed, coming back down to earth with a thud. "They wouldn't let me—"

"They wouldn't let you run free?"

"I—Aunt Ellen is all the relative I've got." It startled her to find herself defending her aunt, even in so small a way. But old habits died hard, and up until the time she married Uncle Henry, three years ago, Aunt Ellen had been as fair and kind and understanding as a bitter woman could be.

"You've got more now," he said enigmatically. "Remember what I told you. Smile a lot, and look pretty, but keep your mouth shut. Right?"

"I—right. Yes, sir. My dad was an Army Colonel. You sound a lot like him."

"I shouldn't be surprised," he chuckled. "Buckle up and prepare to jump." That strong arm came down around her waist again, instilling courage by osmosis, right through the thin linen of her dress. Stacey savoured it, rebuilding her stock of bravery. When Harry turned her loose and picked up the bags instead, she felt bereft, like the little girl who expected a lollipop from the bank teller, and got only a smile.

So they continued towards the outer doors, and the car park. She moved with a mixture of bravado and tremor, putting a good face on things, so to speak, but ready to jump at a second's notice—and praying there would be at least a second.

With both hands full, Harry backed into the glass doors and held them open for her to pass through. She was smiling her thanks when she heard the roar behind her.

"Well, it's about time," growled Uncle Henry. "You've kept us waiting in the hot sun for over thirty minutes!"

Stacey cringed. The first lash of the whip. She knew what he meant. Stacey Bronfield was responsible not only for keeping them waiting, but also for the hot sun itself, and the humidity, and his discomfort at having to drive all the way to Waco from clear on the other side of Gatesville. And there was just a little threat behind it, too. Like, wait until I get you home, girl!

Very suddenly Stacey realised that even this strong man—this Harry—could hardly cope with Uncle Henry. And, dear God, George was right behind him. Uncle Henry's voice had been fine-tuned by years of hell-raising. It had the sharp bray of a startled Texas mule. Uncle Henry. Superimpose what he used to be over what he is now, and see the difference. He's dressed in the best clothes money can buy—my money, Stacey noted grimly. A lightweight white summer suit, boots—as if he ever dared to come near a horse—and an expensive ten-gallon hat. Just under six feet, going to seed at the waistline. A sallow face; despite claiming to be a Texan, Uncle Henry hated to go out in the sun. And behind him, a thinner carbon copy, his son George. Except for the hat. George was proud of his shoulder-length fair hair. And where his father's face was planed and furrowed by life, George's was as smooth as a baby's bottom.

"And so this is your family?" Harry squeezed her shoulders gently, just enough to shake her out of her stupor. He had dropped the bags, and was standing with feet slightly spread, his hawk-eyes scanning the pair in front of them. Under his breath she heard him render the final Texas judgment. "Dudes," he muttered.

He didn't wait for her to answer. He moved directly in front of Uncle Henry, between Stacey and her relatives, close enough so that her uncle was forced to bend his head back a little to look up at him. "I'm Harry," he boomed, extending a hand towards Stacey. "Harry Marsden, you know."

The two other men stared blankly at him. It's the first time I've ever seen Uncle Henry faced down, Stacey thought, and the very idea restored some of her composure. A tiny giggle bubbled in her throat, and almost made it to the outside world. Almost. His next statement rocked her back on her heels.

"Harry Marsden," he repeated in that deep booming voice. "Kitten's new husband."

Uncle Henry stepped back as if he had been stung by a scorpion. He opened his mouth to say something, but only managed to gasp like a gaffed fish. George, who looked like a child watching someone steal his ice cream, took two threatening steps forward. Stacey swallowed her giggle and tried her best not to choke on it—or him.

"You mean you—you and Stacey—" stuttered Uncle Henry. His face was turning a brilliant sunset red. "You two?"

"Right in one gasp," Harry returned, laughing. "Stacey and I. Us two. Isn't it wonderful?" He turned back to her, and pulled her close again, tilting her chin up with one of his huge fingers. "It *is* wonderful, isn't it, Kitten?"

"I—yes. Yes, it's wonderful." Stacey's confidence was improving by leaps and bounds. There was no doubt about it; he could do it. He was doing it! "Magical. It's so wonderful that it's almost unbelievable!" There was a warning twinkle in those dark eyes that shut her mouth with a snap. Look pretty, keep your mouth shut, she commanded. Things were bad enough with two Delanos mad at her, without adding a—what had he said?—a Marsden to the list. And doesn't that sound nice? Harry Marsden. Harry J. Marsden. Mrs Stacey Marsden? It did have a nice ring to it. Where have I heard that name before? she wondered. And then he was lifting up her left hand in front of Uncle Henry's nose.

"There, you see," he stated flatly. "Signed, sealed, and delivered. Until death do us part, and all that." Uncle Henry gasped again. Glaring in the summer sun was one of the largest diamonds Stacey had ever seen—a garish old-fashioned thing, surrounded with diamond chips, set in a platinum ring. Which was an exact match for the ornate platinum wedding ring that squirrelled down next to it on Stacey's finger.

George pushed his father aside, making noises deep in his throat, his arms outstretched as if he meant death to them part at just that very moment, or at least within the next five. Harry watched him come with an inane smile on his lips. Then at the last moment he pushed Stacey to one side, moved both his arms rapidly in front of him, and very suddenly George was sitting down on the sidewalk, his nose slightly bent, and a trickle of blood streaming down from it.

"You hit him!" Stacey gasped at the audacity of this man who had claimed her as his bride.

"Yes, I do seem to have," Harry returned coolly. "Bruised my knuckles, too. A stupid thing to do, but sort of automatic. A karate chop would have been better—knuckles are at best a poor thing to hit out with. I need a little sympathy, Kitten."

"I—you hit George!" Stacey's head was buzzing with the notion. Lord, how many times have I wanted to hit George, she told herself. How many times? And Harry had just put out his hand and—hit him!

"Well, it did seem to be the thing to do," he rumbled. "He was being pretty offensive. Was there anybody else who needs hitting, while I'm in the mood?"

Uncle Henry had lived by his wits for a long time, and he quickly shifted the conflict into the verbal level. "Surely you don't expect us to believe all this nonsense," he stormed. "Stacey was not married when she got on that plane! Get over here, girl, We're going home—immediately! Do you hear?"

Stacey's robot legs almost carried her forward, but Harry's arm intervened, wrapping her up in his protective cocoon again. "She's going home all right," Harry said coldly. "With me. And while we're at it, just who the hell are you?"

"Why—why—" Uncle Henry spluttered, "I'm her uncle, of course."

"Only by marriage," Stacey interjected.

"I'm her guardian," continued Uncle Henry. "I'm responsible for her welfare." And then the older man's courage reasserted itself. "And now I'll ask you to get your hands off her—at once, do you hear?"

"I've got plans for keeping my hands on this girl for the next fifty years," drawled Harry. "And just what makes you think you're Stacey's guardian?"

"Why, I—I'm married to her aunt, her only living relative. She's my wife's brother's daughter."

"You talk as if you thought she was under age, friend. Whatever gave you that idea?"

"Idea? Why, of course she is. She's seventeen." Uncle Henry was caught in the grip of a terrible rage, with no safe outlet in sight. Stacey could see the red gleam in his eyes, but she could not let the untruth stand.

"It isn't so, Harry. I'm eighteen. Three months ago I was eighteen!"

"And so that would seem to put an end to your guardianship, if it ever existed," said Harry grimly. "In fact, it would seem to require an accounting of your stewardship, Mr—?"

"Delano," stuttered Uncle Harry. He's going to burst a blood vessel any minute, Stacey told herself. And as terrible as it sounds, I think I would be glad. "Henry Delano," her uncle repeated. "And I have Stacey's power of attorney, all signed and sealed under the law."

"A waste of paper," Harry told him. "In Texas everything changes when the lady marries. Now, about that accounting?"

"What accounting?"

"You know," snapped Harry. "A legal statement telling us what you've done with her property and money. Pretty simple, isn't it? And as her husband I'll represent Stacey in any future debates of this nature. You do have a lawyer?"

"I don't need a lawyer!" Uncle Henry was still trying to bluster it out, but with only half the fervour he usually employed.

"You need a lawyer very badly, Mr Delano. Here it is Friday. On Monday Kitten and I will come over to check up on your trusteeship. Where do I find you?"

"At Rancho Miraflores," interjected Stacey. "Just west of Gatesville. It's mine. They all just—moved in. They—" Harry raised his hand and stopped her in mid-sentence.

"Then they'd better be prepared to move out just as quickly," he said. Then, without waiting for the Delanos to say anything, he took Stacey's arm and led her in the direction of the parking lot. She found herself staggering, as if her two-inch heels were too high—or as if her shoulders had just been relieved of a massive burden. He felt her wobble, and swept her up in his arms, as if she were a small child. All at once she felt tired. Reaction was setting in from the massive struggle that had taken place within her, and she was worn to the nub. "Don't let it all get to you, Kitten," Harry murmured in her ear.

"I—it's hard not to," she whispered back, feeling a joy at the warmth of him, the strength, the assurance.

It was a Mercedes 280XL into which he ushered her, propping her up on the soft seat and strapping her in with a safety belt. As he walked around the front of the car she settled herself against the back of the seat and watched. That's what it is, she told herself. He doesn't walk—he just seems to flow along the ground like some jungle cat. And I don't really know whether he's done me some good, or just made things worse, do I?

The seat sank as he climbed in. "Just hold on a minute," he said. He started the motor, waited until it was running smoothly, then flipped on the air-conditioner. Moments later cool air flowed out of multiple vents straight at her, ruffling her hair, whispering at the hem of her dress.

"Now then, tell me all about it." His invitation was extended behind a warm smile. It changed his face from a craggy silhouette to something almost good-looking. Almost—the qualification brought a smile to her lips, and set her nose to wrinkling.

"Like Peter Rabbit," he commented. "Tell me."

"You mean about them?"

"Well, more than likely I mean about you, and then about them. Start at the beginning and go forward."

Stacey almost said, "Yes, sir." And she did mentally click her heels. "Well, in the beginning there was my dad and I," she started, then stopped to lick her lips, and think.

"Don't do that," chuckled Harry. "You act like a girl who needs to be kissed. And what happened to your mother?"

She shrank farther into her corner of the car and watched him apprehensively. That second kiss had been so startling that she was afraid of what another might bring!

"I—I didn't do anything on purpose," she said shyly. "I guess I had a mother, but I don't remember her. She died when I was born. It was always just me and my dad."

"All right, I'll settle for that. There was you and your dad. And then what happened?"

"Daddy—he was a soldier, you know. And he owned a ranch. He was an officer in the regular Army. He flew helicopters, and things like that. And when they sent him someplace and I couldn't go, he would take me up to St Anselm's, the convent school in Dallas, and leave me there until he came back. And then he was ordered to Vietnam, and he didn't come back.''

"Oh, wow! How old were you then?"

"I was—I was thirteen when he left. Fourteen when they sent the word that he couldn't come back."

"And then Aunt Ellen came. She was different then. She took me out of the school, and we went to the ranch."

"What school did you go to then?"

"Why, no school. We just lived at the ranch, Aunt Ellen and I. She was my father's sister. Did I say that before? She had no money of her own, and she was—well, you'll see for yourself. I never did understand it. Daddy was a handsome man. Aunt Ellen, she looks like—But it was nice on the ranch. I helped with the stock—we ran beef. It was before they—well, just before. And we were happy, Aunt Ellen and I. Then Henry Delano came along. He took one look at my aunt, two at the ranch, and they got married."

"You don't care for your uncle?" queried Harry.

"I—he—he tried to—touch me," she said reluctantly.

"Oh damn! One of that kind!"

"It wasn't terribly bad. It's a very big ranch, and I could keep out of his sight pretty easily. But then, when I was sixteen, he found out somehow that all the property belonged to me, and Aunt Ellen hadn't anything. That made him terribly angry at both of us. And that's when George appeared."

"Ah! George is Uncle Henry's son—a Delano?"

"Yes. He had been married a good many years before—I think. At least, he said George was his son."

"All right, you needn't tell me the rest. They all decided that you ought to marry George. Right?"

"Yes. How did you know?"

"It wasn't hard." Harry laughed, but it was a cold glittering laugh, with no warmth in it at all.

"They just kept after me, morning noon and night," Stacey went on. "*You ought to marry George, Stacey.* Or, *you have to marry George, Stacey.* Things like that. And then—lord, he would chase me too. Only there was one thing in my favour. George is afraid of horses, so if I could get to the stables I was always safe. And then—" She was fighting to keep the tears out of her voice, and having very little luck. "And then they said I should go to Dallas to sign some legal papers—and when I came back I would have to marry George!"

"So why didn't you just disappear?"

"With what?" she asked scornfully. "You can see what I am. I don't have the courage to go out on my own, and I don't have a penny to my name. Look at me! They laugh and call me the little heiress, and look—" she fumbled in her purse, "I've got ten, twenty, forty-six cents to my name. Where would I run to? What would I do? I don't know a thing about anything except horses."

"And you've not been to school since you were fourteen?"

"Not a day. I read a lot, but that's not schooling." Her words fumbled away through softness to inaudibility, until finally she ground to a halt. Why didn't I run away? she asked herself. Why couldn't I work up enough courage to do something about my own life? Why?

An uncomfortable silence fell over them, with only the purr of the engine and the high-pitched whine of the air-conditioner to fill the void. One of Harry's hands moved across the back of the seat and settled at the nape of her neck, massaging it gently.

"Poor kid." Oh, my God, thought Stacey, now he's going to *pity* me. I don't want that. Anything but pity—anything! I'd almost rather go back to Uncle Henry.

He felt the tension in her neck muscles. "Don't fight it," he said gently. "Relax."

"Why did you say that?" she asked.

"Say what?"

"That we—that—we were married?"

"Hey, that was a little far-fetched, wasn't it?" he chuckled. "But we had to give them some surprise— and you'll admit it worked."

"For the moment." She smiled, reflecting on the look on Uncle Henry's face. And George! "I thought George was going to fall through the ground!" But then the serious side of it came back to her.

"But it only delayed things, you know. Sooner or later I have to go back home. And they'll all be there— and then what's going to happen?"

"A great deal of what's going to happen depends entirely on you, Kitten," returned Harry.

"Why do you keep calling me Kitten?"

"That's another story, Stacey. Maybe I'll tell you about it one of these days. But first, let's stick to you. What do you want to have happen? Would you like me to go with you on Monday and talk to the Delanos again? To get them off your ranch? Can you run the ranch without them?"

"It—it doesn't take any running," she admitted softly. "We don't run cattle any more. Four years ago they—somebody—found oil on our land. Everything is run by Parsons Oil Company now, under a lease. We just have the house, and about three hundred acres. They lease the rest. And—"

"And what?"

"Would you really go with me?"

"Would you like me to?"

Would I like to walk up the front stairs, and see them standing there, and me with my arm through his? Would I like to see him roar at them and make them shiver the way they've made me? Would I like that!

"Yes, I think I would like that very much," she said happily.

"It will cost you something," he chuckled. "There's a fee."

"I—I guess if I—I suppose there must be some money in my bank account, if—you wouldn't charge too much?"

"Oh, I charge a great deal, Kitten. But it's not money I want from you, you know."

"I know? How could I know? But I do want you— I have to have you come with me, or I can't go myself. So tell me, what's your price?"

"Very simple," he said solemnly now, his dark eyes following every movement of her facial muscles. "I want you to come with me to my grandmother's house, and spend the weekend pretending that you're my wife!"

CHAPTER TWO

STACEY looked over at him, her eyes wide, her mouth pursed. "To be your wife? To—I don't understand." Very suddenly the car had become overwhelmingly chilled, as if a cloud had obscured the bright sun. *To be your wife? What he means is he wants me to—to share a bed with him for the weekend. And I thought he was my own true knight. Hah!*

"Did you know your lips move when you talk to yourself?" he asked.

"Hah!" It seemed impossible to find anything else to say. *I'm so tired—so tired. He wants me to be his temporary wife. What a nice name for such a mean position! He wants a weekend mistress, and like all those older men, he wants somebody young. I should feel damn angry about it, shouldn't I? Then how come I just feel—sleepy?? And my ears are buzzing so?*

"What kind of pills were those your aunt gave you?" demanded Harry.

The question was right out of the blue. It was the last subject in the world she expected. "I don't know," she mumbled sleepily. "There were all kinds—some little white ones, and then some yellow ones, and then some blue ones. I never asked the name, because—" *Because I can't hold my head up for another minute. Aunt Ellen gave me two of the blue ones this morning, and I haven't the strength to talk any more.*

Slowly, like the Tower of Pisa, she began to lean over towards him. She was fast asleep when her head finally landed on his shoulder and slipped off. He cradled it with one hand, moving back against the seat to make a little pocket where she could rest. She sighed in her dreaming, and shifted over beside him, both hands wrapped around his upper arm. Her feet came up off the floor and on to the seat. Unconsciously she tucked them up under her, and settled her entire weight on him, in a graceful half-kneeling position. Her lips parted slightly; he could hear the rhythmic passage of air. She wiggled once or twice, squirming closer as she did, then was still.

He sat perfectly still until he was sure she was sound asleep. It was hard to keep the satisfied smile off his face. There was no doubt about it, she was perfect for the part. True, except for the hair, she had only the vaguest similarity to Lisette. But Grandmother was almost totally blind. And it was the aura about her, not her looks, that had struck him. Not that she wasn't a beauty—for that she certainly was. An innocent beauty, full of spirit and loveliness, and that was something that Lisette never was! It *would* work. It had to work. There wasn't time for another search, another replacement.

His left hand tapped at the steering wheel of the car as he assessed her. Five foot seven, perhaps eight? Lovely hair. The hand that had been on her shoulder moved up and toyed with the fullness of it. Strange, he thought, there are lighter streaks in it. I wonder how she does that? Thick curly eyelashes. Eighteen? She'll set the male world on fire by the time she's twenty-one. Green eyes, weren't they? Or grey? It had been hard to tell, with the crying and all. A slender figure, tall for a girl. Nice hips, well rounded. Magnificent breasts! Lord, come on, Harry, the kid's too young for you, and too full of fears. Get on with the masquerade, then get her home. That pair of dudes who thought they could milk the child of all her money were in for some surprise! He had to use his left hand to reach the stick-shift of the automatic drive; using his right would surely wake her up. It cost an extra two dollars to get the parking attendant to put their bags in the back seat of the car. He whistled under his breath as he drove out on to Airport Road, then turned north on Rock Creek road.

Stacey napped for twenty minutes or so, then came brightly awake. The car was bumping down a pot-holed farm-to-market road. For a moment or two, wide awake, she savoured the comfort, and nuzzled closer to him. Then she began to think, and instantly her peaches-and-cream complexion turned a brilliant red. She pushed herself up and moved back into the farthest corner of the car, stammering her apologies.

"No need," Harry laughed softly. "I enjoyed it all." He flexed his right arm a few times. "Even my arm went to sleep. Feel better?"

"Yes. Where are we?" A soft, almost timid request from someone who obviously was not allowed to do much questioning. The tone cut him, leaving behind a swift sweet pain that had nothing to do with pity.

"About a quarter of a mile from my grandmother's home," he answered. "About eight miles north of Waco." He was still flexing his right hand and fingers as he pulled over to the shoulder of the road and stopped the big car. When the emergency brake was set he turned sidewise in the seat to give her his full attention. "You said you couldn't go home alone?"

She nodded agreement.

"And you would like me to go with you to de-louse the place?"

Stacey giggled uncontrollably. "We still have some cattle-dip in the barn," she finally managed to get out. "Is that good on humans?"

"Calm down," he sighed. "It was an unfortunate choice of words." He settled himself back in the seat and watched her face intently. "We'll go over there on Monday, and I'll stay long enough to get everything straightened out to your satisfaction."

"You're a lawyer?' Her eyes widened at the thought. The only lawyers she knew were cold business types who lived in Dallas.

"No," he interrupted her train of thought, "but I have a couple of lawyers working for me. Not to worry—it's the weekend between now and Monday I want to talk about."

"Oh." He could see her face drop. The dimple on her left cheek disappeared, to be replaced by a tic that pulled at the corner of her mouth. "I'm—not sure I can pay your price." The words rattled out at full speed, as if she were eager to get them out and gone. "I—I don't have any experience in this sort of thing." She was trembling, almost uncontrollably.

"Of course you don't, child." There was a snap in his voice that brought her head up. Anger? she thought, I'm the one who ought to be insulted, and *he's* angry?

"Look here," he said, "this is strictly a business proposition, nothing more. You're too young for me, little lady."

For some reason the comment stung her. Too young? Hah! She pulled her shoulders back and took a deep breath. And I hope that bugs your eyes out, her mind shouted at him. But his eyes stayed glued to her face, and how long can you hold your breath just to look sexy? She let the air escape in a wild sigh, and slumped down.

"That's better." There was a paternal chuckle in his voice. "Now, Stacey, I went to Dallas to hire an actress to do an impersonation for me, but I couldn't find anyone suitable. Until I met you on the plane, that is."

"You want an actress? I don't know anything about acting."

"That's what makes you perfect for the part."

She looked up at him, measured what she saw, and was satisfied. "OK," she said, "tell me about it."

"It's my grandmother," Harry began. "She's eighty-five, and living in the old family home just around that bend in front of us. She's dying, Stacey. The doctors tell me that she'll be lucky to make it through the weekend. And she's dying troubled." He stopped long enough to search her face again. Then, apparently satisfied with what he saw, he continued.

"My grandmother raised me from a pup. Me and Lisette Langloise, her godchild. Grandmother always expected Lisette and me to marry, but that never set right with me. Anyway, a bigger fish swam into sight, and Lisette departed, for parts unknown, as they say. That was eight years ago, and Grandmother still grieves. I want her to go with a clear mind. And that's where you come in."

"You want me to make believe we're married, and that I'm Lisette? Do I look like her or something?"

"Not a bit," he chuckled, "which is a mark in your favour, believe me. Don't worry about that—Grandmother is blind, slightly deaf, and completely bedridden. I'll present you to her, you'll wear Lisette's favourite perfume, and we'll play it by ear. Love is what she needs, and you look like what she romanticises Lisette to be. You're almost exactly Grandmother's dream. Well?"

It was a request that Stacey could not possibly refuse, and yet she stalled. "There won't be any—I— being your wife—there won't be any hanky-panky?"

"Hanky-panky?" Harry threw back his head and roared. "I didn't know people actually talked like that these days," he gurgled. "No, Kitten, there won't be any hanky-panky. There are three other people in the house, and outside Grandmother's bedroom everything will be as decorous as one of the Mayor's lawn parties—which are plenty boring, let me tell you. Well?"

She waited a moment, hoping that her mind would throw some well-reasoned excuses. But none came. Her mind remained an absolute blank. And Harry's craggy face had an appeal on it that said more than words. Why he's not actually homely, she told herself. "Yes," she said.

"Yes? No yes but. Or yes and?"

"No. When I make up my mind I don't quibble. It's just yes."

"Thank God for you," he said as he started the engine. "What in the world have I been doing, fooling around with all those other women?"

The car started forward, bumping back on to the road surface. "Waiting around for me to grow up?" suggested Stacey, in that wicked humour that found so few places for expression. He grinned at her, then turned his attention to the road.

A few yards farther on they swept around a bend in the road, and there on a hill in front of them, surrounded by carefully fenced paddocks, was the house. It towered above the landscape in a Victorian mishmash of dormers, gables, and towers, two stories high, with a huge curved veranda enveloping everything.

"I thought you had a ranch!" gasped Stacey. "It looks just like the old Cooper home in the city!"

"An exact copy," he laughed, "built a year later, in 1908. My great-grandfather built it for his immigrant wife. Come on in."

She followed him slowly up the stairs, through the door with the inset stained glass windows, and down the hall. A middle-aged woman, black hair turning white, bustled out of the door behind the stairs. "We're back, Millie," said Harry, and the woman stopped, hiding her hands under her apron.

"I'm all flour and chocolate," she laughed. "And this is—?"

Stacey could hear him take a deep breath, as if preparing to make a steep dive. "This is my wife, Millie. We were married in Dallas. Stacey, this is Millie Fallon, who runs the house. Her husband Frank does everything else that's required."

"Your wife? You mean you finally did it? Oh, Harry, wait until your grandmother hears!" There were tears in the older woman's eyes, and she lifted a corner of her apron to wipe them off. "Welcome home, Mrs Marsden."

"Please, call me Stacey. 'Mrs Marsden' is a little too much for me to handle right this minute!"

"Of course—Stacey. A nice round name. You come from these parts?"

"Over Gatesville way. We have a little ranch over there."

"Harry—you'd better get yourself and your surprise package upstairs," said Millie. "The nurse came down for your grandmother's meal a few minutes ago. Lunch could be ready in—say, fifteen minutes, Stacey?"

"I—" Stacey fumbled for words. Is this what a wife is supposed to do? she thought. I suppose it must be, but what do I say? She looked over to Harry for some signal. He was grinning at her, one eyelid barely dropped, an almost imperceptible wink.

"Oh, that would be fine—Millie?" With both of them beaming at her she felt an access of strength, and was almost jovial as Harry tucked one hand under her elbow and urged her up the stairs.

The ground floor halls and rooms had been bright with light, flashing with colours. Here on the upper floor everything was in shaded darkness, lit by tiny safety lights spaced down the hall about four inches above the floor. He led her down to an empty bedroom at the end of the hall. The curtains were open, so the eternal gloom of the hallway was relieved. Stacey looked around in surprise. Gold on white was the motif—frilly white, loaded with lace. Certainly not a man's room!

"Yours?" she ventured cautiously, and he laughed, an uproarious guffaw. "Not hardly. Now where the devil is that—ah, here." He had been searching the low dressing table in the corner, and came back to her with a perfume bottle.

"This was Lisette's room," he explained. "Grandmother kept it clean and ready for her—being sure she would be back, you know. Here's the perfume."

Stacey took the stoppered bottle from him, still looking around the room. What a disaster of a bedroom! It looks more like a harem than a sleeping place, she told herself.

"Well," Harry interrupted her train of thought.

"I—well what?"

"The perfume—put it on. It's the one thing Grandma will recognise right away."

"Put it on?" she queried.

"Oh, come on now, don't tell me you've never used perfume before!"

"All right," she told him, feeling miserable about it, "I won't tell you that." But I haven't, she screamed silently at him. I don't even know where to start!

He showed his impatience for two minutes, then took the bottle back and pulled out the stopper. "Like this," he sighed. He dabbed at her wrists, the pulse point in her neck, and behind the lobes of her ears, then he stepped back to measure the result. "Okay, you smell fine. Remember, you're Lisette, and she's your godmother, and you've been away for eight years. Ready?"

"I don't think I'll ever be ready," stammered Stacey. "I'm really not an actress—you must know that." And besides, the perfume was almost overpowering her with its musky undertones.

"I know, but don't let that worry you. Just do what comes naturally." His long lean hand swallowed her wrist, and he towed her out into the corridor and down to the third door from the stairs. It opened just as they came abreast of it, and a woman dressed in nurse's uniform came out—a small woman, overly round, with freckles across her nose, and a big smile.

"She's just finished her lunch," the nurse whispered. "I think she'll want to rest for a while. You could have perhaps fifteen minutes, no longer. She's really down in the dumps."

"I've got the cure for that," whispered Harry in return. He patted Stacey's wrist, still entangled in his hand-trap. "Stacey, this is Nurse Wilson—Sara to her friends. Sara, my wife Stacey."

The nurse's smile turned into a broad grin. She stepped out into the hall and closed the door behind her. "Wonderful," she crowed. "Marvellous! Is this the girl she calls Kitten?"

"This is she. She is it—whatever. Why don't you go get your lunch, and let us see what sort of miracle we can concoct up here." The nurse nodded, and pushed them both towards the door. Harry turned the knob and gestured Stacey ahead of him, but she stopped in the middle of the door-jamb. "So that's why!" she hissed at him.

"Why what?"

"Why you keep calling me Kitten. It was *her* name!"

"Yes, it was the name we all used."

"Don't you ever call me that again," she said fiercely. "Not ever again!"

"Why, I do believe you're jealous!"

"No such a thing. But don't you dare call me that again!"

He wasn't prepared to fight, not on the threshold of his grandmother's bedroom. One of his huge hands settled in the middle of her back and pushed her into the room.

A small bedlamp provided the only light. The scent of flowers filled the air. An air-conditioner hummed songs to itself in the corner. The bed was an old four-poster, raised on blocks to the height of a regular hospital bed, and the little stick-figure lay exactly in the middle of it, with back and head raised on double pillows. As the pair of them ghosted across the thick carpet, Stacey studied the recumbent form.

A thin face, almost fallen in, that spoke of past beauty. White hair, growing sparse in spots, but still kept in curl for pride's sake. A long white nightgown, with a choker collar, and a tiny bit of blue ribbon at neck and wrists. Long beautiful hands, translucent skin over thin bones, with touches of brown pigmentation spots. Only the hands moved, clutching and unclutching the sheet that covered her. Occasionally the eyes blinked, but their faded blue saw nothing.

Stacey gasped. Raised without elderly people around her, she was instantly touched by this tiny relic. "Who's there?" the voice quavered—halfway between a handsome contralto and a squeak.

"It's me, Harry," he said quietly, leaning over to drop a light kiss on the clear forehead. "I've brought you a surprise."

"A surprise?" Both eyes popped open, and one thin hand reached out towards his. "Harry, you're enough of a surprise for—what's that smell? Lilacs? Harry!"

"Yes, love." Strange how soft his voice was, Stacey thought as she watched; you could almost feel the caressing love in it. "She's come back, Grandma—Kitten's back. And that's only half the surprise."

"Half?" The hand groped away from him, reaching blindly into the darkness. Compelled by an emotion she had never felt before—not pity, but something deeper—Stacey took the searching hand in her own. The fingers intertwined with hers, strongly for a woman so ill. And then both hands shifted to Stacey's left, and explored.

"Kitten!" The words were like a sigh running down the wind. "It's been so long, my darling. But you've come home. I can go in peace, my love, and—Kitten? You're wearing my mother's rings. You and Harry?"

"Yes," he said, from just over her shoulder. "Lisette and I. Does that make you happy, Grandmother?"

Tiny tears rolled out from under the shuttered eyes and ran down the hollows of the sunken cheeks. "The Lord has been good to me," the old woman muttered, then was silent.

"She's fallen asleep," Harry whispered in Stacey's ear. "That's the way it goes. We might as well go down to lunch."

Stacey made an attempt to free her hand, but met instant objection from the reclining woman. "No," his grandmother whispered. "It's been so long. Stay with me, Kitten."

"Of course," she murmured softly. Some memory, some emotion, drove her to lean over the bed and kiss the tear-stained cheek. "Of course I will." She gestured with her head. Harry brought up a comfortable chair to the bedside, and she dropped into it, still holding the fragile hand in her own. "You go along and have your lunch," she told him. "I'll stay as long as she needs me."

"Sara will be back in an hour," he promised. "Come downstairs when she comes in."

"If your grandmother wants me to," Stacey returned and could not for the life of her reason out why she had said that. At nine o'clock she had been in Dallas, saying goodbye to Aunt Ellen, swallowing her pills *like a good little girl*. And here it was just after midday, and she was sitting in a strange house, at the bedside of a strangely loveable woman. And a man who called her his wife was standing behind her, giving orders. Out of the maze of all this confusion something good might come. So I'll sit here and see if I can sort it all out, she thought. The hand enclosed in hers squeezed lightly. She returned the gesture, and looked around to find that her "husband" had gone.

The nurse did return at one o'clock, but the patient's restless sleep would not allow a disengagement, so it was three that afternoon before Stacey managed the stairs, and found her way into the living room where Harry was waiting. He put down his paper and got up, welcoming her with a brief hug. "Thank you, Stacey," he said, in that same soft caressing voice he had used with his grandmother. "I came up twice to check. It worked! Hungry?"

"I think I'm starving." She flexed her arm and hand to restore the circulation. At the same time Millie bustled in with a plate of sandwiches. "Coffee?" the housekeeper asked.

"Milk?" Stacey suggested timidly, and both of them smiled at each other over her head.

"Milk, of course." Millie smiled again and went back to the kitchen, singing. Stacey consumed two sandwiches in short order, drank down the milk thirstily, then turned around to Harry. "You've got a dribble of milk on your chin," he told her. "Come on, we'll take a walk around the area. You sure need some exercise." Of course I do, she mumbled to herself. I need food, I need exercise, I need—why is the world so full of people willing to tell me what I need? What I really need is—whatever in the world am I thinking of! She made a hasty swipe at her chin, and almost ran to catch up to him. Strange, too—she felt as if she were floating over the ground, never touching.

He led her out of the back door into a lush green world that took her breath away. Long paddocks, fenced in white-painted wood, stretched in all directions. In one, several mares, each with a foal, cropped lazily. In the far opposite, resting in the shade of an old oak tree, a brilliant white stallion took his ease.

"I don't understand any of this," said Stacey, her interest caught both by the animals and the land. "Over most of middle Texas there's hardly a blade of green grass. Everything is sere and brown. And those magnificent animals! Morgans?"

"That's why my great-grandfather built here on the hill." Harry was pointing towards a low concrete structure behind the house, with pipes running out in all directions. "It's a fresh water spring—never been known to fail, in over eighty years, although it does get a little brackish sometimes in the August droughts. And no, they're not Morgans. Those are thorough-bred Arabs, every one of them."

"Arabs? They're so beautiful. So that's what you do for a living!"

"Don't say that too loudly," he chuckled. "There's a spy from the Internal Revenue Service behind every tree these days! Actually, raising blooded Arabs has been a fine tax shelter for many years. People raise them for the tax loss, you understand."

She didn't, but she hated to tell him so. "But you?"

"But, with a little concentration, and a lot of luck, I manage to make a profit. No, little lady, I make my

living downtown in Waco. I have a little building on
Clay Avenue, near the University. All this out here
belongs to my grandfather—except the Arabs.''

"Oh." It wasn't much of a conversational gambit,
but it was all she could muster. Her heart had run out
to the foals, and to the little old woman upstairs, and
to—but I don't intend to think about *that*, she lectured herself. I'll think about that when I get home.

"Funny, isn't it,'' she said, meaning funny-strange,
not funny-ha-ha, "I've got oil on my property, and
your grandmother has water. I wish we could trade.''

He chuckled at her, lifting her chin up with his index finger. "What big eyes you have,'' he teased.
"And that's the problem with a great deal of Texas—
there's plenty of water, but not where we want it.
Come on, let's go down to the stables and look
around.''

They dined together that night, sitting close together at a huge round table that almost filled the
dining room. "It seats twenty,'' he told Stacey when
she enquired. "Steak, mashed potatoes, tortillas? Mrs
Fallon favours Mexican food; most of the hands are
vaqueros.''

"I don't mind,'' laughed Stacey, and thought to
herself, that's the first time I can remember really
laughing since Daddy—since all those years ago! It's
just so—pleasant—being Mrs Harry Marsden. No
wonder Aunt Ellen rushed into marriage! I *must* not
judge Aunt Ellen too harshly. I wonder if I should
have my pills now?

She asked him, right in the middle of a bite, and his
forked clattered down to the table with a thump, and
he leaned over towards her. "I don't think you need
any pills!" he thundered. Oh Lord, she thought, it's

like pronouncements from Mount Sinai. I hope he doesn't throw lightning bolts at people who displease him. Or do I have the wrong mountain?

"I—I just—" she stammered. "Aunt Ellen said I was hyperactive, and had to have them, and I'm getting a very peculiar feeling in—"

"That's enough of that subject!" Harry returned, somewhere between a shout and a roar. And of course that's it, Stacey told herself warily as she ducked her head towards her plate and tried to hide behind her mass of hair He roars—but somehow he doesn't frighten me the way Uncle Henry does. Maybe all men roar at their women? *Their* women? What a lovely thought that was getting to be. She struggled to suppress the secret smile that flirted at the corners of her mouth, as she spooned up the last of the potatoes, and the rich brown gravy that covered them.

After dinner Harry took her back upstairs again, and into the darkened room. A new nurse was on duty, and she held her hand to her lips and shushed them as they came in. "She's asleep," she whispered.

"No, she's not," the voice quavered from the bed. "Kitten? Come and sit by me again."

Stacey laughed at the astonishment written on the nurse's face, and sank down into the same chair she had occupied earlier in the day.

"Harry? Are you here too?"

"Yes, Grandma."

The voice from the bed grew stronger, more positive, and for the first time Stacey could see and hear the dominant force of this pioneer woman. "Harry, you take yourself and that nice little nurse, and go talk to your horses, or something. I want to talk to Kitten alone."

He grinned down at Stacey, his face cast in shadows by the tiny light, then shrugged his shoulders. "So OK," he said softly, "Nurse and I are going. For fifteen minutes, not a second longer."

"Git!" the old lady snapped at him. But there was a smile on her tired face too. "Now, girl." She fumbled on top of the coverlet until Stacey put her hand in the way. It was snatched up in a death-grip.

"You were gone a long time, Kitten. I'd almost given up." There was a silence which Stacey felt driven to fill.

"I—I had to have time to think," she said sweetly. "Everybody was pushing at me to—"

"I know, girl— To marry Harry. That was all my fault. But now you've done it, you must work to make him happy. He's overworked, supporting us all. Promise?"

"I—" Stacey stopped in mid-sentence. Pushing me to marry Harry? Just the way Aunt Ellen was pushing me to marry George? Is that the way it always happens? Have I been wrong all this time, to think I was the only one treated like that? But then how much pushing would it have taken for them to get me to marry Harry!

"He's a good man," the voice from the bed whispered. "We all lean on him, and he has nobody to help him." The old lady's strength was fading. Her eyes were half closed, and she was breathing rapidly.

Stacey squeezed her hand gently. "I promise," she said, "For all my life."

There was a sigh of contentment, then suddenly the hand in hers went limp. Stacey bent over the bed anxiously, but the old woman was still breathing. Lying still, with a smile on her face, but still breathing. Stacey fell back into the chair again, clinging to the fragile hand, repeating all she could remember of the prayers she had learned in the Lutheran Church near her home. The nurse came back silently, after a full half-hour, and looked carefully at her patient.

"She won't wake up again until morning," she whispered. "You might as well get some sleep."

Harry was waiting for her, outside in the hall. "We've got a small problem," he said lightly as he led her in the other direction, around the stairs, and into a separate wing. Things were different on this side of the house. All the window curtains were drawn back, room doors were open, and brilliant lighting banished the dark memories of the wing behind them. As usual, he was going full speed, towing her behind him by her wrist.

"What small problem?" she gasped. "And could you slow down?"

"Oh!" He came to a full stop, with his hand on the knob of the only closed door in the wing. "You'll have to keep reminding me," he said. "You're tall for a girl, and I forget about short legs."

"It isn't the legs, it's my skirt," she snapped at him. He opened the door and almost pushed her into the room.

"I somehow knew there was nothing wrong with your legs," he leered. "That's the first thing I noticed on the plane."

"Stop drooling," she snapped, irritated. "Just tell me what the problem is." But instead of telling her he showed her, with a wide sweeping gesture. The bedroom was as large as three of her own, back at the ranch. The décor was gold and white—a women's room, without a doubt. Three delicate chairs were scattered around a large queen-sized bed, which held pride of position between two bay windows. On a small coffee table at the foot of the bed were three suitcases, two of Harry's, and one of hers. Suddenly she felt a chill.

She looked up at him. He frowned down at her and shrugged his shoulders. "Servants," he said dolefully. "When you grow up with them, they tend to dictate. This is the only room prepared."

"I don't think I'm going to like what you're going to tell me," Stacey said determinedly. "We're going to share a room?"

"Well, almost," he sighed. "Not actually, but we have to give Millie that impression, otherwise there's bound to be some hint of it given to Grandmother."

"So?" She was trembling again, but not from any emotion she had ever experienced before. There was something about this whole affair that gave it the aura of *déjà vu*. Or perhaps It was something of an old Hollywood "B" picture. In any case, she intended to be on her guard, and give him no advantages.

"So we have to make this room look lived in," he sighed, "even though I'm going to sneak down the hall for the night. Right?"

"That all depends," she said cautiously.

"On what?"

"Oh how much 'living in' we're expected to provide," she snapped. "I'm going to bed. You'd better do your act and get down the hall."

"You bet," he said. He was wearing a big smile, a big artificial smile. "The bathroom's there to your right."

With the door locked behind her, Stacey languished in the hot water, using somebody else's bubble bath, and splashing herself liberally with lotion afterwards. Her bag contained only one nightgown, an old cotton ankle-length that she had worn for three years, and had almost outgrown, especially around several interesting places.

Sure that Harry would be a long time, she strolled out into the bedroom again, scuffing her feet in the softness of the thick pile rug. The bedroom lights were off, but there was enough starlight stealing in through the double windows to outline the bed. She hummed as she walked over to it, pulled back the corner of the sheets, and slipped into the softness, the blessed softness. Her bed at home felt like a board. This one sank and rose to meet every curve. She lay down flat on her back, and stretched both arms sidewise, in the sheer joy of it all. The contentment lasted just long enough for the nerves in her left hand to report that somebody else was sharing the bed with her!

She sat up, clutching at the sheets, tensed to scream, when Harry's big hand sealed her mouth. She struggled against him, but the weight of the sheets entangled her. "Hey," he said, "I told you it has to look real!"

She broke away from his grip, and managed to get her feet on the floor. "It doesn't have to look *this* real," she snapped at him. "What the devil do you think you're doing!"

"I'm just setting the scene," he retorted. "My God, why did I have to get a *child* for this!" The comment stung. A child— Lord, she was tired of that classification! She was a long way from being a child, damn him. I'll show him *child!* She sat back, pulled her feet back under the sheets, and stretched out again.

"Okay," she snapped at him, "what's the next act?"

"Well, we have to squirm around, get close, dent the pillows, and everything like that."

"And then you go down the hall?"

"Yup."

"Okay, start squirming." That last sentence ended in a squeak, as he squirmed up close against her, dropping one hand across her stomach. "Now it's your turn," he whispered in her ear.

"My turn to what?"

"Squirm," he chuckled. "Wriggle closer. Put your arms around me."

Stacey bit her lip. "You'd better be sure it's all necessary," she hissed at him, but he made no answer. So squirm, she told herself. She turned towards him, feeling the warmth of bare skin brushing against her barely covered breasts. She gasped at the shock, and almost drew back, but his encircling arms held her close. Gradually she extended a finger in his direction, and it bounced off his hip. Nothing but skin, her sensors reported.

Oh Lord, what do I do next? she asked herself. Nothing she had ever learned had prepared her for this. His arms locked her in—and strangely enough, she was enjoying it! She moved slightly, the change brushing her aroused breasts against the solid warmth of his chest. He lay very quietly. Asleep? She held her breath, trying to monitor his. He was inhaling deeply, just the tiniest bit noisily.

Why, damn the man, he's gone to sleep, she told herself bitterly. He really *does* think of me as a child. Listen to him! But her fractious body was paying no attention. One of her hands came back to his hip, traced a careful line upward, across his narrow waist, up on to his muscular chest, and farther, up into his hair. He stirred slightly, but settled again.

The length and tenor of her day began to catch up to her. It's warm here, she sighed to herself. Warm, and comfortable—nice. And what harm can he do if he's asleep? She snuggled even closer. Her eyelids grew too heavy, and she dropped off to sleep.

When he was sure she was asleep he moved carefully on to his back, a broad grin on his face, and pulled her head into a more comfortable position on his shoulder. Man, have you got willpower! he told himself. His hand moved slowly downward to cup her breast. That's enough, his conscience dictated. Lord, is this *child* loaded! His hand moved gently down to rest on the swell of her hip, and there he managed to rein himself in. Some time later he too fell asleep.

They were both awakened by a knock on the door, and Millie Fallon came, not waiting for an invitation, and not at all abashed by seeing them so close together. The sun was coming in the windows, bright with the promise of a new day. The early morning birds were hard at work, and a slight breeze flavoured the room. "The doctor's been," Millie announced. "I thought you'd like to hear first hand."

She beckoned, and an elderly white-haired man came into the bedroom. Oh, my God, groaned Stacey as she ducked her head under the covers. It's not enough to be caught in his bed, but the darn place is like a train depot!

Harry sat up in the bed, reading Stacey's mind. Under the covers his big hand came down on her well-padded bottom, and gave an admonitory whack. "Doctor Jenkins," he acknowledged. "What is it?"

"The nurse called me a couple of hours ago," the doctor replied. "Your grandmother has slipped into a coma. It might last a day, or a week—maybe even longer. But I think you have to accept the fact that she will never wake up. And I've got to run. The nurse has my instructions."

Mrs Fallon shooed him out of the room, turning back in the doorway before she closed it. "And you two better have some breakfast. Downstairs in twenty minutes." The housekeeper sniffed a couple of times at the tear breaking from her right eye, and went off.

Stacey poked her head timidly out from beneath the covers. "I thought you were supposed to go down the hall," she snapped.

"I seem to have fallen asleep," Harry returned innocently. "I hope it didn't inconvenience you?"

"No—no, not at all," she stammered. Not for the life of her was she going to tell him that she had wakened at three in the morning, and found his hand on the peak of her breast, driving her into emotions she had not ever thought about before. It had been bad enough to feel that nervous shiver that came when her pills were late. But to have—this—on top of it? Not for the life of her would she tell him!

CHAPTER THREE

It was nine o'clock on Monday morning when the big car came out of Gatesville, and turned south on Highway 116, in the direction of Pidcoke. "It's about a mile south from here," Stacey directed from her corner, close against the door of the car, and as far as she could get from Harry without actually getting out. "There's a little sign, and a dirt road: Rancho Miraflores. Dad was stationed in the Canal Zone, you know."

He grunted an answer. His humour hadn't improved since Saturday morning, she told herself. That was the moment he had received the news of his grandmother's aggravated problem, and from then on he had plunged into a round of notifications and instructions, while Stacey had done her level best to keep out of his way. Far out of his way. Waking up in the morning, finding him next to her in bed, not wearing a stitch, had blown her eighteen-year-old mind. Sunday's meals had been catch as catch can. And then, on Sunday night, he had tracked her down on the veranda.

"We'll leave tomorrow—early," he told her. He sounded tired—and no wonder. The doctor had called twice, with worse news each time. There was no hope for his grandmother. "Tomorrow some time, my Aunt

Angela is coming,'' he added. "I want to get you settled before then.''

Translate that to, "I want to get you out of here before she smells a rat," Stacey told herself. He's too
proud to have me meet his aunt. Is it me, or is it his
family? Me, probably. Why would he want to unload
a troubled teenager on his family, at a time like this?
So he'll whisk me home to Aunt Ellen, and run. And
I can't blame him, can I? If I helped his grandmother
at all, it was because she deserved it, nothing else. And
if he stayed in my bed all night—well, nothing really
happened. Did it? That was the question that had
bothered her all during the fifty-mile drive from his
home to the gates of Rancho Miraflores.

She could feel her own disappointment, after
weekending at Rosedale, his grandmother's home.
The ranch house was an unpainted wooden structure,
all on one floor, with two weatherbeaten wings shel-
tering ten rooms and only one bath. It had been great
for herself and her father. But now—she sighed, and
knew that he saw with a rancher's eyes the dried-up
land stretching to the horizon, the battered barbed
wire fences, the empty barns. Despite the fact that the
pumps could be seen in the distance, nodding their
heads over black gold, the house looked as if it hadn't
seen a penny of repairs for years. And the open range
land, even close to the house, barely held down by a
smattering of rough grass, looked promising grounds
for high winds to strip.

"It's not much," she offered in apology.

"All it needs is work," he returned. "Work and
money, and a little water. There should be underground water in these parts; there are all kinds of

creeks in the area, and the Lampassas River isn't too far away. Is that your Aunt?''

Stacey looked up at the house, to where Aunt Ellen was standing on the porch. ''Yes,'' she sighed, then hesitated as Harry came around to open her door. The early morning heat smashed at her as the car's airconditioning died. It was the kind of day depicted in the old Texas joke, where the hawk chased the pigeon, both carrying their lunch, and both walking. She struggled out of the seat and forced her feet to function.

Block your ears, she told herself, as she mounted the two steps to the porch. The first blast from the Delanos will knock you back to Gatesville, and the second will probably take you all the way out of Coreyelle County. But, surprisingly, there was no blast at all. When she reached the door her aunt was standing there, slightly slumped, her shoulders bent, and tears rolling down her face.

''Aunt Ellen?'' she queried.

''They're gone, Stacey. Packed up and gone.''

''You mean Uncle Henry?''

''Yes. What did you say to him? What, Stacey?''

''She said nothing. I said a great deal,'' Harry interjected. ''Are we going to discuss it on the porch?''

''Come in,'' invited Stacey, and her aunt looked up, shocked. ''It's *my* house,'' Stacey said coldly. ''It took me a long time to realise that, but it's my house. Come in, Harry.''

The other two followed her into the living room. Looking with newly opened eyes, she could see that it was a tacky room—old furniture, falling to pieces in places, a worn rug, and dirty curtains at the windows. Harry looked around searchingly, but made no comment. He took the biggest chair, without invitation. Her aunt sat stiffly on the edge of one of the rickety straight chairs.

"And you're the one? Stacey's husband?" There was a trace of defiance in Aunt Ellen's voice, but only a trace.

"Yes, I'm the one," he said. "Stacey, could you get me a cup of coffee while I talk to your aunt?"

"I—I'd rather—" I'd rather stay and listen, she meant to say, but his eyebrows went up, and there was that imperious look on his face, so she retreated into the kitchen. But no amount of looking down Harry's nose would make her close the door behind her. She started on the coffee makings automatically, with an ear glued to the living room. Her hand trembled as she measured the coffee into the pot.

"Now first," he said, "we'll get rid of this idea of yours that you're Stacey's guardian. She's of age, according to Texas law, and you have no powers over her."

"But she gave me her power of attorney—signed legally, and all."

"Tear it up," he snorted. "Since she married after the event, the paper isn't worth a penny. This morning she excuted another power of attorney, superseding yours, and naming me. As her husband I have certain other legal rights. Among them, Mrs Delano, is the right to call for an accounting. Where are her property records for the last two years?"

"Henry—he burned them all last night. And—oh God—the strongbox!" exclaimed Aunt Ellen.

"What about the strongbox?"

"We've been cashing the quarterly oil lease payments, and putting the money in the strongbox. Henry said it was best, in these times, to have the ready cash, rather than tie it all up in a bank vault."

"I'll bet he did," said Harry sarcastically. "Where is it?"

"In his study. I'll—it will only take a minute."

"You bet," Harry said again. "I'll come with you." Their voices faded into the distance, and Stacey shook her head in disgust. Just at the interesting part! That's always the way when you're snooping, she thought. She reached up to the third shelf for cups, and as she stretched to her limits her hands began to shake, and a pain struck in her stomach. Nausea followed, leaving a feeling of weakness and disorientation. The cups in her hands fell to the floor, and in a moment she followed.

When she came to she was lying on the couch in the living room, her head on Harry's lap, while tender hands smoothed her brow with a cold wet cloth. "What happened?" he demanded.

"I—I don't know," she stammered. Her voice was slurred, and her head ached, but her stomach had settled down. "I was reaching for some cups, and I felt sick, and then everything—I just don't know." His heavy hand rested on her forehead, quieting some of the trembling that was still shaking her.

"I don't think you've got a fever," he started to say, and looked across at her aunt. The older woman had never been one to hide her feelings, and now running across her disfigured face was a guilty look.

"You've seen this before, Mrs Delano?" His voice was cold enough to freeze a side of beef. Aunt Ellen shook her head and reached into the pocket of her dress for a handkerchief. When she pulled it out a plastic container of pills came with it, and rolled out into the middle of the floor. Harry was on it before the older woman could make a move.

"My God!" he roared. "Is this what you've been feeding the child? Valium? What doctor prescribed this?"

"No doctor." Aunt Ellen was crying. "Henry got them—he has friends in Dallas. The girl gets excitable, and we had to calm her down."

"Yes, I'll bet you did." His tongue dripped bitter venom, enough to send Aunt Ellen out of her chair, shrinking back against the windowsill. "And how long have you been feeding her this stuff?"

"Two—two years."

"No wonder she's sick!—a perfect case of withdrawal symptoms. Damn you all! Where's the telephone!"

At this point Stacey closed her eyes. She could hear words, endless words. She felt someone pick her up, carry her to her room, undress her, and tuck her in. But beyond that, nothing really penetrated. The voices continued in the distance—roars, followed by weeping. And then in succession, separate cars arriving at the door, and finally the roar of a helicopter.

Shortly after that she could feel cold hands exploring her body, the touch of metal at her chest and back, a peering into her eyes, the slight pain of a hypodermic needle. Then things quieted down, and she slept.

Harry was sitting by her bed when she woke up. Her mouth tasted furry, and her vision was slightly blurred, but her stomach had settled. She smiled weakly up at him. "I seem to be a continual problem to you, don't I?" she asked.

He moved over to the bed and looked down at her. Searching for something, her mind told her. "I brought my own doctor in from Waco," he said. "He says you're going through withdrawal symptoms, a sort of Valium poisoning. He gave you a couple of shots—a sedative, and some B12 vitamins."

"What do I do now?"

"It depends on how tough you are, Kitten—I mean Stacey. Can you take it straight?"

"I—I don't know, do I? I guess I can. Take what straight?"

"If you think you can take it, love, it's like kicking a barbiturate habit cold turkey. All you have to do is stick it out for a couple of weeks, then you're home free."

"Otherwise?" she asked.

"Otherwise is four to six weeks in a hospital facility, while they wean you from it all. Your choice."

"I—I take it straight," she sighed. "I'm really not all that brave, but I would rather try."

"That's my girl! Your best bet is to keep your mind occupied and your stomach empty—relatively, that is."

Stacey watched him, fighting a touch of nausea at the same time. He looked—just a tiny bit more handsome than when she had first seen him. He was never really ugly, she told herself, and now—why, now he's almost handsome! "What else has happened?" she asked.

"Not much." He sat down on the edge of the bed and picked up one of her hands, treasuring it against his cheek to help her control the trembling. The way your husband would, her conscience reminded her. As if—but of course, he couldn't; that would be silly. She tried her best to wipe the wistfulness from her face.

"First of all," he said, "you mustn't take it too seriously, but as best I can figure out, you're broke. Your Uncle Henry made off with all the money in the strongbox, and we don't even know how much that is. I called Parsons Oil, and they'll reconstruct your income account for you. At least that way you'll know how much he stole from you."

She laughed up at him. "You're fooling me, Harry. I've called Parsons a time or two myself, and they won't tell anybody anything. Do you expect me to believe that you just picked up the telephone and—"

"I'm darned if that wasn't just what I did," Harry said solemnly. "They must have mistaken me for somebody else, because I got instant service. How about that!"

"Well—" she was still suspicious, "I suppose it could have been an accident. And then what?"

"And then I called the Texas Rangers. Your uncle is being charged with embezzlement, and other crimes. I also have a lawyer who's looking into this business about him prescribing medicines without a licence, and things like that."

"Oh, wow!" she giggled. "I don't suppose you could think of some reason for arresting George too?"

"I haven't come to that yet," he chuckled. "How about for proposing marriage in bad faith? If I could get him into court and show he's afraid of horses, any jury in Texas would put him away for life."

"And Aunt Ellen?"

"That's not for me to say, Stacey. You have to decide. She's a very shaken lady, with no place to go. Do you want her arrested?"

"Lord no, Harry! Before Delano came she was good to me. I can't have my father's only sister arrested. Leave her here with me."

He smiled and nodded agreement. Why, he's a wonderful man, she thought. Won't he just make some lucky girl a fine husband! "I suppose you'll have to go back," she offered hesitantly.

"In a day or so," he said gruffly. "I'm bringing in a staff of nurses, and a temporary housekeeper for you, but until then, I mean to stick it out here. Okay?"

But in the event, he didn't go in a day or so. He stayed on, spending the whole of that first night comforting her, rushing her to the bathroom when nausea overcame her, changing her nightgown twice, and sponging her down. And when the nurses arrived the next day, he continued waiting on her through those miserable days, when she was too sick to eat, and yet dared not stop, for fear of the pain of the empty stomach. The doctor came twice, with more vitamin shots and considerable sympathy.

For more than a week she was a very sick girl, and he remained at her side, doing everything necessary, until she began to realise that nobody in the world knew her body as well as he did. He seemed—almost—to really be a husband to her. And when she was finally allowed out of her bedroom it seemed only proper that they would breakfast together in the kitchen, she in her robe, drinking her tea, and he reading the morning paper in his shirt sleeves.

She established a shambling sort of peace with Aunt Ellen, too—an aunt who was dogged by a guilty conscience, and was trying her best to make up for it.

At the end of the second week Stacey walked out around the ranch buildings with Harry, happy to see that someone had been taking care of her old quarter horse, Ramona. "You could ride her if you please," she offered, remembering that he had talked about daily rides for exercise.

"Me?" he laughed. "On that critter? What is she, ten—twelve hands high? I hate to ride a horse that's smaller than me."

It tickled her fancy, and she giggled. "Well, Ramona needs the exercise as much as you do," she chortled. "Why don't you let her ride you?"

It was said in all innocence, but Harry retaliated by chasing her around the outside of the stable, her steps wobbly but firm, until she collapsed in a bundle of laughter by the old hand pump that stood in the yard.

He came up behind her, puffing a little, and swept her up in his arms. "You're a sparky little kid, aren't you?" he panted. "Two more laps and I could have had a stroke or something!" His face was just a few inches from hers, his mouth wide, displaying a forest of straight white teeth. Close enough to—but whatever she had been about to say was squeezed out of her as he moved her an inch or two in his arms, and her full strong breasts scraped across his chest, where only his thin cotton shirt and her even thinner blouse separated them. Harry drew in his breath with a hiss, and Stacey was so startled by the impact that she hardly knew what to do next. I hope he'll kiss me, she told herself. But he didn't.

He stared down at her, then gently put her down on her feet. Still holding her close, he tilted up her chin with his index finger, and concentrated on her eyes.

"Whatever made me think you're a kid?" he half whispered. "Don't you ever wear a bra?"

She dropped her eyes and let her hair swing over her face. His hands flexed on her arms, then released her. She stepped back away from him, leaving the question unanswered. "I think we'd better go in," he finally managed. "All this might be too much for you."

There was no room for argument. He took her by the arm and hurried her across the desolate back yard and into the house, where he turned her over to her aunt, and disappeared into his bedroom.

The house was quiet that night. The nurses had been released—happy to go, apparently, since Harry did all the work. And the temporary housekeeper was packing her bags for an early departure in the morning. When he came down to dinner he was a different man, cool, detached, almost as if he had put all the adventures behind him. He made three telephone calls, then came in for the meal.

"I'll bring you up to date," he told Stacey, as the soup came in. "The Rangers have an all-points bulletin out on the Delanos, and the County Sheriff has agreed to have a patrol keep a good watch on the house for the next few days."

Stacey could not meet his eyes. With her attention focused on the soup plate, she spooned at it, and nodded her head, hoping that he would not see the growing despair on her face.

"I've also made arrangements with Parsons Oil," he went on, while Aunt Ellen brought in the steak. Like an armoured assault column, Stacey told herself. He knows I don't want to hear, but he's going to tell me—for my own good, I suppose. He doesn't seem to realise that "my own good" has changed—changed drastically. It's only been three weeks since I met him for the first time, and everything has changed. But he doesn't care. Look at him!

"They'll make your next quarterly payment in advance, two weeks from today. The cheque will go directly to an account in the First National Bank of Waco, and half will be put in a checking account, the other half into an investment fund. You can begin drawing on it on the eighteenth."

"I—I suppose it would be graceless to ask how much?" she managed to get out.

"Not at all. Your quarterly payment comes to seventy-six thousand dollars."

Her spoon clattered as it hit the edge of her plate and bounced on the floor. Across the table from her, Aunt Ellen began to cry, soft soundless tears, that dripped across the huge disfiguring birthmark on her face and dropped into her coffee cup.

At eight o'clock that evening, in the last of a lingering twilight, they heard the roar of the helicopter. It landed in the flat area between the house and the stable. Harry came into the kitchen, where Stacey was hiding—to be truthful about it—and led her out of the house, bag in one hand, she on the other. Halfway between the flying machine and the house he dropped the bag and pulled her around to face him.

"I didn't want your aunt to hear," he said. "It's been a wonderful couple of weeks, Stacey, very different from my ordinary routine. And now I have to go. I thank you from the bottom of my heart for what you did for my grandmother. It meant more than I can say. And it's been a lot of fun, having such a lovely young wife. Some day you're going to meet a man who will welcome you as his *real* wife. And I'll read about it in the papers, and envy him every bit of his good luck. Goodbye, Kitten.''

Stacey struggled to keep a smile on her face, despite the fact that her heart was breaking into tiny little pieces. Yes, I'll make somebody a fine wife, she wanted to shout at him, but dared not. I'd make *you* a fine wife. And you wouldn't even have to ask. Just give me one small sign that you want me. Just one small sign! Or—if you don't want a wife—if you would just say, and I'd come with you, right now. The words were close on her lips, and slipped out. "Do you need a mistress?''

She clutched herself close up against his chest, so he would not see the burning flash of shame that crossed her expressive face. What could a man say to something like that!

"No,'' he said gently, "I don't need a mistress. And you don't need some casual lover, Stacey Bronfield. Go back to the house and give this whole crazy mix-up some thought. I'm much too old for you, little lady. Some day a man will come for you, never fear.''

She backed away from him, into the gathering darkness. Some day a man will come for me? she thought. If he does, he'll find a girl who has already been spoiled, ruined by memories. She wanted to run screaming after him. You're not too old for me, she wanted to shout. I may be too young, but it's something I'll grow out of, if you'll just give me time!

In the vague twilight of sub-tropical Texas his figure wavered as he moved towards the helicopter. The door slammed, the engine reverberated across the empty farmland, and he was gone, transformed from a lean, loving man to a pair of blinking lights in the sky, gradually fading away.

Stacey went back into the house, her face locked in the stiff control she had clamped over it outside. But once inside her bedroom her control failed, and she fell on to her bed, face down, burying her grief in her pillows, so her aunt would not be alarmed by the wailing.

A sort of mutual gloom settled over the house for the next few days. The temporary housekeeper had gone, and Aunt Ellen reigned in kitchen and in house. And gradually, as they both realised that there was no one else to turn to, she and Stacey turned to each other. Small talk, at first, then brief confidences that led, over the days, to a mutual respect which had never existed before.

Stacey spent most of her mornings riding over the ranch, exploring the places she had known as a little girl, the places that had disappeared from her drug-shrouded memory in these latter years. Afternoons she devoted to housework, draining her aunt's mind of those myriad little things that go into making a house run smoothly. And there were countless hours in the kitchen, where Stacey quickly learned those skills which her aunt had long hidden. Stacey had a goal, even though she did not know how to achieve it.

Two weeks after Harry had left Aunt Ellen finally broke down. When Stacey came in from her lonely ride, she found the older woman bent over the kitchen table, crying her heart out. A picture of Uncle Henry lay in the middle of the table. Much wiser in the ways of the world than she had been four weeks before, Stacey offered comfort, but made no effort to shut off the tears. After a good hour of lamenting, her aunt was ready to talk. Stacey made instant coffee, and waited. Somehow, she knew, she must get the older woman talking. A great catharsis, talking; the American woman's escape from reality. The home psychiatrist, so to speak. And it worked.

"I knew it would come one day," her aunt mused. "I knew it from the very beginning, but I just took one day at a time, and tried to avoid all the tomorrows."

"He loved you?" queried Stacey.

"Love had something to do with it, but it wasn't love of me. He fell in love with the ranch, first thing out of the barrel. But I guess it was only fair. I didn't love him, either."

"I don't understand. Why did you marry him if you didn't love him?"

"You don't understand, Stacey. You're young, and all the world is beautiful—and so are you. But I'm not. Life has passed me by already. I had none of the things that other woman have and want—a home, children, love. I wanted it all, and love just really didn't rank at the top." Her light voice held bitterness in its cup, bitterness that overflowed and flavoured her whole life.

"For a beautiful girl like you, Stacey, there's always a beautiful man waiting. For women like me—" her hand unconsciously brushed across her disfigured cheek, "for women like me, there just isn't much available. You have to play the hand God dealt you. Henry wasn't much—I knew that the day I met him, and he never proved me wrong. But he was a man, and I was his wife. There was that feeling—that feeling of belonging. Belonging—that's what it's all about, isn't it?"

Stacey looked down at the bowed grey head, and understanding came. She leaned forward over the table and ran her fingers through the iron-grey hair. "It's all right," she whispered. "I understand. We still have each other."

The next day started off in a companionable warmth between the two surviving members of the Bronfield clan. But it lasted hardly until ten o'clock, when a sheriff's car pulled up in the yard, and heavy boots climbed up the front stairs.

He was a big man, perhaps a little too old for his job, with forty excess pounds around his belly. But the badge was official, and the paper he presented was legal enough to shake Stacey in her boots.

After she had invited him into the living room he doffed his ten-gallon hat, made uncomfortable noises, then came right to the point. "I'm serving papers for the County Tax office," he explained, as he handed her a triple-fold sheet of paper.

"What's this?" she asked in amazement.

"You *are* Stacey Bronfield, the owner of this spread, aren't you?"

She nodded, not able to summon the proper words. Aunt Ellen came into the room at the same time, and stood absolutely still. "I still don't understand," muttered Stacey at the Sheriff's officer.

"Taxes," he explained. "You haven't paid the taxes on this place for the past four years. The county is preparing to take court action to foreclose unless these taxes are paid in the next forty-eight hours."

"Forty-eight hours?" Her mind was moving desperately. It was still another week before payments from the oil company would be paid, and as of that moment she was totally broke. Harry had left two hundred dollars behind. "A feed stake," he had said. "Enough to keep you eating until the royalties come

in.'' But two hundred dollars was hardly enough for—
or was it?

"How much do I owe?" she asked timidly.

The Sheriff's officer looked down at the paper, still
in his hand. "It says here, payments and interest included, twenty-two thousand dollars, ma'am. Land is
still pretty valuable.''

Stacey could feel the ground shake under her feet.
Where in the world was she going to get that kind of
money? Poor little rich girl! Hundreds of gallons of oil
were being pumped out of her land every day, and she
hadn't the money to pay the tax bill. She looked across
at her aunt, the anguish showing on her face. "And I
only have forty-eight hours to pay it up?"

"That's what the judge said, ma'am. Forty-eight
hours, or the county forecloses for taxes.''

"And then what?"

"And then they auction the spread, and apply what
they get to the tax bill. If there's anything left over,
you get it. Although from the looks of the place, you'll
be lucky to break even. Don't you have any friends
you could call?"

"That's it," Aunt Ellen shrieked in her ear. "Call
him!"

Still in a daze, Stacey just could not comprehend.
"Call who?"

"Why, your husband, of course!"

"Your husband?" The Sheriff's officer began to
smile. It made a difference. Coming ten miles to foreclose a place on two women was not his idea of a fun
thing. But if there was a husband—well, that was a
different breed of cat. "By all means call your husband," he offered.

"But I—he'll be working," stammered Stacey. "And I don't know—I don't have his number, and—"

"He left his card," said Aunt Ellen. She was already at the telephone, dialling, "before he went off. He left his card with me and said I was to call if anything went wrong. And what better than this? Hello? Yes, I want to speak to Mr Marsden, please. Who's calling? His wife, of course, Stacey, what is that idiotic name he calls you? No, operator, his secretary won't do. I need Mr Marsden. His wife is in a lot of trouble, and—don't you dare talk to me like that!"

"Let me take it," Stacey intervened. There was a cool secretarial voice on the other end. "And Mr Marsden is definitely not married," it said.

Stacey's dander was up—a compound of foreclosure notices, supercilious secretaries, and a vast need to pound somebody in the mouth. "A lot you know," she snapped down the line. "Please tell Harry that Kitten is on the line. And do it quickly!'

It was her tone of voice, rather than the words, that brought attention. She could hear keys click at the other end, and eventually that deep familiar voice. It cheered her, and all her anger drained out of her.

"Well? Who is it?" he roared.

"It's me," she said very weakly. "If you remember—"

"Kitten?"

"Yes, it's me."

"Why the devil didn't you say so! I'm in the middle of a big meeting. Can't it wait?"

It was hard to keep the tears out of her voice. Lord, he was angry! She fumbled for excusing words. "I—I'm sure it can wait," she cried, "but if it does they're going to foreclose on the ranch and take everything because we didn't pay the taxes for the last four years and the Sheriff is here—no, that's wrong. He says he's only a Deputy Sheriff. But he's here with a paper from the judge and he says if we don't pay twenty-two thousand dollars he—what? Oh. And twenty-six cents, he's going to seize the property and sell it at auction or something, and I've only got forty-eight hours to get— what did you say?''

"I said stop!" Harry yelled down the line. "Stop and take a deep breath. Take two deep breaths. Come on, let me hear them.'' Stacey struggled to master her confusion, breathing deeply, clenching her teeth to keep them from rattling.

"All right now," he said softly. "Follow along. A Deputy Sheriff is there. Right?'' She nodded. "Right?'' he repeated. She nodded again, half paralysed by his anger.

"He can't hear you shake your head," the Deputy suggested. This stop was about to make his day. He had looked forward to a gloomy time, serving four foreclosure notices, and here at the second stop there was entertainment galore.

"No," Stacey stammered, "of course he can't.''

"What did you say?" the voice at the other end asked.

"I said no, you can't hear me when I shake my head.''

She could hear the rattle of his sigh as it came down the wire and reverberated in her ear. "Please—please don't be mad," she begged.

"I'm not, Kitten." His voice still had that soft low caress. "Let's do it again. The Deputy Sheriff is there with a tax notice, and he wants twenty-two thousand dollars for—"

"And twenty-six cents," she interrupted.

"Yes, and twenty-six cents. Or else he's going to foreclose on the ranch. Have I got that right?"

"Yes," she mumbled. "But I suppose it can wait. I really don't want to bother you, and I wouldn't have, but Aunt Ellen—"

"Oh, shut up," he snapped. "I thank the Lord for your aunt. Now, listen closely."

"Yes, sir?"

"Don't *sir* me, damnit! Just listen. Go make the nice man a cup of coffee, and smile at him a lot. I'll be there in thirty minutes."

"Thirty minutes? How can you do that? Where are you?"

"I'm in Waco," he chuckled, "and there's a helicopter on the pad outside. If you'll only stop talking and start moving I'll be on my way. Now what do you have to say?"

"Goodbye? Sir?"

"I'll get you for that!" he snapped, but the threatening tone was missing.

Stacey turned to the Deputy and tried a smile. It was a second-hand sort of smile, but it served its purpose. The big officer, content that a man was coming to talk to him, settled back in the chair next to the window, and was prepared to be entertained.

Harry was wrong, of course. It took him twenty-five minutes, the flight being the easiest part of it. When the helicopter boosted to one thousand feet and moved north to skirt the restricted area around Fort Hood, he was still laying down the law to his accountant about money. And his lawyer, who was supposed to have checked for this sort of thing beforehand.

So he stomped into the house at just a peg below tornado force, and began to express certain strong opinions before the door closed behind him. Stacey dived for her bedroom and slammed her door behind her. She could still hear him giving directions out in the living room. Her eyes searched frantically for some way to bar the door. She pushed with all her might, trying to move the lowboy up against the door panels, but Harry pushed the door, the lowboy, and herself aside as he burst in without knocking.

She stood stock still in the middle of the room, head up, shoulders back. I'll go down fighting, she told herself. Lord, is he angry! His face is all red!

"Come here," he commanded, and all her resolve about going down fighting flew immediately out the window. She took one hesitant step in his direction, then ran the rest of the way, hurling herself into his welcome arms. When he kissed her through all the tears, it was like a reprieve from a life sentence. One touch and he brought comfort. His mouth roamed down her neck, and nibbled at her ear lobe—and back up.

The second touch on her half-opened lips blew the top of her skull off, and left her desperately striving to hold on around his neck. The floor rocked, tensions disappeared. She pressed into him until her feet came off the floor. She was panting when he set her down again. And he was no model of calm concern, either; it did her composure a great deal of good to see that he was shaken, perhaps almost as much as she.

"Good God," he muttered, "I didn't realise marriage was all this tough. What ever in the world am I going to do with you?"

"Pay my taxes?" she offered wistfully.

"What? Is that all you can think of?" he laughed. "One kiss and I pay your taxes? Well, I've got two people out in the other room taking care of that little problem. But what am I going to do about you?"

"I'm growing older terribly fast," Stacey offered hesitantly. "I think I've aged five years in the past five hours. Perhaps you could—"

"Perhaps I could what?"

Love me? she whispered under her breath. But Harry had already turned away to give instructions to the other two men, and apparently missed her comment.

He stayed for lunch. The other two, his lawyer and his accountant, went into Gatesville with the Deputy Sheriff, "to make sure there are no more loose ends," he told her.

After the meal they sat out in front on the worn porch swing, watching a flock of crows squabbling over something in the pasture. They sat comfortably close, close enough for thighs to touch, and for his hand to drape naturally over her shoulder.

"So I guess I must have made a little mistake," he said.

"I can't imagine what you mean," Stacey returned idly. "I never conceived of the Harry Marsdens of this world making mistakes, big or little."

"Hey! A little sarcasm there," he chuckled. "You *are* growing up in a hurry, aren't you?"

"Well," she said meditatively, sticking her tongue out to gently moisten her dry lips, "I'm not a very good judge of such things, but I *feel* older. In fact I feel like a wrung-out seventy-year-old woman right this minute. Does all that have some significance?''

''Hard to say. Look over there—two ducks flying east, a good luck sign. Make a wish.''

''I made one weeks ago,'' she admitted shyly. ''I don't intend to make another until the first one comes true. Why did you say that about you'd made a little mistake?''

''Honest Injun?''

''Please.''

''Now, if you promise not to let this go to your head,'' he began, ''I had a notion a time ago that you and I had done each other a favour, and were quits. So then, I thought, I'll just put this child out of my mind and—''

She stirred restlessly under his hand. ''Child?'' she snapped.

''Well then, this young lady. Let me finish before I forget what I'm trying to say. What I meant was that I found it pretty hard to put this young lady out of my mind. Of course, the story of our marriage is all over Grandmother's property—and the neighbourhood. And it leaked downtown into my office, too. And do you know something? It's added considerably to my stature, having a bride. So I thought—if you have no objection—that perhaps from time to time I might call on you for a little more bridal work, so to speak. If you don't object?''

Stacey did her best to keep from looking at him. Her face was too easily read, she was finding out, and the tear shadowing the corner of her eye was too much of a giveaway. She cleared her throat noisily. ''Sort of like Rent-a-Bride?'' she suggested.

"Yes, short of." Harry sounded so serious that she had to look. His long craggy face was as solemn as a judge. The corners of his mouth were turned down, and he seemed poised—for a rejection. "If you don't mind," he repeated.

"No, I—I don't mind," she said. The tinkling little laugh she had forced out to accompany words—to show him how casual she was about the whole idea—was so timid and so cold it even sent chills down *her* spine.

"Well, I think things are under control here," he said coolly. "And I've got a million things to do at work. By the way, Grandmother is still unchanged, in a coma. I'll keep you posted. And keep my telephone number close by, in case you need to rent a husband again. Right?"

Stacey couldn't get a word out in answer, so she sat stiffly on the edge of the swing and watched as he got up, stretched, and started around to the back of the house where the helicopter waited. Halfway down the path Harry stopped, hesitated, and came back.

"I'm not much up on this husband business," he offered. "I forgot this." He leaned down and kissed her gently on the cheek, right over the spot where her dimple usually sparkled. And again, before she could get out a word, he wheeled around and left.

She was still sitting there rigidly when the roar of the engine announced his departure. Her left hand cupped her cheek where that goodbye salute had touched, and her right hand, on top of the other, twirled and fumbled at the two rings on her third finger, which she had never got around to removing.

CHAPTER FOUR

THE next few days seemed deadly dull. The sky clouded over, although no moisture fell to relieve the drought. Stacey began to ride again, saddling up early in the morning and wandering the far empty reaches of the ranch, where only the perpetually nodding pumps thumped back and forth, moving unseen oil up from the depths, forcing it into unseen pipes, and dispatching it to the Lord only knew where. Funny, she mused, as she dismounted beside one of the million No Trespassing signs, walked through the little gate marked Keep Out, and put her slender foot up on the wellhead cap. All that controlled movement going on beneath her feet, and only the lazy nodding head of the pump itself to indicate.

Wishing it were cattle instead of oil, she kicked at the cap, stubbed her toe, and continued miserably on her ride. She knew as well as anyone could, she told herself, that it wasn't the lack of cattle, or the broken-down fences, or the sere grazing land that made her ache. But I'm not going to think about *him!* she thought. Not at all. If he calls, well—maybe I might go to help him again. Maybe.

On Friday morning she came back to the house just before lunch, to find a gaggle of visitors. One group of three, surrounding an old drill-truck, looked somehow familiar. "Steuben," the elderly man introduced himself. "My two boys." He gestured at the two giants behind him, perhaps thirty-five to forty years old. "We was over this way before your father—died. Water, he wanted, as I remember. I allus said they was water on this spread, you know, and your pa, he agreed with me."

"I don't remember, Mr Steuben," Stacey sighed. "I guess I was too young to think about it at the time." She was finding it difficult to concentrate on the subject even now.

The other two men, lounging on the steps of the porch waiting their turn, were young—in their early twenties, perhaps, and dressed like working cattlemen.

"Well, I remember you, Stacey. Cutest little tyke, you was," Mr Steuben continued. "So I was sittin' to home the other day, business bein' slow like it is, and the telephone rings, and it's this girl from Waco. Mind you, I ain't got nothing agin Waco, there's nice folks over there, and all, but it done growed up from just a cattle town, and puts on airs, you know?"

She nodded. So many times she had listened to such conversations, at her father's side. There is just no hurrying a Texan when he's set in his ways, she thought. He'll talk it out eventually. She smiled at the old man, inviting more.

"Well, anyway, turns out she's a secretary to some big shot in the city, and he comes on the line without no howdo-do or nothing. There's water on Rancho Miraflores, he says. And me, I ain't go no more idea in the world who he is, or what. So I says, is that true? And how do you know? And right quick he come back with, when they drilled the oil wells they found plenty water on the way down!"

Stacey's head shot up. If there was one thing she knew for sure, it was that wildcat oil drillers never, but never, ever told a soul about their drilling. Not ever!

"And?" she prompted.

"And to make a short story longer, as my pa used to say, we talks awhile about drillin', and he gives me a bunch of instructions. And when he hangs up I figure, well, that's the end of that. Some dude in the city pullin' my leg, or something. But the next day, here comes a Special Delivery, and it's got about six sections-charts, all from that Parsons Oil outfit, and they're marked for water. And attached on the front is this whoppin' big cheque—a certified cheque from the bank, mind you—all nice and pretty."

"And that's it?"

"Nope. Underneath the cheque is a permit from Parsons Oil for me to drill anywheres on their leased land—for water. And then there was this note. Look here." He reached into his overall pocket and pulled out a crumpled piece of paper. The heading on it said Marsden Management.

"Tell my wife," the note said, "that I want at least six bores put down."

"And since I don't see no other young girls around, I guess you was her. His wife, I mean," added Mr Steuben.

"Oh, I guess that's right," muttered Stacey, not at all sure. "I—well, what do you want me to say?"

"Not a word," the old man laughed. "We're supposed to begin close to the house, he said. And we'll start now. You just go about your business and don't pay us no mind, y'hear?" He waved at his two "boys", who climbed on the truck without a word being spoken, and rattled around into the area behind the house. Their truck clattered and clanked as if on its last trip.

Stacey watched them, astonished. Water? It was all that was needed to make the land bloom. But who— or rather, why? And without even a word of explanation. How about that! You'd think we really *were* married, the way he gives long-distance orders around here! She backed up to the steps and sat down when she felt the pressure of the risers against her legs. "I think I must be married to a dictator," she said to nobody in particular.

"Seems as if." One of the two young men lounging on the steps had spoken. She turned and stared at him—at them. Young, wiry, sun-creased faces. Cattlemen, and identical twins, for heaven's sake!

"All right," she sighed, "and just what the devil are you two doing here?"

"Can't rightly say," the one closest to her announced. "Morgan. I'm Jim and he's John."

"Or maybe it's the other way around," his twin commented.

"Heaven preserve me, a pair of comedians!" snapped Stacey. "Let me start it off for you. You were sitting in your office and the telephone rang and it was—"

"No, ma'am," Jim returned. "Not like that at all. We work for Westland Cattle on their spread up the Brazos River. What with the drought and all, things have been tough. So the boss cornered us yesterday, and gave us a briefing, and said that tomorrow—that's today—y'all haul—well, I can't rightly say exactly what it was he said. Get over to Rancho Miraflores, is what he meant. Pretty fast too, he said."

"Okay," she snapped, "so here you are. And now what? What did he tell you to do when you got here?"

"Everything that needs doing," replied John—or was it Jim? "Left it up to us, he did. Course, we've had a lot of years experience."

I'll just bet you have, Stacey thought, as she assessed them. Neither one looked to be older than twenty-one. Years of experience? Oh well. "And who's going to pay for all this?"

"Well, ma'am, if you won't take it too poorly, it seems your husband, he arranged it all. Mind if we mosey along and get at it? We brought our own *remuda*."

"Don't ask me anything," Stacey told them. "I don't have any answers. Lunch will be at twelve-thirty, and you'll eat in the house with us. The bunkhouse hasn't been used for eight or ten years, but you can put your horses in the barn—that's been kept up."

She could hardly help smiling at them. Their grins were infectious. But after they had gone she stomped into the house. I'm going to call that man, she told herself grimly, and chew him up one side and down the other. The nerve of him!

Her hand was halfway to the telephone when all the pieces began to fit together. She fell back into her chair and the giggles started to come. What's the matter with me, she lectured, is that I can't stand being done good to! Which, despite the poor English, seemed to sum it all up. She put the telephone down, and was still laughing when her aunt came through from the kitchen. "Can we feed two more?" asked Stacey, still trying to control the giggles. "It seems we've hired a drill-crew and a couple of ranch hands."

"No problem at all," Aunt Ellen responded. "It just might liven things up around here."

"I'll liven things up," Stacey retorted, "just as soon as I can get my hands on Harry Marsden. I'll liven things up, believe me! I wonder why he doesn't call! Darn that man!"

She did hear from him that day, but the message was not one she wanted to receive. It was four o'clock in the afternoon, and the sky was growing darker. Far to the north-west there were flashes of lightning splitting the clouds. The telephone rang—not the series of repetitive sounds that one expects, but rather one long ring, and then silence. Stacey pulled herself away from the window where she had been watching Mr Steuben at work. The old man had consulted charts, inspected gradients, surveyed particular points—and then whipped out a dowsing rod to determine just where to drill. Stacey was still chuckling as she moved towards the telephone. She picked it up and offered a tentative "hello".

"Mrs Marsden?" the coolly modulated voice asked. "Mrs Stacey Marsden?"

"Yes," she responded automatically, "speaking."

"I have a message for you from your husband."

"I—" It took her just a moment to think herself into the right mental posture. I've got to be more careful, she moaned. I'm almost beginning to believe it myself! "Yes, go ahead."

"Mr Marsden is in Houston. He hopes to return immediately, but the weather is bad for flying, and it may take some time. He asked me to call and inform you that his grandmother passed away this afternoon."

"Oh, how terrible!" Stacey returned. A picture of the tiny frail form in the bed, clinging to her hand, fingering her rings, flashed into her mind. And the smile that had fixed itself on the worn face as she closed her eyes.

"Did she ever come out of the coma?" she asked tearfully.

"No." For a moment the voice had sounded as if it cared, but suddenly it became all business again. "Mr Marsden asks that you come to Waco for the wake and the funeral. He also asked me to repeat a peculiar statement. He said I was to tell you that he badly needed support. Does that sound right?"

"Yes," Stacey responded softly, "I understand. Does he want me to come to Waco right away?"

"Oh no, Mrs Marsden. He intends to come for you, and just as soon as he can."

"I understand. If you talk to him again, please tell him I'll be waiting for him."

The thunderstorm broke over Gatesville about six o'clock that evening, and although she peered out the windows at least every fifteen minutes, until Aunt Ellen began to complain, Stacey knew that no aircraft would want to challenge that sky. In between trips to the window, she sorted through her meagre wardrobe, and packed what looked presentable into a single suitcase. She had nothing in black, and that bothered her. The image of that frail old woman, clinging desperately to life until her dreams were fulfilled, stuck in her mind. She knew that no matter what others thought, she would mourn.

There were no large stores in her immediate area. Pidcoke was the nearest, but hardly a major shopping centre. Gatesville, the county seat, was farther away, and on a stormy Friday night it too might have little to offer. Stacey did what she had learned to do over the past few weeks—she put the problem aside, and went for a hot bath.

Steaming hot, this bath, misting the bathroom, fogging the mirrors, colouring her skin a brilliant pink as she slipped into it and relaxed. Bath bubbles played around her, releasing lavender fragrance into the air. She scooped up a handful of the suds, inhaled, then lay back in the tub. Wild dreams. Her hand played sensuously up and down her side, from curve of hip to peak of breast, while she dreamed—of him, of course. Of my husband, she thought, who has rights and privileges no other man has had—and who knows me better than anyone in the world. A man who—suddenly the trend of her thought bothered her, and she sat up primly, rebuking herself for such wild wanderings. Her *temporary* husband! But wouldn't it be nice if it were real, and he were here? Her hand wandered again, stirring emotions she had never expected. Her head dropped back onto the rest, and a smile played at her mouth.

All of which blocked her ears to the sound of heavy footsteps on the stairs. The unlocked bathroom door burst open without ceremony, and very suddenly he was there!

"Well—really!" she spluttered. There was not a towel within reach, and she had left all her clothing in the bedroom. Seething, she sank down under the cover of the soap bubbles. "What in the world are you doing, breaking in here like that!" she shouted at him.

"Hey," he said, with a tired sound in his voice, "your aunt said you were in the tub and would prob-

ably camp out there for another hour unless somebody stirred you. So I'm stirring.''

"You could have knocked!" she snarled at him.
"I'm not selling tickets. This isn't an exhibition!"

"You don't know what you're saying," he chuckled. "It's some beautiful sight, Kitten. Come on—I
had to drive all the way from Houston, and I'm tired.
Millie called to tell me she was being mobbed by calls
and problems. Boy, do I need a wife!" He pulled one
of the huge bath towels from the rack and held it out,
wide-spread. "Come on now, Kitten, into the towel
and let's get you dry so we can hit the road."

There was mutiny in her eyes. "Don't call me that,"
she snarled. "The least you could do is get my name
right!"

Harry paid no attention to the outburst, but jiggled
the towel at her a couple of times, as a matador might
do in the arena. *"Ola, toro!"*

"I'll *toro* you!" she snarled. She scrambled at the
sides of the slippery tub and barely managed to throw
herself on the floor at his feet.

"Well, that wasn't much of a charge," he said solemnly, staring down at her quivering anger without a
twinge of concern.

"Why you—arrogant—conceited—" She was so
angry she stuttered. She tried to get up without using
her hands, which were vainly busied trying to cover her
breasts.

"I do believe you're right," he drawled. "My
grandmother used to say exactly the same things. Pig-
headed, too—one of her favourites. Pig-headed arrogant conceited male!"

"I'm sorry." Stacey could see the torment behind
his eyes, the strain-lines on his cheeks. "I didn't

think," she said quietly, and got up gracefully. With equal grace he enfolded her in the towel, covering her completely from neck to toe. He pulled her back against him and leaned over her shoulder.

"This is no time for tears—that's what she told me, love. She had her time in this life—a long fruitful time—and she was ready to go, convinced there's a better life beyond. So no tears. Now's the time for us to remember what she was, and pray success on her journey. All right?"

"All right," she whispered. There was a great comfort to be gained, leaning back against him, letting his strong muscles take over all the labour of living. She recalled again that frail little body, the parchment face, those eyes boring into her, and the promise she had made just before his grandmother slipped into her final coma. "I'm ready for whatever you want me to do," she sighed.

Downstairs, her bag in his hand, she stopped him. "I won't let you drive all that distance back without something to eat," she insisted. Harry argued, but she stood firm. "It's seven o'clock at night," she nagged at him. "Your grandmother is dead. Surely another hour won't make that much difference?"

He gave in, but not too graciously, sitting at the kitchen table making small talk to Aunt Ellen while Stacey wrestled with a steak, and warmed some chips she had taken from the freezer. With coffee bubbling on the stove, she set a man-sized plate in front of him, and sat back to watch while his temper improved in direct ratio to the disappearance of the food before him.

"Hits the spot," he gasped at last. "Second best meal in Texas, that. Second only to—"

"I know," she laughed. "My father was one of you too. Second only to barbecue. Drink your coffee."

"I keep forgetting that you're a hometown girl," he said. "Some day you must let me throw you a barbecue. How are the Morgan boys doing?"

"I don't know, do I?" His change of subject was too much for her tired mind. "You shift topics faster than a rattler sheds its skin. Darn you, how am I supposed to know how the Morgan boys are doing? The last time I checked they were fixing a leak in the bunkhouse roof. I don't know if they got it done, I don't know if they intend to stay here, I don't know what or when they get to eat—and most of all, Mr Marsden, I don't know what the devil they're doing here!"

"That certainly ought to keep you busy for a while." He smiled wearily, then seemed to shrug his shoulders and get back into high gear. "Come on now, let's get hustling. Aunt Ellen, you can expect her when you see her. And don't you go worrying about the Morgan boys. They've had their instructions. No worries, right?"

Although Aunt Ellen had made her peace with Stacey, she still did not understand the man who had brought about all the change. She stared at his face, as if trying to read some concealed message there. "I don't understand, but I'll try not to worry," she said.

The sky was spitting rain by the time they settled into the big Mercedes. Harry tossed her bag on to the back seat and settled in behind the wheel. "One bag, Stacey? You're travelling light?"

"I don't mean to," she said, watching his skilled hands take them out on to Route 116, heading north towards the junction with Highway 84. "It's just that—well, I never did have many clothes, and I don't have a driver's licence, so I just can't run into town when I want to. And, Harry," she touched his knee to be sure of his attention, "I don't have anything black. I suppose it's proper to be dressed in black?"

"I hadn't thought about that." He took his attention away from the road long enough to smile at her. "Having a wife is very complicated, isn't it?" She returned the smile weakly, wanting to yell at him, *Not half as complicated as having a husband!* But she stifled the words. He lifted one wrist to consult his watch. "Eight-fifteen now. Everything in Waco will be closed at nine, unless—I know. Hand me the telephone, girl."

The instrument was hidden inside a compartment between their seats. Look at this, Stacey told herself. I own oil wells and don't have a dress to wear. He works for a living managing something, and rides around with a telephone in his car! She handed him the instrument, then moved as far away from him as she could.

The downpour was almost obliterating the road markers when they finally reached the main highway. They ghosted through Gatesville as if it were a deserted city. The only lights to be seen were in two drugstores. There was some sign of life at the County Courthouse as they went through the tree-lined square in the centre of the city, and then out the other side, with a straight run to Waco. Harry drove one-handed, carrying on some argument on the telephone. When he put it down there was a smile of satisfaction on his face.

"It's hard to get what you want on a rainy Friday night," he told her.

"I don't really believe that," she returned. "You always get what you want—at least that's the way it seems to me. What now?"

He ran one tired hand through his hair, and shrugged his shoulders to relax the driving tensions. "It's like most everything," he chuckled. "It's not what you know, but who you know. The answer to our problem is Dillards. It's a Department Store at the Richland Mall, right ahead of us, at the intersection of Waco Drive and Franklin Street. The manager and I went to school together. Good old boys—that sort of thing. And he's willing to stay open until we get there. If they don't have a black dress for you I'll eat my hat."

As it turned out, at seventy miles an hour they arrived in the mall shortly before closing time, and found assistance, and a suitable black dress without a bit of trouble. "It's severely simple," the saleswoman told Stacey. "Something for—not necessarily for funerals, you know. It should do."

It did look simple of line, knee-length, with a high demure collar. It was not until she tried it on that she discovered how closely it clung, how tantalising it looked. But Harry, his mind on other things, gave it a quick okay, then insisted on a matching hat and veil.

"But I'm not close family," she protested. "That would be overdoing it."

"How much closer can you get?" he whispered. "You're my wife. I'm her only grandson; all the rest are distant aunts and uncles. Besides, Grandmother was a locally famous woman. The press will be there, and who knows how many friends, and friends of friends. You'll be one of the stars, girl, and don't you forget it."

"How could I?" she groaned. It was almost impossible to win an argument with him while at the same time keeping up with what the saleswoman was saying. "I'm beginning to wish I'd taken up Drama when I went to Saint Anselm's. But you're not fooling me, Harry *dear*. What you want to do is keep me out of sight without actually hiding me. Isn't that it?"

"Women!" He threw up his hands, and gained the immediate support of the store manager. "And besides the hat and veil, while we're at it, how about a few more odds and ends? My wife has come home almost threadbare. If you don't mind?"

"As long as we're here, we might as well go whole hog," the manager returned. "Providing our Mrs Lord here can spare the time?" With visions of commissions running through her head, "our Mrs Lord" was more than willing to spare the whole night. And so when they headed towards the door, and out into the darkened Mall, it took all four of them to carry the packages.

The car started with a grumble. "Wet wiring," Harry told Stacey. "It was a real gully-washer out towards Houston, and hasn't gotten better since. Now, one more stop, and we're off for the house."

"I don't mind," she affirmed. "It's you I'm worried about. Do you want me to drive?"

"I thought you said you didn't have a licence?"

"I don't, but that doesn't mean I can't drive, for goodness' sakes. I've driven all kinds of things around the ranch. I started when I was twelve."

"I just bet you did!" There was a tinge of sarcasm in his answer. She sat back in her seat and folded both hands in her lap. And that's the last time you'll get an offer from me, she muttered under her breath.

"What was that?"

"Keep your eyes on the road. All we need to make my life complete is a road accident."

"Women!" Harry groaned.

"Hah! Men!" She squirmed just a little bit further away to demonstrate her absolute and complete independence, then spoiled it all by giggling at him. He drove with exaggerated care down Franklin, took a slow right turn on 18th Street, crossed the railroad tracks, then made a sharp left on Clay, passing the Municipal Stadium and going on down past 7th Street, where he pulled up in the middle of the block.

"This is it," he explained as he shut off the engine. "Was madame satisfied with my driving?"

"Yes. This is what?"

"Our home," he chuckled, and Stacey looked out of the window. Another gust of rain struck, and his hand restrained her. "No sense running between the raindrops. We'd both drown."

It made some sense—the bit about the rain, that was. But a home? She peered out the window at the building. It was neither new or old, one of the units built in the era when everything had to be glass. Not too big, either, for that matter; eight or nine floors, as best she could guess. Neat, but not ostentatious. Perhaps it might give her some clue as to what Harry did for a living. So why not ask?

"What do you do for a living, Harry?"

"Oh, this and that," he answered lightly. "I manage things. I have a little organisation up on the top floor. We do—well, I guess you might call it odd jobs."

"Oh. You don't use the whole building?"

"No, Stacey, there are other tenants. The rain's letting up. Come on, let's give it a whirl."

He was out of the car and around to her door before she could shape another question. His hand palmed her elbow and hurried her through the drizzle, and in at double doors which gave access to a small lobby. A security guard greeted them at the desk, making small talk about rain and rheumatism as Harry signed the book. While the two of them were busy, Stacey looked around and found a building directory. Floors numbered one through five belonged to Parsons Oil Explorations. Floors six and seven were the property of Westland Cattle Associates. Floor eight belonged to the Federal Electronics Corporation. Floor nine was the property of—ah—Marsden Management Corporation. And then there was a penthouse, with no names attached.

"What's the matter, somebody walking over your grave?" Harry's hand was on her elbow again, as he hurried her over to the elevator bank, pushed a button, and got instant response—of course, she told herself. Even the elevators wouldn't dare make *him* wait!

Don't say a word, she lectured herself. Isn't life crazy enough already with what you know? Why make it worse by learning something more? So he makes a living. It's a nice building, but set squarely between the railroad tracks and an elevated super-highway. Not exactly the classiest neighourhood in the world. And—of course! Parsons Oil. He shares a building with them. No wonder he could get all kinds of information! "I'll bet you a nickel to a doughnut he knows a dozen secretaries in the right places!" she remarked.

She hadn't meant for that to come out—not in the confines of a slow elevator. Harry looked at her quizzically, but before he had time to pursue the subject the elevator stopped and the doors opened. At floor number ten, the blinking light said.

"Did we miss a floor someplace?" Stacey asked cautiously.

"Not that I know of. Downstairs is where I work. This is where I—I mean this is where we live. Come on, I'll only be a minute or two!"

She dragged her feet, wondering just how far into whatever mess there was she had finally stepped. "You—you live here? I thought you lived—Rosedale—your grandmother's house? The servants, the horses, and—"

The door was controlled by some sort of electronic lock. He merely placed his palm on a plate by its side, above the bell, and everything slid open for them. "You're just a little incoherent tonight," he chuckled. "Maybe a drink will settle you down."

"I—" He was pushing her ahead of him through a tiny corridor and into a spacious living room that faced out over the lights of the city. Rain drummed at the wide glass panes. A sunken centre held couches and stuffed chairs. Around the elevated rim were tables, a few occasional chairs, books, and a huge desk. In the near wall, a fireplace sparkled with a gas fire. A pair of wide stairs led up to a half-landing, where other closed doors shut off the view. "If—if you're having one?" she sighed.

"Sure. Scotch on the rocks for me, but something non-alcoholic for you. Alcohol and Valium don't mix, and you'll be another six months getting it all out of your system."

"Which doesn't leave me much choice, does it? How about a Coke?"

Harry fumbled through a stack of papers while she answered. When he looked up his grin was back, that wide infectious grin which had so held her when first they met. "Coke?" he laughed. "Well, I don't think I have any of that. How about a Doctor Pepper?"

"Oh, you!" There was a pillow close at hand. She threw it at him, then dodged around to the other side of the room. "You didn't bring me here to look at papers and offer me drinks," she said. "So just why did we come?"

"Smart," he said solemnly. "Can't pull the wool over your eyes, huh?"

"Watch that talk," she giggled. "This is cattle country."

"You've seen too many John Wayne movies," he returned. "I do have a good reason for bringing you here, Stacey." He came around the room and touched her hand lightly. "This is where I live. This is where you've been living. When we get out to Grandmother's place, as far as all the people out there know, you've just come from this penthouse with me. So I wanted you to have a look around, to get the feel of this place, before we go on. Satisfied?"

"Harry, you are some great conspirator, aren't you? You think of everything. It would never have crossed my mind!"

"Of course not. That's what I'm here for—to do all the devious thinking. Ready for the Grand Tour?" And off she went again, tugging after him as he moved at full speed towards the stairs. She stumbled as her foot missed the first step, but his hand sustained and tugged and urged. Onward and upward, she laughed to herself. Will I ever get to move at a normal speed again?

The first door at the half-landing opened into a massive bathroom, all blue and white tile, with a sunken tub in one corner, and a barrel-shaped hot tub in the other. Stacey took one look and almost swallowed her tongue. For more than two weeks Harry had put up with the old dingy bathroom at the ranch, with a tub whose enamel was cracking, and whose four supporting claw legs were weak enough to rock!

"Care to try it out?" It was a sarcastic offering, she thought, but then again, could she ever be sure of a man like Harry? Just in case, she returned a polite refusal and he led her back to the landing.

The second door opened to another flight of stairs that opened into a single circular bedroom that took her breath away. The room had no walls. Windows completed a great circle around her, allowing three hundred and sixty-degree look at the city. A few scatter pillows occupied strategic sections of the thick-pile carpet. In the middle of the room a huge circular bed was set up on a pedestal. Storage space was provided by low cabinets, built under the windows, and below the level of the bed. There was no other furniture.

"Watch this," he said gleefully—like a kid with a brand new toy, Stacey told herself. Look at how much he enjoys showing me—this what? His finger moved a dial on the wall, and the windows gradually turned opaque, shutting out the driving rain. "There's a control like this on the bed, too. Hop on to the bed, Stacey. Nobody will believe you if you haven't tried the bed."

She looked over at him, confused. Try the bed? Now what? she thought. Is this the old story—lie down on my bed, lady, and we'll have a long talk? Warily she walked around the side of the bed farthest from him and sank gingerly down into the absorbing softness of the thing. It rolled slightly beneath her, readjusting to her form as she moved.

"A water bed?" she gasped.

"Best in the West," he chuckled. "It gives a fine night's rest."

I'll just bet it does, she thought. If it wiggles when you sit down on it, what the devil happens if—if something more athletic takes place? A girl could get seasick in a place like this. Look at him—he's waiting for me to ask, and I'll be darned if I will!

"Lie back," he instructed. "You haven't seen anything yet!"

"I—I don't suppose I have," she offered weakly. Almost automatically her feet came up off the floor and coiled themselves up. She leaned back towards the pillows, just as he joined her from the other side. Keep a respectable distance, her nerves screamed. She crowded over towards the edge. There was no need. The bed was big enough for six. A family could fit in with ease!

She slowly lowered her head back until the pillows supported her. It *was* comfortable. But why was Harry grinning like some jackass, waiting carefully for her to settle down? I won't ask him. Let him be a smart aleck!

He was prone, but his head was held up on one bent elbow. With exaggerated movements, his hand moved to a metal plate under his pillow, and pushed a button. Nothing seemed to happen, until his fingers moved to a dial beside the panel of buttons, and the windows slowly became transparent again. And there was definitely something wrong! The lights of the city were very slowly circling around them—or—no, the bed itself was slowly rotating, so that someone in the bed, on a clear day, could see a panorama of the entire city.

"It's hard to see because of the storm," he said. "But here beginneth the reading from the First Book of Waco, Texas." Before her eyes the city marched very slowly in review. "You're looking south now," he commented, in his best tourist-guide voice. "Those lights are cars on the Kultgen Freeway, Interstate 35, and now—we're moving eastward, those lights are at the campus of Baylor University. My company lives on brain power, and we draw most of that right off the campus graduate school. Now, that's the light reflecting off Lake Brazos, and next to it you can see a tiny part of Fort Fisher, the original Texas Ranger camp in this part of the state. Most of that is a museum now. And there—as we move north, that's the Convention Center, the Municipal Building, the Mall, and then, all the way around our circle, that's the Waco Municipal Stadium. And way beyond that is Baylor Stadium. You'll have to come up some sunny afternoon to see it all. It takes a full fifteen minutes for the bed to make one revolution."

A fierce burst of envy—no, jealousy—struck at her. Obviously he didn't spend his afternoons up here riding his bed around in circles, alone. How many other women had seen this sight—or perhaps had been too busy to see the sights? I'll bet it takes considerably less than fifteen minutes for *him* to complete one revolution. All those poor, poor women. I wish I was one of them!

"Daydreaming?" he intruded.

"I don't know," she stammered, embarrassed by her own thoughts. "It's just—I don't understand who would be questioning me about your—your bed—and your apartment, and things. Am I going to be on the griddle some place?"

"I don't know one way or the other," he sighed. "All this doesn't strike you as the least bit romantic?"

"Not in the least," she lied. "It looks like a move-lot seduction scene. If my lesson is complete, could we perhaps get going?"

"Damn!" Once again she had found the wrong phrase, the wrong answer. But if he had been asking serious questions, she just did not understand them. Very suddenly it became chilly, as if the air-conditioners had been turned up full blast. Harry got up out of the bed, leaving her to rock in the wavelets by herself. He stalked around the bed to where she was barely clinging to the edge.

"If that's not romantic," he said determinedly, "how about this!" He dropped down almost on top of her, and as she opened her mouth to protest, his lips sealed her off. Closed down her entire world, and let in a concentrated circle of spark and flame that chased echoes up and down her spine, and back to her hip, where one of his hands rested. She made a futile effort to struggle against him. He put down the rebellion without a bit of trouble, and returned to the attack.

Stacey closed her eyes, her frame shaking in anticipation. And again the sparks, the flame, the riot of sensation as his warm lips challenged hers, invading her mouth without mercy, without challenge. She stiffened for a moment, then gave it up, relaxing in the fury of the storm he was creating with his lips. When he finally pulled away from her she was unable to move. He watched, like a heron watched the shallows, waiting. When her breathing apparatus finally settled down she ran a nervous hand through her hair, brushing it back from her perspiring forehead.

"How about that?" Harry asked of the room in general.

She stared up at him, having trouble focusing her eyes. How about that? Is that all he can say about the quake that shattered my whole world? How about that? The bitterness crept in under the sweet. Colour me green, for jealousy, she screamed at herself. How many others have there been? One thing's for sure, the scenery is a waste. None of them could ever have looked out the window while *he* was working at his seductive best!

CHAPTER FIVE

IT was after midnight when they drove up to the old house on the hill. The storm had abated, thundering off towards the Gulf Coast, leaving behind it the heady smell of fresh-cleaned air, and the tang of wild sage, damp earth, the fragrance of oleanders, and the dusty dry smell of cedar. One star, no more, peeped through the tail of clouds. One light, a small yellow bug-light, gleamed at the front door.

"They've all gone to bed," commented Harry, sounding as if he were astonished by the whole idea. "We'll have to struggle with this lot by ourselves." He was standing outside the rear door of the car, peering in at the pile of boxes that littered the back seat.

"Well, it was all your idea," Stacey teased. "All I ever wanted was the black dress."

"All right, hush now." He gave an exaggerated sigh, and she searched his face. The closer they came to the house, the more solemn he had become, almost as if the mansion was stretching out dark fingers to embrace him. "Do your darn best best to refrain from being a smart aleck, will you? You go first and open the doors, and I'll struggle with your paraphernalia. And don't make a sound. There's nothing I hate to face worse than an aroused household. Millie is really a witch without her sleep."

"Me, too," she told him, then ducked away as he swung one heavy hand in the direction of her bottom. "OK, I'm going. Are you sure you don't want me to take some of those little boxes?"

"Yes, I'm sure," he snapped back. "Why did I ever get married?" That last statement was addressed to the one bright star.

"How should I know?" she said wistfully. "Probably because I'm so beautiful?" This time she was unable to avoid his hand, and retreated towards the door, rubbing her injured flank.

It took three trips up the stairs, some light squabbling, and one or two minor catastrophes involving furniture being in the wrong places. So that made it two in the morning before she managed to shoo him out of the door, strip off her clothes, and fall wearily into bed. The day had seemed ten years long.

A dream possessed her. Somehow or another she was staked out on a rotating platform, and an unrecognisable monster was about to turn her into a virgin sacrifice, using the knife method. She tossed and turned, woke and went back to sleep, twisted the sheets into knots, and was unable to fall asleep again until just before dawn. And in his next reappearance the monster was using his knife to tickle her nose. Stacey pushed one eye open warily, and the monster became Harry, using a tiny feather rather than a knife.

"It's eight o'clock," he said very solemnly. "Time to get up. There are lots of things to take care of today."

"Nobody gets up at eight o'clock, Harry. And if you think I'm one of those country girls who get up with the chickens—well, think again. My father hated chickens. And I'm a night person." He tickled her nose again.

"Damn you," she said in her grumpiest voice, and rolled over on her side, with her back to him. He came around to the other side of the bed and knelt down on the carpet. His face was barely inches from hers. She managed to get both eyes open. There was no smile on his face. In fact, all the craggy lines were back—worry lines, as she knew by now.

She stretched out one hand from under the sheet and pushed back the lock of unruly hair that kept falling over his forehead. Deep in his eyes she could see the pain, rigidly suppressed. Oh God, she thought, another proud Texan. It just isn't the thing for a Texan to cry, no matter how much pain it alleviates.

Ignoring her skimpy nightgown, she sat up and cradled his head between her hands. "Your grandmother?" she asked hesitantly. The corner of his mouth twitched upward very briefly.

"That's one of the reasons why I've never married, Stacey," he said. "You're too discerning by far. Yes, my grandmother."

"Tell me about it," she offered, hoping to help him find release.

"There's nothing to tell," he said gruffly. He stood up and turned away from her. She slipped out of bed to stand beside him. "My mother and father died when I was young," he continued. "Grandma stepped in and raised me."

"And also your godchild?"

"Yes, and also Lisette. End of story. She was a grand old lady. I've long since adjusted to the idea that I was going to lose her, but it didn't really strike me until last night—until we came on to the property. I had this crazy feeling that she was up there someplace on the turret, watching to see what I would do about things. Oh Lord, this is all nonsense. There are a million things to do, and you're the mistress of the house. Let's go downstairs to the kitchen and have some breakfast first."

End of a confidence! Stacey felt suddenly bereft. For a moment Harry had offered her a part of himself, and then as quickly snatched it away. She watched as he stalked off towards the bathroom. He was wearing only a pair of pyjama bottoms, and his bronze back made him look like a Greek god. Everything brown, except for that line of white at his midriff, above the pyjamas, that marked his slender waist and emphasised his narrow buttocks. He moved like an athlete, graceful, flowing. But not once did he look back as the bathroom door closed behind him.

Stacey sat up in the bed, no longer mindful of her own concerns. He had called on her for support, and she must give it. The clothes she had shed the night before were scattered around the room. She picked them up, slipped into her robe, made a simple selection of undies, jeans, and blouse, and went out into the hall to find another bathroom.

They were both downstairs within fifteen minutes, just in time to catch Millie as she placed two loaded plates on a tray. "Oh my, you startled me!" the elderly housekeeper gasped. "I was going to bring breakfast up. You two have hardly had a honeymoon at all. You need a little pampering."

"But I've already had that," Stacey laughed. "Have you ever seen Harry's apartment?"

"Ah, that!" laughed Millie as she removed the tray and set two places at the kitchen table. "You want to watch that stuff, girl. Sodom and Gomorrah, that's what that's all about. How in the world do you ever get any sleep with that bed going around in circles?'

"We manage," Harry broke in. "Pull up a mug of coffee and sit a spell, Millie. There's a lot of thinking to be done."

He held Stacey's chair for her. She slipped into it and flashed him a thank-you smile. Millie, suddenly very serious, went over to the big gas cooker in the corner and refilled her mug. "You've made all the arrangements downtown?" she asked as she came back and sat down at the table. "Eat before it gets cold."

Almost automatically Stacey's fork came into play. "There's not much outside arranging to be done," said Harry between mouthfuls of scrambled eggs. "It's been expected for so long that we've had all the plans made. No, the big problem will be right here in the house. I expect some of the family members will start to trickle in today. I had my secretary make all the calls last night. And, of course, they'll all demand to be accommodated here at the mansion. And that puts the monkey on your back, Stacey. Yours and Millie's, of course."

"She can do it." The older woman patted Stacey's hand. "Young, but she's got guts, Harry. I still don't know how you lucked out with this one, after those crackpots you usually bring around. The only thing—" She looked Stacey up and down in a critical fashion. "The only thing is that all that family of yours will expect *her* to do things for them. You know, meet them at the door, see to their rooms, preside over meals—all that. And for that, little Mrs, you've got to start wearing dresses."

"I—I have some," Stacey stammered. "And I'll—try. If y'all will help?"

"We'll help," promised Millie. "Fill us in on the general plan, Harry."

"OK. Tomorrow we'll have the family wake. The day after there's a public one scheduled. I understand that the Governor intends to come." He looked over at Stacey's surprised face, and took both her hands in his.

"Grandmother was a famous lady in her time," he told her. "There'll be a lot of her friends come—those that she hasn't outlived. The Governor's father was one of her favourite beaux before she settled on grandfather. Where was I?"

"The public wake the day after tomorrow," Millie threw in.

"Oh, yes. The funeral will be on Friday. She wanted to be buried from her old parish church in town, the one she and Grandfather attended before he made a mint of money and moved out here—the First Lutheran, that is. And the burial will be beside her husband. She wanted it simple."

"So then there won't be any trouble," Stacey asked.

"Oh, there'll be trouble," he sighed. "After the funeral. Grandma was a very rich woman, and there'll be aunts and uncles all over the place, looking for what they can get. They couldn't see their way clear to come and visit when she was alive, but now they'll be in on top of us like a bunch of sharks. Oh yes, there'll be more than enough trouble for all, believe you me. I don't know what it contains, but her will is only one page long. There'll be a gnashing of teeth when it's read. Stick with me, wife!"

The few days went by quickly. Stacey found herself lost in the mass of family that poured in, all demanding rooms in the mansion. She played her part as mistress in style. In the face of the invasion Harry hired two women from Valley View to come in by the day. Stacey pitched in to help in the kitchen, too, in addition to supervising the new help.

Harry commanded her to the public wake. She shrugged herself into the black dress, crammed her hair up under an unaccustomed hat, and sat patiently at his side while mourners in their dozens passed by the bier. By the time the Governor arrived she was too tired to notice what was going on. All the newspapers were on hand, referring to it as "the passing of an era."

The next day, under a bright Texas sun, they buried the old lady in the family plot in the old part of the cemetery, beside the lost lover of her youth, who had preceded her in death by more than twenty years. And then it was over.

So much panoply and ceremony, Stacey sighed to herself as they were driven back to the house. So much, for a tiny woman whom she had seen for scarcely an hour, before she slipped away into a coma. If it had not been love that Harry's grandmother had engendered in her, at least it was respect. She leaned back against the seat, folded her black veil up out of the way, and dabbed at her eyes. His hand came over and covered hers, resting in her lap. A firm squeeze, a signal of shared grief and comfort. She accepted it for what it was, and closed her eyes.

As it turned out, those days of the wake and funeral were the peaceful days, for no sooner were they all back at the mansion than pandemonium set in.

Uncle Clarence—the one with the broken nose and the loud voice—was insisting that the two paintings in the study belonged to him, while three other couples disputed his right. Harry disabused them all, warning that the estate would be distributed according to the will, and in no other way.

"They're both Renoirs," he told her grimly as they made their way up to their rooms to change. "Everybody wants what Grandmother had, but none of them were ever willing to work for it. You're lucky, Stacey, to be from such a small family."

"Am I?" She turned away from him, not willing for him to see the additional tear in her eye. Apart from Aunt Ellen, she told herself fiercely, I've got nobody—and he's complaining because he's got a million aunts and uncles! So maybe they *do* squabble a little. Shaking her head, she snatched up some work clothes and ran into the bedroom so change. She walked by him without looking, and dashed for the kitchen.

"No need for that," Millie reprimanded minutes later. "We got caterers to come in. There's all sorts of food set up in the dining room."

"And all sorts of relatives," muttered Stacey. "Before the funeral they all looked so—nice. And now, Lord love us, I'm afraid to go by one of them for fear they'll bite me."

"If they do you'll get rabies," Millie commented. "What do you really want in here?"

"I need some work, Millie. Some hard physical work, to make me forget."

"Me too," her older companion said softly. "Twenty years I've been in this house. I wasn't much older than you are now when I come. Twenty years;

it's hard to forget. Why don't we clean the silver before one of those—relatives—steals it all.''

And that was the start of another week. A week that progressed from silver polishing to general house-cleaning, despite the crowded conditions. ''Anything to keep your hands busy,'' Millie said. ''A couple of solid weeks at hard labour, and then things will be back to—well, whatever normal is going to be around here in the future.''

Whatever normal is going to be? Stacey thought about that often during the nights that followed. She and Harry had settled into a routine: a display of moderate affection during the day—a few hugs, a kiss or two, a walk hand in hand. Nothing more. And then early retirement behind the closed door of their bedroom suite.

''Where, I suppose, they all think we're living it up,'' grumbled Harry, as he tried to make himself comfortable in one of the spindly chairs. Stacey could hardly suppress a giggle. He was a big man, and looked so out of place in this feminine room. And yet, to foster the image, all his clothes shared the closet with hers. His shaving gear cluttered up the bathroom, and occasionally the smell of one of his cigars would fog the whole room. And there he sat, trying to distribute his weight on the little chair, while he read the day's paper.

Strange, that was, for a man who did—what the devil *does* he do for a living? she asked herself for the hundredth time; somehow she felt it would break her luck to ask *him*. Not raise horses! He had finally admitted that the pure-bred Arabs out in the paddock were his. But not a profitable business. He kept trying to explain to her what a tax loss was, to no avail.

Somehow it all was too much of a puzzle. "A penny saved is a penny earned"— That made sense. But not this other idea.

So Harry gave up explaining, and sat there, running through the pages of the Waco paper, the Dallas paper, and the *Wall Street Journal*. He was a sound-reader; whenever he came across an interesting paragraph he would hum contentedly. A story that displeased would bring a sharp "Hmmmp!" And occasionally a story would be so hard to take that he would rip that page out of the paper and throw it into the waste basket.

My husband, Stacey lectured herself, and the idea brought a wistful sigh. It's only make-believe, of course. And I'm getting good at it, aren't I? Maybe I should start a company? "Bronfield Rent-a-Bride?" That didn't sound too bad.

"You've lost a button on your shirt," she commented.

"Ah." Well, that was better than being totally ignored. She took out her sewing kit and began to match buttons. His paper rattled, and she looked up to find him staring at her over its top. A piercing stare, that seemed all-encompassing, as she fumbled with the needle, licked the end of the thread, and tried for the third time to force it through the needle's eye. I'm out of practice, the practical side of her mind told her. Like hell you are, the other side prodded. Why are your hands shaking so much? Either fish or cut bait, girl. Throw his shirt on the floor and stamp on it, then run across the room and jump on him. That's what you really want!

She fought back the urge, biting at her lower lips. The thread finally condescended to go through the hole, and she picked up the button and started at it, keeping her head lowered so that her hair swung between them. The needle flashed prettily. Almost as if you knew what you were doing, she shouted at herself. Harry's paper dropped into his lap.

"We'll hear the will read tomorrow," he said. "Look at us—we're getting to be a regular pair, aren't we? Darby and Joan?" He tossed the papers aside, came over, and dropped a kiss on the top of her head. "Me for bed," he said, and went through the door into the adjoining room, the one in which he actually slept. Stacey watched his back as he disappeared. Darby and Joan? Who in the world were they? A tiny tear formed at the corner of her eye, ran down her cheek, and fell off on to the shirt clutched in her hand.

She looked down at the shirt, as if it were something she had never seen before. "That's silly," she mumbled to herself. "Why would anyone sew a button on at the elbow?" It took her almost an hour to cut the threads and place the button where it belonged.

So they heard the will read in the morning—the relaties, that was. Stacey managed to fight her way out of bed by seven, and was in the kitchen preparing breakfast by seven-thirty. Practically all the relatives were up, she noticed, as she carried a platter of ham and eggs into the dining room. They all turned to stare at her, as if she were some sort of superior servant. She flashed them a quick smile, and retreated to the kitchen.

"Like a bunch of vultures," she muttered to Millie, who was starting another batch of scrambled eggs. "They look at me as if they think I might inherit something of theirs!"

At nine o'clock Mr Simmons arrived. He looked to be too young to represent the august firm of Herrick, Portnoy, and Simmons. But he had the right papers in hand, and all the family followed him into the big double-parlour. The doors closed behind them.

Less than half an hour later both Stacey and Millie, sharing coffee in a pair of old mugs in the kitchen, heard the uproar. "Forty people, all yelling at once," commented Millie. "It sounds as if the old lady did them *all* in!"

The doors of the parlour slammed open, and disgruntled people stamped their way into the hall. "I'll contest the will," Aunt Marion shrieked. "She can't do this to us—we're family!" Nobody else offered to second the motion. They all seemed lost in their own private agonies. By lunch time every one of them had left, in a mad cacophony of protests and tyre-squealings. Young Mr Simmons stood on the porch with Harry to watch them go, then he flashed a tiny smile, and followed.

Stacey came out of hiding in a dark corner of the hall as soon as the lawyer's car started moving, and joined Harry on the porch. He looked down at her sombrely, then grinned, dropping a friendly arm over her shoulder.

"Thank God for you, my dear," he sighed, and she shifted contentedly under the weight of his arm. "And that's what *family* means."

"You sound so cynical. Was it always this bad?" She wanted to comfort him, but her lack of experience betrayed her effort.

"Bad? I don't really know." His left hand squeezed her shoulder. "But I wish that Grandmother had left the entire estate to charity, or something." There was a touch of bitterness behind his words. She could read the anguish in his eyes. "Do you know what she's done to us?"

Done to *us?* A little shivering thrill ran up Stacey's spine. *Us?* Have we come this far, Harry, you and I? "No, I didn't hear," she said softly. "What?"

"She left the entire estate to be divided equally between myself and her godchild Lisette. I don't even know what her married name is now. Grandmother made her will almost a year ago, when I think she was despairing that I would ever get married. So there we have it. The entire estate to be shared between us, with two provisos. First, I'm charged with finding Lisette. Second, she and I must both live together for three months in the mansion before we can dispose of it. And I haven't the slightest idea where she is. I haven't known for almost five years!"

"I—" Stacey could not find the words. Harry would live in this sprawling house for three months with another woman. The child he had grown up with. The woman he had once loved? Out of the grave his grandmother had laid a commitment on him that could surely only lead to—stop! Stacy screamed at herself. I don't want to think about it! She turned away from him, cramming her fist in her mouth to stifle the sobs.

"Kitten?" His hand touched her shoulder again.

"Don't call me that!" she sobbed, and ran for her room. She stood against the closed door, shaking, her frame rocking back and forth on unsteady feet. The tears came silently, flowing like Niagara, but unable to wash away her woes. When she heard the footsteps in the hall she looked wildly around for a place to hide. The only locks available were on the bathroom door, and at that were only a pair of courtesy bolts. Nevertheless, they were something. Stacey shook her trembling feet loose from the rug to which they seemed glued, and ran for the bathroom. She could hear the bedroom door open behind her as she slammed the bolts home. Harry knocked twice.

"Stacey? Are you all right?"

"Yes," she managed to force out of a hoarse throat. "Please—"

"All right. Lunch will be in an hour. We have a lot to talk about."

She leaned wearily against the wall, one hand clutching the towel rack for support. Yes, we have a lot to talk about, she thought, but only one of us is ready to listen. He thinks he's too old for me. As soon as he finds Lisette—Kitten—he'll fall back into the old pattern. And then they'll live here together, and propinquity will take care of the rest. Lord, I had a chance up to that point. But he has a charge from his grandmother to find that woman, and he will. It's no use. Maybe in fifty years, when I've finally grown up—but I can't wait. I've got to go now, while I've still got the courage!

Given a goal to work to, her mind responded. She put her ear to the door and heard nothing. Cautiously she unfastened the bolts and peered out. The bedroom was empty. Stacey hurried to the closet, pulled out her old suitcase, and opened it on the bed. Only your own clothing, her mind commanded. Her fingers skipped past all the delicate light finery Harry had bought her on that stormy night, and plucked out only her old dresses, dungarees, and slips. She crammed them into the case without thought to proper order, then emptied the drawers of her own plain cotton briefs, ignoring the piles of flimsy lace and silk that he had helped choose. Her heart seemed to block her throat as she shut the closet door against temptation, and locked her case.

She could hear them talking—Millie and Harry and Frank—as she stole down the staircase by the kitchen, and out of the front door. There were three cars parked beside the house. The Mercedes was too much for her, and the little red Sprite standing next to it was just as bad, but the battered old four-wheel-drive jeep was just her style, and the key was in the ignition. It took several minutes for her to adjust the seat. The engine fired at the turn of the key. The gears screeched as she shifted, and she whirled the vehicle around, heading out to the highway.

The commotion from the house came to her ears. The back door slammed shut as someone came charging out. But her eyes were glued to the road. Despite all her boasting, her experience of driving on the farm had in no way prepared her for reality. She clenched her teeth, wrestled the heavy vehicle to the far right side of the road, and careered down it at full speed. As she approached the old cemetery at Keys she slowed down, looking for a way to the main highway. A quick jog at the Bosqueville corners eventually led her to Lake Shore Drive. She slowed down to twenty-five miles an hour, ignoring the host of beeping cars piling up behind her, and did her best to keep the heavy vehicle on the road. Eventually she picked up the Route 35 markers, and followed them up on to the divided highway.

She gave a great sigh of relief when she saw the unencumbered road stretching out in front of her, like a south-pointing arrow. The cars which had been tail-ing her all the way roared by, honking derisively as they went. Stacey wobbled her vehicle to the side of the road and stopped almost underneath the sign which said *No Stopping On Highway*. She was still fumbling for a tissue when the Texas Ranger car pulled up behind her, and an officer ambled over to where she sat, frozen at the wheel.

"I wasn't speeding," she defended herself the moment he came up to the door. "I wasn't!"

"No, ma'am." He grinned a mouthful of white young teeth at her as he took off his dark glasses and whipped out a notebook. "May I see your licence, please?"

Her face turned a brilliant red. "I—I don't seem to have it with me," she mumbled, fumbling in her handbag as if there was something to find.

"But you're supposed to," he responded gently. "Didn't they tell you that when you got your licence?"

"No," she whispered, "they didn't tell me that."

"That's strange," he returned jovially. "They're supposed to tell you. Well, where did you get your licence?"

"I—I don't have a licence," she confessed, ducking her head.

His smile shrank just a bit. "No licence," he muttered to himself as he scribbled something in his book. "But you do have the car's registration, I imagine. May I see that, please?"

"I—I don't have the car registration," she answered in a very small, very timid voice.

"Don't tell me you stole the car?" He was joking, she knew, trying to reduce the tension he could read on her face.

"Yes."

"Oh, brother!" The smile had gone completely. "Please show me some identification."

Stacey reached for her bag again, only to find that he had backed away from the car and drawn his revolver. "I—I was just—I have a credit card," she offered. He extended one hand carefully and took it.

"Stacey Bronfield," he said. "That's you?"

"I—yes, that's me. I—"

"And you live where?"

"In Coryelle County," she responded, more terrified of that huge gun than she would care to admit. "On the highway between Pidcoke and Gatesville."

"And who did you steal the car from?"

"From—" It almost came out. From my husband. Oh Lord, what a confusion that would make! "I don't remember," she said, trying to shrink into invisibility.

"Please step out of the car," he ordered, very watchful now, the gun in a half-raised position. Stacey was mesmerised by that gun. The hole in the barrel looked to be as big as a cannon, and behind it she could see the dull rounded heads of the bullets in its revolving chamber. Her teeth began to chatter.

"Put your hands on the car and spread your legs," he instructed. She turned to comply, just as a squealing of brakes announced that another vehicle had stopped near them. She felt one of the officer's hands begin to pat her shoulder and side, when the voice she least wanted to hear in all the world demanded, "What the hell are you doing to my wife!"

The Ranger was as startled as she was. Out of the corner of her eye she saw him whirl around, gun at the ready, and then stop. "Mr Marsden?"

"Yes—Harry Marsden. You know me?"

"Yes, sir. I was in the guard of honour at your grandmother's funeral."

"Then surely you must know that this little lady is my wife?" Damn them both, Stacey whispered under her breath. Listen to them! The *old boy* network in full swing. This *little lady*—how degrading can they make it sound! Forgive her, officer. She is, after all, only a woman!

"No, I didn't know that," the Ranger returned, holstering his gun. "She was in that black veil. And today she claims to be someone else."

"Ah." Another nail in my coffin, Stacey thought. The poor little lady is confused! I wish I were ten feet tall, so I could mangle both of them!

"Ah." Harry repeated. "Well, you know how it is, officer. We've not been married very long, and we had a—a little misunderstanding. You *do* understand?"

Stacey turned around to face them, a mad glare in her eyes, only to find that they were standing with their backs turned towards her, paying her no attention at all. She swallowed her anger. She was still in a tight spot—but wait until I get you afterwards, Harry Marsden! she raged to herself.

"Then there's this business about the stolen car," the Ranger interjected, gesturing back to the jeep.

"Stolen? Why, that's my car," said Harry. "I was giving her driving lessons in it."

"Then you'd better make sure she gets her licence before she goes out on the highway," the Ranger concluded, shoving his notebook back into its clip. "She drives like she's following a snake down the road. And at her speed we would have had traffic piled up in back of her all the way to Dallas."

"Not to worry," Harry assured him. "I've got everything in hand. I'll just move the jeep off to the side here, and send someone down to drive it back to the farm. And the little lady—well, I guess I'd better take her with me and reason with her."

The Ranger tipped him a salute and went back to his patrol car. Harry, completely ignoring Stacey, walked over to the jeep and moved it off into the breakdown lane. As he walked back to her his hands were in his pockets, and he was whistling a tune that had no real melody. She turned to face him, red anger showing, her fists clenched so tightly that her nails were biting into her palms. He took one good look.

"Not a good time to say anything, is it?" he suggested diffidently. She tried her best to glare him to death. It brought a smile to the corners of his mouth.

"Would you be willing to climb into my car?" he offered, waving toward the Mercedes. She sniffed at him, and stalked around to the passenger side. He was there before her, holding the door open. Stacey inserted herself without even looking at him. He went around to the driver's seat, started the engine, and turned on the blessed air condition.

"We'll go back to the house and talk this over," he said.

"No!" she shouted at him. "I've had enough. Take me home!"

He took another close look at her, noting the flushed cheeks, the sparking eyes, and the marks of strain around her mouth. He shrugged his shoulders, and took the car out into the south-bound traffic.

Not another word was said during the whole trip, until the car pulled up into the front yard of the Rancho Miraflores. Stacey's hand went immediately to the door handle, but it refused to open.

"Unlock the door," she gritted at him.

"No. We have to talk."

"I don't have anything more to talk about," she snapped, pushing feebly against the door. "It was all a farce from beginning to end. I needed you, but you didn't need me. I'm not your wife. I'm not even sure that I like you."

"What a lie that is, Kitten," he returned. One of his fingers rummaged through her hair. The contact was more than she could stand. It jolted her, shook her confidence in herself—and made her admit, at least to herself, that what she had said was the biggest lie she had ever told, in all her life. But she had to fight back. That, at least, was something her father had left her: always be prepared to fight back! She shifted away from him on the seat.

"Take your hands off me!" she snarled. "The game is over. I'm not your wife, I'm not a good enough actress to go on with this lie. Unlock the door and let me out." Out of the corner of her eye she saw the twins sauntering around the corner of the house, becoming interested spectators.

"And that's another thing," she snarled. "Get your cowhands off my ranch, you hear!"

"Oh, I hear all right," Harry said solemnly. "You have a remarkably clear voice when you want to, Stacey. And they're not my cowhands. They work for Westland Cattle Associates. You gave me a power of attorney, you'll remember. Rancho Miraflores hired those two young men, and they stay hired until that power of attorney is revoked. Do you want to do that?"

"I—I—" No, I don't want to do that, she cried silently. It's all too much for me. I need you. I hate you, but I need you. And that's not true either. I love you and I need you, but you're going to live in that house with Lisette Langloise for three months, and what chance do I have? "No, I don't want to cancel."

"Very well, that's one step in the right direction. Now, how about the rest of it?" Harry leaned in her direction and those two huge hands seized her shoulders and pulled her across the seat, hard up against his warm male frame. "Now what's the real reason you're blowing your top?"

"I—you and that damn Ranger," she stormed into his shirt button. "The little lady. The idiot child—she's only a woman, of course. My God, but you've got a nerve!"

"But it did keep you out of jail, didn't it?"

Stacey snapped her head back to get a clear look at his face. Just one glint of amusement, she promised herself, just one glimmer of a laugh, and I'll—I'll— But his face was solemnity itself, betraying not a quiver or a grin.

"So now suppose you just tell me why you ran away from the house?" suggested Harry.

"You didn't need me any more," she sobbed. "You didn't need me at all. It was just a game, and I'm through playing!" To emphasise her point she struggled with the two rings on her left hand, jerking them off at the expense of a little skin. She threw them up on the dashboard in front of him. "And there's your jewellery. It's all over!"

"You really mean that, Stacey?"

"Oh God, please—just unlock the door and let me go." The tears were beyond her control and when she raised her face to him she had no idea of the wild appeal it flashed. Harry sighed and shook his head wearily. His fingers went over to the instrument panel and flicked a switch. Stacey heard the snap as the door unlocked, and fought her way across the seat and out on to the baked earth of the yard.

"Kitten!" Harry called after her, but she turned her back and stamped up to the porch, past the two gawking cowboys.

"Doesn't anyone on this ranch have any work to do?" she snarled at them as she slammed into the house and leaned back against the door. Behind her she could hear the whisper of the engine starting up again, and the tyres of the Mercedes squealed as Harry made an angry U-turn. She rushed out into the kitchen, slamming that door behind her too, and then collapsed across the kitchen table, crying her heart out for everything she had lost. Aunt Ellen hurried into the kitchen behind her, flustered. Stacey got up and fled into her arms, and they cried over each other until their tear ducts were empty. Two lonely women.

Stacey wiped her eyes clear with one knuckle. Her hand wandered lightly over her aunt's disfigured cheek. "You know," she said determinedly, "at least that's something we can do something about, Aunt Ellen. Plastic surgery. Think about it!"

As she went up to bed that night in her tiny, draughty room, Stacey thought about it again herself. They had plenty of money. Plastic surgery could give her aunt another face, another chance. I wonder, she thought, just before she closed her eyes, if I could arrange for a heart transplant to give *me* another chance!

CHAPTER SIX

THE week that followed was a succession of bad days. Stacey kept to her room, coming out only for a quick snack in the kitchen, eating because she knew she had to, rather than because she was hungry. Her aunt shadowed her, but did not try to force a confidence. The sun shone almost every day, but there was no real cheer. She wasted box after box of tissues, and thought. At the weekend, still tired and dispirited, she had her answers, and came out into the world. Aunt Ellen was in the kitchen, up to her elbows in flour.

"You're looking better," her aunt commented.

"Yes," Stacey replied firmly. "I have to get a lot of things done. Harry and I—we—" It was too hard to say.

"I know," her aunt returned. "I talked to him on the telephone a couple of times this week. He wanted to know how you were."

"Did he really?" Stacey snapped up the information, not sure whether it made her happy, or just complicated things more. Don't think about Harry just yet, her mind insisted. Get about your business!

"Is Mr Steuben still drilling?" she asked.

"No, I don't think so," Aunt Ellen responded, after some thought. "They found water—in seven different places. Another company is working down in the south pasture now, running pipes, setting up pumps, watering troughs—that sort of thing. The old well was getting brackish. You can actually drink this stuff right out of the faucet. And they put in a new automatic pump and a new cistern in the attic. Now all we have to do is turn on the faucet to turn on the pump. Isn't that something?"

"That's nice, dear. What are you making?"

"Bread. Those two young men eat it up faster than I can bake it."

"Do they eat at the house?"

"No, not really. They cook for themselves. They're living down in the old foreman's cottage. But I do like to contribute. Nice boys, both of them. What are you thinking about? Your face is all screwed up, and you've been wearing a frown all week."

"What I'm thinking of, Aunt Ellen, is that we two ought to settle down and do something good for ourselves."

"Do something? What, for example."

"Well—I learned while I was living at the Marsden house just how little I really know," Stacey explained. "I've got to find some way to finish my high school education, and maybe even go to college. But I don't know who to contact, or what to say. And I need a driver's licence, and—" She fumbled to a stop. What use was it to blurt out all her secrets? The second greatest want in her life was related to her father, and those crazy helicopters of his. She wanted to fly— to do something to remind herself of Dad. "But I don't even know where to start," she concluded mournfully.

Aunt Ellen stopped her to-and-fro rush and looked at Stacey, as if she wanted to say something but dared not. Then she plucked up her courage. "Why don't you call that nice Miss Moreland?"

"Miss Moreland?" Stacey's mind felt dull, almost as it did when she had been taking all those pills. She shook her head and tried again. "Do I know a Miss Moreland?"

"Well, you ought to, for goodness' sakes. She's your husband's executive secretary. Amie Moreland. By the way, what happened to your rings?"

"I—we—there was a problem with the fitting, and Harry took them back to the jewellers." Which was as good a lie as she could concoct in a hurry. Times had changed considerably between her aunt and herself in the past few weeks, but Stacey could not forget that Harry was the defensive wall behind which she had hidden. And wanted to hide again, if the truth be known. Explanations would be required some time— but if it could all be put off until tomorrow?

"Yes," her aunt continued, "last week, after you had that idea, I called Miss Moreland, and within three days she had all the information. A nice girl, that one. Or perhaps I should say woman?"

"I don't know. I've never seen her. What idea was that that I had?"

"Oh dear, surely you haven't forgotten? About the plastic surgeon?" The older woman's upper lip was trembling. Oh Lord, Stacey thought, what have I done now!

"Oh, I remember that very well," she hurried to say. The lip stilled, and a smile flashed across her aunt's face.

"Well, I thought it over for a time, and it seemed to be such a good idea—so I decided to go ahead. If I can find the money, that is."

Stacey waved a hand carelessly. One afternoon, just before the funeral, Harry had taken her in to the First National Bank in Waco, and stood laughingly at her side while a vice-president explained to her about the contents of her investment portfolio, and her checking accounts. She had been aware for years that she was "in oil," but the size of the quarterly royalty cheque deposited directly into her account by Parsons Oil had taken her breath away. "Are you sure you've got the decimal point in the right place?" she had asked, in all innocence—and then turned blush-red as half the bank employees within hearing started to laugh. Harry had touched her cheek with one finger, and traced a circle there just before he planted a kiss in its centre. She remembered that now, and her hand came up to caress the spot, still marked in memory.

"Don't worry about the money," she said. "There's plenty for everything now. What did you find out?"

"Everything seems to be all arranged, my dear. I'm sorry I didn't talk it over with you beforehand, but once I called Amie, things just seemed to happen—so fast that I haven't caught my breath yet. I'm to go down to the Texas Medical Centre in Houston very soon. I'll stay there for a week or two, for examinations. Then, if they think anything can be done, I'll go back again. Perhaps around the first of the year—if the money is available. They said, over and above our Blue Cross insurance, perhaps twelve thousand dollars. That's a great deal of money, Stacey."

"No, it isn't," she returned, with only half her mind engaged. Miss Moreland, was it? Could it be possible to call her for some advice, without leaning on Harry? Perhaps without him even knowing? Because that was the core of all her dreams. To force-educate herself, to become more sophisticated—to grow older in a hurry. And then go back to Harry and say, "See, I'm all grown up. Now what?"

And of course Harry would sweep her off her feet, and instantly fall in love with her, and then they would be married, and raise cattle and kids. Perhaps not in that order!

"So you think I should go ahead?" Aunt Ellen was clutching at the edge of the kitchen table as if her life depended on it. Their relationship had completely changed. Where once the older woman had ruled the roost, now she had relinquished all authority, and lived in a half-world between acceptance and rejection. Looking at the unmarred side of her face, Stacey could see her father all over again—the same forehead, the strong nose, the dark grey eyes, all there in his sister's face. And deserving of love, she told herself. Who am I to condemn her for snatching at the golden wedding ring? Look what a fool I'm making of myself about Harry. And if I don't condemn her, then I should show her.

Stacey smiled across the table, walked around it and put her arms around her aunt. "We're all that's left of the Bronfields," she said. "We have to take care of each other. I love you for who you are, my dear. Of course you should go ahead. We've some money in the bank, and there'll be more on the first of October. And while we're at it, let's both run in to Gatesville and buy ourselves a few pretties to wear!"

John Morgan drove them out and back, package-laden. But it was not for another hour after they had returned that Stacey was able to sneak off into the living room and make that all-important telephone call. Amie Moreland turned out to be a delight to talk to, and hard to get to. Her call to the Marsden Management switchboard encountered delays, shifts, reconnections, and a succession of young voices repeating, "And what would you like to talk to Mrs Moreland about?"

By the time the correct extension was rung, Stacey learned, to the detriment of her confidence, that Amie Moreland was Mrs Moreland, exceedingly busy, executive secretary to the president of the company, a member of the board of directors in her own right, and a very warm-voiced lady who responded cheerfully to Stacey as "young Mrs Marsden." Which seemed a very adequate summary of things.

Her explanations were slightly fuzzy, coloured by a stammer she thought she had lost in her childhood. The call lasted forty minutes, during which time the "very busy" Mrs Moreland asked questions, made notes, and finally said, "I don't know a single thing about any of this, Mrs Marsden—Stacey. But I do know how to find out. Shall I just go ahead and get things started?"

"If you would—Amie?" Stacey used the name diffidently, having received permission, but not sure that she should. "I'm in a terrible hurry. I've wasted a great many years, and—" And not for the life of me am I going to tell you *why* I'm in a hurry, or what my ultimate goal is!

"Let me check the list again." There was a silence. Stacey could hear voices in the background. A few words filtered through. "It's your wife, Harry. She has a few small problems that—" and then a softer buzz of indistinguishable words. Finally Amie was back at the telephone. "I think I have everything lined up," the soft contralto voice said, "and I don't see why we can't have something going very soon. You'll be at home? Or at the ranch?''

"At the ranch. And I'll be here every day, waiting. Only—Amie—please don't tell—" she was about to say Mr Marsden, until her mind caught up with her tongue—"Harry?"

"No, of course not." The woman on the other end of the line giggled. "What men don't know won't hurt them! I've been married a couple of years myself."

The smile was still on Stacey's face as she hung up the telephone and walked back into the kitchen.

The next morning, after her first good night's sleep since coming back home, Stacey was up early to face a beautiful sun rising over Beaumont way. After a quick breakfast of toast and coffee she strolled out behind the house for her first real look at what had been done while she was away. Jim Morgan—or was it John?—was squatting down on his heels outside the barn, tinkering with a bridle. He stretched himself up as she came over.

"Ma'am." He tipped a finger to the brim of his hat in salute. "This bridle's chewed a fare-thee-well, but I'm fit and determined to stay right here until it's mended." He smiled down at her with a grin that reminded her of Harry, and it was like a stab in the heart. She turned away from him to hide the tears. He noticed her confusion, and repeated himself. "Right here until it's mended." Of course he said it all in that flat Texas drawl that made it come sounding like "raght cheer", but Stacey was accustomed to all sorts of accents in cosmopolitan Texas.

"Tell me what's going on," she prodded him.

"Around these parts, you mean?" She nodded. "Well, my brother, he's gone into town to get that car you ordered. We done got some help last week, and the corral is all built. The barn is in first-class shape, and some men from Waco are building that wooden-fenced paddock for them Arab horses. Whoeee, ain't they something? And—yeah, we done rode the ranch fence-line, Jim and me, and repaired that. The water is flowing all over the place. And—well now, I sort of forget, we been so busy. Oh yeah, the oil company come in one day last week, they did, and fenced around all them pumps, so the cattle won't be trying to munch on them. And I guess that's all. The boss said we was to get everything ship-shape for spring, 'cause that's when the herd will be coming in. And that's all I know for sure, ma'am. Oh, I did forget—them guys was here to measure the house. And that's it for sure."

"It—all sounds so very busy," Stacey commented hesitantly. How in the world does the owner of a spread ask a ranch hand what the devil's going on here? But curiosity outweighed caution. "They came to measure the house?"

"Well, I don't know about that, ma'am. They was talkin' about making it bigger, and a new roof, and paint—and things like that. That's out of my line."

"Mine too," she laughed nervously. He squatted down to his work again, and she joined him, plucking at a blade of grass to nibble on. "And what car was that, the one your brother went to town for?"

"Oh, that. Well, we drawed straws, you know, right after the boss called. Oh yeah, we got us a telephone down to the cottage now. So anyway, the car's all picked out, over to the car place in Gatesville. He done that himself—the boss did—and Jim, he's got nothin' to do all this week but teach you how to drive it, and help you get your licence.''

All of which was plenty to think about as she rode her mare around the perimeter of the ranch, admiring the neat fencing, and the return of green to the landscape after the storm which had broken the back of the drought. The long flat vista stretched out all around her, broken only by clumps of cottonwood trees. In the western distance the hills loomed, outlining the valley of the Lampassas River, but beyond the boundaries of the ranch. Everything in sight seemed to be imbued with new life, new promise. And the only pain in her heart came from the thought that her father could not be there to see it.

It took more than the week before Jim Morgan was satisfied with her performance at the wheel. The car he had brought proudly back was an American Eagle, a four-wheel-drive station wagon, heavily sprung to match the needs of ranch driving. When she finally met his requirements, he took her down to the warehouse district of the huge military post, Fort Hood, where examiners had previously arranged for the testing of several Army officers from other states.

Stacey breezed through the written examination, then went out for the road test. There was just a moment of nervousness as she watched the big husky Ranger come over towards where she was parked. ''If it's him, I'll fall through the floor,'' she mumbled to herself. But when the officer arrived, he was not the same man who had stopped her on that wild day on Route 35! She stalled the engine immediately, and the Ranger laughed.

''Par for the course,'' he chuckled. ''Don't be so nervous, Mrs Marsden.'' And that was enough to take the edge off. She sailed through the parking manoeuvres, the passing test, and the road run. "And you pass with flying colours," the officer said. "Now be sure, always carry your licence with you when you drive!"

Her face was blush-red when they handed her the permit. She had been on a high jag of excitement until that moment, but with the permit in hand, exhaustion hit her so hard she had not the strength to drive them both back to the Ranch. It was the first of her goals accomplished. She checked it off in her mind and wondered when she might start on the next.

Two days later she found out. It was almost as if someone off-stage had been waiting for her to get her licence before turning to the next page of the script. She had awakened happily, bent on going out immediately and driving somewhere—anywhere. Aunt Ellen was in the kitchen, smiling to herself as she put together a real Texas breakfast.

"Steak and eggs?" enquired Stacey, peering over her shoulder.

"Just so," her aunt returned. "I heard from Jim— or was it John?—that you did real well yesterday. You deserve a real breakfast."

"And I'm ready for it," Stacey laughed as she set the kitchen table for two. "But why are you so happy? Not because I got my licence, surely?"

"No, not exactly." Her aunt still wore that secret smile, that expression that lit up the inner woman. "I talked to Mrs Moreland again yesterday, and she says the doctors are ready for me, beginning next Wednesday." She hugged herself, trying to contain her glee. "Oh, Stacey," she sighed, "you'll never know how much this means to me, and after all I did to hurt you!'' The glow produced tears. Stacey hurried over and hugged her. The minute her arms went around the older woman, she knew what she herself had been missing all these days—two warm comforting arms, and the pleasure of touching! They sat down opposite each other at the breakfast table, having cemented one more brick into the structure of their family relations.

Stacey did the dishes while her aunt wandered off in a happy daze. The vacuum cleaner began to hum at about the same time that the doorbell rang. Stacey dried her hands and walked to the front door. It had been so long since anyone had used that door that she could hardly remember the occasion. Everyone came to the side door, in typical farm fashion. An elderly man, barely five and a half feet tall, with white hair and a stringy Vandyck beard, stood waiting.

''Bob Herndon,'' he introduced himself. ''Will you tell your mother that I'm here?''

''My mother?''

''Yes—Mrs Marsden. That is your mother, isn't it?''

Stacey looked down at her denim-clad figure, almost completely covered by a huge kitchen apron—the one with the crimson letters that said ''Texas Beef Barbecues Best,'' her hair combed back under a kerchief that left her looking twelve years old, and laughed. He joined her, obviously not knowing why. ''Come in,'' Stacey giggled, and gestured him into the front parlour. He walked by her, juggling his briefcase from one hand to the other to accommodate his cane.

''Old age,'' he apologised as her eye swung to the cane. ''Old age, and—er—fast living, perhaps.'' He sank down into one of the overstuffed chairs without waiting for an invitation. "Your mother?"

"Oh, yes, my mother. I think there's some mistake," she told him slowly. "My mother has been dead for many years. I'm Mrs Marsden."

"You? Why—" his urbane manner disappeared in the confusion, and then he laughed again, "of course, Mrs Marsden. I've been sent by Federal Electronics." Stacey snapped to attention. Federal Electronics—that *other* company that rented space in the Marsden Management business! "I'm a retired schoolteacher, to be exact. I and a small group of other retired teachers have banded together in a company called Tutorials, Inc. We specialise in High School Equivalency Testing."

"Do you really?" Her mind was on other things. For example, what business was it of Federal Electronics to send someone to *her* door? "What in the world is that?"

"Many states, including Texas," he explained, "recognise that considerable number of adults who didn't finish their high school courses would like to have a diploma. So the Equivalency Test was established. Very simply, if you take the test and pass, the State of Texas will award you a high school diploma. There are no strings attached."

"But I—I haven't been in school for years," Stacey protested. "I don't think I could pass *any* kind of test."

"Not to worry," he told her. "That's what I'm here for—to serve as tutor for you in any weak subjects you might have, and to see that you *do* pass the test. So sure are we in our guarantee that we don't charge a fee until you've successfully taken the examination. Shall we begin?''

And begin they did. First with a diagnostic test that painfully indicated Stacey's need of tutoring in math and Social studies, and then with intensive drills and tutoring, every morning except Saturday and Sunday, until her brain cried out against further stuffing. Stacey kept her nose to the grindstone as the cycle of the year rolled down.

Every afternoon she spent two hours or more with her studies, then saddled her old mare for a brief ride through the changing ranchland.

Suddenly summer had gone. She marked it well. From time to time friends of her father came to adjacent Fort Hood, and came out to the ranch to reminisce. More often than not, in the heat of the season, they would invite her back to the fort to use the outdoor pool at the Officers' Club. And summer's end was announced on October the fifteenth, when the unheated pool was closed for the winter.

During that same month Aunt Ellen went off to Houston for her diagnostic tests. Stacey had planned all along to drive her to Waco Airport to flaunt her seldom-used driver's licence. But that unseen hand that manipulated her life was before her again. When she judged it time to leave for the airport her aunt gave her one of those big smiles, and refused to budge. An hour later a clatter in the sky announced the arrival of a helicopter. Stacey went out on the porch, slipping on a light sweater against the cool wind, and watched the whirly-bird set down behind the house. It was one of those big Sikorsky heavy-duty jet jobs, all blue and white, with WESTLAND CATTLE painted in garish red on one side. The pilot was Jim Morgan—or perhaps John.

He climbed down out of the cockpit and came over to her, ducking under the threat of the rotating blades, even though they were ten feet or more above his head.

"I didn't know you were a helicopter pilot," she yelled in his ear.

"Am I?" he asked, equally loud. "Oh, that, you mean. Yes, I am. Jim too, for that matter. Is your aunt ready?"

"Yes, she'll be out in a minute. The—other one of you is getting her bags together now." She swung both hands behind her back and crossed all available fingers. "I wish I could fly one of those things."

"It takes a mite of doin'," he advised, being just as casual about it as she was. "Nigh on to a hundred hours of just ground instruction, you know." Aunt Ellen came out the door, struggling against the backlash of the helicopter-created wind, and Stacey knew she had very little time to pin down a commitment.

"But you could teach me if you wanted to?" She found it difficult to be coy and little-girlish when she had to shout at the top of her lungs. And in any event, Morgan was having none of it.

"You got one or two words wrong," he yelled in her ear. "I could teach you if *he* wanted to."

"Who are you talking about?"

"The boss man. I work for Westland Cattle. If the boss says teach you, I teach you. If the boss says no, I don't. Makes life simple, ma'am. I gotta run now." And he suited action to words.

Stacey gave her aunt a parting hug, wished her well, then stood back as the chopper took off in another swirl of dust, circled once, and headed eastward. And while she watched, her mind ran around the outside of the problem, trying to find a hole leading into the central core of it. Who was responsible for all this? Amie Moreland? Or somebody she hadn't even met yet? Who, for example, was the head man of the cattle company? That might be a good place to start, but right this minute, as the sounds of the helicopter faded in the distance, she knew that more immediate problems must be faced. Her tutor, Mr Herndon, had agreed to come in the afternoon on this one day, and she had yet to complete the three pages of algebraic equations he had assigned from the day before. She waved at Jim Morgan, in the distance, who was headed for the corral with a saddle slung over his shoulder, and for just a minute entertained a rebellion against her own rules—but quickly passed it up. Her goal was still too distant, and no minutes could be squandered on the road leading there.

The days trudged after each other, one on one, like a herd of elephants in a single line, none different from another, all plodding, driving, skull-shattering. "Your history is good," Mr Herndon had told her, "and so is your English. But there has to be more drill in Maths, and your Spanish is atrocious. Dig in, girl!" And she did.

Aunt Ellen arrived back at the ranch after a two-week absence, happy, with an affirmative report from the doctors. "They want to start skin grafts right after the first of the year," she told her niece. "They say it may take as much as three separate operations, over a period of three or four months."

"Do you want it to happen?" asked Stacey.

"Indeed I do," her aunt chortled. "They had an artist come in, and he drew me a picture of how it

would look when they finish! Oh yes, I want it to
happen!'' The glow that she brought into the house
was enough to last for the remainder of the week.

After Stacey had done her lessons, earning her a
grudging "not bad" from her tutor, she wandered
outside. The helicopter was still there, sitting like an
ugly duck in a little depression behind the house. One
of the Morgan brothers came out of the barn as soon
as Stacey approached the machine.

"I talked to the boss man," he said laconically. "He
says, give the little lady anything she wants. When you
wanna start?''

"How about right now?'' she returned eagerly.
"I'm free every afternoon.''

"Takes a heap of studying,'' he said. "And you
ain't exactly unemployed right now. You sure?''

She was sure, but a little disappointed to find out
that the first hundred hours were practically all theory—communications, navigation, and a dozen other
topics, with only a few familiarisation rides in the
machine to keep up her enthusiasm. But thoughts of
her father drove her—of her father, and Harry. And
of the goals she had set for herself.

November passed into December. The Thanksgiv-
ing turkey was shared by herself, her aunt, and the two
ranch hands. A trip down to Pidcoke to say her thanks
in the church in which she had been baptised, then
back deep into the books again.

The weather changed in December. The arctic winds
began to roar down the Mississippi valley from Can-
ada, straight into the Texas panhandle, then farther
down, to the valley of the Brazos. There was a little
snow, and on December the twentieth, when as much
as half an inch fell, practically all of Coryelle County

seemed to come to a standstill under the unusual threat.

On December the twenty-second Stacey drove herself proudly into Gatesville and sat for her examination. She had gone in demurely dressed, hair carefully brushed, cheeks shining with expectation. She came out bedraggled, tired, drained, surrounded by a dozen or more other adults who had come for the same purpose. They were all in need of conversation. She was so sure that she had made an unholy mess of the affair that she slunk away, backed her Eagle out of the parking area, and had driven home like a madwoman, wondering what she could turn to next.

Christmas was a quiet time. One of the men had cut a small fir tree for them, and the two women set it up in the living room, decorating it with wildly improbable baubles they had picked up at a sale in Killeen. It looked incongruously like a tiny burro trying to bear the load designed for a mule. They had a quiet laugh for themselves, opened two bottles of Lone Star beer in honour of the occasion, and went off to bed.

The Morgan boys went home for Christmas Day, leaving the women alone. They both slept late, and barely made it to church services. When they came back they found a cruiser from the Sheriff's patrol waiting for them at the door.

"Just a check-up, ladies," the young Deputy told them. "We've got orders to keep an eye open for you over the holidays."

"Does that mean you know something about the Delanos?" Stacey hated to raise the spectre, but could not hold back.

"Nope," he replied. "Them two is long gone—north, I suspect. The young one was seen in Chicago a few weeks ago, but got away. Don't you worry none. We'll be keeping a close watch. Merry Christmas!''

They wandered into the house after exchanging greetings. As usual, the side door had been left open, and Stacey knew that someone had been there in her absence. There was a smell of cigar smoke in the air, and an additional present under the tree.

Under the layers of wrapping and packing tissue was a glass box, about twenty inches high, and four to six inches deep. Stacey fumbled eagerly with the wrappings, and managed to get the box out. Inside the glass case, sealed in some preservative, were two long-stemmed roses, intertwined. A key was set into the base of the box. She turned it a couple of times, and began to cry as the music box inside stumbled through ''I Love You Truly.'' There was no card.

For the rest of the day she carried the case around with her, treasured in the crook of her arm. Occasionally she turned the key a few twists, just enough to get the first few bars of the old love song. Aunt Ellen kept to the kitchen, humming to herself as she heard the echo of the music box sounding from all over the house. Stacey took it to bed with her, nestling it on the empty pillow next to her own. At two o'clock in the morning she awoke to moonlight, and stood by the window looking eastward, clutching the encased roses in her hands.

But it was back to work the day after Christmas. She did not expect to see her tutor again until after the New Year, but she felt so badly about the exam that she pulled out all her reference books and buried herself in the work. The only interruption was the sound of the mailman's horn, as he announced a delivery at the roadside box.

"Somebody's got some mail," Aunt Ellen called out to her.

"I heard," she said wistfully. "For you, I suppose. I'll go and get it—I need the air." She struggled into the old sheepskin coat that hung by the side door. It's getting a bit straggly, she noted. And why not? You've had it for four years, girl. How about that? Six months ago she never would have noticed. Now she did.

A blast of frigid air slapped her in the face as she stepped down off the porch and headed for the mailbox. From the barn she could tell from the noise that the Morgans were back. Animals have to eat, no matter what the human holiday. A thin wisp of smoke shot up from the chimney of the house, to be instantly seized by the wind and torn to shreds. Stacey pulled her coat collar up tighter, and headed down the track.

There were four letters and two newspapers in the Rural Delivery box. Stacey crammed them into the capacious pockets of her coat and hurried back to the house. The wind was already finding the leaks between the loose buttons.

That same wind snatched the door from her hands as she came back up the steps, slamming it back against the doorstop with a thud. "You've got some mail," she called out as she dropped the envelopes on the table, shed her coat, and went back to deal with the door, two-handed.

Aunt Ellen brought in a mug of steaming coffee, and she accepted it gladly, using the heat from the mug to warm her hands. She sipped gently at it, daydreaming. Her aunt handed her an envelope. "This one's for you," she said.

The envelope had a return address on it: "School Department, Coryelle County." Stacey almost dropped the cup of coffee in her eagerness to open the letter. Tangled fingers tore at the seal and, after much fumbling, managed to extract the thin single-page letter.

"We are pleased to inform you," the letter said briefly, "that you have passed the High School Equivalency Test with a score of 97.8%. A certificate and a diploma will be mailed to you in due course."

Which meant after New Year, she told herself. Passed! After all that sweat and tears! Passed! She could not hold back. She flashed the letter under her aunt's nose, shrieked a couple of times in glee, and went over to the corner where all her books and work papers were settled. "No more!" she shouted at them, and hurled everything up in the air, to fall where it would. "I did it!"

"You did indeed!" Her aunt came over to join her, and the two of them danced together wildly around the room, until sheer exhaustion forced the older woman to call a halt. "If I get my breath back," Aunt Ellen threatened, "we'll have a celebration. I can make a cake, and—"

The telephone interrupted. It had stood silent for so many days that they were both startled. Stacey hesitantly picked it up and offered a tentative "hello".

"Stacey, this is Amie Moreland." She knew who it was before the name was announced; it was that kind of voice. "I understand that you heard from the school department?"

"Why, I—just this minute," Stacey stammered. "How in the world did you know?"

"Oh, I have spies everywhere," the woman chuckled. "Did you get a good mark?"

"I guess I did. I know I did! 97.8%! I think that's pretty high. And I want to thank you for all your trouble. Everything worked so nicely, and Mr Herndon was a real doll, and I wish you would send me the bill."

"I think it's already been paid," said Amie. "Out of your investment portfolio, or something. Well now, with that out of the way, are you prepared to go on? I mean with the plan you suggested?"

"Yes, more than ever. I suppose there's a waiting period—until next fall, perhaps?"

"No, I don't think so," Amie returned. "I talked to the Dean of Admissions at Baylor University, and he agrees that you could be accepted in probationary status, beginning in the spring term. It starts on January tenth. Too soon?"

"I—no. Wait just a minute, please." Stacey covered the mouth of the telephone. "Aunt Ellen, what's the date you have to go back to Houston?"

"On the sixth of January, dear. Does that make a problem?"

"No, not at all," she answered, and returned to the telephone. "That would be fine, Amie. What do I have to do?"

"On the seventh—that's a Friday—I want you to come to my office. By about nine o'clock, let's say. There'll be a young man here to guide you through the registration. And, Stacey, you'd better plan to stay in Waco during the week, and go home at the weekends. Is that satisfactory?"

"You mean you've already found me a place to stay?"

"Not exactly, dear. The dormitories are already filled to overflowing. But I can't believe that somewhere in this city of a hundred thousand people we can't find room for one girl student. Is that all right?''

"I—I think it's a minor miracle,'' Stacey returned. "I feel as if I'd found a fairy godmother, or something. I do thank you, Mrs Moreland—Amie—With all my heart. I'll be in your office by nine o'clock on the seventh. And thank you again.''

She hung up the receiver and went around for the rest of the day in a state of shock, treasuring her roses. On her way to bed that night, her ears filled with her aunt's congratulations, she changed into a warm flannel nightgown, and stood barefoot in front of the window, tracing star-patterns. You've taken the first two steps, she told herself. And maybe an inch or two more. You've studied, and been rewarded. You ought to be the happiest girl in the world. You should be sitting on top of Cloud Nine, singing two-part harmony with Stevie Nelson. Yes, you should!

She walked over to the bed and sat down on it, feeling the fingers of a dull headache reaching out for her. Yes, I should be the happiest girl in the world, she assured herself, through the dull throbbing pain. So how come I wake up every night, crying?

CHAPTER SEVEN

HER first three weeks as a university coed went by so quickly that Stacey had no time to assess her situation. And she learned a great deal in those weeks. She met Amie Moreland, a roly-poly raven-haired woman of about thirty. "Before I married I was a Lopez," she explained, laughing. "And my husband is of Norwegian descent. If all the children turn out to be blue-eyed blonds my mother will kill me! Are you settled in now?"

Settled in? That was a very large question. As predicted, there had been no rooms available in the dormitories, and nothing "suitable" within two square miles. "So, since Harry is in Europe, and that whole penthouse apartment is sitting there empty, you might as well move in."

She did so hesitantly, not working up the nerve to unpack her bags until the end of the second week. It was convenient, being only a few blocks from the campus, and it provided parking space for her car, and a uniformed guard at the entrance. But that big revolving waterbed carried too many memories with it. For the first week she hardly slept at all, lying back in the bed and letting it rotate across the Waco skyline all night long, until the swishing of the liquid soothed her to sleep.

She found it difficult to make friends at school. All the boys seemed too young, and all the girls were babblers. She was of their age, but not of their generation. Harry had spoiled all that for her. So she stuck her nose in the books, and came out only on Thursdays and weekends. The classes themselves were simple, a typical Freshman college curriculum: History, English, Spanish, Economics, and Accounting. But she found a tremendous problem disciplining herself to the school routines. After all, for more than four years she had been away from such things, on her own, and it was difficult to adjust.

At weekends she found the helicopter available to her, sitting on the pad by the building, with either Jim or John Morgan at the controls. They used the ride to Houston as a continuation of her flying lessons. She had already completed the ground instruction, and was well into flight training.

At the hospital, she found that her aunt was recovering slowly from her first operation, but was in good spirits. She spent all of Saturday there, getting the little odds and ends her aunt wanted, cheering her up, and taking voluminous orders about things to be done at home—which never were finished.

Then it was back to Waco late Saturday night. Sunday was her day of rest. She hardly felt the need of study time; her classes met on Monday, Wednesday, and Friday, with one odd two-hour meeting on Tuesday, and nothing on Thursday. After three months under Mr Herndon's whip, she found the college requirements fairly simple.

So on her day of rest she washed clothes, pottered around, went to church, toured some of Waco's entertainment spots, and thought about Harry. It was almost impossible not to, surrounded as she was by his work, his clothing, his books—everything. That last Sunday night, the first week of February, she ate a TV dinner, took a long bath in the hot tub, and then, physically exhausted, went to bed and fell asleep almost at once.

It was one of those typical Texas winter nights. The moon looked in coldly from the west, and a line of high clouds was edging in from the north. The temperature hovered around the freezing mark, and the wind blew hard.

About two in the morning a noise wakened her. It was the sort of indeterminable noise that one normally puts down to the wind, or a loose shutter. Stacey smiled at her alarm, turned over and started to drift back to sleep, when it struck her. A loose shutter in a penthouse? Come on now, Stacey! Both eyes snapped open, and she turned over on her back, searching the semi-darkness at the head of the stairs. There definitely was a noise.

Footsteps, thumping wearily upward from the apartment below! That's all I need to make my day, she thought—burglars in the middle of the night. It was a tough neighbourhood, trapped between the railroad tracks and the elevated highway, but surely with the guard downstairs—?

She watched, mesmerised, as the footsteps gained a shadow. An arm reached around the corner and snapped the switch that slowly turned the windows from transparent to opaque. Unconsciously she squashed herself up against the head of the bed, knees driven hard into her stomach. Panic rose to engulf her, blocking her throat, straining her breathing. She clasped her arms tightly around her knees, and sat there, shivering.

The shadowy arm moved again, this time to the light switch. The lights came up softly, as if the control knob had barely been turned. Her squeak of recognition alerted the man, and turned him in her direction.

"My God!" he roared. "So this is where you've been hiding!"

Stacey wanted to roar back at him—to roar and rant and rave, and tell him a few home truths. But nothing came out, except for a weak moan which even she could not recognise. And while her dazed mind tried to regroup its scattered senses, her fool body took command. She bounced off the bed and ran at him, smashing deep into the comfort of his arms.

Frantically she pressed closer, trying to be absorbed in him. Her arms snaked up around his neck, and she pulled herself up on to her toes. His shirt, under the unbuttoned gold of his jacket, was soaking up all the tears. Dry sobs hacked at her throat.

"There now, little lady," he crooned into the tangled mass of her hair. "There there now, love—I didn't mean to frighten you half to death."

One of his hands came up and toyed with her soft golden crown, fingering it like a comb, comforting. Gradually the sobs faded and the tears stopped, replaced by hiccups. He bent slightly and swept one arm under her knees, picking her up and cradling her against his chest as he stalked over to the bed and sat down there, with her shivering body resting on his knees.

"I didn't mean to scare you so," he repeated.

"You didn't scare me that much," she managed to get out. "it's just—oh, Harry, I've missed you so! I thought you'd forgotten me. And after the awful things I said, I couldn't blame you. Oh, Harry!" She nuzzled her face into his shirt again, trying to avoid the searching look in those dark eyes.

He pried her loose, forcing her head back so he could examine her face. One of his huge knuckles came gently up under each eye in succession, and wiped away the last hanging tear. "There now," he comforted. "I could never forget you, Stacey, never." He pulled her head against his chest again, resting that firm chin on top of her wild hair. "Better now?"

"I—yes," she managed weakly. "I didn't mean to usurp your apartment, but Amie said—"

"Ah—Amie said! Now there's a woman with a lot of explaining to do! Where the devil is she?"

"Amie? Why, she's on vacation. She and Karl went down to Brownsville. She said something about fishing. Karl loves fishing."

"Yes. And Amie hates it."

"Well, she said it was his vacation and they were going fishing, and besides, you're in Europe, and nobody has heard a word about when you're coming back, and—but you *are* back, aren't you?" Damn the man, she sighed to herself as she bit down on her tongue. Of course he's back. Why is it that whenever I see him I react like a ten-year-old moron? Babbling! Diarrhea of the mouth, her father used to say, teasing her. And no wonder he thinks I'm too young for him!

"Yes, I'm back," he chuckled. "In fact, I've been back for a week or so."

"For a week?" Indignation set in. "And just what the devil have you been doing, not telling anybody!"

"Hey, whoa! I'll tell you what I've been doing, you teasing little minx. I've been looking for you so I could tell you that I'm back. What a run-around you've given me, lady!"

Minx? Teasing? It suddenly came to her that she was dressed only in her nightgown. But it's a warm flannel, she told herself. It covers from neck to ankles, loosely. What the devil does he mean—tease? His free hand came up and perched a finger on the end of her nose, running slowly down across her parted lips, over her chin, into the valley between her half-exposed breasts, where she had failed to fasten any of the six buttons that formed her security guard.

"Oh, my!" Her squeak of alarm brought a laugh from him, and cured her hiccups. Her frantic fingers swarmed to her defence, fumbling at the tiny ivory buttons without success.

"Here, let me help." There was a dollop of sarcasm behind the words. One of his hands imprisoned both of hers, pulling them down into her lap. His other hand, coming completely around her, fumbled with the buttons, inhibited by the wrong angle, but still doing better than *she* had—but not without an occasional brush against the smooth softness of her breasts. Each little touch set her on fire, and she revelled in the feelings, admonishing herself that it was only by casual accident—until she became aware that no more buttons were being closed. Harry's hand had slipped under the yoke of her gown, and was claiming a hardened bronze peak as his prize. Lightning struck at her, a roiling feeling she had never felt before, starting at the captured fortress of her breast and running down into the pit of her being. Vague feelings of alarm were discarded, sent back into the limbo from which they had sprung. His fingers played lightly across her swollen breasts, teasing each one of them in turn.

She felt the coolness as one corner of her gown slipped off a shoulder, to be followed quickly by the other. Now both his hands roved free across her stomach and back, moving in gentle circles from her lips to her breasts, to the tips of her ears. And through it all she trembled more and more as the excitement fed on itself. She had difficulty breathing. Her lungs were no longer able to fill and expand.

She opened her mouth to complain, only to find he had been waiting for the opportunity. His lips came down on hers in the slow gentle movement of a giant wine-press, tantalising at first, then sealing her off from all the outside world. He tasted the honey of her, and strove for more.

Stacey gave herself up to the moment. The searing excitement heated, cooled, and reheated. It was something she had never thought of before, something for which she had never been prepared. This driving passion that demanded she make a gift of herself. A gift of herself? The thought was sobering. Her lips were still sealed by his, but she could feel some movement as one of his hands began to inch the hem of her gown up above her knees and across her thighs—and reason, regrettable reason, intervened.

"No!" she commanded softly as she struggled away from his relentless lips. She pushed herself away, bouncing as the water-bed responded. There was a dazed expression on his face as his hands continued their exploration, and then the stern craggy look returned, his hands made tender farewells. He took a deep breath, lifted her off his lap, and dumped her on the bed.

"No, of course not." His voice was gruff and strained, as if stopping had taken more energy than he had to give. "No, I'm sorry—I should have said it first."

Stacey struggled with her buttons, then moved a few feet farther down the bed, her shaking hands moving to her disarrayed hair, using it to hide her face.

"You don't need to apologise," she said, with a quiver in her voice. "It was as much my fault as yours."

"Don't be a fool," he snapped. "You're only eighteen!"

"Still the same old story, huh?" She glowered at him, biting on her lower lip to keep it from trembling. "Just a kid? Did you know that my mother was seventeen when she married, and only eighteen when I was born? Did you know that?"

"No, I didn't." His face was losing that fixed determined stare. There was even a tiny glint of humour in his eyes. "No, I didn't know that, and you're not your mother. Let's get away from this damn bed. I need to talk to you." He stood up and headed for the stairs leading down to the apartment proper. She watched him move—glide would be more like it. At least he's not mad at me—for the moment! She grabbed her old green robe, shrugging her way into it as she followed behind him. By the time she caught up he was in the kitchen, heating water for instant coffee.

He gestured her into the overstuffed chair on the other side of the coffee table, and sank on to the big couch. She did her best to look adult, brushing her hair away from her face, teasing it with her fingers until it fell in orderly waves down around her shoulders. He sipped once at the too-hot coffee, set the mug down on the low table, and looked at her.

"Well, I found her," he started out.

"Found who?" I don't want to admit an interest, she told herself fiercely. Why should I make it easy for some—good lord, she must be thirty or more—for some old bitch to take my place!

"Lisette," he said slowly. "Lisette Langloise, my grandmother's godchild. You surely remember her?"

"Oh, vaguely," she muttered. That's all I needed, just a little more time. Just enough for him to see that I'm not a child. Just a reasonable time for me to improve myself, to become more sophisticated! That had been the subject of her prayers for the last three months, just before she dropped off to sleep. Let him find her, Lord, but not right away. Give me time, Lord. Let him wait for me!

"Yes, I remember now. It was something about the will, wasn't it?"

"Oh, come on, Stacey." He was laughing at her again, or at least his eyes were. "You remember every single thing about it, don't you?" It wasn't really a question, it was a command.

"Yes," she sighed, "everything. Tell me what happens next?"

"So I brought her home. I found her in Paris, trying to live the good life. And someone else, too—I'll tell you about that later. Lisette is sick—a stupid thing. She says she had tuberculosis, but she won't let me call in a doctor. When I caught up with her she was in a hospital in the eighth Arrondissement. A charity patient, would you believe that!'

And that really pops my cork, Stacey sighed to herself. Had the woman come home beautiful, rich, poor, interesting—any of them I could have put up a fight against. But instead she had come home sick. He wouldn't turn a sick dog away—and now the beautiful Lisette Langloise would really get her hooks into him!

"She looks like death warmed over," Harry continued, musingly. The statement caught Stacey flatfooted. All her wild dreams had been about that moment of confrontation, when the gloriously beautiful Lisette was completely outfaced by the young but sophisticated Stacey Bronfield. She looks like death warmed over? I don't know whether to laugh or cry! So she did neither.

"That's too bad," she muttered, not too convincingly.

"Don't overwhelm me with your grief," he said sarcastically. "The girl is really sick." And how about *that*! Stacey told herself. Thirty years old, and still a *girl*. But also, no matter how much she wanted to, Stacey was unable to wish her opponent more suffering.

"I did mean it," she said, somewhat more convincingly. "What can I do to help?"

"I knew you'd say that!" he exulted. "I hate to keep coming back to you, but I need you again. I need you badly."

"Yes—well—" Almost she blurted out *and I need you too, Harry. Need you badly. I ache all over, from teeth to toenails, from needing you.* "Tell me what you want me to do."

"I don't know how to say it," he muttered, reaching across the table to snatch up her hand. "She's—

different, changed a lot from what she once was. That bastard she married cut her loose—divorced her—in Germany, and left her without a penny. She's had to hold her own without any help, and it's made her— well, hard is the word that fits, I guess. Last week when I brought her back to the house it took no more than two days for Millie Fallon to tell me she would rather quit than work for that woman. And the only thing that kept Frank from packing it in was that he was away most of the time, moving my remuda of Arabs."

"But sick people generally are hard to get along with," Stacey told him. "I'm sure Millie will make adjustments. Surely you don't want me to come out there and be your housekeeper?"

"But that's exactly what I do want," he said. For the first time that night his smile sprawled wide across his face. "With you in charge, there would be no doubt about who Millie was working for."

"Come on now," she retorted. "Look, it's three-thirty in the morning, and this girl has to be at work by eight-fifteen. Lay it on the line, Harry. You know darn well you could hire a dozen competent house-keepers, and ten thousand nurses, if you wanted them. Just what—"

"What the devil do you mean, *you have to go to work?* Has that damned accountant screwed up again? I'll kill that guy! What's happened!" It had taken only microseconds for the smile to disappear, to be re-placed by a glaring rage. I don't know what account-ant we're talking about, Stacey told herself, but he'd better buy a ticket to some faraway place, quickly. Harry looked as if he really *could* kill!

"No, it isn't whatever you're thinking," she snapped at him. "I don't mean I had to go to work to earn a living. I mean I—well, didn't Amie tell you?"

"Didn't Amie tell me what?" he roared again. She put both hands over her ears and ducked.

"Didn't she tell me what?" he repeated, at about forty decibels lower.

"I—I'm going to school," she stammered tentatively, and stopped to see if the tornado was about to strike again. He seemed calm—well, almost calm. A corner of his mouth was still twitching, and there was more red showing on his cheeks than she cared for. She tried one more step. "I—finished High School, and now I'm a freshman probationary student at Baylor." And then she ducked back out of the way. No explosion. In fact the news sent him back against the sofa, relaxed, and the smile returned.

"You're a co-ed?" he chuckled. "Stacey?" She nodded. "You can start breathing again," he added. "You're turning blue. I like the idea—grand!"

"Well," she amended, "it's only a trial, that's all. If I do well by May, then the Faculty Board will evaluate me, and—" Once again caution caught up with her. She was just about to mention that in May also she would be up for her pilot's licence, providing she could get another six hours of flight time in a fixed wing aircraft.

"Well, I'll be double-dyed and dipped in sheep grease!" It was very definitely a grin again, as big and as broad as the Panhandle. "I'm proud of you, lady."

"That's nice," she said, trying to restrain her own glee. "Now tell me why you can't just hire a housekeeper, since I'm not available—except on weekends, and on Thursday."

"That's just fine," he told her, "just fine. The house is near enough for you to commute with me in the mornings, and—"

"And that's stalling," she interrupted, wondering as she did so where she had got the nerve. "So just flat—out tell me what the score is, please."

"The score? Oh yes, the score." Somehow Harry had discovered something very interesting on the floor between them. His eyes refused contact, and she felt the insane urge to reach over, as he had done so often, to tilt up his chin and make him confront her.

"Well, the problem isn't so simple," he told the rug. "Lisette had a few days to think things over before we came home, and now she evidently thinks that both the house and I were left to her in the will. And that's something I don't want to encourage. Look, Stacey— I know it's beginning to sound old hat to you, but I need the protection of a wife in the house again!'

"Oh, no! Not that!" He looked up at her. His face was masked with a hangdog *I wish she would* look, while her fierce stare did its best to carve him up into tiny pieces. Then there was a twitching at the corners of both mouths, and they simultaneously broke out into laughter. At least Harry did. Stacey was caught in the middle of a wild rage of giggles by another massive hiccup, which entirely routed the solemnity. There were giggle-tears in her eyes when she finally was able to settle down again.

"It's four o'clock now," she told him, in her best James Bond imitation. "Synchronise watches. What's our cover story?"

"You read too much of the Fleming stuff," he chuckled. "Well, I think something simple. Millie and Frank have kept asking for you, and I've been telling them that you had to go to Houston to be near your aunt.''

"Oh, you knew about that, did you?'' she snapped, her eyes flashing again.

"Yes, I knew about that,'' he returned. "Cool off, banty hen. I arranged it. Your aunt and I have talked two or three times a week for the last four months. Strange she didn't tell me about your school, though. Well, it's not important. Here's our cover story. You had to be with your aunt last week—there were complications, or something. And you're coming directly back to Waco on Monday. I mean today—and then after school you're meeting me here at the office, and away we go. You're a *bona fide* student, God's in his heaven—and why don't we go get a couple of hours of shut-eye before we both have to go to work.''

They both stood up, and Harry opened his arms invitingly. Stacey accepted immediately, leaning against his shirt again, surrounding herself in the comforting warmth of him. "Your wife shouldn't let you go out with a wet shirt on,'' she murmured softly.

"What?''

"I said you just remember that I'm only a rental bride, not the real thing, Harry Marsden.''

"You mean I'm supposed to keep out of your bed?''

"That, and—and you're not to try to seduce me, whether it's in my bed or not. Right?''

"That's a hard bargain you drive,'' he said solemnly, and she leaned back to see if that sardonic gleam was in his eye. It was.

CHAPTER EIGHT

A COOL shower helped Stacey pry open her eyes in the morning, and killed her predilection to linger. The alarm clock had failed to go off; it was seven-forty-five in the moring. Harry was still asleep in the waterbed, behind that stupid barrier of pillows that had "protected" her from him all through the early hours. Ha! Protect indeed. How can you shut off your mind when he's lying there, not two feet away? She had tossed and turned all the remainder of the night, and cursed him heartily for being able to sleep so peacefully.

She slipped into the typical college uniform—worn blue jeans, a bulky sweater, and loafers. A quick brushing re-established order to her hair. She neglected everything else, stopping only to brush her teeth and steal a quick lingering look at Harry, and then dashed for the elevator. Naturally, on a day when she wanted to hurry, it was raining, a cold winter rain that bore the label "made in Ontario". And the car, sitting in the parking lot beside the building, refused to start.

What do you do with a car that won't start? Stacey knew a great deal more about cars now than she had three months ago, but was not about to be analytical. Either you loved it or you abused it! In her gloomy rain-ridden mind she was not about to spare a little love for an automobile. She banged the steering wheel three or four times, bruising the palm of her hand in the process, then applied half a dozen words she had heard when she was an "Army brat". The car was sufficiently impressed by it all, and started immediately. Her fingers tingled from the impact. She looked down, remembered, and blushed.

Harry had been in the bedroom when she came out of the shower, wearing a nightgown that clung to her now, due to the steamy bathroom. "That's what I forgot!" She held both palms up to her cheeks to hide the blush. "My rings! I—I threw them at you!"

"And I caught them," he chuckled. "I played short stop for SMU in my college days. Now, where the devil did I put them?" He fished in the pockets of his robe, and came out triumphantly.

"You kept them? You carried them around with you?"

"A fellow never knows when he needs a wife," he had said, pompously. "Now, let me see." He picked up her left hand and gently threaded her fingers through the two rings.

"Oh, but that's not—that's beautiful!" She held up her hand admiringly, watching the light sparkle from a delicate diamond-studded band next to the familiar wedding ring she had worn. "It's not—"

"No, it isn't Grandmother's ring," he said softly. "I could see you were upset by that ring. It was too garish—too ornate. But I saw this one in Dallas one day, and it was just like you, slender and sparkling with life. I just had to have it. Do you approve?"

"Oh yes." Her voice was as soft as a sigh running down the wind. His arms came around her, treasuring her. For just a moment she could almost think it was real. But the shadow of Lisette was too dark on her mind. She had to ask.

"Lisette," she questioned. "Did you love her very much?"

"Love her?" There was a stern strange look in his eyes as if he were seeing beyond them both, beyond the walls, beyond the years. "Stacey," he sighed, "I've only ever loved one woman in all my life."

And now, sitting in the car, the motor running, she was sorry she had asked. She shifted into gear, bucked and stuttered down to Fifth Street, drove under the shadow of the expressway, and found not a single parking space available on the campus.

Her bitterness bred defiance. She pulled up in front of the Administration building and parked in the spot marked "Distinguished Visitors". One of the campus police started in her direction, but she fled into the rain before he arrived. All of which brought her into Professor Calnan's class ten minutes late, soaking wet, and fully prepared to be the butt of all the "guinea-pig" jokes. Which she was.

By lunchtime her anger had boiled over twice—once at a perfectly innocent Junior who had been trying to date her for weeks, the other at her History professor, who had a somewhat limited view about the participation of women in the world's scene. The boy backed off quickly enough when Stacey flashed her rings under his nose, and mentioned how big her *husband* was. The professor also retired from the field, under her barrage of feminist responses. It didn't help that the rest of the class cheered her on. They would have done anything to break up a Monday morning lecture.

Which brought her to lunch. She could hardly face the thought of food, so she went back to the car, set-

tled back on one of the reclining seats, and promptly
went to sleep, missing both her afternoon classes.

What woke her up was a sharp movement of the car.
She sat up, startled, to find a tow-truck about to take
her and her car away to the impound centre. And that
was the last straw. She came out of the vehicle like an
avenging angel, stormed at the policeman, then spared
a little vitriol for the driver of the tow-truck. It had
been a long time since the US Army had used mules
for its artillery, but the mule-driving language still
persisted, as any Army brat could testify.

"And I wasn't parked," she finally threw at them
both, her face red with rage. "If you'd looked you
could have seen that I was trying to repair my car! But
you didn't look, did you? You didn't even know I was
in there!" And with that atrocious lie on her conscience she climbed back in the Eagle, waited barely a
moment for them to uncouple the cable, and drove
off. The black rage settled a few blocks away, when she
recognised that she was driving in the wrong direction, and was now in the middle of Oakwood Cemetery.

"Stop here!" she yelled at herself. The car swerved
to the kurb, almost at the feet of a startled mainte-
nance man. Stacey smiled sweetly at him, then started
counting backwards from two hundred down.

And thus back to the Marsden building, driving se-
dately, wondering how she might explain it all to
Harry.

It really didn't matter. Harry was in conference
when she arrived, and she spent another half-hour
reading old magazines in the waiting room. "And just
why am I worried?" she mumbled to herself. "I'm not

responsible to Harry. He's not my father or anything!''

"What's that?'' asked Amie as she came through.

"Nothing," mumbled Stacey. "I was talking to myself, is all."

"Well, he'll be another hour, at least," Amie returned. "He suggests that you go on up and have a nap. He'll come when he can."

But even in the soft comfort of the waterbed Stacey was unable to sleep. By the time Harry *did* come she had managed to convince herself that the whole terrible day was entirely his fault. As a result, the greeting he received was just this side of glacial, and the trip out to the mansion was made in complete silence. When he parked in front of the house he took her arm as she tried to climb out, and she was unable to escape.

"I can see something's wrong," he said, "and we'd better get it settled before we go in. Was it because of last night?"

He pulled her over against him, burying her head in his chest. For a moment she beat on him with her clenched fists. "It's all your fault," she sobbed. "Everything is all your fault!"

"Of course it is," he soothed, stroking her hair. "Everything is my fault. Tell me about your day."

She did, between tears and hiccups. All the details, including the sneer on the professor's lips, and the policeman's threat to have her arrested and locked up. "And he said I was a menace to society, and they would lock me up and throw away the key, and—"

"There, there," he sighed, squeezing her shoulder. "He won't do that—I won't let him. What else happened?'' Stacey poured the rest of her day on to his broad shoulders and then sat up and dried her eyes.

''I'm all right,'' she whispered to him, and knew she was. Nothing could touch her. He wouldn't let them!

''Sure you are.'' He handed her his big handkerchief. ''Blow.''

She sniffed a couple of times, ran a hand through her hair to straighten out the mess, adjusted her blouse, and folded her hands primly in her lap.

''Should I have changed?'' she asked in a very small voice.

''No,'' he returned. ''I doubt if Lisette is up.''

''Did you tell her about me?''

''Well, I—'' It was still light enough for her to see his face, as it flushed under the tan.

''You didn't, did you! I have to do that myself?''

''I'm afraid so,'' he mumbled. ''I seemed to have lost my courage when the time was right. You don't mind?''

''I don't mind,'' she sighed. ''It's just policemen and provosts and cynical professors that scare me.'' And you, when you're angry, she wanted to add, but dared not. ''I'm ready.''

It was like coming home. Harry held the door for her, and it seemed as if the house reached out to welcome her. Everything was as it had been; perhaps a little shabbier, a little more dusty—but home. She saw it all now with new eyes—the dark mahoganies of the panelling, the slightly curved main stairs, the bric-à-brac scattered throughout the hall. Paintings. She had seen them all before, but never noticed them. The Marsden family ancestors? A small sigh of contentment welled up as she looped her hand through the crook of his arm and just stared. He patted her hand like some proud proprietor, and smiled that teasing half-smile that transformed his face.

And that's something else, she told herself. He's becoming more handsome all the time! It must be the weather, or—or what? Lisette? Just the thought was enough to send little spasms of monstrous jealousy coursing through her. Her smile vanished and she withdrew her hand. Harry was about to say something when the kitchen door, under the stairs, banged with a vengeance, and Millie Fallon came surging out into the hall.

"And that's the last straw!" Millie yelled at him, her angular face riven by anger. "Up and down, up and down—you'd think I had a pogo stick, the way she wants and gives orders. Stood right here, she did, ordered her lunch in bed, then walked upstairs like some queen. There's nothing wrong with that girl, Harry, when you're not in the house! Well, not this time!"

She banged the heavy tray down on a side table and folded her arms belligerently across her bosom. And only then did she see Stacey, half hidden behind his frame. "Oh, my Stacey! Lord, it's good to see you back home! It must have been terrible having to nurse your aunt for such a long time. Welcome. Frank will be so tickled that you're back. He always did have an eye for the good-looking girls." She waded forward and embraced the younger woman, smothering her in aprons and love.

"Of course he does," Stacey chuckled. "That's why he married you!"

"When we get to the end of this meeting of the Mutual Admiration Society perhaps someone will tell

me what's going on? I didn't hire you out to wait hand
and foot on Lisette. What happened to the new girl?''

"Quit, that's what happened." Millie stepped back
from Stacey and glared at him. "I hired two of them,
to share the load. The first one quit at noontime, and
the second just walked out a few minutes ago. It seems
that our fair lady said some unpleasant things in very
foul language, then threw a pitcher of water all over
her.''

"But she's sick, Millie." Stacey did her best to pour
a little oil on the troubled waters, but it was plain that
the housekeeper was in no mood to be passified.

"Yeah, sick," she snorted. "She couldn't hardly eat
any dinner last night when Mr Harry was here. And
then as soon as he's out of the house she must have a
double snack, and a midnight supper, as well as half
a dozen drinks. And now look at this! She won't be
down for dinner tonight, she tells me, but will I please
send up—well, take a look.''

The tray was crowded. Harry snorted, and Stacey
giggled. A coffee pot and cup, a Bloody Mary in a
curved wine glass, two hefty roast beef sandwiches,
and a dozen assorted cookies.

"It looks as if she has consumption instead of TB,"
Stacey commented.

"That's a lousy pun," he snapped. "I'm sure there's
some reasonable explanation.''

"I'm sure there is too," grated Millie. "Why don't
you take this tray up and ask her?''

"All right, all right." Stacey stepped between them.
"Retire to a neutral corner, both of you. I'll take it up.
Put my jacket away, Millie?''

"Oh, love," the housekeeper sighed, "I didn't mean to get you into the puddle, and on your first night home, too."

"Don't be a ninny," Stacey returned. "That's my job, isn't it? Who's the mistress of this house?"

"Well—why, of course you are. Here, let me take that. Harry, look at this coat! Aren't you ashamed of yourself, having your wife run around in rags and tatters? And those blue jeans—lordy, I've seen prisoners working on the road gangs in better clothes than that!"

"Don't look at me," Harry laughed. "I don't have a thing to say about what she wears—or much else around here, apparently. But come right back, wife. We'll have our dinner in the—"

"In the kitchen, Millie," Stacey interrupted. "There's no need to carry all those dishes to the dining room when there's only the family. You lay the table, set the food on the stove, then you and Frank go take a night off. I'll take care of everything else."

"Why, indeed you will," the housekeeper chuckled. "How you've changed! You were only a slip of a girl when you first came, and now look at how you've grown!"

Stacey was juggling the tray when the unexpected compliment caught up with her. She looked around quickly to surprise a strange look on Harry's face, a look she could not identify. But it quickly fled, to be replaced by one of his "I am King of the Hill" expressions. She winked at Millie anyway, and started up the stairs.

The tray was heavy, one of the old silver services his grandmother had treasured but had never taken out of the china closet. And that's another problem, Stacey noted. All of a sudden there's a panoply of glory around the place. More of Harry's doings? Are we celebrating the greening of Lisette Langloise? "Well, I hope it chokes her," she muttered, then stopped in midstride to berate herself. "That's the way children talk," she lectured. "If you expect Harry to think you've grown up you have to prove it!" And there's no argument there, she assured herself bitterly. Nevertheless, she rested the tray for a moment on a chair in the hall, ran a quick hand through her hair, brushed down her blouse, and checked all the buttons. Then she plastered a smile on her face, turned the door knob, and carried the tray into the bedroom.

It was the same room that Grandmother Marsden had used for so long, the room in which she had had her first and last look at the indomitable old woman. There had been a massive rearrangement. All the drapes and heavy furniture were gone, replaced by light modern things, flower-sprayed wallpaper, concealed lighting, and a Hollywood type queen-sized bed.

And the queen bee was sitting beside the bed, prepared to sting!

"Oh, good heavens, another ragbag! Don't they have anyone in that kitchen who knows how to dress?" The voice might once have been a lovely soprano, but now it cracked and was hoarse. It emanated from a tiny body, hardly more than five feet tall, slender as a willow, with a dark thin face surrounded by a halo of raven hair. The woman wore the gamine look of a Parisienne, outfitted in harem pyjamas with a light negligee thrown over the whole.

Stacey set the tray down on the table in front of the dormer window and turned around. "Miss Langloise? I'm—"

"Mrs Burnet," the other woman snapped. "Mrs Burnet. Call me ma'am. Doesn't anybody ever teach you girls anything? Don't you own a dress?"

Stacey looked down at her own extended hand and laughed. Six months ago she would have been in tears, terrified out of her mind. But now it was just funny.

"Mrs Burnet? OK. That makes it easier, I suppose." She looked down at her ragged jeans. "Perhaps I should have changed." She smiled, remembering the conversation downstairs. "But then again, I only dress to please Harry, you know, and he was perfectly content with these. The coffee is very warm. Do you want me to pour you a cup? I can only stay a minute, but perhaps that's enough time for us to get acquainted."

"Don't count on it," Lisette snapped. "You don't seem any better than the other two. What happened to them?"

"Oh, they both quit their jobs," Stacey said quietly. "Of course I'll have Harry find them something else to do. Nobody ever loses their job in Marsden Enterprises."

"Whatever in the world are you talking about?" There was more than puzzlement on Lisette's face; there was the beginning of anger. Her rather ordinary face began to glow from the inside, adding a look of sensuous beauty. There! That's what attracted Harry, she told herself. She's beautiful when she's angry, and I expect that's most of the time. I've only ever loved one woman in all my life—isn't that what Harry said? And this must be the one.

"All right, who are you?" Lisette's snarl snapped Stacey back to attention.

"Me? My name is Marsden," she lied. It was becoming easier, much easier. "Stacey Marsden. I thought you knew."

"No, I don't know." Stacey could actually see the wheels revolving in the older woman's brain, as she ran through the geneology of the family. "Stacey? Stacey Marsden? I don't remember anyone by that name in the family, and I knew them all. What the hell is this? Some sort of a con game?"

"I don't think so." Stacey busied herself around the bed, picking up discarded magazines, emptying an over-flowing ashtray into the wastebasket, keeping her head down. "Perhaps you'd recognise me better by my formal name? I'm Mrs Harry Marsden."

The screech that followed shook the heavy windows in their ancient casings. "You're a damn liar!" the other woman shouted. She staggered to her feet, glaring enough to kill. "Nobody does that to me—nobody!"

"Then I guess I don't know what your problem is," Stacey answered quietly. "Harry and I were married just before his grandmother died. It's been some time. We had been hoping that by this time I would be—well—of course, there's no way to guarantee that!" Stop padding your part, her conscience nagged at her. If you get yourself tangled up in the "patter of little feet" routine, there's no telling where it all will end! Keep to the straight and narrow. Uncle Henry had said that once—if you have to lie, keep it simple. And who would know better than Uncle Henry? "Are you not really feeling well, Mrs Burnet?"

"No, I'm not feeling well. Help me get back to bed. I've—I must be having a reaction to the medicine." Sure you are, Stacey chuckled to herself. But you're not taking any! She moved, nevertheless, and helped the other woman under the covers. As she looked down at the troubled little face she felt just a touch of sympathy, but she drew herself up fiercely. It's Harry she wants, she told herself grimly. *My* Harry. Anything goes. All's fair in love and whatever! She patted down the blankets, checked to make sure that the push-bell was near to hand, and started for the door. Behind her in the bed she could hear a mumbling, rising in volume but still incomprehensible. Without looking back, Stacey lengthened her stride and hurried out of the room.

Just in time, apparently. Something crashed against the other side of the door she had just closed behind her. She leaned against it, half in tears, half in laughter, clutching at her stomach to still the aching created by giggles. "The medicine's too strong for you, baby, isn't it?" she commented, and made her way around to the other wing, where her own little suite— and Harry's—waited.

It was a strange evening that followed. Stacey shared a homey dinner with Harry, serving his plate directly from the stove, wishing she could produce as nice a meal as Millie had left. After dinner they stacked the dishes in the dishwasher, and prepared a light tray for Lisette—a vegetable salad, a paper-thin slice of steak, a spoonful of mashed potatoes garlanded with a cherry at its peak, and a pot of tea.

"That looks just what an invalid ought to eat," Harry commented, clapping her on the shoulder. She knew he was being gentle, but her shoulder almost collapsed.

"Then why don't you take it up?" She turned her head away quickly to hide the smile, but it felt as if he were boring holes in the back of her neck, understanding her every ploy before it was executed.

"Don't be sarcastic, Kitten, it doesn't become you. She *is* an invalid, you know."

"I know she is. And don't call me Kitten—I hate that. That's *her* name." Stacey was applying her father's axiom: the best defence is a good offence. But Harry was insufferably unconquered. Damn the man!

"Why not both of us together?" he suggested. "Togetherness? Love and closeness, all that?"

"Why not?" she muttered. Indeed, why not. It ought to be worth the price of admission. She picked up the tray, a light plastic one she had resurrected from under the kitchen counter, and started for the stairs. Harry relieved her of the weight, using one hand, and slipped the other around her waist as they went up the stairs, side by side. His touch startled her, but there was something more than that. Her eye was on the tray as they climbed, and at the very second his hand closed on her waist, the tray in his other hand jumped and almost spilled the teapot off on to the rug. So there, she told herself! He's not all that impervious after all!

They went into the room the same way, he with his arm tightened around her slenderness, she handling the doorknob as if it might explode in her face.

It was an entirely different woman that she saw. Still reclining in bed, with two pillows at her back, Lisette Burnet had changed into a very demure granny gown, high-buttoned and flower-decorated. Her hair sparkled from brushing, her face was carefully and smoothly made up, and she had become the perfect picture of an enticing invalid.

"Harry," she cooed, "how nice of you to go to all this trouble! And your little wife, too. I was so surprised when I met her this evening—she seems like such a lovable child. And you both brought my dinner. I don't have much of an appetite, of course."

Harry busied himself setting up the tray on her knees, all solicitude and charm. Stacey gritted her teeth and went over to draw the curtains. By the time she returned they were deep in conversation, the "do you remember when" type, that filled the air with names and times and places, all strange to Stacey. Once Harry made an attempt to draw her into it, but Lisette quickly manoeuvred around the subject to exclude her again.

Oh well, she told herself, what would you expect? They grew up together. But what an act that is! All love and delight. To give her credit, in the soft light of the lamps the older woman did not look her age. The lighting and her make-up had done wonders. *Now, Stacey,* her conscience tickled, she's ill—you can see the marks of it on her face. Her hair is fading from it. She deserves the comfort. And if I were the Christian I was raised to be, I'd be helping, instead of standing here like a blithering idiot, berating her.

In a blush of guilt Stacey looked around for something to do. They were too engrossed now to remember she was present. The closet doors stood open, and clothes were strewn around in heaps. She didn't just accidentally find that demure little nightgown, Stacey told herself, as her fingers busied at smoothing and sorting and rehanging. And then there was the silver tray to be squared away. Empty, she noted. All the sandwiches and cookies gone, the pot drained—and now she's struggling with the dinner!

"It's just too much for me," Lisette sighed. "I have so little appetite these days, Harry."

"Of course," he returned heartily. "That's to be expected. But you have to keep your strength up. These mashed potatoes are a delight. She puts a little cheese in them, and a touch of some herb that I don't remember. Open up."

My God, he's going to hand-feed her, Stacey muttered to herself. What a glorious act this is! But why does it bother me, that's the question. Why? It wouldn't have taken her more than a minute or two to wrestle with the problem and find an answer. But she also knew it was an answer she didn't want to hear, so she pushed it away.

The pair of them were at it again, bent close to each other in the lamplight. Occasionally Harry would make some soft comment, underlined by his deep bass chuckle. And Lisette would counterpoint with her high shrill soprano. The only interruptions came when Lisette stopped to light another one of her interminable cigarettes. One for my side, Stacey mused; Harry really hates to see women smoking. She hugged that tiny bit of warmth to her as the recollections dragged on. But eventually it all began to get under her skin. The game had sounded fine the first time around, but now its ragged edges were beginning to show. After all, it had been Lisette who had gone away. I wish I knew more about that, Stacey thought, but I've had about as much of this as I can stand for one night.

She tapped Harry on the shoulder. He turned around, looking as if he were startled to see her, as if he had forgotten her existence. "It's been a long day," she said quietly, "and I still have a load of studies to work through. If you two will excuse me, I'll take this tray down to the kitchen and clean up."

"Studies?" Lisette looked up at her with an eager smile.

"Yes," Harry responded. "Stacey is enrolled at Baylor. We thought she ought to finish up, but Grandmother wouldn't hear of delaying the wedding. She wanted so much to see it accomplished." He checked his wristwatch. "And I guess it's late enough for both of us to bustle off. Get your beauty sleep, Lisette. I'm not going in to work tomorrow, so we'll have plenty of time to talk."

"You could stay, Harry," the woman invited. "I'm sure your bride won't be able to do much studying with you around."

"Yes, well—perhaps," he laughed. "But to tell the truth, I—er—help her out. After all, we've only been married a few months, Lisette. You get your rest."

"If you insist, Harry." The words were buttery. Nothing that Harry wants can be wrong! Stacey stumbled for the tray, only to have it taken from her immediately. But before she could sort out the dishes to be carried down, he swept her up in his arms, brooded over her for a moment, then leaned down to seal her lips with his. Whatever it had been meant to be—deception, greeting, whatever—it turned itself into a fiery volcano of passion that left her hanging in his arms, gasping. And over his shoulder she could see a very thoroughly dissatisfied Lisette, glaring at them both.

"Excuse us," Harry called over his shoulder as he helped Stacey to the door with one hand, and balanced the silver tray in the other. "We'll see you in the morning, my dear."

My dear? After withering me with that—that kiss, he calls *her* my dear? Why, I'll— Whatever it was she would, Harry squeezed it all out of her with a massive hug that left fingerprints on her ribcage, and hurried her out of the room and down the hall. She forced him to a stubborn stop at the head of the stairs.

"We're off stage now," she snapped at him. "Let me go, you monstrous—"

Harry put one finger over her lips. "She has remarkably good hearing," he whispered in her ear. "Was there something wrong with that kiss?"

"You know darned well there wasn't, you—you lecher," she snapped. "It was that whole ball of wax in there. Gee, do you remember? What is it she's trying to do—lure you back into your cage, or something?"

"I do believe you're jealous." He chuckled softly, as if the idea were very pleasant to him.

"Jealous be darned," she snarled. "Oh, my dear Harry!" She did her best to mimic Lisette's trill. "And after that you display your gorilla act. What the devil do you think I am, made of cast steel or something?"

"Did I hurt you?" He was all solicitude, but somehow or another she got the impression that it was all a put-on.

"No, you didn't hurt me," she raged. "You only managed to crack two or three ribs, I think."

"Good Lord, did I?"

"Yes, you did!" It was hard not to giggle, even though her side was truly bruised. There was such a twinkle in his eyes, and his voice dripped honey all over the conversation. He set the tray down on the rug and pulled her around to face him.

"Honest Injun?" he asked solemnly.

Stacey nodded her head. Before she could react further Harry swept her off her feet and went stalking down the corridor to the other wing, where their suite was arranged. The door was open. he closed it behind them with a hard click of his heel, fingered the overhead lights on, and carried her over to the four-poster.

"Now what in the world are you doing!"

"Checking up," he said briefly. "It doesn't pay to have an injured member in the cast. Especially when it's the star of the show." He dropped her unceremoniously on top of the bed and watched while she bounced and vibrated.

"That's a rotten thing to do," she snapped at him. "I might have a punctured lung or something. Leave me alone!"

"Maybe," he mused. He put one hand flat on her chest, just below her throat, and held her in place while the other hand tugged the tails of her blouse free from her jeans and began to unsnap the line of buttons that held it closed.

"What are you *doing?*"

"I'm looking for bruises," he replied mildly, as his hands continued on their errand. "No time for a bra today, love?"

"Mind your own business," she retorted stiffly. She was doing her best to discipline a recalcitrant body, and not having a great deal of luck at it. Every spot his fingers touched seemed to catch on fire, the whole feeling gathering together quickly into a massive firestorm that was beyond her control. But control she must! Don't think about it, her conscience dictated.

Count. Count to a thousand! She started off, but lost her place somewhere beyond eleven, when one of his hands turned her on her side, cruising just over the tip of her breast to do so.

"Yes, I *did* do something," he commented, tracing a finger around the sore area. "That's terrible. I just don't seem to know my own strength."

"You can say that again," Stacey gritted through clenched teeth. "Now will you let me be?"

"An ice pack," he continued, as if she had said nothing. "That's what we need."

"I don't need an ice pack," she screeched at him. "What I need is a great deal of privacy!"

"Yes, well, that's something that's hard to come by," he chuckled as he gently pulled her blouse back together and re-buttoned it. "Try a cold shower."

"I don't need a cold shower for my bruises," she stormed at him.

"Not for your bruises, but you do need a cold shower." His fingers tilted her chin up so she was forced to look into his eyes. "You're shaking like a bowl of jelly. Just look at you!"

She jerked away from him. "Please get out of here and leave me alone!" she snapped.

"Of course," he said softly, dropped the teasing tone that had aggravated her so much. He walked over to the door, then came back. "I don't know how you feel about Lisette, but you were surely a shock to *her*."

"I—I did all right? I'm not much of an actress."

"You did more than all right," chuckled Harry. "You were superior. I'm afraid, in all the confusion, I haven't told you often enough how well you play your part, Stacey. You fit in perfectly. It means a lot to me." He sat down at the foot of the bed, and strangely enough, it didn't seem to bother her.

"You and Lisette—you were close?"

"When we were kids, yes. After she got to high school it was a different story. But yes, we were close. She was important to me—still is, I guess."

"Still important to you? So important that you had to hire a bride for protection?" It was hard for her to keep the bitter edge off the words.

"Important, yes. But marriage never entered my thoughts. She and I have often agreed to differ about that subject. No, what I meant was that Grandmother left me a charge in regard to Lisette, and I want to do everything I can to make it all come out right for her. Up to a point, that is. And that's where you come in. You know, Stacey, you *have* changed a great deal in these past few months. Amie told me about your ambitions. It's good to see you take control of your own life. And before you ask, no, I don't think of you as some child cluttering up the landscape. Does that make you feel better?"

"Yes!" She managed a smile. "And you didn't really break my ribs—I was just angry."

"I know. But you'd better get some rest, and do that studying of yours."

"I made that up," she said shyly. "It's English tomorrow—Emerson and the New England poets. I read all that years ago. And Mr Herndon snapped the whip over my head about it just a little time ago. After Mr Herndon, this college material is a snap."

Harry smiled at her enthusiasm. "Mr Herndon?"

"My tutor. I—somebody hired him to tutor me, so I could qualify for my High School Equivalency exam. He's a nice man."

"Oh, I know that," he chuckled. "He was the Assistant Superintendent of schools in Waco before he retired. What other little gimmicks are you working on?"

"Nothing," she half whispered. "I just want to get my degree, that's all."

"Come to think of it," he mused, as he got to his feet, "I made a small mistake there. Amie didn't tell me about your ambitions, she told me about your immediate goals. Which means there's something more behind all this sudden spurt of work, isn't there? Care to tell me about it?"

"No, I don't think I do," she said primly. "I mean there's nothing else—and if there were, perhaps I wouldn't care to tell you about it. I'm entitled to my own secrets."

"Methinks the lady doth protest too much." Harry touched one finger lightly on the tip of her nose. "Get on with it," he concluded. "The world opens up to the educated. And whatever your ambition, I wish you well of it."

Me too, thought Stacey, as he strolled through the door. Me too. And I can't possibly tell you. How do you go about stating your final objective to the one who is it—your final objective, that is?

It's a strange, upsetting household, she mused. But no matter how many troubles there are, I can't help smiling. The world seems—better, over here. And I don't know why. Don't I? She was singing an advertising jingle as she picked up her night things and went into the bathroom. Cold shower, indeed! She giggled at the idea, and after a long warm dousing, gave it a try. The water came out as cold as a Witches' Sabbath, and she was unable to find the faucet handle to turn it down. Shrieking and laughing at the same time, she stumbled out of the shower cubicle into a huge warm towel held by huge warm hands.

"You're red all over," Harry commented solemnly as he rubbed her briskly.

"A real gentleman would never have looked," she snapped at him. But her heart wasn't in the squabble. It's no use fighting against him: that was the one conclusion that the cold shower had brought her to. Let be what will be—that was another saying of her father's. And now Harry bundled her into the towel as if it were a sarong, then pulled another towel from the warming rail and swathed her hair in it.

"What's this all about?" she asked, warm again under the massage that continued through the towels.

"I went downstairs," he said, "and then I remembered something important I'd forgotten to tell you about. As I came back up I noticed that our house guest was out and wandering."

"So you came immediately into my bathroom?"

"Our bathroom," he corrected. "Now come on— show time!"

He pulled her out into the bedroom, teasing and tickling as they went. They fell in a heap on the foot of the bed. Harry was on the bottom, still massaging her hair. Stacey, on top, wiggled to get free, not really meaning it. In her exertions the knot on her towel slipped, and it fell to her waist, leaving her almost nude, sitting in his lap and giggling happily. He took one more swipe at her hair and flicked that towel away on to the floor. His hands came down hungrily on her bare shoulders, manipulating her against his soaked shirt. And at that moment the door opened, and Lisette came in.

They both stopped their game and stared at her. Lisette's eyes inspected them carefully, swung to the mussed bed, and returned. "Well, I *am* sorry," she drawled. "I was exploring the house for old times' sake, and I didn't realise that you—"

"Lisette," said Harry reproachfully, moving one hand to restore Stacey's towel, "surely you can see we're—occupied at the moment. Would you excuse us, please?"

The older woman was definitely not pleased at the tableau. To emphasise the point, one of his hands came around under the curve of Stacey's breast, and hovered there. She did her best to contain her reflex action, but it was a hard struggle. Lisette stared at them both for another moment, then turned slowly and went out, slamming the door behind her.

"Okay, you can breathe now," he chuckled.

"What?"

"You're turning blue, love. Start breathing, or I'll have to apply the kiss of life. Is that what you want?"

"Huh? Oh no—certainly not! Let me down, please, and—" again that telltale squeak of alarm—"I mean *with* the towel too! I'm not running a free peep-show!" She stomped over to the other side of the bed and perched there. "And that's another thing," she stated flatly.

"What? Locks on the doors? No peeking until Sundays?"

"No, silly. That waterbed has got to go!"

"What in the world brought that into the conversation?"

"Never you mind. Just mark it down in your little book. The waterbed has got to go! You hear?"

"I imagine that everybody in McClennan County can hear. Okay, the waterbed has got to go. Seasick, were you?"

"No. You knew she'd come up here to my—to our bedroom, didn't you!"

"Yes."

"Rat! What was it that you wanted to tell me?"

"Oh, I almost forgot again. Seeing little Miss Langloise pussyfooting down the hall knocked it out of my mind."

"Mrs—little Mrs Burnet," corrected Stacey. "She gave me what-for when I used the wrong title."

"Ah. And what did you tell her?"

"I told her that I was big Mrs Harry Marsden. She didn't seem to like that. What was the other thing?"

"The other thing? Oh Lord, yes—the other thing." Harry picked himself up from the bed and moved gingerly over to the rickety chair. "As you must know," he continued, "I hired a firm of international private detectives to run—Mrs Burnet to ground. And while I was at it I had them keep an eye open for your Uncle Henry."

"Henry Delano?"

"The very man."

"And?"

"And I met him in Paris too. We had a long talk. He's not as mean a man as he used to be—having a packet of money seems to have lessened his animosity. Did you know that he took you for almost seven hundred thousand dollars? He's invested it comfortably in French government securities, and is living with a woman near the Paris Opera House."

"What should I say? That's nice? Or something like that? Was George there?" She sounded calm, she thought. Good! How sophisticated did you have to be?

"No, evidently he dumped George, who's still somewhere in Texas, I'm told. But the old man was prepared to make some amends, providing you don't try to get him extradited to stand trial."

"I don't care what becomes of him," Stacey said quietly, "just as long as he stays far away. That's all I want. Aunt Ellen—she hasn't said a great deal, but I suspect she would like to be free of him."

"Yes, I thought so myself. So I took it upon myself, acting as your husband, to assure him that if he co-operated, nothing further would happen."

"If he co-operated in what?"

"Well, he gave me a few papers that I brought back—affidavits, birth certificates, marriage licences—"

"Whoa—say that again! Marriage licences—plural?"

"That's right. Would you believe it, your Uncle Henry married your aunt without getting a divorce from his first wife. I've got it all in writing, at the office."

"And that means?" asked Stacey.

"And that means that if she wants it, your aunt can have her marriage annulled. In fact, I've got a lawyer friend who could take it in hand and get it over with before she finished her last operation. How about that?"

"Oh, you wonderful man!" She jumped up from the bed and threw herself at him, losing the towel in the process. His arms came around her again. "You wonderful man!" she repeated.

"Yes, aren't I?" he said in that wondering voice. He looked down her long lush nude frame, and moistened his lips desperately. "Lord, I've got to get out of here!" he groaned, and ran for the door.

CHAPTER NINE

THAT first week of living at Rosedale with Lisette was like taking up housekeeping on a roller-coaster. Stacey was hardly back from school for more than half an hour on Wednesday before she discovered that her guest had given up being an invalid and was downstairs, dressed in slacks and see-through blouse, giving orders which Millie was decidedly refusing to take.

"I take orders only from Mrs Marsden," Stacey heard as she came down, having showered and changed. "She's the mistress of the house, until I hear different from the mister."

"We'll see about that—oh, hello Stacey." The voice was shrill. Lisette had a half-filled glass of something in her hand, twirling it nervously so that the ice cube rang against the sides. Stacey checked the clock. Four-thirty, time for at least one of the chores she had set her mind on.

"Hello," she offered quietly, then turned to the house-keeper. "You got my note about the upstairs hall? And a new girl?"

"Yes," Millie returned, "I did manage to get a local girl, but she wants to live in. A hard worker, with plenty of references."

"Live in? Sounds like a good idea. But you must warn her that it may only be temporary. These choc-olate chip cookies are delicious, Millie. Well, I've intended to dust that bric-à-brac cabinet of Grandmother's ever since I first saw it, and today's the day. Care to give me a hand, Lisette?''

''Me? What a laugh! No, you go right ahead and get it all cleaned up for me.'' There was a taunting laugh behind the words as she slurped at the glass. ''It won't be long before it's all mine, all this.''

''Well, you're half right anyway,'' Stacey commented grimly. ''Where are those dust-cloths, Millie?''

That had been only the first week. By Friday night of the third week Stacey was totally discouraged. ''I don't think I can last out the whole three months,'' she told Harry that night in the privacy of their room. ''She picks at everything I do, but won't offer a hand to help at all. And you noticed at dinner tonight? Every chance she gets, I'm a child. I just hope for your sake, Harry, that I can hold my temper.''

He shifted his weight in the big chair. That's *one* thing I've accomplished, she told herself—scouring the house to replace the dainty furniture with something substantial for him! ''Don't hold back on my account,'' he said from behind his newspaper.

Funny I hadn't noticed that before, she told herself. Every night he hides behind his paper. I never get to see his face at all. And he pays my complaints about as much attention as they're worth—which is nothing! What is this? Some kind of message he's sending me? Don't tread on my Lisette?

She piled her knitting back into its bag and moved over to the footstool beside his chair, ready to fire a salvo in the war—well, at least the skirmish—for his attention.

"Did you know she spent the entire afternoon today in your study, making telephone calls? The bill this month will be out of this world."

"Uhuh." The paper did not come down, but it did rattle a bit as he changed pages.

"And she keeps asking me about the Delanos. Did you tell her about Uncle Henry?"

"Uhuh."

"Does that mean that you did?"

"Uhuh."

"She was terribly angry when Frank told her she couldn't ride the one Arab mare that's still here. He told her the horse wasn't well, and he was putting a hot poultice on her foreleg. But Lisette wouldn't take that for an excuse. She said she was going to ride the mare anyway."

"Uhuh."

"But I don't think the animal will ever recover. Very few do, after a crocodile bite, you know."

Harry lowered his paper with a great sigh and folded it carefully into its proper sections. "Why are you looking for a fight tonight?" he asked mildly. "The way you keep nagging at me I might as well be married."

Stacey's face turned a brilliant red. The idea had tremendous appeal, even though that wasn't what she had in mind when the discussion started. "You weren't listening to a thing I said," she snapped. "I'm certainly learning a great deal around here. Everything *not to do* when I really get married!"

"I heard every word," he sighed. "Every word. Lisette is running up the telephone bill. Yes, she was present the first time I met your Uncle Henry, but that's all she knows about it. And you don't have to worry about the mare. Frank is taking her over this afternoon.''

''Over where?''

''Over to Rancho Miraflores, of course. Where all the others have gone. Don't you keep in touch with your own ranch?''

''I—I've been busy—you know that! Why to— what's going on?''

''I explained it all once before,'' he said quietly. ''Rosedale is all Lisette has left in the world. That bum she married left her nothing. As soon as the three-month period is up, she'll want to sell Rosedale, and I can't blame her.''

''You mean you'd give all this up? You never explained any such a thing to me, Harry Marsden. That's one of the problems around here. You never explain anything to me—not anything. Tell me about the Arabs!''

''Well, I didn't want to catch them up in all the confusion of changing home pastures in the middle of May, so I've had them all shipped over to your ranch. Westland Cattle informed me that the new barn and paddocks were ready.''

''Without even consulting me?''

''You did give me your general power of attorney,'' he reminded her. ''You want me to tear it up?''

''I—no. Dear Lord, no! I'm not *that* independent-minded.'' Stacey edged her footstool an inch or two closer, and put her folded arms on his knees. ''Harry?'' she asked tentatively. He smiled.

''Harry? What do you really do for a living? *Really,* I mean. How come your offices are in the choice spot at the top of the building, with a penthouse, no less?''

"Mostly because I own the building, Stacey. And a couple of other properties."

"Oh, is *that* it! Of course, I should have guessed—Marsden Management. You manage real estate!"

"I guess you could say that," he chuckled. "Satisfied?"

"I—I guess so." For the moment, you mean, her conscience dug at her. There are a million things more I'd like to know, but haven't the courage to ask. Now if I were a real wife I wouldn't stop until I knew everything about him. Look at me. I know what he likes for breakfast, what size all his clothes are, which silly gossip makes him angry, how his left eyebrow cocks up just the slightest when he's really puzzled. I know everything about him except where he's at. Isn't that silly? I'll never know him better until we share a—but that was asking too much. She pushed away from him and went back to her knitting. He watched her flying fingers, then added, "And by the way, there aren't any crocodiles in the Western Hemisphere, only alligators." And with that he dodged behind his paper again.

Stacey was still making her regular trips to Houston. Jim Morgan brought the helicopter up to the house. She was sure this time—he was wearing a T-shirt with his name scribbled on the chest.

Aunt Ellen was as chipper as one could ask. "I'm ready for the second transplant," she gurgled. "Would you believe it, me looking forward to an operation? They're going to take this little piece of skin from the inside of my arm and replace that little section there—" She gestured awkwardly to the tiny section of her cheek still marked by the raspberry birthmark— "and then maybe that will be that. Stacey, I've met some of the nicest people you ever could see. There's a man who—but of course, that's out of the question.''

''Isn't there a phrase about striking while the iron's hot?'' Stacey laughed as she told her aunt all about Henry Delano. When she had finished she noted a glisten in the older woman's eyes. ''It doesn't please you?''

''It pleases me very much,'' her aunt sighed. ''I thought there might never be a way to be free of him, but then I had no reason to want to be free. I had no other plans, but—does this all sound confusing?''

''Not at all, love. Shall I tell Harry to go ahead full speed?''

''Yes, please, Stacey. My, how much that man has done for us! Your father would have been very pleased with your selection of a husband. You must treasure him, girl.''

That phrase stuck in Stacey's mind all the way back to Waco, flying in the darkness under IFR—Instrument Flight Regulations—in order to complete her licence requirements.

''Bang on the nose,'' Jim told her as she flashed on the landing lights and made an approach to the pasture behind the house. ''Suppose I make an appointment for you for next month?''

''Do you really think I'm ready, Jim?''

''John,'' he corrected. ''I had to borrow Jim's shirt this morning. Our laundry problem seems to be growing, now that you're not around any more. Yes, you're more than ready. Why don't you get in some solo time? There are three choppers and four fixed wings down at the airport. Just go down there and introduce yourself.''

It was the start of a new adventure. On Tuesday, when she had only one early class and one late one, and on Thursday, when she had no classes at all, she fell into a pattern. She took her Eagle to school with her, and in between classes squeezed in a few hours of flight time. There had not been a bit of trouble at the airport, where a separate hangar with the Marsden Management logo over the office door stood at an isolated end of the field. At least there was no trouble after the first few minutes, when a dubious flight manager had been about to turn down her request.

Stacey, with more courage than she had shown in the past five years, ran a bluff on him. She picked up his telephone and dialled Amie Moreland's number. Amie herself answered. Stacey passed the telephone, without a word, to the flight manager.

"There's this woman down here who says she's Mrs Marsden," he started to say, then listened for a time. "Yeah—about five foot ten, blonde hair, young, stacked like a brick—oh, excuse me, Mrs Moreland. And I can what? Anything? It'll cost a bundle in fuel—oh, on the boss's account? And if there's a scheduling problem? First priority? Well, okay, but I'd feel better if I had it in writing. No! No, ma'am, I didn't mean I couldn't take your word—yes, ma'am." He put the handset down very carefully. "She hung up on me," he sighed. "Lord, I hate to work for a woman. Oh—I don't mean nothing by that, Mrs Marsden. You can have anything you want—two of anything. The whole shootin' match, if you want."

Stacey had used the new authority to its fullest, not only to get in her helicopter flight time, but also to take the minimum instruction in fixed wing flight. It was her release valve, that bled off all her bad temper, and allowed her to go back to Rosedale at the end of each day with her chin up.

March came in like a lion, bringing spring with it. Winter's cold grip was pried loose from the midlands, and the world took on a happier look. Even the animals at the Central Texas Zoo, adjacent to the airfield, took on a new life. And then March went out like a lion, and only Lisette had not responded to the change of season.

Instead of improving, she was looking more and more haggard. And more shrewish. Several times she commanded Frank to drive her, and made stops in Waco and Temple. "I dunno what she's doin'," Frank reported. "Them's some strange places she goes to. Got a lot of friends, she says, but I ain't seen any of them."

Lisette always seemed to have a glass in her hand, morning, noon and night. And never a kind word for anyone except Harry. She came back late on the first of April, and was unusually excited at dinner.

"It won't be long, Harry," she announced. "Another month. Have you thought it over?"

"You mean your proposition about Rosedale?"

"Yes. What else is there to talk about?"

"Not now, Lisette. Stacey isn't interested. Find something that we can all talk about."

"With that child, Harry? What in the world were you thinking of!"

"I've had it with that *child* business," Stacey stormed at her. "I'm not a child!" But the look in Lisette's gleaming eyes was enough to tell her that she had blown it all—had demonstrated that she *was* just a child.

"All you need to do is prove it," the older woman answered coldly. "Just how old are you, child?"

"I—none of your darn business," Stacey snapped back. She sat rigidly upright at the table, immersed in her misery, and felt the drops cascading down into her soup. She fumbled for her napkin.

"There's another interesting thing," Lisette continued. "I heard tell you were engaged to someone else—a really torrid relationship—before Harry snapped you up. His name was—well, it just slips my mind at the moment." She patted her lips daintily with her napkin, and turned her guns on Harry.

"You know a funny thing," she gurgled, "nobody seems to be able to find just where it was that you got married. Isn't that a surprise?"

"Don't you think you've had enough target practice for one night?" Harry grumbled at her. "So Stacey is a lot younger than you are—so what? It's a problem she'll grow out of gradually."

"Don't tell me that, Harry Marsden," the woman seethed. "I know you too well, man and boy. If that isn't guilt, I don't know what is!"

"Then you don't know a thing," Harry returned. The lines on his face had reappeared, the craggy stern lines that Stacey had come to understand. Lines of strength. Lines of anger. He pushed his chair back from the table, came around, and tugged Stacey up. "I would think that even a sophisticate like you could read the cards better," he snapped. "Stacey and I have been married for almost six months now, and women in her condition tend to get a little weepy and despondent now and then!"

"Damn you! Damn you both!" Lisette jumped to her feet, upsetting her heavy chair and sending it top-

pling into the corner. "You rotten—" And then in a
high-pitched shriek, "You deserve each other, you pair
of—"

The rest of the conversation was lost as she slammed
the dining room door behind her. Mrs Fallon opened
it, and stuck her head around the jam. "She didn't like
the soup?" she asked whimsically. It was just the right
note. Stacey leaned against Harry, caught up in comfort, and cried until her eyes could shed no more. He
wiped her eyes, furnished a handkerchief for her nose,
then they both resumed their seats and went on with
the meal as if nothing had happened.

But something had crystallised. From that day on
Lisette did her best to avoid Stacey, remaining in bed
until the younger girl had gone off to school, eating
alone from a tray in her room, spending hours locked
up with the telephone.

Something else occurred, too. Harry was worried
about something. He spent a great many hours walking in the empty paddocks, alone by choice. Stacey
would have loved to join him, but he refused her
company. So she spent an equal amount of time at her
bedroom window, looking down at him, wondering
how she might help. And then an even more hurtful
practice began. After dinner almost every night, Harry
began to excuse himself, leaving Stacey downstairs to
help with the dishes. He went up to Lisette's suite—
and closed the door behind him.

In the face of all this, Stacey stubbornly kept her
nose in her books, practised her flying, did the thousand things that the mistress of a house was supposed
to do—and worried. May the tenth would mark the
day when Harry and Lisette had complied with his
grandmother's Will. And then what? she agonised.

Then once again he won't need a wife, and would turn me out to pasture? Would they sell Rosedale? If they did, what would happen to the Fallons? The thought became so strong that, towards the end of April, two days after she had passed all her flight tests and examinations, she went down to the kitchen and asked.

"You mean you're worried about us?" Millie was up to her elbows in dough, and four pie tins were scattered across her work table. "Apple pies—can you imagine that? Springtime, and we have fresh apples for pies! Don't ask me where they come from." She stopped long enough to smile over the tops of her bifocals, which had slipped down to the end of her nose.

"That's all taken care of, you know. Harry didn't tell you?"

Stacey grimaced. One more item to add to the ten thousand that Harry didn't get around to telling her. "No, I suppose it slipped his mind," she said. "Tell me about it." She walked over to the always-filled coffee pot and helped herself to a mug.

"Why, it ain't no big thing," chuckled Millie. "The contractor over to your ranch has finished with expanding the house. When they decide—Harry and Lisette, that is—whatever they're going to do with Rosedale here, me and Frank, we're packing up and moving over to Rancho Miraflores."

"To—to Miraflores? Expanding the house?" Stacey was stunned, and her face showed it.

"You don't want us to come?" Millie asked anxiously.

"Don't want—of course I want you to come," Stacey returned. "It just was so startling that—it—overwhelmed me, that's all. Of course I want you to come—both of you—and the new girl too, if she wants to. Wonderful!'' She skipped around the table and traded a bear hug for a kiss and a covering of flour.

"Now you just get out of here," Millie warned, "or the pies won't be ready for supper, and you know what the mister will say about that!"

Stacey obeyed with alacrity. She needed to think about this. "The mister" was set on improving her property at the expense of his own, it seemed. Or was he expecting to leave Millie and Frank at Miraflores while he looked for a new place of his own, then move out after the pretend-marriage was finished? She felt bewildered, but one thing was sure—she owed the man some favours. He could send his entire staff to Rancho Miraflores if he wanted!

But no sooner was she out of the kitchen than she found herself trapped by Lisette. "I've been meaning to have a talk with you," the older woman said. She was purring, as if the world was finally revolving in her direction. "Come into the living room for a minute."

"That's a lovely little suit you've got on," Stacey managed to get out.

"Sit down." Lisette gestured towards the couch. "Cigarette?"

"No. I don't smoke." There was an uneasy moment of silence, while the older woman lit up, using her ivory holder.

"You don't have many vices, do you?" There was something in her voice that jarred Stacey's teeth, some sort of predatory warning, as if a jungle cat were prowling.

"I—I guess I have as many as most," she answered. "Except smoking."

"Stealing other people's men seems high on your list!"

''What? You mean Harry?'' The other woman was pacing up and down in front of her, and Stacey felt the disadvantage of being seated.

''Yes, I mean Harry. Who else in the world is there?''

''You make it sound as if I came along and picked him up from where you left him. You don't know Harry as well as you think you do if that's what you had in mind.''

''I know Harry a lot better than you'll ever know him, you stupid little bitch. I grew up with Harry. Surely you don't believe we lived together in this house for so long without anything happening?''

''Anything? I don't understand.''

''Of all the—heaven protect me from the innocent! I'm talking about Harry and me. We were lovers for years, right under dear old Grandma's nose. And still would be, if it weren't for you, damn you! What happened? Did he give you a fling and get you pregnant?''

''Why—why—'' Stacey's anger came up and overflowed. ''I don't know what you think you're up to,'' she snarled, ''but I don't believe a word of it. Harry's too—too honest to do something like that. I don't believe it. If it were so, how come you didn't marry him a long time ago, when you had the chance?''

''So I made a mistake.'' Lisette tipped her ash off on to the rug. ''I actually thought Burnet had more money. And he turned out to be as big a four-flusher as Harry. You don't really know why Harry married you, do you?''

''Of course I do,'' said Stacey indignantly. ''We fell in love. He needed me, and I needed him! And I wasn't pregnant—at that time. And I think that's all you and I have to talk about, Mrs Burnet. Just keep away from me. If I really lose my temper you could get kocked on your—lovely foundation!"

"Well, I'm going to tell you anyway, you stupid bitch. Luckily the detectives I hired struck pay dirt on you. You're the sole owner of Rancho Miraflores, aren't you? All that lovely oil just waiting to be sucked up out of the ground."

"So what?"

"So I don't suppose you read the financial pages, do you? Parsons Oil—isn't that the outfit that pays your royalties for the field? Don't bother to deny it, I know it's true."

"Again—so what?"

"So Parsons Oil is in a great deal of trouble. Five dry holes they've drilled in the last six months. The outfit's on the ropes, believe me—the word is out all over Houston and Waco. So what does Harry do? He goes out of his way to play a little game with the poor little orphan girl, the owner of all that lovely oil. How about that?"

"What are you talking about?" The news was more than uncomfortable. Stacey had wondered for all those months. Why had Harry picked her up that first day at the airport? I'm not all *that* pretty, she told herself. And—and since then, he's been running everything. I gave him my power of attorney, and he's been running everything. How do I know how much oil he's been pumping out of my reserves? No, Harry wouldn't do that. How could he? Parsons Oil might do it, but not Harry! There were glinting tears in her wide eyes as she glared at Lisette. "Get to the point. What are you talking about!"

"I'm talking about Harry." The other woman could see how deeply her darts had penetrated, and was moving in for the *coup de grâce*. "Why, you naïve little thing, you! You really don't know. Well, let me draw you a picture. Harry is Marsden Management. And what does he manage? Parsons Oil, of course."

"And Westland Cattle?" The words came out in a whisper of apprehension.

"Yes, of course, Westland Cattle. And Federal Electronics too. Did you think he supported all his pretensions on a fly-by-night management corporation?"

Stacey struggled back to her feet and glared back at the little gadfly. That was what had been the difference in Lisette's appearance—the look of vengeance. It glared out of the sallow cheeks, the glittering eyes, the straight thin mouth.

"So he owns them all," she sighed, wiping the tears away with her fingers. Her mind was racing. Harry. No matter what he owned, how he acted, what he did, she loved him. If he stripped her of all her property she would still love him. If every word Lisette had said was true, her love still would hold.

She patted the other woman sympathetically on the shoulder. "And if he owns all that, and does all that, and thinks all that—I still love him," she stated flatly. "And there's nothing you can do to make me stop loving him. Save your breath." She spun on her heel and walked out of the room, missing the contorted hatred that set Lisette's body trembling in a fit of desperate passion.

CHAPTER TEN

STACEY cornered him at the dinner table a few days later. "Harry, would you tell me something?"

"I don't know. It depends on what it is."

"It's only five more days before the will runs out. What are you going to do?"

"That's more than one question, and I don't have all the answers yet."

"You could tell me about the things that *are* settled?"

"Okay." He stopped long enough to munch on the steak. "Now, first of all, there's Lisette. I guess you know that her so-called illness was a fake. Oh, she felt bad, and suffered from malnutrition, but the basic cause of it is alcoholism. I've argued and raved, but I can't convince her that she needs treatment. And that's the first step with alcoholics—they have to admit that they're sick. Lisette is not ready to admit it. She's sure she can give it up any time she pleases."

"I know," Stacey said hesitantly. "Moving from Army post to Army post, you see them all. That's one of the leading causes of disability in the service—alcoholism. So that's what you've been doing with her every night?"

"That's it." He set both knife and fork down on the plate and stared at her. She did her best to dodge behind the curtain of her hair. "*Is* that all, Stacey? Do I detect a little jealousy behind all these questions?"

"Me? Jealous? Why should I be jealous? I'm only the hired hand around here. And come to think of it, I'm not even sure what the wages are."

"That's fancy footwork, too," he admired. "You can change the subject faster than any girl I've ever met!"

She stared at him. Surely he doesn't think I'll comment on that insult, does he? she thought. I may have been born yesterday, but I've learned a great deal since then.

"You're talking to yourself," Harry said mildly. "Interesting subject?"

"What about Lisette?" she prodded, trying to change the subject again.

"Well, as you say, we're coming down to the wire, and there's no immediate solution in sight. But you understand, she's still my charge."

"And?"

"And I have to discharge that responsibility before I can take on any new ones. You can see that?"

No, I can't, she shrieked inside. "Yes," her well-trained lips responded. Harry gave a sigh of contentment.

"That's one of the many things I like about you, Stacey. You understand things, and react sensibly."

Sure I do, she told herself. I think I'll go jump in Lake Waco. They say that a non-swimmer like me could drown in four minutes. You bet I'm sensible. I wonder if I could hire a hit-man from the mob to get rid of that woman?

"Whatever the reason," he continued, "Lisette is too emotionally insecure to agree that we should sell the estate and split the proceeds. In the end I suspect I'll just have to resign my share and let her take it over, lock, stock and barrel."

"Then on the tenth," she said hesitantly, "I suppose our need for play-acting will be over?" As soon as the words were out of her mouth she regretted them. I don't really want to know, she told herself fiercely. No matter what the answer is, I don't want to know. Please God, don't let him answer!

"Yes," he said slowly, pushing his empty plate away, "I suppose we should say that on the tenth our road show will close down, and we can get on with life. The tenth? There's something else about that date that sticks in the back of my mind."

"It's my birthday," she said flatly. "I'll be nineteen on that date."

"That's it—of course. Your birthday. And you'll be nineteen—a ripe old age. At least I won't feel so much like a cradle—I mean, at least you'll be almost out of your teens, won't you?"

The bitterness blocked her ears, sent tears to her eyes—and he had continued to talk.

" . . . so you can see you can't stay here after that," he was saying. "I think you'd best go back to Miraflores."

"On the tenth?" she asked, trying to hold back the tears.

"Yes, on the tenth," he said. "Didn't I make that clear? When will your classes end for this semester?"

"On the fifteenth," she offered sadly.

"Well then, let's say you leave here and go to the penthouse from the tenth until the fifteenth, and then back to Miraflores. Then in the fall, we can make—"

"I don't think we should plan that far ahead," she said woodenly. "In the fall I think I'll transfer to the University of Texas, at the Austin campus." She forced herself to look straight ahead, trying to avoid his eyes. He got up from his chair slowly, reaching for the dirty dishes.

"Damn it, Stacey, you haven't been listening to a word I said," he complained. "I've got business to tend to. Why don't you go on to bed, and I'll look in before you fall asleep."

She watched the muscles ripple under his silk shirt as he walked to the door. "Yes, Daddy," she muttered rebelliously.

When she awoke to the new day Harry was gone. "There was an emergency call," Millie explained as she piled a plate high with scrambled eggs and honey-cured ham. "I didn't get the particulars—something about a fire. He took off in a cloud of goose-grease. Didn't you hear the helicopter?"

"If I did I must have turned over and gone back to sleep," sighed Stacey. "How can anyone my age sleep so much?"

"There must be a million reasons," Millie returned. "I don't suppose you've been to the doctor lately?" Oh no, not that one again, Stacey sighed to herself. Not that one. I'm not pregnant, damnit! I'm not even—

"Can you keep a secret, Millie?" The housekeeper favoured her with a big smile, and leaned both elbows on the work counter, waiting for an important confidence.

"Of course I can," she replied.

"So can I." Stacey laughed as she cleaned her plate, grabbed for an apple, and headed for school.

The days marched slowly by, and Harry did not come. She haunted the office, looking for news. On the eighth of May Amie Moreland came back. Stacey haunted her until she managed to slip out of her coat, pat her hair, and order up a cup of coffee. As she leaned back in her executive chair she looked at Stacey again. "You mean that rotten devil didn't even tell you where he was going?"

"Well, I was asleep," Stacey started off lamely, then pulled herself up. Why should I defend him? That's exactly what he did, the rotten—"Yes, that's exactly what he did," she grumbled. "And then he hasn't called, or written, or—what is he up to, Amie?" And why do I sound as if I were begging for a handout? I only want to know where my husband is. Is that too much to ask? To know where my husband—

The strain was too much. Tears poured down her face like a spring gully-washer. She was too weak to stand. She backed up slowly until a chair bumped against the back of her knees, and fell into it, making no attempt to mop up the mess.

"Hey, now," Amie comforted, "No man on earth is worth that. Calm down. There's more to this than meets the eye. Have you seen a doctor lately?"

And that was the last straw. Broken, sobbing, bent over to protect against the pain in her stomach, Stacey spilled it all out. Everything, from the beginning, on that early flight from Dallas, to the day before yesterday. By the end of her story Amie Moreland was storming up and down the room, pounding one hand into the other.

"Why, that rotten—" she sputtered. "You mean—just like that—he hired you to be his wife?"

"It really isn't that—well, at first I did it for him as a favour, because he had done me a favour, Amie. And then it—it just grew. I didn't know where to stop. I didn't *want* to stop, can't you see?"

"Oh, I can see all right. You fell head over heels in love with him. No?"

"I—yes. I couldn't help it, Amie. I didn't *want* to fall in love with him, honest!"

"Yes, I can see that, my dear. Here, use my handkerchief. It's a lot bigger than that piece of lace you're fooling with." Amie bustled into the corner of the room and came back with two full shot glasses. "Here, drink this, love. Down the hatch."

"But—but I don't drink."

"Me neither. Down the hatch." They both tilted their glasses and emptied them. The liquor burned its way down Stacey's throat and hit her stomach like a major brush fire. She gasped and choked on it, unable to breathe. Amie was having her own similar problems.

"Now then." The older woman cleared her throat and sat down behind the desk again. "He's down in Galveston—well, not exactly there. There was a fire on Parsons Oil Rig Sixteen, out in the gulf. Naturally we called in trained fire-fighters. But your husband—damn—but Harry is never one to leave things alone. He had to be there. He's still out there on one of the fire ships. I can understand why he couldn't call or write. But he could have told me to call. Damn that man! Now, what are we going to do about you?"

"Nothing, I guess," Stacey muttered, dabbing at her eyes. "I feel better just telling somebody about it.

It's all been building up inside me for months. I'm sure you have enough troubles of your own.''

"One thing you can be sure of is when he gets back, I'm going to give him a piece of my mind. You ought to, too.''

"I can't do that, Amie. I really can't." A distant memory tickled her mind. "My father always said, don't give people a piece of your mind, when you're liable to need it yourself!''

"I'll say one thing for you, Stacey, you've a strong character,'' said Amie. "If I'd been through all this I'd be having a nervous breakdown right about now. Anything you want me to do?''

"I don't think so. The day after tomorrow I'll be leaving the mansion. I'm almost finished with final exams now. I'll come in to the apartment for the remaining five days of school. And then I suppose I'll go back to the ranch, or something.''

"And brood about him, I suppose? You really love him, don't you?''

"I—I guess so. I don't know. I've never been in love before. Maybe it's only an infatuation?'' Stacey sent an appealing look across the desk. Tell me that's what it is, her eyes pleaded. Tell me it will pass away soon. Tell me!

"I don't know what to tell you,'' Amie sympathised. "When I met Karl I knew he was my man right away. But my mother says when she first met my father she didn't even like him. He had to court her for a year before she discovered otherwise.''

"I just—I don't know what to say, Amie. Do you know when he'll be coming home?''

"No, I don't. It could be as early as tomorrow—or it could be as late as next week. The oil business is a funny thing."

"I have to run, Amie," said Stacey. "I have another class, and it's all the way across the campus."

"All right, love. Study hard, and don't worry. Basically, Harry is really a fine man."

The next day, her last at Rosedale, was a Thursday, and Stacey had no classes to account for. She spent an hour in the kitchen helping Millie Fallon, then drove her Eagle down to the airport for another lesson. This time it was a fixed wing solo, in a Cessna Commander. She junketed in a great circle around Waco, sweeping almost a hundred miles in each direction before she came back in, shot several practice landings, and made her way back to the house.

Millie had left her a note on the kitchen table. "Frank and I have gone to Temple. One of our nephews has had an accident. Supper in refrigerator." She poked around in the big cooler and made herself a ham and chicken sandwich. Nothing else interested her. She washed it down with a glass of milk, then went slowly up the stairs. There was packing to do.

She went about it lackadasically, cramming her college clothes into the lightweight flight bag, and saving her big suitcase for the formal wear, the accumulation of her months of living in the big house. Don't leave anything behind, her mind niggled at her. Take everything. You may never come back this way again. The thought was not exactly comforting, and when the sound of a helicopter filled the twilight, and landing lights stabbed down, her first thought was that Harry had finally come home. "Be practical," she told herself. "He's seen you for months in blouse and jeans. Get dressed! Get gussied up!"

Her uncertain hand reached into the bag she had been packing and extracted a lightweight A-line shift in pastel yellow. It fitted her mood, and highlighted her hair, so she dived into it, all the while telling herself to "Hurry, hurry!" The sound of the motor could still be heard, the blades idling, and sending out their familiar "whap—whap—whap" as they rotated slowly. She ran a brush through her hair and, not bothering with make-up, ran for the stairs and out into the dark behind the house.

Her eyes were not adjusted to the dark, but she could see the blurred figure of a tall man moving up from the paddock. This is no time to hang back, she yelled to herself. Go for broke! She ran across the uneven ground towards him, until her right foot slipped on a small rock and she pitched forward into his arms.

"Oh, Harry," she laughed, "I've missed you so much!"

"Have you really?" said the gruff voice above her head.

"You're not—oh, my God! George. George Delano! What are you doing here?"

"Why, I've come to get you, little Stacey. We're going to be married!"

"Let me go!" She struggled in his grip but could not break free. "You must be some sort of idiot," she snapped at him. "I'm already married. Let me go! How in the world did you know I was here?"

"Would you believe it," he laughed, "your house-guest told me. And offered me a bundle to carry you off. Married, are you? Then we'll have to write this off as a kidnapping. And when—or if—your husband gets you back, maybe he won't want you.''

"Why are you doing this?'' she screamed at him as he urged her up to the house and into the hall.

"For money, of course. One way or another, for money.''

"You're a fool, George. If I scream there'll be people around here like crazy. Then what? Let me go!''

"In just a minute. Go ahead and scream. See how many people there are to help you! It took long enough to arrange for them all to be away, baby!'' In the light of the hallway she looked up at him, and did not like what she saw. His face was contorted, his eyes were bright with determination, and she remembered. George, the one who liked to hurt people.

"Hold her still, for heaven's sakes!'' The voice was behind her, a woman's cracked soprano.

"Lisette—get help! He's a madman or something!'' shrieked Stacey.

"I wouldn't be surprised. But you were engaged to him, weren't you?'' The laughter startled Stacey.

"Lisette? Not you! You wouldn't—I'm leaving tomorrow. What harm can I do to you?''

"None at all,'' the older woman laughed. "Not now. Hold her still. Get her mouth pried open.'' George had her in a firm grip, one she could not fight off. One of his hands came around and pulled at her nose, forcing her mouth open.

"There's the little dear,'' laughed Lisette. She tugged at the cap of a bottle she held in both hands, and Stacey could smell the overwhelming odour of alcohol as she came closer. "You're not leaving tomorrow, girl. You're leaving tonight. And after I tell Harry that you ran away with your boy-friend, that ought to be the end of you. Hold her still!''

She shook two pills out of the bottle and forced them between Stacey's lips. "Swallow nicely child,'' she laughed. "It's the pill you're used to.'' George tilted her head back, and it was either swallow or choke. Stacey swallowed.

"A couple more,'' muttered Lisette. Unable to control her own actions, Stacey's fears grew to be more than she could handle. Her struggles ceased, and she fell limp in his arms. Unable to fight back, she swallowed three more pills that the other woman crammed in her mouth.

"That ought to be enough,'' Lisette said. "Now get her out to the helicopter. Where are you taking her?''

"I know a place,'' growled George. "An abandoned spread out by Sweetwater. And the less I tell you, the better off we'll both be. I am to have a little fun out of this.'' He swung Stacey up and threw her over his shoulder in a fireman's carry, and went back to the machine. The pilot waited for them, a puzzled look on his face.

"Give me a hand here,'' George demanded, and between them they slid her into the middle of the bench seat. She was beginning to regain her courage, and the pills had not yet taken effect. The pilot climbed in beside her and revved up the engine. She managed to get both hands on his arm, and he looked over at her. "They're kidnapping me!'' she shouted at the top of her voice.

The startled pilot looked over at George. "Kidnapping? I thought you said she was sick. I'm not flying any kidnapping route, buddy.''

"The hell you aren't," George returned. "Take a look at this, fellow." He displayed an old-fashioned Colt .45 Peacemaker, its long barrel wavering between Stacey and the pilot.

"I'm not flying you anywhere," the pilot insisted.

"So try this!" George screamed at him. The heavy weapon rose, and the barrel smashed down on the pilot's head. He slumped over immediately, losing his grip on the controls. George kicked him out of the aircraft with one foot, then forced Stacey into the left-hand seat. "You!" He gestured with the gun. "You can fly this thing. I've watched you for a month."

"Me?" she returned in surprise. The pills were gradually working. "You want me to drive to my own funeral?"

"Just get it up in the air, or you're a dead chick." He waved the muzzle of the gun under her nose. Up? It was beginning to sound like a logical thing to do. Her ears were buzzing, and nothing seemed important any more. She yanked back on the pitch control and gunned the engine. The helicopter vaulted straight up, snarling to a thousand feet. The sound of waltz music buzzed in her head. She swung the controls right and left to the cadenza of the dance, and the chopper swayed as directed.

"You're turning green, George," she sighed, hating to have the music disrupted. "That's a silly gun. It ought to be in a museum. Does it still shoot?"

"You'll find out if there's any funny business. Go west!"

"West?" She peered at the compass. Her eyes were blurred, and she could barely read the meter. A voice blared at her from the loudspeaker over her head.

"Helicopter K610, you are making an unauthorised crossing of the landing pattern. This is Waco tower. Return to five hundred feet."

Stacey nodded. It certainly was the right sort of order to give. Her hands moved, and the bottom fell out of the world as the machine dropped like a stone to the lower altitude. George, she noted, was still green, and hanging on to a strap by the door. He looked as if he was going to—and he did.

"Helicopter K610." It was the same voice. "Are you in some trouble?"

She fumbled for the microphone switch. "No, thank you," she carolled gaily, "except he's kidnapping me!"

George growled and pulled the microphone wires loose. He raised his hand to hit her, and raised the contents of his stomach at the same time. "Go to Sweetwater," he said hoarsely.

Go to Sweetwater—what a lovely name. Why not? But her eyes could not focus on the map he was waving at her. She smiled gaily at him, and the waltz music surrounded her again. Back and forth the ship swayed as she danced it across the sky in three-quarter time. Sweetwater, I really ought to land. But I could make a horrible mess of it. The fuel tanks have to be empty, right? George was back upright again. He jabbed at her breast with the long barrel of the gun. His gun hand shook, while the other covered his mouth.

"That hurts," she complained in a little-girl voice. The pills were really taking over. Obviously it was a game they were playing, and all she had to do was to fool George. Hide and seek? The first one home wins? Gleefully she blinked her blurry eyes at the compass, set a north-westerly heading, and began a great circle that took her over Hamilton, Stephenville, Clerbourne, and Waxahachie, with one eye on the fuel consumption gauge, and the other on the highways below, which was serving as her real navigational guide. Another pithy remark from her father: "When you really get lost, just follow the railroad or the highway!" Seat-of-the-pants flying. She swept the machine back into three-quarter time, and giggled as George lost control of his stomach again.

"Are you sure we're headed for Sweetwater?" her nervous passenger asked.

"Of course we are, George," she kept repeating. "Why not?"

"How much longer?" he mumbled desperately.

"Not too long," she said in that high little-girl voice. She squinted at the gauge. It was easier to see with just one eye. The needle was bouncing off the bottom peg. The tanks were almost empty, and out of her side window she could see the markers. They were back exactly where they had started.

"George," she said, "I think we have to land here."

"God, I don't care," he groaned. "Land the damn thing before I jump."

"Oh, poor George," she sympathised, deep in the clutches of the pills. "I don't think you'll be a very successful kidnapper, George." And at that moment the motor sputtered, spurted again, and completely stopped. In the instant silence that followed Stacey shifted the blades into the auto-giro position. "You'd better hang on, George," she carolled happily to him. "I can't seem to see the ground, and we might hit something."

But George won't be mad, she told herself. He's very forgiving. She was unable to tell how right she was. When the motor had stopped, George had fainted. And now the helicopter was swinging, lacking motor drive on the stabilising tail rotor. It swung around, slammed into the side of the barn at Rosedale, and the entire fragile aircraft collapsed around her ears.

So she missed all the rest of it. Everything went happily black. She missed the noise, the confusion, the sudden appearance of that angry man, the fire—everything. Even the eventual explosion that spread remnants of the aircraft over a two-hundred-yard circle, and burned the empty barn completely down to the ground.

CHAPTER ELEVEN

"WELL," the soft voice said in her ear, "you've decided to come around, have you?"

"I—I guess so," she returned muzzily. "I—" She was about to utter that old bromide, "Where am I?" when she suddenly knew. She was in her bed, at Rosedale. She struggled mightily to get up, but her arms were slow to respond. "I have to be out of here today," she muttered. "Oh, Millie, today is the tenth, and I've got to go. He said so."

"Nonsense," the housekeeper said gently. "Today's the twelfth, and you don't have to go anyplace. How do you feel?"

"I feel fine—except—why am I so sleepy?"

"Five Valium pills will do that," the housekeeper said cheerfully.

"You said the twelfth? What—lord, I've got a final exam today at nine o'clock! I have to go, or waste the whole quarter's work."

"You're as bad a patient as he is," chuckled Millie. "Amie Moreland took care of all that. The University has granted you an exemption from the rest of your exams."

"As he is?" The gleam had gone from Stacey's lovely eyes. "Harry was hurt?"

"More mad than hurt, love. He came home unexpectedly, not more than twenty minutes after you'd left. You should have heard him give Her Majesty the business—her with that cock and bull story about you running away with the Delano fellow. So he sat there by the telephone and got all the radar stations in the heart of Texas looking for you. Especially after Waco Tower reported that you were being kidnapped. Did you know that the Army had two helicopters trailing you all the way? Harry is a Colonel in the reserve, you know.''

Of course he is, Stacey told herself. ''Oh, how nice. How wonderfully nice.'' And it was. Somebody cared. Somebody important cared! ''But he was hurt?''

''Hey, when you were hovering over the house all that time he was out in the paddock waiting. Boy, was he charged up! 'She'll set it down exactly right', he kept saying—but then you missed, didn't you?''

''It was those pills,'' she protested. ''I couldn't get my eyes focused. Do you think they'll pull my licence?''

''Don't be a fool, Stacey. You're a heroine,'' Millie assured her. ''Well, anyway, you crashed, and he was in there after you like a streak of lightning. You had a little bump on your forehead, and now you've got a dandy black eye.''

''And that's when he got hurt? Carrying me out of the chopper?''

''No, not exactly. He brought you up the hill and left you with us, then he went back for Delano.''

''And that's how he got hurt?''

''No, not exactly. 'Smartest little girl in all the world,' he said when he came back with Delano. 'Ran it till the tanks were empty, shut off all the switches, but there's a gasoline vapour in the tanks. It's bound to blow'.''

"And that's when he got hurt?" Stacey sat up, cramming her hands into her mouth.

"No, not exactly. Wait—you'll laugh."

I'll laugh, she thought. I love him and I'll laugh. He went into the helicopter to get me, knowing it was about to blow up, and I'll laugh! "What happened?" she screamed. "Tell me what happened!"

"OK, OK," the housekeeper laughed. "But don't yell—he's in the next room, sleeping. Well, anyway, he had us all duck down, and sure enough the machine blew up. Like ten thousand Fourth of July celebrations, it was. Skyrockets, firecrackers—oh, my! And then the barn caught fire. All of us, there was nothing to do, so we just sat there and watched. But not your husband. He was raving mad—not about the chopper, or the fire, but because Delano made a nasty remark about you. He pulled that guy up by his shirt tails and almost beat him to death, he did. And broke his hand doing it. That's probably the only reason why he stopped. Now, you get on the outside of this breakfast, and get some more sleep. Y'hear?"

"Oh, I hear all right." But sleep I don't need, Stacey told herself. She tossed down the orange juice, sipped at the hot coffee, and took one bit out of the toast. It was difficult getting up, but the more she moved the better she moved. The girl who looked at her out of the full-length mirror on the bathroom door was a stranger to her. Snarled blonde hair tumbled down where it would around a thin stretched face. Wide trembling eyes, one of them underscored by a discoloured swollen lump. Shaky lips, trying valiantly to be still. Someone had poured her into a see-through nightgown, a little lacy thing that she would never have had the nerve to wear. Oh well, she sighed, what you see is what you get. I owe him—for everything. For saving me from the Delanos, for spurring me into a new life, and most of all, for believing in me instead of Lisette. And then he saved my life. I owe him, and I've only got one thing to give to a man who already has everything: me. And then I'll leave.

Her body responded beautifully as her feet carried her through the connecting door and into his bedroom. His room was not a match for hers. Small, utilitarian, heavy furniture, and a bed almost as big as the waterbed at the Penthouse. He was lying flat on his back under a single white sheet, his right hand resting on top of the sheet and encased in a small plaster cast. Stacey went around the bed, stopped to slip out of her nightgown, and crawled in beside him.

The heat of his body was like an oven. She snuggled up against him, using one finger to push back the unruly lock of hair at his forehead. We just fit, she told herself hysterically. With my toes on his, the top of my head just fits under his chin. I didn't realise that the hair on his chest was so wiry. And does he ever need a shave! It was her wandering hands that were conveying the information to her mind.

Harry stirred, still not quite awake. "Stacey," he muttered. "I love you." Her heart stopped. I love you? Can the subconscious lie? Probably! What do I do next?

She snuggled closer, nibbling at the tip of his ear. He growled in his sleep, and moved an inch or two. Without quite knowing what she was up to, she came up on one elbow and teased the tips of her ripe breasts across the taut skin of his chest. He stirred, squirmed, and opened one startled eye.

"What the hell are you doing?" he rasped. The gruffness of his voice forced her back from him.

"I—I'm seducing you," she half-whispered.

The glare turned into a smile. "Well, you're not doing a very good job of it," he chuckled.

"I'm doing the best I know how," she returned petulantly. "I've never seduced a man before. You could help. I love you."

"I wouldn't be much help to you," he grinned. "I've never seduced a man before myself. And I love you too, Stacey."

"You—you do? For a long time?" The hopeful note overflowed her voice and lit up the room.

Harry struggled to control the laughter, but was not too successful. "Not exactly," he said. "I was going to say since Amie read me the riot act a few days ago. Lord, that woman has got a mean tongue! But truthfully, I fell in love with you when I saw your sensitive loving heart, dealing with my grandmother. I was afraid that with you it was just a teenage infatuation. Until Amie told me, at great length, how wrong I was. What the devil are you doing now?"

"I read in a book once that if you did this—" Stacey grabbed his good hand and pressed it against her breast. "Aren't you—aren't you going to teach me what to do next?"

"You're darn right I am," he returned, "but not until the day after tomorrow."

"I—I don't understand." She could feel the whole weight of rejection fall on her shoulders. "Why not tomorrow? Why not today? Is it because of my oil wells? Are you really trying to steal my oil? That's what Lisette said—that you were trying to steal my oil to keep your company from going bust."

"Nobody can be as naïve as you are," he chuckled. "Of course I'm not trying to steal your oil wells. I'm a big-time thief, not a penny-ante one. I'm trying to steal you!"

She no longer had to hold his hand at her breast; it was doing well enough on its own. And causing a wild war to rage among her senses. A wild unquenchable thirst ravaged her mind, ran rampant over all the Lutheran truths of her upbringing, and smashed square into the wall of her practical curiosity.

"And you're not bound to Lisette any more?"

"After what she did to you? Nonsense! I turned her over to the Sheriff, along with that Delano fool. Did you know she hired a gaggle of detectives to find him? They deserve each other. Next question?"

"And me. Do you still think I'm infatuated with you—that I'm still a kid?"

"Holy Hannah, what a question at a time like this!" His hand was forming and shaping her breast, teasing the bronze tip. "No, I don't think you're a kid, nor do I think you're suffering through an infatuation. My God, this cast makes me clumsy!"

"Well—then—" she stammered, following her own logic to its end, "why do I have to wait until the day after tomorrow?"

"Because that's when we're getting married, you little nut. We're going to take a helicopter, and you're going to fly us as far away from here as we can get, and find us a Justice of the Peace who will perform a very quiet wedding. Two weddings for us would be a mite suspicious, you know. And then after that, I'll teach you all about seduction."

"But that's what I don't understand. I thought we were already married. I've thought so for months.

And so have the Fallons. And everybody in the neighbourhood." As she talked her hands were roaming again, up and down his rib-cage, across his stomach, down his heavily muscled thighs.

"And everybody at the Corporation knows it," she continued grimly, "and almost everybody at the University, and everybody at Rancho Miraflores, and—"

"In fact, I'm the only one who doesn't know, is that what you're saying?" Harry's face was losing its stiffness, his breath becoming sharper. His good hand reached for her shoulder and pulled her forward, flat against him. "Lord, how I want you, girl."

She could feel the tension spread throughout his long lean body, and wild horses rode rampant through her being. "Let this be the time, Lord," she whispered.

"What did you say?"

"I said, why are you so stubborn? Why are you the only one in McClennan County who doesn't believe we're already married?"

He buried his face in the warmth of her hair, nibbled at her ear, then pushed her away so his tongue could touch madly at the tip of her aroused breast.

"I'm beginning to recall the details of the ceremony," he laughed as he pulled her close again. "You were wearing an ivory dress, because you were two days too late for white, and your teacher at the School of Seduction had just given you a passing grade in his course. Right?"

"Oh, I still wore the white dress," Stacey answered dreamily. "I understand that a lot of girls lie about that these days." She laughed and waited, trembling, expectantly, as he began the first lesson.

YOU OWE ME

Penny Jordan

CHAPTER ONE

THE letter caught up with Chris in New York. She had been working there for a month—one of her longest spells in one place in nearly six months—modelling clothes for one of New York's top designers and sandwiching between the shows photographic sessions under her five year contract with a large cosmetics house.

That was the trouble with getting to the top of the modelling profession, she thought wryly, as she let herself into the apartment she had "borrowed" from an American model, for the duration of her assignments in New York—the work came thick and fast, but there wasn't enough time to do it all. She was twenty-six now; and she had promised herself when she took up modelling she would only stay in it four years. She had been twenty then. Grimacing faintly she bent automatically to retrieve the mail that had slipped from her fingers on to the floor. Her needs were not extravagant, but her aunt's final illness had been extremely expensive financially. The illness from which her aunt had suffered had been progressive and terminal involving mental as well as physical destruction, and Chris was only thankful that during those final few years her aunt had retreated into a world of her own where the true nature of her own decline was concealed from her. Two months ago her aunt had died, and although now there was no reason for her to continue earning large sums of money, Chris admitted mentally that it was too late for her to change her career. She could model for possibly another four years if she was lucky, and during that time she should earn enough to keep her in comparative comfort for the rest of her life—if she was careful. But what was she going to *do* with the rest of that life? Seven years ago she thought she had known exactly what course her life would take. Marriage to Slater; children. The smile curving her mouth was totally humourless. So much for dreams. Reality was a far cry from her late teenage hopes.

The midsummer heat of New York had darkened her honey-blonde hair slightly with perspiration. Thank God for air conditioning she reflected as she dropped the mail on the small coffee table and headed for the shower. Being able to lease Kelly Reading's apartment had been a welcome bonus on this assignment, she was tired of living out of suitcases; of moving from city to city, always the traveller. That was never how she had envisaged her life. It was strange really that she, the stay-at-home one, should have a career that made her travel so widely, whilst Natalie, her restless, will o' the wisp cousin should have been the one to marry, to have a child.

Frowning Chris stripped the silk suit from her body, the firm curving lines of it too familiar to her to warrant undue attention. In all her years of modelling she had always refused topless and nude shots. And received a good deal of heat from her first agent for it, she remembered wryly. Things were different now. As one of the world's top models she could pick and choose her assignments and Hedi, her agent, had clear instructions about what she would and would not accept.

As she stepped into the shower stall she swept her hair up into a loose knot. Long and honey-blonde, it was thick and resilient enough to adapt to the different styles she had to adopt. She showered quickly and then stepped out, wrapping her body in a towel before starting to remove her make-up. As always when she had been wearing it for several hours she itched to be free of it. A model girl who hated make-up. She laughed derisively, cleaning eyeshadow from the lid of one sea-green eye. Her beauty lay in her bone structure and her eyes, and was ageless.

Her looks had always been a source of contention between them when she and Natalie were young. Orphaned at five she had been brought up by her aunt and uncle alongside their only child, Natalie, who was two years younger than Chris. Tiny, dainty Natalie, who she had soon learned possessed a cruelly vindictive streak, which she used unmercifully to protect what she considered to be hers, and that had included her parents and all her friends. Chris had not found it easy to accept her unwanted role as "orphan", and many times during those early days she had retreated to her bedroom to indulge in secret tears when Natalie had taunted her about her orphaned status. "You would have had to go in a home if you hadn't come here," had been one of Natalie's favourite taunts, often with the threat tagged on of "...and if I don't like you, you will still have to go there."

Under that threat Chris had weakly, hating herself for her weakness, given in to many forms of blackmail, which ranged from the subtle never-expressed pressure from Natalie that she would always keep herself in the background, to open demands for "loans" from Chris's pocket money.

Sighing Chris moisturised her skin. She could see now that Nat had just been insecure. There had been a bond between aunt and niece that had never truly existed between mother and daughter. Even in looks she had resembled her aunt, Chris acknowledged, and Natalie with the perception that most children possessed had sensed her mother's leaning towards her sister's child and had bitterly resented Chris for it.

Nat, on the other hand had always been her father's favourite. Uncle Roger had adored his small, dark-haired daughter, "his little pixie fairy" as he had called her. His death in a road accident when Nat was fourteen had severely affected her. Funnily enough she herself had never shared Nat's deep resentment of their relationship, and as she had grown older she had adopted a protective instinct towards her younger cousin, knowing without anything being said that she was entering a conspiracy with her aunt which involved a constant feeding of Nat's ego; a never-ending soothing of her insecurities. As a child Nat had grown used to her father describing her as the "prettier" of the two cousins, and with her dark curls and smaller, frail frame she had possessed a pretty delicacy that Chris lacked. When, as a teenager, Chris had started to blossom Natalie had been bitterly resentful.

"Boys hate tall girls," she had told Chris spitefully. And Chris could still remember the occasion when, one very hot summer, she had been sent for by the Headmistress, because Nat had told her teacher that her cousin bleached her hair, strictly against the rules of the school. In point of fact, its extreme fairness that summer had been the result of more sunshine than usual, and when pressed for an explanation as to why her younger cousin should try to get her into trouble deliberately, Chris had leapt immediately to Natalie's defence. She could still remember her headmistress's words on that occasion.

"Chris, my dear," she had told her firmly, "your desire to protect Natalie is very natural and praiseworthy, but in the long run you would be helping her more if you allowed her to take responsibility for her actions. That's the only way we learn to think carefully before we commit them."

Would life have been any different if she had heeded that advice? Grimacing, Chris extracted fresh underwear from the drawer. It took two to commit treachery; Natalie alone could not be blamed for the destruction of all her bright—and foolish—dreams.

It was another half-an-hour before she discovered the letter. She had just mixed herself a cooling fruit drink and sat down, when she caught sight of it, protruding ominously from among a stack of mail, the solicitor's name and address in one corner, the airmail sticker in the centre.

She had grown used to correspondence with Messrs Smith & Turner during the weeks following her aunt's death. On her marriage Natalie had deliberately, and to Chris's mind, quite heartlessly cut off all ties with her mother. "She always loved you best," she had told Chris spitefully, when she tried to talk to her about it. "I never want to see her again."

It had been a couple of years after that that Chris had actually noticed the oddness of her aunt's behaviour and another harrowing seven months before her condition had been correctly diagnosed. The specialist, sympathetic and understanding had told Chris of an excellent nursing home which specialised in such cases, and where her aunt would receive every kindness and the very best of care.

The fees had been astronomical. Chris had written to Natalie, believing that she would want to make her peace with her mother in view of her failing health, but Natalie had never even replied, and it had been more than Chris could have endured to go down to Little Martin and talk to her. In order to pay the nursing home fees she had committed herself to a gruelling number of assignments, and for the last four years she had barely had time to take a breath.

Now it was over, and she presumed the letter from Smith & Turner related to the final details surrounding her aunt's estate, if her few belongings and the house in Little Martin could be classed as that.

It had come as no surprise to Chris to discover that her aunt had left her the house. She had bought it after Uncle Roger's death, selling the larger property and investing the difference. Chris had always loved the thatched cottage, despite its many inconveniences, but Nat had hated it. She had never forgave her mother for selling the larger property, and constantly complained about their drop in living standards. In anyone else Chris would have denounced her cousin's behaviour as brutally selfish, but because of her childhood conditioning Chris was constantly finding mental excuses for her. Although there was one sin she could never forgive her... Idly sliding her nail under the sealed flap she extracted the sheets of paper inside.

Her heart thumped as she read the first line, barely taking in its message, her eyes racing back to the beginning and tracing the words once again. '' ... regret to inform you of the death of your cousin, Natalie James née Bolton, and would inform you that . . .''

Without reading any further Chris lifted her eyes from the paper. Natalie dead! She couldn't believe it. She was only twenty-four. What had happened?

She glanced at the date on the letter and her heart dropped sickeningly. Natalie had been dead for six weeks! Six weeks, during which she had travelled from Nassau to Rio, then on to Cannes and finally to New York.

She dropped the letter on the floor, filled with a mixture of nausea and guilt. How often during the last seven years had she wished Natalie out of existence? How often had she prayed that she might wake up and discover that what had happened was all just a nightmare? Only now could she admit to herself the frequency of such thoughts, generally after she had just had to point out to yet another male that being a model did not mean that she was also available as a bed mate. She had never wanted her present life; it had been thrust upon her in a manner of speaking; a means of salvaging her pride and her dignity, and also a means of . . . of what? Escaping her own pain?

No. Not entirely. Deep inside her had been the unacknowledged thought that by leaving somehow she was giving something to Natalie's unborn child—Slater's child. The child that should have been hers.

The doorbell rang and she slipped the intercom switch automatically, shocked out of her involvement with the past when she heard Danny's familiar New York accent.

''Danny, I'm not ready yet,'' she apologised. In point of fact she had lost what little desire she had possessed to go out with the brash New Yorker, who had forced his way into her life three weeks ago. Tall, fair, good looking, and well aware of his attractions Danny had been chasing her from the moment of her arrival, and was, Chris was certain, supremely confident that in the end he would catch her. She, however, had other ideas. Charming though Danny was he couldn't touch the deep inner core she had learned to protect from the world. No man had touched that since Slater.

Ten minutes later she was down in the lobby with Danny, the poise she had learned over the years covering the innate inner turmoil.

They were dining out with a business associate of Danny's. He wanted to show her off like a child with a new and status-symbol toy, it was an attitude she had grown accustomed to.

They were to go to a chic, "in" restaurant, which would be full of New York glitterati, and Chris's spirits sank as she got into the taxi. Natalie dead! Even now she could not take it in. What had happened? She wished now she had read the letter more fully, but she had been simply too stunned. She supposed it was natural that the solicitors should write to her as Natalie's closest blood relative after her daughter. She knew that Natalie had had a girl, her aunt had told her, wistfully, longing for an opportunity to see her only grandchild, but knowing it would be denied her.

If it hadn't been for Ray Thornton, she herself would have had to stay in Little Martin, enduring the sight of Natalie living with Slater as his wife. She had a lot to thank Ray for. Slater had never liked him. "Flash" he had called him, and in a way it was true. Ray had made his money promoting pop stars. He had been thirty-one to Slater's twenty-five then, fresh from the London "scene" and defiantly brash. She had liked him despite it, although then she had turned down the job he had offered her in the new club he was opening in London. She had then only known him a matter of months and yet he had been the one she had turned to that night, when she had discovered Natalie in Slater's arms. He had comforted her bracingly then, just as he had done when Natalie announced her pregnancy. It was Ray who had told her she ought to become a model. It was Ray who had introduced her to the principal of the very select London modelling school were she had trained. "A little too old for a beginner" was how Madame had described her, but she had more than repaid Ray's faith in her. For a while he had pursued her, but only half-heartedly, recognising that she was still far too bruised to contemplate putting anyone else in Slater's place. They had kept in touch. Ray was married now and lived in California. Chris liked his wife and he had the most adorable two-year-old son.

The evening dragged on interminably. Chris was aware of the sharp, almost disapproving looks Danny was giving her, and made an effort to join in the conversation. The other two men and their wives were obviously impressed both by Danny and the restaurant. Two out of the three wasn't bad averaging, Chris thought cynically, wondering what sort of deal Danny was hoping to arrange with these two very proper Mid-Western Americans and their wives. Danny was a wheeler-dealer in the best sense of the word; he thrived on challenge and crises.

Chris could tell he was still annoyed with her when he took her home. He wanted to come in with her, but she told him firmly in the taxi that he could not. His

brief infatuation with her was nearly over, she recognised when he let her get out of the cab, but then what
had she expected? It was hardly Danny's fault that she
didn't live up to her image. She had grown used to
seeing her photograph plastered over the gossip press,
generally with that of a casual date, nearly always re-
ferred to as her latest "conquest". What would those
editors say if they knew that in actual fact she was still
a virgin?

The thought made her wince. That she was, was
only by virtue of the fact that Natalie had interrupted
Slater's lovemaking. He had cursed her cousin that
day. They had thought themselves alone at his house.
He had rung Chris at home just before lunch, and the
sound of his voice had sent shivers running down her
spine. She had known him a long time. His father had
been friendly with her uncle, but he had been away at
University and then he had worked in Australia for a
couple of years preparing himself for his eventual
take-over of his father's farm machinery company.
His father had died of a heart attack very unexpectedly and he had come home; tanned, dark-haired,
hardened by physical work, Chris had felt an immediate attraction to him.

She had been nineteen, and falling in love with him
was the most exhilarating, frightening thing she had
ever experienced. She had thought he loved her too.
He had told her he did; he had spoken about the future as though it was his intention that they shared it,
but in the end it had all meant nothing.

She ought to have guessed that day when Natalie
suddenly appeared unexpectedly, but she had simply
thought of it as another example of her cousin's bitter jealousy of her.

She had been on holiday from her job in a local travel agents. Slater had rung her at home, suggesting they met for lunch, but when he picked her up, he had told her throatily that the only thing he was hungry for was her. She could remember her excitement even now, she could almost taste the exhilarating fizz of sexual desire and intense adoration. They had gone back to his house—he had inherited it from his father along with the family business; a gracious late Georgian atmosphere that Chris loved. She hadn't considered then how wealthy Slater was; she had simply been a girl deeply in love for the first time in her life. If Slater had taken her to the tiniest of terraced houses she would have felt the same.

They hadn't even waited to go upstairs, she remembered painfully. Slater had opened the door to the comfortable living room, and she had been in his arms before it closed behind them, eagerly responding to his kisses, trembling with the desire surging through her body.

They had kissed before, and he had caressed her, but they had never actually made love. Slater knew that she was a virgin. He had asked her, and she had answered him honestly. She had imagined then there had been tenderness as well as anticipation in his eyes but of course, imagination was all it had been. They had been lying on the settee when they were interrupted by Natalie. Chris's blouse had been unfastened, her breasts tender and aroused by Slater's kisses. Natalie had burst in on them completely unexpectedly, half hysterical as she accused Chris of deliberately misleading her about her plans for the day. The only way Chris had been able to calm her down was to go home with her. Slater, she remembered had been tautly angry, and she had thought then it was because he resented her concern for Natalie. Had he even then been making love to her cousin as well? What would have happened if Natalie had not interrupted when she did? What would he have done if he made both of them pregnant? Hysterical tension bubbled painfully in her throat. Perhaps they could have tossed a coin for him?

The pain grew sharper and she suppressed it from force of habit. Dear God, even now after seven years, the thought of him still made her ache, both emotionally and physically. She had never truly got over him—or more truthfully, she had never truly recovered from the blow of discovering he was not the man she had believed. Not only had she suffered a gruelling sense of rejection, she had also to endure the knowledge that her judgment was grossly at fault.

She would never forget the day Natalie came to her and told her the truth. It was just a week after she had seen her cousin in Slater's arms.

She had been working all day, and normally Slater picked her up after work. On this occasion though, the girl she worked with told her that Slater's secretary had rung and left a message asking her to go straight round to his house.

She had no car of her own, and it was a two mile walk, but Chris had been too much in love to consider that much of an obstacle. At Slater's house they would be alone. Something he had seemed to avoid since Natalie interrupted them. She knew he was having problems with the company; a matter of securing a very important order which was vital to its continued existence and had put his behaviour down to this.

His car had been parked in the drive when she arrived, and for some reason, which even now she could not really understand, instead of ringing the front door bell she had decide to surprise him by walking in through the sitting room and gave her an uninterrupted view of the settee and its occupants. Her whole body had gone cold as she recognised her cousin's dark head nestled against Slater's shoulder, her arms were round his neck, his head bent over hers. Chris hadn't waited to see any more. On shaky legs she had walked away, dizzy with sickness and pain, unable to come to terms with what she had just witnessed.

She went home and rang Slater from there to tell him that she wasn't feeling well, hoping against hope he would mention Natalie's presence; that there was some explanation for what she had seen, other than the obvious, but he hadn't.

Natalie had returned many hours later, her face pale, and her eyes smudged, her whole bearing one of vindictive triumph and Chris knew that somehow Natalie knew what she had witnessed. It was never mentioned by either of them, at least not then, and Chris had determinedly refused to accept any of Slater's calls in the week that followed, too hurt to even confide in her aunt. Later she was glad she had not done so.

Never in a thousand years would she forget her shock and pain when Natalie came home and announced that she was expecting Slater's child. She had only told Chris at that stage, gloating over her pain, violently triumphant, almost hysterical with pleasure. Her cousin had always been volatile, Chris remembered, always subject to emotional "highs" and "lows"; dangerously so, perhaps.

She had not got in touch with Slater. The only thing
left for her now was her pride and her profound
thankfulness that she would not share Natalie's fate;
at least she had told herself it was thankfulness. Even
now pain speared her when she thought of Slater's
child, but she dismissed it, forcing herself to remember the events of that traumatic day.

Just as soon as she could escape from Natalie she
had gone out, simply walking herself into a state of
numb exhaustion, and that was how Ray had found
her. She hadn't even realised how far she had walked
or that it was getting dark. He had taken her home
with him, and although he had questioned her closely,
all she would tell him was that she wanted to get away
from Little Martin. That was when he had made his
suggestion that she should take up modelling as a career. Previously she had only known him casually, but
now she found him a warm and helpful friend. When
Chris mentioned Natalie's name briefly, not wanting
to tell him the truth, Ray had looked angry, and she
had gained the impression that he did not like her.
That alone had been sufficient to underwrite her trust
in him, and it was a trust that had never been misplaced, unlike that she had had for Slater.

She had left that night for London with Ray, and
had written to her aunt the next day, explaining that
she had worried that her aunt might dissuade her from
leaving, giving this as an explanation for her un-
planned departure.

A month later Natalie and Slater were married. Her
aunt was both stunned and concerned. "She's so
young, Chris," she had sighed, "far too young for
marriage, but perhaps Slater..." she had broken off

to frown and say quietly. "My dear I know that you and Slater..."

"We're friends, nothing more," Chris had quickly assured her, hastily changing the subject, telling her aunt about her new life and making it sound far more exciting than it actually was.

She had worked hard for two years, before suddenly becoming noticed, and was now glad that she had not accepted any of the more dubious assignments that had come her way in those early days. No magazine was ever going to be able to print "girly" photographs of her simply because none had ever been taken.

She had heard from Natalie once, that was all. A taunting letter, describing in detail her happiness with Slater, and his with her.

"It was very wise of you to leave when you did," Natalie had written. "You saved Slater the necessity of telling you he didn't want you any more."

Chris hadn't bothered replying and she had never heard from either of them since. Now Natalie was dead.

It took her a long time to get to sleep, images from the past haunting her, and then when, at last she did, the impatient jangling of the telephone roused her.

Her room was in darkness, and for a few seconds she was too disorientated to do anything but simply listen to the shrill summons of the 'phone.

At last she made a move to answer it. The crisply precise English accent on the other end of the line surprised her by sounding almost unfamiliar, making her remember how long it was since she had visited her own country. "I have Mr Smith for you," the crisp voice announced, the line going dead, before Chris heard the ponderous tones of her aunt's solicitor.

"Chris my dear how are you?"

"Half asleep," she told him drily. "Do you realise what time it is here?"

"And do you realise we've been trying to get in touch with you for the last six weeks," he retaliated. "I've practically had to subpoena your agent to get this address out of her. Chris, it isn't like you to be so dilatory... I'd expected to hear from you before now."

He must mean about Natalie's death, Chris realised, suddenly coming awake.

"I only got your letter today," she told him. "It must have been following me round. What happened? How did Natalie...?"

"The coroner's verdict was suicide while the balance of her mind was disturbed," she heard Tom Smith saying, the words reaching her stupefied brain only very slowly. "I did tell you that in my letter, my dear. Your cousin always was a mite unbalanced, I'm afraid. Your aunt recognised that fact and it used to cause her considerable concern. Roger's mother had a similar temperament."

Since Tom Smith had known the family for many years Chris did not dispute his comments. Suicide! The word seemed to reverberate painfully inside her skull, resurrecting all her childhood protective instincts towards her cousin. "Why? Natalie had had everything to live for, a husband, a child..."

"It seems that your cousin had been suffering from depression for a long time." Tom Smith further shocked her by saying. Remorse, hot and sharp, seared through her. Had Natalie needed her, wanted her? Could she have helped her cousin. Pain mingled with guilt; her animosity towards Natalie forgotten, all her bitterness directed towards Slater. Perhaps he had been as unfaithful to Nat as he had her? She should never have blamed her cousin for what had happened; Nat had been an impressionable seventeen, Slater a mature twenty-five. Hatred burned white hot inside her, he had robbed her of everything she thought childishly, all her illusions; her unborn children, and now her only relative. No, not quite her only relative, she realised frowning. There was Nat's little girl...Sophie.

"How is Sophie taking it?" she asked Tom Smith automatically, voicing the words almost before she realised she was going to. She had deliberately held herself aloof from all knowledge of Sophie, unable to contemplate the pain of knowing she was Slater's child—the child she had wanted to give him.

"That's why I'm ringing you," Tom Smith told her, further stunning her. "She's always been a very withdrawn, introverted child, but now I'm afraid there's cause for serious concern. Sophie hasn't spoken a single word since her mother died."

Pity for her unknown niece flooded Chris, tears stinging her eyes as she thought of the child's anguish.

"Natalie wouldn't have named you as Sophie's guardian if she hadn't wanted to do so. I know it's asking a lot of you, Chris, but I really think you should come home and see the child."

Guardian! She was Sophie's guardian? Chris couldn't take it in. Her hand was slippery where it gripped the receiver, all her old doubts and pain coming back, only to be submerged by a wave of pity for Natalie's child.

"But surely Slater..." she began huskily, knowing that Slater could never willingly have agreed to Natalie's decision to appoint her as his child's guardian.

"Slater is willing to try anything that might help Sophie," Tom Smith astounded her by saying. "He's desperate, Chris."

There was a hint of reproach in his voice, and guiltily Chris remembered the unread pages of his letter, which she had discarded. "Did you write to me about this?" she asked.

"I set everything out in my letter," he agreed patiently. "I was surprised when Natalie came to see me nine months ago and said that she wanted to appoint you as Sophie's guardian, but she was so insistent that I agreed. If only I'd looked more deeply into her reasoning I might have realised how ill she was, but she seemed so calm and reasonable. Her own experience of losing her father had made her aware of how insecure a child could feel with only one parent; if anything should happen to her she wanted to be sure that Sophie would always have someone she could turn to.

"I had no idea then of course, that she hadn't discussed her intentions with Slater, or indeed that you weren't aware of them. There's nothing legally binding on you, of course, and naturally Slater will continue to bring up his daughter, but at the moment he seems unable to reach her. She needs help, Chris, and you might be the only person who can help her."

"But I'm a stranger to her," Chris protested, realising fully what Tom was asking of her. How could she return to Little Martin? How could she endure the sight of Slater's child; of Slater himself... but no, she was over that youthful infatuation. She knew him now for what he was, a weak man too vain to resist the opportunity to seduce a trusting seventeen-year-old.

Had he really loved Natalie or had he simply married her because he had had to? She had had a lucky escape Chris told herself. She could have been Natalie, crushed by marriage to a husband who didn't love her, trapped... She was letting her imagination run away with her, Chris told herself. She had no reason to suppose that Slater did not love Natalie, perhaps it was even wishful thinking! No! Never!

"Well, Chris?"

"I'm coming home." It wasn't what she had intended to say at all, but now the words were out they could not be retracted.

"Good girl." Tom Smith's voice approved, and Chris shivered wondering what train of events she had set in motion. She didn't want to go back to Little Martin; she didn't want to see Slater or his child. The past was another country; and one she had sworn she would never re-visit, but it was too late now, she was already committed; committed to a child she had never seen, and remembering instances of Natalie's vindictiveness, she wondered momentarily just why her cousin had named her as her child's guardian. This thought was brushed aside almost instantly by a flood of guilt. If Natalie had been jealous of her, hadn't *she* been jealous too in turn? Hadn't she felt almost ready to kill her cousin when she saw her in Slater's arms. She sighed. All that was over now, Natalie was dead, and in the end, for whatever reason, her cousin had entrusted to her care her child, and she could not in all honour ignore that charge, if only for her aunt's sake.

CHAPTER TWO

Less than thirty-six hours later when she stepped off a 'plane at Heathrow, Chris still wasn't sure quite how she had got there. A brief call to her agent explaining the situation had resulted in cancellation of several of her assignments and the postponement of others. It was a testimony to her success that this was allowed to happen, her agent told her drily when she rang from London to tell Chris what she had done.

London was much cooler than New York. To save herself the hassle of a complicated train journey Chris had elected to travel to Little Martin by taxi. The cabbie raised his eyebrows a little when she explained where she wanted to go. The fare, would she knew, be astronomical, but that was the least of her worries right now. Had she done the right thing? Time alone could answer that. She had acted impulsively, rare for her these days, listening to the voice of her conscience rather than logic. Sophie did not know her and it was almost criminally stupid to imagine the child would respond to her when she could or would not to her own father.

Closing her eyes Chris leaned back into her seat, unaware of her driver's appreciative scrutiny of her through his rear view mirror. Her clothes were simple, but undeniably expensive, and the cabbie wondered what it was that took her to such a remote part of the country in such a rush. She wasn't wearing any rings.

It was three o'clock when the taxi deposited her at Slater's house. She hadn't known where else to go, and since Tom Smith had told her that Slater would be expecting her it had seemed the sensible thing to do. She had only brought one case with her. The local estate had the keys to the cottage she had inherited from her aunt and she planned to collect them later on. The cottage would make an ideal base for her whilst she tried to get to know Sophie and decided what to do. It had at one time been let out but the past tenants had left some time ago and now it was empty.

Her ring on the doorbell produced no response and as she waited for someone to appear Chris acknowledged that at least some of the tension infiltrating her body was caused by the thought of meeting Slater.

The house seemed deserted and she rang again, frowning when there was no response. Tom had assured her that Slater would be there. He wanted to see her before she saw Sophie, so Tom had said. Sighing she tried the door handle, half surprised when it turned easily in her hand.

The moment she stepped into the hall memories flooded through her; she had often visited the house with her aunt and uncle who had been friends with Slater's parents, but most of her memories stemmed from the brief months when she had met Slater here, when merely to cycle down the drive and arrive at the house had sent dizzying excitement spiralling through her veins. It had been in this hall that he had first kissed her the afternoon she had come on some now forgotten mission from her aunt. Slater had taken her by surprise, and she had been too stunned to resist. He had seemed half shocked himself, but he had recovered very quickly, making some teasing remark about her being too pretty to resist. That had been the start of it . . .

She sighed, glancing anxiously round the panelled room. Where *was* Slater? She called his name doubtfully, shivering a little in her thin silk dress. What had been warm enough in New York was far from adequate here at home, despite the fact that it was June.

The sitting-room door was half open and drawn by some force greater than her will Chris walked towards it, almost in a trance. It had been here in this room that all her bright, foolish dreams had been destroyed. Like a sleepwalker she walked inside, surprised to find how little had changed. Natalie had loathed the house's traditional decor and she had half expected to find everything different. The sun shone rosily through the french windows, clearly revealing the features of the man stretched out on the settee and Chris came to an abrupt halt, her breathing unexpectedly constricted, almost unbearably conscious of the air burning her skin, as though someone had ripped off an entire layer and left her exposed to unendurable pain. The shock of seeing Slater was a thousand times worse than she had envisaged, and it mattered little that he was oblivious to her presence, apparently fast asleep. Suddenly the intervening years meant nothing, the sophisticated shell of protection she had grown round her during them dissolving and leaving her acutely vulnerable.

His hair was still unmarked by grey, thickly black and ruffled, his frame still as leanly powerful even in sleep. His eyes were closed, lines she didn't remember fanning out from them. His mouth curled downwards, a deep cynicism carved into his skin that she didn't recall, and that shocked her by its unexpectedness. His face was the face of a man who had suffered pain and disillusionment, or so it seemed as she looked at him, and yet where she should have felt glad that this was so, his appearance made her heart ache. Seven years and God alone knew how many thousand miles, they had been apart, and yet as she looked at him Chris found her reaction to him as intense and painful as it had been so long ago.

She couldn't possibly still love him; that was ridiculous, no, what she was experiencing now was something akin to *déjà vu*... It was only the shock of seeing him so unexpectedly that caused this reaction... She must remember that he was not and never had been the man she had thought him. She had invested him with qualities, virtues that he had never possessed.

Unaware of what she was doing, she moved closer to him. Tiredness was deeply ingrained in his features. As she moved something clinked against her shoe and she glanced downward to see a half-empty bottle of whisky and a glass. Slater had been drinking? She frowned, and then reminded herself that he was a man whose wife had only recently committed suicide, and that whatever his feelings for Natalie, there must be some feelings of pain and guilt inside him. He moved, frowning in his sleep and the cushion on which he was resting his head slipped on to the floor.

Chris bent automatically to retrieve it, balancing herself against the edge of the settee. Her fingers brushed accidentally against Slater's wrist and he jerked away as though the light contact stung. His shirt was open at the throat, and she could see the dark hair shadowing his skin, thicker now than she remembered, or was it simply that at nineteen she had been less attuned to sheer masculine sexuality than she was now.

Her heart started to jump heavily and she began to draw away, grasping with shock as Slater's fingers suddenly closed round her wrist. His eyes were still closed, a deep frown scoring his forehead. His thumb stroked urgently over the pulse in her wrist, and Chris didn't know what shocked her the most; his caress or her response to it. He was still deeply asleep and she dropped to her knees at his side, gently trying to prise his fingers away without waking him. Anger and tension brought a hectic flush of colour to her skin. Seven years when she had learned to defend herself against every awkward situation there was, and yet here she was reduced to the status of an embarrassed adolescent, simply because a man held her wrist in his sleep.

But Slater wasn't simply *any* man, she acknowledged bitterly and her combined embarrassment and pain sprang not so much from the fact that he was touching her, startling though her reaction to that touch was, as from the knowledge that he undoubtedly believed she was someone else; perhaps Natalie, perhaps not. She couldn't release his fingers. She would have to wake him up. Inwardly fuming, outwardly composed, she leaned over him, trying not to admit her awareness of the smooth firmness of his flesh beneath his shirt-sleeve as she touched his arm.

The moment she shook him his eyes flew open. She had forgotten how mesmeric they could be, topaz one moment, gold the next. They stared straight into hers.

"Chrissie…" He started to smile, the fingers of his free hand sliding into her hair and cupping the back of her head. Too startled to resist, Chris felt him propel her towards him. Her eyes closed automatically, her lips parting in anticipation of his kiss. She might almost never have been away. His kiss was tender and powerful; she was nineteen again quivering on the brink of womanhood, wanted him and yet frightened of that wanting and his kiss told her that he knew all this and understood it.

She barely had time to register these facts before his hold suddenly tightened, his eyes blazing burnt gold into hers as he withdrew from her. Chris blinked, slower than he was to make the transition from past to present, until she saw the biting contempt in his eyes and recognised that when he had kissed her he had not been fully awake; not fully aware of what he was doing.

"So you finally came." He released her and was on his feet, whilst she still knelt numbly on the floor. "I suppose we ought to be honoured, but I'm sure you'll forgive us if we don't bring out the fatted calf. What brought you back, Chrissie? Guilt? Curiosity?"

Just about to tell him that she had only just learned of Natalie's death, Chris stumbled to her feet as she heard sounds outside. The sitting-room door opened and a smiling plump woman in her fifties walked in holding the hand of a small child.

Chris breathed in sharply. So this was her niece...Natalie's child. Slater's child. She couldn't endure to look at him as she studied the little girl, and knew instinctively why Natalie had named her as guardian, just as she knew that her cousin's decision had not been motivated by any of the gentler emotions. Natalie had not changed, she decided helplessly, studying the small face so like her own; the untidy honey-blonde hair, and the general air of dismal hopelessness about the child. By some unkind quirk of fate Sophie could more easily have passed for her daughter than Natalie's although unlike Chris she had brown eyes.

Chris frowned. Natalie had had blue eyes, and Slater's were amber-gold. No one as far as she knew in either family had possessed that striking combination of blonde hair and velvet-brown eyes, and yet it was familiar to her, so much so that it tugged elusively at her memory.

"There you are, Sophie," her companion said brightly, "I told you you were going to have a visitor didn't I?"

The child made no response, not even to the extent of looking at her, Chris realised sadly.

"I have to go and get some shopping now Mr James," she added to Slater.

"That's fine, Mrs Lancaster. You've made up a room for our visitor, I take it?"

"The large guest room," Mrs Lancaster told Chris with a smile, adding reassuringly to Sophie. "I'll be back in time for tea, Sophie, and then perhaps tonight your aunt will read your story to you."

Once again there was no response. Chris ached to pick the child up and hug her. She looked so pitifully vulnerable, so lost, and hurt somehow, and yet she sensed that it would be best not to approach her. She frowned as she remembered what Slater had said about a room for her. She must tell him that she would be staying at the cottage. She glanced at her watch, remembering that she still had to collect the keys.

"Bored with us already?" Slater drawled sardonically.

Chris saw Sophie conceal a betraying wince at her father's tone and she frowned, wondering what had caused the child's reaction. Had Slater perhaps often spoken to Natalie in that sarcastic voice? Children saw and felt more than their parents gave them credit for, but she could hardly question Slater on his relationship with her cousin. Did he know why Natalie had appointed her as Sophie's co-guardian?

She glanced at him bitterly. Perhaps he had shared Natalie's resentment that their child should so much favour her. She shuddered to think of the small unkindnesses Sophie could have suffered at Natalie's hands; torments remembered from her own childhood, and then reminded herself that Sophie was Natalie's child, and that as usual she was letting her imagination run away with her.

Chris looked up to find Sophie studying her warily, as she crept closer to her father. His hand reached out to enfold her smaller one, the smile he gave her was reassuring. A huge lump closed off Chris's throat. She had been wrong about one thing at last. Patently Slater did love his small daughter—very much. There was pain as well as love in the gold eyes as they studied the small pale face.

"I can't think why Natalie specified that I was to be her guardian," Chris murmured unguardedly.

Almost at once Slater's expression hardened. "Can't you?" he said curtly. Sophie tensed, and as though he sensed her distress, he stopped speaking, smiling warmly at the child before continuing, "I'd better show you to your room."

"That won't be necessary." Chris was cool and very much in control now. She gave him the same cold brief smile she reserved for too-eager males. It normally had an extremely dampening effect, but Slater seemed quite unimpressed. "I'll be staying at the cottage," she continued. "In fact I'd better get round to Reads and collect the keys. They've been keeping the place aired and cleaned for me."

"Chris!" There was anger and bitterness reverberating in his voice, and Chris saw Sophie tauten again. Slater must have been aware of her tension too, because he broke off to say soothingly, "It's all right Sophie, I'm not cross. We have to talk," he told Chris levelly, "and it would be much easier to do so if you stayed here, but I remember enough about you to realise that you'll go your own way now, just as you did in the past. I'll walk out to your car with you."

No doubt so that he could say the things to her he wanted to without upsetting Sophie. It was strange, Chris reflected painfully. All these years she had deliberately refused to think about Slater's child, and yet now that she had seen her, she felt none of the resentment or pain she had expected. Sophie was simply a very unhappy, vulnerable child whom she ached to comfort and help, but she was sensible enough to know that the first approach would have to come from Sophie herself.

"I don't have a car," she told Slater coolly. "If I can leave my case here for an hour I'll come back and collect it once I've got the keys for the cottage. I can use my aunt's Mini to drive back in."

Slater's smile was derisive. "Please yourself Chris," he drawled mockingly. "I'd offer to take you, but I can't leave Sophie, and she isn't too keen on riding in the car."

Chris frowned, but Sophie's face bore out her father's statement, she looked tense and frightened.

It took her longer than she had anticipated to walk to the village—she had forgotten that she was no longer a teenager and accustomed to the almost daily walk. The estate agent expressed concern when she told him her intentions.

"But my dear Chris, the place has been empty for nearly two years..."

"I arranged for it to be kept cleaned and aired," Chris reminded him frowningly.

"Which we have done, but the roof developed a leak during the winter, it needs completely rethatching. I have written to tell you," he told her half apologetically, and Chris sighed, hearing the faintly accusatory note in his voice. "Using your aunt's Mini is completely out of the question. I doubt you could even get it started. I've got a better idea. My sister has a small car which I know she won't mind you borrowing. She's in Greece at the moment on holiday, and won't be back for several weeks. How long are you intending to stay in Little Martin?"

"I'm not sure yet," Chris told him accepting his offer of the loan of a car, but refusing to allow him to book a room at the village inn for her. However bad the cottage was, she could stay there one night, surely? She was already befuddled with all the decisions she had had to make recently. Tomorrow she could decide where she was going to stay. It would have to be somewhere close to Sophie otherwise there would be no point in her visit.

After she had collected Susan Bagshaw's small Ford and thanked Harold Davies for the loan of it, Chris drove straight back to Slater's house. She had been longer then she expected and her heart thumped anxiously as she approached the house. Unbidden the memory of Slater's warmly persuasive kiss made her mouth soften and her pulses race.

Stop it, she warned herself angrily. He had kissed her almost as a reflex action, his true feelings towards her more then clearly revealed in his attitude to her once he was properly awake. What was the matter with her anyway? She had been kissed by dozens of men since she left Little Martin. But their touch had never affected her as Slater's had done, she admitted tiredly. Perhaps now that she was back in Little Martin, it was time for her to face up to the fact that she had never really overcome Slater's rejection of her; that her feeling for him had never properly died; principally because she had never allowed herself a true mourning period. She had rushed straight from the discovery of his infidelity into the hectic world of modelling, refusing to even allow herself to think about what had happened. Had she really come back simply for Sophie's sake, or had some instinct, deeper and more powerful than logic drawn her back, forcing her to face the past and to come to terms with it, because until she did, she would never really be free to love another man?

She could admit that now, just as she could admit how barren and empty her life was. All the things she had really wanted from life had been torn from her and so she had been forced to set herself alternative goals, but career success had never really attracted her; the values instilled in her by her aunt still held good. At heart she was still that same nineteen-year-old. She wanted a husband and children, Chris admitted, surprised to discover how deep this need was, but Slater stood firmly in the way of her ever forming a permanent relationship with any other man; as did her lifestyle. The men she met were not marriage material. Disturbed by the ghosts she had let loose inside herself, Chris parked the car and walked towards the front door.

It was several minutes after she had rung the bell when Slater appeared. He had changed his clothes and in the checked shirt and jeans he could almost have been the Slater of seven years ago. Chris felt her muscles tense as he invited her in. As he stepped back her body brushed briefly against his in the close confines of the half-opened door. Her nerve endings reacted wildly, shivering spasms of awareness flickering over her skin, whilst she schooled her face to betray nothing.

"What happened to the Mini?" he asked once she was inside.

"Harold didn't think it would start. He's loaned me his sister's car in the interim."

"What did you do? Flash those sea-green eyes at him? You'll have to be careful, Chris, this isn't New York. Husband-stealing isn't acceptable practice down here."

Anger burned chokingly inside her. Who was he to dare to criticise what he assumed to be her way of life? After what he had done to her, how dare he... She bit back the angry retort trembling on the tip of her tongue. Tom Smith had warned her that should he wish, Slater could protest against and possibly overrule Natalie's will. If she wanted to fulfil the role Natalie had cast for her she must try to maintain some semblance of normality between Slater and herself.

"Where's Sophie?" she asked hesitantly, trying to fill the bitter silence stretching between them.

"In bed," Slater told her, adding sardonically, "Children often are at this time of night. It's gone eight, and she's had a particularly tiring day. Meeting strangers always seems to have a bad effect on her."

He had no need to remind her of her status, Chris thought tiredly. No one was more aware of it than she; it made her feel very guilty. There was something about Sophie that touched her almost painfully. Perhaps it was the physical resemblance to herself; the memories of the pain and loneliness of her own childhood, once her parents had died and before she realised the depth of the bond that could exist between her aunt and herself.

"I don't know exactly why you've come here Chris," he added tautly, "But Sophie isn't a toy to be picked up, played with for a while, and then put down when you're bored. She's a very vulnerable, unhappy little girl."

"She's also my only living relative," Chris said unsteadily, "and I feel I owe it to Natalie to do whatever I can for her."

"Is that how you see her?" he jeered unkindly. "As a responsibility? She's a responsibility it's taken you damn near six weeks to acknowledge, Chris. Sophie doesn't need that sort of half-hearted, guilt-induced interest."

"I've only just received Tom Smith's letter," Chris protested angrily.

"Why? Or is it that you only return to your own address at six weekly intervals, just to check that it's still there?"

His inference was plain and dark colour scorched Chris's face. Let him think what he wished, she thought bitterly. Let him imagine she had a score of lovers if that was what he wanted. Why not? It was far better than him knowing the truth. That there hadn't been a single lover, because in her heart she was still aching for his lovemaking…still grieving for what she had lost.

"I didn't want you here," she heard him saying curtly to her, "but Natalie did appoint you as Sophie's joint guardian, although I think we both know that can't have sprung from any altruistic impulse."

Hard eyes impaled her as she swung a startled face towards him. But then why should she be so surprised? Naturally Natalie would have told him how much she hated her. After all in the early days at least they had been deeply in love; in love enough for him to have discarded her in the cruellest and most painful way he could. "I suppose Natalie did resent the fact that she looks like me," Chris agreed bleakly.

Slater's face was grim. "In the circumstances it hardly endeared the child to her," he agreed, and Chris frowned a little. At times he had a manner of speaking about Sophie that seemed to distance her from him, almost as though the little girl were not his daughter, and yet there was such an obvious bond of affection between them. Before she could question him further about his remark he went on to say, "Tom Smith seems to think you might be able to reach Sophie, and so does John Killigrew, the doctor in charge of her case at the hospital. Sarah and I aren't so sure."

Sarah? Chris's heart pounded. Was this the explanation for Natalie's suicide. Did Slater have another woman?

"Sarah?" she questioned lightly, avoiding his eyes, in case he read in them what she was thinking. Much as she had cause to resent her cousin, she could only feel sympathy with her, if she too had suffered the pain of being rejected by Slater. At least in her case all he had destroyed was her ability to love and trust, while in Natalie's...

"Sarah is the psychotherapist in charge of Sophie's case. Such behaviour isn't entirely unknown in children and generally springs from a deep-seated trauma. Until we discover what that trauma is it is unlikely that she will speak, although there are various ways in which we can encourage her, but if you do intend to stay and help, Sarah will brief you on these herself."

Chris stared at him nonplussed. "I thought the trauma was obvious," she said unsteadily. "Sophie has lost her mother in the most distressing way... Surely that..."

"Sarah doesn't believe that is the cause and neither do I." He was almost brusque, turning slightly away from her so that his face was in the shadows. "Sophie and Natalie did not get on. Natalie spent very little time with the child."

Chris was not entirely convinced.

"Why did Nat commit suicide?" she asked him abruptly.

He swung round, the shadows etching the bones forming his face, stealing from it every trace of colour. His eyes glittered febrilely over her as he studied her, his body tense with an emotion she could not define.

"Tom Smith has already told you. She was mentally disturbed."

"You don't seem particularly concerned." It was a dangerous thing to say, and she almost wished it unsaid when he continued to stare at her.

"What is it you want me to say Chris?" he demanded bitterly at last. "Natalie and I elected to go our separate ways a long, long time ago. My main concern now is Sophie. She's already suffered enough at the hands of your cousin. I don't intend to let you increase that suffering. Just remember that while you're here I'll be watching every step you take. Do anything that affects Sophie adversely and you'll be leaving."

"I'm not leaving Little Martin until I see Sophie running about, laughing and chattering as a six-year-old should," Chris retaliated fiercely, the commitment she had just made half shocked her, almost as though she had been impelled to take the first step down a road she hadn't intended to traverse. Slater was still watching her and fantastically, despite his cold eyes and grim mouth she had the impression that he was pleased by her reaction, although she could not have said why. Imagination, she told herself sardonically. Slater could have no reason at all for wanting her to stay.

"That's quite a commitment you just made," he told her softly. "Are you capable of seeing it through I wonder?"

She bent to pick up her case pushing the honey blonde cloud of hair obscuring her vision out of the way, impatiently, as she stood up to face him.

"Just watch me," she told him grimly.

She was outside and in the car before she realised that she had not made any arrangements for the following day. A quick mental check informed her that it would be Friday—how travelling distorted one's sense of time—that meant that Slater would be working. She would call on him early in the morning and tackle him about what access she could have to Sophie. Feeling as though she had cleared at least one obstacle, she put the car in gear and set out for the cottage.

CHAPTER THREE

THE lane which led to the cottage and which she remembered as scenic and rural, was dark, almost oppressively so, the lane itself badly rutted in places, and Chris heaved a small sigh of relief when at last she picked out the familiar low crouching outline of the cottage in the car's headlights.

Parking outside she hurried up the uneven paved path. The lock was faintly rusty and she broke a nail as she applied leverage to the key. Grimacing ruefully she stepped inside, flicking on the light automatically. Her eyes widened in shock as she stared round the sitting room. Damp stains mildewed one of the walls; the cottage felt cold, and even worse, smelled faintly musty. She remembered now that her aunt had always insisted on a small fire even in the summer, and that she had often expressed concern about the building's damp course too. As a teenager she had paid scant attention to these comments, but now she was forced to acknowledge their veracity.

Why had no one written to her; told her how much the cottage was deteriorating? Or perhaps they had and their letters were still following her round the world. Sighing Chris made her way through the living room and into the kitchen. Here too signs of decay and neglect were obvious. The cottage was clean enough but desolate somehow, and so cold and damp that the atmosphere struck right through to her bones. The dining room was no better, more patches of damp marring the plaster. With a heavy heart Chris made her way upstairs. The roof needed re-thatching John had told her, and during the winter it had leaked. He had added that they had made what temporary repairs they could, but all her worse fears were confirmed when she opened the first bedroom door and walked inside. She and Natalie had once shared this room; its contours, every crack in its walls were unbearably familiar to her, as was the faint, but unmistakable perfume, heavy and oriental, at seventeen she was far too young to wear such a sophisticated fragrance, but she had insisted on doing so nonetheless, and its scent still hung on the air. Surely after six years it ought to have died, Chris thought frowningly. Unless of course Natalie had been here more recently. But why? She had flatly refused to take on any responsibility for the cottage when Natalie had been forced to have her aunt moved away from it. It could moulder away to dust was what Tom Smith told her she had said when she asked him to get in touch with her. She touched the cover of one of the single beds absently, withdrawing her fingers as they met the damp fabric. She shivered suddenly, noticing the mildew clinging to the cover. This had been her bed . . . She smiled wryly to herself. She had chosen the quilt herself. Natalie had chosen exactly the same thing, and then had burned a hole in her own with a cigarette while smoking secretly in bed. Absently her fingers smoothed the fabric, tensing as they found the small betraying burn mark. This was Natalie's quilt. What was it doing on her bed?

Memories of Natalie's possessiveness during their shared childhood flooded her. Natalie had hated her ever touching anything of hers. She would never have allowed her quilt to be placed on Chris's bed. That was all in the past, Chris reminded herself. No doubt whoever cleaned the cottage had mixed up the quilts. She turned round and walked out of the room, shutting away the memories and lingering traces of Natalie's perfume. She couldn't possibly sleep in that room, it was far too damp.

Her aunt's bedroom showed the same distressing signs of neglect. Now she knew why Slater had offered her a bedroom she thought wryly. She would have to stay here tonight. She could hardly go back now and wake up the whole household. So where did that leave her? If she wanted to get close to Sophie she would either have to take a room at the pub or... or swallow her pride and ask Slater if his offer of a room was still open. Much as she wanted to help Sophie she didn't know if she could cope with sharing the same house as Slater.

She wasn't nineteen any more she reminded herself wryly. What was she afraid of? That Slater would try to take up where they had left off? Hardly likely. No, tomorrow she would just have to go cap in hand to him and ask for his help, much as she resented the idea. But that was tomorrow. She still had to cope with tonight. Sleeping in either of the bedrooms was out which left only the living room. Shivering slightly at the thought she remembered that her aunt used to keep spare bedding in the airing cupboard. If it was still there, perhaps it might at least be dry. While she was here she would have to get a builder in to check over the cottage and put it to rights; put in a new damp course and renew the roof. Until that was done no one could possibly live here.

As she walked towards the bathroom, she glanced automatically at the small chest in the landing alcove and then frowned. Two cigarette butts lay in the ashtray. The hairs on the back of her neck prickled warningly and she suppressed the desire to turn round and look behind her. Obviously they had been left there by the cleaner. And yet as she entered the bathroom Chris had the distinct impression that something was not quite right... Pushing aside the notion as fanciful she opened the airing cupboard, relieved to discover a pile of bedding there that felt dry to the touch. The house had an immersion heater so at least she would be able to have a warm bath before curling up downstairs on one of the chairs, although she didn't anticipate getting a good deal of sleep. Coming back had resurrected far more memories than she had anticipated, or was it Slater's briefly tender kiss that had stirred up all the tension she could feel inside herself? Why had Natalie committed suicide? Would they ever know? Mentally disturbed was how Slater had described her and whilst it was true that she had always had a tendency towards hysteria, especially when she couldn't get her own way, she had always thirsted for life with a tenacity that Chris simply could not envisage disappearing overnight.

She woke up as she had expected to, cold and stiff, shivering in the early morning light. It was seven o'clock. In the past Slater had always left for the factory at eight thirty, which didn't leave her much time to see him.

Bathing and dressing in fresh clothes, she brushed her hair, leaving her skin free of make-up. Her stomach growled protestingly, reminding her how long it was since she had had something to eat, as she hurried out to the car.

She drove up towards Slater's house slowly, dreading the moment when she must face him. Mrs Lancaster opened the door to her, her kind face creased in concern as she saw Chris's pale set face.

"Is Slater in?" Chris asked tensely.

"He's just having his breakfast," she told her. "You can go straight through. I'll go and get another cup, you look as though you could do with something to drink."

Chris knocked hesitantly on the door and then opened it. Dressed in a formal business suit, Slater looked far more formidable than he had done the previous day. He was drinking a cup of coffee, the cup raised to his lips, his eyebrows drawing together as he saw her. He replaced the cup and folded the newspaper he had been studying.

"Good morning. I trust you slept well." His voice was coolly derisive and Chris had to stop herself from flushing, knowing that he must know exactly how uncomfortable a night she had had.

"Not very," she managed to respond. "I hadn't realised the cottage had become so dilapidated. My own fault I suppose..." She saw Slater flick back a cuff to glance at his watch, the gold band glistening among the dark hairs, and she had to fight down a sense of hostility that he should make it so plain that he was anxious to be free of her company.

"Let's cut the small talk shall we?" he said curtly. "I'm sure you haven't come here at this time of the morning to discuss the work that needs to be done on the cottage. What do you want?"

God how she hated him, Chris seethed, loathing the way he was reducing her to the role of begging.

He must know why she was here; he had to, and yet he was doing everything he could to make it hard for her.

The arrival of his housekeeper with a cup and a fresh pot of coffee provided a welcome break, but as soon as she had gone, his eyes hardened to icy coldness, and he made no move to offer her a drink, Chris noticed, her resentment increasing by the second. If it wasn't for Sophie she would turn on her heel and walk out of here right now.

"Well Chris?" The curt impatience of his voice lacerated her tender nerves.

Her voice husky with anger she said tensely, "I came to ask if your offer of a room was still open. Obviously I can't stay at the cottage..."

The smile he gave her wasn't encouraging. It made her heart miss a beat and then start to thud unevenly. "Well now, I seem to remember yesterday that you were most vehement in refusing to stay here. Quite a change of heart."

"Yesterday I thought I would be able to stay at the cottage." Chris replied as evenly as she could, hating the way he was making her explain what he already knew—and had known yesterday. All the time she had been refusing to stay here he had known the state of the cottage and that she would have to retract. Fury brought a dark flush of colour to her skin as she continued bitterly, "Unlike you I didn't realise the state it was in..."

"What are you trying to do, Chris," he interrupted sardonically. "Blame me for your own rash impulsiveness? That was ever your way wasn't it—to blame others for your own failings?''

The injustice of his comment and the bitter way in which he voiced it took her breath away. Tears stung her eyes, much to her chagrin. That was it. She couldn't take any more. Turning her back on him she was just about to walk out when he said quietly, ''The offer *is* still open, and now if you'll excuse me, it's time I was leaving. Sarah will be arriving just after ten. Mondays, Wednesdays and Fridays, she spends two hours a morning with Sophie. And now if you'll excuse me.''

He was standing up and opening the door before Chris could speak. She wanted to fling his offer in his face, to tell him that she didn't need his room, but she forced herself to hold her tongue. Surely she had learned in the last six years to control her temper? Puzzled she glanced at the closed door. In fact she couldn't remember a single instance when she had lost it, and yet here she was dangerously close to boiling point after the exchange of barely a dozen words with Slater.

Before she could dwell too deeply on her thoughts Mrs Lancaster came in, smiling again. ''I'll just get you some breakfast,'' she offered, ''and then I'll take you up to see your room and Sophie.''

Gratefully Chris sat down. At least Mrs Lancaster appeared not to resent her presence. When the older woman came back with grapefruit and toast, Chris asked her to stay. ''It would help me to know something of Sophie's routine,'' she told her. ''I know so little about her.''

"Poor little mite, it's a shame," Mrs Lancaster murmured. "Bright little thing she was too at one time. Worships her father she does . . ."

"And her mother?" Chris questioned. "Did Sophie get on well with her mother?"

"I couldn't say." The housekeeper avoided her eyes. "Always in and out was Mrs James. Always here, there and everywhere." In other words Natalie had tended to neglect her child, Chris thought reading between the lines, but how did Sophie's inability to speak tie in with that? Perhaps Sarah would be able to tell her more; perhaps it wouldn't be a bad idea to see if she could find something to read on the subject.

While she ate her breakfast Mrs Lancaster outlined Sophie's routine. "I normally get her up about nine; she has breakfast, and then if Sarah isn't coming she goes out to play in the garden.

"In the afternoon if it's fine I take her out for a walk. Mr James normally plays with her for a couple of hours when he comes in—devoted to her he is, and so patient."

"She's almost six," Chris murmured. "What about school?"

"Doing quite well at playschool she was until this happened. She still reads a lot and Mr James gets special books for her; you know, so that he can teach her himself, but they won't accept her at the village school the way she is just now."

Poor Sophie, Chris's heart went out to her. Already she was an outcast—different from her peers; if only she could help her in some way.

Tentatively she asked Mrs Lancaster if it would be possible for her and Sophie to have breakfast with Slater, and to her relief the housekeeper agreed.

"More company is what she needs," she told her, "a proper family atmosphere if you know what I mean. I always thought..." She broke off and looked slightly flustered, and diplomatically Chris didn't probe. The housekeeper must know more about Slater and Natalie's life together that anyone else, and perhaps in time she might be able to learn something from her that would give her a clue as to why Natalie should take her own life.

Finishing her breakfast, she asked if she could accompany the housekeeper upstairs when she went to wake Sophie.

The little girl was awake when they walked into her room—a dream of a little girl's room, decorated in sugar candy pinks and frills.

"Chose all the decorations in here himself Mr James did," Mrs Lancaster told Chris proudly watching her survey the room. "All new it is..."

"Oh... what was it like before?" Chris questioned wondering if it had been a good idea to take away things that were familiar no matter how well-intentioned the action had been.

Mrs Lancaster's lips compressed. She frowned slightly as she looked at Sophie, and then said at last. "Mrs James always said there wasn't much point in doing a room up specially for her, claimed the child wouldn't appreciate it. Downright cruel she was to her sometimes," she added, lowering her voice.

Biting her lip Chris glanced across at the bed. Sophie was lying there watching them, and sudden memory of her own childhood came to her. Without pausing to think Chris went across to her and sat down, picking up a framed photograph off the chest by the bed. In it Sophie was smiling up at her father.

Natalie was not included in the print. "What a lovely photograph of Sophie this is," Chris exclaimed, holding the frame out to Mrs Lancaster. "She looks so pretty when she smiles." It was no less than the truth, but Chris had had a vivid memory of Natalie at six saying furiously that she would not share her bedroom with Chris and that she hated, hated her plain ugly cousin.

Chris had been heartbroken at her rejection, and for years had genuinely thought that she was ugly; a view that Natalie had been at pains to reinforce. Could she have done the same thing to Sophie? It seemed impossible, but the human brain was a strange thing. Natalie would have bitterly resented having a child who looked so much like her, Chris knew and perhaps there had been occasions when she had taken out her hatred of her cousin on her child.

The pansy brown eyes flickered from Chris to the photograph, but the small face remained solemn and stiff. Where had she seen that combination of fair hair and brown eyes before Chris wondered idly. It was so familiar she felt she ought to be able to remember and yet she could not.

"What a pretty pink dress too," Chris exclaimed, refusing to give up. "I used to have a dress like that when I was a little girl. Is pink your favourite colour Sophie?" she asked the little girl, addressing her directly for the first time.

Sophie's only response was to look behind Chris at the housekeeper.

"Mrs James used to dress her in dungarees most of the time," she told Chris. "Said there wasn't much point in dressing her up, although she spent enough on her own clothes." She sniffed disapprovingly and then said to Sophie. "Come on now young lady. Time you were getting up."

Not wanting to overwhelm Sophie Chris got to her feet. "I'll meet you both downstairs, shall I?" she suggested, smiling at Sophie, leaving her with the other woman.

Exactly on the dot of ten a small estate car stopped outside the house. The girl who got out was slim, with chestnut hair and a very self-possessed expression. Chris disliked her on sight and wondered at her atavistic response. It wasn't like her to take an instant dislike to anyone.

Nevertheless she introduced herself pleasantly while Mrs Lancaster went to get Sophie and make them some coffee, trying to make conversation.

"Slater tells me you come here three mornings a week? How is Sophie responding so far?"

"It's too early to say yet," the other girl said dismissively.

Was Sarah slightly defensive? Chris could not tell, but she knew that her dislike was reciprocated when Sarah added curtly, "You know that neither Slater or I want you here? You can't do anything to help Sophie. She needs expert care and attention."

"Her mother appointed me as her co-guardian," Chris interrupted quietly, determined to keep her temper and not allow herself to be rattled by the way Sarah banded Slater and herself together, and firmly placed Chris as their enemy.

"Her mother!" Sarah smiled with derision. "Natalie never gave a damn about the child...she hated her from the moment she was born. If she ever thought of Sophie at all it was simply as a pawn she could use against Slater."

"You seem to know an awful lot about my cousin and her husband." Chris spoke before she could stop herself, hating the triumphant gleam shining in Sarah's too pale blue eyes as she returned, "Slater and I are old friends..."

Old friends and new lovers? Chris wondered, stunned by the spearing pain jolting through her body.

When Mrs Lancaster returned with Sophie, she was glad of the excuse to escape.

"I'll take you up to your room now," the housekeeper offered. "It does have its own bathroom."

On the landing she walked past Sophie's room and the two other doors, hesitating for a second outside one before passing on to a third, and opening the door into a pleasantly decorated guest room. Chris's case was already on the bed; the room had attractive views over the gardens, the adjoining bathroom decorated in a similar style to the bedroom.

How long would she be staying here she wondered? How long could she *endure* to stay here? An unpleasant thought struck her. If Sarah and Slater were lovers, did she stay here?

Why should it concern her, she asked herself hardily. She had no romantic interest in Slater now. That was all dead. But was it?

More to distract her thoughts than anything else she asked Mrs Lancaster briefly, "Slater and Natalie... which room..."

"Mrs James had her own room," Mrs Lancaster told her non-committally—"the door next to this..." She fidgeted for a moment and then added anxiously. "All her things are still in there, I was wondering if you could possibly sort through them..."

"But surely Slater..." Chris protested, still trying to come to terms with the fact the Slater and Natalie had apparently had separate rooms. At whose instigation? Mrs Lancaster had already intimated that Natalie spent a good deal of time away from the house, but how long had Slater and Sarah...

"Mr James just told me to get rid of everything and close up the room, but I felt I couldn't. Some of her clothes were very expensive..."

Chris could understand Mrs Lancaster's dilemma. "Of course I'll go through them," she agreed, thinking that distasteful though the task promised to be, it was something she owed her cousin.

Chris did not see Sarah go. Mrs Lancaster came out into the garden to tell her that lunch was ready and explained that the other woman had left.

Sophie was very subdued over lunch, keeping her eyes fixed on her plate. What had happened that was so traumatic that it had stopped her from talking? And not just from talking, Chris acknowledged, covertly watching her. Sophie was a very withdrawn little girl, flinching away from almost every physical contact, locked up inside herself.

After lunch Mrs Lancaster explained that she was going shopping. Sophie normally went with her but when Chris suggested that the little girl might want to stay behind with her, she was both surprised and pleased to see the fair head nod.

"She's taken to you," Mrs Lancaster told Chris when Sophie went upstairs to clean her teeth. "Apart from those brown eyes she's the spitting image of you too."

"Umm, genes are a funny thing," Chris agreed. She had spotted a pile of children's books in the sitting room. The afternoon was sunny and warm, and after choosing a book for herself from Slater's well-stocked bookshelves she headed back to the dining room, where as she expected, Sophie was waiting. Just because the little girl refused to speak it didn't mean she did not hear—and understand, Chris reminded herself. She couldn't force Sophie to accept her, to give her her confidence, but... Coming to a decision she began speaking, talking, quietly, addressing her comments to herself.

"It's such a lovely afternoon I think I'll go out into the garden. If I can find a deckchair somewhere I could sit down and read. Perhaps I'll find one in the garage."

Without looking to see Sophie's reaction she headed for the kitchen and the back door, pleased to see that the little girl was following her. The drab, oversize dungarees she was wearing did nothing for her thin, tense little body, and Chris made a mental note to go out and buy her some new clothes. Perhaps she might even be able to take Sophie with her.

As she had expected she found some garden chairs in the garage, picking one up, she strolled round to the large back lawn, Sophie at her heels.

All the time she was walking she kept on talking— about the house and village—about the changes she had found—about her aunt and her own childhood, but never mentioning Sophie's mother.

When she finally sat down and opened her book Sophie was still beside her.

"Umm this looks a good story." She flicked a glance at the silent child as she opened one of Sophie's books and started to read aloud from it.

Sophie was standing six feet away watching her. Chris read slowly and patiently, occasionally lifting her eyes from the page to remark on her surroundings. Sophie gave no signs of responding, but she was still there, watching her motionlessly.

Chris was more than halfway through the book before she felt Sophie move. Her heart leapt tensely. Had she got bored and walked away or... She dare not lift her eyes from the printed page, and was only able to expel her breath properly when the child's shadow fell across her lap as Sophie crept nearer. She was still standing beside her chair when Chris came to the end of the story.

At least she had established contact with Sophie if nothing else, she thought elatedly. The little girl had not rejected her as she had feared. What had Natalie told Sophie about her if anything? Had she drawn comparisons between them? Sighing frustratedly Chris picked up another of Sophie's books. There was so much that was a puzzle to her and it was one she had no way of solving without Sophie's co-operation. She had reached automatically for the next book in the pile, and was startled when Sophie's brown fingers pushed her hand away and then extracted another book thrusting it towards her.

The book was old and tattered, and suddenly unbearably familiar. It was one of her own Chris recognised. A book she had received from her parents on her last birthday before they died. Carefully smoothing over the battered cover she remembered how precious the book had once been to her—a symbol of all that she had lost. She had left it behind at the cottage when she left along with all her other treasures. But where had Sophie got it from?

Frowning slightly, she suddenly realised that the little girl was watching her, her eyes imploring. With an unexpected movement she opened the book as it lay on Chris's lap, pointing to where Chris had long ago inscribed her name.

Sophie knew! Somehow the little girl had divined what had been in her mind and this was her way of showing her that she did know who she was. Emotion overwhelmed her, and reacting without thinking Chris did what she had promised herself she would not do, reaching out to hug the tense wiry body braced against her. Too late she remember that she had told herself she would let Sophie be the one to do the approaching. "Oh Sophie..." She released her shakily, brushing the fair hair out of the brown eyes. "Yes that was once my book," she told her, trying to sound calm. "My parents gave it to me when I was a little girl—before I went to live with your mummy, but where did you get it?"

Instantly Sophie tensed, her brown eyes frightened and wary. Dear God, Sophie thought she was going to be cross with her. "No no, darling," she said softly, "I'm not cross. I'm glad you found it. Do you want me to read to you from it?"

The fear retreated and Sophie nodded her head guardedly, leaning against the side of Chris's chair as she started to read. The warmth of her slight body was a reminder to Chris of all she herself had never had.

Slater's child, Chris thought painfully glancing at her downbent head, and yet she could see nothing of Slater in her. Because perhaps she didn't want to?

She stopped reading and looked at Sophie, remarking softly, "You know I think you would be much more comfortable sitting on my knee, What do you think? Would you like that?''

She held her breath, half expecting rejection. She was amazed that Sophie had responded to her as well as she had, but when the fair head nodded she managed to conceal her elation and say very calmly. "Come on then, let me lift you up."

She was still there an hour later when Mrs Lancaster returned, the older woman's eyebrows lifting when she came into the garden and she saw them.

"She's asleep," Chris told her smiling at her.

"My goodness, you're honoured, but then I could tell she'd taken to you right from the start. Never left you, her eyes didn't yesterday."

"I can't help wondering what Natalie told her about me," Chris felt drawn to confide in the other woman. "She and I never got on. She used to say I was ugly…"

"Aye, she had a nasty way with words when she wanted," Mrs Lancaster agreed. "Many's the time I found the kiddie crying after she'd had a go at her."

"Slater doesn't seem to think that Sophie's trauma is as a result of her mother's death. He seems to think there's something else."

"I must admit I didn't expect her to take it so hard. After all she didn't see that much of her, but then you never know with kiddies."

Not wanting to seem too curious about her cousin's private affairs Chris did not ask any more questions, letting the housekeeper continue indoors.

Tomorrow she would make a start on Natalie's room, she decided as she carried Sophie inside a little later on.

She heard the 'phone ring as she walked inside, and then it stopped as Mrs Lancaster answered it.

"That was Mr James," she told Chris ten minutes later. "Said he wouldn't be in to dinner tonight and that you were to eat without him."

"Did he say when he would be back?" Did her voice tremble betrayingly Chris wondered, hating herself for asking the question. What business of hers were Slater's comings and goings?

"No, he didn't."

So Slater wouldn't be eating with them tonight. Why should that make her feel so restless and tense. Was he taking Sarah out to dinner perhaps. White-hot shafts of pain burned through her flesh. What was the matter with her, Chris asked herself. Surely she wasn't jealous?

CHAPTER FOUR

CHRIS woke abruptly from a deep sleep, completely disorientated and not knowing why she had woken until she heard the thin keening sound again. It shivered through her, raising goosebumps of flesh on her body, compelling an automatic reaction that had her on her feet and hurrying towards her bedroom door.

The sound was one of an animal in pain and terror—or a small child and Chris headed instinctively for Sophie's room, not bothering to switch on the lights in her haste to reach the little girl.

A nightmare scene greeted her. Sophie's curtains were open, moonlight picking out the rigid figure of the little girl as she sat bolt upright in her bed; her eyes wide and staring, a tormented almost unearthly sound issuing from her throat, making Chris shudder in sympathetic response.

As she reached the bed, Slater's authoritative voice said curtly from behind her, "Leave her...don't touch her. I'll handle this."

He pushed past her, and sat down on the bed, taking Sophie in his arms, murmuring soft words of comfort to her, until the rigidity left her body. Chris expelled her own breath in reaction, not realising how tense she had been until she did so. Very gently Slater laid the sleeping child back on the mattress, watching her broodingly for several seconds before drawing the covers up over her. Sophie's eyes were closed now, her body relaxed and at peace. For the first time Chris became aware of the thinness of her own muslin nightdress. She had responded automatically to Sophie's distress, not bothering to pull on a robe. Unlike Slater. Against her will her eyes were drawn to the open vee between the white lapels of the loosely belted towelling robe he wore, her pulses thudding out an unmistakable message to her.

The robe stopped short at Slater's knees, the unmistakable shape of his hard thighs easily distinguishable beneath the fabric as he came towards her, ushering her out of the room, and then swiftly closing the bedroom door after them.

"What happened?" Chris asked him in a distressed voice. "I heard the most awful sound..."

"Sophie has these nightmares," he told her in a clipped tone. "It's the only time she ever uses her vocal chords. They *had* been getting more infrequent."

The inference was that somehow she was responsible for their re-appearance and Chris flushed angrily. She had been so thrilled by the rapport she seemed to have established with the little girl, and now Slater was making her feel guilty, as though in some way she were responsible for Sophie's distress.

"The theory is that in her nightmares Sophie comes face to face with whatever trauma prevents her from speaking. During the day she's able to keep her fears at bay, but at night..." he shrugged, pain etching sharp lines alongside his mouth and Chris ached with sympathy for Sophie and her mental agony.

"If she could just talk about it..." she whispered, more to herself than anything else, but Slater caught the words and grimaced sardonically.

"If she could...yes all our problems would be solved and Sophie's with them, but unfortunately she can't."

They had been walking down the passage as they spoke, Chris reluctantly conscious of Slater's proximity as his thigh occasionally brushed against hers. Outside her door she halted, turning to face him, her heart leaping into her throat with a bound that almost suffocated her as she saw the way he was looking at her. The moonlight through her open door had her trapped in its beam, tracing the outline of her body beneath the thin cotton of her nightdress in faithful detail. She held her breath as Slater's gaze slid slowly over her, trying to quell the tension building up inside her. In the past he had never looked at her like that. He had desired her yes, but he had been conscious of her youth and experience. Now he was studying her with a blend of raw sexual appreciation and contempt that urged her to escape.

"That's a very fetching garment you're wearing," he drawled softly at last. "Are you sure you got up purely on Sophie's account, Chris?"

"What do you mean?" The breath hissed from her lungs with the question, her skin colouring with anger as she interpreted his question.

"Oh come on Chris," he continued, watching her, "I may not be a member of the jet set crowd you hang around with but I am well aware of the kind of woman you are. Quite a challenge I should imagine, to see if you could come back and take up where you left off, but I'm afraid your reputation's gone to your head my dear I..."

Too furious to guard her tongue, Chris interrupted him. "You know nothing of the woman I am, Slater."

She virtually spat the words at him, her eyes gleaming bright green in the moonlight, her smooth skin flushing with the onrush of adrenaline to her veins. "And as for what you're implying, I wouldn't touch you if you were the last man on earth. You do nothing for me," she hurled at him recklessly for good measure. "You never have and you never will."

"Oh no?" His fingers gripped her wrist as she reached for the door, imprisoning it almost painfully. He was close enough now for her to be aware of the angry rise and fall of his chest, and of the dark fury burning his eyes to molten amber. "It's high time someone shook that pedestal you've place yourself on lady," he ground out against her ear as he bundled her into her room. The moment they were inside, Chris turned on him, reacting instinctively to the fear racing through her, darting for the door as she sought to evade the punishment she sensed he had in mind, but he was too fast for her, leaning against the closed door as she raced for it and using the impetus of her flight to pull her hard against his body, almost knocking the breath from her lungs. His hand left her wrist to grip her waist. She was trapped between his hands, every angry squirm of her body bringing her into closer contact with his unyielding hardness. She could almost feel the rage vibrating inside him.

"I've waited a long time for this opportunity Chris." His fury almost stunned her. She was at a loss to understand the reason for it. *She* was the one who had been betrayed; who had been so badly hurt that she had had to completely change her life in order to escape the pain, and even then she had not succeeded. "You owe me..."

"I owe you nothing." Somehow she managed to bring out the angry denial, all too aware that the increased pressure of Slater's hands was forcing her breasts against his chest, the roughly angry movements of his breathing exerting a sensual stimulation that hardened her nipples into provocative invitation and increased her pulse rate. Why was she reacting to him like this when so many other men had left her cold?

Why? Because quite simply her body had never forgotten his touch; had never forgotten the promise implicit in his lovemaking; once long ago she had been programmed to react passionately to his touch, and she was no more able to stop what was happening to her than she was able to understand his motivation.

"Like hell." He almost snarled the words into her mouth as he bent his head towards her. "When you left here, you were still a virgin—one of the biggest mistakes I ever made. You won't fool me so easily again Chris."

Her virginity, that was what he believed she owed him? That was what this was all about? In Slater's eyes she was the one who got away and he bitterly resented that fact. Wasn't he content with the fact that he had seduced her cousin and impregnated her with his child? Was his conceit so colossal that he regretted that she had not shared Natalie's fate?

Hard on the heels of wrenching pain came fierce rage...rage against herself because he could still arouse her, and rage against him, because he was so much less than she had once thought him to be.

"Is that what all this is about Slater?" She marvelled at her own ability to appear cool and mocking. He was angry, dangerously so, and somehow she must get him out of her room before his control broke completely. To wound him where he was most vulnerable—in his outsize ego—seemed her best chance she decided quickly, knowing that she could not trust herself to react logically while he still held her in his arms. That was the bitterest pill of all—despite everything she knew; all the pain she had endured; she was still physically very much aware of him; her body still yearned for him, and she knew that she would have to fight not just him, but her physical craving for him as well.

"My virginity?" She forced a mocking smile. "It's long gone I'm afraid."

"And I'll bet you can't even remember the man you gave it to." There was a bitter violence in his voice; that shook her, alerting her to her increasing danger. "What can you remember Chris? This?"

His mouth was on hers before she could escape, searing her skin, moulding her lips to the hard contours of his, his tongue expertly prising its way past their soft barrier. A thousand sensations coursed through her veins, chief of which was the knowledge that no man had ever made her feel like this. She knew she should fight to escape, but her body was too weak to obey her mind. She made a soft sound of need in her throat, instantly translated by Slater, his teeth nipping erotically at her skin until her mouth opened, and her hands of their own volition locked behind his head, her fingers clutching at the thick darkness of his hair, as she gave herself up completely to the overpowering rage of need pouring through her. It was as though her starved sense had suddenly come to life, drinking greedily from Slater's mouth, responding to his kiss with a feverish intensity that blotted out all ability to think. His thumb stroked her throat, finding the spot where the soft sounds of pleasure reverberated against her skin, making her tremble with desire.

Her hands slid from his neck to the open lapels of his robe, investigating the powerful structure of his shoulders, his skin warmly sensual like raw silk, to her touch.

She wanted to touch him all over, to absorb him into her and be absorbed by him. It seemed impossible that she could get close enough to him, and his probing thumb registered the impatience of her softly moaned need, as it stroked her throat.

Which one of them loosened the belt of his robe Chris did not know, but she did know that it was Slater who slid the straps of her nightdress down her arms, until the bodice came free, his body taut with desire as he studied the moon-silvered outlines of her breasts. No man had seen her like this before, not even Slater himself, but there was pride in the way Chris held her body, her breathing quickening as she felt Slater register the burgeoning evidence of her desire as her nipples stiffened into hard peaks and she swayed close to him.

Still leaning on the door he pulled her into the cradle of his hips, the hard evidence of his desire for her something that would have shocked her normally but which now made her ache with excitement and need. Rational thought was impossible. Past and present merged and mingled until they were inseparable. The six long years they had been apart might never have been; Chris's body rejoiced in his familiar touch, her mouth pressing wildly pleading kisses against his skin as his hands cupped her breasts and his dark head descended, his lips making a leisurely exploration of her satin skin.

Neither of them spoke a word, the sound of their mingled breathing the only thing to break the thick silence. Obeying some unspoken command Chris arched back against the support of Slater's hands low on her back. In the moonlight her breasts gleamed milky white, their full curves taut and provocative. Her heart thudded with sledge-hammer blows, an aching need coiling in the pit of her stomach. Against her lower body Slater's thighs felt hard and tense, the heat coming off his skin invading her bloodstream and quickening the course of her blood.

One hand left her back to cup her breast, his thumb stroking slowly over the hard peak of her nipple. Slater's gaze fastened on the flesh he was caressing with a tense absorption that tightened the spiral of need inside Chris, until she wanted to cry out with the agony of it.

With almost unbearable slowness Slater lowered his mouth to her breast, stroking agonising deliberate circles of pleasure round the pale skin just beyond the aureole of her nipple. It was a torment Chris couldn't endure. She lifted her hands to his neck burying her fingers in his hair as she urged his mouth against her body, arching it wantonly against him. Still he continued his sensual play with her nipple, teasing it with light moist strokes that drove her into a mindless frenzy of need, husky sounds of frustration joining the growing tension of their breathing.

"Chris..." The hoarse sound of Slater's voice intruded on her private world of fantasy, shocking her into reality. Slater raised his head to study her, his eyes missing nothing as they slid slowly over her body in sardonic appraisal of its arousal. The heat inside her turned to ice, and Chris shivered, bitterly regretting her lack of self control.

"What was that you said about me doing nothing for you?"

It was a taunt she might have expected, and one that was well deserved in the circumstances, and where she had ached with desire Chris now ached with pain. As Slater released her, she made an instinctive move to cross her arms over her naked breasts. His expression grimly contemptuous he followed the movement.

"All these years I've wondered what it would have been like with you but a woman who's so easily aroused by every man who touches her is like flat champagne—tasteless and unappetising."

"You wanted me." Chris murmured the words in bewildered agony unable to comprehend fully what had happened.

"That was merely a male manifestation of physical desire... there was nothing personal in it Chris, just as there was nothing personal in your desire for me. Your New York studs might not mind being merely one of a crowd, but I'm afraid that's not for me." He opened the door and walked through it leaving her staring numbly after him.

How had it happened? How had he trapped her into betraying herself to him in such a way? Her mind circled endlessly trying to find an explanation, but there was none. Her lips were dry, and she touched them with the tip of her tongue, disturbed by their faintly swollen contours. Like an automaton she pulled on her nightdress, shuddering as deep spasms of self disgust wracked her. She deserved every ounce of the contempt Slater had shown her—not because she was the shallow, self indulgent creature he believed, but because she had allowed her body to betray her mind, to overrule six years of hard work. Originally when she left Little Martin she had told herself that at least she had her self respect; that that was still intact; now she didn't even have that. She had melted in Slater's arms like a lighted candle, like over-dry kindling, and it still shocked her that he had the power to ignite her senses in that way. Viewed from a distance of six years, her adolescent hunger for him had been something she had set aside as unable to happen to her a second time. The intensity of need he could arouse inside her was something she found hard to come to terms with. She knew herself well enough to know that she had never felt like that with anyone else. Slater was the only one who could make her burn with physical hunger. Why? Because of what had happened between them in the past; that must be the answer. Unbidden, another and more serious explanation raised its head, but Chris refused to even admit it. Still in love with Slater? How could she be.

She couldn't hide herself away in her room for ever, Chris told herself sardonically, studying her reflection in the mirror, her make-up was flawless and only an expert could tell how much she had done to conceal the results of her sleepless night. Her hair she had drawn back in a sophisticated knot; her silk separates were specially chosen to enhance her cool, touch me not appearance. It was a little too late to hide behind that façade now, she told herself cynically, but she needed the armour of appearing to be in control when she faced Slater. Her face coloured faintly beneath her make-up as she remembered her abandoned response to him. No, Slater wasn't going to allow her to forget last night in a hurry. Teeth clenched she walked towards the door. She would *have* to face him, for Sophie's sake if nothing else.

He lifted his head briefly in acknowledgement of her presence as she walked into the breakfast room. Dressed for the office, he looked remote and formidable. Trying to stem her inward quivering Chris pulled out a chair and sat down.

"Very impressive." The paper was laid aside as he studied her immaculate face and silk blouse. "But it doesn't fool me Chris. I ought to thank you for last night. It might have taken six years to bring me to my senses, but last night certainly did the trick. There's nothing like a cold dose of reality for banishing impossible dreams is there?"

He was talking in riddles that Chris could not understand. She started to pour herself a cup of coffee and then stopped as her hand started to shake.

"Withdrawal symptoms?" His smile was tauntingly cruel. "You don't have to stay here Chris, you know that. You can leave any time you like."

"That's just what you'd like me to do isn't it." The truth hit her in a blinding flash. Slater was too clever to openly defy Natalie's will, but there were more subtle ways of making sure she never fulfilled her responsibilities towards Sophie. "I'm not leaving here yet Slater," she told him curtly, "Not until I find out what's haunting Sophie . . ."

"Noble sentiments." His face looked austere, his expression shuttered. "You realise of course, that we might never find out. Sophie's trauma could be permanent."

It was a shocking thought. Chris's mind switched from her own problems to the little girl's. "How is she this morning?" she queried worriedly.

"Still sleeping. She often does after a bad night like last night. I've given Mrs Lancaster instructions to let her sleep on. What do you propose to do with yourself this morning?"

Who did he think he was, her gaoler? Chris frowned deeply. "I thought I'd go into the village and see about getting the Mini fixed. I can't keep on using someone else's car."

"Umm..."

He didn't speak again until he got up to leave, by which time Chris's nerves were in shreds. Unlike her he seemed to have suffered no after affects from last night, but then unlike her he had not suffered the most acute mental and physical anguish because of it. The most unpalatable thing of all was that her body still ached for him; still hungered for his possession.

After he had gone Chris went upstairs to look in on Sophie. The little girl was so peacefully asleep that it seemed impossible to connect her peace now with the torment she had suffered during the night. Slater had told her that Sophie rarely woke up during her nightmares, and that on her doctor's advice he did not mention them to her when she was awake.

Explaining to Mrs Lancaster where she was going, Chris got in her borrowed car and drove down to the village. The small garage looked much sprucer than she remembered it and the young man who came forward to help her seemed eager to please. Quickly Chris outlined her problem.

"I'll certainly go up and a have a look at it for you," he agreed when she had finished. "Where did you say you were staying?"

When Chris told him, she was surprised to see that dark colour seeping up under his skin. "You'll be Nat...that is Mrs James's cousin then?" he blurted out.

"Yes." She watched him carefully. Obviously he knew Natalie, but then he would. Little Martin was a very small village. He was quite attractive in a fair-headed, boyish way, probably a couple of years her junior Chris deduced, and possibly something of an idealist.

"You knew my cousin?"

He nodded his head, his colour increasing, his head lowering defensively as he answered. "She brought her car to me for servicing. We got quite friendly." His face twisted into a bitter smile. "If she'd taken my advice she might still be alive now. I knew she wasn't happy, but..." he turned away, and Chris questioned sharply,

"Natalie told you she wasn't happy?"

"We used to go out for a drink occasionally. Her car hadn't been running very well. I couldn't find anything wrong with it, so she suggested we went out for a drive—she thought the fault might show up better. She told me she was very lonely and we got into the habit of going out once or twice a month." He saw Chris's expression and not knowing what had caused it and that her sardonic grimace was more for her cousin's duplicity that because of his response to it, said defensively, "It was all quite innocent...she just needed someone to talk to... I liked her...she said that no one here understood her. She was bored, lonely...

Her husband ignored her; he had other women. The coroner said that she took her own life because she was severely depressed, but it was her husband who was really responsible. If he hadn't neglected her. If he'd loved her as she deserved to be loved.'' He turned to Chris, his face drawn in betraying lines of anguish, and Chris recognised in his expression all his hopeless adoration of her cousin and felt pity for him. ''He refused to sleep with her you know, to be a proper husband to her. It started when she was carrying his child. He said she looked repulsive. He broke her heart.''

His revelations were astounding Chris. She didn't know what to believe. Natalie had always had a penchant for embroidering the truth, but she already knew that her cousin and Slater had separate rooms. Had he perhaps regretted his impulsive marriage to her? Had he ever wished that *she* had been the one he had married? But no, she was letting her imagination run away with her now. Slater had never really wanted her. She knew that Natalie had died from an overdose of sleeping pills and she wondered suddenly if the doctor who had prescribed them had realised how dangerously depressed her cousin was.

Having thanked Natalie's young admirer for his offer to check over the Mini, Chris made arrangements to telephone him in a few days' time to see what progress if any had been made. He had, she learned before she took her leave of him, bought the small village business with a small legacy. Had he and Natalie been lovers? Somehow Chris didn't think so. Richard Courtland did not strike her as the type to involve himself with another man's wife on a physical level. No whatever comfort Natalie had had from him, it had been of a purely emotional nature Chris felt sure.

Before returning to the house she called in at the village chemist in Little Martin, they shared a doctor with three other villages, and old Doctor Goodfellow had never made any secret of his contempt for sleeping tablets and tranquilisers. Chris was nearly sure he would never have prescribed them to Natalie who had always had a tendency towards morbid hypochondria.

On enquiry the chemist told her cheerfully that Doctor Goodfellow had retired, and that they now came under a local Group Practise based in the nearest town. "It's Doctor Howard who nearly always does the house calls," he further amplified. "He lives just outside the village. He used to practice in London, but when his wife became ill they decided to move down here. Shame about her. Only thirty-two and likely to be an invalid for the rest of her life." He explained to Chris that the doctor's wife suffered from a progressive muscular wasting disease, adding that their three children were now at boarding school. "Devoted to his kids Doctor Howard is."

Smiling mechanically Chris left the shop. It wasn't hard to imagine that an overworked doctor, with as many personal problems as Dr Howard apparently had, would prescribe sleeping tablets for someone like Natalie . . . possibly hoping to keep her out of his busy surgery.

Chris wondered if it was worth going to see him. She knew that nothing would bring back her cousin, but she couldn't help thinking if she could discover more about *why* she had taken her own life she might find some clue that would help with Sophie.

It was lunchtime when she got back to the house. Sophie picked lacklustrely at her food, looking heavy-eyed and tired. It transpired that it was Mrs Lancaster's afternoon off, and Chris readily agreed to look after the little girl, suggesting that they went out for a walk.

Sophie nodded her head when the question was put to her, and half an hour later the two of them set along a path Chris remembered from her own childhood. It led across several fields and on to some open ground where gypsies used to camp when Chris was little. At first Sophie seemed quite eager to walk briskly through the fields. The crops were growing well and as they walked Chris talked, not asking for any reply, but trying to monitor Sophie's response to her chatter. It wasn't until they reached the last field that Chris realised the open ground no longer existed. Several houses had been built on it, including a large bungalow whose back garden overlooked the fields. Frowning slightly she was disturbed to discover that Sophie had suddenly gone rigid, her small body very tense.

"Sophie, darling, what is it?" Chris knelt beside her, looking worriedly at her set face. Sophie was staring in the direction of the new development. Puzzled, Chris followed her concentrated attention. There was nothing especially remarkable about the houses; nothing that to her eyes could have given rise to the little girl's intense reaction.

Deciding to take a risk Chris said casually, "Come on then, let's go and look at those houses, I haven't seen them before."

She stood up but before she could take a single step forward Sophie tugged on her hand and refused to move. It wasn't until Chris turned round to face the direction they had come in that Sophie consented to walk.

What had been the cause of her sudden tension? Chris wondered if it was worth mentioning the incident to anyone, reluctant to approach Slater in case he thought she was simply using Sophie as an excuse to draw his attention to her. Her face flamed as she thought about the previous night. She tried to dismiss the memories from her mind, but they kept surging back. The intensity of her own physical response still shocked her; even now she could hardly believe that she had actually experienced such an overwhelming need. It was completely out of character. Completely out of the character she had built for herself since leaving home, she amended slightly. The old Chrissie had reacted in much the same way, only then she had not had the experience to recognise the intensity of her desire.

Sophie looked so tired and drained when they got back to the house that Chris suggested a nap. Although she could not speak Sophie had her own way of communicating and her brief nod confirmed to Chris that the little girl was tired.

With Sophie asleep the rest of the afternoon stretched emptily ahead. It was five o'clock. She had no idea what time she could expect Slater back—if indeed he intended to return for dinner. In the old days he had only worked Saturday mornings. She had a strong suspicion that from now on he would be at pains to avoid her. He had made his point; proved how vulnerable to him she was.

Sighing, Chris remembered her promise to go through Natalie's things. She pushed open the door to her cousin's room, letting out her breath in a faint sigh. The decor was typically Natalie, strong and dra-

matic with lots of rich colours. A bank of wardrobes
filled one wall.

An hour later Chris had accumulated several piles
of clothes on the floor beside her. The air around her
was thick with her cousin's favourite perfume, almost
cloyingly so, and Chris moved back to push open the
bedroom door. Natalie certainly hadn't stinted herself on clothes, but then wasn't clothes buying a favoured occupation of lonely, bored women? *Had* her
cousin been lonely?

A small sound made Chris turn round. Sophie was
standing just inside the open door a look of abject
horror on her face. When she saw Chris she made a
small, inarticulate sound and hurled herself at her, the
force of her small body nearly rocking Chris back on
her heels.

Instinctively she comforted the little girl, hugging
and soothing her. Sophie buried her face against her
breast, breathing in deeply, and it was several seconds
before Chris realised that the little girl was trying to
absorb *her* perfume. Unlike Natalie's it was light and
fresh, and Sophie seemed to find it soothing, because
she stopped trembling and allowed Chris to stand up
with her in her arms.

She was just walking towards the door with her,
when Slater walked in, his eyes a hard, metallic gold.
They raked over her furiously as she stood there, a
pulse beating sporadically at the side of his jaw.

"What are you doing?"

"Natalie was my cousin." Chris replied tautly, for
some reason not bothering to explain to him that Mrs
Lancaster had requested her help. "Isn't it natural that
I should want to know why she should want to end her
life?"

"And you hoped to find explanations in here?" His smile was unkindly derisive. "Natalie spent almost as little time in her own bed as she did in mine. Well," he demanded savagely when she stared mutely at him, "isn't that what you wanted to know? Isn't that one of the reasons why you came back? To see just what havoc you wrought?"

His meaning was lost to her, all she could do was take in the fact that whilst she had assumed Slater's indifference had driven Natalie away from him, he was implying that her cousin never enjoyed being his wife. What was the truth?

CHAPTER FIVE

NOT wanting to meet Sarah again Chris decided the next time the other girl was due that she would spend the morning at the cottage. Before she got estimates for the work that would need to be done she wanted to have another look at the place. Was it simply misplaced nostalgia that made her want to keep it? After all she was rarely in England these days. Still she wouldn't model for ever, she reminded herself and then there was Sophie. The cottage would be a useful base from which she could see the little girl in years to come. She had a sudden and sharply painful vision of Slater with Sarah and perhaps even their children, herself condemned always to be an outsider in his life, tolerated because Natalie had appointed her as her child's guardian. A bitter thought struck her. Natalie had known how desperately in love with Slater she had been; had her cousin appointed her as Sophie's guardian through some Machiavellian desire to cause her further pain? She frowned, trying to dismiss the thought as she drove towards the cottage. She had heard so much that was conflicting recently, it was no wonder she found it difficult to correlate all the facts properly. For instance Richard had claimed that it had been Slater who rejected Natalie because of her pregnancy, while Slater had implied, without saying as much, that Natalie had been promiscuous—unfaithful to her marriage vows, but then might her emotionally unstable cousin have thought she had good reason to be if Richard was right and Slater had rejected her?

When she pulled up outside the cottage Chris was no nearer to discovering exactly what she thought. As a teenager she had found Slater sexually overpowering; he was a man with a strong sex drive as recent events had proved and she couldn't see him absenting himself from his wife's bed unless there was someone else to take her place. Had he perhaps betrayed *her?* Both of them had been young and innocent—perhaps too naïve to hold his interest once the thrill of the initial chase was over.

In the bright early summer sunshine the cottage looked depressingly dilapidated. It would cost a fortune to put it in order, Chris mused as she examined the downstairs rooms. The kitchen, always small and poky needed completely gutting and perhaps even extending, if planning permission could be obtained. The prospect of all the work and expense involved should have been daunting but as she wandered round Chris found herself imagining how the cottage could be; how much she would enjoy being here, looking after Sophie... the two of them spending long evenings talking... If Sophie ever did talk again.

She must, Chris thought fiercely, somehow the little girl must be freed from the trauma trapping her in her world of silence. If only there was some way she could really help her. The impotence of her situation galled her. She wanted so much to help Sophie, already drawn to the little girl in a way she had never expected. Sophie had much of her grandmother in her Chris acknowledged; and that combined with the physical similarity between them had forged an almost instantaneous bond. Soberly she reflected on how that same combination must have affected Natalie, who had loathed *her*, and never truly appreciated her own mother.

Sighing Chris made her way upstairs. The stairs creaked protestingly under the pressure of her weight, the banister rail dangerously rickety. Upstairs Chris made instinctively for her own room, her eyes glancing along the familiar book shelves. There were several small gaps. Did that mean Sophie had more books that had belonged to her? But how had she got them? Chris couldn't see Natalie giving them to her. Natalie had never been a keen reader; indeed Chris had a vivid memory of crying wretchedly under the bedclothes one night because Natalie had mutilated one of her favourite books. Natalie had taken a spiteful pleasure in her distress, she remembered wryly. Could her cousin have changed so much that she had actually wanted to hand Sophie into her care through genuine cousinly love? Chris did not think so. She bit her lip as she stared sightlessly out of the bedroom window. She had a strong conviction that her earlier suspicions had been the right ones. Natalie had made the appointment through sheer malice, knowing how much it would torture her to have to come in close contact with Slater. Knowing...

Chris drew in a sharp breath, trembling as she sank down on to her bed, unaware of the damp seeping from it into her jeans. What was she thinking? What was she admitting? Suddenly she had been brought face to face with something she had tried to conceal from herself for years. There had been no one else in her life simply because she had never completely evicted Slater from it. Oh yes, she had gone away, built a new life for herself, but it had been in many ways a sterile life; and no matter how much she tried to deny it to herself she was still very vulnerable to Slater. She had met many men during her careers as a model—some as sexually powerful, many better looking, but none of them affected her in the way that he did. She still loved him; if love, such a simple word, was the right description from the frightening complexity and range of emotions he aroused inside her; anger; need; pain, sharply acute sexual hunger, and always a terrible aching loss that she should care so much and he should care not at all.

Shivering, she stood up, pacing the small room, angry with herself and bitterly resentful of Natalie who forced this confrontation upon her. The other night when Slater had touched her she had responded blindly, instinctively, her starved sense responding to his touch against her will. He believing her to be sexually experienced had put her response down to sexual hunger—she knew better. Wrapping her arms round her slender waist she told herself that Slater must never, ever discover the truth. If he did he would use it to humiliate and degrade her, to mock her and cause her pain as he had done once before. Like a child burned by fire Chris shrank away from even the thought of such pain, remembering how searing and agonising it had been.

Suddenly the cottage seemed claustrophobic. She walked towards the door, bumping into a small chest in her haste. The impact jarred her hip painfully. It also moved the small chest a few inches and revealed a man's tie lying half concealed beneath it. Idly Chris bent and picked it up. The tie was very traditional;

striped in the fashion of an old school or university tie. She fingered it absently, noting that the fabric was high quality silk. How had it come to be in this room? Perhaps it had been Natalie's father's, although somehow it looked too new. Telling herself that it didn't matter who it belonged to, she put it on top of the chest, and headed for the door.

It was time she returned her borrowed car to its rightful owner and checked up on the Mini's progress. If nothing could be done with it she would have to hire another for the duration of her visit.

A call at the garage elicited the information that the Mini was being overhauled and that there was nothing major wrong with it. It would take two days to fix, Richard told her with a shy smile, asking if she wanted him to continue with the work. Chris said that she did, and then drove on to the small estate agents' office. Harold Davies was delighted to see her, and asked her out to lunch. Remembering the work that would need to be done on the cottage Chris assented. She would be able to pick his brains as to who she ought to employ. When she mentioned the car, he brushed aside her comments. "Keep it until yours is ready. My sister won't be back for some time yet."

"You really are very generous," Chris thanked him. "I don't know how I'm going to repay you."

"By having lunch with me today and dinner one night later in the week," he responded promptly.

They both laughed. Chris recognised his type of approach, and was amused by it. Harold Davies was a man who would always enjoy having an attractive woman on his arm; if she was socially or publicly prominent, so much the better. When he married, it would be a carefully judged step, possibly to someone who was faintly "county". He was a man who would always put his own interests first, but he was pleasant company. Lunching out would be a welcome break from her too intense thoughts, she decided as she followed him out to his car, smiling faintly as she noticed the impressive lines of the new registration BMW, commenting dutifully on it as she slid into the passenger seat.

"A reasonable car is a must in my business," Harold told her with a smile. "Helps impress the clients..."

He took her to a small country restaurant that was new to her, but obviously very popular to judge from the packed car park. Without being told Chris guessed that it was the local "in" place.

"This place hasn't been open very long," Harold told her, confirming her thoughts. "I sold them the farmhouse—a very enterprising young couple, who specialise in nouvelle cuisine. I think you'll like it."

Inside Chris was pleased to see that the farmhouse atmosphere had been retained. The cottage had been skilfully renovated to provide a comfortable, but authentic-looking dining room.

The young woman who greeted them was pleasant and charming. Harold introduced her as Sally Webb, explaining that she and her husband ran the restaurant. "Paul is king of the kitchen." Sally added with a grin. "I'm responsible for the buying and the general running of the place." They chatted for a few minutes, and then went to the bar to order their drinks. By the time they had been served Sally was back to take them to their table. Although busy, the restaurant wasn't overcrowded, and Chris particularly liked the way the other woman went through the menu with them. The selection was quite small, but very varied, and Chris gave her order confident that she was going to enjoy every mouthful.

They were just waiting for their first course, when a tall fair-haired man walked into the restaurant. Broad shouldered, physically, he was very attractive, although Chris had the unmistakable impression that he was under some degree of strain. His blond hair was already streaked with silver, although he couldn't be more than in his late thirties at the most. When he saw Harold he smiled and came quickly towards them.

"John," Harold greeted him warmly. "Are you lunching alone?"

"That was my intention," the other man agreed.

"Well if Chris doesn't mind, why don't you join us?" Harold suggested quickly.

Put like that Chris could hardly have voiced an objection even had she wanted to, but she didn't. Something about the blond-haired man touched her deeply. She had an intuitive sense that he had experienced great pain. Whoever he was, he must be relatively important for Harold to want him to join them, she thought cynically. A prospective client perhaps?

The introduction when it came startled her. "Chris, meet John," Harold smiled, "Dr John Howard. He lives just outside the village..."

"Yes..." Chris's smile was automatic. "Yes, I know..." So this was Dr Howard. The same doctor who had prescribed Natalie's sleeping pills apparently. Was that why he looked so strained? He looked a caring man; one who would suffer from the knowledge that one of his patients had used the drugs he had given for aid, to end her life. And then Chris remembered the story of his wife, and her sympathy increased. Instinctly she put herself out to make him feel at ease, tactfully mentioned in conversation that she was Natalie's cousin, and sensing his controlled start.

"A real tragedy," Harold interrupted, "and that poor little kid. How is she, Chris?"

"It's hard for me to say. I know so little about these things. What are the chances of her regaining speech?" She put the question directly to John Howard, glad of an opportunity to get a qualified medical opinion.

"It depends." He had gone very tense; Chris could plainly see the signs of his tension in his clenched hands and white face.

"On what?" Chris persisted. "Discovering the cause of the original trauma? I'm sure it's connected with Natalie in some way," she continued. "My cousin..." She broke off, startled as John Howard upset his drink, the fluid pouring stickily over the table. His face was almost as white as the linen, and Chris was shocked by his tension.

He apologised jerkily. Harold was frowning, and Chris summoned every last ounce of her social poise to smooth over the awkward moment. She didn't know why John Howard had knocked over his drink like that, but plainly he had more compelling things on his mind than Sophie's trauma. She talked gaily for several minutes about her life in New York, making Harold laugh and even drawing a faint smile from John, and by the time their food arrived the awkward moment might never have been.

John ordered quickly, refusing a starter. He and Harold obviously moved in the same crowd, and Chris listened to them discussing a local hunt meeting with one ear while her other sense quivered tensely in response to some silent, subtle message. At last, unable to stop herself, she turned her head.

Now it was her turn to lose colour. Slater was seated three tables away, with two other business-suited men and an extremely glamorous brunette. All four of them seemed to be engrossed in discussion but as her glance lingered on Slater's face it was as though she had sent out some silent message to him. He moved, gold eyes taunting green, his mouth twisting derisively as he studied her too-pale face. Still acutely aware of the morning's unpleasant discovery that she loved him Chris was the first to look away, hoping that he had not noticed the sudden betraying flood of colour surging up under her skin.

Who was the brunette? In other circumstances she would have found her instinctive jealously almost ridiculous, but now she was held fast in its painfully biting grip, torturing herself on its sharp teeth, as she tried to listen to what her table companions were saying instead of watching Slater.

He was like a magnet, drawing her attention back to him time and time again. On several occasions he looked up to find her watching him, and on one the brunette saw her, and smiled.

"Umm, I hadn't realised Slater was here," Harold commented following her gaze. "He's got the Chief of Executives from Fanchon with him too... Must be negotiating another contract with them."

Fanchon, he went on to explain, were a French company in a similar market to Slater's, to whom he occasionally sold various patent rights.

"And the girl?" Chris asked as lightly as she could.

"Slater's secretary," Harold told her promptly. Chris felt acutely sick. What was the matter with her?

Just because the girl was Slater's secretary it did not necessarily mean that they had a sexual relationship as well as a business one. What about Sarah?

What about her, she derided inwardly, with unusual bitterness. Sarah, like herself and Natalie would no doubt have to accustom herself to sharing him.

She was glad when the lunch was over, and so it seemed was John Howard. There was an almost physical air of relief about him as he stood up. She had not, Chris thought regretfully been able to ask him about Natalie. Moved by sudden impulse she reached out to place a restraining hand on his jacket. "Please..." she asked huskily, "could I see you some time...I want to talk to you about Natalie." Beneath her fingers Chris felt his arm tense. "I...I'll call you," he told her curtly. "I must go now..."

"He seems to be under a lot of strain," Chris commented to Harold as they left the restaurant.

"Yes, well of course, his wife is virtually an invalid. That can't be easy for a man—a normal healthy man, to live with. Of course he would never divorce her," he added, "she comes from an extremely wealthy family. He was in private practice before she became ill; the work he does now can hardly pay as much, and once one has become used to a certain standard of living..."

His comments nauseated Chris, but then Harold would think that way, she told herself as they headed back to his office. That, of course, did not mean that John Howard did. He had struck her as far too sensitive and caring a man to jettison his wife when she needed him the most, but then men as a race rarely thought as women did. Women were capable of great sacrifice on behalf of the men they loved, men seldom returned the favour.

When they returned to his office Chris discussed with Harold the work she believed needed doing on the cottage. As she had hoped he knew of several firms who could carry it out and promised to obtain estimates for her.

"So, it could be that we might see a little more of you in the future," he commented as he walked with her to the car. "I'm very glad." Before she left he asked her out to dinner mentioning that some friends of his were holding a twenty-first party for their daughter and that he would like her to accompany him. The party was on Saturday, and Chris asked him if she could let him know. She hadn't come to Little Martin to socialise, but for Sophie's sake, then again though by Saturday she might be glad of an excuse to escape from the house and Slater's disturbing presence.

Sophie was having a nap when Chris got back to the house. Sarah had left but Mrs Lancaster raised her eyebrows when Chris asked what progress had been made. "Sarah gets too impatient with her. Succeeding with Sophie is very important to her—too important perhaps. I think she hopes to impress Slater..."

Chris was a little surprised that the housekeeper should speak to her so freely, but then no doubt Mrs Lancaster, who couldn't know of the events of the past, considered Chris as a member of Slater's family. Had Natalie envisaged how she would feel; how she would suffer being in such close proximity to Slater. She shuddered suddenly. Could that thought perhaps even have been in her cousin's mind in those last moments before her death? All at once she could almost feel Natalie's malevolence reaching out to touch her. Shrugging aside the unpleasant sensation she went upstairs to Sophie's room. The little girl was fast asleep. She had been drawing, and sheets of brightly coloured paper littered the bed. Almost absently Chris started to pick them up, freezing as she studied the stick figures. In one drawing a small stick figure was confronting a larger one, both, to judge from the dresses Sophie had drawn on them, female. The larger one's face was contorted in an expression of anger so violent, Chris could almost feel it. She couldn't see the smaller figure's face because Sophie had drawn her back view. Quite irrationally she felt that the drawing had some relevance to Sophie's trauma, and she riffled through the other drawings, studying them all carefully, but there were none similar.

Extracting the drawing she bent down to touch the sleeping child's hair. Poor Sophie. If only she was *her* child Chris thought achingly, hers and Slater's. Angry with herself she went into her own room, putting the drawing in the drawer beside her bed. She wanted to show it to Slater, but she was afraid he would dismiss her suspicions as childish.

Restless; pursued by unwelcome thoughts she wandered out into the garden. Beyond the expanse of lawn a winding path led to a secluded summerhouse, built beside an ornamental fish pool. The pool had always entranced Chris; the peace and solitude of the summer house drawing her, and she headed there now. Sheltered from the rest of the garden by a screen of trees, it had a secret, ageless air.

The summerhouse was unlocked and Chris walked inside, noticing that since she had last visited it, new cushions had been made for the seats that lined one wall. She had often imagined Edwardian ladies taking afternoon tea here, swinging gently in a hammock beside the pool perhaps, while fanned by some ardent, but bashful admirer. Lost in daydreams, she jumped tensely when she heard Slater's voice, calling her name, her instinctive, "what are you doing here?" drawing a sardonic smile from his lips. "I live here," he drawled, "What's your excuse?"

She shrugged, striving to steady her racing pulses. "The summerhouse always drew me." Too late she recalled with intense clarity that they had once taken shelter here from a sudden summer storm, her thin cotton dress had been soaked in their impulsive instinctive dash for shelter, and she had not realised why Slater was studying her so intently until she looked down and saw the outline of her breasts clearly delineated beneath the thin cotton. That had been the first time he had kissed her with real passion, his hands molding the firm shape of her breasts, teaching her things about her own burgeoning sexuality she had never dreamed possible. With an effort she dragged her thoughts away from the past.

"Enjoy your lunch?"

Slater was watching her, waiting to trap her, she sensed intuitively. "Very much," she responded coolly. "Enjoy yours?"

"Financially it was extremely rewarding, as no doubt was yours. Two new possible lovers discovered in one day, but that's all they'll ever be Chris—lovers. Harold won't marry anyone less than someone with the right social pedigree, and John Howard will never leave his wife. But then you always did have a penchant for other people's men, didn't you? Those were always the sort of men you wanted.''

She could sense his anger without knowing the cause for it. She could feel it reaching out to envelop her like a blast of heat and she responded to it, driven to goad him by saying mockingly. ''I once wanted you Slater... remember?''

For a moment the folly of her taunt crystallised in her mind and she wanted to call the words back, but Slater was already reacting, his mouth twisted in a bitter parody of a smile.

''Oh yes, I remember all right...'' he agreed smoothly. ''I just wish to hell I didn't,'' Chris thought she heard him mutter under his breath as he came towards her. ''I remember this.'' He reached her before she could evade him, the back of the cushions brushing against the back of her knees as she tried to move away.

''What are you so nervous about, Chris?'' he asked her mockingly. ''Why the timid virgin act? You must have played this scene a thousand times since we first rehearsed it here in this summerhouse. How did it go?'' His voice had an ugly taunting sound that tore at her heart. ''Oh yes... Take one rain-dampened girl... conveniently not wearing a bra.''

''Stop it.'' The words were torn from her throat making it ache with pain. He was deliberately trampling on all her memories, destroying not just her future but her past, turning something that to her at least had been poignantly beautiful into something mundane and even unpleasantly calculated. There had been nothing calculated in her response to him nor in her embarrassment when she found him looking at her. Her breasts rose and fell in quick agitation beneath her cotton shirt, her breath tightening painfully into an explosive knot in her chest when Slater deliberately placed one hand either side of her head on the wall behind her, leaning his torso towards her.

He was close enough for her to catch the scent of his body, male and slightly musky as though tormenting her like this was something that vaguely excited him. The thought made her nauseous, her body trembling with reaction. She was old enough to be able to handle this situation with sophistication, she reminded herself, so why wasn't she doing so? Why was she reacting like an adolescent, torn between escape and desire.

"Stop it?" His eyebrows rose. "I haven't even begun to start yet Chris. And besides you don't really want me to stop do you?"

She turned her head away so that she wouldn't have to look at him, shocked when his fingers suddenly bit into her arms, and he hauled her against his body. "Do you?" he grated, almost shaking her.

"What am I supposed to say Slater?" For a moment she had almost believed the harsh voice held a note of fierce agony, but she dismissed this as sheer imagination, reminding herself of how he had hurt her; of how he must not guess how she felt. Summoning all her courage she threw back her head, forcing herself to meet his eyes. "What do you want from me Slater? What do you want to hear me say? That I want you?"

"Yes...damn you. Yes! You owe me Chris..." His voice dropped slightly over the last few words, his eyes dark with anger.

Chris was too stupefied to respond. *She* owed *him?* How could he stand there and expect her to accept that?

"You owe me..." He repeated the words as though they were some private incantation as he bent his head, the hard pressure of his body against hers making Chris acutely aware of his arousal. It was all so unexpected and inexplicable that she had no defences against him. The pressure of his mouth was fiercely, angrily demanding, savaging the softness of her lips, invoking a response from her that brought thickly muttered sounds of pleasure from his throat.

She was lost, completely and utterly, Chris thought hazily, melting beneath the heat of his kiss, wanting him... loving him...

"Slater?"

Sarah's voice from outside the summerhouse broke into the dreamworld Chris had entered. Instinctively she tensed, breaking away from Slater. He was breathing heavily, the pupils of his eyes dilated, whether by anger or passion Chris could not tell. She was old enough now to know that men did not necessarily love and respect where they desired and she had to turn away as Sarah entered the summerhouse, sickened by her own blind, betraying response to him.

"Oh there you are," she heard the other girl saying peevishly. "I've been looking for you. We're supposed to be going out to dinner tonight..."

"Yes, I know. What progress have you made with Sophie today?"

If she had needed confirmation that Slater cared nothing for her, she had it in his swift reversion to normal; his complete lack of interest in her.

"Not much."

Chris forced herself to turn round, shaken by the open hostility in Sarah's eyes as she studied her. "She seems to be very disturbed by your presence." She looked directly at Chris. "If you want my opinion Slater, you'll get rid of her. Sophie will never make any progress while she stays here upsetting her."

Chris held her breath, almost dizzy with the effort as she waited for Slater to denounce her and agree with Sarah.

"I can't do that," he astounded her by saying. "Natalie chose Chris as Sophie's guardian . . ."

"Heaven alone knows why," Sarah cut in impatiently. "She never had a good word to say for her while she was alive." She turned away opening the summerhouse door. "I'll see you later then Slater . . ."

She went without a word to Chris, who wondered why she had come when she was seeing Slater later on that evening. Perhaps she wanted to reinforce to Chris her involvement with him. Suddenly she felt very vulnerable and insecure. Perhaps Sarah was right? Perhaps she was having a bad effect on Sophie? Her negative feelings made her murmur softly, "I don't know why Natalie appointed me either . . ."

The tension emanating from Slater as she made the admission startled her. His face was pale under his tan, the skin drawn tightly over the bones of his face. "Oh come on, Chris," he said icily. "We both know exactly why . . ."

He turned on his heel and left her before she could say another word, but Chris was glad she was alone. The pain of the blow he had just dealt her was so severe that she would have broken down if he'd stayed. He knew . . . He knew how she felt about him and just why Natalie had appointed her. He *knew* and he was adding to her torment deliberately. He must hate her nearly as much as Natalie had!

Instinctively she wanted to escape, to put as much distance between herself and Slater as she could, but she could not do it, for Sophie's sake. She must simply stay and endure.

CHAPTER SIX

THAT night Chris went to bed early, but sleep eluded her. Of course her wakefulness had nothing to do with the fact Slater was out with Sarah, she derided herself, as she lay tense waiting for the sound of his returning car. All these years she had deluded herself that she was over him; that he meant nothing to her other than bad memories and now in a few short days the protective cover she had built around herself had been blasted away.

Not until she heard Slater's car stop outside the house did she manage to sleep. A glance at her watch showed her that it was nearly two o'clock. Jealousy, fiercely corrosive and painful, overwhelmed her as she pictured Sarah in Slater's arms. Her desire to find out why Natalie had taken her own life was fast being overtaken by an instinctive need to get away from Slater before he haunted her; he knew why Natalie had appointed her Sophie's guardian; he knew exactly how vulnerable she was, but please God he did not know yet *why* she was so vulnerable. If only she could leave, but there was Sophie to consider; Sophie who she sensed needed her. Perhaps she *was* over-dramatising she reflected in the morning as she dressed. Why should Sophie respond to *her* when she did not to Sarah or her own father? She went from her own room to the little girl's and found her getting dressed. Her smile when she saw Chris banished all her doubts, and Chris hugged her instinctively, tensing as the door opened and Slater walked in.

He surveyed them with unreadable eyes for several long seconds. Dressed formally in a business suit he looked so physically attractive that Chris felt her stomach actually clench in fierce desire.

Sophie, unaware of the under-currents flowing deep and fast between the two adults, beamed at her father.

"I'm leaving early this morning," Slater told Chris when she had transferred Sophie into her father's arms, "and I don't expect to be in to dinner tonight."

Sarah again? Chris thought jealously. She had to avert her face so that he wouldn't see what she was feeling. "Oh, I nearly forgot," he added drawlingly, an expression in his eyes that Chris could not define, but which made her shudder with tense dread, "some mail arrived for you this morning."

He reached into his pocket and withdrew a bundle of envelopes. Chris had left his address as her forwarding address with her agent and she took the letters from him in silence. Like most of the others it carried an air mail sticker. Written on pale blue paper, on the reverse side was the sender's name and address and Chris smiled involuntarily as she reached for it, unaware of how much her smile changed her expression.

"You're still in touch with Thornton then?"

The harsh contempt in Slater's voice made her stiffen, her head bowed as she retrieved her letter. "I read that he married . . ."

"Yes . . . He has a little boy now," Chris told him smoothly, unable to understand the reason for his ob-

vious contempt. She knew that he and Ray had not
been particular friends when Ray had lived locally, but
she could see no reason for him to react in the manner he was doing.

"You're a very cool lady Chris." The way he said it
wasn't a compliment. "Does his wife..." He stopped
as the telephone started to ring, putting Sophie down
on the floor. "I'm expecting a call," he told Chris
curtly. "That will be it."

When he had gone Sophie looked uncertainly up at
her. Just because the little girl could not speak, it did
not mean she could not understand, Chris thought
guiltily, forcing a smile and reaching out to take Sophie's hand. Her responsive smile made her heart
ache. There was something so familiar about it, and
yet it wasn't Slater's smile, she realised, with a small
stabbing shock, and it certainly wasn't Natalie's. It
must be Sophie's resemblance to herself that she saw
in her smile Chris reflected, and yet something tugged
at her memory, something elusive that she knew she
should remember but could not.

She read Ray's letter over breakfast. It was teasingly chatty and included an invitation to visit them
later in the year. It was high time she learned to stop
leaning on Ray and Dinah she thought wryly as she
put it back in its envelope and then turned to study the
photographs he had sent her. Both of them were of
Dinah his wife, and Jeremy, now nearly three years
old. The toddler beamed out of the photograph, and
sensing Sophie's curiosity Chris showed it to the little
girl.

"My that's a bonny little boy," Mrs Lancaster
commented, coming in with their breakfast, and
glancing over Chris's shoulder, she put her head on

one side, and ruminated, "Reminds me of someone, but I can't just think who for the moment."

"His father used to live locally," Chris offered, "and Jeremy is very like him facially, although he has his mother's colouring."

They chatted for a while and then Chris offered to take Sophie out into the garden so that Mrs Lancaster could get on with her work.

Chris had brought some more books back from the cottage and she ran upstairs to get one. Half an hour later, she glanced up from the page she was reading to study Sophie's entranced face. *Winnie the Pooh* was obviously as firm a favourite with Sophie as it had been with her.

"I'll just read to the end of this chapter and then we must stop," she told her with a smile. She had fallen easily into the habit of talking to Sophie as though she had expected her to respond. The little girl had her own ways of communicating what she wanted or needed, and Chris sighed faintly when she closed the book, wondering if she would ever talk again.

"Time for my exercises," she told Sophie, standing up. "Want to watch?"

As a model her exercise regime was an integral part of Chris's life, and when Sophie nodded her head she held out her hand to her. "Come on then. We'll do them outside today as it's so nice. Let's go upstairs and get my cassette."

While Chris changed into shorts and a brief top Sophie watched her gravely. An idea suddenly occurred to Chris. "You can do them with me this morning," she told her with a smile. "Let's go and find your shorts shall we?"

When Sophie made no demur Chris took her into her bedroom and helped her to change into shorts and a tee-shirt.

Outside in the garden, she did a few basic warm up exercises and then turned to Sophie, showing her a simpler easy version that would not tax her growing muscles. To her delight Sophie responded enthusiastically. She had a natural physical rhythm that helped her adapt quickly to the exercise routine. Chris had deliberately opted for a "fun" tape with lively music including several "pop" songs that had recently been in the charts. She could miss out on serious exercises for one day, and the physical fun of joining in with her would be good for Sophie she was sure. The child must feel the effect of all the adult concern concentrated on her.

They were halfway through the tape when Chris suddenly became aware of a sound other than that issuing from the tape which was playing a popular hit tune. Hardly daring to believe what she was hearing she kept on moving automatically, edging slightly closer to Sophie. Disbelief made her heart turn over with joy as she discovered that she was right, Sophie was actually humming in time to the song. Chris didn't know what to do. One part of her wanted to hug the little girl and show her excitement and yet another warned her that Sophie's humming was entirely spontaneous, something she herself was probably not even aware of and that to draw attention to it might cause all sorts of repercussions. Suddenly she wished she knew more about Sophie's condition; that she could help her; but not daring to do anything she simply carried on with her exercises, trying not to let Sophie sense her excitement.

She didn't hum with any other songs, and afterwards, thinking about it, Chris realised that that particular tune had been in the hit parade for some weeks prior to Natalie's death. Could there be any connection? She *had* to talk to someone. Slater was unobtainable; Sarah she couldn't bring herself to contact, so that left who? Suddenly she thought of John Howard. *He* lived locally, so surely he must be in the telephone directory.

Telling herself that he probably wouldn't even be at home, Chris nevertheless found his number and dialled it, her heart thudding with tremulous excitement.

To her relief he actually answered the 'phone. Quickly Chris announced herself. "I was wondering if you could come over," she told him breathlessly. "It's about Sophie...the most curious thing...I thought I heard her actually humming just now..." She held her breath dreading hearing him scorn her discovery, but to her pleasure he seemed almost as excited as she was.

"I'll be over right away," he told her.

Replacing the receiver, Chris went in search of Mrs Lancaster. "I'm expecting Dr Howard soon," she told the older woman, surprised when she frowned and looked rather disapproving.

"Is something wrong?" she questioned uncertainly. "I...wanted to talk to him about Sophie..." Quickly she explained what had happened in the garden and at once Mrs Lancaster's expression lightened.

"He'll certainly be the best person to talk to," she told Chris. "Used to specialise in children's ailments before he came down here. Said it took up too much of his time."

"Yes. I can understand that he'd want to spend as much time as he can with his wife," Chris commented. "It must be dreadful for her, poor woman..."

"Aye, but there's them as thinks it's worse for him," Mrs Lancaster told her obliquely, "being tied to an invalid and all... Of course she's secure enough. He couldn't divorce her. He only works part-time now and it's her money that supports them. Comes from a very wealthy family. Her father was extremely well to do and she was the only child..."

"Oh I'm sure that isn't the reason he stays with her," Chris was extremely distressed by Mrs Lancaster's comment although she couldn't exactly say why. Perhaps it was because she had suffered so much disillusionment herself that she couldn't bear to hear of any male betrayal of her sex.

"Maybe not." Mrs Lancaster's voice was noncommittal but the smile she gave Chris extremely warm.

She was just going upstairs to change when the 'phone rang in the hall. She picked up the receiver, surprised to hear an unfamiliar female voice.

"I'm Helen Howard," she introduced herself. "My husband asked me to give you a call. He was just on his way round when he was called out to an emergency—a road accident. He'll be with you as soon as he can. How is Sophie?" she asked in concern. "She was always such a warm, responsive child, I hate to think of her suffering..."

As *she* suffered, Chris thought intuitively, liking the other woman without knowing her. They chatted for several minutes and then Chris hung up, retracing her footsteps to the kitchen to advise Mrs Lancaster of the changed arrangements.

It was after lunch before John Howard finally arrived. Chris was sunbathing in the garden, Sophie asleep beside her.

"Sorry I couldn't get here sooner," he apologised.

He looked tired, Chris realised, getting up carefully so that she didn't disturb Sophie. "That's all right," she told him easily. "Your wife explained when she rang."

Something flickered in his eyes and was gone. Pain possibly Chris decided, suddenly aware of how healthy she must appear in contrast to Helen.

"Beautiful day." He shrugged off his jacket and grimaced. "That's better." He was formally dressed, wearing a striped tie that was vaguely familiar Chris realised, mentally comparing it to the one she had picked up in the cottage. Were they the same? She shrugged aside the thought as unimportant and improbable. What would one of John Howard's ties be doing in her aunt's cottage?

"I'll go and make us some coffee," Chris offered, picking up her robe and tying it. There was nothing indecent about her bikini but nevertheless she felt better a little more covered up.

When she returned with the coffee and some lemonade for Sophie the little girl was still asleep. Encouraged by John Howard she explained what had happened that morning.

"Umm, as you describe it, it sounds like a completely involuntary thing—if nothing else it proves conclusively that there's no damage to the vocal chords, but then we never thought there was. Was Sophie herself aware of what she was doing?"

Chris shook her head. "I didn't dare to draw attention to it. Should I . . ."

He shook his head anticipating her question. "No . . . no you did the right thing. Does Sophie have her own tape or radio?"

When she shook her head, he mused, "It might be an idea to get her one. If we can get her to respond to music it will help . . ." He broke off as Sophie woke up, lifting her head. Chris smiled at her, worried by the look of total terror she suddenly saw in the little girl's eyes. As she picked her up she could feel the waves of tension shuddering through her body, but was at a loss to understand the reason for them. "What is it, darling?" she asked softly. "Did you have a bad dream?"

"Something wrong?" John Howard looked ill at ease.

"She seems terrified of something," Chris told him. "Perhaps she's been having a bad dream."

"Is that what it was, Sophie?" He reached out a hand and Chris was almost overbalanced by the force with which Sophie drew away from him, clinging to her and turning her head into her shoulder. John Howard's hand dropped away. "It seems she doesn't much care for me," he said wryly. "Poor Sophie, I suspect she's grown very wary of all us medical types, and perhaps it's no wonder." He made no further effort to touch the little girl, and Chris was warmed by the expression of guilt and unhappiness in his eyes. He obviously cared very deeply about his patients, but she could understand that Sophie might distrust and perhaps even dislike the medical profession as a body.

"Why don't you go upstairs and choose a book for me to read from?" she suggested softly, putting Sophie down. "Dr Howard is just going . . ."

They both watched her run away. "I'm sorry she reacted to you like that," she apologised ruefully, "but..."

"*You're* sorry?" His expression almost agonised he gripped her forearms, his face contorted with pain. "Chris there's..." He broke off turning to look towards the drive as they both heard the sound of a car.

"Slater," Chris murmured frowning. "But he said he wouldn't be coming home until after dinner." She could still sense John Howard's tension and as Slater stopped the car and climbed out, she reached up instinctively to touch his face in a gesture of commiseration, her smile warmly sympathetic. "It must be difficult for you," she said understandingly, "but..." She had intended to go on to say that he must be used to his small patients reacting against him when they had to endure pain and suffering, but his tortured, "Difficult—my God..." stopped her. Unaware of how close they were to one another, or how their proximity might appear to an onlooker, it took Slater's harsh exclamation to make her step back involuntarily, her nerves tensing in response to his nearness.

Dimly she was aware of John Howard saying goodbye, and something about getting in touch with her, as he hurried away, her sense totally concentrated on Slater.

"You said you weren't coming back until after dinner."

Stupidly she made the words sound like an accusation, and Slater's mouth hardened. "This *does* happen to be my home," he ground out bitterly, "and I won't have you tainting it by filling it with your lovers. What's the matter, Chris?" he demanded thickly when she simply stared at him, totally non-plussed by his accusation. "Came back at the wrong moment did I... Your body still aches for completion, does it? Well I might not be John Howard but I reckon I can satisfy you as well as he could..."

"No..." The panic-stricken word was clawed from her throat.

"Yes..."

She had always known that Slater was strong, but how strong she had not realised until he picked her up, clamping hard arms round her, carrying her over the grass despite her desperate attempts to escape. He was heading for the summerhouse, she realised dazedly gasping as he opened the door and slid her to her feet, securing her wrist with one hand, while the other deftly locked the door. She tried to escape, using her nails on his hand to try and prise them free, but apart from a brief grunt of pain there was no response. Red weals lined his tanned skin, his expression savage as he followed her glance down to them.

"My God I'll make you pay for that," he muttered thickly, and Chris wondered fearfully if he was temporarily deranged. There was no smell of drink on his breath, and in most respects he appeared completely normal, but there was nothing normal about the way he had dragged her in here, locking the door behind and then pocketing the key. Neither was there anything normal about the way he was watching her, the gold eyes dilated, burning with a fever that was mirrored in the dark surge of colour running up under his tanned skin. He was almost savage with rage, Chris acknowledged, shuddering deeply. He reminded her of a wild animal penned up in a cage, secured for the time being but relentlessly determined to escape, infinitely dangerous in his captivity. What was it that held Slater in captivity? The memory of Natalie? Was that why he was here? Did he share her cousin's hatred of her? Was this his way of showing his grief? A sacrifice of her on the altar of his guilt towards Natalie?

His relationship with her cousin had obviously been particularly complex, if *he* was to be believed at least . . . but they had stayed married, and he had tolerated her infidelities.

"Is that what you like, Chrissie?" His voice was almost hypnotic. The purr of the jungle panther before it tore out its victim's throat Chris thought trembling. "Sex mixed with violence? Is that what excites you . . . drawing blood physically as well as mentally?"

His words seared through her, shocking her and making her ache with renewed pain. This was not the Slater she had cherished in her memories; the lover she had dreamed of at night, even though in the morning she had managed to deny those dreams to herself.

"What I *don't* like is being forced against my will, Slater." She managed to utter the words with some semblance of self-assurance, using her model's poise to conceal her fear. "If you just unlock the door, I'll forget this ever happened . . . If not . . ."

"If not, you'll what?" he jeered bitterly. "Cry rape?"

The jibe stabbed right through her body, making her tense in shock and anger, the ugliness of the word bringing a hideous reality to her situation.

"Oh no," Slater muttered savagely. "It won't be rape, Chrissie . . . that wanton body of yours is going to want me just as much as it wanted John Howard. Funny about you and Natalie, how you always wanted the same man . . ."

The cruel taunt robbed her of the ability to speak. She hated him for choosing now to remind her of her vulnerability to him. Of course he felt confident that he could make her want him. He knew how she had responded to him in the past. What she couldn't understand was why he thought she had even contemplated making love with John Howard but that hardly mattered now. Somehow she was going to prove to him that she could resist him and that would take every ounce of will power she possessed.

As he came towards her she refused to move, even though every nerve in her body cried out for her to back away. Her best form of protection was cold rejection. Flight would only increase his belief that he could subdue her.

His hands untying the knot of her robe and then sliding up over her body were a shocking reality. Fiercely keeping her face averted, Chris willed herself not to react. She was simply posing for an ad, she told herself frantically, Slater's hands were simply those of another model... But no other man had ever touched her like this, and her body refused to accept her deception. She shuddered as Slater's fingers bit into her shoulders. "I think we can dispense with this," he told her softly, adding mockingly. "Why are you shivering, Chrissie? You can't possibly be cold."

If anything the summerhouse was over-warm, and his mockery broke through the façade of her control. "Don't call me that," she demanded huskily, referring to his special use of her name.

"Why not? You used to like it... I was the only person who called you Chrissie, you once told me, and you said just hearing my voice saying your name brought you out in goosebumps."

She had said that, Chris remembered achingly and although he had laughed gently at her naïveté she remembered that always after that when they were alone Slater would murmur her name against her skin, savouring her instantaneous response to him.

His hands slid the robe off her shoulders and much as she would have liked to have fought to retain it, Chris let it go. It would be undignified to struggle she told herself, and besides the best way of resisting him was simply not to respond. Her bikini wasn't particularly brief by modern standards, but she felt acutely uncomfortable as Slater studied her.

"You always did have a beautiful body, Chrissie." He murmured the words against the vulnerable skin of her throat. Chris gritted her teeth together, willing herself not to respond, and hating Slater with a wave of feeling so strong that it dizzied her as he laughed gently, his thumb registering the hurried thud of her pulse, his mouth, moving with unerring precision against her skin, closer and closer to the base of her throat.

Wild surges of desire tormented her, every instinct urging her response. It was so tempting simply to arch her throat against his mouth; to curl her fingers into his hair and hold him locked against her while her heated blood pounded out its message against his lips, but she wasn't going to give in.

"Still the same old Chrissie." His mouth left her skin, but his thumb continued to torment the thudding pulse. "Ready to cut your nose off to spite your face. You know you want me, and I know it too..."

"I don't." The hot denial was out before she could silence it, temper glittering greenly in her eyes. To her surprise Slater laughed, a rich, triumphant sound that skittered dangerously over her taut nerves. "Now that's better. Real emotion at last. You're lying, Chris," he added sleekly. "You want me all right. I can see it here." His thumb touched her pulsing throat, in a tormenting caress that forced her to smother an aching groan. "And here."

His hand moved, and Chris closed her eyes in fierce pain as his thumb moved with insolent appraisal over the hardening nub of one breast. She didn't want to open her eyes but something forced her to do so. She didn't want to look down at Slater's lean brown hand where it rested against the underside of her breast, but she felt impelled to. Against the thin cotton of her bikini top her nipples strained in unmistakable arousal, panic clawing in the pit of her stomach, mingling with her aching muscles until she felt she would snap in two with tension.

"You want me," Slater insisted thickly, "and although I'll probably be damned for it, I *ache* for you."

"No..." Her wild moan of denial seemed to unleash something deeply primitive inside him, because Slater's restraint snapped and he pulled her fiercely against his body, brushing her against his chest, his hand trapping hers against his thigh, forcing her to acknowledge his arousal as he muttered rawly. "Yes... Yes... Chris... Feel how much I want you, and you want me the same way... I know you do."

It was useless to keep on resisting him. The heat of his body beneath her hand in those few seconds before he had let her pull away had left her with a suffocating emotional response. She was a fool to be swayed simply by his desire for her; hadn't she learned just how little male desire really meant? And yet the knowledge of his need of her touched off something elemental buried deep inside her that once awakened could not be subdued.

She was barely aware of her own soft moan as Slater untied her bikini top, her sense all too attuned to him; to the hurried rise and fall of his breathing; the darkening glitter of his eyes as he pushed her away from him to study the full perfection of her breasts. Heat rose up in a dark tide under his skin. He thrust off his jacket, wrenching impatiently at his tie, and as though the impatience of his movements were an echo of her own feelings Chris felt the surge of desire sweep tormentingly through her body, including a yearning ache in her lower stomach and making her breasts swell, her nipples rosily erect.

Chris had never posed for any photographs that involved her going even topless, never mind nude, and she was torn between shame and excitement as she saw Slater's reaction to her evident arousal, and discovered the sensual pleasure of knowing he was watching her, his body taut with hunger.

He pulled at the top two buttons of his shirt, abandoning the task to take her in his arms, his voice hoarse and muffled against the smooth skin of her shoulder as he demanded. "Take it off for me, Chrissie. I think I'll go mad if I don't touch you."

As she made a tentative movement towards the small pearl buttons Chris felt the heat of his skin burning into her through the fine material of his shirt. The need to feel that heat directly against her skin was almost terrifying in its intensity. She didn't know which of them was trembling the most she thought hazily as she tried to work the small buttons free one hand flat against the hard wall of Slater's chest as she steadied herself. All the time she was trying to concentrate on her task, Slater's mouth was playing delicately over her skin, caressing the line of her neck and shoulder. Shivers of pleasure raced through her, as the last button came free and she tugged the shirt tails free of his waistband. His body was harder; stronger than she remembered, the muscles of his stomach drawn in sharply as her fingernails accidentally grazed against his chest. The hair that grew there was dark, and oddly smooth, and she gave in to the temptation to run her fingertips lightly through it.

Slater's sharp gasp brought her explorations to a sudden halt, pleasure flooding her body like melted honey as he bit into her skin, pulling her against him so that the fine dark hairs grazed arousingly against her swollen nipples. When he moved, increasing the tormenting contact, Chris moaned huskily in her throat. It arched beneath her tentative caress inciting further exploration. Delicately Chris brushed her thumb over its male outline, feeling Slater's harsh sound of pleasure reverberating beneath her hand. Her lips touched the spot caressed by her thumb and she was startled by the harsh exclamation of sound Slater made, his hand cupping her breast, stroking urgently over its hard tip.

"Chrissie." The sound of her name was lost beneath the savage pleasure of his kiss, their mouths melding and fusing, passion a tangible force enveloping them as Chris wrapped her arms round him, exulting in the fierce abrasion of his body hair against her breasts, pulsing with feverish need that betrayed itself in the compulsive thrust of her lower body against his as it demanded an increasingly closer contact with the hard muscles of his thighs.

They were still standing up, and when Slater released her breast, his hands moving swiftly down her body, to slide inside the cutaway legs of her bikini bottom, and hold her against him so that she could feel the shudders of need pulsing through him she gloried in the intimate contact, pressing wild kisses against his moist skin. A wildness she hadn't known herself capable of entering her blood, her hands stroking feverishly over Slater's torso, her mouth obedient to Slater's muttered urgings, following a path downward over his throat and shoulder until she rested against the hard, almost flat outline of his nipple.

Shock held Chris almost rigid for a moment, the heat of Slater's hands cupping her bottom sending shivers of intense pleasure quivering through her. His body pulsed frantically against hers one hand freeing itself from her lower body to tangle in her hair and then spread against the back of her head. "Yes...Chrissie," she heard him mutter, as she was convulsed with waves of pleasure. "Yes...kiss me..." Feverish sounds of pleasure wracked his body as she let her lips play with the small hard nub of flesh, and feeling suddenly, recklessly responsive, Chris let her tongue play delicately over his tense skin, teasing it with her lips, until Slater gave a harsh moan that demanded fulfilment of the promise her tormenting mouth implied.

The hoarse, almost feverish words ignited her own passions, her body throbbing with aching need as she stroked and kissed as much of his body as she could.

It was the barrier of his waistband and belt that stopped her—that and the sudden sensation of losing her balance, that it took her several seconds to recognise the fact that Slater had lifted her off her feet and was carrying her over to the low cushioned bench against the wall.

"Chris…my God, how you torment me." The thick admission was made as Slater lowered her on to the cushions, Still bending over her, he studied her almost broodingly for a second and Chris shivered lightly under that exploration. She wanted him so much it hurt, and suddenly, she knew that no matter how much she suffered for it afterwards she desperately wanted him to make love to her. It wasn't simply a matter of appeasing her aching body. It was something to hold on to in the lonely future. Something to dream about and to remember. And she always *would* remember that she had aroused him; that she had made him tremble and cry out with pleasure so fierce that she could still see it beating in his body. Instinctively she knew that if she denied him now he would not try to force or coerce her; they had gone far beyond that, and she sensed that he was as taken off guard as she was herself by their explosive response to one another.

This was the coming together they should have shared seven years ago, she thought intuitively; this was why she had never been free of him. Unconsciously she moved, reaching up towards him, the afternoon sun slanting in through the windows and outlining her breasts. There was a clear line where her tan ended and Slater traced it slowly, his dark gaze absorbing the reactions of her body, making her feel that in his mind already he possessed her and filled her.

Her fingers touched his waist, her hair golden against the dark fabric of his pants as she leaned forward and pressed tremulous lips to the firm skin just above his belt.

"Chrissie..." His response was explosive, his head lowering until his mouth touched her nipple. Fierce, almost unbearable pangs of pleasure shot through her at his touch, her teeth unwittingly nipping erotically at his skin, her body clenching beneath waves of fiery pleasure as without any gentle preliminaries Slater's tongue rasped the sensitive peak of her breast, his mouth tugging compulsively, while his hand struggled to release the fastening of his pants, his urgent movements inciting Chris to help him, and to shiver in primaeval female responsiveness at the sight of his naked aroused body.

She wanted to touch him; a desire increased by his fierce possession of her breast, but trembled on the brink of doing so, until he released her tender nipple to mutter a plea against her skin that made her go hot with reaction and response.

As though to underline what he had said, his mouth moved downwards over her body, his tongue circling the smooth indentation in her belly, his fingers deftly untying the strings of her bikini bottom.

Just for a second Chris felt acutely self-conscious. She raised her head, intending to murmur an instinctive protest, but the words died unsaid as Slater looked directly at her, and she trembled beneath the fierce need burning in his eyes.

"You're so very, very beautiful..." He said the words slowly, as though barely aware of having spoken them, his hand pushing away the fabric of her bikini. Just for a second it rested against her body, and Chris was stunned by her muscles' instinctive response; by the tightly coiling sensation building up inside her that made her ache to arch against the hard pressure of his hand, to... She closed her eyes, shivering with the shock of her own sensuality.

"Chrissie..." She felt a touch as light as butterfly wings against her thigh, and then gasped at the intrusive stroke of Slater's fingers, half shocked half thrilled by his intimacy. It was almost as though he had read her thoughts; had known... She opened her eyes to speak to him and was transfixed by the sight of his dark head leaning against her thighs. The gold eyes would not allow hers to slide away, hot colour mounting her skin as he deliberately placed his mouth against her skin. Hot shivers of pleasure surged through her. Her body seem to melt, opening to him and she gasped, shuddering beneath the caressing intimacy of his fingers.

"Touch me, Chrissie," he commanded in a hoarse voice. "Touch me... kiss me, the way I'm touching and kissing you..."

Almost like an automaton she obeyed him, tensely at first, overwhelmed by the intimacy of what she was doing, but the heat of his skin, the sheer pleasure of hearing his raw sounds of desire, the responsiveness of his body to her lightest touch, soon obliterated every trace of shyness.

Her own body was equally responsive to him, arching wantonly to his lightest touch, her mind cast adrift by her body as she gave in to the mindless ecstasy his touched evoked.

His mouth against her thigh made her ache with hunger but when it moved higher she tensed instinctively, thrown into shivering uncertainly.

"Chrissie?" Slater's voice registered her unease, and suddenly fearing that he might withdraw from her, Chris said urgently, "Slater...please...I want you. I..." Tears spurted unexpectedly from her eyes, as he moved—away from her or so she thought, until she realised he had joined her on the cushions, his body hard and warm against her own as he took her in his arms, tracing the course of her tears with his tongue.

"I want you too." His words were confirmed by the aroused weight of his body. Her fears subsiding Chris arched upward instinctively to meet it, gasping as the full intensity of her inner need washed over her, and she responded blindly to the urging of Slater's hands and body, revelling in the rhythmic thrust of his maleness against her, startled by her reaction to the sudden brief spasm of pain that for one second threatened to overcome pleasure. She felt Slater's fingers tighten and opened her eyes to find him looking disbelieving back at her. She had forgotten that he hadn't known she was still a virgin. She thought he was going to speak, to withdraw from her, and pressed herself fiercely against him, holding him to her, kissing him passionately, her teeth catching on his lower lip as she felt his response in the powerful surge of his body into hers.

She knew she cried out—in pleasure not pain, but the sound was swallowed by Slater's mouth, fiercely enmeshed with hers, schooling the fierce tide of need swelling through her just as his body controlled her untutored physical response, nurturing it until she thought she would simply explode, dissolve, with the intensity of it. The power of the spasms of pleasure wracking her made her cry out his name, conscious briefly of his own harsh exclamation of pleasure, and filled with an intensely female sense of accomplishment that she had satisfied him. Even as she tried to register the thought the world started to whirl in a blur round her. She was going to faint Chris realised in stunned disbelief... Slater had just made love to her and she was going to faint. Darkness welled up and claimed her, spinning her dizzily round. She was aware of Slater calling her name, but she could not summon the energy to respond.

Her faint could surely have lasted only seconds, Chris thought muzzily, opening her eyes, blushing furiously as she discovered that Slater was bending over her, once more fully dressed.

"Chris..." His voice was harsh, the expression in his eyes so cold that she shivered beneath it. He had covered her with her wrap, she realised, suddenly glad of its brief protection. "Chris...we have to talk..."

No words of love or praise, she realised bitterly, but then what had she expected?

"No...No..." Panic edged up under her voice and she struggled to conceal it, sitting up and clumsily pulling on her robe. When Slater moved to help her she flinched away from him as though the contact burned. He dropped her arm immediately, backing away, his mouth tense. "Chris..."

"No...no, don't say anything, I don't want to hear." She stumbled to her feet, half stumbling and half running to the door. She had forgotten it was locked and banged on it impotently with her fists, tears streaming down her face. "Let me out of here," she demanded half hysterically, not knowing why she was crying or why she was filled with this impulse to flee, knowing only that she had to get away...that she had to escape Slater's presence.

"Chris..." He came towards her, and she backed away.

"I'm not going to touch you." His voice was terse, his back turned towards her as he unlocked the door and opened it. She bolted through it like a terrified hare, not stopping until she was safely inside her own room. What had caused her flight she didn't know. Now that her sexual hunger was appeased she felt bitter and ashamed. She loved Slater, but he did not love her, and worse still he now knew how she felt—he *must* do—he *must* recognise the reason why she had retained her virginity for so long—and the reason she had been so impatient today to lose it. Shame scorched her skin. If only she could simply disappear she thought helplessly. If only she never had to face him again, but there was Sophie to consider. She simply could not walk out on the little girl now. Surely *her* future; *her* good health was more important than selfish pride? Natalie might not have made her Sophie's guardian for any love of either of them, but she was going to do all she could to carry out her task properly. Somehow she would just have to face Slater and endure his mockery. Somehow . . . but please God not just yet, she thought achingly as she curled up on her bed. She couldn't face him just yet.

CHAPTER SEVEN

SHADOWS were lengthening in the garden when she woke up. Downstairs a door slammed and her body tensed, her eyes fixed on her closed door, in mute dread. When Slater came in she shrank back under the bedclothes.

"Chris." His voice was sharp. "Sophie seems to be missing." The very real anxiety she could detect in his eyes banished any suspicions she might have had that he was making it up.

"Mrs Lancaster gave her tea as usual and she went upstairs to read. When she went to get her ready for bed she couldn't find her."

"I'll help you look."

She pushed back the bedclothes, avoiding meeting his eyes as she swung her feet to the floor.

"I've searched the house and garden already. Now I'll have to ring the police." He was out of the door before she had left her bed. She had dreaded coming face to face with him again but now their mutual concern for Sophie over-rode any embarrassment Chris might have felt.

Dressed and downstairs she was just in time to catch the tail end of his telephone conversation.

"Yes I understand how you feel, Sarah," she heard him saying, "but obviously I can't take you out to dinner tonight . . .

Yes...yes..." He sounded tersely angry and Chris
wondered at the other woman's lack of concern for
Sophie. After all she was Slater's child and she
thought Sarah would have cared about her for his sake
if not for the little girl's own.

Anxious for something to occupy herself with, Chris
went out into the garden. It was very large and parts
of it were almost overgrown. Sophie could easily be
lost in it, but Slater had said he had searched it and
knowing him as she did she owned that that search
would have been a thorough one.

She wandered down the drive and out on to the
road. It made her blood run ice in her veins to contemplate the fates that might have befallen the little
girl. She frowned remembering how distressed she had
been by John Howard's visit. She hadn't even had
time to tell Slater about her humming, Chris reflected
retracing her steps back to the house. She found Slater
in the study, his back was towards her. He was studying a framed photograph he held in his hands. Chris
didn't need to see it to recognise the photograph of her
cousin and Sophie which normally stood on his desk.
Inwardly she wept bitter tears of pain, but outside she
strived to appear calm as she approached the desk.

The naked ache of agony she had discerned in Slater's expression was wiped clean as he saw her, the
photograph restored to its rightful place.

"It might not be important," she began tersely,
"but Sophie seemed very upset this morning while
John was here. He explained to me..."

"He did, did he?" Slater laughed with harsh bitterness. "The Chris I remember wouldn't have... Oh
for God's sake what's the use... Yes, it *is* important," he went on bitterly. "Surely even *you* can re-

cognise that much ... Dear God when I think of what could happen to her..." His voice was suspended and Chris wondered on a shock wave of horror if he blamed her for Sophie's disappearance. His next words seemed to confirm her fears. "Sarah warned me against letting you stay," he ground out savagely, "and I'm beginning to think she might be right..." He strode past her without another word leaving Chris to stare painfully after him.

Could Sophie have run away because of John's visit? Had she perhaps feared that they might be a forerunner to more tests? More visits to hospital which Mrs Lancaster had already told Chris she hated? But where would she go? Unbidden the memory of her book in Sophie's hands tormented her. The cottage! But surely Sophie could not have gone there? A two mile walk or more and all on her own. Someone must surely have spotted her.

No, she was being ridiculous to even think of such a thing as Slater would no doubt tell her were she foolish enough to confide her thoughts to him. But what if she were right ... what if Sophie had ... There was only one way to find out, Chris thought numbly heading for the front door and picking up her keys on the way.

Ten minutes later she was pointing the car down the lane that led to the cottage. Already it was dark enough for her to need headlights and the thought of Sophie walking all alone down this narrow, over-grown lane made her ache with fear for the little girl.

The cottage was all in darkness. Getting out of the car Chris berated herself for her stupidity. She was just wasting valuable time which would have been far better expended in searching closer to home. Sophie could not possibly be here.

The cottage door wasn't locked. Chris remembered that she had not locked it after her last visit anticipating the arrival of the workmen who were to give her the various estimates she wanted.

The door creaked slightly and swung inwards. The sound of tiny scampering feet brought the fine hairs on Chris's skin bolt upright. Mice... Shuddering she found the light switch.

The room looked no different than it had on her last visit. "Sophie..." she called the little girl's name softly, feeling foolish. Of course she was not here... A quick inspection of the kitchen and dining room confirmed this view. Only upstairs to check now, Chris thought wearily already regretting her impulsive action in coming here. The stairs creaked as she climbed them, reminding her of how precarious they were. She hadn't bothered with the light and she cursed softly as one stair gave way beneath her foot. The wood felt soft and rotten and she grimaced anticipating the cost of replacing it. The whole place was probably riddle with damp.

At the top of the stairs she called Sophie's name again. Silence... Her ears stretched to catch the slightest sound registered a faint...what? Shivering faintly Chris hurried into her old room, stopping dead when she saw the small, huddled up figure on her old bed.

"Sophie..." Her relief turned to fear as she reached the bed and discovered how cold the little girl was, her eyes glazed and unseeing as they stared right past her. "Sophie, it's me. Chris..." she said softly, fear touching ice fingers at her heart. What had happened to Sophie to cause this? "I'm going to take you home to Daddy," she said quietly. "Come on now..." Sophie's small body was rigid and tense, so much so that Chris feared to move her. Her eyes, normally alight with warmth were empty, vacant almost, and that more than anything frightened Chris. What should she do? She daredn't risk moving Sophie by force in case her reactions drove her even further into her trauma, and yet she dreaded leaving her here alone.... If only the cottage had a 'phone... There was one at the bottom of the lane, and the lane led only to the cottage. It would take only minutes for her to get there...minutes in which Sophie would surely be safe? As these thoughts raced through her mind Chris tried to appear outwardly calm.

"We've been worried about you," she told the little girl, hoping to see some glimmer of response in her empty eyes, praying that she could make Sophie respond to her; that she needn't leave her here, but could take her with her back to Slater... If only she had told him her suspicions; if only she had not feared his rejection and mockery more than she had trusted her own instincts. It was useless to think of "if onlys" now she told herself. "Please look at me Sophie," she begged. "Let me take you home to Daddy."

"I don't have a daddy...*she* told me I didn't..." The sound of her hoarse, rusty little voice transfixed Chris almost more than the words she was uttering, and then it hit her, Sophie had actually spoken. "Sophie...Sophie darling..." She rushed over to the bed, hugging her, murmuring foolish words of praise, soaking her fair hair with her tears, but Sophie was completely unresponsive. So much so that her elation died. What on earth could Sophie mean? She didn't have a daddy? Slater thought the world of her; he was so gentle and caring with her that often she found herself envying her. Just this evening studying her photograph there had been such pain in his eyes that Chris had ached to have the power to soothe it.

"Sophie, listen to me," she exhorted softly. "You do have a daddy and Daddy loves you very much. I know he does..." There was absolutely no response. She had come out dressed in jeans and a thin tee-shirt and now Chris shivered. The cottage was both cold and damp, the musty scent pervading everywhere creeping into her lungs. What on earth ought she to do? Sophie's almost trance-like state decided her. She daredn't risk moving her forcibly; specially not in view of her extremely disturbed state; she would have to drive down to the end of the lane and ring Slater.

"Sophie, I'm going to go out now and telephone your daddy..." It seemed pointless talking to her, but she couldn't simply leave without an explanation Chris thought numbly and who knew perhaps if she talked she might get some response. "I won't be long," she promised opening the bedroom door. "You wait here for me. I'll be back just as soon as I can."

Her heart thumping painfully she hurried downstairs, in her haste and anxiety forgetting the rotten step. As her foot went down into nothing she cried out and pitched forward into endless darkness, pain exploding inside her skull.

Where on earth was she Chris wondered muzzily opening her eyes. For a second she thought she was still in the summerhouse... but no it was far too cold and there was no sunshine. Heat ran through her body as it remembered Slater's lovemaking. She moved her head restlessly trying to escape the memories, crying out as pain lanced through her temple. She put her hand up to it instinctively, wincing as she felt the warm stickiness there. Now she remembered. She had missed her step and fallen down stairs in the cottage. Sophie... Fresh panic surged through her as she remembered the little girl... At least Sophie could not have left, she reflected glancing at the stairs; half of them had given way as she fell and there was now a gaping hole where the staircase had been. The downstairs lights were on; they might alert someone to their presence.

She must try to get to the 'phone. She tried to get up and bit back a fresh gasp of pain as her ankle buckled underneath her refusing to take her weight. Had she broken it? Chris wasn't sure, but she did have to admit after two more attempts to stand on it that she wasn't going to be able to get out to the car. That meant that she and Sophie were trapped here until someone found them. Thank goodness she had put the downstairs lights on. Someone might see them and be alerted to their plight. It was a faint hope she recognised. No one used the lane and there were no other houses nearby.

Would Slater eventually decide to come and investigate? Grim pictures of herself and Sophie starving to death flooded her mind, firmly rebutted by her common-sense. She was being ridiculous. The most they would have to wait was probably until tomorrow morning when surely one or other of the workmen would be along to survey the cottage. It was scarcely a comforting thought. The night stretched out ahead of them, long and very, very lonely. Sophie! Chris's heart lurched in panic. "Sophie..." she called softly..."Sophie...it's Chris. Can you hear me?"

There was no response. She tried again several times, dragging her throbbing ankle behind her as she moved closer to the stairs.

The pain moving engendered made her head swim. She had barely eaten all day and now the traumas she had endured were beginning to take their toll. Her head throbbed muzzily, and the room went black whirling sickeningly round her. How many times in the hours that followed she slipped in and out of consciousness Chris did not know. She must be suffering from concussion she reflected at one point, trying to sort out her muddled thoughts; thoughts threaded through with tormenting images of Slater. It was just as well she thought unhappily at one point, that Sophie was unaware of their situation. At least the little girl was saved the terror that stalked her. How did *she* know what fears tormented Sophie's young mind, she asked herself achingly. Why had Sophie made that comment about Slater? What was she doing at the cottage? Was it as Chris had once sensed, a place of a refuge for her? Her muddled thoughts ran into one another, pain making her long to give way to tears. Her body felt as though it had been beaten. Her back must have caught on one of the stairs as she fell, it ached so much.

"Sophie..." she called weakly, knowing there would be no response. "Sophie..."

She must have slept because the next thing she knew it was light. Her body ached all over and she was shivering. Exposure, she calculated, almost as though she were an onlooker on her own pain. She looked down at her ankle. It was very badly swollen and bruised black and blue. She couldn't bear to move it. Her head throbbed and her eyes felt gritty.

"Sophie..." Her voice sounded thin and reedy, but her physical discomfort was forgotten as Sophie suddenly appeared at the top of the stairs, looking untidy and grave. But this time there *was* recognition in her eyes—recognition and concern.

"It's all right, Sophie..." she said weakly. "I fell down the stairs. Don't come too near the edge, they're very rotten. Have you been asleep?"

The fair head nodded. No sign of any attempt to speak Chris noticed... Did that mean that Sophie wasn't aware of what had happened last night? It was so frustrating not being able to ask her.

"Did you come here to get another book?" she asked lightly, watching Sophie's small face. For a moment it crumpled and looked puzzled and then Sophie nodded, running back to the bedroom and then reappearing with an old Enid Blyton book.

"Good girl. You sit there and read it," Chris encouraged. "Some men will be here soon and they'll take us home to...to your daddy." Praying that what she was saying was true, Chris watched Sophie's face closely, but her only response to her comment was a brief smile. She was exhibiting none of the emotion she had shown last night when Chris mentioned Slater. She glanced at her watch. Seven... How much longer would they be trapped here? If the stairs hadn't gone she could perhaps have sent Sophie off with a message, but then if they hadn't gone she wouldn't be lying here unable to move.

Time crawled by. Chris tried moving and groaned as pain shot through her body, willing it away as she saw Sophie's worried expression. She must not frighten the little girl... "Throw me down a book Sophie and I'll read to you," she offered, letting out a painful breath as Sophie trotted off into the bedroom.

The book she dropped carefully within Chris's reach was another Enid Blyton. Painfully turning the pages Chris started to read. At times the pain from her bruised body almost suspended her voice. She was shivering badly and her head ached, fine points of light dancing against her eyeballs making her long to close her eyes and give way to oblivion. When she eventually heard a car coming down the lane, she almost didn't believe it...

"Sophie, run to the window and wave," she commanded tensely... It was hardly likely that whoever it was wouldn't stop. The lane led nowhere else, but she couldn't relax until she heard slamming doors and male voices.

"Whose car is that outside?" she heard someone ask as the door was thrust open. Two stunned male faces looked down at her... Trying to smile Chris focused blindly on their faces, and said foolishly, "Thank goodness you're here..."

"Get on the 'phone to Doc Stafford," she heard the older man saying tersely. "We'd best not move her. Come a real cropper she has..."

"Please..." Chris fought encroaching unconsciousness to tug on the man's sleeve. "Please... there's Sophie..." she managed to whisper... "Upstairs..."

"Sophie? Isn't that Slater James's kid? The one that's gone missing?" The sharp query was the last thing Chris heard properly as blackness washed down over her. Vaguely she was aware of comings and goings, of voices, Slater's among them but when she tried to reach out to them she couldn't speak. Someone was lifting her...

"Slater..." she tried to get her tongue round his name, but it felt numb and swollen.

"She's okay, I've given her a pain-killing shot..."

"Okay?" Was that really Slater's voice, sounding so rawly bitter. "Concussion...a swollen ankle... God knows how many bruises and contusions...exhaustion and exposure and you say she's okay..."

She barely had time to absorb Slater's concern before the other voice spoke again. "None of them things that won't mend...and at least Sophie's safe... Wonder what made her come down here... You'll have to ask your friend when she's recovered. Obviously she must have suspected..."

"Then why the hell didn't she tell me instead of coming down here alone?"

The savagery in Slater's voice pierced through her. No doubt he blamed her for the delay in finding Sophie. She started to cry slowly, consciousness receding.

"Chris...Chris..." She knew it was Slater calling to her but she couldn't respond. She dared not for fear of what her response would reveal. It was easier by far to simply slide down into the welcoming blackness that reached out its arms to embrace her; arms far safer than Slater's had ever been.

CHAPTER EIGHT

IT was several days before her doctor pronounced Chris well enough to leave hospital. Although her actual physical injuries had been relatively slight he had been concerned that she might be suffering from concussion. To tell the truth Chris found the events of the evening of her accident very blurred and shadowy. All that she could remember properly was hearing Sophie speak; the little girl's anguished words were carved into her heart, but she was reluctant to mention them to anyone. Although kind and concerned the hospital staff were so brisk that she feared they would believe she was imagining things and perhaps even keep her in hospital for further tests. She was far too thin Dr Stafford complained, and Chris was forced to admit that she had lost weight since coming to England.

Mrs Lancaster had been in to see her, and from her Chris had learned that Sophie had suffered nothing more than a cold after her ordeal. "You know what kids are," she said cheerfully, "although we still haven't been able to find out why she went there in the first place."

Chris herself wasn't sure, but she did know that something that had happened that afternoon had triggered off Sophie's flight, and that something it seemed was somehow connected with John.

Slater came to pick her up. She had wanted to refuse to go with him, but could see no way of doing so
without causing a scene. He walked into the ward, tall
and virilely healthy-looking in jeans and a thin cotton
shirt. Chris could feel her body pulsing in silent response to his presence, and she averted her head unable to bear the pain of looking at him without
betraying how she felt.

"Chris..." He hadn't been to see her during her stay
in hospital, but then why should he? She meant nothing to him. She bit her lip remembering the heat of his
body against hers in the summerhouse and amended
her thoughts. He had wanted her physically, he had
told her that much but there was no desire now in the
golden eyes as they slowly searched her pale face.
"How are you feeling?"

"I'm fine..." A cowardly impulse made her add
huskily, "I really must think about leaving soon...
Sarah was right, I don't seem to be helping Sophie."

She turned away from him not wanting him to see
the defeat in her eyes. She had come to Little Martin
so buoyed up with hopes and ideals, but now they were
all gone. The indifference to Slater she had been so
proud of had been nothing more than a mental sham
erected by her mind to protect her vulnerable heart—
now it had been destroyed. Far from helping Sophie,
all she seemed to have done was to precipitate another trauma. Had she been pushing the little girl too
hard, demanding too much of her? When Slater didn't
speak she continued slowly. "I feel responsible for her
disappearance... It must have been because of something I said or did..."

"Not necessarily." His cool denial made Chris turn
her head and look up at him in surprise. Slater too had

lost weight, she recognised numbly. His face was thinner, revealing hard bones, but then he must have endured agony wondering what had happened to Sophie.

"Why did you invite John Howard to the house?"

Chris closed her eyes on a wave of pain. They'd only been together for five minutes and already he was back to accusing her; condemning her. "Not because I wanted him to make love to me," she assured him bitterly. "No matter what you might think of my morals or lack of them..." She broke off colouring hotly and shivering.

"That's another subject we have to discuss," Slater told her curtly. "I *am* aware that I seem to have been guilty of some error of judgment Chris, but now is neither the time nor the place."

Of course it was only natural that he should be more concerned about Sophie than he was about misjudging her, Chris told herself firmly, and yet there was pain in acceptance of the knowledge and with it came the death of her faint, only just now admitted, hope that somehow the fact that she had had no lover but him would bring about a change of heart within him. What had she expected, she derided herself. A declaration of undying love?

"Well?" His curt tone reminded her that he was still waiting for an answer.

"If you really want to know why don't you ask John himself," she demanded childishly, "I'm sure you'd much rather believe him than me."

"On this occasion I'm quite prepared to accept what you have to say."

The faintly sardonic inflection to his voice made Chris look more closely at him, not sure if it was directed at her or at himself. The gold eyes were shuttered, unreadable, but there was tension in the way he held his body.

"It was because of Sophie," Chris told him huskily. "We were exercising together... just a game really and then I heard her actually humming... I didn't know what to do... I was frightened of provoking the wrong response from her... so I 'phoned John."

"Humming?" The fierce glitter of hope burning his eyes to deep topaz made Chris's heart lurch in sympathy. Whatever else she could accuse Slater of, not loving his child was not among them. "John said it was probably an automatic reaction," she explained shakily. "The tune was one that had been in the hit parade just before Natalie died. Sophie had probably heard it dozens of times," she added, remembering her cousin's predilection for popular music. Natalie had never been able to endure silence of her own company; always she must have noise, activity... Hers had in truth been a restless spirit.

"Why didn't you tell *me* this?" His fingers gripped her arm, darkly tanned against her paler skin. Chris flinched automatically instantly remembering the last occasion on which he had touched her, unaware of how huge her eyes looked in the hospital pallor of her face.

"It's all right, Chris." Slater's voice was clipped and derisive as he removed his hand. "I'm not about to force myself on you..."

She flushed darkly, believing the comment to be a cruel taunt designed to remind her just how little force had been needed—none if she was honest, because she had wanted him with a need that probably over-rode his own. Her need, unlike his, had been fuelled by love.

"I wanted to tell you, but you were at work," she reminded him, "and you said you weren't coming back until late..." She frowned remembering his unexpected appearance. "Why did you tell me that, Slater?" she asked him bitterly. "Was it because you wanted to catch me out? To prove perhaps that I wasn't a fit person to be involved with Sophie? I might have guessed that you'd find some subtle way of getting rid of me...that always was your style wasn't it?"

"*My* style?" He gave a short bark of laughter. "My God that's rich coming from you. Perhaps I came back because I couldn't endure being away from you any longer."

He said it so derisively that for a moment she actually wanted to hit him, but she controlled the impulse saying quietly, "Us quarrelling won't help Sophie, Slater."

"No." He frowned. "I think I know what made Sophie disappear the way she did, but I can't work out why she should go to the cottage. To the best of my knowledge she didn't even know it existed. Natalie never visited her mother there after you left, and once the cottage was empty..."

"You're wrong, Slater," Chris told him positively, "Natalie had visited the cottage—and relatively recently. The first time I walked into it after my arrival I could smell her perfume—it was quite unmistakable, and Sophie must have been with her because she has some books of mine that can only have come from the cottage. Natalie would certainly never have thought to collect them and give them to her."

"No, there never was any love lost between you was there?"

"I can't think why Natalie should go to the cottage," Chris persisted. "She always said she hated it when we lived there." She glanced enquiringly at Slater, surprised to see how brooding and bitter his expression was.

"Can't you?" he said derisively. "I should have thought it was obvious, although in view of recent discoveries perhaps I'm misjudging you again. I suspect Natalie used the cottage as a convenient place to meet her lovers," he told Chris frankly.

She was stunned and completely lost for words, partly because of what Slater had suggested and partly due to his apparent lack of concern at Natalie's betrayal.

"You didn't care?" she whispered, only half aware that she was giving voice to her inner thoughts... "You didn't..."

"Love her?" His mouth twisted. "Natalie and I made a bargain, Chris, and whatever else was involved in it, love most certainly wasn't."

It took her several seconds to grasp the truth. Slater had married Natalie because she carried his child. She ought to have felt pity for her cousin and one part of her did, but the greater feeling surging through her was one of relief. Slater had never loved Natalie... but he had *made* love to her, her brain cautioned, and at the same time as he was making love to you... he might not have loved Natalie, but he didn't love you either, Chris... It was undeniably true.

"Sophie seemed very distressed by John's presence." Chris broke the heavy silence with the first thing she could think of.

"Yes...yes, she would be." Slater's voice was clipped, his expression grim. "What made you think of looking in the cottage, and why the hell didn't you tell me where you were going?" He asked, the question just as the nurse came up to tell Chris that she was free to go.

"It was only a very faint hope—I felt silly telling anyone about it... I didn't really believe it myself..."

"And so instead you damned nearly killed..." He broke off and turned his head away. He was furious with her, Chris acknowledged achingly and he had every right to be. She *had* jeopardised Sophie's life, but must he underline to her how very little *she* meant to him?

The nurse asked him to leave so that Chris could get dressed. He was waiting for her outside the ward, his expression still bleak.

"Are you sure you're okay?"

She must look an absolute wreck, Chris acknowledged painfully, or was it simply that Slater would prefer her to remain in hospital out of his way.

"I'm fine," she told him tautly. "Just as soon as I can make the arrangements I'll be leaving..."

"We'll talk about that later." He was hustling her into his car. "Dr Stafford wants to see you for a check-up in two weeks from now, so I shouldn't make any arrangements to leave before then if I were you."

Chris gasped. "He never said anything to me."

"No?" Slater was plainly bored with the conversation. He leaned across her, deftly securing her seat belt.

"I'm not a child you know." She knew she was being petty, but even the clinical brush of his fingers against her clothed body was a kind of agony she still felt too vulnerable to endure, conjuring up as it did images of other touches, far from clinical and burned into her memory for all time.

"And what about Sophie," Slater demanded. "What about all that pure motivating stuff you came out with not so long ago about having a duty towards her, or was that simply all a pose, Chris? A way of getting at me..."

"No! I love Sophie," she told him shakily, "but I don't think I'm helping her at all."

"Same old Chris," Slater taunted. "You always did want instant results. Sophie needs time, Chris...time to adjust to Natalie's death... She loves you," he told her unexpectedly. "If you leave now it could do her irreparable harm."

Why was he telling her this? Chris's head felt muzzy. He couldn't possibly want her to stay; he had already told her that; proved it to her...unless...she shivered suddenly despite the car's heating... Slater was an extremely sensual man...did he perhaps envision her as a willing bed-partner; someone he could use until such time as he tired of her?

"If I do stay, it will be strictly as Sophie's guardian." The words were out before she could stop them, the sudden screech of car tyres as Slater pulled to an abrupt halt, shocking her. It was fortunate that they were on an empty country road Chris reflected numbly as his hands left the wheel and gripped her shoulders, the bitter fury in his eyes shocking her.

"And just what the hell does that mean?"

"Don't touch me." She was in danger of total collapse, Chris thought weakly. If Slater didn't let go of her soon, she would be babbling her love to him, demanding far more from him than merely the angry grip of his fingers on her skin. "Let me go. I can't bear you to touch me," she lied huskily, desperate to put some distance between them. Slater's face looked grey, only his eyes alive as they burned into her. He released her slowly and sat back in his own seat.

"Don't worry, Chris," he told her sardonically, "I've far more important things to worry about than making love to you. You puzzle me you know, there's so much about you that's contradictory..."

"I'm a woman, Slater..." Somehow she managed to summon a small smile, "It's an attribute of my sex..."

"I think I'm beginning to understand why you and Ray are still 'friends'. What happened, Chris? Did you hold out for marriage and he lose interest?"

Chris was totally nonplussed. "I never wanted to marry Ray," she told him in bewilderment.

"No... I forgot it was your career you wanted to further, wasn't it? And he was the vehicle you used to do it..."

Her heart was thumping erratically. "Yes that's right." For a moment she had almost forgotten the lie she had perpetrated all those years ago to save her pride, going to Slater and agreeing when he accused her of wanting to pursue a career as a model, even boasting a little of Ray's offer to help her. Anything to stop him from guessing how much his betrayal hurt her.

The rest of the journey was conducted in silence, Chris heaving a faint sigh of relief when they reached the house. Her ankle was still slightly painful, necessitating her taking care on stairs, but she was not prepared for Slater to pick her up in his arms when she hesitated at the bottom of them.

"Slater, put me down. I can manage..."

"Why bother, this way's much quicker."

"I'm not an invalid you know," she protested when he carried her into her bedroom and deposited her on the bed.

"Perhaps not, but you have spent the last few days in hospital. Stafford said we were to make sure that you got some rest." He was still bending over her and Chris had a suffocating desire to reach up and touch him ... to feel his mouth against her own.... Perhaps something in her expression communicated her desires to him because she was conscious of a change in his expression, a darkening of his eyes that betrayed his purpose as his head came lower. "Chris..." The way he said her name made her heart turn over; she yearned for him to hold her; to love her. His hand cupped her face, his thumb probing the softness of her mouth.

"Slater!" The sharply imperative sound of Sarah's voice forced Chris back to reality. She jerked away from Slater as though he was fire.

"I need to talk to you about Sophie. She's still extremely distressed." She gave Chris a bitterly venomous look. "You've brought her back then."

No need to guess what Sarah thought about that. It was clear to hear in her voice. It was only when Slater left her room with the other woman that Chris remembered she had not told him about Sophie speaking. There would be other occasions, and anyway perhaps she would be wiser to discuss what had happened with John first. He was more likely to believe her than Slater who might even think that she was making it up, deliberately fabricating something to prove that her presence was of benefit to Sophie, lengthening her stay so that she could be near him. But Slater apparently wanted her to stay... Thoroughly muddled by her thoughts Chris closed her eyes and drifted into sleep.

It was Sophie who woke her. The little girl had crept into her room and was sitting on the end of the bed watching her. Chris gave her a warm smile, and said softly, "Hello..."

The pleasure that shone in her brown eyes as Sophie returned her smile, made Chris's heart swell with love. "Have you come to read to me?" she asked. Sophie had the inevitable book with her, she noticed, taking it when Sophie proffered it, guessing that she wanted her to read.

Half-an-hour later they were interrupted by Slater. "So there you are. Sarah's been looking everywhere for you," he chided Sophie gently. She pulled a slight face, but hopped off the bed in obedience to her father's instructions. Watching them leave, Chris frowned, remembering Sophie's anguished words. There had been no evidence today that she even remembered them, never mind doubted that Slater was her father.

She ate the lunch Mrs Lancaster prepared, dutifully, and was just wondering about getting up when Sarah marched into her room.

"I suppose you think you've been very clever," she hissed without preamble. "Making Slater feel so guilty that he has to keep you here, but it won't do you any good. Oh I'm not fooled even if he is. You don't care about Sophie. It's all a pretext to stay here with Slater. He doesn't want you, you know," she added viciously, "any more than he wanted Natalie. He and I are going to be married." She laughed mockingly when she saw the pain in Chris's eyes. "Surely you guessed?"

"You're not wearing an engagement ring." Chris knew that her voice trembled betrayingly.

"Not yet... we don't want to cause any gossip, besides it's the wedding ring that's the most important. Oh Slater may find you physically attractive," she continued before Chris could speak, "but he'd never let himself get involved with another member of Natalie's family. You're probably all tainted with the same brush... If she was mentally unstable, who's to say that you aren't too... Slater had enough of what that means being married to Natalie..."

"My cousin was not unstable," Chris denied, knowing in her heart that she was lying... Had Slater complained to Sarah about Natalie's difficult temperament? She couldn't endure the knowledge that he must love the other woman. What would Sarah say if she revealed that only days ago Slater had made love to *her*? It was a hypothetical question because Chris knew she would not tell her. She had too much pride, and besides she knew that Sarah would put the same interpretation on his behaviour that she had herself. He had simply wanted her physically. Pain overwhelmed her.

"No?" Sarah's eyebrows arched contemptuously, "Can you think of any other explanation for her...nymphomania...?" She laughed unkindly when Chris blanched. "Oh come on, you must know what sort of woman she was. She couldn't leave any man alone... I'm only surprised that Slater married her."

"What would you have had him do?" Chris demanded bitterly, "Ignore the fact that she was carrying his child?"

"*His* child?" Sarah's mouth twisted contemptuously. "Slater didn't father Sophie. I doubt that even Natalie knew who did, but it certainly wasn't Slater. She told me herself that they had never once been lovers. Slater couldn't bear to touch her, you see."

The shock of what she was saying stunned Chris. "Not Slater's child?... but..."

"Why did he marry her? Natalie once told me they had some sort of pact. Slater doesn't talk about it."

So there were *some* things that Slater didn't tell her, Chris thought numbly. "I don't believe you," she managed to get out finally, "Natalie may have told you these things, but she..."

"Was a congenital liar? Yes I know, but in this instance I believe her. She knew how Slater and I felt about one another... She knew he wanted a divorce... Why else do you think she took that overdose?"

It was horrible, far worse than Chris had imagined... "She was too selfish to let him go," Sarah continued, angry spots of colour burning in her cheeks. "She didn't want him for herself; she didn't love him but she wouldn't let him go..."

"But Sophie..." Chris protested weakly. "He loves her... she loves him..."

Sarah shrugged. "He feels a responsibility towards the child; he's that kind of man, but once we're married, there'll be no place here for Natalie's bastard. If you care so much about her, why don't you go back where you came from and take her with you... Neither of you are wanted round here," she finished callously.

She was gone before Chris could react. She wanted to deny the truth of what Sarah had said, but some deeper instinct than logic warned her that it was true; that Sophie was not Slater's child... And Sophie knew it. Who had told her? Sarah? She was vindictive enough, Chris thought angrily. And what of Natalie? As though it had been yesterday Chris remembered her cousin telling her that she was carrying Slater's baby. After seeing the two of them together she had had no reason to disbelieve her, but according to Sarah they had never even been lovers. And if not Slater, then who... As though an inner door in her mind had unlocked, a picture flashed across her mind. Thrusting back the bedclothes, she walked unsteadily across to the dressing table, quickly extracting Ray's letter. Her fingers trembled as she picked up the photograph. The baby beamed back at her, the resemblance to Sophie so acute that she marvelled that she had not seen it before. She was standing ashen-faced studying the photograph when Slater walked in.

"Sophie's Ray's child." She croaked the words, still only half able to believe them.

"He begot her, if that's what you mean," came Slater's grim response. "It isn't very pleasant discovering that someone you trusted has deceived you is it, Chris?"

"He can't have known," Chris whispered positively, "Natalie..."

"Natalie went to him and begged him to help her. He told her to go and get an abortion," Slater told her curtly. "She was on the verge of a breakdown when she came to me."

"And you married her because..."

"My reasons for marrying her are nothing to do with you. If I were you it would be Ray I wanted to question—not me. What suddenly brought on this flash of insight, by the way?" he drawled tauntingly, and Chris had the nausea-inducing suspicion that he thought she had known all along about Sophie's parentage.

"Sophie spoke when we were at the cottage," she said slowly. "I told her I wanted to take her home to you, and she said to me, 'he isn't my daddy...'"

"That bitch!" Slater's face had gone bone-white, his mouth hard and tense. "Natalie must have told her. God knows she threatened to often enough, but I never thought..."

"It really doesn't matter what you thought." How cool and controlled she sounded, Chris marvelled, watching Slater's face change, alert wariness creeping into his eyes as he watched her.

"All this proves is that Sophie is solely my responsibility. Just as soon as I can I'll make arrangements for both of us to leave..."

"You...now just one minute." He almost snarled the words. "Sophie stays right here with me..."

"Why?" Chris looked directly at him. "You don't want her."

For several tension filled seconds Slater merely stared at her with mingled loathing and contempt, and then at last in a clipped voice he said, "You haven't changed have you, Chris? You always did have this facility for turning things round to suit your own convenience. Well not this time...not this time."

He slammed the door after him, leaving Chris to replace the photograph in its envelope. Even now she could barely take it all in, but she did know one thing. Ray would never have told Natalie to have an abortion. He was a deeply religious person; something that very few people knew. He himself had been illegitimate and often commented that had abortion been freely available in his mother's lifetime, he never would have been born at all. He had been abandoned as a baby and brought up by a succession of foster parents; and for that reason Chris could never see him refusing to acknowledge any child of his own. She *had* to speak to him, but the news that he had a six-year-old daughter was hardly something she could just announce over the telephone. And what about Sophie? Could the knowledge that Slater wasn't her father be the cause of her silence. She had to talk to John.

She wouldn't ask him to come to the house in case seeing him upset Sophie again, she decided. She thought for a few minutes. The cottage, they could meet there... Once she had spoken to him she might be able to evolve some plan for Sophie's future. One thing she was sure of; she wasn't going to leave her here to be bullied and disliked by Sarah once she became Slater's wife. Slater had claimed that he wanted her. Why? Unless of course, it was simply that he wanted to prevent her from having the little girl? Could he really hate her so much? She was the one who ought to have hated him. She frowned. Why had he not *told* her why he was marrying Natalie...why had he not explained? What did it matter now. Nothing was changed. He couldn't have loved her at all; it had been bad enough when she believed he had preferred her cousin to herself, but to know that he had married Natalie *without* loving her; to know that she had meant so little to him that he had so easily and carelessly dismissed her from his life, was bitter gall indeed.

CHAPTER NINE

CHRIS had to wait three days before an opportunity presented itself for her to ring John without being overheard by Slater. It was unsettling, knowing that he was in the house with her, and it made her stay in bed much longer than she had anticipated. On one or two occasions when he had come up to see her, she had the suspicion that that was exactly what he had wanted, and she couldn't help remembering his grim expression on the day they had left the hospital and she had announced her intention of getting back on her feet just as quickly as she could.

It was, she had told herself, just a matter of biding her time, and eventually she was proved right. On the third morning of her enforced stay in bed, Slater walked into her room and announced tersely that he was having to visit the factory.

"Don't even think of attempting to do anything foolish while I'm gone, Chris," he warned her tersely, coming to stand beside her. He hadn't yet put on his jacket and the thin white silk of his shirt lovingly outlined the taut muscles of his chest. She ached to touch him Chris admitted to herself, half shocked by the intensity of her physical desire for him. Seven years ago, she had wanted him yes, but then she had been more than content to let him set the pace of their relationship and to follow his guidance whereas now ... Now she was a woman, not an adolescent, she reminded herself wryly, dragging her eyes away from him, lest they betrayed something of her thoughts to him.

"We still have to talk."

"No." Her response was instantaneous and very revealing. She knew from his expression that Slater had heard the fear in her voice. His mouth had gone hard, his eyes almost amber as he stared down at her.

"Yes, damn you," he contradicted thickly, adding, "What are you so frightened of, Chris? Is it this?"

His mouth was on hers before she could move, his body blocking out the light, his hands imprisoning her shoulders against the mattress.

At first she twisted desperately from side to side trying to escape, but the fierce heat of his mouth; the need that his angry, almost bitter kiss aroused in spite of all her determination not to acknowledge it, overwhelmed her and her mouth softened beneath his, her arms going round his neck, stroking the softness of his hair.

She felt the bed depress under his weight and her treacherous body gloried in having him so close to her; offering no resistance at all when he slid aside one of the delicate straps of her nightdress to cup the rounded firmness of her breast.

The soft sound of pleasure she made in the back of her throat must have reached him. Chris felt him tense, registering her response. A bitter wave of shame flooded over her and she pulled away from him, turning her face into the pillow.

"Running away again, Chris?"

She felt his breath brush her skin, and shivered involuntarily, trying to withstand the stroking probe of his thumb, as it moved over her lower lip.

"All right, I'll let you get away with it—this time. But you can't run for ever, Chris." She felt him get up, her body instantly missing the heavy warmth of his, and as she heard him move towards the door she ached to call him back. Only after the door closed behind him was she able to expel a shaky breath. The sooner she left here the better, she told herself, listening for the sound of his car driving away. She didn't know what game he was playing with her, but what she did know was that if she allowed herself to be drawn into it, she would definitely be the loser.

Once she was sure that Slater was gone she dressed as quickly as she could, taking care not to put too much weight on her injured ankle.

Luckily Mrs Lancaster was out with Sophie, and there was nothing to stop Chris from ringing John.

Nothing apart from her conscience which urged her to tell Slater what had happened in the cottage, before she told anyone else. Why should she, she argued stubbornly with herself, Sophie wasn't even his child; he didn't really want her, he simply looked after her through habit... And yet... she had been so sure she had seen real love and caring in his eyes for the little girl.

John Howard was a doctor, she told herself. He would know far better than Slater what interpretation to put on Sophie's behaviour.

She got through to him straight away, and asked him if he was free for lunch. She didn't want him coming to the house again—not after what had happened last time.

He seemed rather restrained and cool towards her, but Chris urged him to accept. Perhaps he thought she was making a play for him, she thought bitterly. After all, if what Sarah had said about Natalie was common knowledge in the local's eyes, she might already be tarred with the same brush!

Eventually John gave way and agreed to meet her at the same restaurant where they had originally been introduced.

"I wouldn't ask, but it really is important," she told him before ringing off, "and I just don't know who else to turn to."

She was in a fever of tension as she went back upstairs to collect her things, dreading Slater coming back and preventing her from going out. She daren't even leave a note for Mrs Lancaster just in case Slater came after her.

It wasn't until the taxi she had ordered to take her to the restaurant cleared Slater's drive that she was finally able to release her pent up breath. To her relief John was already sitting in the bar waiting for her. He greeted her briefly, looking tense and ill at ease.

"I'm afraid I don't have much time," he apologised, ordering her a drink. "I have a pretty heavy schedule today, and my wife wasn't too well this morning. I want to go home and check up on her before I go back to work."

"I wouldn't have rung you if it hadn't been important," Chris began defensively. "I just didn't know who else to turn to... It's about Sophie..."

Quickly she outlined what had happened; when she had finished there was a long silence. John Howard's face was white, his eyes almost haunted. He looked so ill that Chris was shocked. She had never imagined him reacting so violently to her disclosures.

"Dear God, I've got to get out of here," he told her unsteadily. "Are you desperately hungry?"

Chris shook her head. Her stomach was churning it was true, but not through hunger. She had the sensation of being poised on an unexpected precipice, and it was an extremely unwelcome one.

"Did you drive here?" John asked tersely.

When Chris shook her head again, John took her arm and led her out of the bar. "We'll go for a drive... Come on."

He still looked ill when they were installed in the car, so much so that Chris felt extremely guilty.

"Look," she began uncertainly, "I'm sorry I bothered you with all this. I should have told Slater, but I was afraid he would dismiss it as sheer fantasy... That was before I learned that he isn't Sophie's father, of course." She bit her lip wondering if she had revealed something that John didn't know, but his mind was obviously running on different lines from hers because all he said was, "She promised me she wouldn't do it." His voice sounded thick and strained, almost as though he found uttering the words a huge physical effort.

The road he took was a meandering country one that Chris dimly remembered. He pulled off it by a farm gate, and switched off his car engine. His face was still grey with pain, and Chris felt the nervous tremors of dread inside her building up as he finally turned towards her.

"God it's times like these that I wish I'd not given up smoking," he said tensely. Abruptly he looked at her. "You're sure that Sophie really spoke?"

"Quite sure," Chris confirmed quietly, "although she seems to remember nothing about it."

"No...no she wouldn't do...it would be the trauma of being there in the cottage alone, especially after seeing me...her mind would blot it all out I expect." He took a deep breath and let it out on a shuddering sigh. "None of us really knows what will happen about Sophie. A trauma as great as the one that originally caused her dumbness would be the ideal solution, but such things cannot be manufactured or controlled, and can go dangerously wrong..."

"What was the trauma that originally caused the problem?" Chris asked quietly. "No one seems to know..."

"I know," John told her, "and so does Slater." There was a long, long pause during which Chris held her breath wondering if he would go on and if he did, what he would tell her? Was Slater to blame for Sophie's illness? Was that what John was going to reveal to her?

"Is that why Slater feels so responsible for her?" she asked at last, needing to break the painful silence. "Because he's to blame?"

"No...no." The anguished denial filled the interior of the car with emotion so intense that it was almost tangible. "If anyone's to blame, it's me."

The admission shocked her, robbing her of breath and the ability to rationalise. It took her several stupefied seconds to find the impetus to say huskily, "You...but how could that be possible?"

"Natalie and I were having an affair."

Once again Chris was lost for words. Of all the men to be involved with her cousin, John Howard was the very last she would have thought of.

"But..."

All that she was thinking must have shown on her face because John grimaced slightly and said, "Yes, I know...but there are times in our lives when we all do things we can't explain or analyse. Natalie was the very worst woman for me to become emotionally involved with. Demanding, petulant, selfish, greedy, unstable, she was all of those things—completely opposite from my wife, in fact, and perhaps that's where the attraction lay. It wasn't even a physical thing—at least not at first. She seemed so gay...so pathetically lonely and vulnerable. She came to see me when I was doing some locum work for her regular doctor. She wanted me to prescribe tranquillisers for her. She couldn't sleep, she told me. She was thin, almost painfully so.

"I didn't realise then that her thinness was part of a deliberate campaign to get at Slater. I thought her husband the most selfish inconsiderate brute alive. She rang me up a week later. She needed someone to talk to she told me... I fell for it... It was very flattering to have such a beautiful woman wanting my company.

"We started meeting...lunching together, and then later going to the cottage. I'll never forget the first time we made love there. Natalie seemed to be on an intense high... She kept laughing, gloating almost... I knew there was something wrong, but I closed my eyes to it, by then I was too deeply involved. I refused to see what should have been obvious to me; that Natalie was desperately ill. We kept on seeing one another, and then one day she told me she wanted me to get a divorce. I told her it was impossible. She'd always known that... Whatever my feelings, I couldn't leave Helen.

"She seemed to change completely from the person I thought she was. She screamed and raved, calling me vile names, telling me she'd tell Helen about our affair. On and on it went until she'd exhausted herself. I admitted then that she was seriously mentally ill, but I couldn't break off our relationship—I daredn't. I tried to persuade her to go and see a specialist, but she had such severe hysterics that I tried to take the coward's way out then I'm afraid. I reminded her that she had a husband...a child...

"Her husband loved someone else, she told me and as for her child, Sophie! She hated Sophie she told me. She had always hated her. It was because of Sophie that she was trapped in her marriage with Slater. It was only later that she told me that Sophie wasn't even his child, by which time I was at my wits' end, desperate to prevent my wife from finding out about our affair, and terrified for Natalie who, it was becoming increasingly obvious, was very, very ill. I was caught in a cleft stick. In other circumstances I could have approached Slater and told him my fears, but because of my relationship with Natalie, that was impossible.

"She rang me up at home one evening demanding that I meet her at the cottage the next day. I went to bed that night determined to sort things out once and for all.

"She was jumpy and on edge when I got there. Slater was furious with her, she told me because she'd threatened to tell Sophie that he wasn't her father... She was very wild and distraught. She wanted me to go away with her, to leave my wife. I explained that it was impossible. While we were arguing Sophie walked into the cottage. I didn't know it but Natalie had been taking her there. She had a thing about the place that I couldn't understand. She hated it, and yet she wanted to be there. Before I could stop her Natalie turned on the little girl screaming at her. She actually hit Sophie across the face before I could restrain her. Sophie was crying naturally. She wanted her daddy, she sobbed.''

He broke off, shuddering deeply, his eyes dark with pain, remembering what had happened, and Chris held her breath.

Her own chest felt tight and uncomfortable. If anyone else had told her this she doubted that she would have believed them.

''That was when Natalie told her that Slater wasn't her father... I'll never forget it. Sophie just stared at her, and then she said slowly, 'I hate you and I wish you'd go away and never, ever come back.' She ran out of the cottage before I could stop her and when I started to go after her, Natalie held me back, screaming that she'd go straight to my wife, if I left her. I didn't know what to do. All my instincts, my training, urged me to go after Sophie, but my guilt, the knowledge of what Natalie could and would do to our life together, stopped me. And that's something I'll never cease to regret, never be able to square with my conscience—something I'll have to live with for the rest of my life.

''I never saw Natalie alive again after that night. I eventually managed to calm her down, and I took her home. Slater was away in London.

''He rang me the next day. I think I knew the moment I heard his voice. He asked me to go round. When I got there he told me that Natalie was dead. She'd taken a massive overdose cocktail of tranquillisers and God knows what. She left a letter, blaming me, saying that she was carrying my child, that I'd seduced and then abandoned her.

"I just didn't know what to say to Slater, but he made it easy for me. He knew what Natalie was like, he assured me. He also destroyed the letter. He told me that what had happened—the truth—would remain between the two of us. Natalie had been unwell and unbalanced for a while. Her own doctor could attest to that. He had in fact notified her own doctor the moment he discovered her. As you know they had separate rooms, and apparently it was Sophie who found her. Slater found her standing beside the bed, just staring at her mother. She hasn't spoken a word since."

He laced his hands together and studied their blunt tips. "It's quite obvious that Sophie blames herself for her mother's death. I never want to see you again, she said, and what happens...her mother disappears. Of course we've tried to explain...but she's a child...and also deep inside her there's still hatred there for Natalie. Natalie never showed her any affection. In fact she seemed to hate her, but Slater..." He shook his head. "Some days I wonder how I can live with the burden of guilt I have to carry. I look at my wife... I think of my life, and I wish to God I had the guts to tell her. She's strong enough to take it, much, much stronger than Natalie, much stronger than me, but I'm afraid that if I do tell her, she'll divorce me, and if Natalie taught me anything, it was just how much Helen means to me."

It was all so very different from what she had imagined that Chris had difficulty in taking it all in. Far from being the cause of her cousin's death, Slater had in actual fact been more of a victim, both of her treachery and her unstable nature. In mentally depicting her cousin as desperately unhappy because of the unkind treatment of her husband, she had been about as far from the truth as it was possible to get. But that didn't alter her own vulnerability to Slater; nor the fact that she would be wise to get away from him before she revealed to him more than she wanted to know.

She was still as far away as ever from discovering why Slater had married Natalie in the first place—the only person who was ever likely to find out was Sarah, once they married. As his wife, she would have a right to know. And Sophie? What of her?

That Sarah didn't want Natalie's child to have a place in their lives Chris knew, but would Slater be in agreement to her having sole guardianship of the little girl? She had enough money now to retire from modelling; she could give Sophie a comfortable home, love, care; and perhaps even in time she might be able to introduce her to her real father...

But Slater *was* Sophie's real father, part of her insisted. Slater was the father she wanted; the father who had brought her up. How could Natalie have been so cruel? Instinctively she knew and she blanched at the knowledge, apart from Slater none of them were innocent of hurting Sophie. Natalie couldn't love her daughter because she looked too much like *her*, Chris acknowledged.

"Are you all right?"

She smiled painfully. "I'm fine, just rather shell-shocked. No...please... You don't owe me any explanations or apologies...I'm glad you've told me though... It explains so much...why Sophie should be so upset after your visit."

"Yes, poor child. Slater seems to think she believed that I might take you away from her as, in her eyes, at least, I had taken her mother."

So Slater had talked to him about that. Chris chewed absently at her bottom lip. She needed time to think, time to sort herself out and come out with a concise, workable plan for her own and Sophie's futures—a plan that Slater would agree to.

"Shall I take you back now?"

They were only a couple of miles from Slater's house, as the crow flies, and Chris shook her head.

"No I think I'll walk back through the fields," she told him. "I need time to think—to re-assess things. The walk will help me."

"Well take it easy on that ankle."

As she got out of the car Chris turned to him. "Thank you for telling me," she said softly. It couldn't have been easy for him—she could see in his face that it hadn't. "I think your wife is a very lucky lady," she added encouragingly, "and I think you should tell her—everything."

"Perhaps I will. I want to, but finding the courage is another matter."

Walking slowly back to the house, Chris tried to formulate some sort of plan to put to Slater. Should she simply confront him with her newfound knowledge and demand that he release Sophie into her care? After all there was no blood relationship between them. Or should she approach the matter more subtly; should she say that she knew that Sarah would not want the child once they were married?

And Sophie herself? What would she want? That she loved Slater Chris didn't for a moment doubt, but would that love be able to survive Sarah's hostility?

Would she ever be able to regain her voice if she stayed with Slater? Wouldn't she have a far better chance of recovery in a completely new environment? She would have to take legal and medical advice Chris reflected—and she could be facing a hard and expensive battle, but she felt sure that she could give Sophie more than Slater and Sarah. What would happen when Sarah had a family? Sophie would be totally excluded, Sarah would make sure of that.

Wrestling with her thoughts she was half-way up the drive before she saw Slater's car. It was parked at an angle, tyre marks scored through the gravel as though he had stopped in a hurry. Her heart started to thud in panic. By now he must have discovered that she was missing. Why hadn't she thought about that? Because she had been too concerned with John's revelations and Sophie's future, that was why. He was back early. Had he returned especially to check up on her? Well she was a grown woman she reminded herself nervously, and if she wanted to go out for a walk then she was completely free to do so. Her ankle was virtually fully recovered; it barely ached at all. Slater was being ridiculous in refusing to let her go out.

As she rounded the corner of the house, hoping to walk in undiscovered via the drawing room french windows, she came to an abrupt halt, her pulses racing anxiously as she took in the small tableau on the lawn. Slater was crouching down on his heels, rocking Sophie's small frame in his arms. Mrs Lancaster stood worriedly by, and as she watched them, their voices reached her, Slater's terse as he demanded brusquely, "When did you discover that she'd gone?"

"Just before lunch." Mrs Lancaster sounded extremely upset. "She'd just gone, no note...nothing."

"But all her clothes are still here..."

Did they think she'd left permanently? Chris was horrified to discover what her innocently intended deception had led to. She took a step forward, kicking a small pebble as she did so.

The sound it made as it skittered across the crazy paved path seemed preternaturally loud in the tense silence that followed Slater's awareness of her presence. Across the half dozen or so yards that separated them their eyes met, Slater's topaz and darkly bitter, Chris's green and uncomfortably guilty. She waited for Slater to say something; to voice his smouldering rage, but it wasn't he who broke the thick silence, it was Sophie. Lifting her head she saw Chris, her eyes widening first in disbelief and then in tremulous joy. Racing towards her, she called her name, a thick, choked sound, but quite distinctly her name, Chris thought dazedly, going down on her knees and holding out her arms to catch her.

"Sophie...Sophie..." Tears stung her eyes, as she held Sophie slightly away from her. "Surely you didn't think I'd really go just like that?" Watching the small delicate face, she remembered all that John had told her, and remorse flooded through her. Had Sophie thought that *she* had left her too?

"Sophie!"

Slater was standing beside them, one lean hand resting on Sophie's cheeks as he turned her face up towards his own.

"She said my name," Chris said chokily.

"Yes, I heard her." The quiet calm in Slater's voice warned Chris not to make too much of what had happened. "And a rusty little squeak it was too... It sounded more like a mouse with a sore throat than my Sophie.''

To Chris's great joy Sophie giggled. ''It wasn't a mouse, Daddy...it was me.'' Across her head their eyes met, and for once Chris wasn't ashamed of Slater seeing the emotion glittering there. His own eyes had darkened and looked over-bright.

''Take her inside,'' he told Chris quietly, ''I'll go and ring the hospital. And Chris...'' His mouth was grim as she turned towards him. ''Don't think this means that you and I won't be having that talk.''

CHAPTER TEN

Of course, it was hours before the excitement abated. Sophie, much to Chris's cowardly relief, insisted on sleeping with her and thus ensured that Slater would not be able to talk to her alone.

Once she realised what Sophie had thought, Chris was at great pains to assure the little girl that there had been no question of her leaving without telling her.

"I don't want you to leave here at all. I want you to stay for always," Sophie protested.

They were alone in Chris's room. Downstairs Slater was no doubt making appointments for Sophie to see her specialists, Chris reflected, torn between giving the little girl the assurance she so badly needed and telling her the truth.

"I want you to be with me for always," Sophie continued passionately.

This at least Chris knew she was able to respond to honestly. "And I want to be with you, sweetheart," she told her.

"Daddy said you must have gone back to America," Sophie confided guilelessly. "He said you had your career to think of."

Chris's mouth tightened. She could just imagine how Slater had said that. "There'll always be an important place for you in my life, Sophie."

"Promise me you'll stay with me for always?"

At a loss to know how to respond, Chris was saved the necessity of doing so when Slater rapped briefly on the door and walked in.

"Bed for you, young lady," he told Sophie, "You've got a big day ahead of you tomorrow. We're going to see Dr Hartwell."

Sophie pulled a face.

"He wants to hear this new voice of yours for himself. He didn't believe me when I said you sounded like a rusty mouse," Slater teased.

Watching them like this it seemed impossible to believe that Sophie wasn't his child. He seemed to love her so much. To punish herself for her momentary weakness Chris interrupted coolly, "Have you told Sarah the good news?"

"Not yet." Slater's voice was blandly easy.

"I thought she'd be the first one you'd want to share it with."

"I'll give her a ring later on..."

He seemed so casual, but then perhaps like her he realised that Sarah would not be particularly overjoyed by the news.

"Daddy, tell Chris we want her to stay with us for always," Sophie interrupted. "I want you to."

"Oh, Chris is too big a girl to pay any attention to what I say," Slater responded. "She always goes her own way. I learned that a long time ago."

Chris felt colour tinge her skin. Slater was obviously referring to the time she had told him that her career was more important to her than him; but then she had believed that he loved Natalie, and she had spoken those words to save her pride, knowing that she could not remain in Little Martin to watch as an onlooker his marriage to her cousin. Neither had she wanted him to guess why she was running away, so she had used the convenient excuse of her "career".

How angry he had been the first time she told him that Ray had said she would make a good model! Then she had barely paid any attention to Ray's comment, simply shrugging it aside. Modelling, or indeed any career, had been the last thing on her mind; she had been dreaming of marriage to Slater, bearing his children...

"Modelling? More like posing for girlie magazines," Slater had said scathingly, adding, "Don't you know how many silly little girls fall into that trap every year? And once they're in it, no matter how hard they fight they can't get out."

Now she could see why he had doubted Ray's sincerity, but then she had been puzzled by his dislike of the other man.

And Slater had been wrong about him, of course. Without Ray's help and encouragement she would never have made it to the top.

"Are you happy now, Chris, now that you've achieved your ambition?"

Happy? Unhappiness darkened her eyes momentarily. Of course she wasn't happy in the way that he meant; her career had been a way of filling time, of silencing her thoughts, of keeping at bay the knowledge that she still loved him.

"Of course." How smoothly the lies slipped off her tongue. "I have a healthy bank balance, my independence; some very good friends..."

"But no lover to share your bed at night," Slater taunted.

Sophie, Chris suddenly noticed, had dropped off to sleep in his arms, obviously worn out by the day. Her mind seemed to have gone blank, refusing to provide her with a means of turning aside Slater's question.

"Only because I don't choose to have one," she managed at last.

"Why not, I wonder? It certainly isn't because of any lack of physical desire."

Her face stung with hot colour. "Perhaps I simply prefer my independence to being held in thrall to some male."

"But you can't deny that it is possible that you could be 'held in thrall', as you put it?"

The thrust was soft, but intensely painful.

Chris summoned all the skill she had learned in her years of modelling, all her ability to assume an expression at will.

"Possible," she drawled smiling at him mockingly, "but not probable."

She held her breath waiting for him to react—to retaliate, and expelled it in relief as she heard Mrs Lancaster calling him.

"I'll take Sophie." She held out her arms for the sleeping child. As he passed her over, their hands touched. Tiny electric frissons of awareness shimmered over her skin. The moment he had gone Chris hurried to the door and locked it, thankful for the old-fashioned locks these doors still possessed.

Just as soon as she could she was going to leave Little Martin and take Sophie with her. Slater would see the wisdom of such a course; he must see it. Sarah would certainly agree with her, Chris thought grimly.

It was comforting to wake up and feel Sophie's small body curled into hers, although Chris felt rather embarrassed when she had to pad across the floor to unlock her door at Mrs Lancaster's knock.

"Slater said to let you both sleep in this morning," she announced carrying in a tray of tea. "He's just gone down to the factory, but he'll be back soon. He's taking Sophie into Martin at eleven, to the hospital there."

While he was gone she would ring her agent, Chris decided, she would know the best legal firm for her to employ. Anxiously she bit her lip, would Sophie turn against her for taking her away from Slater? She hoped not.

The little girl was irrepressibly chatty over breakfast, and when Chris helped Mrs Lancaster to clear away the older woman laughed, "I never thought the day would come when I didn't want to hear Sophie talking, but right now..."

"Umm, she seems to have got her voice back with a vengeance," Chris agreed. She put down the plates she was carrying. "I'm so sorry I gave you all such a scare yesterday. I don't know why Sophie should think I'd left. I'd simply gone out to lunch with...with someone."

"Oh, that's all right. Actually it was Slater who decided that you'd gone for good. Fit to commit murder, he looked when he came back and found out you'd gone." Her glance was speculative. "If Sophie hadn't been in the kitchen with me when he came in saying that you'd upped and left, I doubt it would ever have entered her mind. Of course she was disappointed when we got back from the shops and you weren't here..."

"I should have left a note," Chris apologised.

"Well in view of what's happened, it's all worked out for the best," Mrs Lancaster said comfortably.

Chris made a point of staying out of the way when Slater returned to collect Sophie. She very much wanted to go with them, but Slater hadn't asked her to, and besides she wasn't sure if she was up to the ordeal of his company.

Her attempts to get through to her agent were frustrated by the lines being busy. She would just have to wait until tomorrow Chris reflected when she heard the sound of Slater's car returning later in the afternoon.

She went downstairs to meet them. Sophie was glowing with excitement. "Dr Hartwell said I was a miracle," she told Chris proudly, "and he said I didn't sound like a rusty mouse at all."

"He also said you had to rest," Slater reminded her wryly.

"I'll take her upstairs," Chris offered. Looking at him she had suddenly been struck by the lines of pain and tiredness round his eyes. He had always seemed so strong and invulnerable that she had never noticed them before. She wanted to go up to him and draw his head down on to her breast; to comfort him. To combat this momentary weakness she took hold of Sophie's hand and tugged her inside.

Upstairs in her room Sophie was still arguing that she wasn't tired, but within ten minutes of Chris starting to read to her she was fast asleep.

It was a shock to find Slater standing just inside the door, watching them. How long had he been there? Her heart thumping unevenly, Chris got up.

"You really care about her, don't you?" he said quietly. "How does it feel, Chris, to know what you've given up?"

Reaction rioted inside her. Forcing it down she said lightly. "I'm only twenty-six, Slater. There's still plenty of time for me to have a child, if I want one."

"First you've got to find a man." He said the words almost insultingly, and remembering what she had read of artificial insemination and the new scheme in operation in the States whereby a woman could elect to impregnate herself with the seed of some of the best brains in the world, she shrugged, "Not necessarily, you..."

Almost at once his face darkened, his eyes smouldering dark gold. "I what?" he snarled, totally misunderstanding her comment. "I might have already have given you a child! If I have you won't get to keep it. No child of mine is going to be brought up by..."

"By what?" Chris shouted at him, nearly as furious as he was himself. "By someone whose cousin is a nymphomaniac? What's wrong, Slater? Are you worried that I might have inherited the same tendencies as Natalie; that I might corrupt my own child?"

She was barely able to understand her own pain, knowing only that it had sprung from the bitter anger in Slater's eyes when he thought she might be referring to the fact that she could have conceived his child. Did he really dislike her so much? Belatedly she remembered Sophie. A quick glance at the little girl confirmed that she was still asleep. Brushing past Slater, she went on unsteady legs to her own room. Once there she sank down on to the bed, longing to give way to tears, but too wound up to do so.

When the door opened and Slater walked in she could hardly believe her eyes.

"Running away again, Chris," he taunted. His voice sounded odd, thick and husky, as though he was barely able to frame the words. "Well this time there's nowhere to run to. Just answer me one thing honestly, have you ever regretted what you did? Have you ever wished for just one second that you hadn't put your precious career first? Why the hell did you come back, Chris?"

"You know why... I'm Sophie's guardian."

"And that brought you back; a tenuous link with a child you'd never even seen? That's not the Chris I know. She never let emotional ties of any type mean anything to her."

"That's not true!"

"Isn't it? Then how the hell do you explain the fact that you were able to walk out on me, without so much as a single word of regret?"

"All these years and you still resent that?" She could hardly believe it. She had never thought of him as being so egocentrical. He hadn't loved her; he had been planning to marry someone and yet after all this time he could display this almost excessive bitterness because she had left. "I'm surprised you can still remember."

"Oh I remember all right... just as I remember every hour of the nightmare my life's been since. Have you any idea what it was like married to Natalie wondering what the hell she was going to do next? When Sophie was six weeks old Natalie tried to smother her." He watched her go white. "Oh yes. She never loved Sophie; never wanted her. I had to watch her like a hawk, and then later there were men... Never one man for any length of time, until ..."

"Until she met John," Chris supplied for him. "I met him for lunch yesterday. He told me all about it. I'm not Natalie, Slater," she added quietly when she saw the thoughts reflected in his eyes. "I thought when we were trapped in the cottage that Sophie spoke and I wanted to talk to him about it. He told me a lot more than I'd bargained on hearing." She desperately wanted to ask him why he had ever married Natalie, but she didn't have the right. "You might as well know," she continued, "that I want Sophie to come and live with me."

The furious sound he made as he swore, silenced her. "You bitch," he exclaimed bitterly. "You think you can take it all, don't you? Well you're not having Sophie."

"She isn't your child," Chris pointed out, "and Sarah doesn't want her."

"Sarah? What the hell's she got to do with all this?"

"Oh, come on, Slater." She was getting angry herself now. "Sarah told me you and she are getting married. She seemed to think that was why Natalie took her life—she said you'd asked her for a divorce. She doesn't like Sophie, you must know that. You'll have other children but Sophie is related to me by blood. I can give her so much, and I love her."

"And you think I don't is that it? For six years she's been my child, and now suddenly I'm supposed to give her up? Well if you want Sophie, you're damned well going to have to pay for her," he snarled suddenly, slamming the door closed behind him.

"How?" Chris was totally confused. What did he want? Money? Slater had always been relatively wealthy; money had never seemed to be a motivating force in his life. Her mind could not take in what he was saying.

"Like this." He locked the door and came towards her, his intention written clearly in his eyes. Chris tensed and moved back; the eternal moves of prey and hunter. Deep down inside her tension began to coil in spirals of excitement. Slater wanted her; she knew it as instinctively and intensely as though he had said the words out loud to her. Her pulses thudded protestingly as he came closer, so close that she could see the yellow speckles in his irises.

"Slater..."

"Don't say anything," he warned her thickly. "You owe me this, Chris...this and all the thousands of other times you should have been in my arms and weren't. I don't understand it, damn you," he muttered as he reached her and seized hold of her upper arms. "You're not cold, or lacking in passion—just the opposite, and yet all these years there you've remained a virgin..."

Chris tried to summon a cool smile. "Perhaps I just enjoy teasing," she commented brightly, trying to shake free of his grip. "I really don't think this is a good idea, Slater..."

"Really? Now I happen to disagree." The silky softness of his voice shivered across her nerves.

"You're marrying Sarah," Chris reminded him suddenly growing desperate.

"I'm not married to her yet. You owe me this, Chris..."

It was the second time he had voiced the emphatic claim. She didn't owe him anything, Chris thought bitterly; on the contrary, he was the one... Her thoughts became a confused jumble as his mouth touched hers, lingering sensually on the softness of her lower lip. Violence she could have resisted, but this tenderness, this feeling she had that he was willing her backwards in time were things she couldn't compete against. Her body wanted him; yearned for him far more hungrily now that it was aware of all that his possession could mean; than it had done in the old days, when his experience had protected her innocence.

The heat of his mouth as it moved on hers seduced her senses, her body burning where he touched it, stroking lightly over her clothes, until she ached to be rid of their constrictive layers and free to feel the oiled silk of his skin on her own. She felt him move slightly away and instinctively her mouth clung, her tongue tentatively begging him to stay.

"Chris!" The muffled sound of her name, almost tortured as he muttered it against her throat made her heart thud excitedly. She loved him so much she was willing to take even these crumbs, she acknowledged mentally. If Slater wanted to make love to her then she was more than willing for him to do so. In his arms she wanted to be for him all the woman he had ever hungered for; a woman he would remember all his life. She wanted their lovemaking to be something that marriage to Sarah would never be able to obliterate and if that was selfish then she was going to be selfish she decided, anguishedly.

"You don't know how much I want you." The admission seemed to be wrung from him, his skin hot as he pressed his forehead against hers, his fingers tense on her body. The sudden sensation of power was so strong and overwhelming that she didn't even try to resist it.

"Show me." She whispered the words against his mouth, teasing the taut shape of it with soft kisses, sliding her hands along his shoulders until her breasts were pressed flat against his chest.

The frenzied thud of his heart seemed to beat right through her, her insides curling pleasurably with excitement as his hands cupped her face, his mouth devouring hers, absorbing the taste and texture of it, as though it were some magical life force.

The heat of his palm against her breast melted her insides, her need finding some relief in the small sounds of pleasure she made deep in her throat.

"It's like listening to a kitten purring." Slater mouthed the words against her throat feeling the reverberations of the small sounds increasing in volume as he unfastened her blouse and slid his hand inside.

Against the thin silk of her bra her nipples strained provocatively for his touch, her body arched along the length of his, supported by his arm at the back of her waist.

His mouth left her throat, and Chris opened her eyes reluctantly. Heat exploded inside her as she saw the naked desire glittering in his eyes as his gaze rested on the aroused thrust of her breasts.

"Kiss me." The words seemed to come from a woman who was almost a stranger to her; a woman who seemed to know instinctively how to guide Slater's dark head to her breast; a woman who made no secret of the pleasure he gave her when he pushed aside the fine silk and slid his mouth over the hard nub of her nipple.

"Like this?" Slater's mouth caressed her other breast, while Chris murmured her pleasure, her hands clutching at the smooth flesh of his back. Totally engrossed in the sharply erotic sensations flooding her body as Slater's mouth suckled her nipples, Chris was barely aware of him unzipping her skirt until it slid free of her hips, and he lifted her free of it, his hands sliding inside the barrier of her briefs to hold her against him. His harsh groan of pleasure at the intimate contact of their bodies flooded her with love. Her fingers tugged at the buttons of his shirt, her mouth fusing eagerly with his, as her hips strained eagerly against him.

Beneath his shirt his chest was slightly moist, the musky scent of his body enveloping her.

When he dropped down on one knee in front of her to unfasten her stockings Chris quivered with heady anticipation. For once in her life she wasn't going to think or rationalise; she was simply going to feel. But the fierce sheeting of pleasure racing under her skin as Slater's mouth caressed the tender inside of her thigh was something for which she was totally unprepared. She pulled away instinctively, trembling, caught up in coils of ever tightening desire for him, a dark tide of colour storming her skin.

"Chris... Chris... let me love you." Slater's skin was as flushed as her own, his voice thick, barely recognisable.

Quivers of sensation arrowed through her like darts of fire as he took her silence for consent and his tongue wove delicate patterns against her responsive skin, his hands deftly removing the silk stockings. The dainty ribbon of her suspender belt slid to the floor the moment he unfastened it. Chris shivered as she felt the light brush of his fingers against the top of her thigh and then under the elastic of her tiny briefs. Dizzily she closed her eyes, wanting to touch him as he was touching her, aching for him to possess her body, to...

Idiotically, when he had removed her briefs she wanted to hide herself away from him, and as though he sensed the impulse he reached up, grasping her wrists, securing them lightly behind her body with one hand, while the other stroked slowly up the left hand side of her body, his fingers curling round her ankle, exploring the shape of her calf; her knee... Chris was shivering convulsively, long before she felt the gentle drift of his mouth along her inner thigh. His hand cupped her bottom, and she cried out aloud as she felt the intimate brush of his tongue against her body, wanting to pull away and yet too enfeebled by the tumultuous surge of pleasure rushing through her to do so.

The small sounds she had been suppressing clogged up her throat and were expelled in a tormented moan. "Slater, please..." She wanted to make him stop what he was doing; to give voice to her shock at the intimacy of his caresses, but the fevered words of praise and encouragement he was groaning against her skin stopped her. She let him lift her on to the bed, holding out her arms eagerly to him as he removed the rest of his clothing. His body was perfect, she thought breathlessly studying it with open curiosity, unable to stop herself from touching, half in awe...half in love. A man's open physical arousal was something she had never witnessed before, and she was overcome by a feeling of pride that she should have such an effect on him, coupled with a need to show him how much his desire for her meant to her.

When she touched him hesitantly he tensed. Uncertainty flickered through her. In the old days although she had known that she aroused him, all the caresses between them had been initiated by Slater. She had never touched him intimately nor had he indicated that he wanted her to do so. Now she wanted to, for her own sake as much as his, but what if he didn't want her to?

She looked hesitantly up at him, and caught her breath. Desire burned fiercely in his eyes, every bone in his face sharp-etched; his body tensed. He swallowed and she watched the muscles in his throat move, like someone in a dream. Wanting him was the worst kind of agony; an ache that seemed to invade every muscle and cell of skin.

"Slater." She murmured his name, her fingers stroking the firm sinewed surface of his thigh. Unlike her own it was covered in fine dark hairs. He didn't move, neither rejecting nor accepting her caress. She bent her head and touched her lips to his skin.

A thick inarticulate sound shattered the heavy silence surrounding them. Instantly Chris tensed and looked up at him, her heart thumping.

Need; hunger; anger; all were clearly discernible in his eyes. He closed them as she watched, sliding his hands into her hair.

"You make me ache so badly that I think I'm going mad with the agony of it. Don't play with me, Chris," he warned her hoarsely. "You're not nineteen now—you're old enough to know that I want you in all the ways a man can want a woman. I want to caress and arouse your body until I can feel the pleasure flood through it. I want you to touch and caress me in exactly the same way, but not as some sort of experiment you feel you have to embark on; not because it's a reciprocal payment. Do you understand me?"

Of course she did. Her body ached in tune to his harshly spoken words, feeling the pain; the wanting that had given birth to them.

"I've dreamed of you for years," she told him slowly. "Ached for you...cried for you. I love you, Slater," she admitted huskily, bending her head until her hair slid silkily against his thighs and her lips caressed the hard maleness of him. His fierce sounds of pleasure heated her blood, her body pliant and eager for his, revelling in the punitive, urgent rasp of his tongue and teeth against the taut peaks of her breasts as he pulled her away from his body and proceeded to make love to her with an urgency that seemed to match her own aching need for fulfilment.

The thrust of his body against and into her own pierced her with waves of pleasure. Her mouth clung feverishly to his, returning his drugging kisses. Heat filled her and then exploded into waves of pleasure. Beneath his mouth she called his name. His mouth left hers, a harsh cry of fulfillment echoing round the room as his body found release. He kissed her again. Gently this time, his lips pressing tender, almost adoring kisses against her throat and breasts, his arms curving her into his body.

Relaxed and drowsy, Chris was caught completely off guard when he said, "Why did you say you love me? A slip of the tongue... Something you felt you ought to say, or was it simply the truth?"

Reaction rushed over her like a cold spring tide. She tried to move, but he wouldn't let her. Her humiliation was now complete, she derided herself. In her need for him, her love of him she had betrayed herself completely, while Slater had revealed...nothing.

She wanted to lie but she knew she couldn't. The words of an old saying came back to her. "To thine own self be true." Why should she demean herself in her own eyes by lying. What would it achieve now?

"Once long ago I lied to you to save my pride, Slater," she told him quietly, "I'm not prepared to do that a second time. Yes, I do love you." She made herself look at him. "I would think less of myself for making love with you not doing so, than I do for being foolish enough to do so."

She was quite proud of her little speech but Slater didn't appear to have taken it all in. He was frowning. "What do you mean you lied to me once?"

Mentally shrugging, Chris decided he might as well know the complete truth. Perhaps it would help dissolve his bitter distrust of her; help him to see that Sophie's place was with her.

"I'm talking about when I told you that my career came first. That wasn't the truth. I was desperately hopelessly in love with you, but Natalie had just told me that you were going to marry her, what was I supposed to do? I couldn't endure the pain of being rejected by you, so I went to Ray and told him I'd reconsidered his offer to help me become a model."

"You believed Natalie, just like that?"

"Not just like that," Chris admitted candidly. "I saw her in your arms one day. I'd come here to see you. You were in the drawing room together..."

"That must have been the day she told me about the baby."

"She told me she was carrying your child..."

Slater's mouth had thinned, his eyes dark with anger. "She told *me* that you and Ray were lovers; that you'd told her you were tired of me, that you were going to leave Little Martin. She suggested we soothe each other's pride by marrying. I was half off my head with jealousy at the time... I couldn't bear to think that you didn't love me."

Chris sat up, gathering the sheet round her. "She lied to both of us," she said slowly. "Fooled us both...tricked us." Unexpectedly tears started to well in her eyes and brim over on to her cheeks.

"Chris, please don't cry..." Slater's arms came round her, her head resting on his chest. "It's over... the whole thing, and we're free to go on with our lives."

What he meant that he was free of whatever he had felt for her—free to marry Sarah, Chris thought achingly.

"And you'll let me have Sophie?" She winced as he shook his head.

"Let you take away the only thing that's kept me sane these last six years? Do you know why I loved her so much initially, Chris? Well it was because she looked so much like you. I couldn't have you, but I could have a child who reminded me of you—who could have been *our* child."

When she looked at him uncomprehendingly he added thickly. "Chris, Chris, it isn't too late for us. I still love you... you love me..."

"You love me?" She said it wonderingly, despair giving way to joy.

"Of course I damn well do." He tilted her face up to meet his own, kissing her with a depth of emotion that banished all her lingering doubts. "Why do you imagine I was so anxious to get you back here; so disturbed to discover that you were still a virgin; so terrified that I might have hurt or frightened you that I daredn't come near you because I knew that if I did, I'd make love to you again...and again..."

"But Sarah," Chris protested. "She..."

"Sarah lied. I've never discussed marriage with her. I'd never marry her even if you didn't exist, simply because of the way she feels about Sophie.

"Chris, marry me just as soon as we can arrange it..."

"What and give up my successful career?"

She had only been teasing him, giving way to heady, drunken joy but the moment she saw the pain in his eyes she regretted the light words. "Oh no Slater... don't look like that... I'd give up a thousand successful careers to be with you... Of course I'll marry you."

"And Sophie?"

"She'll always be our eldest child. Perhaps one day we can tell her about Ray. I don't believe he can have known about Natalie. He would never have suggested an abortion. Perhaps she knew he wouldn't marry her and used that story to gain your sympathy. We'll never know."

"Seven years of my life your cousin stole from us. Seven years when we could have been together, when I could have woken up with you in my arms. Watched you bear our children... Seven years of loving to catch up on."

"Then we'd better not waste time talking, had we?" Chris murmured archly. She stretched sensuously against him, delighting in his slow appraisal of her body, delighting in the freedom to show her love and know that it was reciprocated. "I love you Slater," she told him softly. "I always have and I always will..."

"I sincerely hope so," he told her thickly, "because without you my life simply isn't worth living."

LOVERS IN THE AFTERNOON

Carole Mortimer

For John, Matthew and Joshua

CHAPTER ONE

WHAT was this man *doing* in her bed!

Dear God, it wasn't even her bed but his, she remembered now. She had been introduced to him at his office only that afternoon, and five hours later here she was in his bed!

She looked down at the man sleeping so peacefully at her side, one strong arm flung back across the pillow as he lay on his back, dark hair silvered with grey, all of his body deeply tanned, from a holiday he had taken in Acapulco he had told her over dinner. And she was well aware of the beauty of all that body, had touched every inch of it, from the broad shoulders, muscled chest with its covering of brown-grey hair, taut flat waist, powerfully built thighs, down long supple legs. The black silk sheet was pushed back to his waist now to reveal the strength of his chest and arms, the thick dark hair disappearing in a vee past his navel and down.

Her gaze returned quickly to his face. It was a strong, powerful face even in sleep, a wide intelligent forehead, widely defined eyebrows, beneath the long-lashed lids were eyes of a piercing grey, a long straight nose, firm uncompromising mouth, and a jaw that was firm as he slept. He was one of the most attractive men she had ever seen, or was ever likely to see, and she had spent most of the evening here in this bed with him, the first man to make love to her since her separation from her husband eight months ago.

But why did it have to be Adam Faulkner, rich industrialist, sixteen years her senior at thirty-nine, and her most recent client with the interior designing company she worked for!

She had gone to work so innocently this morning, had got out of bed at her usual seven-thirty, fed the fish and cat, warned the cat not to eat the fish while she was out all day, got her usual breakfast of dry toast and black coffee, both of which she consumed on her way to the shower as she usually did, applied the light make-up to her heart-shaped face and ever-sparkling green eyes, styled her feathered red-brown hair into its usual mass of uncontrolled lengths to her shoulders before donning the tailored blue suit and lighter blue blouse that made her hair look more red than brown, the white camisole beneath the blouse clearly the only covering to her unconfined breasts.

She had gone down to the underground car-park to her dilapidated VW, sworn at if for the usual ten minutes before it deigned to start. She had then emerged out into the usual helter-skelter of traffic that was London in the rush-hour, dodging the other seasoned drivers as she drove to her office at Stevenson Interiors, cursing the fact that she needed to take the car at all, but the reliable London underground system went nowhere near her flat or the office. Yes, it had been a pretty usual day up to that point in time.

Her breathless entrance on to the sixth floor that housed the employees of Stevenson Interiors, after being stuck in the lift for fifteen minutes was also usual; the lift broke down at least once a week, and Leonie was usually in it when it did. It would have been *unusual* if she weren't!

"The lift again?" Betty, the young, attractive receptionist, asked ruefully.

"Yes," her sigh was resigned. "One of these days I'm going to fool it and take the stairs."

"All twelve flights?" Betty's eyes widened.

Leonie grimaced, running controlling fingers through her flyaway hair. "That would be a little drastic, wouldn't it?" she conceded wryly.

Betty handed her her messages. "In your state of physical *un*fitness it could be suicide!"

"Thanks!" She skimmed through the pieces of paper she had been given, dismissing all of them as unimportant before pushing them into her navy blue clutch-bag. "What's on the agenda for today?" she looked at Betty with her usual open expression.

"The staff meeting at nine o'clock?"

"Nine—! Oh Lord," Leonie groaned, already fifteen minutes late for the meeting David had warned all employees *not* to be late for. "Maybe if I just crept into the back of the room . . . ?" she said hopefully.

"David would notice you if you crept in on your hands and knees and stood hidden for the whole meeting," Betty told her derisively.

The other woman was right, of course. David had picked her out for his individual attention from the moment he had employed her six months ago, and although she occasionally agreed to have dinner with him she made sure it was only occasionally, not wanting any serious involvement, even if David was one of the nicest men she had ever known. An unsuccessful marriage had a way of souring you to the idea of another permanent relationship. Besides, David had little patience with the way things just seemed to happen to her, believing she should be able to have some control over the accidents that just seemed to occur whenever she was around. She remembered another man, her husband, who had also found these accidents irritating, and she didn't need that criticism in her life a second time. She could handle these "incidents" left to her own devices, she didn't need some man, no matter how nice he was, constantly criticising her.

"I'll creep in anyway." She narrowly missed walking into the pot-plant that seemed to be following her about the room. "What do you feed this on?" She looked up at the huge tree-like plant in horror. "It's taking over reception, if not the world!"

"A little love and conversation do seem to have done the trick," Betty acknowledged proudly. "Now shouldn't you be getting to the staff meeting?"

David's office was crowded to capacity as she squeezed into the back of the room, but nevertheless his reproachful gaze spotted her instantly, although he didn't falter in his flow of how well the company was doing, of how good new contracts were coming their way every day.

Leonie yawned boredly, wishing she had been stuck in the lift even longer than she had been, receiving another censorious glare from David as she did, plastering a look of interest on to her face that she had perfected during her marriage, while her thoughts wandered to the Harrison lounge she had just completed, as pleased with the result as the elderly couple had been. She always felt a sense of immense satisfaction whenever she completed a job, knew she was good at what she did, that she was at last a success at something. Although some people would have her believe differently.

"Leonie, did you hear me?"

She looked up with a start at David's impatiently spoken question, blushing guiltily as she realised she was the cynosure of all eyes. "Er—"

"Steady," Gary warned as he stood at her side, deftly catching the papers she had knocked off the top of the filing cabinet as she jumped guiltily, grateful to the man who had taken her under his experienced wing from the day she came to work here.

Her blush deepened at the sympathetic ripple of laughter that filled the room; everyone knew of her habit of knocking and walking into things. "Of course I heard you, David," she answered awkwardly, her gaze guilelessly innocent as she looked at him steadily.

"Then you don't mind staying for a few minutes after the others have gone back to their offices?" he took pity on her, knowing very well that she hadn't been listening to a word he said.

"Er—no, of course not," she replaced the papers on the filing cabinet that Gary had caught for her, wondering what she was guilty of now, feeling like the disobedient child that had been asked to stay in after school. It couldn't be her lack of attention to what was being said that was at fault, she never did that anyway, and David knew it.

She moved to sit on the edge of his desk as the others filed out to go back to work. "Good meeting, David," she complimented brightly.

"And how would you know one way or the other?" he sighed, looking up at her, a tall loose-limbed man with wild blond hair that refused to be tamed despite being kept cut close to his head, the rest of his appearance neat to precision point. He was only twenty-eight, had built his interior designing business up from a two-room, three-man operation to the point where he had a dozen people working for him. And Leonie knew she was lucky to be one of them, that Stevenson Interiors was one of the most successful businesses in its field, and that it was all due to David's drive and initiative.

She grimaced. "Would it help if I were to say I'm sorry?" she cajoled.

"You always are," David said without rancour. "I wanted to talk to you about Thompson Electronics."

A frown marred her creamy brow. "Has something gone wrong? I thought they were pleased with the work I did for them. I don't understand—"

"Calm down, Leonie," he ordered impatiently at her impassioned outburst. "They were pleased, they *are* pleased, which is why the new President of the company wants you to personally design the decor for his own office suite."

"He does?" she gasped.

"Don't look so surprised," David mocked. "It was a good piece of work. Even I would never have thought of using that particular shade of pink—indeed any shade of pink, in a group of offices."

"It was the brown that off-set the femininity of it. You see I had—"

"You don't have to convince me of anything, Leonie," he drawled. "Or them either. You just have to get yourself over there at four o'clock this afternoon to discuss the details."

She was still relatively new at her job, and tried to make every design she did a work of art, something personal; she was more than pleased to know that someone else had seen and appreciated some of her completed work enough to ask for her personally. It was the first time it had happened.

"Mrs Carlson will be expecting you," David continued. "She phoned and made the appointment first thing this morning. And she'll introduce you to the President then."

"Ronald Reagan?"

He gave a patiently humouring sigh. "Where do you get your sense of humour from?"

She grinned at him. "It's what keeps my world going."

David frowned at the underlying seriousness beneath her words. Except for the friendly, and often loony façade she presented to everyone here, he knew little about the real Leonie Grant. Her employee's file said she had been married but was now separated from her husband, but she never spoke of the marriage or the man she had been married to, her openness often seeming to hide a wealth of pain and disillusionment.

But it never showed, and Leonie found as much humour in her clumsiness as everyone else did, able to laugh at herself and the things that happened to her.

His mouth quirked into a smile. "I have to admit that when Mrs Carlson said the President would expect you at four o'clock the same thought crossed my mind!"

"Naughty, David," she shook her head reprovingly, her eyes glowing deeply green.

For a moment they shared a smile of mutual humour, and then David shook his head ruefully. "Try not to be late for the meeting," he advised. "From the way Mrs Carlson was acting he sounds pretty awesome."

Leonie grimaced. "Are you sure you want to send me, I could walk in, trip over a matchstick, and end up sliding across his desk into his lap!"

"He asked for you specifically." But David frowned as he mentally envisaged the scene she had just described. "I'll take the risk," he said without enthusiasm.

"Sure?"

"No," he answered with complete honesty. "But short of lying to the man I don't know what else I can do. Just try not to be late," he warned again.

And she did try, she tried very hard, but it seemed the fates were against her from the start. She caught her tights on the door as she got into her VW, drove around for another ten minutes trying to find somewhere to park so she could buy some new ones, getting back to the car just in time to personally accept her parking ticket from the traffic warden, making a mad dash to find somewhere to change her tights, laddering that pair too in her haste, although it was high enough up her leg not to show. By this time she in no way resembled the coolly smart young woman who had left Stevenson Interiors in plenty of time to reach Thompson Electronics by four o'clock. It was already five to four, and she was hot and sticky from her exertions with the tights, her make-up needing some repair, her hair having lost its glowing bounce in the heat of the day. She was already going to be a few minutes late; taking time to refresh her make-up and brush her hair wasn't going to make that much difference now.

It was ten minutes past four when she entered the Thompson building, her slim briefcase in her hand, and except for the fact that she was late, looking like a self-contained young executive. Ten minutes wasn't so bad, she could blame that on the traffic. She certainly didn't intend going into the story of the ripped tights as her excuse, or the parking ticket either! It was—

Oh no, she just didn't believe this, it couldn't be happening to her! But she knew that it was as the smooth-running lift made a terrible grinding noise and shuddered to a halt somewhere between the eighth and ninth floors. She was stuck in a lift for the second time that day! And as usual she was alone. She was always alone when the damned things broke down, never had anyone to help calm the panic that she felt. This was a large lift, not like the one at Stevenson Interiors, but she would still rather be on the other side of those steel doors. Oh well, at least the floor was carpeted if she had to spend any amount of time here, so she could be comfortable. But it wasn't likely that she would be here for long, this was a big and busy building, someone was sure to realise sooner or later that one of the lifts was stuck between floors. And she hoped it was sooner!

She sank to the floor after pressing the emergency button, knowing from experience that people rarely took notice of that bell. God, what a day it had been, worse than her usual string of mishaps. If she didn't know better she would think— But no, she wouldn't even think about him. God, this was a hell of a place to start thinking of the disastrous effect her husband had had on her, his disapproval of almost everything she did making her more nervous, and consequently more klutzy, than ever.

She determinedly opened her briefcase, going through the fabric book she had brought with her, wondering what sort of colour scheme the President of the company would favour. She had thought of a few ideas, but basically she just wanted to hear what his tastes were.

She became so engrossed in matching paints and fabrics, the books strewn over the floor, that for some time she managed to forget she was marooned in a lift eight-and-a-half floors up. It was almost five-thirty when she heard the sound of banging from above, a voice that sounded strangely hollow calling down that the lift would be working shortly.

Leonie stood up, her legs stiff from where she had been sitting on the floor for over an hour, losing her balance as the lift began moving almost immediately, jerking for several feet before moving smoothly, Leonie flung about in the confined space, falling to the ground in a sprawled heap as it shuddered to a halt and the door miraculously creaked slowly open.

The first thing Leonie saw from her floor-level view was a pair of well-shod feet, the man's black shoes made of a soft leather, a meticulous crease down the centre of the grey trouser legs. Before she could raise her gaze any further Mrs Carlson was rushing into the lift to help her to her feet, the black shoes and grey-covered legs turning away.

"Bring her into my office as soon as you've helped her tidy up," ordered a curt male voice.

Leonie turned sharply to look at the man as the other woman fussed around her, but all she saw was the back of the man's head as he entered a room at the end of the corridor.

"Have you been in here long?" The middle-aged woman helped her pick up her sample books from the floor, a tall capable woman who had been secretary to the last President of the company for over twenty years. Leonie had met her when she worked here last, and although the other woman tried to be distant and authoritative, her warm brown eyes belied the role.

Leonie liked the other woman, but she wasn't sure she liked anyone seeing her sprawled on the floor in that undignified way. "An hour or so," she dismissed distractedly, pushing the books into her briefcase, anxious to get out of the lift.

Stella Carlson followed her out into the corridor. "In all the years I've worked here I've never known any of the lifts break down before," she shook her head.

Leonie grimaced, brushing her skirt down. "I have a strange effect on lifts."

"Really?" the other woman frowned. "Well as long as you're all right now . . . ?"

"Fine," she nodded dismissively. "I'm too late for my meeting, so perhaps you could explain the reason for my delay to your boss and I could make another appointment for tomorrow?"

"Didn't you hear, you're to go in as soon as you feel able to."

She thought of the man with the black shoes and grey trousers. "*That* was the new President of the company?" she dreaded the answer, although she knew what it was going to be.

"Yes," Mrs Carlson confirmed.

Oh David, Leonie mentally groaned, I didn't trip and slide across his desk into his lap, but I did lie sprawled at his feet on the floor of a lift that *never* broke down! David would never understand, things like this just didn't happen to him. They didn't happen to *any* normal person!

"Now seems as good a time as any," she said dully, knowing her dignity was past redemption. "I'm sure I've delayed you long enough already."

"Not at all," the other woman assured her as they walked side by side down the corridor. "Things have been a little—hectic, here the last few weeks."

The new boss was obviously giving the employees a shake-up, Leonie thought ruefully, her humour leaving her as she realised she would probably be in for the same treatment. After all, if she hadn't been ten minutes late in the first place she wouldn't have been in the lift when it broke down. Or would she? As she had told Mrs Carlson, she had a strange effect on lifts. She had a strange effect on most inanimate objects, things just seemed to happen to them whenever she was around.

She smoothed her skirt down as Mrs Carlson knocked on the office door, unaware of the fact that her hair was sadly in need of brushing after her fall, that the fullness of her mouth was bare of lipgloss where she had chewed on her lips as she looked through the sample books. Not that she would have worried too much about it if she had known; she couldn't possibly make a worse impression than she had as she grovelled about the lift floor!

Mrs Carlson opened the door after the terse instruction from within for them to enter. "Miss Grant, sir," she introduced quietly.

Leonie stared at the man seated behind the desk, the man that belonged to the black shoes and grey legs, the rest of the dark grey suit as impressive, the waistcoat taut across his flat stomach, the tailored material of the jacket stretched across widely powerful shoulders, the white shirt beneath the suit making his skin look very dark.

But it was his face that held her attention, a harshly attractive face, his chin firm and square, the sensuality of his mouth firmly controlled, his nose long and straight, ice-grey eyes narrowed on her beneath darkly jutting brows, silver threading the darkness of his hair at his temples and over his ears. Anyone who was in the least familiar with the business world would recognise Adam Faulkner from his photographs in the

newspapers, one of the most successful—and richest—
men in England today. He was also—

"Miss Grant," he stood up in fluid movements, the
coldness instantly gone from his eyes, his voice warm
and friendly, his hand enveloping hers in a grip that
was pleasantly warm, not too firm and not too loose;
the exactly right handshake for a businessman to in-
stil confidence in the person he was dealing with.

But why he should waste his time on such a gesture
with her was beyond her, she was—

"I hope your unfortunate delay in our lift hasn't
disturbed you too much," he continued smoothly, releasing her hand slowly, leaving the imprint of his
touch against her flesh.

Leonie was stunned at his obvious concern. "I—I
have that effect on lifts," she mumbled the same lame
excuse she had given Mrs Carlson, conscious of the
other woman still standing in the room with them.

Dark brows rose questioningly. "That sort of thing
happens to you often?"

Colour heightened her cheeks. "Yes," she bit out.
"Look, I don't think—"

"Don't worry, I'm not expecting you to conduct our
business meeting after your ordeal in the lift," he assured her. "I suggest we make another appointment
for tomorrow," he looked at Mrs Carlson for confirmation. "Some time in the afternoon," he instructed
as she left the room to consult his appointment book.

"Please, I—"

"Please sit down, Miss Grant," Adam Faulkner
instructed when he saw how pale she had become.
"Let me get you a drink. Would you like tea or coffee, or perhaps something stronger?" He pressed a
button on his desk to reveal an extensive array of
drinks in the cabinet situated behind Leonie.

Leonie just kept staring at him, too numb to even answer.

"Something stronger, I think," he nodded derisively at her lack of response, striding across the room to pour her some whisky into a glass. "Drink it down," he instructed her firmly as she made no effort to take the glass from his lean fingers.

She took the glass, swallowing without tasting, reaction definitely setting in.

Adam Faulkner moved to sit on the edge of his desk in front of her, dangerously close, the warmth of his maleness seeming to reach out and engulf her. "Terrible experience, getting caught in a stationary lift." He took the empty glass from her unresisting fingers, seeming satisfied that she had drunk it as instructed. "I've been caught in several myself in the past," he added dryly. "Although not lately."

"It's my second time today," Leonie mumbled dully, feeling the alcohol in her bloodstream, remembering too late that she hadn't had any lunch, that the piece of dry toast she had eaten for breakfast wasn't enough to stop the effect the whisky was having on her. That was all she needed to complete her day, to be roaring drunk in front of this man! "The one at work has always been unreliable," she added in defence of her clumsiness in getting stuck in two lifts that had broken down.

"Maybe you have too much electricity in your body," Adam Faulkner suggested softly. "And it has an adverse effect on other electrical things."

She looked up at him sharply, and then wished she hadn't as a wave of dizziness swept over her. She was going to get up out of this chair to make a dignified exit and fall flat on her face, just to *prove* what an idiot she was! If this man weren't already aware of that!

"Maybe," she nodded, swallowing in an effort to clear her head, having a terrible urge to start giggling. In one part of her brain she could logically reason that she had little to giggle about, and in another she just wanted to start laughing and never stop. There was so much about this situation that was funny.

"Miss Grant?"

She frowned up at him. "Why do you keep calling me that?"

He shrugged. "It's your name, isn't it?"

"Leonie Grant, yes," she nodded in exaggerated movements. "I—Hic. I—Hic. Oh *no,*" she groaned her humiliation as her loud hiccups filled the room. She really was making a fool out of herself—more so than usual, if that were possible! She should never have got out of bed today, should have buried her head beneath the bedclothes and stayed there until fate decided to be kind to her again. If it ever did, she groaned as she hiccuped again.

"Maybe the whisky was a bad idea," Adam said in amusement, going over to the bar to pour her a glass of water.

Leonie gave him a look that spoke volumes before swallowing the water, almost choking as a hiccup caught her mid-swallow, spitting water everywhere, including over one black leather shoe as Adam Faulkner's leg swung in front of her as he once again sat on the edge of his desk. "Oh dear," she began to mop at the shoe with tissue from her bag, becoming even more agitated when several pieces of the tissue stuck to the wet surface.

She closed her eyes, wishing the scene would evaporate, that she would find it had all been a bad dream. But when she opened her eyes again the black shoe dotted with delicate yellow tissue was still there, and the man wearing the shoe was beginning to chuckle. Leonie looked up at him dazedly, liking the warmth in his eyes, the way they crinkled at the corners as he laughed, a dimple appearing in one lean cheek, his teeth very white and even against his tanned skin.

Mrs Carlson entered the room after the briefest knock, breaking the moment of intimacy. "I've checked your appointment book, Mr Faulkner, and you're free at twelve o'clock or three o'clock."

"Twelve o'clock, I think," he still smiled. "Then Miss Grant and I can go out to lunch afterwards."

"Oh but I—"

"Book a table, would you?" He cut across Leonie's protest, smiling at his secretary, much to her obvious surprise. "My usual place. And you may as well leave for the evening now, Miss Grant and I are just going to dinner."

"Er—yes, Mr Faulkner." The older woman gave Leonie a curious look, seeming to give a mental shrug before leaving the room.

"She's wondering why you could possibly want to take me to dinner," Leonie sighed, wondering the same thing herself. But at least the suggestion had stopped her hiccups!

Adam stood up after dusting the tissue from his shoe. "It's the least I can do after your ordeal in the lift."

"But that was my fault—"

"Nonsense," he humoured.

Leonie blinked at the determination in his face. "Why should you want to take me out to dinner?"

"Miss Grant—"

"Will you stop calling me that!"

Would you prefer Leonie?'' he queried softly, locking his desk drawers and picking up his briefcase in preparation for leaving for the evening.

"Yes," she snapped.

"Then you must call me Adam," he invited huskily.

"I'm well aware of your name," she bit out impatiently. The whisky may have gone to her head but she wasn't that drunk! And she had no idea why this man should want to take her out to dinner, they—

"Then please use it," he urged, as his hand on her elbow brought her to her feet.

Leonie swayed slightly, falling against him, flinching away from the hard warmth of his body. "Please, I don't want to go out to dinner," she protested as he propelled her from the room at his side, the top floor of the building strangely in silence, Mrs Carlson having followed his instruction and left for the evening, the other employees having left some time ago.

Adam didn't release her arm. "When did you last eat?" he asked pointedly as she swayed again.

"I had some toast for breakfast this morning. I need to diet," she defended heatedly as the grey eyes looked her over disapprovingly.

"You're too thin," he stated bluntly.

"I'm a size ten," she told him proudly.

"Definitely too thin," he repeated arrogantly. "I happen to be one of those men who prefers his woman to have some meat on her bones."

His woman? *His* woman! Just who did he think he was? "I happen to like being thin," she told him irritably.

He arched dark brows. "Do you also like starving to death?" he drawled.

It was her weakness for good food that had pushed her up to a size fourteen in the past, and she had no intention of giving in to that weakness again, not when it had taken so much effort to lose the excess weight. "I'll survive," she muttered.

"Will you be okay in the lift now that it's working properly?" Adam asked as the lift doors opened to them invitingly.

"I'll be fine," she dismissed his concern. "Although the way today is going so far it could break down on us again," she said ruefully.

Adam smiled down at her as they were confined in the lift together. "I can't think of anyone I would rather be stuck in the lift with," he said throatily.

Leonie gave him a sharp look, expecting sarcasm but finding only warm invitation in the dark grey eyes. He was flirting with her, actually *flirting* with her!

"Pity," he drawled as they arrived safely on the ground floor, stepping into the carpeted reception area, nodding to the man on night security, guiding Leonie to the parking area, opening the passenger door of the sporty BMW for her, the top to the pale blue car back in the heat of the day. He took her briefcase from her and threw it in the back with his own before climbing in next to her, starting the engine with a roar. "Would you like the top up or down?" he enquired politely.

She touched her hair ruefully. "I think it's beyond redemption, so down, please."

Adam glanced at her as he drove the car towards the exit. "You have beautiful hair."

Leonie tensed at the unexpected compliment, her breath held in her throat.

"The style suits you," he added softly.

The tension left her in a relieved sigh. "Thank you."

Conversation was virtually impossible as they drove to the restaurant, although the fresh air did clear Leonie's head somewhat, giving her time to wonder what she was doing on her way to dinner with this man. She should have been more assertive in her refusal, shouldn't have allowed herself to be manoeuvred in this way. And yet she knew she was curious, couldn't think what possible reason Adam had for wanting to take her out to dinner. And his tolerance with the mishaps that just seemed to happen to her was too good to last!

She had been to the restaurant before that he took her to, but it had been a year ago, and hopefully no one would remember that she was the woman who had tripped on her way back from powdering her nose and pushed some poor unfortunate diner's face into his dinner!

"Good evening, Mr Faulkner," the maitre d' greeted warmly, his eyes widening warily as he saw his companion. "Madam," he greeted stiffly.

He remembered her! It had been over a year ago now, and this man still remembered her. He probably didn't have many people who came here and assaulted another diner for no reason!

"Do we have to eat here?" she demanded of Adam in desperation as they followed the other man to their table.

His brows rose. "You don't like the restaurant? Or perhaps the French cuisine isn't to your liking?"

"I love it," she sighed. "I just don't feel—comfortable here, that's all," she mumbled.

"Thanks, Henri," Adam dismissed the other man, pulling out her chair for her himself. "Just relax, Leonie." His hands were warm on her shoulders as he

leant forward to speak softly in her ear, his breath
gently ruffling her hair.

She felt strangely bereft when he removed his hands
and went to sit opposite her, their table in a quietly
intimate part of the restaurant. As the waiter poured
the wine that had been waiting for them, she could feel
the tingling of danger along her spine, wary of this
romantic setting, wary of this game. Adam was playing with her.

"Adam—"

"Try the wine," he urged huskily.

"When are we going to discuss the work on your
office suite?" she asked determinedly.

"Tomorrow. Before lunch."

"About lunch—"

"Don't worry, I'm sure you'll like the restaurant
I've chosen for us," he sipped his own wine. "Please
try it," he encouraged throatily.

She sighed her impatience, ignoring the glass of
wine. "Why are you doing this?"

"This?" he prompted softly.

She shrugged. "The charm, the restaurant, dinner,
the wine. Why, Adam? And don't say to atone for the
lift breaking down with me in it because I won't believe you."

"You're right," he nodded, perfectly relaxed as he
leant back in his chair, dismissing the waiter as he arrived to take their order. "I had this table booked for
us tonight before I even realised you were stuck in the
lift."

"Why?"

"Don't you usually go out for business meals with
your prospective clients?"

"Of course," she sighed. "But it's usually lunch,
and so far we haven't discussed any business."

"We will," he promised. "Tomorrow."

"Why not now?"

He shrugged at the determination in her face. "Maybe after we've eaten," he compromised.

This time he didn't wave the waiter away when he came to take their order, and with the arrival of their first and consequent courses there wasn't a lot of time for conversation. And by the time they got to the coffee stage of their meal Leonie had to admit that she didn't give a damn if they ever discussed business, feeling numb from the head down, the wine one of her favourites, her glass constantly refilled as soon as she had taken a few sips, the food as delicious as she remembered, forgetting her diet for this one night.

"You look like a well-fed cat," Adam eyed her appreciatively.

"I feel like a *very* relaxed one, if you know what I mean," she smiled happily.

He grinned. "I know exactly what you mean."

He was so handsome, so ruggedly good looking, that he made her senses spin. Or was that the wine? No, she was sure it was him. And he had been so patient with her when she knocked a glass of wine all over the table, had dismissed the anxious waiter to mop up the surplus liquid himself, had got down on the floor and helped her pick up the contents of her handbag when she accidentally opened it up the wrong way and it all fell out, had even chuckled a little when she knocked the waiter's arm and ended up with a potato in her lap. Yes, he had been very charming.

"Shall we go?" he suggested throatily as she smiled dreamily at him.

"Why not?" She stood up, narrowly avoiding another table as she turned too suddenly. "I never go back to the same place twice if I can avoid it,'' she assured him happily.

"It must be difficult finding new restaurants," he smiled, a smile that oozed sensuality.

"I rarely eat out," she dismissed. "It's safer that way, for other diners, I mean," she explained as they went outside, surprised to see it was already dark, a glance at her watch telling her it was almost ten o'clock. They had been in the restaurant hours!

His mouth quirked. "I noticed you have a tendency to—well, to—"

"Drop things, knock things, bump into things," she finished obligingly. "My husband found it very irritating," she added challengingly.

"Really?" Adam sounded non-committal.

"Yes. He—Where are we going?" she frowned as she realised they were in a part of London she didn't know very well, the exclusive residential area.

"My apartment."

Leonie blinked as they entered the underground carpark. "You live here?" she frowned.

"Since my separation," he nodded, coming round to open her door for her.

Things were happening too fast, much too fast she realised as they entered the spacious apartment, barely having time to notice its elegant comfort before Adam swept her into his arms, his eyes glittering darkly with desire.

"I've wanted to do this ever since the lift doors opened and I saw you grovelling about on the floor," he announced raggedly before his mouth claimed hers.

She wanted to ask him what he found so romantic about a woman making a fool of herself, but the magic of his kiss put all other thoughts from her mind, drawing her into him with the sensuous movement of his mouth, his arms beneath the jacket of her suit, his hands warm through the thin material of her blouse and camisole, his thighs hardening against her as his hands moved down to cup her buttocks and pull her into him.

The effects of the brandy and wine miraculously disappeared to be replaced by something equally as heady, sexual pleasure. She had heard all the old clichés about women who were no longer married, had scorned the idea of falling into that sexual trap herself knowing how little pleasure she had found in her marriage bed, and yet she knew that she wanted Adam. And he wanted her, there could be no doubting that.

Her lips parted beneath the assault of his tongue, knowing it was merely a facsimile of the lovemaking they really wanted, Leonie feeling filled and possessed by that moist warmth, drawing him deeper into her as she returned the attack.

Adam's breathing was ragged as he pulled away to kiss her throat, peeling the jacket expertly from her shoulders, throwing it to one side, beginning to release the buttons to her blouse, his hands sure in their movements, although they trembled slightly with anticipation.

It was this slight crack in his supreme self-confidence that encouraged Leonie to do some undressing of her own, his own jacket joining hers on the floor, his waistcoat quickly following, her fingers hesitating at the buttons of his shirt.

''Please,'' he encouraged achingly.

Her own hands shook as she revealed the muscled smoothness of his chest, the dark hair there silvered with grey. He was beautiful without the trappings of the successful businessman, wearing only tailored trousers now, his arousal barely contained.

"Leonie!" His mouth captured hers again as she caressed his bared chest, moving fiercely against her, pulling her into him as the tip of her tongue tentatively caressed his lips.

They left a trail of clothes to the bedroom, both naked by the time they lay down together on the bed still kissing, Adam's hands at her breasts making her gasp with pleasure, the nipples hardening and aching, asking for the tug of his mouth. They didn't have to wait long.

Leonie didn't stop to question her complete lack of inhibitions, inhibitions that had made her marriage such an agony, only knowing that this man, with his gentle caresses, held the key to her sensuality in his hands.

Adam kissed every inch of her body, found pleasure in the secret places no other man had ever known, making her tremble uncontrollably as his tongue rasped the length of her spine to her nape, quivers of excitement making her arch back into him as he homed in on the sensitive flesh there.

She lost all lucidity as Adam's caresses brought her again and again to the edge of a fulfilment she had never known, as he always pulled her back from the edge before she could reach the pinnacle she craved, her movements beneath him becoming more and more desperate as he refused to let her escape him even for a second.

"Please, Adam. Please!" Her eyes were wild as she looked up at him.

"*You* take me," he encouraged raggedly, his eyes black with desire.

"What—?" But she understood what he meant even as he pulled her above him, going to him eagerly, gasping as he lowered her on to him, filling her in every way possible before bringing her mouth down to his.

It was so right that it should be this way, that he should allow her the freedom to be the one to choose their pleasure, a pleasure she had never known during her marriage.

She was heady with delight, kissing the dampness of his salt-tasting shoulders and throat, quivering her own satisfaction as he groaned at the invasion of her tongue, feeling his movements quicken beneath her as he could hold back no longer, the hardness of him stroking her own desire until she felt the explosion begin in the depths of her being, beginning to shake as the warm aching pleasure ripped through her whole body in a climactic holocaust.

"My beautiful Leonie," Adam gasped as he reached the summit of his own pleasure, exploding in a warmth of warm moistness. "I knew it could be this way between us!"

And it hadn't stopped there, their strength and desire returning within minutes, their second lovemaking even more intense than the first, the pleasure seeming never-ending.

Leonie looked again at the face of the man who slept beside her, wondering what on earth she had done. Oh God, what had she done!

He stirred slightly as she moved from beneath the curve of his arm, her movements stilling until she realised he was still sleeping. She blushed as she found her clothes scattered in a disorganised path from the bedroom to the lounge; she had never been so carried away by passion before. She hastily began to dress.

"What do you think you're doing?"

She balked only slightly in the movement of pulling the camisole over her head. "What does it look like I'm doing?" she said sourly; at least he had had the decency to put on a brown towelling robe before following her from the bedroom!

"Isn't it usual to spend the whole night in circumstances like these?" he drawled, his dark hair still tousled, his jaw in need of a shave now. "I didn't expect you to go sneaking off while I was asleep!"

"I wasn't sneaking off," she told him resentfully. "And there's nothing *usual* about these circumstances!" She tucked her blouse into the waistband of her skirt.

"I want you to stay the night."

She shot him an angry glare, resentful that he could look so at ease, his hands thrust casually into the pockets of his robe, his stance relaxed. "Why?"

His mouth twisted. "I'm sure I've just shown you two very good reasons why."

"Sex!"

"And what's wrong with that?" He arched dark brows.

"Nothing, you know I enjoyed it," she snapped, knowing it would be useless to deny it, brushing her hair with angry movements, whether at Adam or herself she wasn't sure.

"So stay," he encouraged softly.

"I can't, Adam," she sighed impatiently. "I don't know what game you've been playing with me this evening—"

"A game you were quite happy to go along with," he reminded gently.

She shook her head in self-condemnation. "It seemed the easy way out at the time, so much easier for me to be Leonie Grant and you to be Adam Faulkner,'' she said shakily.

He shrugged broad shoulders. ''Why not, that's who we are.''

''Because until our divorce becomes final I'm still officially Leonie Faulkner, your wife, and you're my husband!''

''And now I'm your lover,'' he gave a slow smile of satisfaction. ''It was your idea, Leonie, you're the one that said we shouldn't have married each other but just have been lovers. And after tonight that's exactly what we're going to be!''

CHAPTER TWO

SHE vividly remembered shouting those words at Adam before she had walked out on him and their marriage eight months ago, remembered everything about her disaster of a marriage to this man. And she didn't intend becoming involved with him again in *any way*.

She was fully dressed now, straightening the collar of her jacket. "Tonight was a mistake—"

"I have another name for it," Adam drawled.

Her eyes flashed her resentment. "I'm well aware of the fact that you planned what happened—"

"Don't pretend you didn't want it, too," he warned her softly.

She blushed at the truth of that; from the moment she had seen him seated across the desk from her at the Thompson building her senses had become alive with wanting him. And the fact that he had acted as if it were the first time they had ever met had added to the excitement. But she had a feeling, knowing Adam as she did, a much less charming and relaxed Adam, that he had realised exactly what effect his behaviour was having on her, that it had been effected to get the response from her she had refused to give him during their marriage.

"It was certainly better than anything we ever shared during our marriage," she snapped waspishly, waiting for the angry explosion she had come to expect from him when they discussed the failure of the physical side of their marriage.

"I agree." Once again he disconcerted her; he had been doing it all evening, from the time she had discovered that her estranged husband was the new President of Thompson Electronics, during dinner when he had had such patience with her "accidents", to the infinite care and gentleness he had shown her during their lovemaking. "You were right," he continued lightly. "We're much better as lovers than as husband and wife."

"We are not lovers!" She looked around desperately for her handbag so that she might get out of here. "I've left my handbag in the restaurant," she finally groaned in realisation. "And that damned man—"

"Henri," Adam put in softly, his mouth quirked with amusement.

"He already thinks I'm some sort of escapee from a lunatic asylum." She hadn't missed his covert glances in her direction during the evening. "I just can't go back there," she shuddered.

"You don't have to—"

"And I don't need any of your high-handed interference either," she cut in rudely. "Why should one more visit to that place bother me!" she told herself defiantly.

"Because it does," Adam soothed. "And there's no need to torture yourself with the thought of having to do it; your handbag is in my car."

Her eyes widened. "Are you sure?"

"Very," he replied with satisfaction. "You were so eager to get up here that you left it next to your seat."

"I was not eager to get up here," she defended indignantly.

"Maybe I should rephrase that," he said thoughtfully. "*I* was so eager to get you up here that I didn't give you a chance to think of such mundane things as a handbag. Better?" he quirked dark brows in amusement.

It was that amusement that confused her; there had been little to laugh about during their marriage, Adam always so grim. But no one knew the deviousness of his mind as well as she did, and she wasn't fooled by this charm for a moment.

"What are you up to, Adam?" she demanded impatiently. "Why are you doing this?"

He strolled across the room to her side, his movements gracefully masculine, as they always were. "I want a lover, Leonie," he told her softly, only inches away from her as he stood with his hands thrust into the pockets of his robe. "I want *you*."

She shook her head. "You had me for a year, and it was a disaster," she recalled bitterly.

Adam nodded in acknowledgment of that fact. "Nevertheless, I want you."

"You've only just got rid of me!" she reminded desperately.

"Of the marriage, not you, Leonie."

"It's the same thing!"

"No," he smiled gently. "We both found the marriage stifling, the sort of relationship I'm suggesting—"

"With me as your mistress!" she scorned.

"Lover," he insisted. "We would be lovers."

"No!"

"Why not?" his eyes had narrowed, although he remained outwardly relaxed.

"I don't want a lover!"

His mouth quirked. "You just proved, very effectively, that you do."

Colour heightened her cheeks. "That was sex—"

"The best sex we ever had, admit it," he encouraged.

She drew in a ragged breath. "Yes."

"And as I said before, what's wrong with that?"

She sighed her exasperation. "You just don't understand—"

"I understand perfectly," he cut in soothingly. "This has all come as a bit of a shock to you—"

"That has to be the understatement of the decade!"

Adam chuckled, at once looking younger. "Poor Leonie," he smiled. "What's shocking you the most, the fact that we found such pleasure in bed together for the first time, or the fact that I want it to continue?"

She couldn't deny that she was surprised at the amount of pleasure she had known with Adam tonight, a pleasure she had known beyond all doubt that he felt too, his responses open and complete. Their sex-life during their marriage, as with everything else during that year, had been a disaster. Adam had been so experienced that in her innocence she had felt inadequate, and she had resented the way he had tried to control her body, her responses automatic and emotionless, refusing to be dominated by him. But the lovemaking they had shared tonight hadn't been restricted by any of that resentment, had been uninhibited. But that Adam should want such a relationship to continue she couldn't accept, not when the breakdown of the marriage and subsequent separation had been such a traumatic experience for her. They simply couldn't pretend they were two people they weren't.

"The first shocks me," she replied coolly. "The second surprises me. Do you honestly not remember what it was like between us, the bitterness, the pain of knowing we were all wrong for each other from the start?"

"As a married couple, not as lovers," he insisted forcefully.

"Have you forgotten what *that* was like between us?"

"Didn't this evening prove that it doesn't have to be that way?" he reasoned.

"I'm still the same person, Adam," she told him with a sigh. "I'm still sixteen years younger than you are, with the same inexperience—no matter what happened here tonight," she added pointedly. "I'm still the same klutzy person I was when we were married—"

"That's a new name for it," he laughed softly.

"I read it in a book somewhere," she dismissed impatiently. "It seemed to suit me perfectly."

"It does," he nodded, still smiling, his eyes a warm grey, crinkled at the corners.

"Don't you remember how angry all those "incidents" used to make you!"

"You're right, I was intolerant—"

"You're missing my point, Adam," she said frustratedly. "It would take a saint to put up with all the things that happen to me in one day—and that's one thing I know you aren't!"

"Have I been angry tonight at all?"

"That was only *one* night," she sighed her impatience. "It would drive you insane—it *did* drive you insane, on a regular basis."

"Haven't you heard, lovers are more tolerant?"

"Adam!"

"Leonie?"

She glowered at him. "You aren't listening to a word I've been saying."

"Of course I am," he placated. "You're young and klutzy." He smiled. "I really like that word, it describes you exactly." He sobered. "As a husband I was rigid and intolerant, lousy at making love to you. As a lover I will be generous and understanding—and very good in bed."

"In your experience," she snapped waspishly.

He raised dark brows. "You sound jealous, Leonie."

She felt the heat in her cheeks. "I most certainly am not!"

"It's all right if you are." His arms came about her as he moulded her body to his. "From a wife it would sound shrewish, from a lover it sounds possessive. I like that," he stated with satisfaction.

That wasn't all he liked from the feel of his body pressed so intimately against hers, aroused for the third time tonight. Leonie couldn't pretend not to be shocked by this evidence of his renewed desire; their sex life had deteriorated so badly at the end of their marriage that it was an effort for them to make love once a week; Adam had never wanted her *three* times in one night before!

"Adam, please stop this." She pulled agitatedly away from him as her own body quivered in reaction to his. "You've had your fun—"

"It was mutual," he drawled confidently.

"Not that sort of fun!" she snapped. "God, I can't believe this is really you proposing this preposterous arrangement! Have you thought of the consequences of your actions?''

''I already know you're on the pill to regulate your periods.'' He dismissed the idea of pregnancy.

''Not those consequences!'' It was embarrassing how intimately this man knew the workings, and malfunctions, of her body! ''We both have families, Adam, have you thought of their reactions to the relationship you're suggesting?''

''My father and your sister.'' The amused glow to his eyes left for the first time that evening. ''I'm thirty-nine and you're twenty-three, do you really think either of us needs their permission?'' he ground out.

''Your father hates me.'' She deliberately didn't mention her sister's feelings towards Adam, although she was sure they were both aware of those feelings; it had been one of the reasons their marriage had proved such a failure.

''My father doesn't understand you,'' Adam corrected gravely.

''There's nothing to understand,'' she dismissed scornfully. ''I am what you see. A little more accident-prone around you and your father, but otherwise I'm a open book.''

''Then a few of the pages must have got stuck together, because I never felt that I knew you completely either!'' He gave a deep sigh. ''I don't intend to argue about the past with you now, Leonie.''

''Lovers don't argue?'' she mocked.

His mouth quirked. ''Only when they know it will take them back to bed to make up.'' He took her back in his arms, his mouth claiming hers.

Her lips parted of their own volition, allowing access to the thrust of his tongue, trembling as desire claimed her, clinging to the broad width of his shoulders as she swayed weakly against him.

"Stay tonight, Leonie," he urged against the creamy warmth of her throat.

She was tempted, God how she was tempted. But she couldn't do it. It had taken her eight months to put herself back together after the devastation of loving this man; she couldn't leave herself open to that sort of pain again.

"No, Adam." She pushed away from him, breathing hard, knowing by his own ragged breathing that he was as aroused as she was. "There's something else lovers can do," she told him tautly. "They can end the relationship at any time; I'm ending it." She turned on her heel.

"Where are you going?" Adam asked softly.

"Home!" She didn't even turn.

"How?" his gentle question halted her. "Your car is still at Thompson Electronics, your keys to the car are in your handbag, your money, too, in case you were thinking of taking a taxi home, and your bag is in *my* car downstairs," he reminded softly.

She had done it again! "So much for my grand exit," she said dully as she turned around.

His smile was sympathetic. "It really was very good."

"Don't humour me, Adam," she snapped.

"Lovers—"

"We are not lovers!" she bit out between clenched teeth. "And we never will be. Now if you'll give me your car keys for a few minutes I'll go down and get my bag."

"No."

"You can't keep me here by force, Adam!" There was an edge of desperation to her voice.

"I don't intend to," he soothed. "I'm going to get dressed and drive you home."

"My car—"

"Will be locked into the car park by this time of night," he pointed out.

She looked at her wrist-watch; it was after midnight! "If you will just let me get my bag I can get a taxi home."

Adam shook his head. "I can't let you do that this late at night."

"That doesn't sound possessive, Adam, it sounds autocratic," she taunted him.

He smiled. "It's concern for your welfare," he mocked. "Lovers are like that," he told her softly before going back into the bedroom.

Leonie stared after him frustratedly; she should have known that today was going to end as disastrously as it had begun. She should also have known Adam would have something to do with it, had felt a premonition of his presence while waiting to be rescued from the lift, her clumsiness always more pronounced whenever he was around.

She had been too stunned, too conscious of Mrs Carlson's presence, to do any other than follow Adam's lead of it being their first meeting when the other woman introduced them in his office. And once she recovered from the shock of seeing him again after all this time she was too intrigued by his behaviour to do any other than go along with the pretence. And as she had admitted to him, it was easier too. But the pleasant atmosphere of their evening together had seduced her into doing something she would rather forget, something that she wouldn't allow to be repeated, her reaction to Adam totally unexpected, given their history together.

Her breath caught in her throat as Adam returned to the room, the business suit replaced with a fitted black shirt and black cords. Adam *never* dressed this casually!

"Changing your image, Adam?" she taunted to hide her reaction to him.

"Like it?" he smiled, not fooled by her attitude for a minute.

She more than liked it, she wanted him again! It was ridiculous when she had been married to this man for a year, when they had been separated for over eight months, to feel the same instantaneous flood of emotion towards him as she had when she first met him almost two years ago. And yet looking at him now she did feel it, her mouth dry, her palms damp.

"You look very handsome," she told him primly. "Now could we please leave?"

"Certainly." He picked up his car keys.

"Lovers are obliging too, are they?" She couldn't resist taunting as she preceded him out of the apartment and into the lift.

"Any time," he said suggestively, his body pressed up against the back of hers. "Just say the word," he encouraged throatily.

She frowned her irritation, moving gratefully away from him as they walked over to the car, their footsteps sounding loud in the black stillness of the night. Adam proved to be right about her bag, it lay on the floor of the car as he opened the door for her to get in.

"You can pick your car up tomorrow," Adam suggested during the drive to her home, the car roof up now in the cool of the night.

"Tomorrow?" she frowned.

"When you come for our meeting," he nodded.

Her eyes widened. "You don't seriously expect me to still come to that?"

He glanced at her, his brows raised. "Of course."

"But I— Wasn't that just a set-up?" she frowned.

"I wanted to see you again," he acknowledged. "And it seemed a good way to arrange it in view of the way *you've* felt about seeing me again, but I do also want my office decorated."

"Not by me," she shook her head determinedly, quivering at the thought of having to see this man on a day to day basis in connection with her work.

"By you," he said firmly.

"No!"

"Yes," he insisted softly. "I really was impressed by your work on the lower floor."

"Adam—"

"Yes, Leonie?"

She drew her breath in sharply at his tolerant tone. "I am not going to work for you," she told him stubbornly.

"Yes, you are," he nodded confidently.

"You can't force me!"

"I wouldn't even attempt it," he assured her mildly. "But I think you might find it a little awkward explaining to your boss, David isn't it, the reason you won't work for me."

"You wouldn't make me do that?" she groaned.

Adam shrugged. "I don't see what else you can do."

"But David has plenty of other designers, much more capable ones than me!"

"I don't want them," he stated calmly. "I want you."

"Please don't involve my career in this, Adam," she pleaded desperately.

"All I want is my office decorated, is that too much to ask?"

His innocence infuriated her! "You aren't just asking *anyone* to do it, I was your *wife!*"

His expression softened into a reminiscent smile. "I'm not likely to forget that."

"But I've been trying to!" She was twisted round in her seat as she tried to reason with him. "I've put my life back together, made the career for myself that I gave up when I married you. I am not about to let you jeopardise that."

"But I don't want to." He shrugged broad shoulders.

"You're forcing me into a situation I don't want. You deliberately sought me out for this job, didn't you," she accused.

He nodded. "I bought the company because I knew you had worked there once."

"You—you did *what?*" she gasped.

"Well, I had to have a valid reason for seeing you, I knew you would flatly refuse to go anywhere where you knew I would be." He shrugged. "So I bought Thompson Electronics."

It was an example of the arrogance she had always associated with him in the past; if he wanted something then he went out and bought it. He had once bought her with that same wealth and self-confidence that had blinded her to how wrong they were for each other.

"Then you wasted your money," she told him tautly. "Because nothing would induce me to work for you."

"I didn't waste my money, the company is a very profitable one," he announced calmly. "And I don't intend to induce you into doing anything; surely you're adult enough that you could design something for my office suite without letting personalities enter into it?'' he raised dark brows.

''It isn't a question of that,'' she said stiffly. ''I just don't want to work for you. Wasn't one member of my family enough for you?'' she added disgustedly.

''You mean Liz?''

''Who else?'' she scorned.

''Liz was the best personal assistant I ever had.''

She had been a little too ''personal'' as far as Leonie was concerned! They had met because of her sister's relationship with Adam, and they had parted for the same reason. ''Look, I'll talk to David tomorrow,'' she told him tautly. ''I'm sure he'll be only too glad to send someone else over to work with you.''

''I don't want anyone else,'' Adam said flatly. ''I wondered about you and him for a while, you know,'' he added softly.

She looked over at him with startled eyes. ''David and I?''

''Mm,'' he nodded.

Her mouth tightened resentfully. ''And what stopped you wondering?'' she snapped.

He shrugged. ''Your dates were too occasional for them to be anything more than placating the boss who has designs on you,'' he dismissed.

Leonie's eyes widened. ''You've been having me watched!'' she realised disbelievingly.

''You are my wife—''

''Was,'' she corrected tightly. ''We're legally separated, and once the appropriate time has elapsed our divorce will be finalised.''

''I was just seeing if we couldn't speed up the proceedings,'' he explained.

Leonie blinked at him for several timeless minutes, unable to believe what she was hearing. "Are you trying to say you were after evidence of adultery against me?" she said with disbelief.

Adam shrugged. "I thought you might feel more comfortable about our new arrangement if we were already divorced. I knew that I couldn't wait three years for you."

"I'm sorry I couldn't oblige!" Somehow the knowledge that he had done such a thing hurt her unbearably. God knows she had enough evidence of adultery against *him!* But she had chosen not to subject any of them to the embarrassing ordeal of revealing their personal lives in public. Knowing that Adam had considered doing it to her made her angry.

"Maybe I should have had *you* followed," she glared at him.

"Oh, I've been living very quietly since you left me," he dismissed.

"Quietly doesn't necessarily mean alone," she snapped.

"In this case it does."

And she knew the reason for that; Liz had continued to stay with her husband Nick. "Look, we're getting away from the subject," Leonie sighed. "You'll have to have someone else do your work for you."

"No."

"Adam, I will not be bullied by you into doing something I don't want to do."

He held up his hand defensively. "Have I tried to bully you? Did I bully you into anything tonight?" he added throatily.

Her mouth tightened. Tonight had been incredible, there was no denying that, and plenty of women would be only too agreeable to the sort of non-committal relationship Adam was now offering her. But not her. She had made a fool of herself over this man once, she wasn't going to do it again.

"Admit it was everything you thought it could be," he encouraged softly. "No complications of marriage, other people, just you and me making beautiful love together."

Just talking about the experience made her body tingle. "But it couldn't stay that way indefinitely," she reasoned impatiently. "Sooner or later one of us would expect more—"

"Not me," Adam assured her with finality. "I've tried being married to you; it didn't work out."

She swallowed down the pain his casual admission of their year together caused. It *hadn't* worked out, she would be the first to admit that, but to hear Adam talk so casually about the commitment they had made caused a constriction in her chest, as if someone had physically struck her.

"You?"

"Sorry?" she frowned as she realised she had missed what he had said next.

"You wouldn't want more either," he shook his head. "After all, you were the one that ended the marriage in the first place."

"Someone had to make that decision," she bit out abruptly.

"Oh don't worry, I'm glad that you did." He shrugged. "I'm just not husband material."

She hadn't thought about that at the time, although perhaps she ought to have done, Adam was already thirty-seven, had had several serious relationships, and even more that weren't serious, and before meeting her he had shown no inclination to marry any of those women, had enjoyed his freedom to the full.

It was difficult enough for any man of thirty-seven to suddenly accept the changes marriage made to his life, to a man like Adam, who could have his pick of women no matter what his marital status, it was impossible. And she hadn't known about Liz then either.

"You think you would do better as a lover?" she derided.

"Haven't I?" he quirked dark brows.

She put a hand up to her aching temples. "It's late," she sighed. "And I'm too tired for this conversation right now."

"There's no rush." He turned to smile at her after stopping his car outside the old three-storey Victorian building that housed her flat. "Are you going to invite me in?"

"Harvey wouldn't like it," she shook her head.

There was a sudden tension about him. "Harvey?"

He had been amused at her expense all evening, and now she couldn't resist a little amusement herself. "Dick wouldn't be too pleased either."

Adam frowned. "I didn't know you were sharing your flat with two men."

"Didn't your private investigator tell you that?"

"No," he ground out. "He—What are you laughing at?" he questioned suspiciously when she couldn't contain her humour any longer.

"Harvey's my cat," she explained between giggles.

"And Dick?"

"Moby Dick."

"You have a *whale* in there?"

Fresh laughter convulsed her. "A goldfish," she finally managed to choke out. "But I thought the name might deter Harvey from eating him; so far it's worked."

Adam shook his head tolerantly. "Klutzy, insane, *adorable* woman," he groaned as he pulled her over to his side of the car before fiercely claiming her mouth. "Life has been so dull since you left me," he rested his forehead on hers as he held her easily in his arms.

"Even a steady diet of caviar can get boring after a while; and I'm *nothing* like caviar!"

"You never, ever bored me; I never knew what you were going to do next!" he smiled.

"That isn't practical for a wealthy industrialist's wife. And I wouldn't stay hidden out of sight as a lover either," she told him before he could point out that he wanted a lover not a wife. "Not that I'm considering becoming one," she added hastily as she realised it sounded as if she were.

"You *are* one." His quick kisses on her mouth stopped her protest. "Sweet dreams, Leonie," he finally released her. "I'll see you tomorrow."

She didn't argue the point with him; so far it didn't seem to have got her anywhere. He would find out soon enough that if he really did want his office decorated that someone else would be in charge of it.

"Good night, Ad— Ouch!" She groaned as her hair seemed to be caught on the button on his shirt. "Adam, help me!" she pleaded, tears of pain in her eyes.

"Sit still, woman," he instructed with patient amusement, his lean fingers working deftly to free her hair. "There you go," he released the last strand, his eyes gleaming with laughter. "I've heard of giving your lover a lock of hair, but this is ridiculous!"

"You're the one that's ridiculous," she snapped, getting out of the car, her exit foiled somewhat as she had difficulty unlocking the door. Her cheeks were red with embarrassment as she turned to speak to him through the open window. "Good night, Adam. Thank you for tonight, it was an interesting experience."

His smile didn't even waver at the coldness in her voice. "One of many," he promised huskily.

Her mouth tightened before she turned on her heel and walked over to the huge front door that was the entrance for all the tenants of the building. She was aware that the BMW hadn't moved away from the side of the pavement, of Adam watching her, congratulating herself on reaching the door without mishap when the keys fell out of her hand straight into the empty milk bottle standing out on the doorstep waiting for collection in the morning.

For a moment she just looked down at her keys inside the bottle in disbelief. Someone ought to lock *her* up for her own safety and throw away the key!

"Are you all right?"

She turned reluctantly to acknowledge Adam's concern at her delay in entering the building. "Fine," she answered brightly as he now stood outside the car, leaning on the roof to look over at her.

How could she nonchalantly pick up a milk bottle and start shaking the daylights out of it! But how could she get in to the building if she didn't God, she felt so *stupid*.

"Leonie, are you sure you're all right?" Adam sounded puzzled as she still hesitated.

"Yes, of course," she answered waspishly, trying to unobtrusively pick up the bottle, the keys inside rattling loudly in the still of the night as she tried to furtively shake them loose.

"What on earth are you doing?"

She was so startled by his sudden appearance at her side, having been so intent on her keys in the bottle that she had been unaware of his approach, that she dropped the bottle. Adam caught it deftly before it could hit the ground, looking down at the keys inside.

"Isn't this a strange place to hide keys?" he frowned as he tipped the bottle up and was rewarded by them falling smoothly into the palm of his hand.

Leonie snatched them from his hand. "I wasn't hiding them," she snapped. "I dropped them."

"Ah."

Her eyes blazed deeply green as she turned on him. "What do you mean 'ah'?" she challenged. "'Ah, I should have guessed'? Or, 'ah, that such an unfortunate occurrence should have happened to me'?"

"Ah, that such an unfortunate occurrence should have happened to you, of course," he said tongue-in-cheek.

Her movements were agitated as she unlocked the door. "I wonder why I have difficulty believing you," she muttered.

"Darling, calm down." He took her in his arms once more. "I really don't mind these little accidents that happen whenever you're around," he soothed.

"I don't remember your saying that the time I caught the bodice of my gown on your father's tie-pin and it took you half an hour to separate us!" She strained away from him, but his superior strength wouldn't allow her to move far, his thighs pressed intimately against hers.

"Dad was the one that was so annoyed, not me," he reminded with amusement. "Look at it this way, Leonie, at least he was a captive audience for that half an hour; you always did say he didn't listen to you!"

She looked up at him in surprise; she had never heard him talk about his father so disparagingly before. "He used to look straight through me," she said slowly.

"Well he didn't that evening!"

"That gown cost a fortune, and it was ruined," she reminded him.

"It was worth it just to see the expression on Dad's face. Every time I thought about the incident afterwards I burst out laughing," he was grinning even now.

"You never told me that," she accused. "I thought I had embarrassed you once again."

He sobered at the admission. "You've never embarrassed me, Leonie," he shook his head. "You never could."

She was more puzzled than ever now, some of that emotion showing on her face as Adam let her go this time when she moved out of his arms. "I have to go in; Harvey hasn't had any supper yet," she told him in a preoccupied voice.

"You'll have to introduce me to him some time," Adam straightened. "I've always liked cats."

"I didn't know that," she frowned.

"Maybe you don't know as much about me as you thought you did."

She was beginning to realise that, she thought as she slowly went up the stairs to her second-floor flat. She would never have dreamt Adam could behave as light-heartedly as he had this evening, that he could laugh at himself as well as his father, that he could find her mishaps so amusing. She had been married to him for over a year, and he was still an enigma to her.

Harvey was sitting on the window-ledge outside when she entered her flat, coming in through the small open window as soon as he saw her, miaowing plaintively.

"All right, all right," she cut off his reprimand mid-stream. "You aren't the only one that can spend a night out on the tiles, you know," she told him as she opened a tin of food for his supper, groaning as she realised what she had said. "Oh, Harvey, what am I going to do?" She bent down to pick up the bundle of ginger and white fur, burying her face in his side. "Tonight was so perfect," she told him achingly.

The cat gave a loud screech of indignation before jumping to the ground.

"All right," she snapped at his lack of sympathy. "I can see you're more interested in your stomach than in my problems." She put his plate down on the floor, the cat immediately pouncing on it. "I know you catch mice outside so you can stop acting as if you're starving to death," she told him crossly, suddenly rolling her eyes heavenwards. "God, I'm having a serious conversation with the cat now!" She sat down dejectedly in one of the armchairs, oblivious to the passing of time as, his appetite appeased, Harvey jumped up into her lap and instantly fell into a purring sleep, Leonie absently tickling behind his ears as he did so.

Her first meeting with Adam had been totally unexpected. She knew of him of course, her sister Liz having been his Personal Assistant for the last year, but he wasn't at all what she had expected of the wealthy industrialist.

Liz and Nick had been away on holiday for two weeks, still had a week to go, and Leonie was house-sitting for them when Adam paid his surprise visit. The sisters had been close in those days, Liz the senior by eight years, having been like a second mother to Leonie since their parents' death three years earlier.

Leonie had opened the door in all innocence that evening, had fallen in love the moment she looked up into that harshly beautiful face, the grey eyes warm, strangely luminous with the black circle around the iris. She hadn't heard a word he said as he spoke to her, having to ask him to repeat himself. He had wondered if Liz were at home even though it were her holiday, had needed to talk to her. Leonie had invited him in as she explained that Liz and Nick had gone away on what they called a "second honeymoon".

She had been shy with him, had wished she were wearing something a little more glamorous than an old dress that did little to improve her already plump proportions, her long hair in need of brushing. And then she had cursed herself for the fool that she was, from what little Liz had told her about this man's love-life he was hardly likely to be attracted to a cuddly redhead who barely reached his shoulders no matter what she was wearing!

But Adam had seemed reluctant to leave that evening, even though he knew Liz wasn't there, the two of them talking for hours, until Leonie suddenly realised it was after twelve and she had to go to work in the morning. She had been speechless when Adam asked her out to dinner the next evening.

There had been a week of dinners together, of talking into the early hours of the morning, and each time Leonie saw him she fell a little more in love. Although Adam gave away little of his own feelings, treating her more like an amusing child as he guided her through one mishap after another.

The night before Liz and Nick were due to return home was a magical one, Adam taking her to the ballet, something she loved but could only rarely afford to attend, taking her back to the house he shared with his father. It had been after eleven when they arrived, but even so the lights were on all over the house, the butler greeting them at the door, a maid bringing them a tray of coffee and sandwiches. Leonie had been so nervous she promptly knocked over the plate of sandwiches.

But even that had seemed unimportant as Adam dismissed the incident after helping her put them back on the plate, his eyes almost black as he followed her down on to the rug in front of the fire, his mouth fiercely claiming hers. It was the first time he had done more than give her a polite brush of his lips on hers at the end of an evening, and after her initial surprise at how fierce he was with her she opened her arms and her heart to him.

He could have taken her right then and there on the rug and she wouldn't have cared. But he didn't, his breathing ragged as he pulled away from her.

"Marry me, Leonie," he had groaned. "Marry me!"

"Yes," she gasped her acceptance, on fire for him.

"Soon," he urged.

"As soon as you want me," she promised eagerly.

When her sister and Nick returned the next day she told them she and Adam were getting married, the following Saturday. Liz had been stunned, and Leonie had thought it was because Liz was surprised at her young sister managing to capture such a handsome and sophisticated man. That was what she had *thought* it was, she should have probed deeper!

Adam had taken over her life from the moment he put the engagement ring on her finger that evening, a huge emerald that he said matched the colour of her eyes. She had been happy with his decision that she give up her job, wanting to be with him whenever he could get home from the empire that consumed such a lot of his time, knowing her career would make that difficult. She had even agreed to live in the apartment Adam had always occupied at the top of his father's elegant London home. She had agreed to anything Adam asked of her.

Within two weeks of meeting him she found herself married to a man she barely knew and who she was soon convinced didn't know her. Her wedding night was a fiasco, with her acting the frightened virgin that she was despite Adam's understanding gentleness with her. The pain had been incredible, too much to bear, until finally they had to stop. Leonie had huddled miserably on her side of the bed while Adam slept. The next night had proved as disastrous, and the night after that, until the fourth night Adam didn't even attempt to touch her. She came home from their honeymoon still a virgin, too embarrassed to discuss her problems with anyone. Adam had had so such qualms, making an appointment for her to see a gynaecologist and ordering her to attend when she protested. The doctor had taken away all the embarrassment of her problem, had explained that it was something that occasionally happened, and within a short time the problem had been alleviated.

But the damage had been done, and she resisted all Adam's efforts to get her to join in his passion, until finally he lost all patience with her one night, pinning her to the bed as he held her arms at her sides, ignoring her cries for him to stop as he brought her to the peak of ecstasy. After that night he always made sure she had pleasure too, but he always had to fight her first, to break down the barriers of resistance that she had built up against him. In the end he became tired of the fight, hardly ever touching her even though they shared a bed every night.

She tried to make up for her inadequacies in bed by being the perfect wife in other ways, but Charles Faulkner made no secret of his contempt for the young girl his son had made his wife, and she didn't even have Liz to turn to for support, feeling too embarrassed to discuss the failure of her marriage even with her sister.

Her tendency to clumsiness became more pronounced as the months dragged on, so much so that she became nervous of leaving the apartment and going downstairs for fear of earning the derision of Adam's father. It was enough of an ordeal that she had to sit down to dinner with the elderly man every night, usually managing to knock something over. She and Adam had intended eating their meals in their own apartment, but after a week of burnt offerings Adam had decided his digestion couldn't take any more and suggested they go downstairs and join his father for their evening meal. She had been hurt, especially as she was usually such a good cook, but for the sake of peace—and Adam's digestion—she had agreed. It was just another brick falling out of the already crumbling foundations of her marriage.

Adam began to stay late at the office, working he said. They also stopped going out, a way of stopping her embarrassing him in front of his friends, she felt sure. But it just left her more and more to her thoughts of what had gone wrong between them. It was easier to try and find something that had gone *right*. The answer was nothing!

But she decided she wouldn't be a nagging wife, would make the most of the life they had together. Much to the disgust of her father-in-law she had offered to organise the decorating and refurbishing of the house; his reply to that was to call in the most well-known interior designing company in London. Next she tried to take an interest in Adam's work; that was met with blank dismissal. After only a year of marriage she was bored, and she was sure—when she wasn't attempting to break one of the family heirlooms or tipping wine over someone—boring! The marriage had been a mistake, and she knew that even if Adam didn't. She had finally had enough after a solid month of not seeing Adam any other time than when he fell into bed beside her, deciding to go to his office and confront him with the fact that she couldn't go on like this any longer.

She had wondered why Adam's secretary tried to stop her going in to his office, especially after telling her he only had Liz in with him. What she had seen and heard had told her exactly why Adam wasn't even trying to make a success of their marriage, and why her sister had been so stunned that he was marrying her at all!

Adam had tried to reason with her when he followed her home, but she had required only one answer to one question; had he been sleeping with Liz just before they met. His answer made her leave him immediately, telling him that he should never have married her, that if he had only wanted a replacement for her sister then an affair would have been a much better idea—and much less complicated to them all. For that was what she was sure she had learnt when she came upon them unwittingly, Liz in Adam's arms, that their decision to end their affair and for Liz to attempt a reconciliation with Nick, had been a failure. And now they were both trapped in marriages they didn't want. But Liz was expecting Nick's child, couldn't leave him now, and Adam was stuck with her young and klutzy sister.

He hadn't been stuck with her for long, although Liz was still married to Nick, their daughter Emma three months old now. And Adam was proposing that they, Leonie and he, had the affair she had once told him they would be better having!

CHAPTER THREE

"BUT, David," she protested the next morning. "I told you how badly everything went."

He shrugged off her argument. "Faulkner couldn't apologize enough about your ordeal in the lift. I didn't like to tell him you made a habit of it!"

She had arrived at work this morning all set to tell David how disastrously her appointment with the new President of Thompson Electronics had gone, sure that when he heard all the details that he would be only too glad to put someone else on that job, only to find Adam had already been on the telephone to David this morning, taking all the blame on his own shoulders!

Her pleas with David had been to no avail; he was adamant she work for Adam. And she was just as adamant that she wouldn't, had sworn when she left Adam that she wouldn't take anything from him ever again, and that included this boost to her fledgeling career. "David, I don't want to work with him," she told him flatly.

His eyes narrowed. "Why not?"

She had no intention of telling David that Adam was her estranged husband. Much as she liked the other man, she knew how ambitious he was, and having the wife of Adam Faulkner working for him could give his company the boost into êlite London society that he had been looking for.

"I—I don't like him," she frowned as she knew that was no longer true either. When she had left Adam eight months ago she had never wanted to see him again, had hated him for his behaviour with her married sister. But last night, the pleasure they had finally shared, giving and taking from each other rather than Adam having to force her response, had changed all that. She couldn't hate a man who had given her that sexual freedom.

Some of the remembered sensuality must have shown in her face. "Did he make a pass at you?" David frowned.

A pass! Adam had never made a *pass* at a woman in his life! He was much too controlled for that. "No, he didn't do that," she answered tautly.

David looked relieved to hear it. "Then where's your problem?"

"I've just told you, I don't want to work for him!"

"But he sounded very charming on the telephone."

She grimaced, well aware of how charming Adam could be when he wanted something. He had once wanted her so badly in his bed that he had married her; how ironic that the one thing he had wanted from her had been so disastrous. "Anyone can be charming for the few minutes of a telephone call," she dismissed.

"Then he wasn't charming to you yesterday when you did eventually meet?" David probed.

"Yes, he was," she sighed. "Very charming." Colour heightened her cheeks as she remembered just *how* charming he had been later that evening.

"Then why don't you want to work for him?" David repeated again in exasperation. "I can tell you, he was very impressed with you."

"I made such a fool of myself," she said desperately. "I feel embarrassed."

David shrugged. "You always make a fool of yourself sooner or later."

"Thanks!"

He grimaced. "But you do," he reasoned. "I've never known you to get through a day yet without something going wrong; and it's usually your own fault!"

"That's what I like, a little sympathy and understanding," she glared at him.

He smiled at her anger. "Trouble just seems to follow you around. Look, I'll tell you what I'll do, I'll call Faulkner's secretary and tell her I'll be joining the two of you for lunch. If I can see any reason, any reason at all, why you shouldn't work for him I'll put someone else on to it. All right?"

It was the best she was going to get, she could see that. And surely she could make Adam drop the tolerant charm for the few minutes it would take David to realise he would be better sending Gary or Sheila on this job, if only for the sake of his company's reputation.

"I'll drive over with you," she nodded agreement, feeling a little happier.

David frowned. "What's happened to the VW, has it broken down again?"

"It's still at Thompson Electronics," she told him awkwardly. "Mr Faulkner insisted on driving me home after my ordeal in the lift," she invented.

David smiled. "He doesn't know you very well if he thinks a little thing like that will shake you up!"

She gave him an exasperated look. "Actually, I did some work while I was waiting."

"See," he laughed.

She went back to her own desk, her nerves becoming more and more frayed as twelve o'clock neared. Then just as she was tidying her desk in preparation for joining David a deliveryman arrived from a nearby florist's. The single long-stemmed red rose took her by surprise, the bold black script on the accompanying card telling her that Adam had in no way changed his mind about where their relationship was going. "For an interesting experience—one of many", the card read. She crumpled the cryptic message in the palm of her hand, would have done the same with the rose if David hadn't arrived at her office at that moment.

"A new admirer?" He raised blond brows as she thrust the rose into a sadly inadequate glass and pushed it to the far corner of her desk.

She shook her head. "Another apology from Mr Faulkner." There was no point in lying about the sender; knowing Adam he would ask if it had arrived!

"Nice gesture." David helped her on with the fitted jacket to her brown suit, the pale green blouse she wore beneath alleviating its sombre colouring.

"A pity he didn't feel generous enough to send the other eleven," she said with uncharacteristic waspishness.

David's brows rose. "I'm sure he— Watch out!" he had time to call out as the sleeve of her jacket caught the perfection of the single red bud, overbalancing the too-short glass, smashing the latter on the floor, the rose crushed among the heavy glass.

Leonie looked down at the ruined perfection with tears in her eyes, instantly regretting what she had done. For the first time in her life she had committed a deliberately destructive act, had knocked against the flower on purpose, not wanting that reminder of Adam facing her when she got back.

"Careful!" David warned as she bent to pick up the crushed flower, sighing his impatience with her as a large jagged sliver of glass stuck straight into the palm of her hand.

Leonie gasped, automatically pulling out the piece of glass, the blood that instantly flowed from the wound the same colour as the rose she still held. She knelt and watched as it continued to bleed.

"You're dripping blood all over the carpet," David snapped impatiently, taking out a handkerchief to wrap it about her hand, pulling her to her feet. "We had better get you cleaned up before we go anywhere." He led her into his office, the First Aid box kept there.

He took the rose she still clutched and threw it in the bin, concentrating on washing her hand and applying a bandage as the small but deep wound continued to bleed.

Leonie felt sick, and not because of the pain in her hand but because of her deliberate destruction of such innocent beauty. It wasn't in her to deliberately hurt anything. Even when she had discovered how Liz and Adam had deceived her she hadn't wanted revenge or retribution, had felt sorry for her trapped sister, although Adam seemed to be continuing with his life as if it had never happened.

"Are you all right?" David frowned at how pale she had become. "Maybe we should cancel this meeting with Faulkner, you look as if you should go home and rest."

She shook her head determinedly, not intending to delay this confrontation any longer than was necessary; she had already spent one sleepless night, she didn't intend having any more because of Adam Faulkner. "I'll be fine," she insisted, flexing her hand under the bandage; it was a bit sore, but workable.

"Sure?" David still looked concerned.

"Yes," she smiled brightly, standing up. "Shouldn't we leave now, Mr Faulkner is going to think unpunctuality is normal for us."

"For you it is," David mocked as they went down to his car, a white Cortina that he drove with the usual reserve he had to the rest of life.

The cut on her hand was only a throbbing ache by the time they reached Thompson Electronics, the bandage showing no sign of heavy bleeding.

Mrs Carlson greeted them with a smile, instantly informing Adam of their arrival, ushering them straight in to his office.

"Sorry we're late," David greeted the other man, their handshakes firm. "I'm afraid a little—accident, delayed us."

Leonie hung back behind David, feeling uncomfortable about seeing Adam again. The flesh and blood masculinity of him was much worse than she had imagined after the passion they had shared the previous evening, the royal blue three-piece suit and lighter blue shirt he wore making him look devastatingly attractive, his eyes more blue than grey.

His gaze moved surely past David to her flushed face. "What did Miss Grant do this time?" he drawled.

Leonie's blush deepened as David grinned. "A collision with a glass, I'm afraid," he explained.

"The rose you sent me was in it," she put in quickly, challenge in her eyes as she realised he wasn't about to reveal their marital status to David either. "It had to be put in the bin, I'm afraid," she added with satisfaction.

For timeless seconds Adam held her gaze, transmitting a message that made the colour burn in her cheeks. "The rose can easily be replaced," he finally said softly. "There's only one Leonie Grant."

"Thank God for that," David said thankfully, missing the undercurrent of tension between them, taking the conversation at face value.

Leonie was perfectly aware of the double meaning to Adam's words, her mouth firming frustratedly as she longed to knock that smile off his lips.

"We may as well talk over lunch," Adam decided arrogantly. "If that's all right with you?" he consulted the younger man as an afterthought.

"Fine," David agreed eagerly, seeing nothing wrong in this man taking charge of the meeting.

It was embarrassing how easily David had been taken in by Adam's charm, Leonie thought angrily. He was supposed to be romantically interested in her himself, and yet he seemed to find nothing wrong with the way Adam's fingers closed possessively over her arm as they left the office together, seemed not to notice when Adam moved his thumb erotically against her inner arm.

"What have you done to your hand?" Adam frowned as he noticed the bandage for the first time, his fingers entwining with hers as he lifted her hand for closer inspection.

"She cut herself with a piece of the broken glass." It was left to David to answer for her, her breath catching in her throat at the intimacies Adam was taking with her hand in full view of the other man.

Adam's gaze bored into hers. "Have you seen a doctor?"

She swallowed hard, shaking her head to clear the spell he was casting over her. "Only David," she dismissed lightly, putting her other hand into the crook of the other man's arm. "But he knows how to take care of me," she added pointedly.

Dark brows met over suddenly icy grey eyes. "Indeed? You have some experience in taking care of Miss Grant, Mr Stevenson?" the question was put innocently enough, but Leonie could feel the tension in the hand that still gripped hers.

"A little." Once again David was innocent of the innuendo behind Adam's words. "I took her to the hospital when she got high using glue in her office one afternoon, and another time when she stuck her letter-opener in her leg."

Adam's eyes twinkled with suppressed humour as Leonie's ploy to imply intimacy between David and herself failed miserably. "I wondered how you had acquired that scar," he said throatily.

Leonie blushed as she remembered the way his caressing fingers had explored the half-inch scar above her knee, how they had explored the whole of her body, pulling out of his grasp to move closer to David. "He's always rescuing this Damsel in Distress," she gave David a warm smile. "I don't know what I'd do without him."

David looked pleased by her encouragement, having received little enough of it the last six months.

"We'll take my car," Adam decided abruptly, striding over to the BMW. "You don't mind if Miss Grant sits in the front next to me, do you, Stevenson, she gets car sick in the back," he said smoothly.

David looked surprised. "I didn't know that."

Neither did she! But short of calling Adam a liar, and possibly alienating him as a client for David she couldn't very well say so, getting ungraciously into the car next to Adam while David sat in the back. She almost gasped out loud when Adam took advantage of their relative privacy in the front of the car to guide her hand on to his thigh, keeping it there with his own hand when she would instantly have pulled away.

His leg felt firm and warm through the material of his trousers, and she could feel the heat rising in her cheeks as both of them acted as if the intimacy weren't taking place, Adam coolly conversing with the unsuspecting David.

By the time they arrived at the restaurant Leonie's nerves were in shreds, her senses in turmoil as she fought against the desire Adam had deliberately instigated. His gaze was silently mocking as he helped her out of the car, although she flushed as she saw his body wasn't quite as controlled, looking away quickly from the evidence of his arousal, her cheeks burning as they entered the restaurant.

She could see David was impressed by the other man, and the restaurant he had chosen, as they studied the menus. She was going to have to do something, and fast, if she wanted David to take her off this job.

"So," Adam sat back after they had ordered their meal. "Is there some problem with Miss Grant coming to work for me?"

David looked disconcerted by the other man's bluntness. "Problem?" he delayed.

Adam shrugged. "Does the owner of Stevenson Interiors usually go to a routine business meeting with his employees?"

"Er—Well—No," David answered awkwardly. "But Leonie is rather new at her job. Not that she isn't good at it," he put in hastily. "She is. But she—we, wondered if you wouldn't rather have someone more experienced.''

''Just how much experience does Miss Grant have?'' Adam asked softly, his hand somehow locating her knee beneath the table, his fingers caressing.

Leonie's mouth tightened at the—to her—unsubtle double-meaning behind the question. ''Not enough for you, I'm sure,'' she bit out, drawing in a pained breath as his fingers tightened in rebuke.

''I'm sure you'll satisfy me,'' he told her blandly.

''And I'm equally sure I won't,'' she grated.

''I'm not a demanding man, Miss Grant,'' he drawled. ''I simply know what I like.''

So did she after last night, having explored the hard planes of his body then more thoroughly than ever before, Adam encouraging her to do so, to both their delight.

''I like what you've done for me already,'' he continued softly. ''I'd like it to continue.''

Her mouth thinned. ''I don't think I can—work, for you, Mr Faulkner.''

''Leonie!'' David gasped. ''What Leonie means is that she does have a couple of other little jobs that need her attention,'' he quickly invented. ''And anyway, this conversation might be academic.''

Adam looked at him. ''And why should it be that?''

David gave a nervous laugh at the other man's quiet intensity. ''Well, *I* know we're the best, but I'm sure you'll have other quotes in for the work, and—''

''No other quotes,'' Adam told him arrogantly. ''I want Miss Grant to do this for me.''

David flushed with pleasure, and Leonie could understand why. Interior designing was a competitive business, and they lost as many prospective jobs as they won, other companies often undercutting them. If only Adam only had work on his mind!

"In that case," he beamed, "I can get someone else to clear up Leonie's odd loose ends."

"I would appreciate it," Adam drawled. "I need Miss Grant right away."

And he wasn't lying either! His hand had captured hers as she tried to pry his fingers from her knees, guiding it to the throbbing hardness of his thighs. She flinched away from him as if he had burnt her, glaring at him furiously for this subterfuge.

"And, of course, if her work proves as satisfactory this time as last I would consider using her when I have my apartment refurbished," he added challengingly.

"It's a brand new apartment!" She almost groaned out loud as she realised she had revealed to a shocked David that she had been to the other man's home. "Mr Faulkner insisted on taking me home to give me a drink to steady my nerves last night before driving me to my flat," she quickly explained.

"Leonie has a habit of walking into one catastrophe after another," David smiled.

"I've noticed," Adam said dryly. "I feel that my apartment lacks the homely touch at the moment, I'm sure Miss Grant could help me create that,"

She was so angry with him at this moment that if he didn't stop baiting her in this way she was going to pick up his soup and tip it over his head! But maybe if she could show David how Adam kept flirting with her he would realise she couldn't possibly work for the other man; the cold treatment certainly hadn't worked!

"I'm sure there must be a woman in your life who could do a much better job of that than I," she suggested throatily.

His eyes widened questioningly, and then he smiled knowingly. "I always think this sort of thing is better accomplished by someone who knows what they're doing."

She blushed as he turned the innuendo back on her. "I'm sure you're just being modest, Mr Faulkner," her voice was husky.

"On the contrary, since my wife left my life has been lacking in a woman's—touch."

She glared at him in silent rage. And if he really expected her to believe there had been no woman for him since their separation he was insane! Liz might be out of his reach at the moment, but there were plenty of other women who weren't, and God knows he had found little enough satisfaction during their brief marriage.

"How about you, Stevenson," Adam turned to the other man. "Does your life have that special woman's touch?"

"I'm not married," David answered in all innocence, receiving a frustrated glare from Leonie at his candid reply.

"Neither am I—now," the other man told him in amusement. "But one doesn't have to be married to have a special woman in one's life."

David glanced awkwardly at Leonie. "I suppose not," he muttered.

"Just as one can have a special woman in one's life even if one *is* married," Leonie put in with sweet sarcasm, looking challengingly at Adam as his expression remained bland.

"Leonie!" David was shocked at the turn the conversation had taken.

She gave him a scornful look. "We're all adults here, David," she bit out. "And the sanctity of marriage does seem to have lost its meaning to some people. Don't you agree, Adam?" she added hardly.

He shrugged, completely relaxed. "Divorce has been made too easy," came his reply.

"Easy?" she repeated disbelievingly. "You'll excuse me if I disagree!" She glared at him, remembering that she had only been able to be legally separated from him without actually revealing the reason she could no longer live with him, had to wait two years to be free of him.

He gave an acknowledging inclination of his head. "It seems to me that at the first sign of trouble in a marriage now one of the partners runs to the nearest lawyer rather than trying to work the problem out with the logical person, their spouse."

If Leonie could have spoken immediately after that arrogant statement she would have told him exactly what he could do with his theory. As it was, by the time she had overcome her rage enough to be able to talk she had also controlled the impulse, conscious of David even if Adam wasn't. "You believe that's what your wife did, hm?" she prompted hardly.

"Oh no," he denied easily. "My wife was perfectly right to leave me, I was lousy husband material."

Having expected a completely different answer Leonie was once again left speechless. Adam certainly knew how to disconcert her. And he knew it, damn him.

David coughed uncomfortably, obviously finding the conversation embarrassing.

"You'll have to excuse us," Adam turned to him with a smile. "Both being statistics in marriage failure I'm afraid Leonie and I got carried away comparing notes. We'll have this conversation some other time, Leonie," there was a promise in his voice. "I'm sure you must have been a much better wife than I ever was a husband.''

Had she been? She doubted it. She had been too young and unsophisticated to cope with the trauma of her honeymoon, had made no effort to bridge the gulf that had arisen between them because of it, had found the physical act between them embarrassing. Then why had last night been so different? Could Adam be right, the lack of a commitment between them made it all so much more uncomplicated, easier to relax and enjoy what they did have?

She looked up to find silver-grey eyes on her, realising he was still waiting for an answer. ''No,'' she sighed. ''I don't think I could have been.''

His gaze held hers for long timeless moments before he turned to signal for the bill, breaking the mood, his hand finally leaving her knee as they all stood up to leave.

''So when do you think Miss Grant will be able to start work for me?'' he asked David on the drive back to his office, the other man once again in the back of the car, although this time both Adam's hands remained on the steering-wheel; and why shouldn't they, he had no further reason to torment her, he had won. She was going to work for him.

''Monday,'' David answered firmly, ignoring Leonie's dismayed expression. ''Is that suitable for you?''

''Very,'' Adam nodded, his mouth quirking triumphantly at Leonie.

She glared back at him. ''You will, of course, have to move out of your office once the work begins,'' she told him tightly.

''I understand that. But you will be supervising the operation personally, won't you?''

"It's the usual practice," she conceded grudgingly, knowing that she had to give in, that she had to subject herself to several weeks of working for Adam. But working for him was all she intended doing. If he expected anything else from the arrangement he was going to be disappointed!

"YOU NEARLY LOST us that contract!"

She had been expecting the rebuke from David ever since they had parted from Adam half an hour ago, but he had remained silent as they went down to the car park to their respective vehicles, had waited until they reached the privacy of his office before turning on her angrily.

"All that talk about not being good enough to do the work," David continued furiously. "The man will think I employ amateurs!"

"David—"

"And I could have sunk through the floor when you started talking about the sanctity of marriage. The man's private life is none of our business, Leonie," he told her disgustedly.

"I—"

"And just how long did you stay at his apartment last night?" he added with a frown.

All colour left her face. "I— What do you mean?" she forced casualness into her voice.

"The two of you seem pretty familiar with each other's private lives. I've been seeing you for the last six months and yet in one evening that man seems to know more about you than I do!" he accused.

He had given her the perfect opening for her to tell him that Adam was her estranged husband, and yet she couldn't take it. It was much too late for that. The time to tell him had been this morning, before she and

Adam acted like strangers for a second time, before
David would be made to feel too foolish by the
knowledge. He would never forgive her if he was told
the truth now.

"I knew you were separated from your husband,"
David continued forcefully. "But I had no idea you
were actually divorcing him."

She shrugged. "It's the usual conclusion to that sort
of mistake."

"But don't you see, I didn't know," he said heatedly. "And yet you told Faulkner after knowing him
only a few hours!"

"I—er— Maybe the fact that he's separated too
gave us a mutual interest in the subject," she invented.

"How mutual?" David asked suspiciously.

She sighed. "Did I seem as if I wanted to see him
again, even professionally?"

"No," he acknowledged slowly. "But that wasn't
just because you're embarrassed about yesterday."

She stood up, moving restlessly about the room,
wondering what explanation she could give David that
would sound plausible. "I think we have a clash of
temperaments," she spoke softly.

"In what way?"

"In every way I can think of," she snapped. "I despise everything about the man!"

"Leonie!"

She sighed at her unwarranted vehemence. "He's a
rich playboy who buys and sells everything that he
wants and then doesn't want, including women," she
said more calmly. "I despise that type of man."

"Are you sure he didn't make a pass at you?" David frowned, still not understanding.

"Yes," she bit out.

"Disappointed that he didn't?" David sounded puzzled.

Her mouth twisted. "I don't think that question even deserves an answer," she dismissed disgustedly. "Look, I know the type of man he is, David, because—because I was married to one," she admitted gruffly.

His expression softened at the admission. "I'm sorry, Leonie," he said gently. "I had no idea. If you really think you can't work with the man..."

"And how would you explain the change to him after assuring him I was definitely available?" she mocked.

"I could always tell him you broke your neck!"

"Now *that* I'm sure he would believe!" she returned David's smile. "But I won't have you jeopardise the contract in that way. I'm just being silly, of course I can handle Adam Faulkner!"

There was another cellophane-wrapped box from the same florist lying on her desk when she returned to her office, and she opened it with shaking fingers, this single red rose made out of the finest silk, so delicate it looked as if it had just been cut from the garden. The card read "*This* rose won't be crushed—and neither will I." Again it was unsigned, but Leonie knew the sender, only too well.

"An admirer?" Gary grinned at her from the doorway.

She sighed. "You could say that."

Gary sauntered into the room, a few inches taller than her, with sandy hair and light blue eyes. The two of them had been friends since she first came to work for Stevenson Interiors. He touched the rose. "He has good taste," he murmured, looking at her and not the flower.

Ordinarily she wouldn't have minded his teasing, was always refusing the invitations he made her, both of them knowing that he had been happily married for the last five years. But today she wasn't in the mood for his lighthearted flirting. "It's been a long day," she said abruptly, turning back to her work.

With a shrug Gary left her to it. Leonie sighed, angry with Adam for upsetting her so much that she had been rude to a man who, although a flirt, had always been kind to her. She stood up to go and apologise to him.

CHAPTER FOUR

"FOILED you, didn't we?" she looked triumphantly at Harvey as he sniffed the silk rose in puzzlement, sitting on the dining-table to eye what looked like a delicious-tasting flower but wasn't. "You won't be able to chew this one beyond recognition," she crowed, as with a disgusted tilt of his nose Harvey jumped down on to the floor.

She had brought the rose home with her, too impressed by its beauty to throw it away as she had the last one. And much to her delight she had found that Harvey, who usually demolished any flowers she brought into the house, had no interest in the delicate bloom.

"Out you go," she opened the window for him. "No, I'm not going out on the tiles again tonight myself," she told him as he hung back reluctantly, obviously not intending going anywhere if he was going to be left on his own for hours again. "Once was enough," she muttered as she left the window open for him.

She stared broodingly at the rose as she tried to reconcile herself to working for Adam as from Monday. The second—indestructible—rose, had been a warning that he was still intent on having an affair with her. Why couldn't he— She looked up sharply as the doorbell rang, instantly knowing who it was. David was her only, rare, visitor here, and he had gone away for the weekend.

"Adam," she greeted resignedly as she was proved correct.

"Leonie," he returned lightly. "Am I interrupting anything?" he arched dark brows.

"Yes."

"Oh good," he walked past her into the room beyond, his denims fitted tautly to his thighs and legs, his black sweat-shirt doing nothing to hide the bulge of muscle in his arms and chest. He looked about the empty flat, his gaze returning to hers. "I thought you said I was interrupting something?"

"You are," she closed the door forcefully before joining him. "My privacy!"

He grinned, thrusting his hands into the back pockets of his denims. "Nothing is private between us," he dismissed, looking about him appreciatively.

Leonie tried to see the flat through his eyes, knowing the soft peach and cream decor, and the low-backed furniture and fluffy carpets, wouldn't be to everyone's liking. But it was to hers, was all her own work, and she didn't welcome any comments Adam might care to make.

His gaze returned to hers. "I think Dad should have let you decorate and refurnish the house, after all," he drawled. "Maybe then it wouldn't look and feel like a mausoleum!"

"You agreed with the suggestion when he said he wanted to bring in professionals!" she was stung into accusing.

He shrugged broad shoulders. "It was his house. But I didn't come here to discuss the past," he frowned.

"Then why are you here?" she demanded resentfully.

"To take you out."

She flushed. "It's usual to ask first," she snapped.

He shook his head, smiling. "I knew what your answer would be if I did that."

"I'm sure you did," she bit out.

"You'll enjoy yourself," he promised encouragingly.

She blushed. "I'm sure I won't!"

Adam chuckled softly. "Are they very naughty thoughts, Leonie?" he mocked.

"Let's leave my thoughts, naughty or otherwise, out of this," she said sharply. "I have no desire to go anywhere with you."

"Oh yes you do," he contradicted huskily. "And maybe later on I just might take you there. But right now I have it in mind to take you skating."

"Skating!"

"Mm," he nodded.

She frowned. "What sort of skating?"

"Well, hopefully, the sort where we manage to stay upright," he grinned. "Although I have no objection if you get the urge to fall on me!"

"Adam, have you been drinking?" she looked at him suspiciously.

He shook his head. "I'm simply acting like a—"

"Lover," she completed resignedly.

"Exactly. Lovers take their lovers out on mad escapades like this all the time."

"Who told you that?" she derided.

"I read it somewhere," he said with suppressed humour.

"You still haven't told me what sort of skating it will be," Leonie frowned.

"Roller-skating."

"But I can't roller-skate!"

"Can you ice-skate?"

"No." Her sense of humour couldn't be repressed any further, not resisting as Adam pushed her in the direction of the hall to get her jacket. "Can you?"

"Roller or ice?" he quirked dark brows.

"Either!"

"No," he informed her happily. "But just think of the fun we'll have trying!"

And they did have fun, Leonie couldn't ever remember laughing so much in one evening in her life before, let alone with the man who had always seemed so rigidly correct to her. Her tendency to be clumsy wasn't so noticeable with everyone else falling over too, in fact she had almost mastered the sport by the end of the evening while Adam still landed in an undignified heap on his bottom most of the time, and that for a man who had always seemed *so* dignified!

This new irrepressible Adam was impossible to resist, laughing at himself and her in a way she would never have thought he could. If this evening was an example of his indulgence as a lover she didn't know how she was going to continue to say no.

"I'm coming in," he told her when they reached her flat, his expression suddenly serious.

"Adam—"

"I want to look at your hand."

The statement startled her; it wasn't what she had been expecting at all. "My hand?" she repeated incredulously.

"Well I'd like to take a look at all of you," he told her huskily. "But I think we'll start with the hand. Did you think I wouldn't notice the discomfort it's given you tonight?" he chided as they entered her home.

She had hoped that he hadn't, but she should have known better; Adam noticed everything! Her hand had been aching most of the afternoon but she had put that down to the healing process. The increased pain she had been suffering the last couple of hours seemed to indicate it was more than that, her falls at the rink only aggravating it.

She took off her jacket, holding out her hand for Adam's inspection.

"You may as well sit down," he shrugged out of his own casual jacket. "I'm not going for a while yet." He came down on his haunches in front of her, compellingly attractive.

He was very gentle with her as he peeled off the bandage, removing the gauze dressing to reveal a very red and angry-looking cut. Leonie grimaced as he unbuttoned the cuff of her blouse to show that the redness extended in a line up her arm.

"It's infected," he mumbled, looking up at her. "You'll have to go to hospital for treatment, I'm afraid."

"Couldn't it wait until morning?"

"It could," he acknowledged softly. "But why suffer all night when you could get some relief now from the pain I'm sure you must be feeling?"

His logic always made sense, and he was right, the pain was bad; she doubted she would be able to sleep tonight without something to dull the pain.

"I'll just put a fresh bandage on it and then we'll go," Adam stood up decisively as he sensed her consent. "Do you have a medicine cabinet?"

"In the bathroom," she pointed to the appropriate door. "With my penchant for accidents I'd be insane to be without one," she added self-derisively.

Adam grinned. "I know you can't be feeling too bad when you still have your sense of humour. It was one of the things I always liked about you."

One of the only things, Leonie thought ruefully as he went into the bathroom. The statement had reminded her of exactly who they were, of the fact that they were in the process of divorcing each other; she had been in danger of forgetting that fact with Adam being so boyishly charming.

He was still in the bathroom when the telephone began ringing. God, she had forgotten it was Friday night, hadn't realised it was already eleven-thirty!

"Yes?" she grabbed up the receiver, not in the least surprised when she recognised the caller's voice, giving a mental groan as Adam came out of the bathroom, frowning when he saw she was on the telephone. "Oh yes?" Leonie answered her caller faintly. "How interesting. Look, I'm sorry," she cut in hastily as Adam approached. "But I can't talk just now." She slammed the receiver down, smiling brightly at Adam.

He frowned down at her. "Who on earth telephones at this time of night?" he asked slowly.

She shrugged. "I remember you did a couple of times during the two weeks before we were married."

"That was different," he dismissed.

"Why was it?"

"Because if I couldn't be in bed with you then I wanted to at least talk to you while you were in bed," he told her absently, his thoughts obviously still on the call she had just taken.

"Maybe my caller felt the same way," her voice was shrill at the irony of that statement.

"Is he the one that owns the man's razor in the bathroom?"

Her mouth tightened. "*I'm* the one who owns the man's razor in the bathroom," she bit out resentfully. "For some reason they happen to be cheaper and easier to find than the so-called women's razors are. And please don't ask why I need a razor," she glared at him.

His mouth quirked. "I won't.

"Then let me say I don't appreciate your prying into my bathroom cabinet. The medicine chest is next to it," she snapped.

"And the scissors were conspicuous in their absence," he pointed out softly.

She remembered now, she had used them to cut a broken fingernail, and must have put them back in the wrong cabinet. "Well I don't see that it's any business of yours even if the razor *had* belonged to a man," she told him huffily.

Adam shrugged. "I'm a very possessive lover."

"You aren't—"

"Just as I expect you to be," he continued softly, his gaze compelling.

"Being possessive didn't do me much good while I was your wife," she reminded waspishly.

He shrugged. "I've already admitted what a lousy husband I was."

"And assured me you're a fantastic lover!" she derided harshly.

"And very possessive," he nodded, his eyes narrowed. "Which means I want to know who would call you this time of night?"

She had hoped to divert him off the subject, she should have realised he wasn't a man to be diverted. "A friend," she dismissed. "I— They work nights," she added desperately.

Adam frowned. "Is that supposed to explain why they would call at eleven-thirty at night?"

"It goes on the company's telephone bill?" she suggested with a grimace for her inadequacy at lying.

"Not good enough, Leonie," he shook his head. "I want to know—" he broke off as the telephone began to ring again, picking up the receiver before Leonie had a chance to do so.

Leonie paled, knowing that the person on the other end of the line wouldn't realise from Adam's silence that it wasn't her he was talking to. She could guess what Adam's reaction was going to be.

"That's very interesting," he suddenly ground out fiercely. "Now let me tell you what I'd like to do to you—" his teeth snapped together as the caller obviously rang off, slamming his own receiver down with suppressed violence. "How long has this been going on?" he demanded to know.

She pulled a face, knowing she couldn't evade answering him. "Ever since I moved in here."

"And how long is that?"

She shrugged. "Six months or so."

Adam's mouth compressed into a thin line. "And is he always so—so—"

"Obscene?" she finished with a grimace. "I think that's how those sort of calls got their name!"

She knew exactly what Adam would have heard when he picked up the telephone, had heard the same revolting filth only minutes earlier. The first time she had received such a call she had felt so sick she was almost physically ill, had felt so threatened she had moved into a hotel for the night. The second time she had been angry, so angry she called the police. They sent someone round to talk to her, but in the end all they could advise was that she change her telephone number. But the calls had still continued. She still felt sick at the disgusting things he said to her each week, but she no longer felt threatened, was sure after all this time that whoever he was he preferred to violate her over the telephone, that he wouldn't actually come to her home and carry out the things he threatened.

"Have you done anything about it?" Adam grated, the nerve pulsing in his jaw telling of his anger.

Leonie sighed. "I've changed my telephone number twice, but it's made no difference."

Adam frowned. "He got your new number both times?"

She nodded. "Even though they're unlisted."

"How often does he call?" Adam's eyes were narrowed.

"Every Friday night at eleven-thirty," she sighed. "There's nothing we can do, Adam, and as long as he stays on the other end of that telephone I can cope with it. Actually, he's getting a little boring now," she grimaced. "His fantasy seems to be stuck in a groove."

"I heard," Adam rasped.

"Interesting idea, isn't it," she dismissed with bravado. "I've told him I think we could do ourselves a mischief, but he—"

"Leonie!" Adam cautioned tightly. "Can't you take anything seriously?"

"I thought you always liked my sense of humour!"

"Not about something like this," he said grimly, his hands thrust into his denims pockets. "The man's a damned fruit-cake, how can you make jokes about it!"

"How?" her voice cracked emotionally. "I'll tell you how! Because every Friday night I live in dread of those calls, and every Friday night at eleven-thirty he calls without fail. In a way it's a relief when he does call, at least then I can relax for another week. You see, I have a theory,'' her voice was shrill. ''That while he continues to call he won't actually come here.''

''You think he knows where you live?'' Adam frowned.

''I would say it's a logical assumption,'' she nodded. ''If he can get my telephone number three times he can certainly get my address!''

''Then you can't stay here,'' Adam decided arrogantly.

''Oh but I can,'' she told him. ''I thought about moving, but don't you see,'' she reasoned at his furious expression, ''I'm as safe here as I can be anywhere. This man obviously has the means at his fingertips to find out anything he wants to know about me. If I move he'll know that too, so why go through the bother of it?'' She shrugged.

''Then you can't stay here alone,'' Adam told her grimly.

''Are you offering your services as bodyguard, Adam?'' she mocked.

''And if I were?''

She shook her head. ''I don't need, or want, a live-in lover.''

''Have you been to the police about this?''

''There's nothing they can do. The man doesn't threaten me, he just talks dirty!''

''He *talks* about violating you!''

''And do you realise how many obscene telephone calls are received and reported each year? I can tell you that it's thousands,'' she said wearily. ''The police don't have enough people to follow up on all of them. They asked me all the usual questions, did I know of anyone who would want to do this to me, did I recognise his voice? I don't, and I didn't! It's all I can do to stop myself being sick when he calls. Now can we drop the subject, hm?" she said brittlely.

His mouth tightened. "I think you should move from here," he stated stubbornly, his jaw rigid.

"There's just no point to that," she sighed. "And except for his telephone calls, which will probably continue wherever I live, I like it here. No, Adam, I'm not moving," she told him firmly. "And one of these days he's going to get tired of calling me."

"And what do you think will happen then?"

"Hopefully he'll leave me alone," she shrugged.

"Hopefully!" Adam repeated raggedly. "What if he decides to come here and act out his fantasy?"

She shivered as he put into words what she had tried not even to think about. "The percentage of those that actually carry out the things they talk about is very low," she dismissed.

"You could be one of the victims of that percentage! God, Leonie," he groaned, taking her into his arms as she began to tremble. "I don't mean to frighten you, but I can't bear the thought of some maniac wanting to hurt you."

Her face was buried against his chest, and for a few minutes she allowed herself the luxury of leaning against his strength, of feeling protected. Then she moved back to smile at him brightly. "Maybe the fact that you answered the telephone tonight will frighten him off," she suggested derisively. "I'm sure he didn't get the same satisfaction whispering those things in your ear!"

"No," Adam agreed grimly, shaking off his worry with effort. "Let's hope you're right. Now we had better get you to the hospital— What the hell was that?'' he jumped nervously as there was a noise at the window.

Leonie laughed softly. ''It's only Harvey wanting to come in.'' She moved to open the window for the ginger and white tabby-cat to come inside.

Adam looked at him with relief. ''After that call my imagination is running riot!'' he admitted ruefully, bending down on his haunches to stroke the cat's sleek fur as Harvey strolled over to inspect him.

''Stroking a cat is supposed to be good for the heart and blood pressure,'' Leonie mocked him.

Adam glanced up at her. ''I can think of another redhead I would rather stroke!''

Leonie gave a rueful laugh. ''I think I walked right into that one!''

''You did,'' he straightened. ''Any offers?''

She shook her head. ''I think one lecher per household is enough—and judging by the amount of females that wait outside for Harvey every night he's it!''

Adam laughed softly, his tension momentarily forgotten. ''Bit of a ladies' man, is he?''

''You could say that,'' she grimaced. ''I certainly get the impression the cat population in the area could be on the increase in the next few months!''

''Is he going to need anything before we leave?''

She shook her head. ''He's already been fed, he's just home to rest after his exhausting evening out.'' She moved across the room to check the wire mesh on top of the goldfish bowl that stood on the sideboard.

''So this is Moby,'' Adam stood at her side watching the fish as it swam into the weeds at the bottom of the bowl.

"I think he snubs his nose at Harvey sometimes," she smiled. "A sort of 'Hah, hah, you can't get me!' look."

Adam chuckled, helping her on with her jacket, careful of her aching hand and arm. "This household is like you; crazy!"

"I like it," she shrugged.

"So do I," he said throatily. "Leonie—" He stepped back as she winced. "Is your hand getting worse?"

"It's—painful," she conceded. But not half as painful as the casual way he kept taking her into his arms! He had been doing it all evening, first at the skating-rink, when he took every opportunity he could to touch her, and now, when the situation was much more precarious, her bedroom all too close.

Somewhere during the evening she had lost sight of the fact that they were adversaries, not lovers. After his disgusting behaviour at lunch today she shouldn't even have been talking to him, let alone have agreed to go out with him. Admittedly, with Adam in this irrepressible mood it was a little difficult to remain angry with him, but she shouldn't have actually enjoyed herself! The same problem still applied to any relationship between Adam and herself; Adam's feeling for her unattainable sister still standing between them.

"Shall we go?" she said sharply. "It's very late, and I have to go out in the morning."

"Where?"

She looked at him coolly as they went downstairs together. "I always visit Liz and Nick on Saturday mornings," she informed him distantly. "Nick would think it a little strange if I didn't make the effort to visit my niece."

"And Liz?"

"I'm sure you're well aware of the reason that I find it difficult to be with my sister," she bit out, coming to a halt as they got outside. "Thanks for a nice evening, Adam," she dismissed. "Even if I didn't quite manage to skate properly."

"I'm coming to the hospital with you."

"I'm not a child," she snapped at his arrogance. "I'm quite capable of taking myself to the hospital."

"And driving yourself there?" he reasoned softly. "With only one hand?"

She blushed at the truth of that. Unlike his own car hers wasn't automatic; she definitely needed two capable hands for driving, and she certainly couldn't use her injured one. "I can get a taxi," she insisted.

"As I told you yesterday, not at this time of night you won't. Especially now that I know there's some sex-pervert with his eye on you," he added grimly.

God, had it only been yesterday that she and this man had shared so much passion! It seemed as if he had never been out of her life, as if they hadn't been separated for eight months, although she knew this was a different Adam from the one she just couldn't live with any more. This Adam had the power of seduction, a power he wasn't averse to using whenever she proved difficult; which was most of the time!

He took complete charge when they reached the hospital, declared himself her husband as he stood at her side and watched as they cleaned her wound, gave her tablets to fight the infection, and others to kill the pain.

Like this he was more like the Adam she had first fallen in love with, and as they left the hospital together she decided to make it plain to him exactly where they stood in this relationship he had decided he wanted with her. "I accepted your offer to drive me to the hospital, but that's all I accepted," she told him abruptly.

"Why, what do you mean?" he asked with feigned innocence as he opened the car door for her, quickly joining her as he got in behind the wheel.

"I mean you are not spending the night with me," she looked at him with steady green eyes.

"Did I ask if I could?"

"Adam," she sighed. "I may not live with you any more but I do know that you aren't a man that asks; you take."

His expression sobered. "I took because you wouldn't give freely," he rasped.

"And I wouldn't give freely because the more I gave the more you took!"

"I wanted to make love to my wife, I don't consider that a bad thing. Most wives complain their husband doesn't pay enough attention to them in bed!"

"The sexual act didn't hold the same pleasure for me as it did for you," she snapped.

"But that's no longer the case, is it," he reasoned calmly. "Last night you demanded as well as gave."

She blushed at the mention of her wanton responses the night before. "Last night I wanted you too," she admitted. "Wanted to know if I could respond to you."

"And you did."

"Yes."

"Then there's no problem, is there," Adam dismissed.

"Yes, there's a problem," she told him angrily. "The problem is *you*, Adam, I can't deny that last night was a success, but I don't want to repeat it. I don't want to work for you, I don't want to be with you.''

"Too bad, the contract is already signed. And as for being with me, you enjoyed yourself tonight, didn't you?''

She had, she couldn't deny the fun they had had together. ''But it wasn't you, Adam,'' she protested impatiently. ''You're the man who owns an empire—''

"Several companies," he corrected softly.

"It doesn't matter how many," she sighed. "You're rich, successful, sophisticated. You aren't really the man that took me roller-skating tonight.''

"Then who was he?" Adam asked her quietly, not expecting an answer.

And Leonie couldn't give him one. The man she had been with tonight, been to bed with last night, was a man she could like all too much. And she didn't want to like him, knew that if she ever came to truly like Adam rather than just have fallen in love with him that she would be lost.

"I'll see you at nine-thirty on Monday morning," he told her as they parted at her door. "You're sure you're going to be all right on your own?''

"My hand is fine now—''

"I wasn't thinking of your hand," he said grimly.

"The telephone calls?" she realised, shaking her head. "He only ever calls that once, at eleven-thirty on a Friday night.''

And it wasn't until she lay in bed that night, Harvey curled up against her side, that she realised that for the first time since the calls began she hadn't even thought about or dreaded tonight's call, that she had been so fascinated by Adam that she had forgotten all about it!

CHAPTER FIVE

LIZ was as beautiful as ever. No, more beautiful. Since Emma had been born three months ago Liz had possessed an inner glow of beauty that far outshone her obvious physical beauty. Her blonde hair was styled attractively close to her head, kept shorter now for convenience sake, having little time to fuss over her appearance now that she had a baby to care for. Her widely spaced hazel eyes were often more green than brown, glowing with the happiness she felt in her new role, her mouth curved into a perpetual smile, her figure having returned to its previous sylph-like elegance, although she wore little that emphasised that fact, her clothes loose and comfortable rather than fashionably styled as they used to be.

Yes, to an outsider Liz looked the perfect wife and mother, ecstatically happy in both those roles. And if Leonie hadn't seen her four-month pregnant sister in Adam's arms she may even have been fooled into believing that image herself.

But she had seen Liz in Adam's arms, had heard her sobbing about when they had been together. Adam had looked up and seen Leonie's stricken face as she watched them from the doorway, but he hadn't come after her straight away, had continued to hold Liz as she cried. In that moment Leonie had realised what a fool she had been, what fools they had all been to think that any marriage other than with the person you loved could possibly work out.

When Adam returned to the house over an hour later her suitcases were already packed, and she was waiting for the taxi to arrive that would take her to a hotel until she could decide what to do with her life now that her marriage was over, the Porsche Adam had given her when they returned from their honeymoon parked outside the house, the keys left on the dressing-table for Adam to pick up, all of the clothes he had given her still hanging in the wardrobe. She wanted nothing he had given her.

He had tried to reason with her, to explain what she had seen, but she had only one question she wanted answered; had he slept with Liz. The guilt on his face had been answer enough. Not that she could altogether blame him for that, Liz was a very beautiful woman, what she couldn't forgive was the fact that he had involved her in their triangle of misery.

She may have left Adam but Liz remained with Nick, both of them adoring the beautiful child they had created between them. But Leonie couldn't help wondering how long that would last, when Liz would decide she had shared Emma with Nick long enough and went back to Adam. Worst of all she wondered how Nick would react to knowing that his wife no longer loved him, that she had stayed with him only because she was expecting his baby. Nick adored Liz, had been in their lives ever since Leonie could remember, his love for Liz evident in everything that he did.

Leonie watched him now as he played on the floor with Emma, the little baby gurgling up at him, her huge green eyes glowing. Nick wasn't a handsome man, but he was strong, in body as well as mind. Having just passed his fortieth birthday he still remained remarkably fit, his blond hair peppered with silver giving him a distinguished air. He had lived next to them since their parents died, had been ecstatic when Liz accepted his proposal.

Leonie loved him like a brother, wished there were something she could do to prevent the pain and disillusionment he would feel when Liz tired of playing house and decided to leave him. But he was happy now, deserved that happiness after the long wait he had had for Liz; why end that happiness prematurely?

"You'll stay for lunch, won't you, Leonie?" Nick looked up to smile.

"Er—no, I don't think so," she refused, finding even this two-hour duty visit per week a strain.

He grinned, straightening, Emma in his arms. "I can assure you that Liz's cooking has improved since she's been home full time," he mocked.

"Just for that, Nick Foster, I may decide not to cook your Sunday lunch tomorrow," Liz pretended to be offended, but she couldn't help smiling.

"You wouldn't do that to a starving man," he protested.

Liz grimaced at him. "You look as if you're starving," she looked pointedly at his muscular physique.

Leonie's heart ached at the way Liz was able to banter and share her life with a man she no longer loved; *she* certainly hadn't been able to do the same once she knew the truth about Adam and Liz.

"Your mummy is implying I'm putting on weight," Nick spoke to his daughter of his indignation at the suggestion.

"She isn't implying anything," Liz laughed softly, taking the baby from him. "She would tell you if you were. I can't have you running to seed after only a few years of marriage." She began to feed Emma.

There was nothing more natural than a woman with a baby at her breast, and yet the sight of Liz and Emma together in that way twisted a knife in Leonie's heart. She had suggested to Adam that they have a baby, had hoped it might help draw them closer together, to give her the confidence in herself as a woman that she so sadly lacked with the failure of the physical relationship. But Adam had turned down the idea, had told her children didn't fit into his plans for some time to come. No doubt Liz's child would be a different matter!

She wondered if Liz would feel quite so content if she knew that Adam was trying to have an affair with her. Why didn't Liz just go to him now and save them all a lot of heartache! She stood up jerkily, unable to take any more. "I really do have to go now."

Liz frowned. "But you've only just arrived."

"I— My hand is aching," she didn't exactly lie, her hand did ache, despite the pain-killers she had been taking to ease that.

"How did you do it?" Liz looked concerned.

She shrugged. "Just another of my little 'accidents'," she dismissed.

Nick gave her a teasing smile. "I'm glad you've never come to me for insurance, it would be embarrassing having to turn down my sister-in-law as too much of a risk!"

She returned his smile. "I don't think I could have afforded the premium anyway on my record!"

"You never used to be quite as bad as this."

Her smile became brittle at her sister's observation. "No," she acknowledged tightly.

"I remember Adam always used to have the effect of making you worse," Nick mused.

"Have you seen anything of him?"

How casually her sister made her interest sound! She had no idea if Liz saw Adam at all, rarely discussed anything personal with her sister, least of all Adam. But she assumed that they would meet occasionally, despite Liz's act of the devoted wife. "I saw him yesterday as a matter of fact," she replied lightly. "He's looking very well."

"He always does," Liz observed affectionately. "Have the two of you—resolved your differences?"

The look she gave her sister was scathing to say the least. "We never will," she said dully, knowing Liz must know that above all people. "Our marriage is over."

"I'm sorry, I assumed because you met yesterday . . . ?"

"I'm going to be working for Adam for a few weeks, nothing more than that," she dismissed.

Hazel eyes widened. "Adam has hired you to work for him?"

"Yes," she bit out. "I may not be any good as a wife but I'm a damned good interior designer."

Liz looked taken aback by her bitterness. "I'm sure you are, it just seems an—odd, arrangement."

Not half as odd as the other arrangement Adam was suggesting! She shrugged. "Adam isn't a man that cares how things look. And I have little say in the matter, David decides who will do what."

"How is David?" Nick asked interestedly.

"Very well." Some of the tension left her at this more neutral subject, looking gratefully at Nick, knowing by the compassion she could see in his deep blue eyes that he understood she would rather not talk about Adam. She had brought David here to dinner one evening, had found him the exact buffer she needed to help her get through an evening with Liz, and the other couple had liked him immensely.

"You see rather a lot of him, don't you," Liz said conversationally.

Leonie at once stiffened resentfully. "I work for him," she reminded abruptly.

"I meant socially, silly," her sister chided.

She looked at Liz with suspicion. What was Liz up to now, trying to absolve her conscience by making sure Leonie had a man in her life when she went to Adam? She was over her own shock and humiliation, needing no man in her life, it was Nick who was going to be devastated.

"I see him occasionally," she dismissed. "Very occasionally. Do you see anything of Adam?" she challenged.

Was it her imagination or did Liz suddenly become very engrossed in feeding Emma?

"Occasionally," Liz replied distractedly, seeing to the baby.

"He came to dinner last week, as it happens," Nick put in lightly. "Strange, he didn't mention that he intended seeing you."

"He meant it to be a surprise," her voice was sharp. "And it was definitely that."

"It must have been," Liz nodded.

Her mouth firmed. "I really do have to be going," she told them determinedly. "I'll see you again next week."

It was Nick who walked her to the door, Liz still busy with Emma. Leonie was just relieved at being able to leave, dreaded these duty visits, sure that both she and Liz were aware of the reason they could no longer get on even on a polite social level.

Somehow knowing she was to see Adam first thing Monday morning made the weekend pass all too quickly. But at least he didn't pay her any surprise visits during those two days; she had half expected that he would, had felt a sense of anti-climax when he didn't.

Her hand was a lot better by Monday morning, the red line of infection having faded up her arm, the wound feeling more comfortable, so much so that she felt able to leave off the sling she had been instructed to wear over the weekend.

"Damn, who can that be?" she muttered as the doorbell rang as she was brushing her teeth, grabbing up her silky robe to pull it on over her lacy bra and panties.

Adam eyed her mockingly. "Either that's toothpaste, or you're foaming at the mouth."

Colour flooded her cheeks as she belatedly remembered to remove the toothpaste from her mouth with the towel in her hand. She had just been so stunned to see him; it was only eight-thirty in the morning. "What are you doing here?" she said ungraciously.

He shrugged, strolling past her into the flat. "You need a lift to work, I'm here to provide it."

Leonie followed him in to the lounge, scowling as Harvey lingered long enough on his way out to rub against Adam's trouser-covered leg, leaving ginger hairs on the dark brown material. "I can drive myself to work," she snapped.

He frowned as she freely used her right hand to prove her point. "You're supposed to rest that."

"I did. I have," she added impatiently. "It's better now. Or perhaps you don't take my word for it and would like to inspect it yourself?" she challenged.

"I can see from here that it's in working order again," he said dryly, making himself comfortable in one of her armchairs. "Did you have a good weekend?"

"Did you?" she returned.

"Very good," he nodded. "Did you visit Liz?"

Her mouth tightened. "Yes."

"How is she?"

"Don't you know?"

"If I did, would I be asking?" he reasoned mildly.

"Probably," she scorned. "After all, you have to keep up appearances. It's Nick I feel sorry for, he just has no idea does he?" she added disgustedly.

"Leonie, you don't know what you're talking about, so just drop it, hm," he was still pleasantly polite.

"I know you were having an affair with my sister when we were married—"

"You know I went to bed with her, it isn't the same thing." Steel had entered his voice.

She gave a disbelieving laugh. "Of course it's the same thing!"

"No," he shook his head, his eyes narrowed. "And one day you're going to want to hear the truth. In the meantime I'd like to concentrate on our affair."

"I—"

"What did you have for breakfast this morning?"

The question took her by surprise. "Toast and coffee," she answered automatically.

"Dry toast and black coffee?" he guessed, standing up. "The more sophisticated hair-style is an improvement, Leonie, but the loss of weight isn't," he told her as he went through to the kitchen.

Leonie followed him. "What do you think you're doing?" she demanded as he took butter, milk and eggs out of the refrigerator.

"Getting our breakfast," he answered dismissively.

"Haven't you eaten?"

He shook his head. "I thought I'd wait and eat with you."

"But I told you, I've already eaten."

"Rubbish," he decided, beating the milk into the eggs. "Go and finish dressing and then come and eat."

"Adam—"

His gaze was steady. "I prefer you as you were before you dieted."

"So you intend fattening me up," she protested.

"That's the idea," he nodded. "I should hurry and dress, Leonie, the eggs will be ready in a few minutes."

"I'll be late for work!"

"I'm your first appointment, and I don't mind if you're late," he dismissed with a smile. "Now off you go," he gave her bottom a playful tap.

Leonie gave him an indignant glare before leaving the room. How dare he ignore her all weekend and then calmly turn up here again this morning and attempt to take over her life once again!

Her movements quieted as she wondered whether she were more angry at being ignored the last two days or at the fact that Adam was taking command of her life. The answer made her wince.

"Very nice. Very professional," Adam complimented when she rejoined him in the kitchen. "Now take off the jacket and put it over that chair with mine;

I'd like to eat breakfast with a lover, not a business-woman.''

He had effectively robbed her of her line of de-fence! She had donned the formal oatmeal-coloured suit and brown blouse in an effort to remain distant from the situation he was trying to create. But he had discarded his own jacket and waistcoat, looking rug-gedly attractive. With her own jacket removed they looked like any other couple having breakfast to-gether before leaving for work.

"That's better." Adam divided the scrambled eggs on to two plates, putting them on the table with the rack of toast and pot of coffee. He poured a cup of the latter for both of them as he sat down opposite her, adding milk and sugar to Leonie's.

"No—"

"You know you love milk and sugar in your cof-fee," he stubbornly added another teaspoonful of the latter.

"But it doesn't love me," she grimaced. "Adam, I can't eat that," she protested as he liberally buttered a slice of toast for her.

"Then I'll feed you," he told her throatily, holding the toast temptingly in front of her mouth.

"Something else lovers do?" she rasped irritably.

"All the time," he grinned.

The toast looked so delicious after the strict diet she had kept herself on the last few months. She closed her eyes so as not to be tempted, although the smell tor-mented her. "I've only just given away all my size fourteen clothes to charity," she pleaded raggedly.

"So I'll buy you some new ones," he dismissed.

Her lids flew open at the arrogant statement. "You most certainly will not!"

"Independent as well as fiery," Adam smiled at her. "Eat, Leonie." The smile didn't leave his face but his tone was firm.

With an irritated glare in his direction she took a bite out of the slice of toast, savouring every morsel; it seemed so long since she had allowed herself the luxury of butter, only keeping it in the refrigerator for guests. But after tasting the toast oozing with butter it was all too easy to eat the fluffy eggs and drink the sweet syrupy coffee.

She frowned as Adam ate his own eggs. "Why didn't she provide you with breakfast?" she mocked.

"She?"

"The woman you spent the weekend with."

"Ah, that she," he nodded, lifting one of her hands to lace her fingers with his. "I spent the weekend in business meetings, Leonie," he told her reproachfully.

"That's a new name for it!" She glared at him as he refused to release her hand.

He smiled his appreciation of her humour. "Would it bother you if I had spent the weekend with another woman?"

"Would it bother you if I had spent the weekend with another man?"

"Like a knife being twisted inside me," he answered without hesitation.

Leonie gasped, meeting his steady gaze. "Did you really spend the weekend working?" she asked uncertainly.

"Yes."

"Why?"

"So that I had time to spare this week to concentrate on my reluctant lover," he teased.

"And did you spend the weekend alone?"

"My personal assistant—"

"Ah."

"Jeremy," he finished pointedly. "Accompanied me."

"I see," she chewed on her bottom lip. "I spent the weekend alone too."

"I know," he nodded, standing up to clear away the debris from their meal before shrugging back into his waistcoat and jacket.

Leonie glared at him. "If you're still having me followed—"

"I'm not." He held out her own jacket for her.

She shoved her arms into the sleeves, turning to frown at him angrily. "Then how did you know I spent the weekend alone?"

He grinned. "Harvey told me."

"Adam!" she warned tightly.

He bundled her out of the door. "The only man you've been seeing since we separated is David Stevenson, and he mentioned at lunch on Friday that he was going away this weekend."

"Oh." She looked at him resentfully as they emerged out into the street, the BMW parked behind her orange, and rusty, VW. The difference in their cars seemed to echo the difference in themselves, Adam a man of caviar and fresh salmon, Leonie fish and chips and McDonald's. "I'll meet you at your office," she told him abruptly.

"Leonie?" he probed her sudden withdrawal even from arguing with him, frowning heavily.

"We're already late, Adam," she sighed wearily. "And my car isn't the most reliable of machines." She unlocked the door.

"Is that yours?" excitement tinged Adam's voice as he walked over to the VW, touching one fender al-

most reverently. "I used to have one exactly like it. I
kept it until it just about disintegrated on me," he
chuckled reminiscently. "You're lucky to have found
one in such good condition."

"Adam, the car is ten years old! And when did you
ever have an old jalopy like this?" she scorned.

"When I was at college. Dad wanted me to buy
something more prestigious," he recalled dryly. "But
I'd worked in a bar in the evenings to buy my VW, I
wasn't giving it up for anyone."

He knew exactly how she felt about this rusty old
car! He had given her the Porsche during their marriage, and there could be no doubting that it was a
fantastic car, but even though she moaned and
groaned about the unreliability of the VW she
wouldn't exchange it for the Porsche at any price, had
worked hard to buy this car for herself. And Adam
knew how she felt. Why couldn't he do something,
anything, so that she could dislike him once more!

"I'll meet you at your office," she repeated lightly,
climbing into her car.

With a shrug of his broad shoulders Adam strolled
back to the BMW, sitting inside the car as he waited
for life to spark in her engine. As usual the VW played
up, and Leonie was hot with embarrassment by the
time the engine roared into life, instantly stalling it and
having to start the process all over again.

Mrs Carlson's brows rose questioningly as they entered the top-floor suite together, and Leonie blushed
at what the other woman must be thinking about
them; she had last seen them going to lunch together
on Friday. She felt sure the secretary imagined they
had spent the weekend together!

"Mr Spencer is waiting for you in your office," she
informed Adam coolly, obviously disapproving of the

relationship between her boss and an employee, albeit an indirect employee.

"Thanks, Stella," Adam dismissed. "Could you bring in coffee for three?" he requested arrogantly as he ushered Leonie into his office.

A young man stood up at their entrance, his smile warm and friendly as he looked at Adam, cooling slightly as his gaze passed to Leonie, looking her over critically.

Leonie did some "looking over" herself! The slightly overlong blond hair was deliberately styled that way, she felt sure, the face too good looking to be called handsome, his body slender, wearing the cream suit and brown shirt well, his hands long and thin, the nails kept short—and manicured.

Adam met her questioning gaze with suppressed humour. "Leonie, this is Jeremy Spencer, my Personal Assistant," he introduced softly. "Jeremy, this is Leonie Grant, the young lady who is going to transform these offices into something approaching comfort."

Leonie was aware of his amused gaze on them as she and Jeremy continued to eye each other critically.

"Miss Grant," Jeremy Spencer made no attempt to shake hands with her. "I hope you won't attempt to change the decor too much, I think this is exactly Adam already."

She looked around the austere room, knowing that it needed light, that perhaps it would have suited the man she had been married to, but not the Adam she now knew, not the Adam that was her lover. "It is very—masculine," she agreed.

Jeremy Spencer turned back to Adam. "I brought these contracts in for you to sign."

Leonie was ignored by both men during the next few minutes as they discussed the contract that had obviously been decided upon during the weekend, unable to resist making a comparison between them as they bent over the desk. Jeremy Spencer didn't attract her at all!

He nodded to her abruptly when it came time for him to leave, and Leonie had trouble holding in her laughter until the door had closed behind him. "Really, Adam," she finally spluttered with laughter. "What on earth made you employ *him?*"

Adam shrugged dismissively. "He's harmless. Now come over here, we haven't had our morning kiss yet," he invited huskily.

"Were we supposed to have one?" she delayed mockingly.

"But of course." He strolled over to her, his arms about her waist as he moulded her body to his. "After a weekend apart we shouldn't be able to keep our hands off each other!"

"Then how have we managed to?" she taunted.

"After the way you greeted me this morning I was afraid to touch you until I'd fed you!"

"You aren't afraid of anything," she scorned. "You never have been."

"I'm afraid that if you don't kiss me I'm going to burn up with wanting you," he groaned.

Her breath caught in her throat, her head tilted back to receive his kiss, her lips parting beneath his, her arms moving about his waist beneath his jacket. He felt warm and solid, his smooth jaw smelling faintly of limes.

"Adam, I forgot— Oh." An astounded Jeremy Spencer stood in the doorway, staring at them in disbelief.

"Yes, Jeremy, what is it?" Adam's voice was terse as he kept Leonie in his arms, the evidence of his arousal pressed against her.

"I—er—I forgot to get your signature on these letters." Jeremy ignored Leonie as he placed the letters on the desk for Adam. "I had no idea I was interrupting—something," he added.

Adam eyed him warningly. "Nothing that can't be continued after you've gone," he dismissed. "I'll sign the letters later," he drawled as the younger man made a hasty departure.

"You've shocked him," Leonie reproved.

Adam scowled. "That's nothing to what he just did to me!"

She laughed softly at his obvious discomfort. "You'll get over it."

"Maybe—for a while," he added warningly. "But it will only be a delay, Leonie, not a reprieve."

She blushed at the promise behind the words. "Isn't it time we got down to business, I do have other clients besides you, you know."

"None that can't wait," he announced raggedly. "I have no intention of discussing anything until I've received a proper good-morning kiss, with a certain amount of feeling."

"That's blackmail," she protested.

Adam grinned. "Terrible, isn't it?" He didn't sound in the least repentant.

"Both lovers have the same physical power," she warned as she moved into his arms, she the one to initiate the kiss this time, moving her mouth erotically against his, feeling the accelerated thud of his heart beneath her hand, moving sensuously against him as he groaned low in his throat, squirming away from him as he would have caressed her breasts. "Good morning, Adam," she greeted throatily.

He let out a ragged breath. "That was with a 'certain amount of feeling' all right," he said ruefully.

She smiled. "I thought so."

His eyes narrowed. "Enjoyed it, did you?"

She was well aware of how aroused he was. "Immensely," she nodded.

"Hm," he muttered. "Let's get down to the business of choosing the decor for this office."

Leonie worked happily at his side for the remainder of the morning, a satisfied smile to her lips for the whole of the hour it took him to put his desire from his mind—and body; meeting his scowls with a bright smile.

The decisions made about colours and fabrics she had to get back to her office and begin the ordering and arranging, the part Leonie liked the best—apart from the finished result, of course.

"Lunch, I think," Adam stood up decisively as she packed away her sample books.

She frowned. "I hope I haven't delayed you." It was after one o'clock.

"I meant lunch for both of us," he pulled on his jacket. "Together," he added pointedly.

"Oh I don't usually bother with lunch—"

"I'm fattening you up, remember." He closed her briefcase and picked it up, taking hold of her arm with the other hand.

"I'm still full up from breakfast," she protested as he marched her out to the lift, blushing as she realised Mrs Carlson had heard her protest. "Now she must have completely the wrong idea about us," she muttered crossly as they went downstairs.

"The right idea," he corrected with a smile.

"My car," she protested as he led her to the BMW.

"You can come back for it."

"I haven't forgotten what happened the last time I intended doing that," she glowered at him.

His only answer was a mocking smile. Leonie seethed all the way to the restaurant, resentful of his high-handedness, feeling as if all decisions were taken from her whenever she was in his company. She had found her independence the last eight months, she didn't need him taking over her life a second time. He—

"Come on, dreamer," he chided, the car parked, Adam having opened the car door for her and now waiting for her to join him.

She got out resentfully. "I wasn't dreaming, I— Adam, this isn't a restaurant." She looked up at the tall building that was almost a national monument.

"No, it's a hotel," he acknowledged, guiding her into the plush foyer.

"But they won't serve us here," she whispered fiercely.

"Of course they will," he dismissed.

"No—"

"Have you ever heard of room-service?" he taunted as he led the way over to the reception.

"Room—? Adam!" She came to a shocked halt.

He turned to look down at her with mocking eyes. "I've booked us a room for the afternoon," he announced calmly.

CHAPTER SIX

"You've done *what?*" she gasped disbelievingly, staring up at him in horror-struck fascination.

"I've booked us into this hotel for the afternoon," he repeated softly.

Leonie looked about them self-consciously, sure that everyone must know they were here for an afternoon of illicit sex; no one appeared to be taking any undue notice of them. "Adam, you can't be serious," she muttered.

"I am. Very."

"But I—We—I thought only married people sneaked off to hotels for the afternoon!"

"We are married."

"I mean people who aren't married to *each other,*" she glared up at him frustratedly. "Surely you have your apartment for this type of thing?"

"I don't know what you mean by 'this type of thing'," he said softly. "But I have my apartment to live in," he corrected reprovingly.

"But you took me there last time," she said desperately as she noticed one of the receptionists eyeing them curiously, sure they must look very conspicuous as she argued with Adam.

"But isn't this more exciting?" he teased.

It was exciting, there was no denying that. She felt deliciously wicked, could feel the heat in her veins at the thought of spending the afternoon in bed with

Adam. But they couldn't just disappear for the afternoon, they both had responsibilities. "Adam, I have to get back to work, and so do you," she protested.

He shook his head. "I told you, I intend concentrating on my reluctant lover; I cancelled all my appointments for this afternoon so that I could spend the time with you. I also told Stevenson I would need you all day. He agreed."

"Oh, Adam, you didn't," she groaned, sure David would be curious as to why Adam should need her for the whole day when they were only discussing colour and fabrics.

"It's the truth," Adam told her huskily. "And that need is getting out of control," he added pointedly.

Heat coloured her cheeks at his verbal seduction of the senses. "I feel embarrassed even being here," she muttered self-consciously.

"Come on, Mrs Smith," he chuckled as he took her hand firmly in his and strode the short distance to the desk. "Or would you prefer to be Mrs Brown?" he paused with his pen over the registration card.

"I'd rather leave," she groaned uncomfortably.

He shook his head, filling in the form before handing it to the waiting receptionist.

"Good afternoon, Mr Faulkner," the beautiful young receptionist greeted after glancing at the card. "The 'Bridal Suite' has been prepared as per your instructions," she continued warmly. "And if you should need anything else please don't hesitate to call." She held out a key to him.

"I won't," he nodded curtly, taking the key, not glancing at Leonie as she would have pulled away at the other woman's mention of the Bridal Suite.

"Do you have any luggage?" the receptionist asked as they turned away.

"It's following on later," Adam told her smoothly. "A mix-up at the airport."

"Oh, how annoying for you," the young woman sympathised.

"Very," Adam smiled. "Come along, darling," he urged Leonie as she stood numbly at his side. "I know you would like to lie down after the exhausting day we've had."

"Adam, how could you?" she demanded as soon as the lift doors closed smoothly behind them, breaking out of the numbed surprise that had possessed her. She couldn't believe this was happening to her!

"With a telephone call," he deliberately misunderstood her.

"I meant how could you pretend to that woman that we've just got married," she accused. "What are you going to tell her when our luggage doesn't arrive and we leave in a few hours?"

Adam unlocked the door marked Bridal Suite, pushing the door open for her to enter. "I could always tell her you left me," he said softly.

Leonie was too engrossed in the beauty of the suite to detect the rasping edge of truth to his words. Vases of flowers filled every available surface, the olde-worlde decor adding to the feeling of this all being a dream.

"Oh, Adam, it's beautiful," she told him breathlessly.

"You haven't seen the best part yet," he assured her, pulling her towards the bedroom.

"Adam, I know what a bedroom looks like," she blushed at his eagerness to occupy the wide double bed.

"Not just the bedroom," he mocked, throwing open the adjoining door.

The room was as big as the lounge in the flat, two walls completely covered in mirrors, a huge sunken bath dominating the room. But it wasn't that that held her attention. "Champagne," she was already intoxicated without it! "Isn't that a little decadent in a bathroom, Adam?" she teased.

"Very," he confirmed with satisfaction, bending down to turn on the water to the bath.

"Champagne next to the bath is hardly in keeping with the modesty of a newly married couple," she said dryly, wondering what the hotel management had thought of these "instructions" of Adam's. "I— Oh, Adam," her cry of surprise was a mixture of despair and choked emotion. "It's a jacuzzi." She watched as the depth of the water foamed and whirled at the flick of a switch.

Adam sat back on his haunches to watch her reaction. "I think I must have telephoned almost every hotel in London, trying to find a Bridal Suite that had a jacuzzi; most of them thought the 'sweet young things' wouldn't have progressed to sharing a bath just yet!"

"A telephone call" he had said was all it took to arrange this magical afternoon, and yet he had now revealed it had taken a lot of planning, planning she was sure he hadn't consigned to the easily shockable Mrs Carlson. "Why, Adam?" her voice was a husky rasp.

"Well I suppose they thought the bride and groom would be a little shy with each other to start with—"

"Not that, Adam," she spoke quietly. "Why have you done all this?" She hadn't realised at first, had been too fascinated by the idea of an afternoon in bed with Adam to notice the similarities to their failure of a honeymoon. Admittedly they hadn't stayed in a ho-

tel then, but Adam's house in the Bahamas had also
been filled with flowers at their arrival, a bottle of
champagne cooling in the bedroom, a jacuzzi in the
adjoining bathroom.

That night she *had* been embarrassed at the idea of
sharing a bath with Adam, her inhibitions making her
shy about revealing her body to him so blatantly.
Adam didn't have an inhibited bone in his body, had
walked about naked almost from the time of their arrival, teasing her when she wouldn't join him in nude
bathing on their private beach.

"We have a few ghosts to put to rest." Adam stood
up as he saw the painful memories flickering in the
bottle-green depths of her eyes.

"Not this way." She shook her head, the memories
too vivid to be denied.

"Exactly this way," he nodded firmly, taking her in
his arms. "I should never have married you," he
murmured. "Another man may have been more understanding about your shy inexperience, may have
given you the confidence in yourself as a woman that
I never could."

She turned away. "It wouldn't have made any difference," she reminded gruffly.

"Sex isn't everything between a man and woman."

"On their honeymoon it is!" she scorned.

He sighed. "We're here to put those memories to
rest, Leonie. Won't you let me try?"

She shook her head tearfully. "I can't be seduced
into forgetting that—that fiasco with champagne and
a—a damned jacuzzi," she told him sharply.

"I admit it would have been better if we could have
returned to the villa, but I had enough difficulty getting you here without arousing your suspicions; the
Bahamas would have been impossible!"

"Why should you want to try, Adam?" she sighed wearily.

"I want to replace the bad memories with good ones, erase the bitterness of the past—"

"And can you also erase your affair with Liz?" she scorned.

"There was no affair—"

"Your sleeping together, then," she amended impatiently.

"No, I can't erase that," he acknowledged heavily. "But I would like to explain it one day, when you're prepared to listen. Not today," he refused as she would have spoken. "We'll erase one memory at a time, and today we're starting with our honeymoon."

"I want to leave," she said stubbornly.

"Without testing the jacuzzi first?" he teased.

"Without testing anything," she looked at him coldly.

He shook his head. "I can't let you do that."

"You can't stop me," she derided.

"And what's that starry-eyed receptionist going to think when you walk out after fifteen minutes?"

"That I did leave you," she bit out. "A year too late. If I'd had any sense at all I would have walked out after the honeymoon."

"This is the honeymoon of our affair," he told her huskily, not releasing her.

"Affairs don't have honeymoons," she scoffed.

"This one does," he insisted. "It also has a ring." He took a brown ring-box from his jacket pocket.

"A Woolworth's special, to convince the gullible?" she scorned.

"A Cartier special," he drawled, flicking open the lid to the box, revealing a flat gold band studded with diamonds.

Leonie gasped at its delicate beauty. "I can't take that, Adam," she shook her head.

"Of course you can." He lifted her resisting left hand. "I noticed you no longer wear the rings I bought you," he pushed the diamond ring on to her third finger. "I want you to wear this instead."

She swallowed hard, the ring looking even more delicately beautiful on her slender hand. "Why?" she choked.

"It's an Eternity ring," he told her softly.

"Affairs are usually short-term, Adam," she shook her head.

"Not this one," he said with a return of arrogance. "I want you to move in with me, stay with me."

"We're getting a divorce, Adam," she reminded exasperatedly.

"After the divorce then, if you think that living together might make that difficult. I think I can wait that long, if I can see you every night at my apartment or yours."

"Adam, living together would be like being married!" she protested.

"It would be nothing like it," his voice was harsh. "You hated being married, remember?"

"Yes," she shuddered at the memory of how much pain it had caused her. "I did hate it," she confirmed vehemently.

He nodded. "But you've enjoyed the last few days we've been together, haven't you?"

She would be lying if she said she hadn't; it had been the first time she had felt really alive since she left him. 'Yes...' she answered guardedly, knowing she was walking into a trap.

"Then wouldn't you like it to continue?"

"It couldn't," she shook her head. "Not indefinitely."

"We could try," he insisted.

"Adam, you and Liz—"

"I'm sick of feeling guilty about Liz and I!" His mouth was tight.

"But what would happen to us when she finally finds the courage to leave Nick?"

"Leave Nick?" Adam looked astounded. "She isn't going to leave Nick!"

"Never?" Leonie frowned.

"Never," he repeated firmly.

"But I thought—"

"I don't care what you thought," he bit out. "Liz is one of those women who make their marriage vows for a lifetime!"

Leonie looked at him sharply, wondering if she had imagined the rebuke behind the words; Adam's bland expression seemed to say she had. "So I'll do as second-best, hm?" she said bitterly.

"You aren't second-best." His voice was harsh. "You never were, you never will be. What happened between Liz and I was already over when I met you. God, I've already admitted I should never have married you, but that doesn't mean we can't be together now. The other night was incredible, you can't deny that!"

"No..."

"And can you deny that you want me now?"

She knew she couldn't, knew he must be as aware of the pounding of her heart as she was. She did want him, the non-committal affair he was offering very enticing.

"Come on." Adam sensed her weakening and took advantage of it, beginning to unbutton her blouse.

"Or the bath will be cold and the champagne flat," he drawled as he slipped the blouse down her arms and moved to the fastening of her skirt. "And we wouldn't enjoy it then—the way I intend us to enjoy it," he added with relish as he stripped her naked.

Colour flooded her cheeks as reflections of herself appeared all over the room, looking very pale next to Adam's dark colouring and the dark suit he still wore. "Are you sure this is a Bridal Suite?" she asked irritably.

"Yes," he laughed softly. "But I think it's for the more—experienced, bride and groom."

"Shouldn't you undress too?" she suggested awkwardly.

"Yes." He looked at her pointedly.

She had had little experience with undressing men, never taking such an initiative during their marriage, their undressing the other night having taken place in a darkened apartment, not broad daylight, with images of them reflected everywhere! Her fingers fumbled a little at first, but her confidence grew as she saw the effect she was having on Adam, her hand trustingly in his as they stepped down into the water together.

It was such a big bath that they could quite easily have sat facing each other, but Adam had other ideas, sitting down to pull her in front of him, pulling her back to lean against his chest, his arms around her waist.

He nuzzled against her throat. "We forgot the champagne," he muttered, the ice-bucket and glasses out of their reach.

"It isn't important." She already felt intoxicated just from his touch, gasping as his hands moved up to cup the fullness of her breasts. "Oh, Adam, I—"

"No, don't move," he instructed as she would have turned in his arms. "I haven't washed you yet." He took the soap in his hand and began to lather her body.

By the time they had finished washing each other the bath was filled with bubbles, all inhibitions gone as they frolicked in the water, Leonie facing him now, leaning against his chest as she lay between his legs. "Do you think we would drown if we made love in here?" The idea had been tantalising her the last few minutes, knowing Adam was as aroused as she was.

"It's too late even if we do," he groaned as his mouth claimed hers.

They didn't drown, but the carpet around the bath did seem very wet when they stepped out on to it, not bothering to dress but wrapping towels around themselves as they carried the champagne through to the bedroom.

Adam dipped a finger in his champagne to trail it between the deep vee of her breasts.

"Oh, Adam...!" she groaned as he licked the wine from her heated flesh, turning in his arms, gasping her dismay as *all* the champagne from her glass tipped over Adam's stomach, dripping down on to the bed. "Oh no," she groaned. "And I was doing so well too!"

"You were," he agreed seductively.

She blushed. "No, I meant—"

"I know what you meant," he chuckled, making no effort to mop up the champagne with the towel he still had draped about his hips. "Care to reciprocate?" he invited. "Your clumsiness may be to my advantage this time."

She knew what he meant, eagerly drinking the champagne from his body, tasting Adam at the same time, feeling the rush of need that engulfed them both as she removed his towel.

"We really should do something about ordering lunch," Adam mumbled contentedly a long time later. "I need to keep up my stamina if you're going to keep attacking me in this shameless way."

"If I'm going to—!" She turned to look at him indignantly, only to find him watching her with one sleepy eye, his mouth quirked in amusement. She relaxed. "Of course, if your age is going to slow you down," she began mockingly. "Maybe I should find myself a younger lover."

There was a deep threatening rumble in his chest as he rolled over to trap her beneath him. "Maybe *I* should just smack your bottom for you," he growled. "My age hasn't slowed me down so far, and—Leonie, did you mean what you just said?" he suddenly asked sharply.

She frowned at his sudden change of mood from lighthearted bantering to serious intensity. "What did I just say?"

"That I'm your lover."

She blushed. "Well you are, aren't you?"

"You didn't seem to think so this morning."

She shrugged. "That was this morning."

"And now?"

"We're in bed together," she stated the obvious.

"And am I your lover?" he persisted, his hand cupping one side of her face preventing her turning away from him.

"Adam, what we just shared was very pleasant—"

"It was toe-curling," he corrected emphatically.

"For you too?" she asked shyly. In her inexperience it had been very special to her, but surely to

Adam, a man with many affairs behind him, it couldn't have meant the same thing.

"Especially for me." His thumbtip moved across her slightly swollen lips. "It was the way I always wanted it to be between us, before a marriage licence and a wedding ring fouled things up."

She looked down at the eternity ring on her finger. "I won't make any demands on you," she told him huskily.

"You never did," he said grimly. "Not even sexual ones."

Her mouth curved teasingly. "Those weren't the demands I was promising not to make," she drawled.

"Thank God for that!" He returned her smile.

She laughed throatily. "Now that I've discovered the—delights of being in bed with you I may never want to get out!"

"Suits me," he murmured as his mouth claimed hers again.

It was after four when they ordered lunch, Leonie groaning at the amount of food Adam had ordered. "I'll get fat," she grimaced.

"I hope so," he nodded. "I really meant it when I said I preferred you more—rounded."

"You mean I really can start to eat again?"

"Please," he said fervently.

They fed each other like starry-eyed lovers, and every time Leonie saw the diamond ring glitter on her finger she felt a warm glow. She wasn't altogether sure what the ring symbolised, they could hardly remain lovers indefinitely, but somehow the ring made her feel as if she really were Adam's lover, and not just a chattel that he took out for display every now and then. Because that was what being his wife had been like; surely being his lover had to be better than that. It *was* better!

"You like the ring?" Adam saw her glowing gaze on it.

"If it enables me to play the part of Mrs Smith, I love it!" she smiled across the table at him.

He laughed softly. "You can play the part of Mrs Smith any time you want to, it's a two-way arrangement."

"You mean if I want to spend another afternoon like this I can just call you and you'll meet me here?"

"Well, not here," he smiled. "We can only play the newly married couple once, but I'll meet you anywhere else that you suggest."

It sounded like heaven after the misery of their marriage. "I think I'm going to like this arrangement," she smiled her anticipation.

"Didn't I tell you that you would?"

"Now don't go and spoil it by saying I told you so," she reprimanded. "I love the ring, and I'll wear it proudly, but it gives you no rights over me other than the ones I choose to give you," she warned.

"Right," he nodded.

She eyed him suspiciously, never having known him be this agreeable in the past. "I won't give up my job."

"No."

"And I won't move in with you."

"Why not?" he frowned, although he made no objections.

She shook her head. "It wouldn't work, Adam. When I lived with you before you swamped me, I became a nervous wreck, terrified of leaving the apartment in the end in case I did something wrong."

"I didn't know that . . ."

"No," she flushed. "We didn't talk a lot in those days."

"Then we'll make sure we talk now. Do I swamp you now?" he asked slowly, all laughter gone.

"Not while I have my own home to go to whenever I want to. I just couldn't live with you again, Adam."

"Okay," he shrugged. "If that's the way you feel."

"You—you don't mind?"

"No, because I'll move in with you," he stated arrogantly.

"That isn't the idea, Adam," she sighed. "I knew this wouldn't work out," she shook her head. "I think we should just forget the idea, it was a stupid one, anyway."

"If you want us to maintain separate households, then we will—"

"Oh, thank you, Adam," she glowed. "I would prefer it. I don't—"

"—for the time being," he finished pointedly. "Leonie, I can't keep going between two households when I reach sixty!" he said exasperatedly as she looked dismayed. "The strain would probably kill me!"

"Sixty...?" she repeated dazedly. "You expect us to still be together then?"

"Why not? Eternity is a hell of a lot longer than the twenty-one years it's going to take me to reach that age! At least, I hope it is," he frowned.

"Adam, if you think an affair between us will last that long why did our marriage fail after only a year?" she reasoned. "After all, I didn't know about Liz until that last day."

"No, but I did," he answered grimly. "Our marriage never really started, Leonie. I rushed you into it, made all the rules and expected you to abide by them the way that my mother did. But that isn't a marriage, Leonie, it's just legalising the sexual act—and even that didn't work between us then.''

''Is that why you married me, for sex?''

''I married you because I wanted to be with you,'' he rasped.

''Did you ever love me?'' she asked dully.

''What difference does it make,'' he dismissed. ''I couldn't make you happy.''

It was a bitter irony that they could now make each other happy, that they were now closer than they ever had been.

''I loved you,'' she told him softly.

''I know,'' he acknowledged harshly. ''And I hurt you. This way is much better, isn't it?''

She supposed it was— Of course it was! She just couldn't understand how they could make an affair work when their marriage had failed. Unless their expectations were lower, their demands less.

She had married Adam expecting forever, had thought him the man of her dreams, with no faults or blemishes. Hadn't finding that he couldn't banish all the problems of life for her, couldn't reach her physically when she put up a frightened barrier, made him less of a Knight in Shining Armour? She had forgotten she was married to a mere man, that he had needs and fears too, had thought only of herself when the marriage began so badly and continued on its downward slide. Adam wasn't responsible for what had gone wrong on their honeymoon, just as he wasn't solely responsible for the end of their marriage. She had taken his involvement with Liz as the easy way out, when in fact she should have realised she was the one he had married, the one he was trying to share his life with.

Poor Adam, no wonder the idea of marriage had been soured for him; the woman he had chosen for his wife just hadn't been woman enough to try to be his partner in life, to give him the same considerations he gave her.

But she was that woman now, could look back on their marriage with perspective, believed Adam when he said he hadn't slept with Liz after their marriage. Yes, she believed him now, when it was too late, when all he wanted was an affair. But if that was all that could work between them then it was what she wanted too, wanted Adam in her life.

"Much better," she assured him huskily, standing up to take off the towel that was her only clothing. "Shall we go back to bed and see just how much better," she invited suggestively.

Adam needed no second invitation, his own towel discarded long before they reached the bedroom.

CHAPTER SEVEN

"No, Adam," she said firmly.

After two more days together she had gained enough confidence in their relationship to say what she liked and disliked, and the idea of joining Adam's father for dinner that evening she disliked intensely!

"Why not?" came Adam's calm query over the telephone.

"You can ask me that?" she gasped. "After the way he always treated me?"

"I was as much to blame for that as he was," Adam reminded. "I should have made sure he understood how things are between us."

"And how are they?" she demanded tautly.

"If he wants to continue seeing me," Adam told her softly, "he'll accept you."

Leonie was well aware of Charles Faulkner's love for his only child; she had often felt jealous of the closeness between them in the past. If Adam refused to visit his father because of her it would break the older man's heart.

"Adam, men don't introduce their lovers to their fathers," she derided.

"This man does."

She sighed at his stubbornness. "And what are you going to tell him about us?"

"Nothing."

"Nothing?" she frowned. "Adam—"

"It's sufficient that we're together," he explained arrogantly.

"Adam, I don't want to see your father again," she told him the simple truth behind her objection.

"I'm sure he feels the same way," he sounded amused. "He certainly sounded surprised when I told him you would be accompanying me."

"Then why put either of us through what can only be an embarrassing experience?" She put her hand up in acknowledgement of the night security guard as he passed by on his rounds. She was working late tonight, felt as if she were the only person in the building; it felt good to know Mick was about.

"I thought you said you wouldn't stay hidden as a lover," he reminded softly.

"And I haven't been!" She was angry with him for reminding her of that; the two of them hadn't exactly been keeping a low profile the last few days, Adam calling for her at the office for lunch, a rose, a real one now, continuing to arrive daily. She wasn't trying to hide their relationship, but neither was she willing to hypocritically sit down to dinner with Charles Faulkner; they both knew their dislike was mutual. "I'm not going to have dinner with your father, Adam," she repeated emphatically.

"He's expecting us."

"Then you go on your own," she snapped. "You had no right accepting the invitation without first consulting me."

"You would have said no," he reasoned.

"Obviously," she bit out. "Now could we end this pointless conversation, I have work to do."

"It's after seven," he pointed out.

"And thanks to an insatiable man I know that kept me awake most of the night I didn't get to work until after ten this morning," she reminded dryly, smiling at Mick as he passed by her open office door on his way back downstairs.

"Are you complaining?" Adam's voice had lowered sensuously.

"No." She could still feel the warm glow whenever she remembered their nights together, magical nights when they couldn't get enough of each other, seeming intent on making up for the time they had wasted. "But I am saying I have to work late tonight. I don't expect to be able to leave much before eight o'clock, and I am certainly not going to feel in the mood to cross swords with your father when I do!"

"I can tell that," he drawled. "Okay, I'll call him and change it to tomorrow."

"Adam—"

"And I won't come to your apartment tonight so that you can get a good night's sleep and won't have to work late tomorrow," he added huskily.

To say that she felt bereft at the thought of not seeing him tonight would be an understatement, the rest of the evening and night stretched before her like a long black tunnel. But she had a feeling Adam knew exactly how she felt, and she wouldn't give him the satisfaction of knowing how much she would miss him.

"That sounds like a good idea," she agreed lightly. "I can also get a few jobs done around the flat that I've neglected the last few days. And I'm sure Harvey would welcome my undivided attention for a few hours."

"You sound as if you're looking forward to an evening without me." Adam sounded annoyed.

She smiled to herself. She would spend a miserable evening without him, but it would be worth it to know that he didn't realise that. "Well we did agree we would have a certain amount of freedom in this relationship, Adam," she reminded brightly. "And the idea of putting on an old robe, curling up on the sofa with a good book, sounds like heaven."

"It sounds awful," he rasped.

"Only because you don't have an old robe," she mocked. "And you never relax enough to read."

"I prefer other methods of relaxation."

She could just picture the scowl of his face, almost felt it was worth the night without him to have turned the tables so neatly on him. Almost. But she had become accustomed to curling up against him at night, and she knew she would sleep badly tonight. "Take a hot bath and read for a while, Adam," she advised mockingly. "It's just as relaxing."

"Like hell it is!" he exploded. "Is that really what you would compare our lovemaking to, a hot bath and a read?" he demanded angrily.

"I didn't say it was as good," she was enjoying baiting him. "Only that it's as relaxing."

"It's the same thing, damn it," he snarled.

"Is it?" she asked with feigned vagueness, almost laughing out loud at his indignation. "Adam, are we having our first lovers' argument?" She instilled disbelief into her voice.

"Yes," he rasped coldly. "I'll call you tomorrow." He rang off abruptly.

Leonie put her own receiver down more slowly, knowing she had won that round, but at what price. She had denied herself a night with Adam, and the mood he was in now she couldn't even be sure he would call tomorrow. But she wouldn't go to him, had given in to him too much in the past to follow that pattern again. She looked at the ring on her finger; a long-lasting affair he had said. And she believed him. One little argument wouldn't spoil what they had now.

But that knowledge didn't cheer her up at all, and she had little enthusiasm for work now, her concentration level down to nil. She packed up after a few minutes, deciding she would be better off coming in early in the morning.

"Had enough for one day?" Mick sympathised as he unlocked the door for her to leave.

"More than enough," she grimaced at the middle-aged man. "I'll see you early in the morning," she told him lightly, knowing he would still be on duty when she got to work at seven-thirty tomorrow. It must be a long boring night for him.

It was a long boring night for her too. Her bath was relaxing, so was Harvey's decision to spend the evening in with her for a change, but the book might as well have been written in Chinese for all she understood it, putting it down after several minutes; her favourite romance author deserved a more avid reader than she could provide this evening.

Had she fallen into the trap so quickly, wanting more from Adam than he wanted to give? There could be no doubting that they came together as equals now, but would marriage make so much difference to their relationship? Their approach to each other was different this time around, would a wedding ring and marriage licence really "foul up" the relationship, as Adam had claimed it had last time. Couldn't he see that it wasn't those things that had ruined their marriage at all, that it had been their attitudes that were all wrong?

Was she saying she wanted to be married to him again? She knew she had changed since their separation, that she was more self-confident now, had independence in her career if not in her emotions, felt more able to meet Adam on an equal footing, both intellectually and emotionally, and certainly physically. God, how quickly she had changed her mind about being married to him, how she wished she didn't have to spend evenings apart from him like this! Could she accept just an affair now, when she knew she wanted so much more?

THE INSISTENT RINGING of the doorbell woke her up, and with a bleary-eyed glance at the bedside clock she saw it was after three o'clock in the morning. She came instantly awake. She had told Adam that she was sure her obscene telephone caller wouldn't come here while she continued to take his calls, but suddenly she wasn't so sure. And she was very much alone here.

Should she call the police before answering the door, or try to find out the identity of her visitor first? The police certainly wouldn't be very thrilled with her if it turned out to be a false alarm. She decided to do the latter, moving warily to the locked and bolted door, knowing that if someone were really determined to get in that they could break the locks with one blow to the door.

"Who—who is it?" she demanded in a hushed voice, trembling from head to foot.

"Who the hell do you think it is?" rasped an all-too-familiar voice.

"Adam!" Her hands shook as she quickly unlocked the door, almost falling into his arms in her relief, barely noticing he wore casual denims and shirt, his jaw in need of a shave. "Thank God it's you!" she groaned, her face buried against the warm column of his throat.

His arms tightened about her convulsively as she continued to tremble. "Who did you think— Oh no," he groaned, holding her closer. "You thought it was him, didn't you?" he realised, closing the door behind them.

"Yes," she shuddered.

"I'm sorry, baby. God, I'm sorry," he muttered over and over into her hair, holding her until the trembling stopped and she pulled out of his arms.

"Sorry!" she glared at him. "You frighten me half to death and all you can say is you're *sorry!*" After the relief came her anger, and she was truly furious!

"I'm *very* sorry?" he said hopefully.

"That doesn't make up at all for the scare you gave me," she snapped. "Just what do you think you're doing here at three o'clock in the morning anyway?" she demanded to know.

He sighed, thrusting his hands into the back pockets of his already tight denims. "I couldn't sleep—"

"Well you can take your damned insomnia somewhere else!" she told him angrily.

"You don't mean that."

"Oh don't I?" she challenged recklessly. "You just turn around and walk out that door. And if you want to see me again you can call at a reasonable time!"

"Have you been able to sleep?"

"Of course, why shouldn't I?" In fact it was because she had only eventually fallen asleep about an hour ago that was making her so bad-tempered, feeling nauseous with the suddenness of her wakening.

"Because you missed me," he suggested huskily.

"Don't flatter yourself," she said heatedly. "I slept before you came into my life, and I'll sleep the times you aren't with me!"

His mouth tightened. "You really want me to leave?"

"Yes!" She glared at him, still badly shaken from her imaginings of him being her obscene caller. "What we have is a *relationship,* Adam. I'm not some available body you can take to help you fall asleep!"

He recoiled as if she had struck him. "It wasn't like that—"

"Wasn't it?" she accused. "Can you deny you came here to make love with me?"

"That was part of it—"

"I'm beginning to think that might be all of it," she scorned. "Now that I'm not such a non-event in bed you can't do without it, can you?"

A white line of fury ringed his mouth. "You have improved in bed," he bit out contemptuously. "But I've had better," he added woundingly. "I thought this," he twisted up her left hand with his eternity ring glittering on her finger, "meant we had more than a physical relationship. I thought we had respect and liking, maybe even loving. But I was obviously wrong," he thrust her hand away from him. "I came here because I couldn't sleep until I'd apologised for the senseless argument we had earlier," he ground out. "But you obviously haven't been plagued by the same need. I will leave now, I'm sorry I troubled you!"

The colour had come and gone again in her face as they hurled the hurtful words at each other, knowing she had provoked this scene, a scene that could be the end of them. And suddenly the idea of Adam walking out of her life became too unbearable to contemplate.

"Adam!" She ran to him as he stopped at the door, her arms about his waist from behind as she rested her cheek against his back. "I'm sorry," she said breathlessly. "I shouldn't have said those things."

He didn't move. "The point is, did you mean them?"

"No," she sighed. "I've just woken up after lying awake for hours aching for you," she admitted gruffly. "I'm a bad-tempered witch, and I'm sorry."

The tension left his body in a ragged sigh. "Can I stay?"

"Please," she groaned her need.

He turned to take her in his arms, holding her tightly. "Have you forgiven me for frightening you like that?"

"Of course." She snuggled up against him.

"Has he called again?"

She shook her head. "No, I told you, only Fridays at eleven-thirty."

"I wonder why that is," Adam frowned.

"Maybe that's his night out with the boys away from his wife," she dismissed.

"You think he's married?" Adam's frown deepened.

"I try not to think about him at all," she told him firmly. "And I wish you wouldn't either. He's a sick man who vents his frustration on life by telling me dirty things."

"If I ever find out who he is I'll kill him," Adam ground out.

She smoothed the anger from his face. "We'll probably never know, so let's forget him."

"Yes." He did so with effort. "Shall we go to bed?"

She smiled up at him encouragingly. "I thought you would never ask!"

Their lovemaking was different again tonight, as enjoyable as it always was, but no more so than the closeness they shared afterwards as they lay in each other's arms. As she lay next to Adam Leonie knew that their relationship had transcended the physical, that even though she had no idea of Adam's feelings for her that she loved him, doubted she had ever stopped.

SHE COULD FEEL the tension rising within her as they neared Adam's father's house, wished with each passing minute that she had stuck to her decision not to go there with him for dinner. But her closeness to Adam that morning had compelled her to change her mind, sure at that time that she could survive the ordeal of meeting his father again.

She had changed her mind back again since then, had picked up the telephone a dozen times during the day to tell Adam to cancel the dinner, only to replace it again without speaking to him, sure he would find her cowardly behaviour less than attractive.

Getting herself ready had been a disaster, not realising her nail-polish wasn't dry, finding out that fact when her tights got stuck to it as she tried to get dressed. Then she had torn the hem of her dress with her evening shoe, having to change her make-up tones with the dress, realising at the last minute that she had grey shadow on one lid and green on the other!

By the time Adam arrived to pick her up at seven-thirty she was feeling hot and flustered, telling him she couldn't possibly go out, that she thought she might be going to come down with something. His method of persuasion had left her even more hot and flustered—but with a decided glow to her eyes.

The fact that they were now going to arrive very late didn't seem to bother Adam in the slightest, the intimate smiles he kept directing her way reassuring her that she had his support, that he wouldn't let her down as he had so much in the past.

The Faulkner staff must have been aware of the break-up of Adam's marriage, and yet the haughty butler didn't so much as bat an eyelid at Leonie accompanying Adam to dinner, his manner very correct as he took her jacket.

"Dad doesn't eat little girls for breakfast," Adam teased her as she hesitated about entering the lounge where she knew the senior Mr Faulkner was waiting for them.

"That's only because he knows I'd give him indigestion!" she muttered ruefully.

Adam was still laughing when they entered the lounge, although Leonie sobered as she sensed the disapproval emanating from the rigid-backed man standing across the room from them. Charles Faulkner was an older version of Adam, still very good looking despite being over seventy, although the lines of harshness beside his nose and mouth weren't quite so noticeable in his son yet. And if Leonie had her way they never would be!

"You're late," Charles Faulkner bit out critically without greeting.

"Are we?" Adam dismissed unconcernedly.

"You know you are," his father said harshly, cold grey eyes turning to Leonie. "What have you been up to now?" he scorned.

In the past she would have cowered away from such open contempt, but somehow tonight she knew Adam was on her side, and that gave her the confidence to steadily meet those critical grey eyes. "Good evening, Charles," she deliberately used the informality she had been too nervous to take while living in this house. "I hope you're well," she added politely.

The older man scowled. "I'm as you see me."

Her perusal of his rigidly held body was deliberate and slow. "You're looking very well—considering your age." Her expression remained deceptively innocent, although she could sense Adam was having difficulty containing his amusement.

"And what does age have to do with it?" Charles frowned heavily at the backhanded compliment.

"Well, I remember your once telling me you're just an old man who wants to see his son happily settled before you die," she reminded him of the argument the two of them had had just before she left Adam; it had been one of many occasions when Charles Faulkner had verbally attacked her without Adam's knowledge. She didn't intend to bring those arguments to Adam's knowledge now, she just wanted to warn Charles Faulkner that she wouldn't stand for it a second time. From the look on the older man's face it was working.

"Oh?" Adam sounded suspicious.

"Don't worry, darling," she gave him a bright reassuring smile, enjoying Charles Faulkner being the one to feel uncomfortable for a change; in the past she had never dared to mention his father's cruelty to Adam. "I assured your father I only wanted the same thing."

Adam looked across at the older man with narrowed eyes. "It sounds an—interesting conversation."

"Oh, your father and I had a lot of interesting conversations," she dismissed with feigned innocence. "I've missed them the last few months."

"I'll bet you have," Adam sounded angry.

"Shall we go through to dinner?" his father rasped. "It's been ready almost an hour."

"Then it should be nicely cooked, shouldn't it," his son dismissed hardly.

"Ruined more like," his father muttered, shooting resentful glances at Leonie, which she promptly ignored.

"I've never known Mrs Simmonds to ruin a meal," Adam insisted.

"Always a first time," his father bit out.

The meal was delicious, as they had all known it would be. Emily Simmonds was as taciturn as her employer, but her food melted in the mouth, and it was always perfectly cooked, the Beef Wellington, asparagus tips, and tiny new potatoes that followed the home-made pâté better than could be bought in any restaurant. But the food didn't seem to have improved Charles Faulkner's mood at all.

"You never did tell me why the two of you were so late arriving," he snapped as they were served the chocolate meringue for dessert.

Delicate colour heightened Leonie's cheeks as she left it to Adam to reply; after all, *he* was the one who had delayed them. Even if she had enjoyed it.

"I took Leonie to bed and made love to her," he stated calmly, continuing to eat his dessert in the midst of the furore he had created.

"Adam!" Leonie gasped her dismay, not expecting him to be quite so candid.

His father's mouth was tight. "In my day a man didn't discuss taking his wife to bed."

"Only other women, hm?" his son mocked, the elderly man spluttering his indignation. "But Leonie is no longer my wife." His hand clasped hers, his smile warm.

"You're back together," his father pointed out abruptly.

"And we're staying that way," Adam nodded. "But not as husband and wife."

"You—you mean you're just going to *live together?*" Charles made it sound decadent.

"Not even that yet," his son replied happily. "Not until Leonie is ready for it."

"Leonie!" his father snorted. "In my day a man didn't ask his wife's permission to do anything!"

"I know that," Adam nodded. "And for a while I followed your example. I walked all over Leonie as if she were a piece of the furniture, didn't ask her opinion on anything, didn't even care if she wanted to make love or not. I did, and that was good enough for me."

"Adam . . . !" She looked at him pleadingly.

"No, Leonie, I have to make my father understand that things are different now." He turned to the older man. "Leonie is a person, with feelings and desires. It took me a long time to realise there was more to a marriage than putting a ring on some lucky woman's finger. Lucky!" he scorned. "Leonie never knew a day's happiness after I married her. I was so busy being the strong man you had taught me to be that I killed the love Leonie had for me. I realise now that mother was just as unhappy with you as Leonie was with me."

His father flushed with rage. "Your mother wasn't unhappy! I gave her everything, cars, jewels, furs, this beautiful house, the servants, *you!*"

"You didn't give me to mother," Adam contradicted impatiently. "You created me together. And instead of giving things to mother you should have spent more time with her, talked, *laughed.*"

"I had a business to run," his father scowled. "I didn't have time for that."

"Then you should have made time!"

The two men glared at each other, the similarity between them at that moment unmistakable.

"And I suppose that's what you intend doing, so that you can pander to this—to this—"

"To Leonie, yes," Adam bit out.

"And the business will suffer because of it!"

"The business will do just fine," Adam corrected. "That's what delegation is all about."

"I'm surprised you haven't decided to sell everything off," his father scorned.

"I thought about it—"

"Adam!" Leonie gasped her shocked dismay.

"And decided against it," he finished gently, squeezing her hand reassuringly. "There would have been no point," he shrugged. "I would still have been the same selfish man, and a richer but unemployed one too. So I decided that it was *I* who had to change, not my life."

"There's nothing wrong with you," his father told him tautly. "At least, nothing that can't be straightened out as soon as you're over this infatuation you suddenly have for your own wife!"

Adam shook his head, his smile sympathetic. "There's nothing sudden about my feelings for Leonie, I was just too busy to express them before. Never show any sign of weakness, that's your motto, isn't it, Dad?"

"It's never failed me," the older man ground out.

"Oh it's failed you," Adam contradicted gently. "Mother was never completely happy, never really sure of your love, and I've turned out to be made from your own image."

"There's nothing wrong in that," his father bit out. "You're a successful man, well respected in the business world."

"The respect of complete strangers doesn't mean a lot," Adam told him impatiently.

"I suppose you're going to tell me next that all you want is Leonie," his father derided coldly.

"Yes," Adam answered quietly. "That's exactly what I want. I also want *your* respect for her, and until you can give her that we won't be coming here again."

"Adam." She looked up at him pleadingly.

"It's all right, Leonie," he assured her with a gentle smile, pulling her to her feet at his side. "I'm sure my father knows I mean what I say." The last was added challengingly.

"You're acting like an idiot, Adam," his father rasped. "Can't you see she's a little simpleton? Why, all she's been able to do for the last half hour is gasp your name in varying degrees of incredulity!" he added contemptuously.

"Good night, Father," Adam told him flatly, guiding Leonie to the door.

"Adam!"

He turned slowly at the anguished cry. "Yes?" he bit out coldly.

His father was standing too now, looking more disturbed than Leonie had ever seen him. "Can't you see you're making a damned fool of yourself, and over a young slip of a girl who isn't worthy of you?"

Adam gave his father a pitying smile. "If this is making a fool of myself I hope I never stop!" He opened the door for Leonie to precede him out of the room.

"Adam...!"

He ignored his father's second plea, his arm about Leonie's waist as they left the house together.

CHAPTER EIGHT

LEONIE sat quietly at his side as he drove them back to her flat, all of their nights spent there together, Adam an integral part of her life now.

She was stunned by the evening with Charles Faulkner, had had no idea Adam meant to issue his father such a challenge because of her. She knew Adam had changed since their separation, but she hadn't realised just how much.

And he had done it for her, he had revealed tonight, that was what she found so incredible. He wanted her so much that he was willing to change his whole life for her. Surely that must mean he loved her? It was a word that remained conspicuously absent from their relationship.

But she loved him, more than ever after his defence of her in front of his father, knew that she had never really stopped loving him. And she believed him when he said Liz was out of his life for ever. But she wanted to be his wife again more than anything, wanted the children with him even a long-term affair couldn't give them. Maybe in time...

"Thank you, Adam," she huskily broke the silence.

"For what?" He heaved a ragged sigh. "For subjecting you to even more unpleasantness from my father?"

She put her hand on his thigh. "I've known worse from him."

"I'm sure you have," he ground out. "Just how often did he used to make those digs at you without my knowledge?"

"It's over now, Adam—"

"How often, Leonie?" he demanded stubbornly.

She sighed. "Whenever he could," she admitted. "It was very demoralising." She had no intention of widening the gulf between father and son by telling Adam how often his father had reduced her to tears.

"You should have told me what was going on," he rasped.

Leonie shrugged. "He never said anything that wasn't the truth. It really doesn't matter now," she assured him.

"It matters to me," Adam bit out. "I was such a lousy husband I couldn't even see what a bastard my father was to you!"

"You were not a lousy husband," she defended.

"Yes, I was," he nodded grimly. "God, I hope I'm a better lover than that!"

She felt any hope she may have had of persuading him to resume their marriage slipping away from her. It was obvious that Adam preferred things the way they were. "Yes," she told him softly. "You're a better lover."

She fed the cat when they got in, Adam watching her with brooding eyes as he sat on one of the armchairs. He still seemed very disturbed by the incident with his father, and she sat down on the carpeted floor in front of him as she turned to talk to him.

"He'll come around," she said softly.

He looked startled. "You mean Dad?" His brow cleared. "Yes, he'll come around," he acknowledged heavily. "And I hope he's a wiser man for it."

"But you weren't thinking about him, were you?" she probed.

"No," he admitted flatly. "I was just wondering how you could have stayed with me as long as you did, and what damned arrogance made me assume I could just walk back into your life and get you to accept me as your lover!"

"But I did, didn't I?" She smiled up at him.

"Yes, you did." He shook his head in amazement. "I thought I had changed after you left me, you see I tried to do exactly that, but now I realise I'm still as arrogant, that I haven't changed in that respect at all. What right do I have to expect you to waste one day of your life on me after what you went through when you were married to me?"

"It isn't wasted," she assured him huskily.

"And if I hurt you again?" he rasped.

She shook her head. "You won't."

"How can you be sure?"

"Why should I want to be?" she cajoled. "One thing I've learnt from our marriage, Adam, is that the whole of life is a risk. You simply have to live it the way that is best for you."

He pulled her up to sit on his knees. "And this is best for us, isn't it, Leonie?" he said fiercely.

"Yes," she said softly, hope completely gone. "This is right for us."

She met his kiss halfway, their emotions spiralling rapidly, standing up in unison to go to her bedroom, needing more than just caresses.

They had barely reached the bedroom when the telephone began to ring, Adam frowning heavily as he glanced down at his watch. "Friday, eleven-thirty," he muttered darkly. "He's consistent, isn't he," he ground out, turning to pick up the receiver.

"No, Adam, let me—"

He easily shrugged off her attempt to take the receiver from him, listening to the man in silence for several seconds. "As I said before, it all sounds very interesting," he finally cut in gratingly. "But if you don't stop these calls I'm going to do some heavy breathing of my own—down your damned neck! Do I make myself clear?" He shrugged, putting down the receiver. "He hung up."

"Wouldn't you?" she teased, relieved that the call was over for another week.

Adam sighed. "Leonie, he worries me. I know you say he's harmless, but—"

"He is," she insisted. "And maybe now that he realises I have an aggressive lover he'll stop calling."

"Maybe..." But Adam didn't sound convinced.

"Darling, let's not think about him now," she moved sensuously against him. "Can't you see this is exactly what he wants?" She sighed as she received no response. "Adam, don't let one sick person ruin everything that we have."

He looked down at her with pain-darkened eyes. "If anything happened to you...!" His arms came about her convulsively, carrying her over to the bed to make love to her until she begged for his possession, until neither of them had a lucid thought in their head other than pleasing each other.

Adam still lay next to her when she woke the next morning, and with a contented sigh she realised neither of them had to go to work this morning. She looked down at the man at her side, remembering the incredible night they had jus· spent together, a night when Adam seemed determined to possess her time and time again, and had.

"Adam...?"

His lids opened instantly she spoke his name, almost as if her voice were all that were needed to wake him. A light glowed in his eyes as he saw the sensuality in her face. "Again, Leonie?" he said huskily.

"Please," she encouraged throatily.

It was after eleven when they woke the next time, Leonie resisting Adam's caressing as she insisted they needed food rather than more lovemaking. It was while they were eating the brunch Adam had prepared that she remembered she should have visited Liz and Nick that morning.

"What is it?" Adam was sensitive to her every mood, fully dressed as he sat across the table from her, although he had told her he intended bringing some of his clothes here the next time he came, sick of dressing in the same clothes he had worn the evening before. He did look rather out of place in the tailored black trousers and white evening shirt, although he had dispensed with the dinner jacket that completed the suit.

"Nothing," she dismissed, not wanting to do or say anything that would dispel the harmony of the morning.

"Leonie?" he prompted reprovingly.

She shrugged narrow shoulders, wearing denims and a cream cotton top. "I should have visited Liz and Nick this morning, but it isn't important. I can call them later."

"There's still time—"

"I'd rather stay with you," she said huskily.

"I have an appointment myself at twelve-thirty." He sipped his coffee.

"Oh?" she frowned, had imagined they would spend the day together.

"Yes." He didn't enlarge on the subject. "And I have to go home and change first," he added ruefully. "So you can still go to Liz's if you want to."

It seemed that she might as well when he put it like that. But she couldn't help feeling curious about who he was seeing at twelve-thirty; he wasn't exactly keeping it a secret, but he didn't seem anxious to talk about it either.

"Well, if you're sure," she frowned.

"I am," he nodded. "I'll come back here around six, okay?"

"Okay."

His sharp gaze narrowed on her. "What's the matter?"

"Nothing," she dismissed with a bright smile.

Adam smiled. "I know you well enough to realise when you're sulking—"

"I do not *sulk!*" she claimed indignantly.

"Yes, you do," he chuckled. "Your bottom lip pouts—like that," he touched the passion-swollen redness with the top of his thumb, "and your eyes get stormy." He looked into the glittering green depths. "Like that. Yes, you're definitely sulking. What is it, Leonie?" he prompted softly.

She shrugged. "I thought we were going to spend the day together, that's all," she admitted moodily.

Pleasure glowed in his eyes. "Tomorrow we won't even get out of bed," he promised. "But today we have our courtesy visits to make, you to Liz and Nick's, I to a business meeting."

"On a Saturday?"

"Sometimes it's the only time that's convenient. But if you would rather I didn't go...?"

"Oh no," she denied instantly, not wanting him to think she was acting shrewish, as he had once claimed a wife's possessiveness could be. "I'll cook us dinner this evening." That way they could spend more time alone together.

"It's about time *you* cooked me a meal." He mocked the fact that he was the one who had once again done the cooking.

"You never used to like my cooking," she reminded softly.

"That isn't true," he sobered. "You used to get yourself in such a state about it if something went wrong that I thought you would prefer to eat with my father. I couldn't have given a damn if some of the food was a bit burnt around the edges!"

"It was usually burnt all over," she grimaced.

"Didn't you know that I didn't give a damn if it was charcoaled?" he rasped. "I didn't even notice what I was eating, I was too busy looking at my wife!"

"Oh, Adam," she choked. "Tonight I'll cook you something really special," she promised. "It's just that I've been too exhausted the rest of the week to be able to crawl from my bed, let alone cook you dinner in the evenings," she teased lightly.

"Tomorrow you won't have to bother," he promised, standing up to pull on his jacket.

"I may starve," she warned.

"You won't." His gaze held hers before he bent to kiss her.

"Man—or woman—cannot live on love alone," she told him.

"We can try," he murmured throatily, shaking his head as he moved away from her. "If I don't leave now, *I* may not have the strength to get out the door."

He gave her a quick kiss on the lips. "I'll see you this evening, darling."

Her flat seemed very empty once he had left, not even Harvey's presence as he jealously followed her from room to room helping to dispel the feeling of loneliness as he usually did. Accustomed to sleeping on the bottom of her bed at night he wasn't too happy about being relegated to the sofa in the lounge this last week.

To Leonie's dismay Nick was out when she arrived for her visit, feeling awkward at being alone with Liz, something she had pointedly avoided since the day she had seen her sister in Adam's arms. But she could hardly leave again just because her brother-in-law was out.

But she didn't know what to talk about to Liz, had felt uncomfortable with her sister since knowing she and Adam had been lovers. Luckily feeding Emma and putting her upstairs for her nap filled the first half an hour, although without the distraction of the baby Leonie felt even more awkward.

"That's a lovely ring." Liz reached her hand across the kitchen table as they sat in there drinking coffee together, admiring the diamond-studded ring on Leonie's slender hand. "It's new, isn't it?" she looked up enquiringly.

Leonie put the offending hand out of sight under the table. "Yes, it's new," she mumbled, wondering why on earth she hadn't thought to take it off before visiting her sister.

"It looks expensive," Liz sipped her coffee.

"I— It probably is," she acknowledged awkwardly.

Her sister's eyes widened. "It was a gift?"

"Yes," she admitted reluctantly.

"Well don't be so secretive, Leonie," Liz laughed reprovingly. "Who's the man?"

She shrugged. "No one important." She instantly felt disloyal for dismissing Adam in that way. "That isn't true," she said quietly, her head going back proudly. "Adam gave me the ring."

"You're back together?"

She wished she could tell more from her sister's expression how she felt about the idea, but Liz was giving nothing away, her expression guarded. "In a way," she finally answered.

Liz frowned at the evasion. "What does that mean?"

She moistened suddenly dry lips. "We're together, but not *back* together if you know what I mean."

"No, I don't," Liz looked puzzled.

"Our marriage was a failure, being with Adam now is nothing like that."

"But you are—together?" Liz persisted.

She drew in a deep breath, not wanting to hurt her sister as Liz had hurt her in the past, their roles somehow reversed now. "Yes," she confirmed abruptly.

Liz let out a long sigh of relief. "You don't know how happy that makes me," she said shakily.

Leonie frowned. "Happy?" It was the last thing she had expected her sister to feel about her reconciliation with Adam. "You realise I know of your involvement with Adam before we were married?"

"Yes," Liz nodded. "I always felt that it was partly that involvement that parted you and Adam."

Partly! It was her sister's involvement with *her* husband that had ended the marriage!

"I'm so glad Adam has at last explained to you what really happened between us," Liz said happily. "He has, hasn't he?" she hesitated.

"I know about it," she acknowledged curtly.

"Adam always said that knowing wouldn't make things any better between you, that you had other problems that couldn't be worked out."

"Yes." But they had worked those problems out now! So what was the secret behind Liz's involvement with Adam, how did her sister think Adam could ever condone their actions so that she could forgive them both?

"I couldn't imagine what they were," Liz frowned. "And it wasn't my business to ask. I know how kind Adam is, I couldn't think what could be wrong between you, but Adam insisted that knowing the truth about the two of us would serve no purpose, that things were over between you. I'm so glad he was wrong!"

Leonie had no intention of correcting her sister's assumption that Adam had explained everything to her, knowing that Liz was going to reveal it without realising she was doing so.

"Adam so deserves to find happiness, he was so kind to me. When Nick went through what I can only assume to be his mid-life crisis a couple of years back and had an affair with a young girl at his office I felt so—so humiliated, so—so unfeminine, so unattractive, that I just wanted to crawl away and hide."

Nick's affair? This was getting more complicated than she had imagined! She made a non-committal noise in her throat, encouraging Liz to continue.

"Adam made me feel like a woman again, a beautiful woman," she recalled emotionally.

"Wasn't going to bed with you a little drastic?" Harshness entered Leonie's voice. "Offering you a shoulder to cry on might have been just as effective— and less complicated."

"*I* was the one who instigated our lovemaking," Liz admitted heavily. "It could have been any man, I just wanted to prove, to myself, that I was still an attractive woman."

"If it could have been any man why did you have to choose *Adam!*"

She shrugged. "Because I knew he was too kind to rebuff me. He knew I couldn't take any more rejection, acted as if it were what he wanted too, but afterwards we both knew it was a mistake. I still wanted Nick, not Adam, and the only way to get Nick back was to fight for him, to show him how important he was to me, not have an affair myself."

"You obviously won," Leonie said dully, the involvement she had believed to be an affair not an affair at all. Then why hadn't Adam told her that! Because he didn't care enough about her to explain himself...? Somehow his actions now disproved that.

"Yes, although it wasn't easy," Liz smiled tremulously. "Knowing Nick had slept with another woman, was perhaps comparing me to her, was a difficult hurdle to cross."

Leonie didn't need to be told about that torment, she had *lived* it!

"And I knew I could never tell Nick about the night I spent with Adam," she sighed heavily.

"But he had an affair himself!"

"Yes," Liz nodded. "But to be told that I had spitefully slept with another man because he had betrayed me was something I knew he could never accept. Besides, Adam was married to you by this time."

"All the more reason for the truth to come out, I would have thought!"

"And what was the truth?" Liz reasoned. "That Adam had loaned me his body for a night so that I might feel a whole woman again? Why ruin five lives just to ease our consciences?'' she shook her head.

Because Leonie had a feeling it was that guilty conscience that had ruined her own marriage, *Adam's* guilty conscience that he had once gone to bed with his sister. ''You were never in love with Adam?'' she probed.

''No,'' Liz denied instantly. ''Or he with me. He took one look at my baby sister and fell like a ton of bricks,'' she added ruefully. ''I'd always teased him that it would happen that way for him, and he had always scorned the idea. When I came back from my reconciliation holiday with Nick to be told the two of you were getting married I didn't know whether to be ecstatic for your sake or nervous of losing the happiness I had just refound with Nick.''

''*That's* why you were less than enthusiastic by our news.'' She had thought it was for completely a different reason!

''Yes,'' Liz grimaced. ''I should have known Adam would never break his promise to me. But when I knew I was expecting a baby it somehow seemed important that he reassure me Nick would never find out about that night I had spent with him. Adam assured me no one would hear of it from him.''

And she had walked in on that scene, had misread it completely. Could Liz be right, *had* Adam fallen deeply in love with her the first time they met? And if he had, did he love her still?

''He told me your marriage wasn't working out,'' Liz looked sad. ''That he expected you to leave him any day. I couldn't understand it, the two of you had seemed so much in love. But Adam assured me my behaviour with him had done nothing to cause the rift.''

And he had lied. He had risked their happiness for the sake of her sister's! She knew it as surely as if Adam had told her so himself. But he never would. He *was* kind, had never deliberately hurt anyone in his life. Not even her, she realised now. Two years ago she had been too immature, too starry-eyed, to accept and understand what had prompted him to make love to Liz, a new maturity gave her the insight to realise he had been helping a friend cope with her pain. He couldn't have had any idea at the time that he would fall in love with Liz's young sister, that he would want to marry her even though he knew that, like Nick, she couldn't have taken the truth about him and Liz. When she had found out about the two of them she had acted predictably, hadn't cared that what she had thought to be their affair had taken place before their marriage, that Adam had been completely faithful to her since that time. All she had seen were the black and white facts; Adam had slept with her married sister!

But had he really sacrificed their happiness for Liz's sake? Eight months after their separation they were back together, happier than ever.

And suddenly she needed to tell him she understood the past, that she wanted a future with him, a permanent future, with a wedding ring. There would be no more evasions of the truth between them, she wanted to be his wife, and she intended telling him so.

"He was right." She stood up to kiss her sister warmly on the cheek, seeing Liz's surprise to the first instantaneous show of affection she had given her in a long time. "We had other, much more serious problems." Such as not talking to each other about what was bothering them. She intended remedying that straight away!

"I'm so glad you're back together again," Liz hugged her.

"So am I." She gave a glowing smile.

"I hope it works out this time. Adam loves you very much, you know."

Yes, she finally believed that he did. He had been brought up in a household where love was never expressed openly, found it difficult to show love himself as a consequence, even when he knew it was pushing them apart. While they had been separated he had set about changing a lifetime of emotional repression, of sharing his feelings and fears with another person. The despair he had shown last night when they got back from his father's because he thought he had failed was evidence of that.

It also made her question the affair between them now. What was it he had said the first night they had slept together since their separation, that the affair had been her suggestion? He believed it was what *she* wanted!

It was time they sorted out this mess, to tell each other of their true feelings, for the past and for each other. If an affair were really all he wanted then she would accept that, but she had a feeling they were both living a lie. God, she could hardly wait to see him again!

CHAPTER NINE

THE telephone was ringing as she entered the flat, and after falling over an awkwardly reclining Harvey as he lay in front of the doorway, she ran to pick up the receiver, sure it was Adam.

"Leonie?"

Her hand instantly tensed about the green-coloured receiver. "Yes?" she sounded breathless.

"You sound as if you've just got out of bed."

"I—"

"Is he still there, Leonie?" that taunting voice interrupted. "Is your lover still in your bed?"

This couldn't be happening. This was Saturday, he never called on a Saturday!

"Leonie?" The man's voice had sharpened angrily as she remained silent.

"Yes! Yes, I'm still here," she gasped, realising that something else was different about this call too. He was using her name! He had never done that before either.

"Did your lover stay the night, Leonie?" he rasped.

"Look—"

"Is Faulkner still there with you?" he cut in furiously.

Leonie felt numb with shock. Not only did this man know *her* name, he also knew about Adam! She felt an uncomfortable tingling sensation down her neck, as if someone were watching her. How else could this man know so much about her and Adam? God, it made her feel sick—and frightened. It was a long time since she had felt physically threatened by this man's calls, but today was different, *he* was different, not talking about the sick things he would like to do to her as he usually did, sounding menacing as he questioned her.

"I said is he there, Leonie?" he grated again.

"I—er—Yes, he's here," she invented desperately, suddenly feeling trapped, out of control of her own life.

"Liar!" the man gave an unpleasant laugh. "He isn't there, is he, Leonie?"

"Of course he is," she insisted. "He—He's in the shower."

"I saw him leave, Leonie."

"You saw—!" She swallowed hard. "Where are you?" Her voice rose shrilly.

"Wouldn't you like to know," he taunted. "Get rid of him from your life, Leonie. You're mine, do you understand?" he growled. "I stood by while that wimp Stevenson tried his luck with you, but Faulkner is a different matter. Get rid of him, Leonie, you won't like what will happen to him if you don't."

"Wh-what?"

"I could love you much better than he ever could," he told her softly.

"What will you do to Adam?" she repeated shrilly.

There was silence on the other end of the telephone, but she knew he was there, knew he hadn't rung off, could sense him there even though he didn't say a word.

"You're in love with him!" The man suddenly exploded.

"No!" she denied desperately. "I just—"

"Yes, you are, damn you," he rasped harshly. "And I can't allow that, Leonie. I would have given you everything, everything," his voice rose. "But you weren't interested, were you? Oh no, you chose Stevenson over me, and now you're in love with Faulkner. You shouldn't have done that, Leonie. I'll never allow another man to have you. Never!" He slammed the receiver down with such force it hurt her eardrums.

She couldn't move, daren't move, felt frozen, her breathing constricted, her hunted gaze darting about the room like a cornered animal.

She had told Adam the man never threatened, but he had threatened just now. She had told Adam she didn't know the man, and yet she obviously did for him to know so much about her. But *who*, who could it be? Every man she had ever met came crowding into her mind, a jumble of male faces that suddenly all looked menacing.

And then she dismissed the majority of them as being too ridiculous; she hadn't seen most of them for years. But that still left so many friends, acquaintances. Two men she knew she could exclude from that list, Adam and David. It couldn't be Adam, she knew that without a doubt, and the man had been so scathing about David he couldn't possibly have been talking about himself.

But there was Tony, the boy she had been seeing casually before she met and married Adam so quickly, several friends of Adam's she had come to know, the man in the upper flat, and the man in the lower one, the men she worked with, the men she had worked for. God, the list was endless, and she couldn't begin to guess which one of them could be this sick.

But she did have to get out of the flat, couldn't stay here and just wait for him to arrive on her doorstep. She had to call Adam, that was what she had to do. It was almost three now, he would be coming to see her soon, and she couldn't possibly let him walk into a trap.

She let his telephone ring and ring, but received no reply, becoming more and more agitated as she didn't. Surely he couldn't still be at his business meeting?

She had to get out of here. She could wait for Adam at his apartment, didn't care how long she had to stand outside; she wasn't staying here.

She moved about the flat picking up her bag and jacket, pushing an unsuspecting Harvey, as he lay asleep on her bed, into his travelling basket; she didn't intend returning here, would have the rest of her things, and Moby Dick, moved to Adam's apartment as soon as she could.

She was just giving one last frantic look round to make sure she had switched everything off when the doorbell rang shrilly. Her breath stopped in her throat, and for a moment she couldn't move. Dear God, what was she going to do? What *could* she do!

She thought of pretending she wasn't here, but the sudden trip she made over the coffee-table, dropping an indignantly screeching Harvey, put lie to that idea. She righted Harvey's basket before moving cautiously to the door, pressing her ear against the white-painted wood. She couldn't hear anything—but what had she expected, heavy breathing!

The doorbell rang again. "Leonie, are you in there?" called a familiar voice. "I heard a thump, have you hurt yourself?"

Relief flooded through her as she ripped open the door. "Gary!" she hugged him before quickly pulling him inside. "Thank God you're here." She felt like crying at the sight of a friendly face after her imaginings.

"I just thought I'd drop by for a coffee while Joan does her shopping," he dismissed in a preoccupied voice, frowning at how pale she was. "*Did* you hurt yourself?"

She shook her head. "Only Harvey's dignity when I dropped him."

Gary looked down at the cat in the travelling basket. "Are you going away?"

"Just to Adam's—Adam Faulkner," she explained with a blush, although Gary must be as aware as the rest of the staff were at Stevenson Interiors that she was seeing Adam. "You see, I've been having these calls, nasty calls," she grimaced. "I think I told you about them once...?"

"Yes," he nodded.

"Well, I was sure he was harmless. But then he called just now, and he never calls on a Saturday, and I—"

"Hey, calm down," Gary chided, his smile gentle. "Why don't you sit down, let me make you a cup of coffee, and then you can tell me all about it."

"No, we can't stay here." She shook her head frantically. "You see, when he called just now he was— threatening. I'm sure he's going to come here," she shivered.

"With me here?" Gary soothed. "I doubt it."

He was a dear, but with his five-foot-eight-inch frame she didn't feel confident she could depend on him if it should come to violence with the obscene telephone caller. But she couldn't say that to him without hurting his feelings.

"I really don't think we should stay here, Gary," she tried to sound calm. "Look, why don't you come over to Adam's with me, he's sure to be back by the time we get there."

"He isn't at home?"

"He had to go to a meeting, and he doesn't seem to be back yet." She was speaking quickly in her agitation. Didn't he realise how dangerous this situation was! "Please, Gary, we have to go," she urged desperately.

"I don't think so."

"But he could be here any minute! He—" her voice trailed off as she watched him walk over to the door, check that it was locked before putting the key into his pocket. "What are you doing?" she asked—but she had a dreadful feeling she already knew!

He looked at her calmly. "Stopping you from leaving."

She swallowed hard. "Gary, this isn't a time to play games. He could be here soon, and—"

"He's already here."

She had guessed that as soon as he pocketed the key—and she had actually *let* him in here! Gary was the man who called her every Friday night, who whispered obscene things he wanted to do to her. She couldn't believe this nightmare, had always believe the two of them were friends.

"Why, Gary?" she asked faintly, feeling weak with nausea that it was him that said such disgusting things to her every week, that he had done so for the last six months, while still continuing to be so friendly at work. God, she had even told him about those calls!

"Why do you think?" he scorned, his eyes narrowed unpleasantly.

"I—I don't know." She watched him warily, but he seemed to be making no move to cross the room to where she stood poised for flight.

"Because I want you, you little fool," he derided mockingly. "I always did, from the moment you came in to my office with David that first morning and promptly fell over the waste-paper basket. You made me feel protective, very much the man as I helped you to your feet. You looked so delicate and defenceless, and I wanted to take care of you." There was a smile to his lips as he recalled the morning they had met. "That month I worked so closely with you was the most enjoyable four weeks of my life," he added flatly.

"I enjoyed it too," she infused enthusiasm into her voice.

His eyes hardened angrily. "You barely noticed me!" he rasped.

"You were married—"

"Yes," he acknowledged harshly. "But so were you."

"I was separated from my husband."

"I remember. I was jealous of any man who had had you and not had the sense to hold on to you. I hated your husband," he stated coldly. "I wanted you, no other man could have you."

"No other man did," she assured him quickly.

"David—"

"We've only ever been friends, nothing more."

"Faulkner?"

She swallowed hard, paling even more, knowing after what he had just said about her husband that she daren't tell him Adam was the man she was married to. "Adam and I are friends too," she dismissed lightly.

"Very good ones from the amount of nights he's spent here with you," Gary scorned.

"How did you— Have you been watching me?" she asked dully.

"I didn't need to," he derided. "Your face when you came into work every morning this week has been enough to tell me just *how* friendly you and Faulkner have become."

"Gary, you don't understand—"

"Oh, I understand," he sneered. "Like all women you need a man, any man, to make love to you and tell you how beautiful you are one hundred per cent of the time!"

"It isn't like that—"

"That's what Joan said when I found out about the little affair she had been having with a doctor at the hospital," he cut in hardly. "I'd been working hard, just wanted to sleep when I finally fell into bed at night, but the bitch couldn't understand that. Oh no, she had to go and find herself a lover to give her what I wasn't!"

She had met Gary's wife at the Christmas dinner, had found the other woman to be shallow and flirtatious, had been surprised to learn she was a nurse, the wine she had consumed with the meal making her silly and giggly, demanding kisses from all the men in the party, her willowy beauty making them all willing to comply.

"You could have left her," she said softly.

"She would take Timmy with her." He looked bleak as he spoke of his young son.

"Gary, can't you see that what you—what you're doing now is wrong?" she pleaded with his common sense—if he still had any!

"I haven't done anything—yet."

She shivered in apprehension at the threat behind that last word. "You made those calls," she reminded.

"Not at first," he shook his head.

She frowned. "What do you mean?"

"I didn't make the first couple," he sneered. "And I wouldn't have made any of them if you hadn't started seeing David. You were really upset when you got the first call, remember, told me all about it. But it was David you let comfort you," he added harshly. "David who took you in his arms and told you everything would be all right. And for a couple of weeks the calls stopped, didn't they, Leonie?" he derided.

"And then *you* began making them," she realised dully. She hadn't noticed a change in the voice, had been too disturbed by the first few calls to notice what it even sounded like!

"Yes," he admitted with satisfaction. "It felt strange at first, I didn't quite know what to say. But after a while it just came naturally," he smiled his relish.

As he became more and more emotionally disturbed! It was his mentally disturbed state that made him so unpredictable now. She didn't quite now what to do next, or what *he* was going to do either!

"You always made such a joke about asking me out, Gary," she tried to smile, although her face felt stiff. "I didn't realise you were serious."

"And if you had you would have accepted, hm?" he scoffed at her attempt to placate him.

"I may have done," she answered sharply.

"You may have done," he repeated derisively, his gaze mocking. "Don't lie to me, Leonie." His eyes hardened to blue pebbles. "Joan is always lying to me." His hands clenched into fists at his sides. "And I don't like it!"

She could see that, swallowing hard at the anger emanating from him. "I'm sure she loves you, Gary," she encouraged. "Every marriage has its problems, I'm sure Joan regrets her lapse with the doctor."

"She still sees him."

"Oh." Leonie chewed on her bottom lip.

"Once a week," he spoke almost to himself, not seeming to see Leonie at all at that moment. "She tells me she's working at the hospital that night, but I've checked; she's seeing him."

"Fridays," Leonie realised weakly.

"Yes," he bit out, focusing on her again.

"She can't really care for him, Gary, otherwise she would have left you to go to him," she pointed out desperately.

"He's married too," Gary scorned. "This way they both have the best of both worlds!"

And Gary's jealousy and pain had acted like a sickness, growing, spreading, until he latched his unwanted love on to another woman—who also turned out not to want him.

"For a while I thought about killing both of them," he continued matter-of-factly. "But then I met you, and realised I could have the same arrangement Joan has. You should have gone out with me, Leonie, I would have been so good to you. Now all we'll have is this one night together."

"Wh-what do you mean?"

"Well you know who I am now," he shrugged.

"You—you're going to leave London?"

He seemed amused by the idea. "No," he drawled.

Leonie felt faint as his meaning became clear to her. She couldn't believe this were really happening—it happened on television, in films, *not* in real life!

"Gary, you're making a mistake," she told him breathlessly. "I—I'll forget all about this if you—if you'll just leave," she urged desperately.

He shook his head. "As soon as I got out the door you would call the police."

She would too, knew she would have to. Gary was a danger to other people as well as to himself. But by the sound of it she wasn't going to get the chance to call anyone.

"It would be your word against mine," she reasoned.

"And Faulkner's," he grated. "It was him who answered the last two calls, wasn't it?"

She flushed her guilt. "Gary—"

"We've talked enough," he snarled. "I didn't come here to talk!"

She knew exactly what he had come here for, and the thought of it terrified her. "Gary, can't you see this is wrong?" she pleaded. "Do you really want to make love to a woman who doesn't love you?"

"Why not?" he scorned. "That's what I do at home!"

"But that's Joan, Gary," she said softly. "Things could be different between us. We—"

"Don't try the psychological approach, Leonie," he scoffed. "I've seen those bad films too!"

"I've always liked you, Gary," she insisted.

"Then you're going to get the chance to prove it, aren't you?" he taunted. "And for God's sake shut that cat up!" he rasped as Harvey scratched frantically at the basket to be let out.

Leonie weighed up the possibility of winning a fight against Gary, instantly knowing that she wouldn't, not even with desperation on her side. Gary may be short and stocky, but muscles bulged in his arms and legs. He could overpower her in a few minutes, possibly sooner.

She moistened dry lips. "If I let him outside he'll stop," she suggested desperately. "He— He's likely to keep scratching if I leave him in the basket."

Gary's mouth twisted. "By all means throw the damned cat out. But don't try and scream," he warned gratingly. "You wouldn't like the way I silenced you," he promised.

Leonie had a feeling *he* would enjoy it immensely, her hands shaking as she carried the wicker basket over to the window, all the time measuring the distance between herself and Gary, a plan formulating in her mind. He was too close, although as Harvey clambered thankfully out of the window the empty basket in her hand gave her an idea.

"Hey, Gary," she called, at the same time launching the basket at him, knocking him momentarily off-balance, his language voluble as she climbed outside on to the ledge that Harvey used to get to the neighbouring buildings.

Only it wasn't as easy for her to balance there as it was for Harvey, the nine-inch-wide ledge that seemed more than adequate for his wiry frame suddenly seeming too narrow for her to negotiate with any degree of safety.

"What the hell do you think you're doing?" Gary's furious face appeared at the open window, his hand reaching out to clasp her ankle.

She had seen the move coming and scuttled a short distance along the ledge, sighing her relief as she realised she was out of his reach, leaning back against the rough brickwork of the wall behind her as she swayed giddily, the ground seeming a very long way down.

"You stupid bitch," Gary's face was contorted with fury. "Get back in here."

"Are you joking?" she gave a shaky laugh, her eyes still closed as she fought back feelings of faintness. "You *have* to be joking, Gary!"

"You'll fall and break your damned neck!"

She turned to look at him, breathing heavily in her anger. "Surprisingly enough," sarcasm sharpened her voice, "I would find that infinitely more preferable to being attacked by you. Isn't that strange!" she bit out contemptuously.

Some of the bravado left him as he realised she was serious, taking on the look of a man who just didn't know what to do next. "Leonie, please come back in here," he encouraged softly.

"No!"

"I promise not to touch you, damn it!"

"You think I believe you?" she derided harshly. "I wouldn't trust you—Oh!" she gasped as dizziness washed over her once again.

"Are you all right?" Gary sounded desperate. "Leonie, for God's sake get back in here."

"I can't," she shook her head, pushing into the wall behind her, biting her lip as she became afraid to look anywhere but straight ahead.

"I won't hurt you," he promised vehemently.

"Don't you understand," she grated between clenched teeth. "I can't move!"

"What is it? Is your foot stuck somewhere? Maybe if I—"

"No!" she cried her panic as she heard him attempting to climb out on to the ledge. "Don't come near me," she warned desperately.

"But if you're stuck—"

"I'm not," she shuddered. "I—I have vertigo!" Two floors up, and she was terrified! Heights had never bothered her before, although she did have to concede that the circumstances of her being out here on a nine-inch ledge may have contributed to the fact that she now couldn't move back into the window and couldn't attempt to reach the neighbouring building either! The thought of moving at all terrified her, frozen to the spot.

"Then let me help you—"

"Don't come near me," she warned as Gary would have joined her out on the ledge. "If you come out here I—I swear I'll jump!"

"But you can't stay there!"

"Why can't I?" she was near to hysteria.

"Leonie, you have to come in some time," he encouraged.

"And face a raving sex-maniac?" she shook her head vehemently. "No, thank you!"

"It was only a game—"

"Remember, Gary," she bit out grimly, "I watched the same bad films."

"You would rather stay out there, possibly fall, than come back in here with me?" he sounded exasperated.

"In one word, *yes!*"

"You stupid—"

"Bitch," she finished curtly. "I've noticed that seems to be your favourite word for a woman who won't do things your way," she scorned. "No wonder Joan found herself another man!"

"You know nothing of my marriage to Joan," he snarled.

"I know that the failure of it has involved me," she bit out. "And I—" she broke off as the telephone in her flat began to ring. "It's Adam," she breathed. "It has to be Adam. If I don't answer that Gary, he'll know there's something wrong."

"Why should he?" he dismissed logically. "He'll just think you're still out."

He was right, of course, but she had to try. "No," she insisted. "He said he would call me. If I—if I don't answer he'll think something has happened to me."

"Then come in and answer it," Gary invited softly.

God, the phone would stop ringing in a minute, with the caller—*possibly* Adam, thinking she just wasn't at home!

"I didn't think you would," Gary said smugly.

"You—you're insane!" She told him angrily as the telephone stopped ringing, the silence it left unnerving.

"I thought you had already concluded that," he dismissed. "I'll be waiting inside if you should change your mind about coming in," he told her conversationally.

When she finally dared to turn her head it was to find him gone from the open window. "Gary," she called sharply. "Gary?"

There was no answer. Was he playing a game with her, waiting for her in silence inside her flat? If he thought she was lying about the vertigo, that believing him gone, she would climb back inside, he was wrong. She really couldn't move!

"Gary," she called again. "Gary, please answer me."

He had gone, she was sure of it. God, what could the time be, about three o'clock? That meant she had another three hours before Adam was due to arrive. She wasn't sure she could balance on this ledge for that amount of time. But if she couldn't, that left only one way off it, and that was down!

CHAPTER TEN

IT was amazing how traffic could pass by and not even realise there was a young woman balancing precariously on a second-floor ledge above them! It was a street that had little or no pedestrians, and the people in their cars were too engrossed in their own lives to look up and see Leonie.

One really bad moment came when Harvey decided to make his way back along the ledge, rubbing against her legs in greeting, not understanding when she wouldn't move out of his way and allow him into his home. He became quite agitated by her refusal to move, and with his usual stubbornness refused to go back the way he had come. Leonie vehemently decided that his wandering days were over if she ever got off this ledge.

And so were someone else's if she survived this! Her fury turned to Adam. If they had been living together as husband and wife instead of conducting this ridiculous affair this wouldn't have happened to her. And if an affair were all he wanted he could find some other woman to have it with, she would be his wife or nothing!

What time was it now? She felt as if she had been on this ledge for hours. Surely it must be almost six by now? She was too afraid to even raise her arm and look at her wrist watch! But as if in answer to her question she could hear a clock striking the hour, one, two, three, four, five—she waited for the sixth bell—nothing happened. Five o'clock, it was only five o'clock! She wasn't sure she could stay balanced here for another hour.

Suddenly she heard a noise in the flat behind her, freezing, almost afraid to breathe. Gary had been playing a game with her all along, he was still in there waiting for her.

"What the—! What the hell are you doing out there?"

She turned sharply at the sound of that voice, regaining her balance with effort, feeling shaken as the world swayed up to meet her.

"Be careful, damn it," Adam rasped. "You almost fell then."

"You don't say," she scorned shakily. "You aren't supposed to be here for another hour," she accused.

"What?" he frowned his disbelief, in the act of climbing out of the window.

"It's only five, you said you wouldn't be here until six," she stupidly reminded. Had she lost her mind? What did it matter what the time was, he was *here!*

"Well if that's the way you feel about being rescued," he ground out, climbing back down. "I'll come back in an hour!"

"Adam!" she screamed her fear that he would really leave her alone again out here. "Oh, Adam," her voice broke on a sob. "Don't leave me. Please, don't leave me!"

"It's all right, Leonie," he soothed, sounded closer now. "I'll be with you in a second, and we'll go in together."

"We might fall," she cried.

"We won't," he told her calmly.

She felt his fingers on her arm, clasping her hand now as she clung to him, feeling his strength flow into her. "Adam," she sobbed, still not turning. "Oh, Adam!" Sobs wracked her body.

"That bastard!" he grated feelingly. "He didn't tell us he had left you out here."

"Gary? You mean Gary?" she prompted. "Did you get him?"

"We got him—"

"How?" she breathed raggedly. "I had no idea it was him, I even invited him in thinking he could help protect me after the man called again. Oh God, Adam, I've never been so scared in my life!"

"I can imagine," he cut in harshly. "And once I have you safely inside you can tell me exactly what happened here this afternoon. But right now I have to get you inside."

"I can't move," she shook her head.

"Of course you can." he soothed.

"No."

"Leonie, you will move," he instructed coldly. "Do you understand me?"

Her bottom lip quivered emotionally. "There's no need to shout at me."

"I'll shout at you a lot more than this if you don't soon get yourself moving," he rasped. "It's damned windy out here."

She turned to glare at him. "Do you think I don't know that?" she snapped furiously. It may have been a warm day but the wind had started to blow about an hour ago, increasing in intensity the last ten minutes or so. "I've been stuck out here for hours," she told him angrily. "I've probably caught pneumonia."

"You probably deserve to," Adam said callously.
"No one in their right mind balances on a ledge like
this one for hours!"

"That's just the sort of remark I should have expected from you," Leonie eased along the ledge behind him, glaring at him as she allowed him to catch
her under the arms and lift her inside. "You don't—
Oh!" Her legs gave way as she realised where she was,
Adam catching her deftly before she fell.

"It's all right now, Leonie," he soothed, smoothing her hair as he held her. "I have you safe."

She shuddered as she realised she was at last off the
ledge. "You deliberately made me so angry that I
didn't know what I was doing," she accused between
her tears.

"As long as it worked I don't care what I did,"
Adam was trembling. "I've never been so scared in my
life as when I came in and saw your open window and
realised you were out there."

"I tried to use psychology with Gary," she remembered with a quiver. "It didn't work."

Adam's arms tightened about her. "He's safely in
police custody now."

"When? How?" she frowned.

Adam led her over to the sofa, sitting her down before pouring her a drink, standing over her while she
drank the brandy. He took the empty glass from her
fingers, sitting down beside her to pull her into his
arms. "Did he hurt you?" he asked gruffly.

She knew exactly what he was asking. "No," she
assured him softly. "Now tell me how you knew it was
Gary? Is he really in police custody?"

"Yes," Adam sighed his relief. "The police arrested him when he arrived home two hours ago. I was
with them, and when they knocked on the door he just

crumpled. He told them everything when they took him to the police station. But he didn't tell us he had left you perched out on a ledge,'' he frowned his anger.

"It's over now, Adam,'' she touched his thigh.

"Thank God,'' he breathed. "Having you followed told us nothing—''

"You're still looking for the grounds to divorce me?'' she pulled away from him, her expression pained. "I hope your detective told you that you're my only visitor! Can you be named in your own divorce?'' her voice rose shrilly.

"Leonie—''

"I don't think you can, Adam.'' She stood up, moving away from him. "So we had better stop our affair so that I can find a lover you *can* name. Maybe I should have just let Gary do what he wanted to do after all,'' her voice broke. "Then you could have named *him*.''

"Leonie—''

"Silly me thought that climbing out on that ledge was better than being violated,'' she said self-derisively. "If I had just let him go ahead I could have saved us all a lot of trouble. You really should have told me—''

"Leonie, if you say one more word, *one more word*,'' he repeated icily, "I'll put you over my knee and beat the living daylights out of you.''

"I wonder why I never realised how gallant you are.'' Her eyes flashed. "I've just escaped attack by a sex-maniac by balancing on a ledge for more than two hours and you intend to beat me!'' She gave a choked laugh. "And to think I'd decided, if I ever got off that ledge, that I was going to talk to you about what went wrong in our marriage. It looks as if I needn't bother.

Although you'll have to provide the evidence for the divorce, the thought of taking a lover nauseates me!''

"Leonie...?"

"Although I know it won't be Liz," she looked at him accusingly. "All this time you've let me believe the two of you were lovers, and you were lying! Liz told me the truth today."

"If she said we didn't sleep together then *she* lied," he bit out.

"I know you went to bed together, before we were married. I also know now that it only happened the once. And Liz told me it wasn't done out of love on either of your parts."

"I still slept with your sister," Adam told her flatly.

"You helped a friend when she needed it," Leonie amended abruptly.

"By making love to her!"

"Do you want a whip to beat yourself with?" Leonie scorned. "What you did wasn't wrong." She shook her head. "Misguided, perhaps, but not wrong. I've believed all this time that you were in love with Liz."

"I never was," he denied softly.

"I know that now!"

He sighed. "The night I made love to her should never have happened, I knew that. Never more so than when I met you," he rasped. "I think I fell in love with you on sight, and yet my guilt about Liz stood between us."

Leonie moistened suddenly dry lips. "You *did* love me?"

"Yes."

"You never once told me that."

He frowned. "Didn't I? But surely it must have been obvious," he dismissed impatiently.

His emotionally repressed childhood again! "I ought to hit you over the head with something!" she snapped.

"Why?" he looked dazed.

"Because I loved you from the moment we met too," she glared at him. "But my inexperience, my clumsiness, my naiveté, seemed to be driving you away!"

He shook his head. "Your inexperience enchanted me, your clumsiness amused me, and your naiveté enthralled me!"

"Then why couldn't you bear to be near me!"

"Because of Liz," he admitted heavily. "I was terrified that one day you would find out about that night I spent with her, and that you would hate me for it."

"Why couldn't you have just told me about it before we were married?" she sighed.

"I'd promised Liz. Although, believe me, if I had thought you could accept what happened I would have broken that promise," he added grimly.

"You thought me too immature to understand," she nodded. "I believe I was," she acknowledged heavily. "But I understand now."

His eyes were narrowed. "You do?"

She gave a ragged sigh. "Liz told me about Nick, his affair, how you tried to help her through it."

His mouth twisted. "I'd like to say it was all a question of helping Liz, but it wasn't. I couldn't have made love to her if I hadn't desired her."

"I understand that too," Leonie nodded. "But you didn't love her, or want to marry her."

"God, no."

"I thought you did, you see. That day I saw you together at your office, I thought you had married me because Liz had decided on a reconciliation with Nick

rather than marriage to you, that you both now realised your mistake, but that it was too late for you to be
together, because Liz was expecting Nick's child. I
believed I was a very second, second-best," she admitted miserably.

"You were never that." Adam shook his head.
"The night I met you I was driving past Liz's house
and saw the lights on. My first thought was that it was
burglars. Then you opened the door!" He gave a tight
smile. "I fell, God how I fell. And yet Liz stood between us. I rushed you into marriage before I could
talk myself out of it, knew I had to have you even if I
lost you later. But our problems began straight away."

"I was a failure in bed," she sighed.

"You weren't a failure," he rasped angrily. "You
were a very young girl with a problem you were too
embarrassed to even talk about. And by the time we
had dispensed with that problem your barriers were
well and truly up, you were self-conscious about lovemaking to the point where you didn't even like me to
touch you. You can't know what that did to me! But
my own guilt about Liz made it impossible for me to
reach you. I knew I was driving you further and further away from me, but I didn't know how to stop it.
When you decided to end the marriage I knew I
couldn't stop you."

"And now?"

"Now I'm giving you what you want," he shrugged.
"An affair."

"While you divorce me," she said bitterly.

"For God's sake, I wasn't having you followed so
that I can divorce you!" Adam grated. "I was pro-
tecting you, because of those telephone calls."

"A lot of good that did me," she scorned, not believing him.

Adam flushed at the rebuke. "There was a flaw in the plan. On Saturdays I met with the detective to get his report. We met at twelve-thirty today for lunch."

"So that was who you were meeting?" she realised.

"Yes," he bit out. "And while he was telling me that he had followed through investigations into the two men that live here, into the people I work with, and the people you work with, coming up with Gary Kingsfield as the caller, *he* was here threatening you! No one was here watching you, damn it," he admitted tersely.

Leonie could see the humour in the situation now that she knew Adam wasn't trying to divorce her. "That was the flaw?" she couldn't hold back her smile any longer.

"It isn't funny," Adam growled. "He could have— could have—"

"But he didn't," she soothed. "And unless I'm mistaken, he's done me a favour."

"I can't think what," Adam scowled.

She walked into her bedroom without answering, coming back seconds later, opening her hand in front of him to reveal a thin gold band, and another ring with the stone of an emerald. "Will you marry me,?" she invited softly.

His startled gaze was raised to hers. "The affair...?"

"Is not what I want," she said with emphasis. "I only said that in the heat of the moment, because I was hurt. I'll grant you the last couple of weeks have been exciting, that first night, the afternoon at the hotel, the rose every day. But can't we still have that and be married?"

Adam looked confused. "I don't understand."

"Do you still love me?"

"Yes," came his emphatic answer.

She felt the glow begin inside her. "And is an affair really all you want?"

He flushed. "I thought after an appropriate time, when you'd got used to my being around all the time, that I would ask you to be my wife again."

That's what she had thought, had finally come to know the workings of her husband's devious mind. "I want to be your wife now," she told him softly. "And I want you to be my husband."

"Are you sure?"

"As sure as I was when you first asked me to marry you," she smiled. "We've made mistakes, Adam, terrible, destructive mistakes, but we still have so much, still love each other so much. Don't you agree?" she looked at him anxiously.

"Gary Kingsfield will never hurt you again, you know. He should go to prison for some time once the police know how he threatened you today."

"I don't care about Gary," she dismissed impatiently. "I'm talking about us. *Will* you marry me?"

"Give yourself time to get over the shock of this afternoon—"

"That does it!" she glared at him, pushing the two rings on to her finger next to the eternity ring herself. "Now we are officially married again," she told him crossly. "And you will be a good, and always *truthful,* husband," she warned.

He raised dark brows. "I will?"

"You will," she told him firmly. "I'll continue to work, we'll lunch together when we can, you'll come home to me at five-thirty every evening, and we'll live together at your apartment. Your new one, I mean. I don't think we would be welcome at your father's again," she grimaced.

"He called this afternoon and invited us over for dinner next week," Adam put in softly.

Leonie became still. "Did you accept?"

"I thought I'd ask you first—"

He was learning, this arrogant husband of hers! "Then accept," she instructed. "I hadn't finished with the outline of our future," she reproved sternly.

"Sorry," he said, but there was a devilish glint in his eyes.

"Apology accepted," she said primly. "Now I will decorate your apartment as you once suggested I should, and one of those rooms will be a nursery—"

"Children," he said softly. "Are we going to have children?"

"Three," she nodded.

"Why three?" he frowned at the odd number.

"Why not?" she frowned.

Adam shrugged. "Why not? And when do you plan to have the first of these offspring?"

"Well I thought I needed a bit more practice at the basics first," she told him thoughtfully.

"Believe me," he drawled, "you don't need any more practice."

She smiled. "But it might be fun, don't you think?"

"I'm sure it will," he nodded, taking her into his arms. "Oh, Leonie, I do love you," he groaned. "I'm sorry I was such an idiot when we were together last time."

"And I'm sorry I was so stupid and left you," she sighed.

"I'm not," he shook his head. "We needed the separation," he explained at her frown. "Otherwise we might never have realised how much we love each other."

She rested her head against his chest as they held each other silently for a very long time, each cherishing the fact that they had at last managed to find happiness together.

"Oh, Adam," Leonie greeted him at the door, her face glowing. "It's triplets!"

The briefcase slipped out of his hand, his face paling. "Are you sure?"

"Of course I'm sure," she said impatiently, pulling him into the house they had shared with his father for the last four months, since Leonie had become pregnant and Charles Faulkner had humbly asked them to. "I've seen them."

Adam swallowed hard. "You have?"

"Yes," she laughed exultantly. "Your father is delighted."

"He is?"

"I must say, you seem less than pleased," she told him crossly.

He looked dazed. "I just never thought— One seemed enough to start with," he finished lamely.

"One?" she frowned. "I don't think that's very usual, they usually come in four or fives."

Adam frowned. "Leonie, what are you talking about?" he sounded puzzled.

"Suki has had her kittens," she sighed her impatience with him. "Harvey is proudly sitting next to the basket, as if he did it all himself, and your father gave a cigar to Chambers." She giggled as she remembered the look on the butler's face when Charles Faulkner pushed the cigar in his breast pocket.

"Dad is excited about his prize Siamese giving birth to Harvey's kittens?" Adam sounded disbelieving.

She nodded. "He says he's going to keep one of them," she announced triumphantly. "Adam," she frowned. "Just what did you think I was talking about when you came in?"

He looked down at her slightly rounded stomach. "Well..."

"Adam!" she gave a shocked laugh. "I've had a scan, there's only one in there."

He took her into his arms. "One can never tell with you," he nuzzled into her hair. "That one came as a complete surprise."

"I think we practised too much," she mocked.

"What shall we call it now?" he said as he led her up the stairs to their bedroom.

"Well, we can't allow all that expertise to go to waste," she teased as she began to undress him.

"No," he agreed as he undressed her.

"So we'll just say we're practising for the next one," she murmured as they sank down on the bed together.

"By the time we're ninety we should be perfect," Adam groaned.

Leonie giggled. "We're perfect now, but so what..."

Everything was perfect, their love for each other, the fact that Charles Faulkner seemed to have accepted her as a member of his family since she was carrying his grandchild.

"By the way," she caressed his chest. "I've booked Mr and Mrs Smith a room at The Savoy tomorrow afternoon."

Adam gave a throaty chuckle. "I think we're going to have to stop being afternoon lovers soon." He looked down at her with tender eyes, one hand lightly cupping her rounded stomach. "As it is our baby was conceived in a hotel room."

"I remember," she smiled. "I remember every minute we spend together."

"So do I," he told her gruffly. "So do I—and I thank God for all of them! I'm so proud to have you for my wife, darling."

And his pride and love for her were all that mattered.

Back by Popular Demand

Janet Dailey
Americana

A romantic tour of America through fifty favorite Harlequin Presents, each set in a different state researched by Janet and her husband, Bill. A journey of a lifetime in one cherished collection.

In August, don't miss the exciting states featured in:

Title #13 — ILLINOIS
      The Lyon's Share

  #14 — INDIANA
      The Indy Man

Available wherever
Harlequin books are sold.

HARLEQUIN

Romance

This September, travel to England with Harlequin Romance FIRST CLASS title #3149, ROSES HAVE THORNS by Betty Neels

It was Radolf Nauta's fault that Sarah lost her job at the hospital and was forced to look elsewhere for a living. So she wasn't particulary pleased to meet him again in a totally different environment. Not that he seemed disposed to be gracious to her: arrogant, opinionated and entirely too sure of himself, Radolf was just the sort of man Sarah disliked most. And yet, the more she saw of him, the more she found herself wondering what he really thought about her—which was stupid, because he was the last man on earth she could ever love....